ROCKFORD PL

P9-CCE-221

3 1112 01404046 9

E LOB
Lobel, Arnold
Days with Frog and Toad

WITHDRAWN

022706

ROCKFORD PUBLIC LIBRARY

Rockford, Illinois

www.rockfordpubliclibrary.org

815-965-9511

Days With Frog and Toad

by Arnold Lobel

An I CAN READ Book

■ HarperCollins*Publishers*

ROCKFORD PUBLIC LIBRARY

For Liz Gordon

HarperCollins®, 🦉®, and I Can Read Book®
are trademarks of HarperCollins Publishers Inc.

A portion of this book previously appeared in *Cricket*.

Days with Frog and Toad
Copyright © 1979 by Arnold Lobel
All rights reserved. No part of this book may be
used or reproduced in any manner whatsoever without
written permission except in the case of brief quotations
embodied in critical articles and reviews. Printed in
the United States of America. For information address
HarperCollins Children's Books, a division of HarperCollins
Publishers, 10 East 53rd Street, New York, NY 10022.

Library of Congress Cataloging in Publication Data
Lobel, Arnold.
    Days with Frog and Toad.

    (An I can read book)
    SUMMARY: Frog and Toad spend their days together, but
find sometimes it's nice to be alone.
    [1. Frogs—Fiction.   2. Toads—Fiction.   3. Friend-
ship—Fiction]   I. Title.
PZ7.L7795Day   [E]   78-21786
ISBN 0-06-023963-8
ISBN 0-06-023964-6 (lib. bdg.)
ISBN 0-06-444058-3 (pbk.)

Contents

Tomorrow

Toad woke up.

"Drat!" he said.

"This house is a mess.

I have so much work to do."

Frog looked through the window.

"Toad, you are right,"

said Frog. "It is a mess."

Toad pulled the covers

over his head.

"I will do it tomorrow,"

said Toad.

"Today I will take life easy."

Frog came into the house.

"Toad," said Frog,

"your pants and jacket

are lying on the floor."

"Tomorrow," said Toad

from under the covers.

"Your kitchen sink

is filled with dirty dishes,"

said Frog.

"Tomorrow," said Toad.

"There is dust on your chairs."

"Tomorrow," said Toad.

"Your windows need scrubbing," said Frog.

"Your plants need watering."

"Tomorrow!" cried Toad.

"I will do it all tomorrow!"

7

Toad sat on the edge

of his bed.

"Blah," said Toad.

"I feel down in the dumps."

"Why?" asked Frog.

"I am thinking
about tomorrow,"
said Toad.

"I am thinking about
all of the many things
that I will have to do."

"Yes," said Frog,

"tomorrow will be
a very hard day for you."

9

"But Frog," said Toad,

"if I pick up my pants

and jacket right now,

then I will not have to

pick them up tomorrow, will I?"

"No," said Frog.

"You will not have to."

Toad picked up his clothes.

He put them in the closet.

"Frog," said Toad,

"if I wash my dishes right now,

then I will not have to

wash them tomorrow, will I?"

"No," said Frog.

"You will not have to."

Toad washed and dried his dishes.

He put them in the cupboard.

"Frog," said Toad,

"if I dust my chairs

and scrub my windows

and water my plants right now,

then I will not have to

do it tomorrow, will I?"

"No," said Frog. "You will not

have to do any of it."

Toad dusted
his chairs.

He scrubbed
his windows.

He watered
his plants.

"There,"

said Toad.

"Now I feel better.

I am not

in the dumps anymore."

"Why?" asked Frog.

"Because I have done

all that work," said Toad.

"Now I can save tomorrow

for something that I really want to do.'

"What is that?" asked Frog.

14

"Tomorrow," said Toad,

"I can just take life easy."

Toad went back to bed.

He pulled the covers

over his head

and fell asleep.

The Kite

Frog and Toad went out
to fly a kite.
They went to
a large meadow
where the wind was strong.
"Our kite will fly up and up,"
said Frog.
"It will fly all the way up
to the top of the sky."

"Toad," said Frog,

"I will hold the ball of string.

You hold the kite and run."

Toad ran across the meadow.

He ran as fast as his short legs
could carry him.

The kite went up in the air.

It fell to the ground with a bump.

Toad heard laughter.

Three robins were sitting in a bush.

"That kite will not fly,"

said the robins.

"You may as well give up."

Toad ran back to Frog.

"Frog," said Toad,

"this kite will not fly.

I give up."

"We must make a second try,"
said Frog.

"Wave the kite over your head.
Perhaps that will make it fly."

Toad ran back across the meadow.

He waved the kite over his head.

The kite went up in the air
and then fell down with a thud.

"What a joke!" said the robins.

"That kite will never
get off the ground."

Toad ran back to Frog.

"This kite is a joke," he said.

"It will never get off the ground."

"We have to make

a third try," said Frog.

"Wave the kite over your head

and jump up and down.

Perhaps that will make it fly."

22

Toad ran across
the meadow again.
He waved the kite
over his head.
He jumped up and down.
The kite went up in the air
and crashed down into the grass.
"That kite is junk,"
said the robins.
"Throw it away and go home."

Toad ran back to Frog.

"This kite is junk," he said.

"I think we should

throw it away and go home."

"Toad," said Frog,

"we need one more try.

Wave the kite over your head.

Jump up and down

and shout UP KITE UP."

Toad ran across the meadow.

He waved the kite over his head.

He jumped up and down.

He shouted, "UP KITE UP!"

The kite flew into the air.

It climbed higher and higher.

25

"We did it!" cried Toad.

"Yes," said Frog.

"If a running try

did not work,

and a running and waving try

did not work,

and a running, waving,

and jumping try

did not work,

I knew that

a running, waving, jumping,

and shouting try

just had to work."

The robins flew out of the bush.

But they could not fly

as high as the kite.

Frog and Toad sat

and watched their kite.

It seemed to be flying

way up at the top of the sky.

Shivers

The night was cold and dark.

"Listen to the wind

howling in the trees," said Frog.

"What a fine time for a ghost story."

Toad moved deeper into his chair.

"Toad," asked Frog,

"don't you like to be scared?

Don't you like to feel the shivers?"

"I am not too sure," said Toad.

Frog made a fresh pot of tea.

He sat down

and began a story.

"When I was small," said Frog,

"my mother and father and I

went out for a picnic.

On the way home we lost our way.

My mother was worried.

'We must get home,' she said.

'We do not want to meet

the Old Dark Frog.'

'Who is that?' I asked.

'A terrible ghost,'

said my father.

'He comes out at night and eats

little frog children for supper.' "

Toad sipped his tea.

"Frog," he asked,

"are you making this up?"

"Maybe yes and maybe no,"

said Frog.

"My mother and father
went to search for a path,"
said Frog.

"They told me to wait
until they came back.
I sat under a tree and waited.
The woods became dark.
I was afraid.
Then I saw two huge eyes.
It was the Old Dark Frog.

He was standing near me."

"Frog," asked Toad,

"did this really happen?"

"Maybe it did

and maybe it didn't,"

said Frog.

Frog went on with the story.

"The Dark Frog pulled

a jump rope out of his pocket.

'I am not hungry now,'
said the Dark Frog.
'I have eaten too many
tasty frog children.
But after I jump rope
one hundred times,
I will be hungry again.
Then I will eat YOU!' "

"The Dark Frog tied one end

of the rope to a tree.

'Turn for me!' he shouted.

I turned the rope for the Dark Frog.

He jumped twenty times.

'I am beginning to get hungry,'

said the Dark Frog.

He jumped fifty times.

'I am getting hungrier,'

said the Dark Frog.

He jumped ninety times.

'I am very hungry now!'

said the Dark Frog."

"What happened then?"

asked Toad.

"I had to save my life,"

said Frog.

"I ran around

and around the tree

with the rope.

I tied up

the Old Dark Frog.

He roared and screamed.

38

I ran away fast."

"I found my mother and father,"
said Frog.

"We came safely home."

"Frog," asked Toad,

"was that a true story?"

"Maybe it was

and maybe it wasn't,"

said Frog.

Frog and Toad sat

close by the fire.

They were scared.

The teacups shook

in their hands.

They were having the shivers.

It was a good, warm feeling.

The Hat

On Toad's birthday

Frog gave him a hat.

Toad was delighted.

"Happy birthday," said Frog.

Toad put on the hat.

It fell down over his eyes.

"I am sorry," said Frog.

"That hat is much too big for you.

I will give you something else."

"No," said Toad. "This hat

is your present to me. I like it.

I will wear it the way it is."

43

Frog and Toad went for a walk.

Toad tripped over a rock.

He bumped into a tree.

He fell in a hole.

"Frog," said Toad,

"I can't see anything.

I will not be able to wear

your beautiful present.

This is a sad birthday for me."

Frog and Toad
were sad
for a while.
Then Frog said,

"Toad, here is what you must do.

Tonight when you go to bed

you must think

some very big thoughts.

Those big thoughts will make

your head grow larger.

In the morning

your new hat may fit."

"What a good idea," said Toad.

That night when Toad went to bed
he thought the biggest thoughts
that he could think.
Toad thought about
giant sunflowers.
He thought about tall oak trees.
He thought about high mountains
covered with snow.

Then Toad fell asleep.

Frog came into Toad's house.

He came in quietly.

Frog found the hat

and took it to his house.

Frog poured some water on the hat.

He put the hat

in a warm place to dry.

It began to shrink.

That hat grew smaller and smaller.

Frog went back to Toad's house.

Toad was still fast asleep.

Frog put the hat back on the hook
where he found it.

When Toad woke up in the morning,
he put the hat on his head.

It was just the right size.

Toad ran to Frog's house.

"Frog, Frog!" he cried.

"All those big thoughts

have made my head

much larger.

Now I can wear your present!"

Frog and Toad went for a walk.

Toad did not trip

over a rock.

He did not bump into a tree.

He did not fall

in a hole.

It turned out to be

a very pleasant

day after Toad's birthday.

Alone

Toad went to Frog's house.

He found a note on the door.

The note said,

"Dear Toad, I am not at home.

I went out.

I want to be alone."

"Alone?" said Toad.

"Frog has me for a friend.

Why does he want to be alone?"

Toad looked through the windows.

He looked in the garden.

He did not see Frog.

Toad went to the woods.

Frog was not there.

He went to the meadow.

Frog was not there.

Toad went down to the river.

There was Frog.

He was sitting on an island

by himself.

"Poor Frog," said Toad.

"He must be very sad.

I will cheer him up."

Toad ran home.

He made sandwiches.

He made a pitcher of iced tea.

He put everything

in a basket.

Toad hurried

back to the river.

"Frog," he shouted,

"it's me.

It's your best friend, Toad!"

Frog was too far away to hear.

Toad took off his jacket

and waved it like a flag.

Frog was too far away to see.

Toad shouted and waved,

but it was no use.

Frog sat on the island.

He did not see or hear Toad.

A turtle swam by.

Toad climbed on the turtle's back.

"Turtle," said Toad,

"carry me to the island.

Frog is there.

He wants to be alone."

"If Frog wants to be alone,"

said the turtle,

"why don't you leave him alone?"

"Maybe you are right," said Toad.

"Maybe Frog does not

want to see me.

Maybe he does not want me

to be his friend anymore."

"Yes, maybe," said the turtle

as he swam to the island.

"Frog!" cried Toad.

"I am sorry for all

the dumb things I do.

I am sorry for all

the silly things I say.

Please be my friend again!"

Toad slipped off the turtle.

With a splash, he fell in the river.

Frog pulled Toad

up onto the island.

Toad looked in the basket.

The sandwiches were wet.

The pitcher of iced tea was empty.

"Our lunch is spoiled," said Toad.

"I made it for you, Frog,

so that you would be happy."

"But Toad," said Frog.

"I *am* happy. I am very happy.

This morning

when I woke up

I felt good because

the sun was shining.

I felt good because

I was a frog.

And I felt good because

I have you for a friend.

I wanted to be alone.

I wanted to think about

how fine everything is."

"Oh," said Toad.

"I guess that is a very good reason for wanting to be alone."

"Now," said Frog,

"I will be glad *not* to be alone.

Let's eat lunch."

Frog and Toad
stayed on the island
all afternoon.
They ate wet sandwiches
without iced tea.
They were two close friends
sitting alone together.

64

A HISTORY OF MINNESOTA

BY

WILLIAM WATTS FOLWELL

IN FOUR VOLUMES

VOLUME 1

LIBRARY, FSU

OCT 20 1988

FLA. STATE UNIVERSITY LIBRARY
TALLAHASSEE, FLORIDA

ST. PAUL

THE MINNESOTA HISTORICAL SOCIETY

1956

F
606
F679
V.1

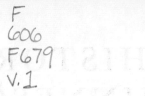

Revised edition
Copyright © 1956 by the
MINNESOTA HISTORICAL SOCIETY
St. Paul

Second Printing 1966

LIBRARY
FLORIDA STATE UNIVERSITY
TALLAHASSEE, FLORIDA

LIBRARY OF CONGRESS CATALOG CARD NUMBER: 21-20894

. . . for historians ought to be precise, faithful, and un-prejudiced, and neither interest nor fear, hatred nor affection, should make them swerve from the way of truth, whose mother is history, the rival of time, the depositary of great actions, the witness of the past, example to the present, and monitor to the future. — Don Quixote, *chapter 9.*

INTRODUCTION

THIS book, which was first published by the Minnesota Historical Society in 1921, remains the best single source for the history of Minnesota from its beginnings to the organization of the state in 1857. Although the volume has some shortcomings, a substantial portion of it has stood the test of time. Perhaps it may now be considered a classic.

All four volumes of William Watts Folwell's *A History of Minnesota* have long been prized by scholars and collectors, but volume 1 has earned a special place in their affections. It has been out of print for many years and has commanded a substantial price in the second-hand market. Although many new source materials have turned up in the thirty-five years since the volume was first published, much that it contains is still useful and pertinent. Thus it seems appropriate, on the eve of the state's centennial, to issue this reprint edition. No attempt has been made to incorporate newly discovered sources or to bring Folwell's interpretations up to date in the light of subsequent research. Only minor errors have been corrected, and new maps and illustrations have been added. The maps were redrawn by Chester Kozlak, associate museum curator of the Minnesota Historical Society, from those executed by Warren Upham for the original edition. Much of the editing on the original manuscript of this volume was the work of Mary Wheelhouse Berthel, the Society's associate editor until May 1, 1956.

When this pioneer work appeared in 1921, Dr. Solon J. Buck, the distinguished superintendent of the Minnesota Historical Society, contributed an informative "Editor's Introduction" in which he provided a biographical sketch of the author. He called attention to Folwell's birth at Romulus, New York, on February 14, 1833; to his graduation from Hobart College at Geneva, New York, in 1857; to his appointment as adjunct professor of mathematics in that institution a year later; to his travels and studies in Europe during 1860–61; and to his return to the United States "in order to be available for service" in the Civil War. "Dr. Folwell served as an officer of engineers in the Union army from February, 1862, to the end of the war," Dr. Buck wrote, "rising from the rank of lieutenant to the brevet rank of lieutenant colonel."

After the war, Folwell spent four years "in business and in the study of economics and politics," Dr. Buck continued, "and in 1869 he was called to the presidency of the incipient University of Minnesota. During his presidency at the university Dr. Folwell not only laid broad and firm foundations for that institution, but also took the lead in promoting the development of high schools and in building up a unified system of public education in the state . . . . After his resignation from the presidency of the university in 1884 Dr. Folwell rendered notable services to that institution as professor of political science and as librarian until his retirement in 1907."

But, as Dr. Buck pointed out, Folwell's contributions were "by no means confined to scholastic matters. He could always be counted on to aid in any movement for the advancement of culture and the public welfare." Thus as "a result of his foresight and initiative," the Minnesota Geological and Natural History Survey was established in 1872; "he was one of the founders of the Minneapolis Society of Fine Arts and served as its president from 1869 to 1884; from 1888 to 1906 he was an active member of the Minneapolis park commission; and from 1896 to 1902 he served on the state board of charities and corrections."

Folwell began work on his four-volume history of Minnesota after retiring from the university. He died in 1929 just as the fourth volume of his monumental work went to press. In his original introduction, Dr. Buck said: "It is difficult to conceive of any one better equipped than Dr. Folwell to write a comprehensive and critical history of Minnesota. In the first place, he is by training and inclination a scholar . . . . In the second place, his half century of public service in the state has brought him into intimate association with many of the men about whom he writes—the builders of the commonwealth—and indeed he himself has been one of the builders. This personal knowledge of men and events has added vividness and accuracy to his interpretation of the basic documents. And, finally, Dr. Folwell has a literary style. He has demonstrated, as did the great Parkman, that scientific history need not be dull and uninviting."

One of the most attractive features of this book is the author's style. Folwell writes candidly and with understanding. An engaging modesty pervades these pages. As a good historian, Folwell conscientiously did the best he could with the materials available. The scope of his scholarship is impressive. Both text and notes remain tremendously valuable to students of Minnesota history. Although the notes and appendixes provide the most reliable and thorough bibliography yet available on certain subjects, they frequently call attention to problems needing further investigation. Thus, Folwell pointed the way for future historians.

Inevitably, manuscripts and other hitherto unknown historical sources have come to light, and numerous studies based on such materials have been published in the years since Folwell wrote. For example, the original journals of Jonathan Carver have been discovered and are now available in the British Museum. Recent scholarship has illuminated wide avenues in the history of exploration and the fur trade—two fields in which this volume is perhaps especially vulnerable to re-examination. The subject of Catholic missions, largely ignored by Folwell, has drawn the attention of later scholars, and useful and significant studies have since contributed to our knowledge of many other features of Minnesota's past—its archaeology, Indians, settlement, economic and political development, and the lives of its builders. It is interesting to note that only three volumes of the infant magazine, *Minnesota History*, had been published when Folwell wrote this book. Now in its thirty-fifth volume, the quarterly contains a wealth of information on Minnesota's backgrounds that was not available to the pioneer historian.

The compelling theme of this work is the building of a commonwealth and the establishment of the political institutions necessary for its functioning. Folwell apparently chose to stress the political origins of the state even at the expense of other important phases of his story, and in the opinion of this writer, that is fortunate. The political decisions chronicled here have influenced and will continue to influence the development of Minnesota. Folwell traces the currents of national politics as they affected the local scene, and he delineates well the unique political alliances that characterized Minnesota Territory.

Like the research underlying his work, Folwell's perspective is broad and deep. Three and a half decades later his book remains unsurpassed. That it has endured is a tribute to this wise and learned scholar, who demonstrated so clearly that the writing of a state's history could be a rich and challenging adventure.

RUSSELL W. FRIDLEY

MINNESOTA HISTORICAL SOCIETY
August, 1956

AN APOLOGY

SOME years ago I contributed to a jubilee number of a local newspaper a sketch of Minnesota history. It was that which led probably to an invitation to prepare a volume for the *American Commonwealths* series of state histories. The narrative was an agreeable recreation for which I trust to be forgiven. In the course of that undertaking a large amount of material was accumulated which could not be used in a compendious volume. Upon my later retirement from university service with an assured subsistence and a prospect of continued working strength, instead of confining my study and production to my proper field, that of political science, I allowed myself to ramble again in that congenial one of Minnesota history. The results of the excursion will be found in this and following volumes. To what degree I have been able as an amateur to conform to the canons of historical authorship my tolerant readers will judge. I wish they may share in my pleasure.

As the work was taken up without expectation of monetary compensation the idea occurred to me to offer the manuscript to the Minnesota Historical Society. I thought that I might thus crown a long life of public service by a much-needed contribution to the historical literature of the state which has given me a home for more than fifty years.

I take the occasion to say that this volume could not have been written but for access to the treasures of the Minnesota Historical Society — its books, its maps, its great collection of Minnesota newspapers beginning with the first issue in 1849, and its manuscripts, containing the papers of Lawrence Taliaferro, Henry Hastings Sibley, Alexander Ramsey, Edward Duffield Neill, John Harrington Stevens, Franklin

Steele, and others. The seventeen published volumes of the society's *Collections*, rich in narratives, reminiscences, biographic sketches, and memorials, have been freely drawn on. Exceptional in character and value, and therefore deserving separate mention, is volume 4, *A History of the City of Saint Paul and of the County of Ramsey*, by J. Fletcher Williams, secretary and librarian of the society for a quarter of a century. The nearly complete congressional set of public documents, with the serial numbers marked, in the general library of the University of Minnesota has been of very great service, and notably so have been many volumes of early travels and explorations acquired by the university with the library of Colonel Daniel A. Robertson. The work could not have been so agreeably carried on without the aid and inspiration of the society's personnel. To Dr. Warren Upham, secretary and librarian for many years, I am indebted for much in the way of counsel and encouragement, and in particular for the execution of the maps. Dr. Solon J. Buck, superintendent of the society, himself an experienced historical scholar and author, was good enough to read the manuscript critically, to point to some better corroborating sources than I had discovered, and to propose occasional changes in diction, some of which I had grace enough to adopt. He also relieved me of most of the proof reading and all the drudgery of making the table of contents and the index.

From a large body of acquaintances formed during my long residence in Minnesota, including all her governors but two, I have been able to derive much information, which if not always exact was indicative of truth. Many correspondents are cited in footnotes and there are numerous references to recorded notes of interviews with persons named; but I must content myself with a general expression of gratitude to others, excepting to a small number to whom I am under exceptional obligations: Mrs. Marion R. Furness, for access to the papers of her father, Alexander Ramsey, before her gift of them to the Minnesota Historical Society; Samuel W. Pond Jr. and Mrs. Frances Pond-Titus, for use of the original papers of the Pond brothers; William Pitt Murray, for inside information on early politics; and Judge William Lochren, my next-door neighbor, for almost daily consultations during two years on Civil War matters, legislation, and public men and measures.

WILLIAM W. FOLWELL

UNIVERSITY OF MINNESOTA
January, 1921

CONTENTS

LIST OF ILLUSTRATIONS

MAPS

A HISTORY OF MINNESOTA

VOLUME I

I. FRENCH EXPLORATIONS

THE first Europeans to penetrate to the area of Minnesota, after a series of adventures, were Frenchmen. French fishermen were taking cod and mackerel off the banks of Newfoundland within a dozen years after the first voyage of Columbus. The French king, Francis I, who ruled from 1515 to 1547, was not content to leave to Spaniards, Portuguese, and English the exploitation of the new world and the glory of opening the passage to Cathay. Giovanni da Verrazano, Italian born, dispatched by him in 1524, coasted from the Carolinas to Labrador, resting some days in the bay of New York. His report encouraged the monarch to patronize further explorations, and ten years later, 1534, Jacques Cartier, under a royal commission, penetrated the Gulf of St. Lawrence. In the year following he ascended the St. Lawrence River and reached Hochélaga, the site of Montreal. Fishing and desultory trade with the natives continued through the sixteenth century, but no settlements were effected.[1]

[1] Pierre François Xavier de Charlevoix, *Histoire et description générale de la Nouvelle France*, 1: xiii, 3, 5, 8–15 (Paris, 1744); or reference may be made to the six-volume annotated edition of this work, in English, brought out by John G. Shea (New York, 1866–72). See also George Dexter, "Cortereal, Verrazano, Gomez, Thevet," and Benjamin F. De Costa, "Jacques Cartier and His Successors," in Justin Winsor, ed., *Narrative and Critical History of America*, 4: 4–9, 47–55 (Boston, 1886–89), and Reuben G. Thwaites, *France in America*, 5–9 (*American Nation*, vol. 7 — New York and London, 1905). Verrazano's report of his voyage is contained in a letter to Francis I, dated July 8, 1524, two Italian versions of which are extant. One of these, accompanied by an English translation by Joseph G. Cogswell, was printed for the first time in the *New York Historical Collections*, second series, 1: 37–67 (New York, 1841); the other, translated by Richard Hakluyt for his *Divers Voyages Touching the Discouerie of America and the Ilands Adiacent* (London, 1582 — reprinted by the Hakluyt Society, London, 1850), may also be found in his *The Principal Navigations Voyages Traffiques & Discoveries of the English Nation*, 8: 423–438 (Glasgow, 1904). English versions of accounts of Cartier's three voyages of 1534, 1535, and 1541, based largely on *The Principal Navigations*, may be found in Henry S. Burrage, ed., *Early English and French Voyages*, 4–102 (*Original Narratives of Early American History* — New York, 1906). See also James P. Baxter, *A Memoir of Jacques Cartier* (New York, 1906), which, in addition to new translations from the original manuscripts in the case of the first and second voyages (pp. 75–215), contains a facsimile of the manuscript of the first voyage (pp. 263–296) and a Cartier bibliography (pp. 395–418).

Soon after the opening of the seventeenth century a company of French merchants was formed to plant a colony in New France, and in 1603 an expedition was sent out to select a suitable location. In the year following, 1604, the company dispatched a body of colonists to Nova Scotia. The important personage in these two expeditions was Samuel de Champlain, then about thirty-five years of age and already experienced in travel and in civil and military affairs. He held at that time the office of royal geographer and was charged with recording the results of all explorations made under French auspices. He not only explored the St. Lawrence and its tributaries up to the Lachine Rapids, but he traced and charted the coasts of Nova Scotia and New England for a thousand miles and more, giving three years to that service.[2] His maps and reports revived interest at home, and a new project was formed of establishing a colony on the St. Lawrence. On July 3, 1608, he staked out the city of Quebec.[3]

The affairs of that settlement were, however, of too little magnitude to deter Champlain from the work of exploration so much to his taste. Attaching himself the very next year to a war party of Montagnais, Huron, and Algonkin Indians in a march against their hereditary enemy, the Iroquois, he discovered the lake which bears his name. In a battle

[1] Accounts of Champlain's voyages may be found in the writings of the explorer himself, published from time to time during his life. A complete and accurate edition of these works, in six quarto volumes, was issued under the patronage of Laval University by the Abbé C. H. Laverdière in Quebec in 1870. For English translations of some of the Champlain narratives, see William L. Grant, ed., *Voyages of Samuel de Champlain* (*Original Narratives of Early American History* — New York, 1907), and the three-volume edition of *Voyages of Samuel de Champlain*, translated by Charles P. Otis and published by the Prince Society (Boston, 1878–82). Citations are to the continuous pagination of the second Laverdière edition in two volumes (Quebec, 1870). For accounts of the first two expeditions, see Champlain, *Œuvres*, 65–127, 154–281, 702–704, 706–764. See also Charlevoix, *Nouvelle France*, 1: 111–121. The first volume of Champlain, *Œuvres*, contains a journal of his voyage to the West Indies in 1598 and 1599 (pp. 1–48), in which may be found his suggestion of a Panama Canal: "One may judge that if these four leagues of land [*between the heads of two waterways*] . . . were cut through, one could pass from the southern sea to that on this side and thus shorten the way by more than fifteen hundred leagues . . . so that all America would be in two isles."

[3] Champlain, *Œuvres*, 283, 296, 783–786, 792. For interesting gossip about Quebec and Champlain see *The Champlain Tercentenary* (New York Lake Champlain Tercentenary Commission, *Report* — Albany, 1911).

which took place on July 30, 1609, near Ticonderoga, by opening upon the foe with three muskets carried by himself and two white companions, he put two hundred terrified Iroquois to indiscriminate rout. It was their first experience of gunpowder. Like punishment was repeated in the following year.[4]

A third expedition, undertaken in 1615, did not result so favorably. A grand campaign of the northern tribes against the Iroquois had been planned, and the rendezvous was at the head of Georgian Bay. To reach this point, Champlain, accompanied by two Frenchmen and ten Indians, voyaged up the Ottawa River through Lake Nipissing and connecting waters — a long and laborious journey. It made him the discoverer of Lake Huron.[5] The line of movement brought him to the north shore of Lake Ontario near the issue of the St. Lawrence River. This lake was crossed, and a march was made to an inland post in the state of New York, probably near the east end of Oneida Lake. Here the enemy was found intrenched in a strong position. A spirited but ill-organized attack was made thereon, which was vigorously repulsed. No better fortune attended the invaders in the days following and presently they were compelled to retreat. Had this fort been captured and the military power of the Iroquois been destroyed or greatly weakened, the history of North America might have been far different from that recorded. The Iroquois, when supplied with arms by the Dutch and English, became the most effective check to French discovery and settlement. In later times they actually drove the tribes engaged in the campaign just mentioned, some to the shores of Lake Superior, others even

---

[4] Champlain, *Œuvres*, 321–348, 355–373; Charlevoix, *Nouvelle France*, 1: 141–151. See also Francis Parkman, *Pioneers of France in the New World*, 2: 161–186 (Frontenac edition, Boston, 1907). Parkman follows closely Champlain's journal.

[5] Consul W. Butterfield, in his monograph entitled *History of Brûlé's Discoveries and Explorations, 1610–1626*, 12–28, 128, 138 (Western Reserve Historical Society, *Miscellaneous Publications* — Cleveland, 1898), assigns to Etienne Brûlé, who was with Champlain as interpreter, the distinction of being the first white man to see Lake Huron. He believes that Brûlé discovered the lake during his stay with the Hurons in 1610–11.

to, if not beyond, the Mississippi.[6]   Champlain, wounded in one of the attacks on the Iroquois fort, was carried off in a litter and was not able to return to Quebec for a year. Meantime he passed the winter with the Hurons on Lake Simcoe, learning their language and recording his observations on their mode of living with great fidelity.[7]   He was now more than ever filled with the desire to ascertain what truth there might be in reports which reached him of a "grand lac," on the distant shores of which the nuggets of copper occasionally shown by the Hurons were said to have been found.   He heard rumors also of a great river flowing to a sea, over which he naturally conjectured must lie the route to Cathay.[8]

It is related that Champlain had adopted a scheme of stationing young Frenchmen with different tribes or bands of Indians to learn their languages and customs, and, if possible, to extract the secret of the untraveled West.[9]   One of these, Etienne Brûlé, reported to the Recollect priest, Sagard, in 1623 or 1624 the existence of a vast body of water beyond Lake Huron, discharging into the latter by a great waterfall.   According to his Indian informers it required thirty days to pass over the two lakes in canoes.   Brûlé gave the length of the great lake, as of his own knowledge, as four hundred leagues.[10]   Another, Jean Nicolet by name,

---

[6] Historians who believe that Groseilliers and Radisson penetrated in 1655 to an island in the Mississippi River between Hastings and Red Wing suggest that they were there entertained by Hurons who had been driven west by the Iroquois. See Warren Upham, "Groseilliers and Radisson," in *Minnesota Historical Collections*, 10: 462 (part 2 — St. Paul, 1905).

[7] Champlain, *Œuvres*, 502–596, 897–965. See also Parkman, *Pioneers of France*, 2: 217–244, and Edmund F. Slafter, "Champlain," in Winsor, *America*, 4: 124–126. Charlevoix's account in his *Nouvelle France*, 1: 153–155, is meager.   For a critical review of the opinions held by various authorities as to Champlain's route and the site of the battle, see the note by Winsor in his *America*, 4: 125.

[8] Slafter, in Winsor, *America*, 4: 123.

[9] Champlain, *Œuvres*, 368, 397.

[10] Gabriel Sagard-Théodat, *Histoire du Canada*, 3: 589 (Paris, 1866).   On page 716 Sagard states that Brûlé showed him an ingot of copper which he had brought from a region eighty or one hundred leagues from the Huron country.   Butterfield, in his *Brûlé's Discoveries*, 105–108, 154–163, declares that it is "reasonable certain" that Brûlé reached the Sault de Ste. Marie, and probable that he paddled along the north shore of Lake Superior to the mouth of the St. Louis River, returning by way of Isle Royale. See *post*, n.13.

who had lived among the Hurons on the Ottawa River, easily lent himself to the purpose of Champlain and set out in the summer of 1634 on a journey beyond Georgian Bay. He paddled his canoe through the archipelago at the north end of Lake Huron, passed the Straits of Mackinac into Lake Michigan, and, holding along the northern shore, entered and passed on to the head of Green Bay. Here he met with a friendly reception by the Winnebago, whose language he found strange. Confident that he would make his way to China, he had provided himself with a gorgeous silken robe like those worn by mandarins. Arrayed in this, he harangued the multitude, and, concluding his peroration by discharging his pistols, he made an immense impression on the savages.[11] Nicolet added the Straits of Mackinac, Green Bay, and Lake Michigan to Champlain's map.[12]

The great lake of which Champlain had early learned and which he had sketched in his map of 1632 was yet to be seen

[11] Reuben G. Thwaites, in his *Wisconsin: The Americanization of a French Settlement*, 24 (*American Commonwealths* — Boston and New York, 1908), following Justin Winsor, *Cartier to Frontenac; Geographical Discovery in the Interior of North America in its Historical Relations, 1534-1700*, 150 (Boston and New York, 1894). Consul W. Butterfield, in his *History of the Discovery of the Northwest by John Nicolet in 1634, with a Sketch of his Life*, 51-54 (Cincinnati, 1881), expresses the opinion that Nicolet reached the Sault de Ste. Marie and rested there at the foot of the rapids. He suggests that the explorer may have ascended the St. Mary's River far enough to view the end of Lake Superior, but he admits that evidence to support such an assumption is lacking. The accounts of Nicolet's explorations as related by Father Vimont may be found in *Jesuit Relations*, 18: 233, 237; 23: 275-279. In the latter narrative (p. 279) occurs the following description of Nicolet's arrival among the Winnebago: "He wore a grand robe of China damask, all strewn with flowers and birds of many colors. No sooner did they perceive him than the women and children fled, at the sight of a man who carried thunder in both hands, — for thus they called the two pistols that he held."

The Jesuit Relations, so called, are the annual reports of the Jesuit missionaries in New France to the provincial or to the general of the order in Paris, which were published by the Cramoisy press between 1632 and 1673. Reference is here made to the monumental edition in seventy-three volumes, *The Jesuit Relations and Allied Documents* (Cleveland, 1896-1901), edited by Reuben G. Thwaites, which, in addition to the Relations, contains the Journal of the Jesuits, private letters from the missionaries to their friends or to officials of the order, and other miscellaneous documents. The work is an exhaustive account of the "Travels and Explorations of the Jesuit Missionaries" during the entire period of their activities in New France, from 1610 to 1791. For bibliographical data, see Winsor, *America*, 4: 295-316; Charles W. Colby, "The Jesuit Relations," in the *American Historical Review*, 7: 36-55 (October, 1901); and Thwaites, in *Jesuit Relations*, 1: vii-xiii. For a list of the Jesuit missionaries in New France, see *Jesuit Relations*, 71: 120-181.

[12] Full-sized reproductions of Champlain's map of 1632 are in Champlain, *Œuvres*, 1384, and in his *Voyages*, 1: 304 (Prince Society, *Publications*); a reduced facsimile is in Winsor, *America*, 4: 386.

by white men, unless it had been seen by Brûlé.[13] The date of its unquestioned discovery was 1641, when two enterprising Jesuit missionaries, Charles Raymbault and Isaac Jogues, made their way to the Sault de Ste. Marie to labor with the local band of Algonquian Indians, called in French, from their headquarters at those falls, Saulteurs or Sauteurs. These missionaries saw the lake, of course, and were told of a great river on which dwelt the nation of the Nadouessis eighteen days' journey distant.[14] Their reports justified Champlain's expectations in regard to a "grand lac," and the whole system of the Great Lakes was now known to the French.

Champlain died on Christmas Day, 1635. His immediate successors were less interested than he in exploration, and they were greatly occupied with the affairs of the settlements on the St. Lawrence and with the defense of their Indian allies against the Iroquois. For a quarter of a century or thereabouts the extension of explorations was left to independent fur-traders, called *coureurs de bois*, whom the government, after vain attempts to suppress, was compelled to tolerate.[15] Of the directions and extent of their

[13] In 1603 Champlain, making inquiries as to the extent of the St. Lawrence River, was told by Indians of the waterway through Lake Ontario, the Niagara River, and Lake Erie, beyond which lake "there is a sea of which they have not seen the end, nor heard that any one has." Again in 1610 specimens of copper taken "from the bank of a river near a great lake" were brought to him. *Œuvres*, 109, 111, 359.

The claims made for the discovery of Lake Superior by Brûlé and Jean Nicolet rest on records too vague and uncircumstantial to warrant acceptance. Both were emissaries of Champlain and must have known his desire to get at the truth of the stories about the "grand lac" told him by the Indians. Both were experienced explorers aware of the prestige accorded to great discoverers. It is not easy to believe that either would have been content to rest at the foot of such rapids as those of the Sault de Ste. Marie and not make a journey of a few hours to see where so much water ("une grandissime courant d'eau") came from. Had either of the men seen Lake Superior he would not have failed to report his discovery to Champlain. That Champlain, having learned of such a discovery, should fail to make mention of it in his narrative of 1632 is also not easy to credit. So voluble and gossipy a chronicler as Sagard should have made a lively chapter out of Brûlé's canoe trip the whole length of Lake Superior and back.

[14] *Jesuit Relations*, 23: 225. The Saulteurs were Ojibway (Chippewa), and the Nadouessis were Dakota (Sioux). In the passage cited, a possible confusion of the Mississippi and the St. Louis rivers is suggested.

[15] Francis Parkman, *The Old Régime in Canada*, 2: 102–115 (Frontenac edition, Boston, 1907); William Kingsford, *The History of Canada*, 1: 75 (Toronto and London, 1887–98); George Stewart, "Frontenac and his Times," in Winsor, *America*, 4: 330.

excursions no adequate record remains. It was their interest to conceal rather than to advertise the regions in which they drove their trade. There can be little doubt that the north shore of the great lake was coasted by the middle of the seventeenth century and that the waters tributary thereto were entered and examined for ores and peltries. Rumors of a great river to the westward and of a mighty people dwelling on its banks multiplied and persisted.

In this period appear two names of importance to the chronology of Minnesota, those of Médard Chouart and Pierre d'Esprit. These men had titles, inherited or assumed; Chouart is better known as the Sieur des Groseilliers; D'Esprit, as the Sieur de Radisson. Both were born in France. Groseilliers, the older, came out to Canada about 1641, when twenty years of age. After spending five or six years as a *donné* or lay helper in the Jesuit mission to the Hurons, whose language he learned, he engaged in the fur trade.[16] Radisson arrived in Canada in 1651, a boy of fifteen or sixteen years. In 1652 he was made captive by the Iroquois, who held him on the Mohawk River about a year. Escaping by way of Albany to New Amsterdam, he got a passage to Holland, whence he returned to France. In the spring of 1654 he was again on the St. Lawrence. During Radisson's absence Groseilliers had married his sister, and the two men became firm friends. It did not require much persuasion to attach the young man to the fortunes of his brother-in-law.

Between 1654 and 1660 these traders appear to have made two expeditions into the remote West.[17] Knowledge of these

---

[16] Upham, in *Minnesota Historical Collections*, 10: 450. According to Benjamin Sulte, Groseilliers was born in 1625 and came to Canada in 1642 or 1643 at the age of seventeen or eighteen years. See Sulte, "Découverte du Mississipi en 1659," in Royal Society of Canada, *Proceedings and Transactions*, 1903, section 1, p. 12. Narcisse E. Dionne follows L'Abbé Cyprien Tanguay, *Dictionnaire généalogique des familles canadiennes*, 1: 129 (Montreal, 1871–90), in giving 1621 as the date of the birth of Groseilliers and places the time of his arrival in New France as 1637. "Chouart et Radisson," in Royal Society of Canada, *Proceedings*, 1893, section 1, p. 117.

[17] In regard to the dates of these expeditions there is much difference of opinion. Sulte and Dionne assign the first voyage to the years 1658–60 and the second to 1661–63 or

expeditions is derived mainly from a narrative written by Radisson, confirmed and corrected in some important particulars by the writings of the Jesuit fathers.[18] The circumstances under which this narrative was written deserve notice. At the close of the second of the two western expeditions, in the summer of 1660, the traders returned to Montreal with a stock of peltries immense in amount and value for the time. The French governor took it upon himself, under pretense that the traders had gone west without his license, to put Groseilliers in prison, and under color of fines to confiscate a large part of their skins. Incensed by such treatment, the two, after a fruitless attempt to obtain redress from the French home government, went over to England. As a result, in part at least, of their representations and efforts, the Hudson's Bay Company was chartered in 1670. There is reason to believe that Radisson originally produced the main parts of his narrative about 1665 for the purpose of promoting this enterprise and securing the patronage of Prince Rupert and King Charles II.[19] In order to gain their support he did not scruple to interpolate an extended story of an imaginary voyage to Hudson Bay, drawn doubtless from the journals of Jesuit fathers who had actually

1662–64. See Royal Society of Canada, *Proceedings*, 1893, section 1, pp 115–135; 1903, section 1, pp. 3–44. See also Edward D. Neill, "Groseilliers and Radisson, the First Explorers of Lake Superior and the State of Minnesota," in the *Magazine of Western History*, 7: 412–416 (February, 1888). With two voyages of Radisson "in the lands of the Iroquoits," and two others in 1682 and 1684 "in the north parts of America," the reader need have no present concern.

[18] Radisson's journals escaped the notice of scholars and remained unpublished until 1885, when the governors of the Bodleian Library and of the British Museum, into whose possession they had come, permitted Gideon D. Scull to transcribe them for the Prince Society of Boston. The manuscript was printed in that year by the society under the title *Voyages of Peter Esprit Radisson, Being an Account of His Travels and Experiences among the North American Indians, from 1652 to 1684*. The story is in the language of an unlettered Englishman without French idiom or quotation. It is the opinion of the editor that the clear and excellent handwriting of the manuscript is evidence that the writer must have been a person of good education; but the recovered manuscript may easily have been the work of a copyist. For a history of the manuscript, see Scull's introduction to the *Voyages*, 22, and *Wisconsin Historical Collections*, 11: 64, n. For a Radisson bibliography complete to October, 1904, see Upham, in *Minnesota Historical Collections*, 10: 568–594. This contains 107 titles with useful explanatory notes.

[19] Radisson, *Voyages*, 240–245; Upham, in *Minnesota Historical Collections*, 10: 451, 516; George Bryce, *The Remarkable History of the Hudson's Bay Company*, 7–11 (Toronto, 1900).

traveled thither.[20] This falsification and another account of a pretended journey to the Gulf of Mexico have discredited, in no small degree, Radisson's whole work.[21] Nevertheless there is good internal evidence for believing that the author and his companion and leader underwent some of the experiences and visited some of the places described.

It will promote clearness if attention is first directed to the second western expedition of Groseilliers and Radisson already mentioned.[22] The narrative represents it as covering a period of two years, but there is good reason for restricting it to one year and that closing with the summer of 1660.[23] It was in midsummer of 1659, therefore, that the Frenchmen set out from Quebec. They took the well-known canoe route by way of the Ottawa River, the Georgian Bay of Lake Huron, and the St. Mary's River, which brought them to the Sault de Ste. Marie, whence they proceeded along the south shore of Lake Superior. In his narrative of the expedition Radisson notes such well-known features as the sand dunes near Point au Sable, the Pictured Rocks, the Grand Portal, and the Keweenaw Peninsula. He relates the making of a carriage across that peninsula, remarking that the "way was well beaten because of the commers and goers, who by making that passage shortens their passage by 8 dayes." The canoe voyage ended at the head of Chequamegon Bay, where the two explorers

[20] The description of this overland voyage to Hudson Bay extends from line 19, page 224, to line 27, page 228, of Radisson, *Voyages*. Both the beginning and the end are obscurely placed in the body of paragraphs. For a critical analysis of the account, see Bryce, *Hudson's Bay Company*, 4–7. See also Upham, in *Minnesota Historical Collections*, 10: 508–513, and Henry C. Campbell, "Radisson's Journal: Its Value in History," in Wisconsin Historical Society, *Proceedings*, 1895, p. 106.

[21] The journey to the Gulf of Mexico is described in Radisson, *Voyages*, 151–153. For discussions as to the reliability of the Radisson narrative on this point, see Upham, in *Minnesota Historical Collections*, 10: 459–561; and Campbell, in Wisconsin Historical Society, *Proceedings*, 1895, p. 114, and in his *Exploration of Lake Superior: The Voyages of Radisson and Groseilliers*, 25 (Parkman Club, *Publications*, no. 2 — Milwaukee, 1896).

[22] Numbered fourth by Scull.

[23] See Upham, in *Minnesota Historical Collections*, 10: 479, 515–519, and Campbell, *Voyages of Radisson and Groseilliers*, 21, for citation of passages in the Relations and the Journal of the Jesuits fixing the dates of the duration of the expedition.

built a " fort of stakes . . . in 2 dayes' time " and cached a part of their merchandise. Escorted by a party of Huron warriors, they marched inland four days through the woods to a village " by watter." Conjecture and a faint Indian tradition point to Lac Courte Oreille in Sawyer County, Wisconsin, as the " little lake " of the narrative.[24] At the first snowfall the Indians dispersed in small parties for their fall hunting to rendezvous after two months and a half at a certain " small lake " where the Frenchmen were to meet them. Eight ambassadors " from the nation of the Nadoneseronons " came to the rendezvous, bringing a calumet of red stone. The Frenchmen stampeded them by throwing some powder in the fire and made them believe they "weare the Devils of the earth." Large delegations of tribes attended a great convocation held in the spring of 1660, among them "30 yong men of ye nation of the beefe . . . having nothing but bows and arrows," the "foreguard" of a large company which arrived the day following "wth an incredible pomp."[25] Conjecture and tradition again conspire in locating that meeting place at or near Knife Lake in Kanabec County, Minnesota, seven miles due north of the railroad station of Mora.[26] Should this conjecture be confirmed as fact, there would be no doubt that Groseilliers and Radisson were the first white men to tread the soil of Minnesota. Wherever that rendezvous may have been, it is clear from the narrative that the adventurers came in contact with the Sioux or Dakota people, mentioned as the "nation of the beefe" — buffalo, of course.

In a brief paragraph of the narrative mention is made of a visit to the "nation of ye beefe, wch was seaven small Journeys from that place." A liberal construction of the paragraph gives the wanderers credit for an excursion far into the heart of Minnesota. The belief has been expressed that

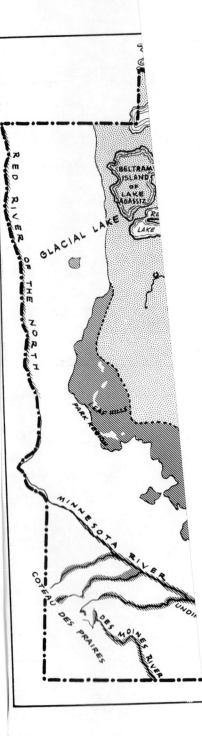

[24] Upham, in *Minnesota Historical Collections*, 10: 486.
[25] Radisson, *Voyages*, 190–219.
[26] Upham, in *Minnesota Historical Collections*, 10: 491.

they penetrated as far as Shakopee and, possibly, New Ulm.[27] The account, however, is so empty of incidents and so full of the improbable and the trivial as to warrant a suspicion that it is founded on information derived from the natives and not on actual observations.

Groseilliers and Radisson appear to have made another trading journey to the West, in regard to which there is wide difference of opinion.[28] It is of record in the Jesuit Relations that on August 6, 1654, two young Frenchmen, "full of courage," with the permission of the governor, Jean de Lauzon, began a journey to the West of more than five hundred leagues, in little gondolas of bark, and that they returned toward the end of August, 1656. Although Radisson himself apparently places this voyage in a later period, there is better reason than any statement of his for believing that the Jesuit record is true, that the two young Frenchmen were none other than he and his brother-in-law, and that the journey took place within the years shown by that record.[29]

Radisson heads the story of what will here be called the first voyage thus: "Now followeth the Auxoticiat Voyage into the Great and filthy Lake of the Hurrons."[30] It is into this account that he injects the relation of a mythical journey down to the Gulf of Mexico, an interpolation which compelled him to add an impossible third year to his chronology. The claim has been set up with great confidence that in the course of this first voyage these enterprising traders reached the Mississippi River, ascended it for a long distance, and made a landing on the area of Minnesota in the spring of 1655. This claim rests mainly on the following

[27] Radisson, *Voyages*, 219; Upham, in *Minnesota Historical Collections*, 10: 502–505, and in *Minnesota in Three Centuries*, 1: 181–185 (New York, 1908).

[28] See *ante*, n. 17.

[29] *Jesuit Relations*, 42: 219; 45: 233–239, 272, n. 23; Upham, in *Minnesota Historical Collections*, 10: 456–458; Campbell, in Wisconsin Historical Society, *Proceedings*, 1895, pp. 108–116.

[30] Radisson, *Voyages*, 134. "Auxotaciac voyage" on page 172. No clew to the meaning of this word has been found.

passage in Radisson's narrative: "We . . . thwarted a land of allmost 50 leagues before the snow was melted. . . . We arrived, some 150 of us, men & women, to a river side, where we stayed 3 weeks making boats. . . . We went up y^t river 8 dayes till we came to a nation called Pontonatenick & Matonenock; that is, the scrattchers. There we gott some Indian meale & corne from those 2 nations, wch lasted us till we came to the first landing Isle. There we weare well received againe."[31]   The author of a most interesting monograph on Groseilliers and Radisson[32] derives from this passage and the context the following movements: the arrival of the party at Green Bay, Wisconsin, in the fall of 1654; the passing of the winter thereabouts; a march in the early spring on snowshoes across the state of Wisconsin to a point on the Mississippi near the southeast corner of Minnesota; a delay there of three weeks for making canoes; the ascent of the river to Indian villages, possibly near Winona, Minnesota, where corn and corn meal were obtained; further ascent of the Mississippi to the "first landing isle." This isle is identified as Isle Pelée or Bald Island, now known as Prairie Island, lying between Hastings and Red Wing.[33] Here the Frenchmen are presumed to have remained more than a year, Radisson spending the summer hunting and exploring. His statement that they "went into ye great river that divides itselfe in 2 . . . because it has 2 branches, the one towards the west, the other towards the South, w^{ch} . . . runns towards Mexico"[34] has led to the

---

[31] Radisson, *Voyages*, 157.

[32] The learned scientist and bibliophile, Dr. Warren Upham, former secretary of the Minnesota Historical Society. His monograph is published in *Minnesota Historical Collections*, 10: 449–594; the same material somewhat condensed appears in *Minnesota in Three Centuries*, 1: 136–156.

[33] Upham, in *Minnesota Historical Collections*, 10: 462–467, 561. Jacob V. Brower, in his *Minnesota: Discovery of Its Area*, published as volume 6 of his *Memoirs of Explorations in the Basin of the Mississippi, 1540–1665* (St. Paul, 1903), dissents from the conclusions reached by Upham as to the identification of Prairie Island with "the first landing isle." Note especially his maps opposite pages 34 and 113. The minor channel of the Mississippi, which separates the western shore of Prairie Island from the mainland, is known locally as the Vermilion River.

[34] Radisson, *Voyages*, 167.

expansive surmise by other writers that Radisson followed the Mississippi River down to the point where it is joined by the Missouri.[35]

The present state of the inquiry does not warrant the ascription to Groseilliers and Radisson of the discovery of the Mississippi. For a generation rumors of a great river which did not flow north nor east had been rife among the French. To open the road to the Indies had been the fond dream of Champlain and his successors. If these traders had any ambition to figure as discoverers, they must have hoped to reach this unknown stream believed to lead thither. They could not have been ignorant of, nor indifferent to, the glory which would crown its discoverer. The Mississippi is no common stream: between Red Wing and Prairie du Chien it flows down a colossal valley flanked by bold and lofty bluffs; for forty miles below Red Wing these banks expand to form a lake a mile in width. It is not credible that intelligent explorers or even ordinary fur-traders who had reached this great watercourse should prosaically record that they came "to a river side," and nothing more. It is also highly incredible that, if these men had actually made the excursion into the Sioux country in the spring of 1660, as conjectured, they could have missed the Falls of St. Anthony, or have failed to report so capital a discovery. If Groseilliers and Radisson had struck the Mississippi either above or below these falls they would have known it; and, unless restrained by most extraordinary inducements, they would have published their discovery at Montreal, won the approval of the governor-general at Quebec, and posed as heroes of the hour at their home in Three Rivers. These

[35] Katharine Coman, *Economic Beginnings of the Far West: How We Won the Land beyond the Mississippi*, 1: 222 (New York, 1912); Captain Russell Blakeley, "History of the Discovery of the Mississippi River and the Advent of Commerce in Minnesota," in *Minnesota Historical Collections*, 8: 303–375 (1898). It may be noted that, in regard to the farthest points reached by Groseilliers and Radisson in their two western expeditions, Captain Blakeley is of the opinion that in the spring of 1655 they descended the Mississippi to the mouth of the Missouri (p. 329); that the "first landing isle" was an island in Lake Saganaga on the Canadian boundary (p. 335); and that the place where they received the eight Sioux ambassadors was at the foot of Rainy Lake (p. 351).

men, who made no claim and left no record, can not be credited with the discovery of the great river.[36] That distinction must still belong to the intrepid Louis Jolliet and his companion, the devout and daring priest, Father Jacques Marquette.

The time was at hand when the French government was to assume direct control of Canadian affairs. In the fashion of the age those interests had at first been committed to a series of trading companies. One of these was organized by Champlain in 1612 with a prince of the blood at its head. Its membership was open to all merchants desiring to subscribe, which disinclined many to venture. This company, reorganized in 1614–15, never became strong and was virtually suppressed in 1622. Another, organized in 1627, was headed by Richelieu, who had become grand master of the navigation and commerce of France. He was not disposed to tolerate private monopolies and therefore substituted a company to be under his own control. Its membership was limited to one hundred, and from this circumstance the organization is best known as "The Hundred Associates," its proper style being "The Company of New France." Champlain was named its active manager with the title of governor and lieutenant general of New France. His first undertaking was to strengthen the settlements on the St. Lawrence and transform them into genuine colonies. A fleet of transports, laden with emigrants, stores, and artillery, sent out the next year, 1628, was captured by a British squadron, and a year later Quebec was surrendered. Champlain, after some detention, was allowed to return to France. For nearly three years Canada was in British hands. In March, 1632, the French recovered possession, and the Hundred Associates resumed their activities. In 1633 Champlain, with a new commission as governor of New France, was at his post. The constant warfare with the

[36] Compare Campbell, *Voyages of Radisson and Groseilliers*, 24–27, and in Wisconsin Historical Society, *Proceedings*, 1895, pp. 112–116.

Iroquois, the demoralization of the fur business by independent traders, a lack of continuity and wisdom in management and of native capacity in the French to build states from the bottom up by settlement and cultivation, were the chief causes for the only moderate success of the company. In 1663, much reduced in members and consideration, desperate of any further profit or usefulness, the company gladly surrendered to the French king all its franchises.[37]

New France thus became a royal province, and according to French usage its affairs were placed in the control of a pair of officials, one holding the sword, the other the purse, an arrangement highly favored by the centralized paternal government at Paris. A governor-general was appointed to be head of the state and representative of the king; he commanded the armed forces. An "intendant" had independent control of the revenue and finances, of commerce, and of justice. Each official reported to, and corresponded with, the home government. Rarely were the two on friendly terms; it was expected they would not be.[38] The first intendant of New France was a man of both ideas and culture, Jean Baptiste Talon by name, who arrived in Quebec in 1665 and at once devoted himself to a study of the nature and resources of the country; he drew up for the eye of Colbert, the French premier, a full account, in which he stated the needs of the colonies and the policy which should be maintained.[39] It is highly probable that Talon was influenced and inspired by the reports of the Jesuit missionaries,

---

[37] Champlain, *Œuvres*, 885–1327; Charlevoix, *Nouvelle France*, 1: 152–176, 370; Henry P. Biggar, *The Early Trading Companies of New France*, 85–166 (University of Toronto, *Studies in History* — Toronto, 1901); Edmund F. Slafter, "Memoir of Samuel de Champlain," in Champlain, *Voyages*, 1: 110–114, 122, 144–158, 187 (Prince Society, *Publications*).

[38] Parkman, *Old Régime*, 2: 62–65; Régis Roy, "Les Intendants de la Nouvelle-France," in Royal Society of Canada, *Proceedings*, 1903, section 1, p. 65.

[39] Winsor, *Cartier to Frontenac*, 191; Edward D. Neill, "Discovery along the Great Lakes," in Winsor, *America*, 4: 172. There is a sketch of Talon's official career by Roy, in Royal Society of Canada, *Proceedings*, 1903, section 1, pp. 69–71. For Talon's commission and instructions, and his report of October 4, 1665, to Colbert, see *Documents Relative to the Colonial History of the State of New York*, 9: 22–36 (Albany, 1855). This volume contains numerous documents relating to the Northwest. The set, which was edited by Edmund B. O'Callaghan, will be referred to hereafter as *New York Colonial Documents*.

who had already pushed their journeys to the West. In 1665 Father Claude Allouez had established a mission at La Pointe, near Ashland, Wisconsin, on Chequamegon Bay. On an excursion to the head of Lake Superior he had seen men "dwelling to the West of this place, toward the great river named Messipi," in a country without wood, who gave him some "marsh rye" — doubtless wild rice.[40] Father Jacques Marquette, who succeeded Allouez four years later, reported rumors of a river nearly a league in width flowing to the south. He thought it must have its mouth in California, and he resolved to explore its course if the savages should provide him with a canoe.[41]

Before leaving France, Talon had proposed that the English should be confined to the Atlantic Coast and the Spanish to the Gulf of Mexico; and that the political power of the French should be extended to the northwest and visibly established at some convenient point. Later he wrote to King Louis: "Since my arrival I have dispatched persons of resolution, who promise to penetrate further than has ever been done. . . . These adventurers are to keep journals . . . and reply . . . to the written instructions I have given them; in all cases they are to take possession, display the King's arms and draw up *procès verbaux* to serve as titles."[42] The governor-general easily concurred in the policy, and the two united in choosing as a proper advance agent a *voyageur*, Nicolas Perrot by name, who in the service of the Jesuits had traveled to many tribes and learned their languages. Perrot, dispatched to the West with a suitable outfit, visited no less than fourteen tribes, mostly Algon-

[40] *Jesuit Relations*, 50:273; 51:53, 289. According to Thwaites this is the first mention of the river by this name in the Relations.

[41] *Jesuit Relations*, 54:189.

[42] *New York Colonial Documents*, 9:64; Pierre Margry, ed., *Découvertes et établissements des Français dans l'ouest et dans le sud de l'Amérique septentrionale, 1614–1754*, 1:82. This collection of documents relating to French affairs in America, in six octavo volumes, was published between 1876 and 1886 by Pierre Margry, archivist of the marines and colonies in Paris. The first three volumes relate mostly to La Salle; the later volumes are devoted to Iberville and to the explorations and settlements of the eighteenth century. The publication was made possible by a subscription of the United States government for five hundred copies. Winsor, *America*, 4:241.

quian, and persuaded the chiefs to assemble in council at the
Sault de Ste. Marie at an appointed time. Perrot was followed by Simon François Daumont, sieur de St. Lusson,
delegate of the intendant Talon, commissioned to take formal possession of seas and lands. It was on June 14, 1671,
on a height overlooking the Indian village, that St. Lusson
and his retinue, sumptuously arrayed, opened the function
in the midst of the assembled nations. A great wooden
cross was planted and blessed, while prayers were said and
anthems were chanted by the priests. The French king's
arms were displayed on a pole above the cross. The central
act was the proclamation by St. Lusson of the sovereignty of
the French king, Louis XIV, over "Lakes Huron and
Superior . . . and all other Countries, rivers, lakes and tributaries, contiguous and adjacent thereunto, as well discovered
as to be discovered . . . bounded on the one side by the
Northern and Western Seas and on the other side by
the South Sea." The Jesuit Father Allouez, already mentioned as having met at La Pointe members of the Sioux
nation from whom he had learned of the mysterious river,
followed with a speech in which he glorified the French
king, invoked the obedience of the Indians, and exhorted
them to be at peace with one another. St. Lusson made
a short address "in martial and eloquent language," giving the reasons for the ceremony, and at nightfall there
was a great bonfire. So far as a dramatic performance
could establish dominion, the French rule was in force
to the shores of the seas, wherever they might be. The
title was as good as any early European title. The *procès
verbal*, never neglected by a French official, was duly drawn
out, signed, and sealed by the principals and witnesses.
The paper domain of the French empire included nine-
tenths of North America.[43]

⁴³ Charlevoix, *Nouvelle France*, 1: 436–439; *Jesuit Relations*, 55: 105–115; communication of Talon and the *procès verbal* drawn up by St. Lusson, in *New York Colonial Documents*,
9: 72, 803, and in Margry, *Découvertes*, 1: 92, 96–99. Perrot's account of the expedition is given in his *Mémoire sur les mœurs, coustumes et relligion des sauvages de l'Amérique*

It was also part of Talon's policy to extend French explorations and to bring under actual control the regions known and unknown over which the royal sovereignty had been declared. In particular he was keen to ascertain what truth there might be in the reports of the wild men of the West as to that great river, called by them "Mechassipi" or "Micissipi," which ran neither north nor east.[44] For his purpose he selected two men. One was Louis Jolliet, a native of Quebec, whom the Jesuits had educated and ordained to some minor orders; he had some knowledge of mathematics and had won honors in philosophy in the schools; he had thrown books aside, renounced the priestly life, and given himself to the seductions of the fur trade. Already at Talon's command he had conducted an expedition to Lake Superior in search of copper mines.[45] As companion to Jolliet, Talon picked out the Jesuit priest, Jacques Marquette, from the north of France, at that time in his thirties. He had been in nearly all parts of Canada, and such was his linguistic talent that he had learned to speak six Indian languages. Probably inspired by Allouez, he was desirous to reach the great river and carry the gospel to the Sioux dwelling in its valley. He records his promise that should the Holy Virgin, whom he fervently worshiped, be so gracious as to favor their enterprise, he would name

septentrionale, 126–128, 290–295. This work was edited by the Reverend Father Jules Tailhan and published in Leipzig and Paris in 1864 as part 3 of *Bibliotheca Americana: Collection d'ouvrages inédits ou rares sur l'Amérique*. An English translation is to be found in Emma H. Blair, *Indian Tribes of the Upper Mississippi Valley and Region of the Great Lakes*, 1: 25–272 (Cleveland, 1911). See also Neill, in Winsor, *America*, 4: 174; Winsor, *Cartier to Frontenac*, 202–206; and Francis Parkman, *La Salle and the Discovery of the Great West*, 48–56 (Frontenac edition, Boston, 1907). Father Allouez's speech is reported in the Relation of 1671 cited; this account gives the date of the ceremony as June 4. The present writer ventures the surmise that Perrot was the principal agent in the convocation; St. Lusson was the titled figurehead.

[44] Charlevoix, *Nouvelle France*, 1: 445.

[45] Margry, *Découvertes*, 1: 81; *New York Colonial Documents*, 9: 787; Winsor, *Cartier to Frontenac*, 234; Kingsford, *Canada*, 1: 399. For sketches of Jolliet, see *Jesuit Relations*, 50: 324, n. 19, and Parkman, *La Salle*, 57, 76, n. 2. The name of the explorer has customarily been spelled with one *l*. Reasons for preferring the form "Jolliet" are presented by Dr. Louise P. Kellogg in a "Memorandum on the Spelling of 'Jolliet,'" in the *Wisconsin Magazine of History*, 1: 67–69 (September, 1917). For a facsimile of Jolliet's signature, see Ontario Historical Society, *Papers and Records*, 4: xl (Toronto, 1903).

the river "The Conception."[46] These men Talon had chosen, but it was not for him to give them the word "go." De Courcelles, the governor-general, resigned in 1671 and was succeeded by Louis de Buade, comte de Frontenac, the greatest figure in Canadian history.[47] Talon soon saw that there was not room enough in the colony for both this ambitious and tireless official and himself. He accordingly requested and was granted his recall.[48] Frontenac, however, had listened eagerly to Talon's suggestions concerning interior exploration and occupation, and promptly commissioned Jolliet and Marquette to proceed with their expedition.[49]

On May 17, 1673, the two resolute explorers, attended by five *voyageurs*, embarked from Mackinac in two birch-bark canoes furnished with a provision of hulled corn and smoked meat and a supply of goods suitable for presents to the natives. They coasted to the head of Green Bay, then worked up the Fox River, traversed the carry near the site of Portage, Wisconsin, and, after four days' paddling with the current of the Wisconsin River, on June 17, 1673, to their inexpressible joy, saw their canoes afloat on the "Missisipi," the "great river" of their quest.[50] They knew what they

[46] *Jesuit Relations*, 50: 322, n. 13; 59: 89–93; Kingsford, *Canada*, 1: 400.

[47] For an estimate of Frontenac's character and services, see Winsor, *Cartier to Frontenac*, 232; Stewart, in Winsor, *America*, 4: 317; and Francis Parkman, *Count Frontenac and New France under Louis XIV*, 458 (Frontenac edition, Boston, 1907). A more adequate study of Frontenac and of the period covered by his administration is Henri Lorin, *Le Comte de Frontenac: Etude sur le Canada français à la fin du xvii⁰ siècle* (Paris, 1895).

[48] Colbert to Talon, June 4, 1672, in *New York Colonial Documents*, 9: 89; Charlevoix, *Nouvelle France*, 1: 444, 450; Kingsford, *Canada*, 1: 392.

[49] Frontenac to Colbert, November 2, 1672, in *New York Colonial Documents*, 9: 92.

[50] The Fox-Wisconsin route remained for a century and a half the most frequented northern passage from Lake Michigan to the upper Mississippi. See Reuben G. Thwaites, *The Story of Wisconsin*, 254–261 (*The Story of the States* — Boston, c. 1891); and *Report of the Select Committee on Transportation-Routes to the Seaboard*, 1: 222–228, and appendix, 114–136, especially the accompanying map facing page 117 (43 Congress, 1 session, *Senate Reports*, no. 307 — serial 1588). William Windom, United States senator from Minnesota, was chairman of this committee, and the document is known as the Windom Report. The Senate committee was of the opinion (1874) that a well-built canal together with adequate improvement of the two rivers would, when one-half of the area of Minnesota should be under cultivation, save the farmers of that state twenty-one million dollars a year on the transportation of their wheat alone to market (p. 227). For a recent and very interesting account of the Fox-Wisconsin route, see Reuben G. Thwaites, *Historic Waterways*, 143–293 (Chicago, 1888).

had been seeking, and that they had found it. Eager to learn where its outlet might be, they took the downstream way. For a month they floated with the powerful current for the most part through unbroken solitudes. By this time they had drifted down to the mouth of the Arkansas River. They were persuaded that the Mississippi could empty nowhere but into the Gulf of Mexico, which they believed to be but a short distance below. They did not wish to fall into the hands of the Spaniards who might be encountered at the gulf, and they found the Indians less friendly as they proceeded. On July 17, therefore, they turned their bows upstream. The return voyage was a tedious one, but after many days the explorers found themselves at the mouth of the Illinois. Under the guidance of a native chief they paddled up this river through a region of promise, carried over the Chicago portage, and were soon afloat on Lake Michigan. They proceeded without event to Green Bay. Here Marquette remained. Late in the next season he returned to the country of the Illinois to establish a mission. An inveterate dysentery rendered him incapable of prosecuting his work, and two faithful Canadians who had attended him undertook to carry him back to Mackinac. At a point near Ludington, on the east shore of Lake Michigan, death overtook the devoted missionary, May 18, 1675, and his faithful followers buried him, as he had charged them to do. Under a modest tombstone —it can hardly be called a monument—in the little Catholic cemetery of St. Ignace on the north shore of the Straits of Mackinac, the bones of Marquette, transported from their first resting place, are believed to lie.[51]

Jolliet returned to Quebec. In the Lachine Rapids, within sight of Montreal, his canoe was upset, and all his

---

[51] The account of the second journey and of the death of Marquette is given by Father Claude Dablon in *Jesuit Relations*, 59: 185–211. See also Thwaites, *Father Marquette*, 221–233 (New York, 1902), and Parkman's graphic account in his *La Salle*, 77–82. Newspaper accounts of the discovery of Marquette's grave are cited in *Wisconsin Historical Collections*, 14: 7. The tombstone was seen by the author.

journals and other papers were lost. He promptly submitted, however, a report to Governor-General Frontenac with a map, which has been preserved. It shows the Wisconsin, the Iowa, the Illinois, the Missouri, the Ohio, and the Arkansas, all emptying into the Mississippi, called by Jolliet the river "Buade" in compliment to the Comte de Frontenac, and the great river itself flowing into the Mexican Gulf.[52] Here is a capital example of true exploration. The expedition was planned by enlightened officials and was intrusted to capable agents, who, after complete prosecution of their undertaking, rendered their accounts of it. Marquette before his death wrote out from memory in two or, perhaps, three forms his recollections of that long journey of more than twelve hundred leagues. Except in trifling details his story agrees with that of Jolliet.[53] Should it hereafter be shown by unimpeachable records that any traveler or missionary had casually reached the great river without recognizing it or, recognizing it, had concealed his knowledge, there will still belong to Jolliet and Marquette

[52] A facsimile of the map in colors precedes Marquette's journal in *Jesuit Relations*, 59: 86. Note the letter to Frontenac on the tablet on the left-hand portion, giving Jolliet's brief account of the voyage. It is related that his reports were not believed until they were confirmed by Marquette's narrative. As a bounty for his explorations, Jolliet was granted the whole island of Anticosti, famed for its valuable fisheries. Parkman, *La Salle*, 76, n. 2.

[53] Marquette's narrative of this voyage first appeared under the title "Voyage et découverte de quelques pays et nations de l'Amérique septentrionale par le P. Marquette et Sr. Joliet," in a volume called *Recueil de voyages*, published by Melchisédech Thévenot in Paris, 1681. It was probably taken from a copy sent by Father Claude Dablon to the provincial of France in 1678. The original manuscript of Marquette, edited and prepared for publication by Father Dablon, may be found in the archives of St. Mary's College, Montreal. It was first published in 1852 by John G. Shea in his *Discovery and Exploration of the Mississippi Valley*, 3–52, 231–257 (Benjamin F. French, ed., *Historical Collections of Louisiana*, part 4 — New York, 1852). It is reprinted in *Jesuit Relations*, 59: 85–163, where, facing page 108, is to be found a reduced photographic copy of Marquette's map. For a history of the Marquette manuscripts, see Henry Harrisse, *Notes pour servir à l'histoire, à la bibliographie et à la cartographie de la Nouvelle-France*, 121, 140–143 (Paris, 1872). The contributions of Jolliet to the narrative are his letter to Frontenac mentioned in note 52, *ante*; the letter of Frontenac to Colbert, dated November 11, 1674, giving Jolliet's verbal report to the governor, in Margry, *Découvertes*, 1: 257; a letter by Jolliet dated October 10, 1674, given by Harrisse in his *Nouvelle-France*, 322; and the accounts which were given "de mémoire" to the writer of "Détails sur le voyage de Louis Jolliet" and "Relation de la descouverte de plusieurs pays situez au midi de la Nouvelle-France, faite en 1673," in Margry, *Découvertes*, 1: 259–270. See Parkman, *La Salle*, 76, n., and Winsor, *America*, 4: 209. On page 217 Winsor assigns the last two oral accounts to Marquette, overlooking apparently his previous crediting of them to Jolliet.

the glory of a splendid enterprise. They made the upper Mississippi known to the world, and they ought to be and will be considered its discoverers.[54]

The report of Jolliet inflamed the desire of Frontenac to know the sources and the mouth of the Mississippi, to establish the domain of France throughout its course, and to extend the fur trade, about which he had a concern not wholly disinterested. His attention was at first given to the upper Mississippi regions. Within two years he sent his engineer Randin to the head of Lake Superior to distribute presents to the Indians and to invite their trade.[55] A company of Quebec and Montreal merchants organized an expedition to open trade with the Sioux and chose for its leader one Daniel Greysolon, sieur du Luth. This selection for the leadership was approved by Frontenac, who, as is evident from certain acts, clothed him with public authority. The energy displayed in this and in following expeditions, the trust reposed in him by his superiors, the fact that he was consulted by the ministry at Paris on civil affairs, and the brilliant military campaign in which he led Indian warriors from Lake Superior in Denonville's expedition against the Iroquois in western New York in 1678— these mark Du Luth as a man of ability and enterprise, deserving a wider fame than has been accorded him.[56] On September 1, 1678, Du Luth departed from Montreal on his journey of trade and exploration. It is not clearly known where he passed the following winter, but in the spring of

---

[54] Until recently it has not been understood that Jolliet, and not Marquette, was the leader of the expedition. Charlevoix, in his *Nouvelle France*, 1: 445, assigns the leadership to Marquette, and other Jesuit writers have been accused of unduly emphasizing Marquette's share in the enterprise. See Frontenac to Colbert, November 2, 1672, in *New York Colonial Documents*, 9: 92, 121; Winsor, *Cartier to Frontenac*, 236; Thwaites, *Story of Wisconsin*, 60, n.; Henry C. Campbell, in *Wisconsin in Three Centuries*, 1: 196–210 (New York, 1906); and Neill, in Winsor, *America*, 4: 178.

[55] Margry, *Découvertes*, 2: 252.

[56] For an account of Du Luth and his various enterprises, see Margry, *Découvertes*, 6: 19–52; Denonville's narrative of the expedition against the Seneca, in *New York Colonial Documents*, 9: 358–369; and Parkman, *La Salle*, 274–282. The spellings are various: Du Luc, Du Lud, Du Lude, Du Lut, Du Lhu, Du Lhut, Dulhut, Du Luth. In this work the spelling "Du Luth" is adopted for the man, "Duluth" for the city.

1679 he wrote a letter to Frontenac, from a point near the Sault de Ste. Marie, and declared it to be his steadfast purpose to prosecute his errand to the Sioux.[57] Proceeding naturally along the south shore he reached Fond du Lac, and, no Indian war hindering, he struck out into the wilderness for the principal Sioux villages reported to lie some sixty leagues to the southwest. Whether he chose the canoe route, later so much employed, by way of Sandy Lake or marched overland by a trail already ancient, has not been determined. It is certain, however, that Du Luth and his party penetrated the region of the "Thousand Lakes" and reached a great village of the Sioux on the southwest margin of the one lake which now bears the name Mille Lacs. He called it "Buade," the family name of Frontenac, and gave the name of the village as "Izatys," a word which was early distorted into "Kathio," probably by the misreading of manuscripts.[58] Here on July 2, 1679, the leader planted the arms of the king of France in token of a claim by right of discovery. This ceremony was repeated in at least two other quarters, as he relates in a memoir addressed to Seignelay.[59] Du Luth long had the credit of being the first white man on Minnesota soil, and he may still be justly entitled to it. Returning to the head of Lake Superior, the enterprising explorer-trader continued his coasting voyage along the north shore as far as Thunder Bay. There he established himself for the winter in a post called Kaministiquia, probably on the site where old Fort William was later established.[60]

[57] Margry, *Découvertes*, 6: 26–34.

[58] "Kathio" has no congeners in the Dakota language. "Izatys" is evidently a variant of "Issati," the name used by Hennepin. A nasalized *a* gives "Issanti."

[59] In Margry, *Découvertes*, 6: 20–25; translated in the appendix to Louis Hennepin, *A Description of Louisiana*, 374–377 (Shea edition, New York, 1880), and in Edward D. Neill, *History of Minnesota: From the Earliest French Explorations to the Present Time*, 813–817 (fourth edition, Minneapolis, 1882).

[60] The claim has been made that Du Luth's post of 1679 was situated on the American side of the Pigeon River, where the village of Grand Portage is now located, and that it was, therefore, the first permanent trading post established by the French in the region now known as Minnesota. See Newton H. Winchell, *The Aborigines of Minnesota*, 582 (St. Paul, 1911). The reader who desires to pursue the question further may consult

For some reason not yet revealed, Du Luth was not satisfied with the results of this year's excursion into the Sioux country, so far at least as exploration was concerned. He had not reached the great river. Accordingly, the next season he resolved on another venture, exclusively of exploration. Early in the summer of 1680 he left his post with four Frenchmen and an Indian guide in two canoes. The Bois Brulé River empties into Lake Superior on the south shore some thirty miles east of Fond du Lac, Minnesota. This rapid stream, broken by numerous beaver dams, he ascended to a point in Douglas County, Wisconsin, where a short portage brought him to the considerable lake which is the source of the St. Croix. Down this he proceeded with repeated portages around falls and rapids to the beautiful lake of its lower reach. A few hours' paddling brought him to a river which he doubtless recognized as the "Misi-sipi." His further progress is connected with that of another character.[61]

Perrot, *Mémoire*, 132, 133, 299; Louis A. Lahontan, *New Voyages to North America*, 1: 315 (Thwaites edition, Chicago, 1905); Elliott Coues, ed., *New Light on the Early History of the Greater Northwest: The Manuscript Journals of Alexander Henry and of David Thompson*, 1: 217, n. 19, 219, n. 22 (New York, 1897); "Mémoire du sieur de la Verendrye," in Margry, *Découvertes*, 6: 586; Neill, *Minnesota*, 809; Upham, in *Minnesota in Three Centuries*, 1: 210; and Parkman, *La Salle*, 275, n. The great northwestern emporium of the Northwest Company was without doubt established soon after the organization of the company in 1783–84 near the mouth of the Pigeon River, on the American side. Here it remained until after the jurisdiction of the United States was extended to the region, when, about the year 1801, it was removed to the Kaministiquia. In 1807 the post was named Fort William after William McGillivray, one of the leading members of the company. Lorin, *Frontenac*, 277 and map; *Wisconsin Historical Collections*, 19: 166, n.; J. W. Foster and J. D. Whitney, *Report on the Geology and Topography of a Portion of the Lake Superior Land District, in the State of Michigan* (31 Congress, 1 session, *House Executive Documents*, no. 69 — serial 578).

[61] On August 8, 1683, Du Luth, lately returned from Paris, where he had consulted with the minister of marine on the subject of trade, set out from Mackinac with men and goods for the Sioux country of the upper Mississippi. There is a tradition, needing confirmation, that he built a trading post on upper Lake St. Croix, where the portage is over to the Bois Brulé. A Fort St. Croix, so situated, is marked on Franquelin's map of 1688. See Father Enjalran to Governor de la Barre, August 26, 1683, in *Wisconsin Historical Collections*, 16: 111, and Neill, in Winsor, *America*, 4: 186, n. 2. A section of the Franquelin map of 1688 was first reproduced as a frontispiece in the first edition of Neill, *Minnesota* (Philadelphia, 1858). Compiled with much skill from the best materials available at the time, it is the basis of all the later cartography of this region. See Winsor, *America*, 4: 226–230; and Neill, *Minnesota*, 798 (fourth edition). Students of this period will be interested in "Rough Notes for an Introduction to a History of Minnesota," by Dr. Thomas Foster, in the *Minnesota Pioneer* (St. Paul), July 15, 22, 1852.

II. FRENCH OCCUPATIONS

A NEW character here appears upon the scene: Robert Cavelier, best known by the title Sieur de la Salle, a man of unbounded ambition, self-confidence, and courage.[1] Born in 1643, the son of a rich merchant of Rouen, he became connected with the Society of Jesus to an extent which cut off his right of inheritance.   At the age of twenty-three he withdrew from that body and, with an allowance of four hundred francs, set out for Canada, whither an older brother had preceded him.   His fertile imagination was already teeming with projects of exploration and conquest.   He devoted himself at once to the study of the Indian languages, and the tradition is that within three years he had "mastered" seven or eight, including the Iroquois.   Such traditions may always be taken with some grains of allowance. Doubtless he obtained a working knowledge of several allied dialects.

La Salle's passion was to trace out the great river upstream and down.   He believed it to empty into the Vermilion Sea, or the Gulf of California, whence the distance to China must be short.   In 1669 Talon was still in office.   He and the governor-general, De Courcelles, gave La Salle their sympathy and encouragement, but they could give him nothing more.   He sold a land grant which had been made him by the Sulpicians of Montreal, and with the proceeds fitted out an exploring expedition, which left that place on July 6.[2]

[1] For an account of La Salle and his explorations the interested reader will do well to read Parkman, *La Salle*.   This work, the first edition of which appeared in 1869 under the title *The Discovery of the Great West*, was revised and in part rewritten in 1879 after the publication of Margry, *Découvertes*.   See *ante*, p. 16, n. 42.   The twelfth edition appeared in Boston in 1883, and a later one, the Frontenac, in 1907.   In *Nouveau Larousse illustré* (Paris, 1898–1904) La Salle's name is given without the "Réné," commonly prefixed.

[2] Although educated under Jesuit influences, La Salle became alienated from that society and he believed that it was inimical to him.   On his first expedition he was accompanied by François Dollier de Casson and Réné de Bréhant de Galinée.   Dollier de Casson

The record of La Salle for the following two years is almost a blank. The scanty materials do not justify a contention that he was on the Ohio River and followed it down to Louisville, Kentucky, and, as claimed by some, as far as its junction with the Mississippi.[3] When La Salle returned, Frontenac was at the head of affairs, and in the young explorer, then under thirty, he found a man after his own heart. He at once placed him in command of the fort recently established at the foot of Lake Ontario to repulse the Iroquois and, incidentally, to skim the cream off the fur trade. In 1674 La Salle was in France on some errand of Frontenac's, and did not lose the opportunity to secure for himself a grant of Fort Frontenac and lands adjacent as a seigniory.[4] Three years later, on a second visit, he obtained what he had failed of in 1674, the royal permission to explore the unknown West.[5] This concession meant a secured credit, advances of money, and the adhesion of many young men of enterprise.

Late in the fall of 1678 his expedition, fully equipped, left Fort Frontenac. We must refuse ourselves leave to dwell upon the details of this journey full of incident and accident.[6]

had already completed arrangements to explore the West for the purpose of furthering the interests of the Sulpician order, and he was persuaded by the governor-general to join forces with La Salle. La Salle parted with his two companions near the head of Lake Ontario on October 1. A record of the expedition is preserved in an account by Galinée entitled "Récit de ce qui s'est passé de plus remarquable dans le voyage de MM. Dollier et Gallinée," in Margry, *Découvertes*, 1: 112–166, translated in Louise P. Kellogg, ed., *Early Narratives of the Northwest, 1634–1699*, 167–209 (*Original Narratives of Early American History* — New York, 1917).

[3] For critical studies of the evidence upon which some historical scholars have based their belief that La Salle during this period explored the Ohio, the Illinois, and the Mississippi rivers, see Parkman, *La Salle*, 28–35; Winsor, *Cartier to Frontenac*, 222–228; and Winsor, in his *America*, 4: 206, 241–246. Clarence W. Alvord, in his recently published work, *The Illinois Country*, 78 (*Centennial History of Illinois*, vol. 1 — Springfield, 1920), cites an unpublished thesis by Frank E. Melvin which is said to prove that the conclusions of these authors are incorrect.

[4] Margry, *Découvertes*, 1: 277, 283; *New York Colonial Documents*, 9: 122, 123.

[5] For the memorial addressed to Frontenac by La Salle, and the patent granted La Salle by Louis XIV to "discover the western part of New France," see Margry, *Découvertes*, 1: 329, 337, and *New York Colonial Documents*, 9: 127. According to Margry, *Découvertes*, 2: 25, La Salle organized a company for the exploitation of his concession.

[6] A detailed narrative of the expedition to the Illinois River is given by Father Louis Hennepin in his *Louisiana*, 65–188 (Shea edition, New York, 1880). A briefer account is contributed by Henri de Tonti, another member of the party, in a report to the French

After battling with discouragements which would have utterly defeated any ordinary man, La Salle, in January, 1680, found himself intrenched in a fort situated on the Illinois River a little below the site of Peoria. It was part of his plan to explore the upper Mississippi, which, so far as was then known, had not been seen above the mouth of the Wisconsin, a point reached five years before by Jolliet and Marquette. As circumstances rendered necessary a long delay and a return trip by himself to Montreal, La Salle determined to send a small party northward to trace the great river upstream as far as practicable. As head of the party he chose Michael Accault, a *voyageur* of judgment and experience, "prudent, brave and cool," as La Salle relates.[7] Antoine Auguelle, sometimes called Picard du Gay, was Accault's lay comrade. The third member was an ecclesiastic, Father Louis Hennepin, a Franciscan of the Recollect Order, who came out to Canada in 1675 in the same ship which brought La Salle back from his first visit to the home country.[8] Hennepin had been able already to gratify a native passion for adventure which the asceticism of his order could not quench. He had begged alms in the coast cities of northern France and had listened surreptitiously to the recitals of Spanish sailors. At the famous battle of Seneff, fought near Brussels in 1674, he had shrived many dying soldiers. Arriving in Canada, he was gratified with a mission at Fort Frontenac, whence he roamed through the native settlements, and even ventured across the St. Lawrence into the Onondaga country. With such experience and with a burning desire for further wanderings he joined

minister of colonies in 1693, entitled "Mémoire de Henri de Tonty sur la découverte du Mississipi, par Robert Cavelier, sieur de la Salle," in Pierre Margry, *Relations et mémoires inédits pour servir a l'histoire de la France dans les pays d'outremer*, 5–8 (Paris, 1867); translated in Kellogg, *Early Narratives of the Northwest*, 286–290.

[7] "Lettre de Cavelier de La Salle," in Margry, *Découvertes*, 2:246.

[8] An account of the missions of the Recollects in Canada may be found in Margry, *Découvertes*, 1: 3–33. For an exhaustive biography of Hennepin, see Reuben G. Thwaites's introduction to his edition of Father Louis Hennepin, *A New Discovery of a Vast Country in America*, i–xlii (Chicago, 1903). See Neill, *Minnesota*, 136 (fourth edition), for an incomplete bibliography.

La Salle's detachment for the expedition of 1679–80.[9] There was, in his experience of life in the woods and on the voyage, some ground for the assumption running through his narrative of the journey that he was the leader, and that his lay companions were mere attendants.

At Fort Crèvecœur, two days before his departure for Montreal, on the last day of February, 1680, La Salle saw the little party launched with some ceremony and with a benediction from a brother priest.[10] The canoe glided smoothly enough down the Illinois, but floating ice hindered its progress up the Mississippi. On the eleventh of April, at a point not ascertainable,[11] the party encountered a fleet of thirty-three canoes, carrying 120 Sioux warriors out for the scalps of the Miami of the Illinois country. By means of signs and marks on the sand, the Frenchmen made the Sioux understand that their intended prey had departed westward. Having no further business down river, the Sioux began a retreat. They took the three Frenchmen along ostensibly as guests, but presently managed to rob them of most of their goods, the priest losing his brocade vestments and portable altar. As they traversed Lake Pepin one of the headmen howled and wept so continually day and night, in spite of the good father's contributions in the way of tobacco, knives, and beads, that Hennepin gave to that beautiful water the name "Lake of Tears," which

[9] The present brief account of Hennepin's journey up the Mississippi River is based on his own first published narrative, *Louisiana*, 195–253, translated and edited by John G. Shea. See *post*, p. 31. For a description and identification of the route followed by Hennepin northward into the interior of Minnesota, see Upham, in *Minnesota in Three Centuries*, 1: 232–236.

[10] Father Gabriel de la Ribourde, who concluded his exhortation with the words, "Viriliter age et confortetur cor tuum." Hennepin, *Louisiana*, 192.

[11] Various conjectures have been made, all of little value. As the Indians had to hunt and fish for food, no estimate can be formed of the time spent in actual travel. Bad weather may have delayed them. Shea, in his edition of Hennepin, *Louisiana*, 205, fixes the meeting place at about the mouth of the Des Moines River; Parkman, in his *La Salle*, 245, at the mouth of the Wisconsin; Thwaites, in his edition of Hennepin, *New Discovery*, xxx, near Lake Pepin; Winsor, in his *Cartier to Frontenac*, 276, near the mouth of the Black River; Upham, in *Minnesota in Three Centuries*, 1: 229, about fifteen miles above Rock Island and Davenport. The author's guess is that it was not far from the present city of Savanna, Illinois. For his estimate see a memorandum dated May 16, 1918, in the Folwell Papers.

was not replaced for a long time. After nineteen days' navigation the party made a landing five leagues below the Falls of St. Anthony at a point on the east bank generally supposed to be the little bay at the mouth of Phalen Creek in St. Paul. Why the canoe route was here abandoned is not revealed; but for some reason a choice was made of the rather less direct overland route, which brought the party after a five days' march to the chief Dakota village on Mille Lacs. After some contention over the division the three Frenchmen were separated and carried off to as many villages.

Hennepin's story of his experiences of the next two months is full of incident. In spite of some horseplay practiced on him for amusement, the father was treated kindly enough. He began the study of the language and got the interested assistance of some of the warriors. He was adopted by a chief who had five wives, and who generously offered to provide his lonely son with one or more according to his pleasure. On one occasion he baptized a child, and he records the great satisfaction with which he viewed its almost immediate death, which occurred before it could fall from a state of grace. About July 1 the warriors, 250 in number, departed, as was their custom at that time of the year, to hunt the buffalo on the prairies of southeastern Minnesota. The rendezvous was at the mouth of the Rum River opposite Anoka. Here Hennepin and Auguelle got leave to go down to ascertain whether the supplies and reënforcements promised by La Salle had reached the mouth of the Wisconsin. Accault preferred to remain with the hunters. Eight leagues of paddling brought the two Frenchmen to the Falls of St. Anthony.[12] The father's account of the beautiful scene is altogether prosaic, and his guess of their height as from forty to fifty feet was a little wild. No rivals lay counterclaims to the discovery of these falls. He christened them, under the name they still bear, after his patron saint,

---

[12] The French league is equal to 2.76 English miles.

Anthony of Padua.[13] The movements of Hennepin and his companion for the next few days are inexplicable from his narrative. Why they did not then return to La Salle's Illinois fort is not explained. In a short time the priest and Auguelle found themselves with a band hunting along the river, and Accault among them. When the hunt was concluded, the whole company set out for home, the Frenchmen with them.

We left Du Luth at the mouth of the St. Croix. Here he heard that certain "spirits," as the Sioux were then calling white men, had passed downstream. They might be English or, less probably, Spaniards. To resolve his suspicions he manned a single canoe and sped rapidly down river. On July 25, 1680, he met the hunting party laboring against the current and found the "spirits" to be his countrymen.[14] For reasons not apparent both exploring parties continued with the returning hunters till they reached their villages on Mille Lacs on the fourteenth of August. This time the Indians traveled by canoe up the Mississippi and Rum rivers.

Late in September the French leaders proposed a return to their homes, promising their hosts to come again to trade. The principal chief drew a map to guide their course. The eight Frenchmen set out in canoes and after many haps and mishaps reached Green Bay by the Fox-Wisconsin route and passed on to Mackinac, where they stopped for the winter. Early the next spring Hennepin made his way by the Great Lakes to Montreal. Du Luth we hear of as pursuing his fur-trading. His later history, full of adventure, both in peace and war, closing with his death at Montreal in 1710, cannot be followed here.

---

[13] Not after St. Anthony the Egyptian, sometimes called "the Great." Hennepin, *Louisiana*, 200.

[14] Hennepin, *Louisiana*, 253. Du Luth's story of the meeting is given in "Mémoire du sieur Greyselon du Lhut adressé à Monsieur le Marquis de Seignelay," in Margry, *Découvertes*, 6: 20–25, translated by Shea in Hennepin, *Louisiana*, 375. The reader of the passages cited cannot fail to note the discordant statements in the accounts of Hennepin and Du Luth.

THE FALLS OF ST. ANTHONY IN THE 1840S

Engraving from a drawing by Seth Eastman in Mary H. Eastman, Chicora and Other Regions, 1854

FATHER LOUIS HENNEPIN
Oil painted about 1694 by an unknown artist

Father Hennepin went back to France in 1682 and obtained leave to print his narrative in book form.[15] On January 5, 1683, it was issued from the press under the title *Description de la Louisiane, nouvellement découverte au sud' ouest de la Nouvelle France*. It is generally agreed that this original narrative, which was not well translated into English until 1880, is, in the main, truthful.[16] It is certainly a well-told story, and nothing is omitted which can redound to the credit of the writer. He makes no allusion to Du Luth's visit to the Sioux the foregoing summer. Du Luth, in a memoir submitted to the French minister for the colonies, after relating his meeting with Hennepin, adds some unimportant observations and lightly disposes of the matter by saying that he put the reverend father and the other two Frenchmen in his canoes and brought them to Michilimackinac.[17] Whoever looks for candor and generosity in the writings of the early explorers, clerical and lay, will be disappointed.[18] Their writings may be said to contain truth.

In 1697 there appeared in Utrecht a work entitled *Nouvelle découverte d'un très grand pays situé dans l'Amérique* with Hennepin named as author. It was soon translated into English, and mostly through it Hennepin has been known to American readers. It contains all the matter of the *Louisiane* and some one hundred and fifty pages of additions. These are so inconsistent with the original narrative and so evidently absurd in themselves as to cause one

[15] Victor H. Paltsits, in Thwaites's edition of Hennepin, *New Discovery*, xlv–lxvi, has furnished a bibliography of the works of Hennepin, together with critical notes on the earlier Hennepin bibliographies.

[16] Parkman, *La Salle*, 137, n. 1; Winsor, *Cartier to Frontenac*, 282–287; Shea, in Hennepin, *Louisiana*, 25–53*; Thwaites, in Hennepin, *New Discovery*, xxxii–xxxv; Upham, in *Minnesota in Three Centuries*, 1: 238.

[17] Margry, *Découvertes*, 6: 24; Hennepin, *Louisiana*, 377.

[18] As an instance of this lack of candor, note La Salle's account of Hennepin's expedition in a letter, probably authentic, dated August 22, 1682. Referring to Du Luth, he says, "Moreover the country of the Nadouesioux is not a country which he has discovered. It has long been known, and the Rev. Father Hennepin and Michael Accault were there before him." In the same letter La Salle remarks of Hennepin: "It is necessary to know him somewhat, for he will not fail to exaggerate everything; it is his character." Margry, *Découvertes*, 2: 253, 259, translated in Hennepin, *Louisiana*, 367, 371.

leading American historian to pronounce them impudent falsehoods and Hennepin an impostor.[19] If he did authorize the publication of the Utrecht edition, he well deserves the compliment. An eminent critic has undertaken to show by internal evidence that Hennepin could never have been the author of the inserts, and that some editor, both ignorant and audacious, interpolated them.[20] The question of Hennepin's veracity is still open, but we may easily give him the benefit of the doubt. Little is known of his later life, and he may here be dismissed with the remark that he has had a fame beyond his deserts.[21] He was but a subordinate emissary of La Salle, who, in a report dated August 22, 1682, months before Hennepin's *Louisiane* was published, recognized Accault as the leader of the expedition.[22]

La Salle returned from Canada to Fort Miami on the St. Joseph River late in the fall of 1680 and devoted the following winter to conciliating the surrounding Indian tribes, mostly Algonquian.[23] His desire was to unite them

---

[19] Parkman, *La Salle*, 242–249. See also Edward D. Neill, *The Writings of Louis Hennepin*, 10 (Minneapolis, 1880), and his *Minnesota*, 135.

[20] Shea, in the introduction to his edition of Hennepin, *Louisiana*, 46*–49*. On page 49* he says: "This intrusive matter cannot therefore absolutely be ascribed to Hennepin, and he be called a liar because it is false." Shea holds that notable peculiarities in the mechanical composition of the volume tend to prove that it was printed in different printing offices; Paltsits is of the opinion, however, that these peculiarities are not of such nature as to preclude the book's being printed in one office; and Thwaites is confident that a careful study of the content of Hennepin's later work will lead one to the conclusion that the blame for the introduction of this additional material "must rest upon the shoulders of Hennepin, quite as much as upon those of his publishers." Hennepin, *New Discovery*, xxxvii, liii.

[21] On July 3, 1880, the Minnesota Historical Society celebrated on the grounds of the University of Minnesota the two-hundredth anniversary of the discovery of the Falls of St. Anthony. From the stage erected on the westerly side of the old Main Building, the falls, not yet obliterated by engineering constructions, were in plain view. The principal address was made by ex-Governor Cushman K. Davis. General William T. Sherman was heard in some remarks of congratulation and encouragement. Archbishop John Ireland contended in advance of Shea's publication for the theory that Hennepin could not be held responsible for obvious interpolations in his *Nouvelle découverte*. For an extended report of the proceedings of this celebration, see *The Hennepin Bi-Centenary* (St. Paul, 1880), a pamphlet containing a reprint of the account in the *St. Paul Daily Globe*, July 4, 1880. The greater part of this account is also published in *Minnesota Historical Collections*, 6: 29–74 (St. Paul, 1894). The writer was present at the celebration.

[22] "Lettre de Cavelier de la Salle," in Margry, *Découvertes*, 2: 245–260.

[23] A detailed narrative of this expedition of La Salle is to be found in "Relation des descouvertes et des voyages du sieur de La Salle, seigneur et gouverneur du fort de

into a strong confederacy, which, backed by French muskets and artillery intrenched in a chain of forts, would be able to resist all attacks of the terrible Iroquois, even though that tribe was supported by the English. He believed that he had succeeded, and again he put his thoughts to the prosecution of his principal enterprise; but another journey of a thousand miles back to Montreal was found necessary, and a year went by. November 3, 1681, found him at length at Fort Miami, where he organized a force of fifty-four persons, twenty-three of whom were French, well armed and provisioned. On December 21 he dispatched his lieutenant, Tonti, with some of the party in advance, and on January 4 followed with the remainder.[24] Reaching Fort Crèvecœur, he decided not to make use of the vessel, the construction of which had been begun in the winter of 1679–80, but to stick to his canoes. By February 6 he was at the mouth of the Illinois, and exactly two months' travel with the current of the Mississippi brought him to one of the islands at its mouth. On the ninth of April La Salle, claiming to act under royal commission, proceeded to proclaim the sovereignty of his king. He erected a wooden column on which were traced the French arms and the inscription "Louis le Grand, Roy de France et de Navarre, règne le 9ᵉ Avril 1682." In sounding phrase he took possession of the whole valley of the Mississippi, including all the land washed by all its tributaries, under the name of "Louisiana." The priests chanted the *Vexilla Regis* and

Frontenac, au delà des grands lacs de la Nouvelle-France, faits par l'ordre de Monseigneur Colbert. — 1679–80–81," in Margry, *Découvertes*, 1: 500–543. See also the account by Father Zenobius Membré, in Chrétien le Clercq, *First Establishment of the Faith in New France*, 2:153–157 (Shea edition, New York, 1881).

[24] The following sources may be consulted for La Salle's expedition of 1682: La Salle, "Relation de la découverte de l'embouchure de la riviére Mississipi dans le golfe de Mexique, faite par le sieur de la Salle, l'année passée 1682," in Raymond Thomassy, *De La Salle et ses relations inédites de la découverte du Mississipi*, 1–8 (Paris, 1859); letters by La Salle in Margry, *Découvertes*, 2:115–159, 164–189; Membré in Le Clercq, *First Establishment of the Faith*, 2: 161–185; "Mémoire de Henri de Tonty," in Margry, *Relations et mémoires inédits*, 14–21; Nicolas de la Salle, "Relation de la descouverte que M. de la Salle a faite de la rivière de Mississipi en 1682, et de son retour jusqu'à Québec," in Margry, *Découvertes*, 1 :547–570.

other appropriate canticles, the soldiers fired volleys of musketry, while the natives wondered what it all could mean. A notary duly recorded the transaction in a protocol and attested it with his name and seal.[25] On this document rest most of the land titles in Minnesota. De Soto, the Spaniard, in 1541 had been on the banks of the Mississippi between Helena and Memphis, and the year after he had been buried beneath its waters near the mouth of the Red River. But no Spaniard had undertaken to colonize in the valley, and the claim of France to dominion by right of discovery confirmed by occupancy, under the law of nations, was never successfully disputed.[26]

At this point the intrepid La Salle might pass from the stage but for the interest which attaches to the inquiry as to what might have been the history of the Mississippi Valley had he lived to see his far-reaching plans for himself and France realized. In September he is back at Mackinac. In December he, with his able lieutenant, Tonti, is building a strong fort on the lofty height now known as Starved Rock, on the Illinois River. It is in the fall of 1683 that he returns to Quebec, whence he hastens to Paris. Here he is the hero of the hour. His modest but inspiring memorials are read by the ministers and perused by the king himself.[27] He proposes a colonizing expedition to the mouth of the Mississippi and a possible raid on the Spanish in Mexico. He asks for men, money, and ships. He is given double what he asks. A fleet of four ships with a company of nearly four

[25] "In the name of . . . Louis the Great . . . I, this ninth day of April, one thousand six hundred and eighty-two . . . do now take . . . possession of this country of Louisiana, the seas, harbors, ports, bays, adjacent straits, and all the nations, peoples, provinces, cities, towns, villages, mines, minerals, fisheries, streams, and rivers . . . along the river Colbert, or Mississippi, and the rivers which discharge themselves thereinto, from its source beyond the country of the Nadouessioux." See Parkman, *La Salle*, 306, and Margry, *Découvertes*, 2:191. The reader will note that La Salle's proclamation did not cover that part of Minnesota north of the Hudson Bay watershed.

[26] See Johnson *v.* McIntosh, 8 *Wheaton*, 543, for the recognition by the United States Supreme Court of the right of discovery.

[27] For the text of these memorials, see Margry, *Découvertes*, 2: 359–369; 3: 17–28; translated in French, *Historical Collections of Louisiana*, 1: 25–34, 37–44. Fort St. Louis was the original name of the establishment on Starved Rock.

hundred soldiers, artisans, gentleman adventurers, and even young women desiring probable matrimony, set sail July 24, 1684.[28] After a tedious voyage and a considerable delay in the port of San Domingo, the expedition passed the Straits of Florida and sailed into the Gulf of Mexico. La Salle, at the time of his occupation in April, 1682, had no means of taking the longitude of his monument. Running by dead reckoning, the fleet passed the mouth of the Mississippi and cast anchor in February, 1685, in Matagorda Bay, Texas, which La Salle mistook for one of the mouths of the Mississippi. Here a dissension with the naval commander of the fleet culminated in the departure of that official, leaving La Salle and his colony on a desolate shore of sand and marsh. Satisfied at length that he had landed to the west of the river, he set out overland with a selected detachment to reach its shores. La Salle was never a gracious personage and was frequently in trouble with his associates and subordinates. There was in his company a little group of miscreants, some of whom he had threatened to chastise. Seizing their opportunity, these wretches murdered their chief, together with his servant, his favorite Indian hunter, and his nephew. A small remnant of the adventurers, after suffering almost incredible hardships, found their way to Fort St. Louis on the Illinois and thence to France. So ends the career of the most picturesque figure in early American history.[29] Doubtless his vast conceptions were

[28] The most authoritative account of La Salle's last expedition is that of Henri Joutel, whose narrative was first printed in full in Margry, *Découvertes*, 3:91–534. An abridged version had previously been published in Paris in 1713 with the title *Journal historique du dernier voyage que feu M. de la Salle fit dans le golfe du Mexique, pour trouver l'embouchure du Mississipi*. A translation of this latter work, issued in London in 1714, entitled *A Journal of the Last Voyage Perform'd by Monsr. de la Sale, to the Gulph of Mexico, to Find out the Mouth of the Missisipi River*, is reprinted in French, *Historical Collections of Louisiana*, 1:85–193. See also Jean Cavelier, *Relation du voyage entrepris par feu M. Robert Cavelier, sieur de la Salle, pour découvrir dans le golfe du Mexique l'embouchure du fleuve de Missisipi* (Shea's Cramoisy Series, vol. 5 — New York, 1858), translated in John G. Shea, *Early Voyages up and down the Mississippi*, 15–42 (Munsell's Historical Series, no. 8 — Albany, 1861), and Father Anastasius Douay in Le Clercq, *First Establishment of the Faith*, 2:229–283. All three writers were members of the expedition.

[29] For Parkman's appreciation of La Salle, see his *La Salle*, 430.

impossible, but had he been able to make but the beginning of colonization, he would have changed the course of events in no small degree.

The current of events has brought us near to the close of the seventeenth century. La Salle was not alone in the conception of a great French empire in the new world. Frontenac shared it; Colbert and his son Seignelay, who succeeded him, were inspired with it; and Louis the Great, although past his prime, occupied with European projects, and swamped with debts, was by no means indifferent to the extension of his dominions. The only way the French knew to accomplish this and probably the only plan they could, under their circumstances, carry out, was to establish fortified trading posts in the wilderness in the expectation that they would become the nuclei of settlement and cultivation. The traders were willing enough to coöperate in founding the posts, but they had no intention of encouraging the aggregation of colonists, who would clear off the woods and drive the game and the Indians into the forest.

In 1685 Nicolas Perrot, the experienced trader and explorer who had been present at the council of nations at the Sault de Ste. Marie in 1671, was commissioned commandant of the West by the governor-general of Canada with instructions to conduct an expedition to Green Bay and the Mississippi Valley.[30] He was licensed to trade with the Indians, and was required to pay the expenses out of his profits, a condition to which he could have no objection. Without delay he pushed his way westward by the Fox-Wisconsin route and ascended the Mississippi to a point about eight miles above the mouth of the Black River, near the present site of Trempealeau, Wisconsin, where he passed the winter of 1685–86. In the following spring he made his

---

[30] For a sketch of Perrot based on Bacqueville de la Potherie, *Histoire de l'Amérique Septentrionale* (Paris, 1722), Margry, *Découvertes*, and Perrot's own narrative (see *ante*, p. 17, n. 43), consult Neill, *Minnesota*, 832–839. See also Gardner P. Stickney, *Nicholas Perrot: A Study in Wisconsin History* (Parkman Club, *Publications*, no. 1 — Milwaukee, 1895), and Blair, *Indian Tribes*, 2:249–256.

way up the Mississippi to Lake Pepin. On the east shore
of the lake, not far from its lower end, he located and built
a fort.[31] The site of this primitive establishment, Fort
St. Antoine, has been identified by careful investigators as
being about two miles below the railroad station of Stock-
holm, Pepin County, Wisconsin,[32] in a portion of that state
which, had scientific considerations — not to say good
political sense — prevailed, would now be part of Minnesota.

Receiving orders to return to Green Bay, Perrot left his
post in the fall of 1686; he took part in the campaign against
the Iroquois and was with Du Luth at the battle in the
Genesee Valley, July 13, 1687.[33] In 1688 he was again dispatched to his post on Lake Pepin and no doubt resumed
his trading. He seems, however, to have been given larger
and truly political powers, for on the eighth day of May in
the following year, 1689, we find him at his fort proclaiming
the French king's sovereignty over the surrounding region,
by virtue of his own discoveries. This is the substance of
his protocol: "Nicholas Perrot, commanding for the King
. . . commissioned by the Marquis de Denonville Governor . . . of all New France, to manage the interests of
Commerce among all the . . . Western Nations of the
Upper Mississipi, and to take possession in the King's name,
of all the places where he has heretofore been, and whither
he will go. We this day, the eighth of May one thousand
six hundred and eighty [-nine] do, in presence of [*eight*

[31] For discussion as to the location of Perrot's posts, see Dan E. Clark, "Early Forts
on the Upper Mississippi," in Mississippi Valley Historical Association, *Proceedings*, 1910–
11, pp. 93–97; Eben D. Pierce, George H. Squier, and Louise P. Kellogg, "Remains of a
French Post near Trempealeau," in Wisconsin Historical Society, *Proceedings*, 1915, pp.
111–123; Lyman C. Draper, "Early French Forts in Western Wisconsin," in *Wisconsin
Historical Collections*, 10: 321–372 (Madison, 1909); and Edward D. Neill, "Early Wisconsin
Exploration, Forts, and Trading Posts," in *Wisconsin Historical Collections*, 10:299–301.
Perrot's posts are clearly indicated on Franquelin's map of 1688. See *ante*, p. 24, n. 61.

[32] Clark, in Mississippi Valley Historical Association, *Proceedings*, 1910–11, p. 94;
Draper, in *Wisconsin Historical Collections*, 10:368–371.

[33] Perrot, *Mémoire*, 138–143, translated in Blair, *Indian Tribes*, 1: 244–252; Marquis
de Denonville, "Memoir of the Voyage and Expedition against the Senecas," in *New York
Colonial Documents*, 9: 358–369; Neill, *Minnesota*, 836.

witnesses named, Le Sueur being one]; Declare to all whom it may Concern, that . . . we did transport ourselves to the Country of the Nadouësioux . . . to take possession for, and in the name of the King, of the countries and rivers inhabited by the said Tribes and of which they are proprietors. The present Act done in our presence, Signed with our hand, and subscribed."[34] So far as proclamations and recorded evidence of the same could go, the French dominion was by this time pretty well established over Minnesota. In the following year, 1690, Perrot visited the lead mines around Dubuque and Galena and pronounced the ore rich but hard to work.[35] The remaining fifteen or more years of his life appear to have been occupied in important public duties in Montreal. Perrot's *Mémoire* is a work of much importance to historians.

One of the witnesses of Perrot's proclamation of 1689 was Pierre Charles le Sueur, who was born in Artois in 1657 and came to Canada with his parents while still in his youth. He soon became interested in the fur trade, and it is probable that before his participation in the ceremony at Fort St. Antoine he had passed some time in the upper Mississippi region.[36] In 1693 he was appointed com-

[34] *New York Colonial Documents*, 9:418; Margry, *Découvertes*, 5:33.

[35] La Potherie, *Histoire de l'Amérique Septentrionale*, 2:251, 260, 270, translated in Blair, *Indian Tribes*, 2:59, 66, 74. See also Tailhan in his edition of Perrot, *Mémoire*, 326, 328, and "Relation de Pénicaut," in Margry, *Découvertes*, 5:412.

[36] There is a statement in the *Journal historique de l'établissement des Français a la Louisiane*, 43 (Paris and New Orleans, 1831), that: "C'est par la rivière des Ouesconsins que M. Le Sueur pour la première fois dans le Mississipi, en 1683, pour aller dans le pays des Sioux, où il a demeuré sept ans en diverses fois." Margry, in his *Découvertes*, 6:72, n. 1, 90, suggests a copyist's error and refers to a memorial written in 1702 in which the writer states that "Lesueur explore le haut Mississipi depuis quinze ans." Neill, in his *Minnesota*, 844, suggests that the date 1683 is a misprint for 1685, when Le Sueur may have been with Perrot on his first visit.

The *Journal historique* is an anonymous narrative drawn largely from the journals of La Harpe and Le Sueur and is usually cited as "La Harpe." A memorial signed by Bernard de la Harpe is appended. Margry, in his *Découvertes*, 5:549, attributes its authorship to "le Chevalier Beaurain, géographe du roy." Winsor, in his *America*, 5:63, regards it as an important document. In 1851 Benjamin F. French published a translation from a manuscript copy in the possession of the American Philosophical Society at Philadelphia. See his *Historical Collections of Louisiana*, part 3, pp. 8–118. Neill, in his *Minnesota*, 144–175, follows the *Journal historique* closely. La Harpe was a notable figure in Louisiana from 1718 to 1723. In a letter to John Law written August 1, 1720, Jean Baptiste de Bienville commends him as "un parfaitement bon officier . . . intelligent dans les affaires." See

mandant at Chequamegon and was instructed to maintain peace between the Sioux and the Chippewa and to keep open the Bois Brulé–St. Croix canoe route.   In pursuance of these ends Le Sueur established in 1695 a fort on Isle Pelée, now called Prairie Island, about nine miles below the present city of Hastings.   During the summer of the same year he returned to Montreal with his winter's accumulation of furs, taking with him a Sioux chief, the first of that nation ever seen in Lower Canada.   At an audience with Frontenac this Indian, after much ceremonial howling and weeping, begged that Le Sueur might be sent back to the Sioux country with plenty of iron and promised that the twenty-two villages of his nation would be obedient.   Le Sueur did not return to his post but went at once to Paris, where he boldly applied to the king for a permanent command on Lake Superior with jurisdiction over the region of the upper Mississippi and its tributary waters, a monopoly of the fur trade for ten years, and permission to work mines.   A license to mine for copper was the only one of his petitions granted. Le Sueur set out for Canada in June, 1697, was captured by the English, and was held as a prisoner for a year or more. A new commission, granted him in 1698, was revoked in consequence of a policy of the government to abandon trade with the Sioux.   The principal reason for such a policy was the opposition of the Fox Indians and of their allies, whose trade was of great value.   They controlled the Fox-Wisconsin route to the Mississippi, and insisted that the

the *Journal historique*, 232. A translation, doubtless made by Neill or at his instance, of the part taken from Le Sueur's journal is printed in the *Minnesota Pioneer*, October 10–24, 1850.

   It is of interest to note here that about 1690, or perhaps even earlier, Le Sueur made a canoe trip above the Falls of St. Anthony of which a brief account may be found in the "Extrait des mémoires de Le Sueur (13 Aoust 1701)," in Margry, *Découvertes*, 6:171.   In the judgment of Upham, this was the "first recorded exploration" of the Mississippi through the central part of Minnesota. See *Minnesota in Three Centuries*, 1:249. Jacob V. Brower thinks that Le Sueur ascended as far as the outlet of Sandy Lake. See his *The Mississippi River and Its Source: A Narrative and Critical History of the Discovery of the River and Its Headwaters, Accompanied by the Results of Detailed Hydrographic and Topographic Surveys*, 89 (*Minnesota Historical Collections*, vol. 7 — Minneapolis, 1893).   In the absence of a relation of the excursion by Le Sueur himself or of other evidence, it must remain a matter of conjecture.

French, who claimed brotherhood with them, thus ought not to furnish guns and ammunition to their ancient enemies, the Sioux. Le Sueur persisted, however, and, supported by the then powerful influence of his kinsman Iberville, was finally given permission to undertake his enterprise, but from Louisiana as a base of operations rather than from Canada.[37]

Soon after La Salle's assassination his loyal friend Henri de Tonti applied for leave to make an establishment at the mouth of the great river, but his influence at court did not correspond to his merit. That opportunity was given to Pierre le Moyne, sieur d'Iberville, a native Canadian, who had made a great reputation in Canada. With a fleet of two frigates and two transports he sailed from Brest on October 24, 1698, for Louisiana. The little colony which he founded at Biloxi in April, 1699, was the first in the whole valley of the Mississippi, and, transplanted to New Orleans, has had continuous existence till the present. Iberville returned to France in May, 1699. On his second voyage to Louisiana he was accompanied by Le Sueur.[38] They arrived at Biloxi on December 7, 1699. Le Sueur passed the winter and spring in preparations for an expedition into the Sioux country; and in April, with a sailing craft and two canoes manned by nineteen men, he began his ascent of the Mississippi. Heedless of various reports and warnings of danger awaiting him from hostile natives, he toiled patiently against the mighty current and on September 19 reached the mouth of the St. Peter's or Minnesota River. Doubtless he had a definite destination in view, for he immediately proceeded up that river to the mouth of the Makato or Blue Earth

---

[37] *Journal historique*, 22–25; Margry, *Découvertes*, 6: 55–59.

[38] *Journal historique*, 38–53. This account is an extract from Le Sueur's own "Relation de son voyage." Shea in his *Early Voyages*, 89–101, includes a translation of the extract, which has been reprinted in *Wisconsin Historical Collections*, 16: 177–186. Le Sueur's journal as quoted in the *Journal historique* leaves off abruptly with the entry of the twelfth of December, 1700. The remainder of the narrative is supplied by Pénicaut, one of his party, whose "Relation" was first published in Margry, *Découvertes*, 5: 375–586; it is translated in *Wisconsin Historical Collections*, 16: 194–200, and in *Minnesota Historical Collections*, 3: 4–12.

River, and, turning into it, was obliged to end the voyage because of ice, although it was still September. He immediately set to work on a fort, which, when completed, he named Fort L'Huillier, after an official in Paris who had befriended him.

The occupation of this post was greatly objected to by the Sioux of the East, who complained that they could not come there to trade without danger of attack by the Sioux of the West, the Iowa, and the Oto, who claimed possession of the region. Le Sueur did not, however, choose to move, and conciliated the complainants with presents, which perhaps were what they were seeking. His hunters killed four hundred buffaloes and placed the quarters on scaffolds near the fort. Before spring the whole company had to come down to buffalo meat without salt. It was nauseous at first, but at length their appetites so improved that, as Le Sueur relates, "at the end of six weeks there was not one of us that could not eat six pounds of meat a day, and drink four bowls of the broth." He states in his narrative that on the twenty-sixth of October, 1700, he proceeded to his mine some two miles away with three canoes which he filled with green and blue earth. Pénicaut, a member of Le Sueur's company, in an extant journal, postpones the work on the mine until the beginning of April, 1701, when twelve laborers and four hunters were employed. "We took from the mine in twenty-two days more than thirty thousand pounds weight of ore, of which we only selected four thousand pounds of the finest, which M. Le Sueur, a very good judge of it, had carried to the fort." The discrepancy of dates is not material and both accounts may be substantially true. With a shallop carrying the precious ore and three canoes laden with furs taken in trade, Le Sueur left in the spring of 1701 and, after reaching Iberville's settlement without accident, sailed for France in the company of his relative in April, 1702. We hear no more of Le Sueur's copper ore. It is presumed that the assayers at Paris gave

him a great disappointment.[39]   With his later history we
have no concern.   It only remains to add that the detachment which he left behind at Fort L'Huillier, after waiting a
year, followed Le Sueur to the gulf, and reported the non-
arrival of promised ammunition and the murder of three of
its number by Fox Indians.

Frontenac died in office November 28, 1698.   Charlevoix
concludes his appreciation of him by saying, "New France
owed to him all she was at the time, and he left a great
void behind him."[40]   The Mississippi had by this time
been navigated from its mouth to the Falls of St. Anthony,
and the French king's sovereignty had been proclaimed by
La Salle and Perrot over all the lands drained by the river
and its tributaries.   But many of the hopes and plans of
Frontenac had not been fulfilled.

No serious attempt had been made as yet at settlement
on the area of Minnesota.   Her territory, lying remote from
the Great Lakes, could be reached only by tedious canoe
transportation over elevated divides and along streams
obstructed by beaver dams, sand bars, and rapids, or by
laborious marches. The northern route by the Savanna
and St. Croix portages had been closed by the incessant

---

[39] George W. Featherstonhaugh, an English geologist, visiting the supposed site of
Fort L'Huillier in 1835, found no traces of a building nor of anything looking like copper ore,
and pronounced the story of the mine "a fable." See his *A Canoe Voyage up the Minnay
Sotor*, 1: 301–304 (London, 1847).   His map is on file in the bureau of Indian affairs at
Washington.   The late Professor Newton H. Winchell, state geologist of Minnesota, exploring in 1873, was obliged to leave the location and nature of Le Sueur's find in uncertainty.   He did not doubt the honesty of Le Sueur, but he discredited Le Sueur's knowledge
of copper ores.   See the Minnesota Geological and Natural History Survey, *Final Report*,
1: 17, 428, 435 (St. Paul, 1884–1901).   In 1904 Mr. Thomas Hughes of Mankato, after
repeated inspections, ascertained the location of the sites of the fort and the mine beyond
reasonable doubt.   The former was on an elevated bluff on the east bank of the Blue
Earth River just below the point where the Le Sueur River empties into it.   Early settlers
remember traces of an excavation thereon and a copious spring of water.   About two miles
up the Blue Earth Mr. Hughes came upon an outcrop of a stratum of bluish-green earth,
and he could find no similar deposit in the region.   See his "The Site of Le Sueur's Fort
L'Huillier," in *Minnesota Historical Collections*, 12: 283–285 (St. Paul, 1908).   There is an
important contribution in William H. Keating, *Narrative of an Expedition to the St. Peter's
River, Lake Winnepeek, Lake of the Woods, &c., Performed in the Year 1823, Under the Command of Stephen H. Long, U. S. T. E.*, 1: 329–331 (London, 1825), in which the author cites
La Harpe and refers to a manuscript in the library of the American Philosophical Society.

[40] *Nouvelle France*, 2: 237.   See also Kingsford, *Canada*, 2: 324–330.

warfare of the Sioux and Chippewa. Allouez's mission at
La Pointe, established in 1665, was abandoned six years
later, when the Sioux swept the Hurons and Ottawa eastward along the lake shore, Marquette with them.[41] The
devoted priest at once reëstablished himself on the Straits
of Mackinac, whither the mission and the military post at the
Sault de Ste. Marie were removed in 1689.[42] That removal
was made partly because of local Indian troubles, and
partly for the better protection of the Wisconsin and Illinois
trade; but still more to repel the English traders with their
cheap goods, who, in spite of Du Luth's fort at the foot of
Lake Huron, built in 1686, were swarming in the lower
peninsula of Michigan.[43] The Fox-Wisconsin road to the
upper Mississippi was always threatened and sometimes
closed by the hostile Foxes and their powerful allies, among
whom the indomitable Iroquois were numbered.[44] It had
become difficult and costly to protect the regular Indian
trade and the missions by maintaining garrisons and armed
parties. The regular traders had become discouraged by
the lawless competition of the *coureurs de bois,* by whose evil
influences the missionaries found their labors neutralized.
As reported by Charlevoix, these adventurers "ruined commerce, introduced frightful libertinage, made their nation

[41] *Jesuit Relations,* 55 : 171. See also Reuben G. Thwaites, "The Story of La Pointe,"
in his *How George Rogers Clark Won the Northwest and Other Essays in Western History,*
243–247 (Chicago, 1904).

[42] Edward D. Neill, "History of the Ojibways," in *Minnesota Historical Collections,*
5: 417 (St. Paul, 1885).

[43] Du Luth's post, Fort St. Joseph, was located on the site of the later Fort Gratiot.
See Denonville's letter to Du Luth, June 6, 1686, in Margry, *Découvertes,* 5: 23, translated
in *Wisconsin Historical Collections,* 16: 125; memoir addressed to Pontchartrain, in Margry,
Découvertes, 5: 186; Henry M. Utley and Byron M. Cutcheon, *Michigan as a Province,
Territory and State,* 1: 66 (New York, 1906); and Parkman, *Frontenac,* 133. Cadillac's fort
on the site of the present city of Detroit, Fort Pontchartrain, begun July 24, 1701, was
established for the same purpose as Du Luth's post. It marked the first attempt to found
a permanent colony west of Montreal. Margry, *Découvertes,* 5: 187–190; Parkman, *Half-
Century of Conflict,* 1: 22–28 (Frontenac edition, Boston, 1907); Clarence N. Burton, *The
Building of Detroit,* 7–9, 13 (second edition, Detroit, 1912).

[44] Thwaites, *France in America,* 97. For an explanation of the raids of the Iroquois
into the Ohio and Illinois countries see Alvord, *Illinois Country,* 84–92. They were no
doubt encouraged by the English, on whom they had become dependent for a market
for their furs.

despised, and placed unsurmountable obstacles to the progress of religion."[45] In vain both missionaries and traders invoked the protection of the French and Canadian governments.

The French king, advised of this state of things and of expected raids by the Iroquois, as early as 1696 decided to order the abandonment of all the western posts and to concentrate the Indian trade in Montreal. The French and Canadians in and around Mackinac were accordingly ordered to depart, and a few years later the garrison was withdrawn.[46] During the whole period of Queen Anne's War, 1702 to 1713, known in Europe as the War of the Spanish Succession, Canadian affairs, neglected by the home government, languished. Such neglect may have been due in part to the uncertainty that France could hold her Canadian and other transatlantic possessions. The treaty of Utrecht, however, resulted in the loss to France only of Newfoundland, Nova Scotia, and her claims to the territory about Hudson Bay.[47] In the spring of 1715 a garrison was sent to Mackinac, and not long afterwards the trade on Lake Superior was resumed.[48] In 1717 Du Luth's old fort on the Kaministiquia River was reoccupied.[49] Ten years more

---

[44] *Nouvelle France*, 1: 532, 533; 2: 161; 3: 89. See also *New York Colonial Documents*, 9: 140, 152; Kingsford, *Canada*, 1: 375; Parkman, *Old Régime*, 2: 109–115; Thwaites, *France in America*, 133; and Winsor, *America*, 4: 330.

[46] Charlevoix, *Nouvelle France*, 2: 161; *New York Colonial Documents*, 9: 637, 662, 663, 684, 695. A letter of Governor Calliéres to the Comte de Pontchartrain, October 16, 1700, indicates that the order to the French traders to leave Mackinac was not fully enforced. See *New York Colonial Documents*, 9: 712. See also a letter of the Jesuit Father Carheil, August 30, 1702, in Parkman, *Old Régime*, 2: 242–248. Intendant Bégon, in a memorial dated September 20, 1713, quoting Father Joseph Marest, Jesuit missionary at Mackinac from 1700 to 1714, says that the garrison at Mackinac was withdrawn after the establishment of the post at Detroit. *Wisconsin Historical Collections*, 16: 295.

[47] See George Chalmers, *A Collection of Treaties between Great Britain and other Powers*, 1: 340–390 (London, 1790), for the text of the treaty; sections 10–15, relating to the loss by France of territory in America, are on pages 378–382. See also James W. Gerard, *The Peace of Utrecht*, 284–286 (New York, 1885).

[48] *Wisconsin Historical Collections*, 16: 314. The Sieur de Lignery had been dispatched to Mackinac as commandant in 1712 by Governor Vaudreuil; from a letter of De Lignery's dated July 20, 1713, it is evident, however, that he was not accompanied by a detachment of soldiers. *New York Colonial Documents*, 9: 865; *Wisconsin Historical Collections*, 16: 295.

[49] Margry, *Découvertes*, 6: 504.

passed, however, before any organized attempt was made to establish trade on the upper Mississippi.

Charlevoix, the now well-known historian of New France, who was in Canada in 1720 and descended the Mississippi the following year, on his return to France strongly advised an establishment among the Sioux as a point of departure from which to push an exploring expedition to gain the shores of the Pacific Ocean.[50] His recommendation was so well thought of that in 1723 the French government authorized the establishment of the post and asked the Jesuits to detail two priests of their order as missionaries at the contemplated station.[51] The continued hostility of the Foxes and reports of the murder of Frenchmen by the Sioux and, perhaps, other considerations delayed from year to year the carrying-out of the project. At length on June 16, 1727, an expedition in command of Réné Boucher, sieur de la Perrière, a Canadian officer who had served in the raids on the New England villages in 1708,[52] left Montreal. The two Jesuit fathers selected to accompany the expedition as missionaries were Michel Guignas and Nicolas de Gonnor, and it is from writings of the former that our slight knowledge of the expedition is derived.[53] Traveling by the Green

[50] See the official report of Charlevoix to the Comte de Toulouse, January 20, 1723, and his letters to officials of the French government, in Margry, *Découvertes*, 6: 521–538. Charlevoix published in 1744, as volume 3 of his *Nouvelle France*, a *Journal d'un voyage fait par ordre du roi dans l'Amérique Septentrionale*. This is a narrative of his travels during the years 1720–23, written in the form of letters. An English version of the journal in two volumes was issued in London in 1761. The Sieur Pachot, who was for a time interpreter of the Huron language at Detroit, in a letter to the French government, October 27, 1722, had also recommended an establishment among the Sioux of the St. Croix region, preferably near the Falls of St. Anthony. Margry, *Découvertes*, 6: 513–517.

[51] *Wisconsin Historical Collections*, 16: 427, 441; 17: 4, 7–9; Margry, *Découvertes*, 6: 541–543.

[52] Thomas Hutchinson, *The History of Massachusetts, 1628–1750*, 2: 156–158 (third edition, Boston, 1795); Elihu Hoyt, *Antiquarian Researches, Comprising a History of Indian Wars*, 198 (Greenfield, Massachusetts, 1824); Neill, *Minnesota*, 183.

[53] For an extract from a letter written by Guignas to Beauharnois, May 29, 1728, see Margry, *Découvertes*, 6: 552–558; it is translated in *Wisconsin Historical Collections*, 17: 22–28, and in Shea, *Early Voyages*, 167–175, under the title "Guignas's Voyage up the Mississippi." A letter of Beauharnois, April 30, 1727, transmits a request of the Jesuit missionaries for astronomical and surveying instruments, an example of the conceded enthusiasm of that society in scientific pursuits. The list embraced a case of mathematical instruments, a universal astronomic quadrant, a graduated semicircle with its support, a spirit level, a chain

Bay route, unmolested by the Foxes, who were temporarily quiet after a severe punishment by the French, La Perrière and his party reached Lake Pepin on the seventeenth of September and at noon made their landing on the west bank about two miles from the site of the railroad station of Frontenac, Minnesota.

A substantial fort was erected, consisting of a stockade one hundred feet square of tree trunks set on end twelve feet out of ground, "with two good bastions," each of which gave a flank fire on two sides of the work. Within were three log buildings, all sixteen feet wide, one thirty feet long, another thirty-eight, the third twenty-five. Upon the completion of the work the garrison celebrated in November the birthday of Beauharnois, the governor of Canada, whose name was given to the post.[54] It is interesting to note that the first Christian mission on Minnesota soil was established at Fort Beauharnois by the priests mentioned. They called it "The Mission of St. Michael the Archangel." The mission, as well as the military establishment, however, was short lived.[55] The plan of starting an expedition from this base to the western ocean was not prosecuted. The Sioux were found inhospitable, and the Foxes often closed the homeward road. Game was found unexpectedly scarce, and the French were too much occupied with gathering peltries to clear and cultivate land. After some ten years of

and pins, and a telescope six or seven feet long. Margry, *Découvertes*, 6: 544; *Wisconsin Historical Collections*, 17: 9.

[54] The priest Guignas gives a piquant account of the effect of some skyrockets discharged by the French. "Quand ces pauvres gens virent ces feux d'artifice en l'air et les étoiles tomber du ciel, femmes et enfans de s'enfuir; et les plus courageux d'entre ces hommes de crier merci et demander très instamment qu'on fît cesser le jeu surprenant de cette terrible médecine." Margry, *Découvertes*, 6: 558.

[55] Neill, *Minnesota*, 183; Parkman, *Half-Century of Conflict*, 2: 7. De Gonnor returned to Montreal in the following summer with La Perrière, who left the post in charge of his nephew, Pierre Boucher, sieur de Boucherville. See *Wisconsin Historical Collections*, 17: 30. The continued hostility of the Foxes and the scarcity of provisions led the commandant with eleven other members of the garrison, including Father Guignas, to leave Fort Beauharnois. On October 3, 1728, they began the descent of the Mississippi, planning to reach Montreal by way of the Illinois River. De Boucherville's account of their experiences, which included several months' captivity among the Kickapoo, was published by Michel Bibaud in volume 3 of *La Bibliothèque Canadienne* (Montreal, 1826); it is translated in *Wisconsin Historical Collections*, 17: 36–57.

desultory occupation the project of maintaining an establishment among the Sioux was abandoned.[56]

There remains to be mentioned one other and the last effort of the French to extend exploration and dominion, if not settlement, to the west of the Great Lakes, and to gain the shores of the ocean which converging traditions located in the sunset land. Pierre Gaultier de Varennes, sieur de la Vérendrye, was a native of Canada.[57] He entered the military service, went to France in 1707, became a member of a Brittany regiment, and fought with distinction at the battle of Malplaquet, September 11, 1709. He returned soon afterwards to Canada and later proceeded to the Lake Superior country, where he was in command of the post at

[56] Edward D. Neill, *The Last French Post in the Valley of the Upper Mississippi near Frontenac, Minn., with Notices of Its Commandants* (St. Paul, 1887); the same material appears in the *Magazine of Western History*, 7:17–29 (November, 1887). See also the documents in Margry, *Découvertes*, 6: 559–580, and in *Wisconsin Historical Collections*, 17: 64–274, and "Remains of a French Post near Trempealeau," in Wisconsin Historical Society, *Proceedings*, 1915, pp. 120–123. The exact location of the site of this original Fort Beauharnois has not yet been clearly identified. Guignas places it "about the middle of the Northern [*western*] shore upon a low point." See *Wisconsin Historical Collections*, 16: 25. Pike says that "the French . . . built a stockade on Lake Pepin on the W. shore, just below Point de Sable." See Zebulon M. Pike, *Expeditions to Headwaters of the Mississippi River, through Louisiana Territory, and in New Spain, during the Years 1805-6-7*, 1: 308 (Coues edition, New York, 1895). The location was not a suitable one, since it was likely to be inundated during periods of high water. When Réné Godefroy, sieur de Linctot, was dispatched in 1731 to reëstablish the post, he erected the new fort and mission on higher ground near the old site. A short distance from the point near the mouth of what Nicollet calls "Sandy Point R.," now Wells Creek, in Florence Township, Goodhue County, Neill notes that there is "an elevated plateau," and adds that "there is evidence that there has been long ago a clearing made there, and as it is the most suitable spot in the vicinity . . . it was probably the site of a French post." See his *Last French Post*, 21. At the present time this site is occupied by the Ursuline Convent and Academy of Villa Maria of Frontenac. "The convent chapel very properly bears the name of its historic predecessor, St. Michael, the Archangel." See Ambrose McNulty, *The Diocese of St. Paul: The Golden Jubilee, 1851-1901*, 20 (St. Paul, 1902), and Francis J. Schaefer, "Fort Beauharnois, near Frontenac, Minn.," in *Acta et Dicta*, 2: 111–113 (July, 1909). In the early years of the eighteenth century the French were more interested in extending explorations and settlements in the lower than in the upper Mississippi Valley. See Alvord, *Illinois Country*, ch. 7.

[57] Some three hundred pages of volume 7 of the *South Dakota Historical Collections* (Pierre, 1914) are devoted to La Vérendrye and his sons. The principal article, "The Verendrye Explorations and Discoveries" (pp. 99–322), is by Charles E. De Land, president of the South Dakota Historical Society from 1910 to 1913; and Doane Robinson, secretary of the society and editor of the *Collections*, gives on pages 94–98 a convenient "Verendrye Calendar" and later certain footnotes indicative of dissent from De Land's conclusions. See also the documents in Margry, *Découvertes*, 6: 583–632; Neill, *Minnesota*, 855–863; Parkman, *Half-Century of Conflict*, 2: 8–42; and Lawrence J. Burpee, *Pathfinders of the Great Plains: A Chronicle of La Vérendrye and His Sons* (*Chronicles of Canada*, vol. 10 — Toronto, 1915).

Lake Nipigon, north of Lake Superior, from 1727 to 1730. Here he speculated on the problem, still unsolved, of gaining the Pacific. Natives assured him that there was an almost unbroken waterway thither. One of them, Ochagach by name, made for him a rough map, said to be still in existence.[58]

The Canadian governor was so impressed with the intelligence and enthusiasm of this officer that he strongly urged the French king to lend his aid in the fitting-out of an expedition. The king, however, went no further than to authorize La Vérendrye to embark on the venture at his own expense, granting him a monopoly of the fur trade in the territory to be explored. With a company of some fifty men La Vérendrye left Montreal on June 8, 1731, accompanied by three of his four sons and his nephew, La Jemeraye. The party proceeded to the mouth of the Pigeon River, whence a detachment under La Jemeraye pushed on along the chain of lakes and rivers which later became part of the boundary between the United States and Canada until, toward the close of the year, it reached the foot of Rainy Lake. Fort St. Pierre was built there on the north bank during the ensuing winter. The main body under La Vérendrye resumed its journey westward in June, 1732, and arrived in early fall at the Lake of the Woods, where, on the southern shore of the Northwest Angle Inlet, about two miles west of American Point, was erected Fort St. Charles. The occupation of this post on Minnesota soil during a period of twenty years may perhaps justify the mention of the La Vérendrye explorations in this chapter.[59]

---

[58] For a reduced facsimile, see Neill, *Minnesota*, 800; or *Wisconsin Historical Collections*, 17: 102. This map may have suggested the "Long Lake" which later figured in the controversy regarding the northern boundary of Minnesota.

[59] The location of Fort St. Charles was identified beyond doubt in August, 1908, by an exploring party of professors from St. Joseph's College at St. Boniface, Manitoba. See Francis J. Schaefer, "Fort St. Charles," in *Acta et Dicta*, 2: 114–133 (July, 1909), and maps between pages 240 and 241 (July, 1910). See also Elliott Coues, *New Light on the Early History of the Greater Northwest*, 23, n. 28. Coues states that Fort St. Charles was abandoned before 1763. The "Memoir of Bougainville, 1757," translated in *Wisconsin Historical Collections*, 18: 185, indicates that the fort was occupied at the time it was written

The extensive wanderings of La Vérendrye and his sons for twelve years in regions remote from Minnesota need not here be followed in detail. It may be noted, however, that in 1742 a small party under the command of the son of La Vérendrye known as the Chevalier set out from La Reine at the forks of the Assiniboine River to explore the regions beyond the Missouri River and, if possible, to reach the western ocean.[60] The main directions of the march are obvious, but there is much dispute as to the ultimate point reached — the "mountains, very high and well-wooded," where the Chevalier was obliged to end his westward march owing to the hostility of the Snake Indians.[61] Thus culminated two centuries of French effort to reach the great ocean beyond which should lie Cathay.

Neither the Canadian government nor that of France had much money or many men to spare for the settling of the upper Mississippi Valley. The expeditions of Le Sueur, Perrot, and the few others resulted in nothing more permanent than trading posts and mission stations, all of which

[60] See "Journal du voyage fait par le Chevalier de La Verendrye," in Margry, *Découvertes*, 6: 598–611, translated in *South Dakota Historical Collections*, 7: 349–358. For a controversy concerning the identity of the son of the Sieur de la Vérendrye known as the Chevalier, participated in by Auguste H. de Trémaudan, L'abbé Ivanhoe Caron, and Pierre-Georges Roy, see *Le Canada Français*, 2: 109–117, 170–182; 3: 286–293, 294–295. The arguments of Trémaudan are also presented in English in the *Manitoba Free Press* for April 10, 1920.

[61] Parkman, in his *Half-Century of Conflict*, 2: 29, places it in sight of the Big Horn Range of the Rocky Mountains, 120 miles east of Yellowstone Park. See also Burpee, *Pathfinders of the Great Plains*, 83–85, and Justin Winsor, *The Mississippi Basin: The Struggle in America between England and France, 1697–1763*, 202 (Boston, 1895). Robinson and De Land dissent from this view, and think it unlikely that the Chevalier went farther west than the Black Hills. De Land's careful and exhaustive analysis of the theories advanced as to the explorer's route is found in *South Dakota Historical Collections*, 7: 201–260. Further discussion of the disputed points is to be found in Orin G. Libby, "Some Verendrye Enigmas," and Robinson, De Land, and Libby, "Additional Verendrye Material," in the *Mississippi Valley Historical Review*, 3: 143–160, 368–399 (September and December, 1916). On February 16, 1913, one of a party of children at play on a hillside in Fort Pierre, South Dakota, picked up a piece of metal with inscriptions on its two sides. The South Dakota investigators have identified it as a leaden plate deposited there on March 30, 1743, by the last of La Vérendrye's parties returning from the West. The journal of the trip mentions the leaving of such a memorial. See Margry, *Découvertes*, 6: 609. Its discovery determines a point of the return journey. See *South Dakota Historical Collections*, 7: 100, 101, 375, for photographs of the plate and for the inscriptions. Libby questions whether it can be assumed with any degree of certainty that the plate was deposited by La Vérendrye in the spot where it was unearthed. *Mississippi Valley Historical Review*, 3: 155.

had disappeared by the middle of the eighteenth century. It is probable that independent traders continued to thread the streams of this region with their canoe loads of merchandise and to gather the beautiful peltries, nowhere more abundant. The French planted no colony on Minnesota soil. If they were indifferent about the establishment of permanent settlements on the upper Mississippi in the eighteenth century, it may have been because they had more important interests elsewhere to safeguard. It was the ambition of the Canadian governors to hold the Great Lakes, which they regarded as French waters, and to keep the English out of the Ohio Valley, to which, they contended, the proclamation of La Salle had given France good title. Early in the century they had strung a line of posts along the south shores of Lake Ontario and Lake Erie, and had erected a permanent fortification at Detroit to cover the upper lakes. The English based their claim to the "Ohio rectangle" chiefly on alleged conveyances from the Iroquois, who had pushed their forays to the Mississippi.[62] Neither party had much respect for the pretended title of the other, and the controversy, long debated in cabinet councils, came, as it must have come, to the arbitrament of the battle field. The French took the initiative by sending an armed expedition down the Ohio in 1749.[63] Four years later a second expedition was sent out and forts were established at Presqu' Isle, on French Creek, and at the mouth of the Allegheny. These activities of the French awoke the British government to action. In 1755 the unfortunate Braddock was sent

---

[62] This transfer of title was effected by the famous treaty of Lancaster in 1744. See Winsor, *America*, 5: 245, 487, 564–566, 611, and authorities there cited, and Thwaites, *France in America*, 150. A detailed report of the Lancaster council is in *Pennsylvania Colonial Records*, 4: 698–737 (Harrisburg, 1851).

[63] This expedition was under the command of Céloron de Bienville, whose "Journal de la campagne" is in Margry, *Découvertes*, 6: 666–726. Extracts from this journal are included in Orsamus O. Marshall, *Historical Writings*, 237–273 (*Munsell's Historical Series*, no. 15 — Albany, 1887). See also Francis Parkman, *Montcalm and Wolfe*, 1: 40–56 (Frontenac edition, Boston, 1906), and Kingsford, *Canada*, 3: 396–408. The expedition accomplished little else than to bring home to the French how slight a hold they had on the Ohio Valley; the Indian tribes of this region were friendly to the English and were not inclined to enter into relations with the French.

over, and the French and Indian War opened. The tedious and wavering course of this contest cannot here be traced. Montcalm triumphed at Ticonderoga in the summer of 1758 and doubtless felt sure that the Canadian front could not be broken. The capture of Fort Frontenac, near the foot of Lake Ontario, late in August of the same year, by a small army of "provincials," cutting off communication and supplies from Fort Duquesne, compelled the French to abandon that strategic post before the end of the year. A year later Quebec was assaulted by the heroic Wolfe, who survived only long enough to hear the shout of victory from his exulting troops. On September 8, 1760, Montreal was surrendered to the British-American forces, and thus closed the French and Indian War in America.[64] During the next two years the French garrisons were replaced at Detroit and Mackinac and generally throughout the Great Lakes region.[65] The English were now in military possession of all Canada.[66]

Whether such military possession should ripen into political dominion was dependent on the outcome of a great European war, that Seven Years' War in which Frederick the Great, backed by England and certain petty continental states, with a force of two hundred thousand men contended against most of western Europe with armies aggregating seven hundred thousand. The result is well known. The Prussian monarch held his own, and the coalition, wearied at length of the undecisive contest, went to pieces. France had to settle not only with Frederick the Great but with England, and in a separate treaty, concluded at Paris on February 10, 1763, accepted such terms as her ancient enemy chose to exact. The part of the treaty important for the present history is that by which the French ceded to the

[64] See Parkman, *Montcalm and Wolfe*, in three volumes, and Kingsford, *Canada*, 3: 445–568; 4: 1–433, for detailed accounts of the war.

[65] See documents in *Wisconsin Historical Collections*, 18: 221–249.

[66] For the Articles of Capitulation of Montreal, September 8, 1760, see Adam Shortt and Arthur G. Doughty, eds., *Documents Relating to the Constitutional History of Canada, 1759–1791*, 8–28 (Canadian Archives, *Reports*, 1907).

English all their possessions on the continent of North America east of the Mississippi River, except the island on which New Orleans is situated.[67] Doubtless the English would have taken over all the former French possessions west of the Mississippi had not the French government taken the precaution the year before to cede them by a secret treaty to Spain.[68] While the treaty of Paris was pending, the question was much debated in the British ministry whether Canada should be retained or France stripped of her rich West Indian possessions. The former policy was advocated by Benjamin Franklin in a pamphlet published in 1760. It has been conjectured that this writing influenced the decision.[69]

[67] For the text of the treaty of Paris, February 10, 1763, see Chalmers, *Treaties*, 1: 467–494, or Shortt and Doughty, *Constitutional History of Canada*, 84–90. Sections 4–7 relate to the cession of French territory in America to England. For an excellent account of the negotiations see Clarence W. Alvord, *The Mississippi Valley in British Politics: A Study of the Trade, Land Speculation, and Experiments in Imperialism Culminating in the American Revolution*, 1: ch. 2 (Cleveland, 1917).

[68] For a translation of the text of the act of session of Fontainebleau, November 3, 1762, see United States Congress, *Register of Debates*, vol. 13, part 2, appendix, p. 226.

[69] The pamphlet, entitled *The Interest of Great Britain Considered with Regard to Her Colonies and the Acquisitions of Canada and Guadaloupe to Which are Added Observations Concerning the Increase of Mankind, Peopling of Countries, &c.* (London, 1760), is reprinted in Franklin, *Writings*, 4: 32–82 (Smyth edition, New York and London, 1905–07). While Franklin had a share in the production of this pamphlet, the greater part of it was written by Richard Jackson. Alvord, *Mississippi Valley in British Politics*, 1: 57; 2: 258; Franklin, *Writings*, 1: 138.

III. THE BRITISH DOMINATION

THE British garrisons sent to the West after the surrender of Montreal received no friendly receptions from the Indians. That at Detroit was shut up for months by Pontiac and his warriors in their heroic attempt to recover their ancient hunting grounds. The Chippewa surprised the little band holding the fort on the south side of the Straits of Mackinac and murdered a lieutenant and twenty men. The detachment left at Green Bay was frightened away.[1] The competition of the French traders from the lower Mississippi was so keen that the British for a long time made no attempt to establish trading or military posts west of Mackinac. Doubtless the bushranger might have been seen in many Chippewa and Sioux villages within the boundaries of Minnesota. In some instances it was found, on the reappearance of the white men, that the Indians had resumed their garments of skins and furs, and had returned to their old ways of life.

During the British domination over Minnesota East no attempt at new settlement was made. One enterprise in the way of exploration, that of Jonathan Carver, has obtained greater notoriety than it deserves. Carver was born in Weymouth, Massachusetts, in 1710 but was raised in Canterbury, Connecticut. Since his father was a man of wealth and of prominence in the community, it may be assumed that the son had the best opportunities the town afforded.[2] In 1755 he enlisted for military service in

[1] Francis Parkman, *The Conspiracy of Pontiac and the Indian War after the Conquest of Canada*, 1: 179–381; 2: 115–124, 366 (Frontenac edition, Boston, 1907). Two valuable contemporary accounts are Robert Rogers, *Diary of the Siege of Detroit in the War with Pontiac; also a Narrative of the Principal Events of the Siege* (Munsell's Historical Series, no. 4 — Albany, 1860), and *Journal of Pontiac's Conspiracy, 1763*, published by Clarence M. Burton (Detroit, 1912). See also *Wisconsin Historical Collections*, 18: 223–269.

[2] William Browning, "The Early History of Jonathan Carver," in the *Wisconsin Magazine of History*, 3: 291 (March, 1920).

Massachusetts for the expedition against Crown Point, and he served throughout the ensuing campaigns of the French and Indian War with some distinction, rising to the rank of captain.[3] Carver's account of the inception of his idea of engaging in western exploration is as follows: "No sooner was the late War with France concluded, and Peace established . . . in the Year 1763, than I began to consider . . . how I might continue still serviceable. . . . It appeared to me indispensably needful, that Government should be acquainted in the first place with the true state of the dominions they were now become possessed of. To this purpose, I determined, as the next proof of my zeal, to explore the most unknown parts of them."[4] It was not until the month of June, 1766, however, that he was able to carry out his plans. He set out from Boston, making his way by the usual lake route to Mackinac; "this being," as he says, "the uttermost of our factories towards the north-west, I considered it as the most convenient place from whence I could begin my intended progress, and enter at once into the Regions I designed to explore."[5] At

[3] The biographic sketch by Dr. John Lettsom entitled "Some Account of Captain J. Carver," prefixed to the third London edition (1781) of the *Travels* (see *post*, p. 58), which was formerly relied on for the principal facts of his early life, is not at the present time regarded as entirely trustworthy. See Reuben G. Thwaites, in *Wisconsin Historical Collections*, 18: 280, n. 98; Edward G. Bourne, "The Travels of Jonathan Carver," in the *American Historical Review*, 11: 287–290 (January, 1906); and John T. Lee, "A Bibliography of Carver's Travels," in Wisconsin Historical Society, *Proceedings*, 1909, p. 147. A careful search through the Massachusetts archives has, however, furnished substantial evidence that the generally accepted facts in regard to Carver's military career are correct. See Lee, "Captain Jonathan Carver: Additional Data," in Wisconsin Historical Society, *Proceedings*, 1912, pp. 89–94, 107–109. A certificate of Carver's character signed by General Page is on page 113. The latest word on Carver, published just as this book goes to press, is Milo M. Quaife, "Jonathan Carver and the Carver Grant," in the *Mississippi Valley Historical Review*, 7: 3–25 (June, 1920). This is based in part on hitherto unused manuscript material recently acquired by the State Historical Society of Wisconsin.

[4] *Travels*, i (London, 1778). Quoting an item from the *Boston Chronicle* of August 8, 1768, in which mention is made of a letter from Carver printed in a previous issue, "communicated to us by a gentleman of distinction in this province," Lee remarks that "the *true* reason for Carver undertaking his westward journey may never be known; but if we knew who this 'gentleman of distinction' was, we might have a clue." See Wisconsin Historical Society, *Proceedings*, 1909, p. 152. Quaife, in the *Mississippi Valley Historical Review*, 7: 8, asserts that Major Robert Rogers was the "real father" of Carver's project. See also Allan Nevins, "The Life of Robert Rogers," in Rogers, *Ponteach; or the Savages of America, a Tragedy*, 119–123 (Chicago, Caxton Club, 1914).

[5] *Travels*, 17.

Mackinac he found that versatile New Hampshire gentleman, Major Robert Rogers, in command. Whether Carver had known Major Rogers previously is not a matter of record. Both had been in service in the Lake Champlain region during the late war. An acquaintanceship between the two is not unlikely. Be that as it may, Carver received from the commandant an appointment to make "discoveries and surveys of ye interior parts of North America, expecially to ye West and North west of that Garrison [*Mackinac*]," for which service he was to be allowed eight shillings a day "together with other incidental Charges."[6] In the absence of any evidence to the contrary, it must be assumed that Carver was unaware that Rogers was exceeding his authority in granting the commission and that he accepted the appointment in good faith.

Furnished with a credit on some French and English traders for goods which served as currency among the Indians, Carver departed from Mackinac in the beginning of September, traveled by way of Green Bay, Prairie du Chien, and the Mississippi, and found himself on the seventeenth of November at the Falls of St. Anthony. He describes the falls with reasonable accuracy and records his pleasing impression of their charming surroundings.[7] After a

---

[6] "Report to the Lords of the Committee of Council for Plantation Affairs on the Petition of Captain Jonathan Carver, July 10, 1769," in Wisconsin Historical Society, *Proceedings*, 1912, pp. 110–112. Failing to receive from Major Rogers or from his superior officer, General Gage, the compensation agreed upon, Carver presented a petition to the English government asking for payment for the services which he had rendered in the way of exploration. Although the committee was of the opinion that legally Carver had no claim against the government, since he had undertaken a commission for Major Rogers which "that officer was by no means authorized to grant," it, however, regarded the case as one "of compassion," and as such submitted it to their "Lordships to act thereupon, either for his Relief, or otherwise as . . . shall seem meet." No suspicion of complicity in the treasonable intrigues of Major Rogers seems to have attached to Carver.

[7] "This amazing body of waters, which are above 250 yards over, form a most pleasing cataract; they fall perpendicularly about thirty feet, and the rapids below, in the space of 300 yards more, render the descent considerably greater; so that when viewed at a distance they appear to be much higher than they really are. . . . In the middle of the Falls stands a small island, about forty feet broad and somewhat longer, on which grow a few cragged hemlock and spruce trees. . . . The country around them [*the falls*] is extremely beautiful. It is not an uninterrupted plain where the eye finds no relief, but composed of many gentle ascents, which in the summer are covered with the finest verdure, and interspersed with little groves, that give a pleasing variety to the prospect. On the whole . . . a more pleas-

short excursion on foot up the Mississippi he returned to the mouth of the Minnesota.[8] In his canoe, which had been left there "on account of ice," he ascended this river, as he says, two hundred miles.[9] His rough estimate of the distance covered, like those of other early explorers, may be cut in two.[10] He found himself at the end of his journey on December 7 in the country of the Sioux of the Plains, who received him in a friendly way, and with whom he passed the winter. He claims to have learned their language perfectly in seven months, a statement which, like the foregoing, may be considerably discounted. If he learned the name "Dakota," by which those Indians called themselves, he did not note it in his journal.[11] In April, 1767, he went down the Minnesota with a large party of the Sioux, who were carrying their

---

ing and picturesque view cannot, I believe, be found throughout the universe." *Travels*, 69. Carver's drawing of the falls, facing page 70, is probably the first that appeared in print.

[8] *Travels*, 71. He claims to have reached the River St. Francis, now Elk River, "near sixty miles above the Falls." The record of the excursion is meager.

[9] Only eight days had intervened since the abandonment of the canoe, yet Carver apparently found no difficulty in navigating the Minnesota, which he describes as being "clear of ice by nature of its western situation." See his *Travels*, 66, 74. These statements arouse inquiry by any one acquainted with the local climate. In an extraordinarily open season both rivers might be free of ice late in November, but it would be the comparatively sluggish Minnesota which would be the first to close.

[10] *Travels*, 75. On the map entitled "A Plan of Captain Carvers Travels in the interior Parts of North America in 1766 and 1767," facing page 17 of the *Travels*, the "utmost extent" of his exploration of the Minnesota is indicated by a group of three Indian tepees on the north side at a point which Upham places "nearly opposite to the site of New Ulm." See *Minnesota in Three Centuries*, 1: 290. What opinion Carver's contemporaries held as to the extent of his explorations may be learned from the journal of Peter Pond. Pond, who was a native of Connecticut, and who was on the Minnesota about eight or nine years after Carver visited it, says: "As we Past up St Peters River about fourteen miles We Stopt to Sea Carvers Hut whare he Past his Winter when in that Countrey. . . . This was the Extent of his travels. His Hole toure I with One Canoe Well maned Could make in Six weeks." See *Wisconsin Historical Collections*, 18: 340. Keating, in his *Narrative*, 1: 336, ventures the opinion that Carver "professes too much." He thought that the journey probably extended as far as the Falls of St. Anthony and that Carver saw the St. Peter's River and may have entered it but did not believe that he spent five months in the country of the Sioux.

Carver reports the Minnesota as about a hundred yards wide all the way he sailed upon it. He was charmed by the delightful country watered by it. Although it was the beginning of winter, he relates that "every part is filled with trees bending under their loads of fruits, such as plums, grapes, and apples; the meadows are covered with hops, and many sorts of vegetables; whilst the ground is stored with useful roots, with angelica, spikenard, and ground-nuts as large as hens eggs." In a similar manner is described the region bordering Lake Pepin. *Travels*, 55, 100.

[11] "A Short Vocabulary of the Naudowessie Language," included in the *Travels*, 433-438, is the earliest printed vocabulary of the Siouan tongue, according to the well-

dead to be deposited in their cemetery at St. Paul, near the cave which to this day bears Carver's name.[12] He describes the funeral rites which took place and reports the oration of the chief speaker.[13] In a council held at the cave Carver claims to have exercised his gift of oratory in the Dakota tongue and he records his speech in English. It is in the proper traditional form of an address to Indians. Its purpose was to impress the audience with a due respect for and awe of the English and with the dignity of the orator.

The explorer met with a disappointment in not receiving a consignment of goods which, as he alleges, Major Rogers had undertaken to forward from Mackinac to the Falls of St. Anthony. He hastened down to Prairie du Chien, then an important neutral trading mart for many tribes, where he got no tidings of the expected merchandise. Still eager to

known ethnologist, James C. Pilling, in his *Bibliography of the Siouan Languages*, iv (Bureau of American Ethnology, *Bulletins*, no. 5 — Washington, 1887). A "dictionary of the Naudowessie language," fuller than that printed in the *Travels*, is among the Carver papers in the British Museum. Lee, in Wisconsin Historical Society, *Proceedings*, 1912, pp. 102, 120.

[12] Carver explored this cave on his outward journey. See his *Travels*, 63. Early settlers in St. Paul were familiar with the cave, as a resort of boys and tramps. On May 1, 1867, the Minnesota Historical Society celebrated the centenary of Carver's council with the Indians by a trip to the cave in the afternoon and a reunion in the rooms of the society in the evening. An account of the celebration published as a pamphlet with the title *The Carver Centenary* (St. Paul, 1867) is reprinted in *Minnesota Historical Collections*, 2: 257–284 (St. Paul, 1889). About 1869 a railroad cutting took a slice off the overhanging (Dayton's) bluff and falling débris so covered the entrance that the cave was lost from sight. In the winter of 1913 the Dayton's Bluff Commercial Club and the Mounds Park Association became interested in locating the historic cavern. John W. Armstrong, county surveyor, aided by old survey notes preserved by him, ascertained the approximate location of the entrance. It was not till about the middle of November of the same year that the débris was removed and the imprisoned waters were drained out. On November 16 two thousand persons visited the spot. The writer saw it on November 20 and decided that Beltrami's calculation of a depth of a mile was somewhat exaggerated. See Giacomo C. Beltrami, *A Pilgrimage in Europe and America*, 2: 191 (London, 1828); " Capt. Jonathan Carver, and His Explorations," in *Minnesota Historical Collections*, 1: 355, n.; and *St. Paul Pioneer Press*, January 8, November 12, 13, 17, 21, 1913. In the *Pioneer Press* for January 31, 1867, there is a letter signed "F." (probably Dr. Thomas Foster), describing the cave after a recent exploration. T. M. Newson, in his *Pen Pictures of St. Paul, Minnesota, and Biographical Sketches of Old Settlers*, 5 (St. Paul, 1886), in describing the cave, says, "Its capacious chamber is filled with beer barrels."

[13] This recital, coming under the eye of the German poet Schiller, was made by him the burden of his "Song of the Nadowessee Chief," pronounced by his contemporary Goethe to be one of his finest compositions. Sir Edward Bulwer-Lytton and Sir John Herschel both made metrical translations of the poem. The original "Nadowessissche Totenklange" may be read in any complete edition of Schiller's poems, and the translations are quoted by Neill, in his *Minnesota*, 89.

prosecute his journey, he resolved to make his way to the Grand Portage near the mouth of the Pigeon River, hoping to obtain from traders there the goods necessary to further progress on the journey he had planned.[14] He reached that rendezvous late in July only to be disappointed the second time; the traders there could furnish no goods. As further travel to the west was impossible without supplies, he abandoned his enterprise and headed his canoe toward the Sault de Ste. Marie, following the north shore of Lake Superior. From that point he proceeded to Mackinac, where he arrived in the beginning of November, 1767. Here he was obliged to tarry until the following June "on account of ice." He says that he passed these months very agreeably and that one of his "chief amusements was that of fishing for trouts." He makes no allusion to Major Rogers.

In the summer or fall of 1768 Carver returned to Boston.[15] Leaving a wife and seven children behind him, he proceeded after a short delay to England, where he endeavored to interest the government in his explorations and projects. The Lords of Trade were not disposed to publish the reports he offered, but accorded him some gratuity.[16] They did not interfere with the publication in London in 1778, on his own account, of his journal and observations. His *Travels through the Interior Parts of North-America, in the Years*

---

[14] *Travels*, 92, 93, 99, 102. Carver journeyed to Lake Superior by way of the Chippewa and St. Croix rivers and an intervening portage. His plan at the time was to pursue his journey from Grand Portage by way of Rainy Lake, Lake of the Woods, and Lake Winnepeg "to the Heads of the river of the West, which . . . falls into the straits of Annian," his intended destination. *Travels*, xi.

[15] In his *Travels*, 177, Carver gives October as the month of his arrival. From an item in the *Boston Chronicle* of August 8, it appears that he arrived in Philadelphia July 24. Lee, referring to this issue of the *Chronicle*, states that Carver returned to Boston in August. In an advertisement in the *Chronicle*, September 12, 1768, Carver "offered proposals" for the publication of his "Travels" and asked for subscriptions. Apparently he did not, however, succeed at that time in getting money enough to publish the journal. Wisconsin Historical Society, *Proceedings*, 1909, pp. 143–155.

[16] In a memorial of February 10, 1773, Carver states that he was granted "a Sum of Money on his giving up his Journals Draughts and plans . . . tho the sum Received was but a little more than Equivolent to the Expences he was at." According to a schedule submitted with his memorial of June 7, 1770, his expenses were estimated at £1,129 15s. 3d. See Wisconsin Historical Society, *Proceedings*, 1912, pp. 116, 118. See also Carver, *Travels*, xiii.

1766, 1767, and 1768 has ever since been a much-read book. It was soon translated into German, French, and Dutch, and English editions have been multiplied.[17] The first part, 180 pages, contains Carver's introduction and journal; the second part, nearly twice as voluminous, is devoted to the "origin, manners, customs, religion, and language of the Indians." That the second part was largely plagiarized from previous writers, Charlevoix and Lahontan in particular, has been proved beyond doubt. In regard to the first part, critics assert that Carver was incapable of such composition and that it was written by a certain Dr. Lettsom, who became his friend in his adversity. Others, to the contrary, contend that Carver was qualified for the task and probably performed it. There is no occasion in this place to enter into the controversy. It is not denied by any that the story is Carver's, whether he himself put it on paper or not. The book added but little to existing information, but it popularized widely what already was known of the upper Mississippi region.[18] It need not be doubted that Carver performed the journey described, or the greater part of it. It should be remembered to his credit that this journey was but preliminary to the greater undertaking he had planned, that of crossing the "Shining"

[17] For an elaborate bibliography of the *Travels*, compiled by John T. Lee, see Wisconsin Historical Society, *Proceedings*, 1909, pp. 155-183; 1912, pp. 121-123. Copies of the original edition (London, 1778) are to be found in the libraries of the University of Minnesota and the Minnesota Historical Society. The third edition (London, 1781), containing a biographical sketch of Carver, is the one best known. For a convenient résumé see John G. Gregory, *Jonathan Carver, His Travels in the Northwest in 1766-8* (Parkman Club, *Publications*, no. 5 — Milwaukee, 1896).

[18] Perhaps the judgment of Peter Pond, as recorded in his "Journal," in *Wisconsin Historical Collections*, 18: 334, fits the case. "He Gave a Good a Count of the Small Part of the Western Countrey he saw But when he a Leudes to Hearsase he flies from facts in two Maney Instances." It may be suggested that Carver's account of his journey is not properly a journal, but is rather a narrative, which might have been written up from memory. It contains no day-to-day entries. The reader who desires to follow up the controversy may consult Coues, in his edition of Pike, *Expeditions*, 1: 59, n. 60; Bourne, in the *American Historical Review*, 11: 287-302; Daniel S. Durrie, "Captain Jonathan Carver and 'Carver's Grant,' " in *Wisconsin Historical Collections*, 6: 224, n. (Madison, 1908); Lee, in Wisconsin Historical Society, *Proceedings*, 1909, pp. 143-155; 1912, pp. 87-123; Clarence W. Alvord, "Travels of Captain Jonathan Carver," in the *Nation*, 97: 184 (August 28, 1913); and Milo M. Quaife, "Critical Evaluation of the Sources for Western History," in the *Mississippi Valley Historical Review*, 1: 169-175 (September, 1914).

or Rocky Mountains and descending to the shores of the then unknown ocean separating Asia from America.

On reaching England Carver at once set about the formation of a company to send an overland expedition to the Pacific. His plan was to build a fort on Lake Pepin as a base of supplies, to ascend the Minnesota, to make portage to the Missouri — a short distance in his belief — to follow the Missouri to its sources in the mountains, to cross the mountains and descend to the Pacific by the Oregon River. The Revolutionary War, then impending, rendered this enterprise impossible.[19] Of the feasibility of such an undertaking, Carver had no doubt. His conception of the resources and possibilities of the region he had traversed was notable. Not only did he conceive of a passage westward to China and the East Indies, but he suggested an open water route by way of the Great Lakes to New York.[20]

Carver remained in England, where he died in poverty in 1780. Further account of his activities might here be dismissed but for one transaction of more than local importance. There is doubtful testimony to an allegation that at the time he asked for money compensation Carver also sought from the king of England the confirmation of a grant of certain lands which the Sioux Indians had bestowed on him. He makes no reference in his journal to such conveyance. Some time after his death a purported deed was produced, dated "at the great cave, May the first, one thousand seven hundred and sixty-seven," signed by two Sioux chiefs, conveying in return for "many presents, and other good services" to their "good brother Jonathan" a tract of land lying on the east bank of the Mississippi River from the Falls of St. Anthony to the south end of Lake Pepin and back a hundred miles eastward, embracing, as estimated, some two hundred thousand square miles.[21] Carver married

[19] Travels, 541–543.
[20] Travels, 74.
[21] Dr. John C. Lettsom included in his biography of Carver, prefixed to the 1781 edition of the Travels, the text of the deed, which, in 1834, he certified was copied from the original

a second time in England and had two children, one of whom, a daughter, grew up and was married.   On the day after the marriage, she and her husband sold their claim under this ostensible deed to a London mercantile firm, which evidently believed it valuable.   The firm's agent, sent out to America, by some misadventure lost his life.   This claim was not prosecuted further.[22]

In January, 1806, a Reverend Samuel Peters, a loyalist in the Revolution, appeared before a committee of the United States Senate in support of a petition of one Samuel Harrison on behalf of all the heirs of Carver, both American and English, for the confirmation of the grant.   In his testimony, Peters alleged that in 1775 the king of England sanctioned Carver's claims by ordering a frigate and a transport carrying 150 men to be furnished him to take possession of the land; but "that, when things were in a state of preparation, the news of the battle of Bunker's Hill was received, which entirely prohibited the projected voyage."[23]   This claim, which was acquired by Peters through purchase from the heirs in November, 1806, was kept before Congress for more than twenty years.   It was at length entertained with enough seriousness to induce the House of Representatives on January 29, 1822, to request President Monroe to communicate available information relative to the claim of Jonathan Carver to certain lands of

instrument in the possession of Carver's widow. The exact description of the Carver tract is given therein as follows: "From the fall of St. Anthony, running on the east banks of the Mississippi, nearly south-east, as far as the south end of Lake Pepin, where the Chipeway river joins the Mississippi, and from thence eastward five days travel, accounting twenty English miles per day, and from thence north six days travel, at twenty English miles per day, and from thence again to the fall of St. Anthony, on a direct straight line."

[22] Testimony was given before a committee of the United States Senate in 1806 that "Mr. C——— & Co." persuaded Carver's daughter Martha to marry a sailor clandestinely, and induced the husband and wife to take out letters of administration on her father's estate and later to sell and convey the same to the said firm. See 18 Congress, 2 session, *House Reports*, no. 44, p. 12 (serial 122), or *American State Papers: Public Lands*, 4: 86. In the addenda to the 1838 edition of the *Travels* (see *post*, n. 26), the name of the firm is given as Conly and Company (p. 347). This transaction took place about 1798. Durrie, in *Wisconsin Historical Collections*, 6: 240.

[23] 18 Congress, 2 session, *House Reports*, no. 44, pp. 2, 19. This report is reprinted in *American State Papers: Public Lands*, 4: 82–89. See also Quaife, in the *Mississippi Valley Historical Review*, 7: 15.

the United States. On the twenty-fourth of April following, the president transmitted an opinion of the commissioner of the general land office to the effect that the claim was in violation of the king's proclamation of 1763, of which Carver, as a former British officer, must or should have had knowledge. The commissioner added to his report, and made a part of it, a letter from Colonel Henry Leavenworth, former commandant at Fort Snelling, dated July 28, 1821. Partly from his own knowledge and partly from what he had "understood from the Indians of the Sioux Nation," Leavenworth stated that (1) the Sioux of the Plains, by whom the grant purported to have been made, "never owned a foot of land east of the Mississippi"; (2) the Indians knew of no such chiefs as those whose names were signed to the pretended deed; (3) they "never received anything for the land"; and (4) "they have and ever have had, the possession of the land, and intend to keep it." The papers were referred to the committee on public lands, from which, so far as can be learned, they did not emerge.[24]

On December 27 of the same year, 1822, however, a petition of Samuel Peters requesting confirmation of his claim was laid before the Senate and referred to the committee on public lands. Two weeks later, January 9, 1823, another petition for confirmation of the grant, signed by Samuel Harrison on behalf of the heirs, was referred to the same committee. The report of that committee, adverse to the claim, was submitted January 23 and was adopted by the Senate six days later. The committee found that neither the original deed nor any proper evidence of its execution had been exhibited; that there were no subscribing witnesses to the purported copy; that there was no proof that the names signed thereto were those of chiefs competent to convey; that Carver could not legally have taken any such conveyance because of the proclamation of 1763; and

[24] 17 Congress, 1 session, *House Journal*, 493 (serial 62); *House Documents*, no. 117 (serial 69). This document is reprinted in *American State Papers: Public Lands*, 3: 551.

that, Carver having rendered no services to the United States, the claim could not lie against the United States government.[25] Peters was not so much discouraged, however, as to abandon further pursuit. His petition was again laid before the House of Representatives in the session of 1824–25. The committee on private land claims on January 28 presented an "unfavorable report," which was laid on the table, whence it does not appear to have been taken. This elaborate report added to the objections of the Senate the further one that the United States had never recognized any Indian right to the soil, and consequently an Indian deed was necessarily void.[26] Congress has not been further

[25] 17 Congress, 2 session, *Senate Journal*, 52, 75, 102, 115 (serial 72). For the text of the report, see 17 Congress, 2 session, *Senate Documents*, no. 20 (serial 74), or *American State Papers: Public Lands*, 3:611.

[26] 18 Congress, 2 session, *House Journal*, 74, 179 (serial 112). For the full text of the report, see 18 Congress, 2 session, *House Reports*, no. 44, or *American State Papers: Public Lands*, 4:82–89. Peters appears to have succeeded in interesting a company of New York merchants in his scheme to establish settlements on the Carver grant, and in company with John Tuthill, Constant Andrews, and Willard Keyes, he left Toronto in July, 1817, and reached Prairie du Chien late in August. There Peters did his utmost to secure support for his claim, but "the authorities" refused to allow him to "open his business," and he departed in May, 1818. Andrews and Keyes remained at Prairie du Chien and even after Peters left tried to secure from the Indians confirmation of the deed. See letters and documents submitted with his petition, in 18 Congress, 2 session, *House Reports*, no. 44; pp. 9–19, and Willard Keyes, "Diary of Life in Wisconsin One Hundred Years Ago," in the *Wisconsin Magazine of History*, 3:339–363 (March, 1920). According to the *Illinois Intelligencer* of December 30, 1818, Peters arrived in Albany in November of that year "from his residence" at the Falls of St. Anthony, whither he was to return shortly "to spend his days in his new settlement." It is further stated that the settlement had been established for about seven years, but that the "number of adventurers" and "the present population or prospects of the new colony" were not known.

In his *History of Wisconsin*, 3:265 (Madison, 1854), William R. Smith calls attention to the fact that for a period of approximately fifty years cartographers indicated on their maps the bounds of the territory known as Carver's tract in spite of the fact that the rights of its claimants were unrecognized by the government; he intimates that in this way they knowingly aided in the deception "of the ignorant and unwary, who might be inclined to make purchases of land in this region of country." John Melish, for example, in his *Geographical Description of the United States, with the Contiguous British and Spanish Possessions, Intended as an Accompaniment to Melish's Map of These Countries*, 52, 134* (Philadelphia, 1816), says that in the Northwest Territory the United States government held "all the unsold lands ceded by the Sac and Fox Indians; and the pre-emption right of all the rest, except that space marked Carver's Grant; which is claimed by Captain Carver's successors"; and that plans were under way for the settlement of that grant. Another writer on Wisconsin openly accuses Peters of having engaged in a "swindling scheme." See J. N. Davidson, *In Unnamed Wisconsin: Studies in the History of the Region between Lake Michigan and the Mississippi*, 181 (Milwaukee, 1895). Smith declares also that the reprint of the 1781 edition of Carver's book, brought out under the title *Carver's Travels in Wisconsin* by Harper and Brothers in New York in 1838, shortly after the organization of the Territory of Wisconsin, was issued in the interests of claimants of the Carver tract. A number of

molested, but the Carver claim has not been forgotten. If the present governor of Minnesota has not been addressed by some person believing himself a rightful beneficiary of the claim, his experience is exceptional.

For fourscore years the area of Minnesota east of the great river had been part of New France. For another score it was to be a part of the British Empire. On October 7 of the same year of the treaty of Paris, 1763, was issued the proclamation of King George III, establishing the government of Quebec.[27] The bounds prescribed did not include the Northwest. That indeterminate region was reserved for the time being for the use of the Indians under the sovereignty and protection of the king. All persons were forbidden to purchase lands of the Indians, and any who had squatted on lands were ordered to remove forthwith.[28] Trade with the Indians was made free to British subjects obtaining licenses from colonial governors and giving bonds. Fugitives from justice were to be returned by

documents in support of the title of the "Mississippi Land Company of New York" to the land in question are contained in the "Addenda" of this reprint, which comprises pages 345–362.

Major Stephen H. Long, in his *Voyage in a Six-Oared Skiff to the Falls of St. Anthony in 1817*, 10 (St. Paul, 1860 — reissued as *Minnesota Historical Collections*, vol. 2, part 1), mentions two grandsons of Carver, named King and Gun, who set out in his company on July 9, 1817, from Prairie du Chien, to identify their grandfather's claim. See page 43 for a later meeting. These men are also mentioned in Keyes, "Diary," in the *Wisconsin Magazine of History*, 3: 349. Major Forsyth's opinion of Carver and his claim is contained in his "Journal of a Voyage from St. Louis to the Falls of St. Anthony, in 1819," in *Wisconsin Historical Collections*, 6: 211 (Madison, 1872). This journal, slightly abridged, is reprinted in *Minnesota Historical Collections*, 3: 139–167 (St. Paul, 1880). A deed, dated April 6, 1836, conveying a tract in the Carver grant is in the possession of the Minnesota Historical Society. There is a letter in the Sibley Papers from Dr. Hartwell Carver, dated Philadelphia, November 13, 1848, in which the writer says that he had been at enormous expense in searching out the claim, and that he had spent three days with Cass and borrowed of him thirty thousand dollars for the express purpose of buying out the heirs — all of which is more than doubtful. According to Harriet E. Bishop, *Floral Home; or First Years in Minnesota*, 26 (New York, 1857), this Dr. Carver visited the upper Mississippi region sometime in 1848. There is a letter in the Folwell Papers from Fred B. Chute to the author, March 7, 1919, attached to which is a copy of a claim made by Odessa University, Odessa, Washington, for three hundred acres of land in Minneapolis as part of the Carver grant, deeded to the university in 1904. The Minnesota Historical Society has a manuscript "Plan of Carver's Grant" drawn apparently about 1817, on which the area is divided into about three hundred townships; numbers or names are given to about half the townships.

[27] *Annual Register*, 1763, p. [208] (seventh edition, London, 1796); Shortt and Doughty, *Constitutional History of Canada*, 119–123 and map; Kingsford, *Canada*, 5: 133–145.

[28] It was this which the Senate committee held made Carver's claim invalid.

military and Indian officials to the colonies where the alleged crimes had been committed. This proclamation gave to a portion of Minnesota an inchoate constitution and government. According to its terms the lands of the Northwest were, in point of tenure, British crown lands.[29]

The act of Parliament of 1774, known as the Quebec Act, extended the bounds of the province westward and southward to the banks of the Mississippi and the Ohio, adding that region known later as the Northwest Territory, and gave to Minnesota East a political constitution, the first written constitution nominally in effect in Minnesota.[30] This act provided for a governor and an executive council of not more than twenty-three nor fewer than seventeen members, to be selected by the king. The representative legislature provided for Quebec in the Proclamation of 1763 was eliminated. The criminal law of England, established by the proclamation, was continued, but the old French civil law, the *coutume de Paris*, was permitted, in deference to the wishes of the French colonists, to remain in force. Thus trial by jury was restricted to criminal cases. Although the Protestant religion was to be encouraged, the act provided for more than toleration for the Catholic by guaranteeing to the clergy their accustomed dues and rights. This constitution never operated west of Lake Michigan. Its only importance here is that it was regarded by the American colonists as an example of the tyranny which the British government was preparing to impose upon them. The address by the Continental Congress of 1774 to the Canadians was expected to induce them to make common cause

[29] For a critical study of the sources of the different clauses of the proclamation and of the purposes and motives which actuated the men who formulated them, see Clarence W. Alvord, "Genesis of the Proclamation of 1763," in *Michigan Pioneer and Historical Collections*, 36: 20–52, or his *Mississippi Valley in British Politics*, 1: 183–210.

[30] The text of the Quebec Act is printed in Shortt and Doughty, *Constitutional History of Canada*, 401–405. See Kingsford, *Canada*, 5: 224–261; 7: 191–193, for a full account of the debate in Parliament, the provisions of the act, and the opposition to it in the colonies. In the case of Dutcher v. Culver, 24 *Minnesota*, 584, decided October 10, 1877, the question was raised and argued pro and con, whether the Quebec Act carried the English common law into Minnesota East.

with the Americans.[31]   But the Canadians were quite content with a government not much modified from that to
which they had been subjected from the beginning.   The
Quebec Act remained the constitution of Canada till it was
replaced by the Constitutional Act of 1791.[32]

The willingness of the British government to hold its grip
on the Northwest was stimulated by the silent but very
effective influence of the Indian trade interest.   The Indian
trading of the French had never been well organized, chiefly
for the reason that the independent trader, the *coureur de
bois*, could drive a good business on very small capital.
With his single canoe he could reach the Indian villages,
exchange his trinkets for peltries, and return to his market.
Before the conquest a change was coming on.   Game,
slaughtered for skins and not for food, had already become
scarce, and this made the Indians unfriendly.   The traders
could not safely venture far from the military posts.   Capital and coöperation were becoming necessary.   Some years
elapsed after the British occupation of Canada before the
Indian trade west of the Great Lakes was revived.   Among
those who then ventured upon it were thrifty Scotch merchants residing in Canadian cities.   They presently found
their profits unsatisfactory owing to the conditions just
described and to excessive competition.

It was not left to the mercantile genius of the last quarter
of the nineteenth century to invent the "combine," whether
in the form of a trust or otherwise.   The Frobishers,
McTavishes, McKenzies, and other shrewd Highlanders of
Montreal got together and came to an understanding intended to discourage cutthroat competition.   An earlier
"gentlemen's agreement" took the form of a partnership in
1783 and in 1787 ripened into the famous Northwest Com-

[31] *Journals of the Continental Congress*, 1: 105–113 (Library of Congress edition, 1904).

[32] Shortt and Doughty, *Constitutional History of Canada*, 694–708; Kingsford, *Canada*,
7: 306–323.   It was during the debate in Parliament on this bill that the memorable quarrel
between Burke and Fox occurred.   For full discussions of the purpose, passage, and operation of the Quebec Act see Alvord, *Mississippi Valley in British Politics*, 1: 204; 2: 235, 247.

VOYAGEURS ON LAKE SUPERIOR

Colored steel engraving by Frances Ann Hopkins

A VOYAGEUR

Oil by Mrs. Samuel B. Abbe

pany.[33] Doubtless its articles were modeled on those of the Hudson's Bay Company, which had been in existence since 1670, except that no political powers were assumed. The Northwest Company promptly and efficiently organized the Indian trade of the Great Lakes and the region westward. The headquarters of the company were established at Montreal, where the older and wealthier of the members resided. Other members were placed in charge as factors at principal distributing and collecting posts, such as Grand Portage, Mackinac, Green Bay, and Prairie du Chien. Grand Portage, near the mouth of the Pigeon River, in what is now Minnesota, was for a long time the distributing point for a chain of trading stations reaching to the Saskatchewan and the Yellowstone. The annual conferences, held here in July, of proprietors, traders, agents, *voyageurs*, Indians, and half-breeds are a favorite subject of chroniclers. For days there was music and dancing, revelry and feasting on viands prepared by French cooks brought from Montreal. Subordinate trading posts were established far and wide in the Indian villages, from which agents followed the Indians to their hunting grounds with canoe loads or packs of goods. The company adopted the wise policy of diverting the French traders with their *engagés* and *voyageurs* from illicit traffic by taking them into its employ. The better educated of the *coureurs de bois* became interpreters and agents at "jackknife" stations.[34]

[33] For a careful study of the development of the fur trade during the British régime, with some comparison with the conduct of the business under the French administration, see Wayne E. Stevens, "The Organization of the British Fur Trade, 1760–1780," in the *Mississippi Valley Historical Review*, 3: 172–202 (September, 1916). See also Bryce, *Hudson's Bay Company*, 91–93, 114–122; Kingsford, *Canada*, 9: 103–107; and Gordon C. Davidson, *The North West Company* (University of California, *Publications in History*, vol. 7 — Berkeley, 1918).

[34] William W. Warren, "History of the Ojibways, Based upon Traditions and Oral Statements," in *Minnesota Historical Collections*, 5: 379 (St. Paul, 1885). Although Grand Portage was on American soil, the Northwest Company maintained a great distributing post there for many years. About the year 1801 the movement to transfer the post to a point near the site of Du Luth's old post on the Kaministiquia River was begun. The new fort was in process of construction in 1803, when Alexander Henry arrived at that point from the West. See his journal in Coues, *New Light on the Early History of the Greater Northwest*, 1: 219. The name "Fort William," bestowed upon it in 1807 (see *ante*, p. 23

The Northwest Company presently acquired a virtual monopoly of the fur trade and proceeded to extend its operations into regions which the French had never effectively exploited. In 1792 Jean Baptiste Cadotte, well known in the history of the fur trade, conducted a journey of exploration far into central Minnesota. His relations of the regions visited by him were such as to inspire the Northwest Company to get possession of that trade. The following year a depot, of which vestiges may still be traced, was established at Fond du Lac, near the mouth of the St. Louis River. A year later, 1794, a stockade post was built on Sandy Lake in the central part of Aitkin County. The inclosure, one hundred feet square, was formed by hewn trunks about a foot in diameter stood on end in a trench and extending thirteen feet above ground, with loopholes for musketry at convenient intervals. At two corners were salients giving opportunity for a flank fire along the sides. Within the inclosure were the necessary buildings; without, a potato patch of four acres was fenced in. But a few years later a similar and larger post was established at Leech Lake, and white men have since continuously resided there. The company now rapidly extended its trading operations to every Sioux and Chippewa village in western Wisconsin and northern Minnesota.[35]

n. 60), now attaches to a town on the site of the old post, traces of which are said to be still visible. For a very graphic description of Fort William and the life there, see Gabriel Franchère, "Narrative of a Voyage to the Northwest Coast of America in the Years 1811–1814," in Reuben G. Thwaites, ed., *Early Western Travels, 1748–1846*, 6: 386–389 (Cleveland, 1904–07). Washington Irving's vivid account in the first chapter of his *Astoria, or Anecdotes of an Enterprise beyond the Rocky Mountains* (New York, 1849), is probably based on Franchère's narrative. Bryce, in his *Hudson's Bay Company*, 95, describes Grand Portage as it appears to the visitor today. A valuable narrative which throws considerable light on the operations of the fur-traders in the upper Mississippi and Chippewa river regions from 1783 to 1820 is that of Jean Baptiste Perrault. His "Narrative of the Travels and Adventures of a Merchant Voyageur in the Savage Territories of Northern America, Leaving Montreal the 28th of May 1783 (to 1820)," found by John S. Fox in 1905 among the Schoolcraft manuscripts in the Smithsonian Institution, is in *Michigan Pioneer and Historical Collections*, 37: 508–619 (Lansing, 1909–10).

[35] Warren, in *Minnesota Historical Collections*, 5: 279–303, 379. He gives 1796 as the date of the establishment of the post at Sandy Lake. Pike, who was there in January, 1806, says, however, that the establishment "was formed 12 years since," or in 1794. See his *Expeditions*, 1: 139. From the Perrault narrative it is learned that Charles Bous-

As a matter of law the British title to Minnesota East terminated with the consummation of the definitive treaty of peace of September 3, 1783. Title did not, however, at once vest in the United States. The colony of Virginia had long asserted a claim covering this area. By her charter of 1609 she had been granted a territory having four hundred miles of frontage on the Atlantic and extending "from the Sea Coast . . . up into the Land throughout from Sea to Sea, West and Northwest."[36] This grant was reënforced by a deed given by the Iroquois in 1744, at Lancaster, Pennsylvania, "recognizing the King's right to all the Lands which are or shall be by His Majesty's appointment in the colony of Virginia."[37] The claim of Virginia was not to remain merely on paper. In 1738 her legislature had created the County of Augusta, bounded on the east by the Blue Ridge and on the west and northwest by the "utmost limits of Virginia."[38] It was a Virginia not a United States army which, led by that indomitable frontier commander, General George Rogers Clark, in 1778 captured Kaskaskia and Vincennes from the British, and took possession of the Illinois country.[39] In the same year, on December 9, the Virginia

quet, an employee of the Northwest Company, was stationed at Sandy Lake from 1794 to 1797. See *Michigan Pioneer and Historical Collections*, 37: 570, 573, 574. The date of the establishment of the post at Leech Lake is not definitely known. William Morrison found a Northwest Company agent there in 1802. See his letter to Allan Morrison, January 16, 1856, in *Minnesota Historical Collections*, 7: 122, n. 1. For a description of the posts at Sandy Lake and Leech Lake as they were in 1806, see Pike, *Expeditions*, 1: 281, 282. See also Perrault, in *Michigan Pioneer and Historical Collections*, 37: 568, 569, for an account of the construction of the buildings comprising Fort St. Louis at Fond du Lac. Perrault was engaged by the Northwest Company to superintend the work.

[36] Francis N. Thorpe, ed., *The Federal and State Constitutions, Colonial Charters, and Other Organic Laws of the States, Territories, and Colonies*, 7: 3795 (Washington, 1909). See Burke A. Hinsdale, *The Old Northwest*, 73–75 (New York, 1888), for ingenious illustrations of the Virginia claim.

[37] *Pennsylvania Colonial Records*, 4: 689–737. The theory of the Iroquois was that, having acknowledged themselves subjects of Great Britain, they acquired title to all lands covered by their extensive forays. See George Bancroft, *History of the United States*, 3: 455 (twenty-second edition, Boston, 1866). See also Hinsdale, *Old Northwest*, 59. Conflicting claims of other colonies need not be considered here.

[38] William W. Hening, ed., *The Statutes at Large; Being a Collection of All the Laws of Virginia*, 5: 78; 6: 258 (New York, 1823). By an act of February, 1752, to encourage settlements on the Mississippi, Protestants were exempted from all taxes for ten years.

[39] General Clark's account of his Illinois campaign, contained in a letter to George Mason, November 19, 1779, is included in James A. James, ed., *George Rogers Clark Papers,*

legislature created the County of Illinois, and Governor Patrick Henry commissioned Colonel John Todd Jr. of Kentucky county lieutenant to exercise civil government in that county, Clark retaining military command.[40] A Virginia land office was opened west of the mountains in 1779.[41] When, in 1784, the United States accepted Virginia's deed of cession, Minnesota East became the property of the United States; and later it was merged into the Northwest Territory, to which the Ordinance of July 13, 1787, gave a constitution and a government.[42]

A generation was to pass before these events could have any practical effect on Minnesota soil. The treaty of 1783 obligated the British government to withdraw its garrisons from all military posts south of the Canadian boundary and to leave the United States in peaceable possession. This withdrawal was long postponed, and there is good reason for the belief that the hope of the British government was that some turn of events might leave the Ohio and Illinois countries in its hands, or at least allow those regions to remain as Indian country in which British influences might operate.[43] Accordingly the garrisons at Oswego, Niagara, Detroit,

1771-1781, 114-154 (*Illinois Historical Collections*, vol. 8 — Springfield, 1912). See also Thwaites, *How George Rogers Clark Won the Northwest*, 3-72, and Alvord, *Illinois Country*, 326-333.

[40] Hening, *Statutes*, 9: 552. For a history of the County of Illinois, see the introduction, by Clarence W. Alvord, to *Cahokia Records, 1778-1790*, xiii-clvi (*Illinois Historical Collections*, vol. 5 — Springfield, 1907); Alvord, *Illinois Country*, 329-357; and Arthur C. Boggess, *The Settlement of Illinois, 1778-1830*, 9-54 (Chicago Historical Society, *Collections*, vol. 5 — Chicago, 1908). Pages 213-256 of the latter work contain an extensive bibliography.

[41] This office was at Wilson's Station in Kentucky, about two miles from Harrodsburg. James, *Clark Papers, 1771-1781*, cxii, n. 2.

[42] *Journals of [the Continental] Congress*, 9: 47-49 (Folwell edition, Philadelphia, 1801).

[43] A proposition to that effect was made in 1814 by the British commissioners at Ghent. They suggested "a barrier between the British Dominions and the United States, to prevent them from being conterminous to each other, and that neither Great Britain nor the United States should acquire by purchase any of these Indian lands. For the line Great Britain was willing to take the Treaty of Greenville for the basis." In reply Adams said: "To condemn vast regions of territory to perpetual barrenness and solitude that a few hundred savages might find wild beasts to hunt upon it, was a species of game law that a nation descended from Britons would never endure." John Q. Adams, *Memoirs; Comprising Parts of His Diary from 1795 to 1848*, 3: 6, 18, 25, 28, 37, 60, 67, 70 (Philadelphia, 1874-77). See also *A Great Peacemaker: The Diary of James Gallatin, Secretary to Albert Gallatin, 1813-1827*, 31-35 (New York, 1914).

Mackinac, and elsewhere along the border were maintained from year to year. The British commandants of these posts continued to exercise jurisdiction over the adjacent regions and even forbade the navigation of American waters to American traders. The moribund Confederation government of the United States was in no condition to undertake effective protest, and it was not until after the government under the Constitution had been organized and put into operation that the matter could be taken up. Thomas Jefferson, the first secretary of state, in 1791 brought the subject to the notice of the British government in so forceful a way as to secure its attention. The British minister, Hammond, offered no apology for his government, pleaded no laches, but complacently informed Jefferson that his government was purposely holding the posts and the territory dominated by them in retaliation for infringement by the United States of the fourth and following articles of the treaty of 1783. By these articles the United States was bound to place no legal impediments in the way of the "recovery of the full value in Sterling Money" of debts due British subjects incurred before the Revolution and to give loyalists opportunity to recover their possessions and dues throughout the country. A letter from Hammond to Jefferson, March 5, 1792, contains an elaborate arraignment of the United States. The gravamen of the charge was that the several states had confiscated the property of loyalists, had thrown obstacles in the way of British subjects seeking collection of debts, and in some cases had provided that their paper money should be good tender for such debts.[44] This open disagreement, with other grave difficulties, was composed by the treaty of 1794, commonly called Jay's treaty, in which it was stipulated that the British garrisons

---

[44] The correspondence between Jefferson and Hammond, including Jefferson's famous reply of May 29, 1792, is in *American State Papers: Foreign Relations*, 1: 188–216. See also Jefferson's notes of his conversation with Hammond, June 3, 1792, in his *Works*, 1: 219–227 (Federal edition, New York and London, 1904–05), and Andrew C. McLaughlin, "The Western Posts and the British Debt," in American Historical Association, *Annual Reports*, 1894, pp. 413–444.

should be withdrawn on or before June 1, 1796.[45]   Soon after
this date the forts along the border were occupied by American forces; but the Northwest Company kept the British
colors over its trading posts in Minnesota twenty years
thereafter.

[45] *Treaties, Conventions, International Acts, Protocols, and Agreements between the
United States of America and Other Powers, 1776–1909,* 1: 590–606 (61 Congress, 2 session,
Senate Documents, no. 357 — serial 5646).   As late as 1794 a new British fort was built on
the Maumee River and garrisoned by British infantry; it was in the vicinity of this post
that General Anthony Wayne won his victory over the Indians in an engagement known
as the battle of Fallen Timbers, a battle which has been, not inaptly, regarded as the real
conclusion of the Revolutionary War.   In the words of Rufus King, "in an hour the pride
and power of the Indian confederacy and the scheme of re-annexing the Northwest Territory to the British Dominions were broken.   It was every way opportune that Mr. Jay,
at this time, was negotiating with the English ministry. . . . This victory secured the
surrender of Detroit, the fort on the Maumee, and all other posts or dependencies within
the boundary of 1783."   *Ohio, First Fruits of the Ordinance of 1787,* 255 (*American Commonwealths* — Boston and New York, 1888).

IV. MINNESOTA WEST ACQUIRED—NATIVE TRIBES

FROM the time when La Salle descended the river St. Louis, as he called the Mississippi, and took possession of the whole vast region drained by it in the name of Louis le Grand in 1682, to the surrender of Fort de Chartres, the last post held by the French on the left bank of that stream, by Captain Louis St. Ange de Bellerive to a British commissary in 1765, the Mississippi had been a French river. Early in the eighteenth century a considerable body of Canadians emigrated to the Illinois country and planted such settlements as Kaskaskia, Cahokia, and Vincennes. In 1718 old Fort de Chartres was built, sixteen miles above Kaskaskia. This work, rebuilt in stone toward the middle of the century, was the strongest French fortification on the continent. By this time a population of perhaps two thousand had gathered about such centers as those mentioned and was shipping flour, pork, corn, tallow, and hides to New Orleans.[1] From the time when the original colonists of New Orleans migrated from Biloxi to the present site of New Orleans, the Mississippi was the thoroughfare of exploration, trade, and missionary effort between that city and Quebec.

By the treaty of Paris, February 10, 1763, France ceded to Great Britain "Canada, with all its dependencies," or, as expressed in a later article, "every thing which he [*Louis XV*] possesses, or ought to possess, on the left side of the river Mississippi, except the town of New Orleans and the island in which it is situated."[2] Bitter as this humiliation

---

[1] *Illinois Historical Collections*, 2: xiii–xxvii; 10: xxix–xxxii, 209; 11: 91–122 (Springfield, 1907–16); Alvord, *Illinois Country*, 114–119, 132, 153, 192, 208–211, 264.
[2] Shortt and Doughty, *Constitutional History of Canada*, 85, 86; *Annual Register*, 1762, pp. [233]–[242] (fifth edition, London, 1787).

was, it was less so than Louis XV and his ministry had feared. They had had good reason to suspect that the victorious English would insist on the delivery of all French holdings on the western continent. As already briefly stated, to forestall such a demand the French king a year before concluded a secret treaty with the king of Spain, his ally in the Seven Years' War, by which France conveyed to Spain all her lands west of the Mississippi River, together with New Orleans and the island cut off by the Iberville and the lakes. There was a nominal consideration in the compensation of Spain for her loss of Florida to the British, but the real motive of the transaction was to put the trans-Mississippi out of the reach of Britain;[3] and Britain, uncertain whether she cared to hold Canada after the conquest, was indifferent about exacting the uttermost acre from her humbled adversary. Both nations had by this time found American colonies a costly investment. The French king was quite content to shift his burden onto the back of his brother of Spain.

By the operation of this Franco-Spanish treaty of November 3, 1762, the area of Minnesota west of the Mississippi and south of the Hudson Bay watershed passed from the dominion of France to that of Spain, and France virtually retired from the mainland of the western continent. This alienation, precipitated by defeat in a European war, must have taken place at no distant time. The English colonies in America had become at least ten times stronger than the French in wealth and population. The Frenchman had attached himself but slightly to the soil; he was looking out for the Indian trade, for mines, for buffalo wool, and for pearls. The Englishman cleared the forest and opened farms. His towns and villages depended on and were tributary to a fundamental agriculture. Let it be that the two peoples were equals in talent and patriotism; still the

---

[3] See the statement of the French minister, the Duc de Choiseul, in Charles Gayarré, *History of Louisiana — the French Domination*, 2: 130 (New York, 1854).

diversity of institutions which they brought with them must have led them into diverse careers. The paternal hand of his king was ever over the French colonist. Every settlement was a little French parish governed from above. The English settler, left to work out his own career, consulted with his neighbors, and organized the town meeting, careless of what might be going on at Whitehall. The confederated townships set a pattern for a union of colonies, which at length ripened into a national bond, stronger than the centralized power of the French could ever have become. Democracy and the Protestant religion must at some time have driven the gallant, the amiable, the romantic Frenchman from the field.

During the forty years of the Spanish proprietorship of Louisiana few events occurred which need detain the readers of this narrative. It was not until 1766 that a Spanish governor arrived in New Orleans. Two years later the reluctant French inhabitants drove him out. After another year a more vigorous Spanish official appeared with a force sufficient to secure obedience.[4] Spanish law superseded French, but as both codes were, substantially, modernized Roman law, no inconvenience resulted. Upper Louisiana was set off as a separate district by a shifting line which at length settled in the latitude of Memphis. A lieutenant governor was appointed to exercise all powers of government over it, subject to the approval of the authorities at New Orleans. The population of this district down to the end of the Spanish domination was confined to a few settlements in the Missouri region, the chief of them being St. Louis, which was founded as a trading station in 1764, when the lieutenant governor established his residence there. French families in considerable number at once abandoned their old homes on the east side of the river and settled about this post. For the first quarter of a century thereafter St. Louis remained essentially a French village. The Ordinance of

---

[4] Gayarré, *Louisiana — French Domination*, 2: 157–356.

1787, prohibiting slavery in the "Old Northwest," had the effect of diverting to Upper Louisiana a considerable emigration of people who desired to hold slaves. This movement was encouraged by a very liberal land policy, under which any settler could take up a farm of eight hundred acres for forty-one dollars, the bare cost of surveying and administration. And this trifling payment was not exacted in advance. At the close of the Spanish period there were upwards of ten thousand people in and about St. Louis, sixty per cent of whom were from the United States.[5]

In the first years of the nineteenth century Napoleon Bonaparte the Corsican, though wearing the modest title of first consul of the republic of France, was the absolute autocrat of that ancient state. Already aspiring to the purple, he was occupied with schemes for the aggrandizement of an empire. To be in fashion he must have great colonial possessions. San Domingo, which had made successful revolt, he would recover.[6] The cession of Louisiana in 1762 to Spain had not been approved by the French colonists, who had never ceased longing for reunion with their beloved France.[7] As matters then stood between Napoleon and the Spanish government, a mild suggestion of retrocession by Spain would doubtless have been sufficient. But for appearance's sake a consideration was nominated in the way of a guarantee to a Spanish prince of certain principalities in Italy, then in virtual possession of the victorious French.[8]

There were several reasons why Spain was so easily reconciled to retrocession. The maintenance of her government

[5] Lucien Carr, Missouri: A Bone of Contention, 36–62 (American Commonwealths — Boston and New York, 1888); Alvord, Illinois Country, 266, 372.

[6] François de Barbé-Marbois, Histoire de la Louisiane et de la cession de cette colonie par la France aux Etats-Unis de l'Amérique Septentrionale, 182–184 (Paris, 1829); James K. Hosmer, The History of the Louisiana Purchase, 45 (New York, 1902).

[7] George W. Cable, in United States Census, 1880, vol. 19, pp. 231–234.

[8] By the treaty of Madrid, March 21, 1801, France agreed to establish the Prince of Parma as king of Tuscany. Annual Register, 1801, p. 299 (new edition, London, 1813). For a carefully studied account of the Spanish occupation of Louisiana, see William R. Shepherd, "The Cession of Louisiana to Spain," in the Political Science Quarterly, 19: 439–458 (September, 1904).

over Louisiana had been a considerable pecuniary burden. By a foolish obstructive policy in violation of her treaty obligations, the Spanish intendant in 1802 cut off the trade of the Ohio Valley by way of the Mississippi to the gulf. There were more than half a million people in that valley who believed that nature had given them an unquestionable right to navigate the great river to its mouth, and they were ready to make good that claim by force of arms.[9] In such a contest Spain would naturally be at a disadvantage. It may also be noted that Spain was not unwilling to see a power friendly to herself and less likely to be obtrusive sandwiched between the United States and her Mexican territories. Accordingly by a secret treaty, called that of San Ildefonso, concluded October 1, 1800, Spain retroceded to France the "Louisiane" which, in 1762, France had put in trust with her.[10]   Napoleon had a good reason for having this treaty kept a secret, or at least for making a pretense of secrecy. His hope was to land, without the knowledge of England, a considerable army on the American continent.[11]   This was a plan easier to conceive than to execute. His expedition to San Domingo had aborted.[12]   He recoiled from the rashness of once more exposing a fleet of transports to the mercies of the British navy, and abandoned his scheme.

The treaty of San Ildefonso was not a year old when its secret provisions had leaked out. The United States government was apprised by its diplomatic officials at London, Paris, and Madrid. Protest was filed against the change of ownership as threatening American interests. Robert R. Livingston was sent to Paris to lodge the protest and to offer

[9] Cable, in *United States Census*, 1880, vol. 19, pp. 234–237; Barbé-Marbois, *Louisiane*, 231–235.

[10] *Register of Debates*, vol. 13, part 2, appendix, p. 228; Alexander J. de Clercq, ed., *Recueil des traités de la France*, 1: 411 (Paris, 1880–1904).

[11] Robert Livingston to James Madison, April 24, 1802, and Madison to Livingston, May 1, 1802, in *State Papers and Correspondence Bearing upon the Purchase of the Territory of Louisiana*, 23, 24 (57 Congress, 2 session, *House Documents*, no. 431 — serial 4531).

[12] Barbé-Marbois, *Louisiane*, 201–219.

about two million dollars for the island of New Orleans and the two Floridas. To his surprise the French ministers offered the whole of Louisiana for a round sum in cash, then much needed by Bonaparte for an impending campaign. James Monroe, appointed United States minister extraordinary to France, having opportunely reached Paris, the bargain was concluded. For a consideration of fifteen million dollars, including the assumption of certain French liabilities to American citizens by the United States, Louisiana became American territory by a treaty dated April 30, 1803.[13]

Napoleon, after finding it impossible to occupy Louisiana with a sufficient force to hold the province, had slight reasons for assuming government over it. He had therefore left the Spanish authorities in possession till after the consummation of the treaty of 1803. It was not until November 30 of that year that the Spanish governor at New Orleans formally gave place to a French successor. And that official twenty days later gave livery of seizin to the United States commissioners, Claiborne and Wilkinson. The upper province was not handed over until the following spring, when the United States troops crossed over to St. Louis. On March 9, 1804, the Spanish commandant delivered the district to Captain Amos Stoddard, U.S.A., commissioned by the French government to act for it. On the next day that

[13] The interested reader may pursue the story of the Louisiana purchase in such works as Henry Adams, *History of the United States*, vols. 1 and 2 (New York, 1889–1891); Binger Hermann, *The Louisiana Purchase and Our Title West of the Rocky Mountains, with a Review of Annexation by the United States* (Washington, 1898); Nathaniel P. Langford, "The Louisiana Purchase and Preceding Spanish Intrigues for Dismemberment of the Union," in *Minnesota Historical Collections*, 9: 453–508 (St. Paul, 1901); James A. Robertson, ed., *Louisiana under the Rule of Spain, France, and the United States, 1785–1807* (Cleveland, 1911); *State Papers and Correspondence Bearing upon the Purchase; American State Papers: Foreign Affairs*, vol. 2; *Annals of Congress*, 8 Congress, 1 session; and the writings of Jefferson, Madison, and Monroe. Consult also Barbé-Marbois, *Louisiane*, 247–335, 351. Barbé-Marbois conducted the proceedings of the negotiation on the part of France. He was secretary of the French legation to the United States in 1779 and later resided in Philadelphia and married an American woman. A report written by Senator Charles Sumner, printed in 38 Congress, 1 session, *Senate Reports*, no. 41, pp. 1–43 (serial 1178) and as 41 Congress, 2 session, *Senate Reports*, no. 10 (serial 1409), is a full and learned account of the French spoliation claims. For the French text of the treaty of April 30, 1803, see De Clerq, *Recueil des traités*, 2: 59; for the convention of the same date see page 63.

officer transferred the possession to the United States. So
ended the Spanish dominion in the valley of the Mississippi.
The whole area of Minnesota West, about fifty-eight thousand square miles, became by this delivery American soil
on March 10, 1804.[14]

After the Louisiana purchase the United States held a
legal title to the whole area of Minnesota, but such title was
subject to that right of occupancy which it had been the
policy of Europeans to concede to the aborigines. At this
time, two Indian nations occupied Minnesota in unequal
portions, separated by an unstable boundary. The Siouan
people, at the time white men appeared in the Mississippi
Valley near the close of the seventeenth century, held
possession of that valley from its head to the Arkansas
River, and from Lake Michigan to the Rockies. There are
reasons which justify ethnologists in believing that they
were at some remote period migrants from an Atlantic
habitat lying between the Potomac and the Savannah, but
their immemorial establishment in the valley warrants us in
regarding them as holding it against other tribes by indisputable possession.[15] The northeast part of their territory
was occupied by the most numerous and powerful of the
Siouan nations, the Dakota, better known as the Sioux.[16]
Groseilliers and Radisson in 1660, Du Luth in 1679, and
Hennepin in the following year found a large tribe of these
Indians dwelling in large villages on and about Mille Lacs.

[14] Barbé-Marbois, *Louisiane*, 351-358; Carr, *Missouri*, 81. The boundary between
Minnesota West and the British possessions to the north remained in question, however,
until 1818.

[15] Cyrus Thomas, in his introduction to Charles C. Royce, *Indian Land Cessions in
the United States*, 527-538, 639-643 (Bureau of American Ethnology, *Eighteenth Annual
Report*, part 2 — Washington, 1899); W. J. McGee, *The Siouan Indians*, 157-204 (Bureau
of American Ethnology, *Fifteenth Annual Report* — Washington, 1897); Stephen R. Riggs,
Dakota Grammar, Texts, and Ethnography, 168-194 (United States Geographical and Geological Survey of the Rocky Mountain Region, *Contributions to North American Ethnology*,
vol. 9 — Washington, 1893); Winchell, *Aborigines of Minnesota*, 63-76.

[16] This name was the white man's contraction of *Nadouessioux*, "adder," a spiteful
Chippewa nickname. See Warren, in *Minnesota Historical Collections*, 5:72, 83, and Charle-
voix, *Nouvelle France*, 3:83. It would long ago have given way to the more euphonious
"Dakota" but for its persistent use by the government.

As yet they were in the stone age of culture, using stone hatchets, knives, arrows, and spearheads. Their clothing was of skins; their dwellings were of earth and bark when in the villages, of mats and skins when in the field for hunting or war. The archeological survey of Brower about Mille Lacs warrants the conclusion that these settlements were of great antiquity. From such a center it was not difficult for this tribe to dominate the hunting grounds reaching to the headwaters of the Chippewa, the St. Croix, the St. Louis, the Mississippi, and the tributaries of the Red River of the North.[17]

It became the fortune of the Sioux, who for long ages had held possession substantially of the whole area of Minnesota, to be disturbed by an intruding people which came against them with the steel knife and the terrible musket of the white man. The Chippewa or Ojibway nation, of Algonquian stock, was one of a number which, originally residing on the St. Lawrence River, were driven from their homes by the all-conquering Iroquois about the middle of the seventeenth century, to find new homes and hunting grounds beyond Lake Huron. Their earliest establishment was about the Sault de Ste. Marie, where by reason of the great abundance of food and freedom from hostile attack they appear to have greatly multiplied. One division continued the westward march along the north shore of Lake Superior and disappears from our view. The other, apparently the main division, followed the south shore of the great lake, at first in occasional hunting parties, later to establish permanent villages. In 1662 they were trading with Frenchmen at Keweenaw and three years later Allouez noted them as occasional visitors there. In 1692 the French established a permanent trading post at La Pointe, about which the

[17] Jacob V. Brower, *Kathio* (*Memoirs of Explorations in the Basin of the Mississippi, 1540–1665*, vol. 4 — St. Paul, 1901); Frederick W. Hodge, *Handbook of American Indians*, part 2, p. 577 (Bureau of American Ethnology, *Bulletins*, no. 30 — Washington, 1910); Samuel W. Pond, "The Dakotas or Sioux in Minnesota as they were in 1834," in *Minnesota Historical Collections*, 12: 319–501.

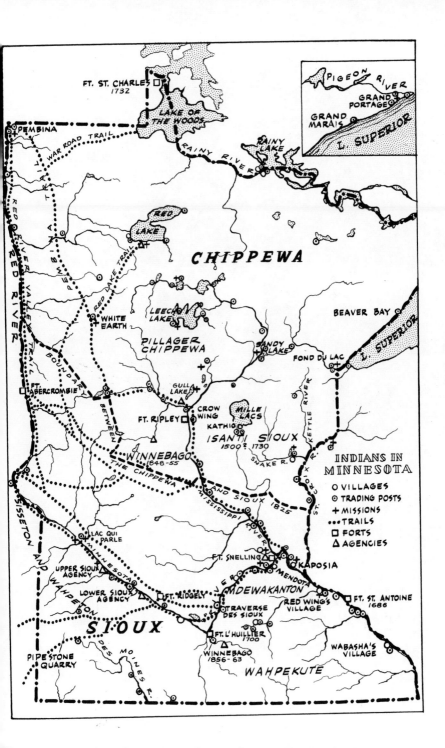

Chippewa concentrated in large numbers; and in that year Le Sueur was sent there to establish peace between them and the Sioux. By the middle of the eighteenth century the intruders, equipped with the white man's weapons, had seized upon the headwaters of the Chippewa and the St. Croix rivers in Wisconsin and had made lodgments to the west of Lake Superior. They then pushed rapidly to the south and west from the head of that lake and occupied Sandy, Leech, and Red lakes; by the close of the Revolutionary War there was not a single Dakota village left east of the Mississippi River above the Falls of St. Anthony. Thus were the Sioux, with an exception to be noted later, crowded to the west of the Mississippi and to the south of the Crow Wing.

This advance of the Chippewa was not accomplished without a half century of bloody warfare. Warren, the Chippewa half-breed who compiled the traditions of his Indian ancestors, could not conceal a note of triumph when recording their victories; but he was compelled to admit that the conquered lands were "strewed with the bones of his fathers, and enriched with their blood." This warfare, like that of all Indian enemies, commonly consisted of desultory forays repeated from year to year; but there were movements which reached the dignity of campaigns, and contests which may be called battles. Such were, mentioned in order of time, those of Mille Lacs and Point Prescott in the seventeenth century; of Sandy Lake, Crow Wing, Elk River, and St. Croix Falls in the eighteenth; and of Cross Lake in 1800, according to Chippewa chronology.[18] Separate descriptions of these battles would be unprofitable, but it may be permitted briefly to sketch from Chippewa tradition the campaign which culminated in the battle of Crow Wing, and

[18] Henry R. Schoolcraft, *Historical and Statistical Information Respecting the History, Condition, and Prospects of the Indian Tribes of the United States*, 5: 142–152 (Philadelphia, 1851–57); Neill, in *Minnesota Historical Collections*, 5: 395–450; Warren, in *Minnesota Historical Collections*, 5: 76–193, 222–246, 344–348; Alexander Ramsey, in 31 Congress, 2 session, *House Executive Documents*, no. 1, pp. 82–92 (serial 595).

resulted in the final expulsion of the Dakota from their lands east of the Mississippi.

This enterprise was probably undertaken within a year after the English conquest. The Sioux by this time had come into possession of firearms; and the bands which had been driven from Mille Lacs, now residing on the Rum River, were ambitious to recover their ancient hunting grounds from the invading Chippewa. They summoned to their aid the bands beyond the Mississippi, and the detachments assembled at the Falls of St. Anthony. Between four and five hundred warriors responded and joined in the dances and incantations preliminary to a raid on the foe. The campaign proposed was no ordinary dash of a raiding party content merely to gather in a few scalps. Not Hannibal nor Napoleon conceived a bolder or happier piece of strategy than that of the unknown savage commander. In essence it was to move a flying corps rapidly past the enemy's front, turn his right flank, and carry his central stronghold by surprise. The party embarked in canoes and moved up the Mississippi to the Crow Wing, and thence by Gull, White Fish, and a chain of smaller lakes, separated by a series of short portages well known to the Sioux, who had hunted thereaway for generations, into Leech Lake. After traversing the broad expanse of this lake, the expedition proceeded to Cass Lake, over two hundred miles from the starting point. Having entered the main stream of the Mississippi, which flows through this body of water, the eager warriors passed rapidly down with the current, hoping to fall upon the great Chippewa village on Sandy Lake unexpected and put out its fires forever. In this they were disappointed. Two Chippewa hunters saw them some distance upstream and paddled with might and main to carry the news to their people. The Sioux followed closely and, had they not stopped to capture a party of Chippewa women picking huckleberries, might have rushed pell-mell into the village and taken possession. The Sandy Lake Indians were ill prepared for defense. A party of their braves had taken the warpath for the Dakota country. The annual delegation to the Sault and Mackinac had just returned bringing enough fire water to disqualify the remaining braves for battle. Most of them were dead-drunk. The squaws were sober, and by a plentiful use of cold water they soon had some of the men in condition to fight. These made a stand against the Sioux and delayed their disembarkment. As others sobered up, their ranks were lengthened and filled, and so bravely did they do battle that the Sioux were forced to withdraw down river with a few female captives.

The Sioux had failed of the main object of the campaign, but a worse calamity awaited them. The absent Sandy Lake braves had reached the junction of the Crow Wing with the Mississippi after the Sioux expedition had passed up and there learned its magnitude and destination. It was too late to return to their village and share in its defense. The leaders resolved to await the enemy on their return and fall upon them from an ambush. Opposite the lower of the two mouths of the Crow Wing is an elongated hill or bluff some fifty feet high and five hundred feet long, running parallel with the Mississippi and sloping to the shore. Just above is a sharp curve nearly equal to a quarter circle, which throws the current against the east bank. On the crest of this hill the Chippewa dug a line of what in modern war books would be called "rifle pits," each deep enough and large enough to hold a half dozen or more men. While waiting for their prey, they hunted in the neighborhood for meat. Early one morning one of their scouts brought word that the enemy was near, and presently the leading canoes of the Sioux were seen emerging above the bend.

Unappreciative of the danger which awaited them, the Sioux made a landing in plain sight of the Chippewa trap and made their morning meal—for many of them the last. The captive women were rudely compelled to cook and serve. Embarking after the meal and a scalp dance for the last day's journey, within their own country, the Sioux formed their flotilla as if for parade. The canoes bore the feathered war ensigns and the Chippewa scalps on feathered poles. Drums were beating and the air was filled with yells of triumph. When they were fairly abreast of the ambuscade, the Chippewa leader gave the longed-for signal to fire. At the short range the fire was fatally effective, and many brave Sioux dropped dead. Many also were drowned; this because a wise old Chippewa woman captive had instructed her companions how to behave under circumstances which she thought might occur. At the flash of the guns, they capsized the canoes and swam off to their friends, leaving their captors to struggle in the water. As long as there were any Sioux in sight, the Chippewa continued their fire, killing and wounding the helpless foemen. The astonished Dakota rallied at a point out of range of the enemy's fire. Believing the Chippewa to be no more than a hunting party, they made an ineffectual effort to dislodge them. Next morning the Sioux renewed the attack, making use of successive lines of cover of logs and earth. They pushed their advance so near to the Chippewa pits as to be able to pitch stones into them. A famous Chippewa chief was thus wounded. The principle of this assault was none other than that of the latest firing tactics of modern infantry. Ammunition failing, the contest was waged with clubs and knives. The Chippewa, however, held their fort, and the Sioux with thinned and shortened ranks departed for their villages. Well aware that such a campaign as this would be followed by a countermovement on the part of the enemy, they soon after abandoned their villages east of the Mississippi and established themselves on the Minnesota River.[19]

[19] Warren, in *Minnesota Historical Collections*, 5: 222–232. For a map of the battle ground and vicinity, see Brower, *Minnesota*, 40. Consult Alfred Brunson, *A Western Pioneer: or, Incidents of the Life and Times of Rev. Alfred Brunson*, 2: 203 (Cincinnati, 1879), for an account of the battle given him by the trader William A. Aitkin in October, 1843. Brunson noticed "holes, apparently rifle pits and inquired what they meant." The account is rather circumstantial. See also Gideon H. Pond, "Dakota and Chippewa Wars," in the *Minnesota Chronicle and Register* (St. Paul), May 4, 1850.

These two Indian nations, the Dakota and the Chippewa, which divided between them the territory of Minnesota at the time the United States established her jurisdiction, were no strangers to the white man. For a hundred and twenty years at least they had been under his influence. He had revolutionized their industries and their warfare, and had profoundly affected their social life. These peoples were too remote to be much influenced by the military commanders of the Canadian government and had little concern about the annexation of their territory by proclamation. It was the missionary and the trader who came into immediate association with them. Of the missionaries it needs only to be said at this point that they were those of a generation later than the heroic Jesuits whose martyrdom is a glory of that society. These later missionaries were not infrequently interested in exploring the country and in learning the Siouan languages, content to evangelize by the way. Their influence on and among the French trading people and their half-breed descendants was no doubt for good so far as it was effective.

The influence of the trader on the Indian can hardly be overestimated. For knives and hatchets of stone the trader gave him those of steel. The earthen cooking pot he replaced with one of iron. To men accustomed to constant exposure of their bodies to the elements, the blanket was a most acceptable wrapping for extremes of cold and wet, and at night a most comfortable covering. To the squaw the trader brought the awl and the needle, and thread and glass beads which she soon learned to combine into really beautiful decorations for moccasins, girdles, and ceremonial belts. The firearm, however, was of first importance. The bow was no mean weapon. Its invention excites a wonder that the inventive power thus displayed did not find a larger scope in the use of native copper and in the smelting of iron ore, both so abundant in the Northwest. The gun — *mazawakan* (magic metal) as the Sioux called it — changed the Indian from a hunter providing for the needs of his family to a "pot hunter" slaughtering for the skins the trader was waiting to buy.   This occasioned a rapid and continuous decrease in game animals; and this increasing scarcity had the effect of rendering migratory people who in previous ages had been sedentary.   The intrusion of tribes in search of new hunting grounds changed the character of war.   Occasional forays to win the eagle plume gave place to bloody encounters between men defending their country and invaders seeking to escape starvation.

In many ways the white man's arts and goods and ministry were beneficial to the Indian.   It is equally true that ruin and death followed him to the native villages.   The multiplication of half-breeds had much to do with breaking up the totemic system of the Indians and other safeguards against endogamy.   The half-breed in many cases had all the vices and few of the virtues of both races.   Eminent exceptions to this general fact go far to atone for ancestral incontinence.   With the white man came smallpox and measles, which at times virtually exterminated villages and tribes.[20]   But among all the contributions of the paleface to Indian degradation and misery, the most potent was his intoxicating liquor, the deadly *miniwakan* of the Sioux. The white man through many generations had become to a degree immune to the full effects of the drugs.   The Indian constitution was highly susceptible to intoxication and possessed but slight resistance.   To the profit of the trader, a little liquor went a great way with Indians when first initiated.   From the beginning to the end of the fur trade it was understood among traders that the Indians must and would have liquor.[21]   If not supplied by the traders, it

[20] Warren states that the Ojibway lost in one epidemic of smallpox, probably in 1782, fifteen hundred or two thousand of their number.   The Sandy Lake village was reduced to seven wigwams.   *Minnesota Historical Collections*, 5: 260–262.

[21] "The traders . . . practise it [*the sale of liquor to the Indians*] without scruple whenever opportunities occur, and he who has the most whiskey generally carries off the furs. . . . The neighborhood of the trading houses where whiskey is sold, presents a disgusting

CHIPPEWA TRAVELING IN WINTER

CHIPPEWA TRAVELING IN SUMMER

*Water colors by Peter Rindisbacher, owned by the United States
Military Academy, West Point, New York*

INDIANS TRAVELING

SIOUX ENCAMPMENT

*Water colors by Seth Eastman, owned by the James Jerome Hill
Reference Library, St. Paul*

would be smuggled to them by a nefarious secret commerce. The Indian would not trade when the means of gratifying his darling passion was not to be had. The Hudson's Bay people, trading along our northern boundary, had liquor for sale. A journey of two hundred miles to get a taste of whisky or rum was joy to a Sioux or a Chippewa. The Northwest Company might as well have gone into liquidation as to have attempted trading without spirits. While it was the policy of this organization to place bounds to the supply of liquor to the Indian and not to take advantage of his passion for it to rob him, still results ensued from this moderation only preferable to the horrors which would have attended unlimited supplies by irresponsible dealers. The management of the "Old Nor'west" was so fair and liberal as to secure the good will of the Indian tribes with which it traded, and the most faithful service of its large body of employees.

For twenty years after the evacuation of the northwestern posts in 1796 the powerful Northwest Company maintained its influence and authority, and it may be considered that in the absence of United States military and civil agents it was better that it did. It is not important that the story of the internal dissensions of this company be told here, nor that of its quarrels with its powerful rival, the Hudson's Bay Company, which more than once occasioned bloodshed. Shut out from its business south of the Canadian border by the act of Congress of 1816, the company dwindled, and in 1821 it was merged into the Hudson's Bay Company, which is still in existence as a trading corporation. This company surrendered its political authority in 1870, precisely two hundred years after its incorporation.[22]

scene of drunkenness, debauchery, and misery. . . . In my route from St. Peters to this place [Detroit], I passed Prairie du Chiens, Green Bay, and Mackinac; no language can describe the scenes of vice which there present themselves. Herds of Indians are drawn together by the fascinations of whiskey, and they exhibit the most degraded picture of human nature I ever witnessed." Colonel Josiah Snelling to James Barbour, secretary of war, August 23, 1825, in 19 Congress, 1 session, *Senate Documents*, no. 58, p. 11 (serial 127).

[22] Bryce, *Hudson's Bay Company*, 24–44; Neill, *Minnesota*, 300–318. See also Wayne E. Stevens, "Fur Trading Companies in the Northwest, 1760–1816," in Mississippi Valley Historical Association, *Proceedings*, 9: 283–291 (1918), and Davidson, *North West Company*.

In 1804 the United States came into legal possession of nearly the whole area of Minnesota. Technically Minnesota East was part of Indiana Territory; Minnesota West was part of Upper Louisiana. In fact, there was no effective governmental authority, civil or military, in existence. The Chippewa Indians held all the country west of the Mississippi north of the Crow Wing and all east of the Mississippi except a narrow strip along the great river, claimed but hardly occupied by the Sioux. They recognized the authority of the Northwest Company, which had its chief trading post in Minnesota at Fond du Lac. The Sioux held all the remaining territory and were under the influence of British traders operating from Mackinac and Prairie du Chien. For all practical purposes the whole territory might as well have remained a part of Canada.

V. MINNESOTA EXPLORATIONS

IN THE year 1783 Thomas Jefferson, writing to George Rogers Clark, tells him of a large subscription being raised in England "for exploring the country from the Missisipi to California," and then asks, "How would you like to lead such a party?"[1] Three years later, in Paris, Jefferson encouraged John Ledyard of Connecticut to undertake his abortive journey, which would have carried him from the Pacific Coast eastward across the continent.[2] In 1792 he induced the American Philosophical Society, of which he was vice president, to finance a transcontinental expedition, to be conducted by his protégé Meriwether Lewis and the distinguished French botanist André Michaux. The recall of the latter by the French minister rendered this enterprise impracticable.[3] To such a mind as Jefferson's the problem which had allured and defied great spirits for nearly three hundred years must have been one of predominating interest. On January 13, 1803, as president, he is writing James Monroe urging him to accept the post of minister extraordinary to France in order to coöperate in the purchase of New Orleans and the Floridas. "All eyes, all hopes," he says, "are now fixed on you . . . for on the event of this mission depends the future destinies of this

[1] Reuben G. Thwaites, ed., *Original Journals of the Lewis and Clark Expedition, 1804–1806*, 7: 193 (New York, 1904–05).

[2] Ledyard, who had planned to embark at Kamchatka for Nootka Sound and thence to make his way to the sources of the Missouri, was arrested in far eastern Russia and was obliged to abandon his journey. See Jefferson, *Works*, 1: 103–105 (Federal edition), and Jared Sparks, *The Life of John Ledyard, the American Traveller; Comprising Selections from his Journals and Correspondence* (Cambridge, 1828); for a review of the latter volume, see the *North American Review*, 27: 360–371 (October, 1828).

[3] Thomas Jefferson, "Life of Captain Lewis," in Paul Allen, ed., *History of the Expedition of Captains Lewis and Clark, 1804-5-6*, 1: xlv (Hosmer edition, Chicago, 1902). See also Jefferson's letter of instructions to Michaux, January, 1793, in which the latter is directed to find "the shortest and most convenient route of communication between the United States and the Pacific ocean," proceeding by way of the Missouri River. Jefferson, *Works*, 7: 208–212.

republic."[4]   Did the vision of this dreamer span the continent then?   Five days later, January 18, Jefferson sent to Congress a confidential message which is a curiosity of statesmanship.   He proposed an appropriation of twenty-five hundred dollars to defray the costs of an expedition which, under guise of expanding our Indian trade in a region still foreign, should ascend the Missouri River, pass "possibly with a single portage" to some westward-flowing stream, and thereon descend to the western ocean.[5]   Congress agreed to the proposition and voted the money.   The absorbing story of the Lewis and Clark expedition cannot here be followed.   As the whole territory to be covered then belonged to France, President Jefferson obtained from the French minister a passport for the party.[6]

The exploration of the Missouri River would naturally suggest that of the main stream of which it was regarded as a tributary.   Although Jefferson made no mention of such an enterprise to Congress, it need not be doubted that he embraced in his great scheme for "advancing the geographical knowledge of the continent" an exploration of the upper Mississippi.   Instead of ordering personally the dispatch of an expedition he remitted that duty, after frequent communications on the subject, to General James Wilkinson, commanding at St. Louis.[7]   On July 30, 1805, that officer issued his order to First Lieutenant Zebulon M. Pike of the United States Army "to proceed up the Mississippi with all possible diligence."   This officer was then twenty-six years old and had been in the service since the age of fifteen.   His

[4] Jefferson, *Works*, 9: 419.

[5] Jefferson, *Works*, 9: 433.   See also Jefferson's instructions to Captain Lewis, June 20, 1803, in his *Works*, 9: 423–429, n.

[6] Jefferson, *Works*, 9: 424, n.   An understanding was had with the Spanish and English ministers before the issuance of the passport.

[7] *American State Papers: Miscellaneous*, 1: 463, 944; Henry R. Schoolcraft, *Summary Narrative of an Exploratory Expedition to the Sources of the Mississippi River in 1820, Resumed and Completed by the Discovery of Its Origin in Itasca Lake in 1832*, xi (Philadelphia, 1855); James Parton, *Life of Thomas Jefferson*, 629 (Boston, 1874); Edward D. Neill, "Occurrences in and around Fort Snelling from 1819 to 1840," in *Minnesota Historical Collections*, 2: 102; Henry H. Sibley, "Reminiscences Historical and Personal," in *Minnesota Historical Collections*, 1: 471 (St. Paul, 1872).

school education was obviously very slender. Little is known of his conduct up to this time, but his later history abundantly justifies his selection for this expedition.[8]

His brief instructions were: to record his topographical observations in a diary; to note the "population and residence" of the Indians, and to spare no pains to conciliate them; to look for positions suitable for military posts; and to ascend the main branch of the Mississippi to its source. Into a postscript General Wilkinson throws an item of much interest to Minnesotans. "In addition to the preceding orders, you will be pleased to obtain permission from the Indians who claim the ground, for the erection of military posts and trading houses, at the mouth of the river St. Pierre, the Falls of St. Anthony, and every other critical point which may fall under your observation."[9] The policy of maintaining government trading houses, repeatedly commended by Jefferson, was still entertained.[10] The commander expected the return of the subaltern before the river should be frozen up.

The first entry in Pike's diary, religiously kept to the end, is: "Sailed from my encampment, near St. Louis, at 4 p.m., on Friday, the 9th of August, 1805, with one sergeant, two corporals, and 17 privates, in a keel-boat 70 feet long, provisioned for four months."[11] On September 4 Pike

[8] A brief, authoritative sketch of the life of Major Pike is Coues, "Memoir of Zebulon Montgomery Pike," in Pike, *Expeditions*, 1: xi–cxiii. See also Henry Whiting, "Life of Zebulon Montgomery Pike," in Sparks, *Library of American Biography*, 15: 217–314 (Boston, 1845), and William J. Backes, "General Zebulon M. Pike, Somerset-Born," in the *Somerset County* [New Jersey] *Historical Quarterly*, 8: 241–251 (October, 1919).

[9] *American State Papers: Miscellaneous*, 1: 942.

[10] Information on government Indian trading houses or factories may be found by consulting, under Furs, Trade, Traders, and Trading houses, the index to *American State Papers: Indian Affairs*, vol. 2. See also Frederick J. Turner, "The Character and Influence of the Fur Trade in Wisconsin," in Wisconsin Historical Society, *Proceedings*, 1889, pp. 52–98; Neill, in Minnesota Historical Society, *Annals*, 1856, pp. 96–99; Solon J. Buck, *Illinois in 1818*, 17–21 (Illinois Centennial Commission, *Publications*, introductory volume — Springfield, 1917); and Lawrence Taliaferro, "Autobiography," in *Minnesota Historical Collections*, 6: 228.

[11] This journal was first published in Washington in 1807 with the title *An Account of a Voyage up the Mississippi River from St. Louis to its Source*. It was republished under the direction of the author in Philadelphia in 1810, in his *An Account of Expeditions to the Sources of the Mississippi, and through the Western Parts of Louisiana, to the Sources of the Arkansaw, Kans, La Platte, and Pierre Juan Rivers, during the Years 1805, 1806, and 1807*.

passed Prairie du Chien, then a village of about 370 people, where he changed his keel boat for two bateaux.[12] He reached the mouth of the Minnesota on the twenty-first, and made camp on the western margin of the island now known by his name. In the late afternoon of the next day a party of 150 Sioux warriors arrived, having given up a raid on the Chippewa to see what the white man might have for them. This party was led by Little Crow, grandfather of that Little Crow who headed the Sioux Outbreak of 1862. On the twenty-third at noon there was a council. Pike opened it with a speech, which he reports in full. It was in the traditional vein of Indian-council eloquence, but no little good sense was injected. He stated the object of his expedition, with some variation from his instructions; gave notice that the American nation was free and independent of the English; stigmatized the Canadian traders who kept the Chippewa stirred up against the Sioux as "bad birds"; advised the chiefs to prevent their men from paying debts to traders who sold them rum; gave notice of the intention of the government to establish factories at the trading posts, where Indians would be able to buy cheaper than of the traders; and exhorted the Sioux to make a permanent peace with the Chippewa. Principally he asked the Sioux to release two pieces of land, one at the mouth of the St. Croix, the other at the Falls of St. Anthony.[13] As the

It is a proper journal and not a narrative written up at leisure from memory. In a letter to General Wilkinson, Lieutenant Pike tells of "the daily occurrences written at night, frequently by firelight . . . and the cold so severe as to freeze the ink in my pen." A reprint of the 1810 edition was brought out in New York in 1895 under the editorship of Elliott Coues, whose elaborate and learned notes are diversified by gratuitous displays of his private opinions on politics and religion. Citations are to this edition. See Coues's bibliography of the editions of Pike's journal and of the "books to which his expeditions gave rise," in *Expeditions*, 1: xxxiii–1. Note is herein made of the version prepared by Neill which appeared in Minnesota Historical Society, *Annals*, 1856, pp. 64–96. Under the title "Pike's Explorations in Minnesota, 1805–6," this version, somewhat abridged and with annotations by J. Fletcher Williams, was reprinted in *Minnesota Historical Collections*, 1: 368–416.

[12] Pike gives a detailed description of Prairie du Chien, which was at this time the extreme frontier post in this region. After the establishment of Fort Snelling its importance lessened. At the time of Long's expedition of 1823 its population numbered only 150. Keating, *Narrative*, 1: 245.

[13] For Pike's speech, see his *Expeditions*, 1: 226–230. His report of the council is given fully in a letter to Wilkinson, dated September 23, 1805, in his *Expeditions*, 1: 232–244.

lieutenant had privately fed two of the chiefs beforehand, and was presumed to be ready with the usual presents, there was no delay in securing verbal assent; but some persuasion was necessary to induce the Indians to touch the pen to the written treaty. As this was the first conveyance of an interest in land executed in Minnesota it is well to give the text.[14]

Whereas, at a conference held between the United States of America and the Sioux nation of Indians, Lieut. Z. M. Pike, of the army of the United States, and the chiefs and warriors of the said tribe, have agreed to the following articles, which, when ratified and approved of by the proper authority, shall be binding on both parties:

ARTICLE 1. That the Sioux nation grants unto the United States, for the purpose of the establishment of military posts, nine miles square at the mouth of the river St. Croix, also, from below the confluence of the Mississippi and St. Peter's, up the Mississippi, to include the falls of St. Anthony, extending nine miles on each side of the river. That the Sioux nation grants to the United States, the full sovereignty and power over said districts, forever, without any let or hindrance whatsoever.

ART. 2. That, in consideration of the above grants, the United States

ART. 3. The United States promise, on their part, to permit the Sioux to pass, repass, hunt, or make other uses of the said districts, as they have formerly done, without any other exception but those specified in article first.

In testimony hereof, we, the undersigned, have hereunto set our hands and seals, at the mouth of the river St. Peter's, on the twenty third day of September, one thousand eight hundred and five.

Z. M. PIKE, *first Lieutenant,*   [SEAL.]
    And Agent at the above conference.
LE PETIT CORBEAU, his X mark.   [SEAL.]
WAY AGA ENAGEE, his X mark.   [SEAL.]

On April 16, 1808, the Senate ratified this treaty and filled the blank in article 2 by adding after "States" the words: "shall, prior to taking possession thereof, pay to the Sioux

[14] *American State Papers: Indian Affairs,* 1:754. The Senate committee, to which the treaty was referred, estimated the amount of land acquired at 155,520 acres (103,680 acres at the Falls of St. Anthony, the remainder at the mouth of the St. Croix), and the price paid at about 1.28 cents an acre. See *American State Papers: Indian Affairs,* 1:755. Pike's estimate is "100,000 acres for a song." See his *Expeditions,* 1:240.

two thousand dollars, or deliver the value thereof in such goods and merchandise as they shall choose."

An ingenious critic has pointed out that this pretended conveyance is defective in the following respects: The parties concerned were incompetent, Pike not being an agent of the United States authorized to negotiate such a treaty and these Indians being warriors of one band only of the lower Sioux; the descriptions are hopelessly indefinite; no consideration is specified; no witnesses are named.[15]   To these criticisms may be added another; namely, that the United States had no need to stipulate for sovereignty, because it was already vested with that.   The only Indian title known to our law is and was that of occupancy, terminable by negotiation.   As soon as the instrument was signed, however, Pike distributed presents worth two hundred dollars; the traders and he gave out sixty gallons of liquor; and in half an hour the savages had dispersed to their villages.   If the transaction was not technically legal, all was well meant, and later all its irregularities were healed.   None of the chiefs questioned the sale at the time it was made, but many years afterwards a claim for additional compensation was allowed.[16]

On September 26 Pike was at the Falls of St. Anthony, which he describes with accuracy, although he wastes not a word of sentiment upon scenery.[17]   Here he was delayed five days by sickness among his men and in passing his

[15] Coues, in Pike, *Expeditions*, 1: 232, n. 6.   It should be noted that one of the seven bands of the Mdewakanton tribe assumed to convey the rights not only of the other bands but also of the other tribes which made up the Sioux nation.

[16] See the manuscript journal of Lawrence Taliaferro, the Indian agent, for September 7, 1830, for the demand.   The Indians claimed that "they only gave Pike . . . as far as can be seen around the Fort without *elevating the eyes*."   The agent's entries for June 22, October 11, 12, 14, and 15, 1838, indicate that four thousand dollars were paid.   There is reason for suspecting that the payment or the promise of payment was a parol inducement to secure the signatures of the chiefs to the treaty of 1837.   On March 11, 1850, Philander Prescott wrote Sibley that the Indians were talking a good deal and "say they never sold the reserve to the Gov^t."   Sibley Papers.

[17] Pike's descriptions of the falls are found in his letter to Wilkinson, September 26, 1805, and in "Observations on the Soil, Shores . . . Islands, Rapids, Confluent Streams . . . and Settlements on the Mississippi," in his *Expeditions*, 1: 244, 311.

boats and their cargoes by the "usual portage" on the east bank. The navigation above the falls he found difficult. Rapids and shoals alternated with unexpected frequency. Much of the time his soldiers were in the water dragging the boats over these and other obstructions. His invalids marched as flankers on the banks.[18] On the sixteenth of October a heavy snowstorm overtook the party near the site of Little Falls in Morrison County. The boats were leaking and the prospect of wading the chutes at the Little Falls up to the neck was discouraging. Pike now gave up his design of reaching the Crow Wing River before ice should form, and returned to a beautiful and convenient spot where he had bivouacked the night before, situated four miles south of Little Falls on the west bank of the Mississippi, eighty rods below the mouth of the Swan River. The rapids of the Mississippi immediately above still bear Pike's name. On the seventeenth his men were slashing the splendid pines at hand and rolling up a log house forty feet square. This and other constructions he later inclosed with pickets and thus made so good a fort that he "would have laughed at the attack of 800 or 1,000 savages."[19] Pike himself seems to have continued lodging in his tent, which his men "raised with puncheons" to form a floor. Having thus secured a sure base, Pike was impatient to continue his march.

[18] In his introduction to the journal Pike says, "I literally performed the duties (as far as my limited abilities permitted) of astronomer, surveyor, commanding officer, clerk, spy, guide, and hunter; frequently preceding the party for miles in order to reconnoiter." *Expeditions*, 1: ii.

[19] The position of the fort has been positively identified by Judge Nathan Richardson of Little Falls, Minnesota. "The location is on the West bank of the Mississippi River on Government Subdivision described as Lot No. 1, Sec. No. 7, in Township No. 128 North, of Range No. 29 West, of the 5th Principal Meridian, near the S. E. corner of said Lot No. 1, and near 80 rods south from the mouth of the Swan river and four miles south of this city." See his letter to Coues, February 24, 1894, in Pike, *Expeditions*, 1: 106, n. 21. See also Nathan Richardson, "History of Morrison County," in the *Little Falls Transcript* (weekly), February 27, 1880. On September 27, 1919, the Minnesota Society of the Daughters of the American Revolution placed a bronze tablet, properly inscribed, on the face of a cairn which had been erected on the site of one of the fireplaces of the fort. See the *Minneapolis Tribune*, September 28, 1919; the *Little Falls Daily Transcript*, September 29, 1919; and the *Minnesota History Bulletin*, 3: 229 (November, 1919). Judge Richardson had previously established a large bowlder as a marker.

On October 28 he loaded two dugouts, which his men had
made, with provisions and ammunition at the head of the
rapids.   Leaking through an unseen wind-shake, one of
these, containing ammunition, almost immediately sank to
the bottom.   While his choppers were working on another
pirogue Pike undertook to dry his powder by spreading it
on blankets and building fires around them.   An experiment in drying some of it in iron pots came near blowing up
two or three men.   It was now too late to think of navigation.   The ingenious lieutenant resolved to await the closing
of the river and meantime to build wooden sleds for the
carriage of his supplies on the ice.   The season so far seems
to have been an unusually mild one, and the river did not
close.   Impatient to reach his goal, the sources of the great
river, he at length resolved "to embark by land and water."
On December 10 he left the post with sleds and one pirogue
"towed by three men."   The march was slow and toilsome.
The snow melting, he was obliged to cache portions of his
loads.   Still his sleds broke through the ice.   One of them
took down his own baggage and all the ammunition.   Fortunately the water-tight kegs of powder were saved, or Pike
would have been marching for St. Louis.   His tent took fire
in a bitter night.   The sentry's alarm enabled the men to
rouse the lieutenant and get him and his three kegs of powder out.   He lost "leggins, mockinsons, socks, etc. . . . no
trivial misfortune."   A cold snap came down so that the
men had to halt and build fires every three miles.   Fingers,
noses, and toes were frozen.[20]   Snow fell to the depth of
three feet.   On January 8, 1806, Pike, with Corporal Bradley marching in advance, after a weary tramp stumbled late
at night upon the open gate of a stockade, the Northwest
Company's post at Sandy Lake.   The agent, Grant, received them with the "utmost hospitality."   It was five
days later when the remainder of the detachment came in,

[20] Pike's record shows no temperature below zero (Fahrenheit) in the whole winter.
Expeditions, 1: 216–220.

to be housed in an excellent room, supplied with potatoes, and regaled with *fille*, the local French cant for a dram of whisky. Pike found the superintendent and his employees living in tolerable comfort. They had horses, plenty of Irish potatoes grown by themselves, and an abundance of game and fish. Still their main diet was "wild oats" (probably wild rice) bought of the Indians for a dollar and a half a bushel. Even the principals could not indulge themselves lavishly on flour at half a dollar, salt at a dollar, pork at eighty cents, and tea at four dollars and a half a pound. During a rest of twelve days spent at Sandy Lake, the thrifty commander rearranged his transportation. He set his men to sawing stocks for *traîneaux de glace*, or toboggans, constructed after the manner of the country.

It was the twentieth of January before Pike resumed the trail, taking the Willow River route to Pokegama Falls and thence following the Mississippi to the Leech Lake fork. On the evening of the first of February the tireless explorer, with a single soldier, was ceremoniously welcomed to the Leech Lake post of the Northwest Company.[21] It was with keen delight, no doubt, that he relished the "good dish of coffee, biscuit, butter, and cheese for supper." Although his legs and ankles were so swollen that he could not wear his own clothes, Pike was a happy man. He had "accomplished his voyage" by reaching the "main source of the Mississippi." He was nearly right, although he had not penetrated to the ultimate source of the great river. With characteristic reticence he devotes less than three lines to the record of this first-rate exploit. His learned editor with justice suggests that Leech Lake with its tributaries be known as the "Pikean source of the Mississippi."[22]

Pike devoted one day to composing an elaborate letter to Hugh McGillis, his host, director of the Fond du Lac department of the Northwest Company. In courteous but direct

[21] For Pike's descriptions of the Northwest Company's establishments at Sandy and Leech lakes, see his *Expeditions*, 1: 281, 282.
[22] Coues, in Pike, *Expeditions*, 1: 151, n. 56.

terms McGillis is told that British goods must not be introduced till after payment of duties at Mackinac; that the English flag must on no pretense whatever be hoisted over his trading posts; that no political dealings shall be had with the Indians; and that the commerce of the company shall be regulated by American law, upon which he is advised to inform himself.[23]　Pike estimated the loss of revenue which the United States had been suffering at twenty-six thousand dollars annually.[24]　In a communication equally diplomatic, McGillis replied to Pike's "address" a week later, conceding every point and promising, so far as he could, the conformity of his principals.[25]　Up to the date of Pike's letter to McGillis, February 7, 1806, the "English yacht [*Jack*]" had been flying over the post.　On the tenth the lieutenant had it shot away by the Indians and his riflemen, and the peace of 1783 thereupon took symbolic effect in northern Minnesota.

While still lame Pike set out on the twelfth for Upper Red Cedar Lake, thirty miles to the northwest, the same body of water reached by Cass's expedition in 1820 and since that time known by his name.　This lake Pike thought to be "the upper source of the Mississippi."　Cass's geographer, Douglass, in 1820 believed it to be the ultimate source.　But three days were given to this excursion.　On the sixteenth a council was held at Leech Lake with the chiefs and warriors of the Chippewa of Leech and Cass lakes.　Pike's injunctions were that they should keep peace with the Sioux, give up their English flags and medals, pay their debts to the traders, and give up the use of liquor.　As for the liquor the traders had on hand, he consented that they might sell it, and thus enable the Indians to "forget it by degrees"; but no more was to be brought into the country.[26]

[23] *Expeditions*, 1: 247.
[24] *Expeditions*, 1: 280.
[25] *Expeditions*, 1: 251.
[26] For Pike's address and the replies of the Chippewa chiefs, see his *Expeditions*, 1: 254–261.

The medals and flags were immediately turned in without apparent reluctance. Every Indian present solemnly smoked from the pipe of Wabasha, a great Sioux chief, which Pike had brought up for the occasion. The next day Pike paraded his army of eleven men, put them through the manual of arms, and fired some blank cartridges, thus doubtless impressing the savage imagination with the power and dignity of their Great Father at Washington.

The return journey, begun on February 18, is mostly without interest for the ordinary reader of this narrative. Pike decided to abandon the stores left at Sandy Lake and to descend in a general southward direction by way of White Fish Lake to the Mississippi. As he passed down, he recovered his cached provisions. It was fortunate that he did so, for, on arriving at his Swan River fort on the fifth of March, he found that his trusted sergeant left in charge had been squandering flour, pork, and liquor upon the men of his command and upon Indians. In particular, a keg of whisky — "for my own use," says the diarist — this faithless subordinate had publicly sold. Very properly was he put into confinement and four days later reduced to the ranks. A month was passed at this fort while the expedition waited for the river to open. On the seventh of April the party took leave of the fort. On the eleventh the portage around the Falls of St. Anthony was completed. "The appearance of the Falls," in the words of the explorer, "was much more tremendous than when we ascended." The same evening on the site of Fort Snelling a council with the Sioux of the local bands was held, with the result that much good tobacco was burned, all in Chippewa pipes which Pike had brought down from Leech Lake. The final entry in the journal is: "*Apr. 30th.* . . . Arrived about twelve o'clock at the town [*St. Louis*], after an absence of eight months and 22 days."

In taking leave of this interesting character, it may be remarked that his success in this undertaking led to his detail in the same year, 1806, for a similar expedition to the sources of the Arkansas and other southwestern rivers, which unexpectedly extended into an enforced tour into New Spain, lasting nearly a year.[27] During his absence he was promoted to the rank of captain, and in due order he became major and lieutenant colonel of infantry. At the outbreak of the War of 1812 he was colonel of the Fifteenth Infantry, which he disciplined and drilled in an original fashion. In March, 1813, he was made brigadier general. He commanded in the successful attack on the British position at Toronto, Canada, then known as York, April 27, 1813. As the enemy were retiring and the Americans were entering the place, the British commander ordered the principal magazine blown up. Among the two hundred and more American casualties was the mortal wound of General Pike.[28]

Since Pike's expedition to the head of the Mississippi was not followed up, it had no effect other than to add to geographical knowledge. It is not likely that the treasury was enriched to any degree by the duties on Indian goods which McGillis had promised to pay. Doubtless the cross of St. George continued to float over every trading post of the Northwest Company, which remained in undisturbed possession of the territory west of Lake Superior. When the War of 1812 came on, the company's leading agents received commissions in the British army and gathered considerable bodies of Indians for the western campaigns.[29] All Minne-

[27] Pike's account of this journey may be read in his *Expeditions*, 2: 357–715.

[28] In an address delivered at the Pike centennial celebrations at Fort Snelling, September 23, and at Little Falls, Minnesota, October 16, 1905, Dr. Warren Upham gave a brief sketch and appreciation of Pike, which, under the title "The Life and Military Services of Zebulon M. Pike," is in *Minnesota Historical Collections*, 12: 302–304.

[29] Neill, *Minnesota*, 278–289. Joseph Rolette and Joseph Renville are among the agents named. See also *Wisconsin Historical Collections*, 13: 11, 33, 88; 18: xix, 468.

Colonel Robert Dickson had his headquarters at Prairie du Chien for some thirty years before the evacuation of that post by the British in 1815. He led a party of Indians, composed of Sioux, Winnebago, and Menominee, in the capture of Mackinac by the British, July 17, 1812, and coöperated in the recapture of Fort Shelby or Prairie du Chien, July 17, 1814. See Louise P. Kellogg, "The Capture of Mackinac in 1812," in *Wisconsin Historical Society, Proceedings*, 1912, pp. 124–145, and Ernest A. Cruikshank, "Robert Dickson, the

sota virtually remained British territory till May 24, 1815, when the British flag came down at Prairie du Chien, eight months and more after the signing of the treaty of Ghent.[30]

The rapid march of Pike in the winter of 1806 to Sandy and Cass lakes gave few opportunities for recording topography, and almost none for observations on the physiography and resources of the region traversed. The upper Mississippi wilderness remained untraveled except by fur-traders and savage war parties. Their accounts were such as to arouse curiosity, both private and official, for fuller knowledge. To reach and identify the source of the Mississippi had, by the time of the establishment of Fort Snelling in 1819,[31] become the ambition of at least one public man of enterprise and foresight. Lewis Cass, born in New Hampshire in 1782, after practicing law some ten years in Zanesville, Ohio, entered the army as a colonel of volunteers in 1812, and served under the unfortunate Hull at and about Detroit. His conduct was such as to lead to his promotion to the rank of brigadier general the following year, and to his appointment as governor of Michigan Territory at the close of the war. He held this office for eighteen years and discharged it with great intelligence and fidelity. Few, if any, men of his day had a better talent for managing a mixed population of Indians, Frenchmen, half-breeds, and pioneer settlers. It is almost a pity that his brilliant career in this office has been eclipsed by later services in senatorial, cabinet, and ambassadorial positions.[32]

Indian Trader," in *Wisconsin Historical Collections*, 12: 133–153. Pike, on descending the Mississippi in the spring of 1806, found Dickson at a trading post below St. Cloud and he records his infinite indebtedness to him. See Pike, *Expeditions*, 89, 90. Neill, in his *Minnesota*, 289–291, states that as late as 1817 Dickson was living at Lake Traverse and was believed to be alienating the Indians from the United States. Dickson is reputed to have exercised an unbounded influence over the Indians of the Northwest and to have established a neutral zone of a radius of twenty-five leagues (about seventy miles) with Prairie du Chien as its center. John Shaw, "Indian Chiefs and Pioneers of the Northwest," in *Wisconsin Historical Collections*, 10: 213.

[30] *Wisconsin Historical Collections*, 11: 259; Thomas G. Anderson, "Narrative," in *Wisconsin Historical Collections*, 9: 201.

[31] See *post*, pp. 134–140, for an account of the establishment of Fort Snelling.

[32] Andrew C. McLaughlin, *Lewis Cass*, 33–129 (*American Statesmen* series — New York and Boston, 1891); McLaughlin, "The Influence of Governor Cass on the Develop-

The legislation of 1818 added to Michigan Territory all the land lying north of Illinois between Lake Michigan and the Mississippi River.[33] Governor Cass of Michigan was naturally interested in this extension of his jurisdiction. Accordingly, we find him in the following year applying to Secretary Calhoun for authority and means to lead an expedition to its western confines, suggesting as proper objects a better acquaintance with the Indian tribes of the region and a further detachment of them from British influences, which had not even yet ceased; the "extinction of Indian titles to the land in the vicinity of the Straits of St. Mary's, Prairie du Chien, Green Bay, and upon the communication between the two latter places"; an investigation of reported mineral deposits in some variety and of great richness in the Lake Superior region; and the preparation of "a correct chart for the information of the Government." The authority was granted, with instructions, however, that there was to be no attempt to obtain title to Indian lands except at the Sault de Ste. Marie; and preparations were made for an expedition to leave Detroit early in the spring of 1820. An engineer officer, Captain David B. Douglass, afterwards distinguished in military and civil life, was detailed to conduct the geodetic and topographical work. Henry R. Schoolcraft, whom we are to encounter in the sequel, was employed as the mineralogist at a salary of a dollar and a half a day.[34] The journal which Schoolcraft kept and published is a charming narrative of an expedition which turned out to be rather uneventful.[35]

ment of the Northwest," in American Historical Association, *Papers*, 3: 311–327; Dwight G. McCarty, *The Territorial Governors of the Old Northwest*, 125–141 (Iowa City, 1910).

[33] See *post*, p. 231.

[34] *American State Papers: Indian Affairs*, 2: 318–320.

[35] Schoolcraft's journal was published at Albany in 1821 under the title *Narrative Journal of Travels through the Northwestern Regions of the United States Extending from Detroit through the Great Chain of American Lakes to the Sources of the Mississippi River . . . in the Year 1820*. The present narrative follows this work. Another account of the expedition in narrative form comprises the first part of Schoolcraft, *Summary Narrative*, 39–177. The official journal of the Cass expedition was kept by James D. Doty and was published for the first time in *Wisconsin Historical Collections*, 13: 163–219 (Madison, 1895).

The party of thirty-eight, including ten Indians, seven soldiers, and ten Canadian *voyageurs*, left Detroit on May 24, 1820, in three birch-bark canoes. Fourteen days' paddling brought them to Michilimackinac, the "northwestern metropolis," where Ramsay Crooks and Robert Stuart were the local managers of the American Fur Company. At the Sault de Ste. Marie, which was reached on June 14, an affair of no slight interest occurred. Governor Cass was more fully aware than any man in office of the pertinacity with which the British authorities continued after the War of 1812 to draw the Indians to Drummond's Island in Lake Huron by annual distributions of presents, in order to keep them in the habit of looking to the English as their ancient and trusted protectors. On June 16 he called a council of the Saulteur Chippewa and proposed a cession by them of sixteen square miles of land, the same area which both the French and the English had occupied for military purposes.[36] After a stormy debate the principal chief kicked out of his way the presents which had been laid before him and stalked off to his lodge, followed by his companions. A few minutes later a British flag appeared over the Indian encampment. Governor Cass instantly ordered his guard under arms and, taking his interpreter, walked boldly to the lodge of the Indian chief before whose door it had been raised. He pulled down the British colors and, in an address to the assembled chiefs, told them that but one flag could wave over them, that of the American Great Father, and that any attempt to hoist another would result in severe punishment.[37] Later in the day, under advice of older chiefs who had not been present at the council, the treaty of cession was signed.[38]

[36] The United States could rightfully claim this land under the third article of the treaty of Greenville, August 3, 1795, confirmed by the later treaties of Spring Wells, September 8, 1815, and Fort Harrison, June 4, 1816. United States, *Statutes at Large*, 7: 49, 131, 145.

[37] An account of this incident as given by Charles C. Trowbridge, who accompanied the expedition, is in *Wisconsin Historical Collections*, 5: 410–416.

[38] *Statutes at Large*, 7: 206.

It was the fifth of July when the expedition, having coasted
the south shore of Lake Superior, reached the post of the
American Fur Company on the St. Louis River.[39]   On the
following day the party proceeded up the river to the principal falls, where the two larger boats were exchanged for
four smaller ones, and on the ninth the journey was resumed
in seven canoes.   Navigation was rendered difficult by falls
and rapids, and the canoes were crowded.   After four days'
travel Governor Cass detailed sixteen of the party to make
a journey overland to the American Fur Company's post at
Sandy Lake.   With the remainder he pushed on up the St.
Louis to the mouth of the East Savanna.   He ascended this
tributary, took the six-mile portage to the West Savanna,
paddled down it, and reached Sandy Lake on July 15 to
find that the overland party had been waiting for him two
days.   Here a council was held on the sixteenth with the
local Chippewa.   The speeches of the chiefs, delivered with
a great show of eloquence, were pitiful appeals for knives
and blankets, guns and powder, lead and cloth, kettles and
tomahawks, tobacco and whisky.   They agreed to send
along with the returning expedition a delegation to treat
for peace with the Sioux.

From Sandy Lake, Governor Cass with a detached party
proceeded up the Mississippi to the lake called by Pike
Upper Red Cedar but named Cassina on Captain Douglass'
chart at Schoolcraft's suggestion.   Shortened to Cass Lake,
the name still appropriately stands on succeeding maps.
Schoolcraft states in his journal that "this [lake] may be
considered the true source of the Mississippi River."   He
proceeds at once, however, to mention two inlets, one flowing
from a lake forty miles distant, the other from one "which
lies six days journey, with a canoe, west-northwest."   We
shall see later that Schoolcraft did not place much confidence
in the statement which, out of deference to his chief, he had
felt obliged to make.   He even adds that the largest inlet of

[39] This post was on the site of the present village of Fond du Lac.

the lake, the River La Biche, was called Mississippi by *voyageurs*.

Having spent two hours on July 21 at the supposed "true source of the Mississippi," the party returned to Sandy Lake after an absence of one week. The united expedition embarked without delay and, aided by the current, reached the Falls of St. Anthony on the morning of the thirtieth. Of the falls Schoolcraft merely remarks on their pleasing simplicity, but he records the exceeding beauty of the prairie on both banks about them. The command reached Fort Snelling at 3 P.M. on the same day and was received with an appropriate salute of artillery.[40] The journal is silent as to the hospitality shown by the garrison but expresses satisfaction at presents of "green corn, peas, beans, cucumbers, beets, radishes, lettuce, &c." from the post garden. About ninety acres of bottom and prairie land were under cultivation, mostly in Indian corn and potatoes. Wheat was already ripe. Members of the garrison spoke in high praise of the climate, but the surgeon refused to exhibit his meteorological records except under promise of secrecy. On August 1 the Sioux residing in the neighborhood, who had been summoned for the purpose, and the Chippewa brought from above were induced to go through the farce of a treaty of peace, which they understood better than the white man would last only till the first chance for taking a scalp by one party or the other. On the following day the flotilla was headed down the Mississippi and on August 5 it reached Prairie du Chien, a village of five hundred people exclusive of the garrison of Fort Crawford. After a short delay the homeward journey began by the Fox-Wisconsin route, and on September 23 the last of the party — the escort of soldiers and the Indians having been dismissed at Green Bay — landed at Detroit. This true journey of exploration, judiciously planned and successfully executed, was well worth

---

[40] Doty states that the party reached Fort Snelling during the afternoon of the thirty-first. *Wisconsin Historical Collections*, 13: 212.

all it cost, although later observations revealed much that was defective and mistaken in its record.[41]

The courses of the Mississippi and its tributary, the Missouri, had now been charted from their supposed sources to their confluence. Between them lay a vast, fan-shaped area, little known except to the savages and their parasites, the traders. The meager reports of the resources of this region were conflicting. Traders desiring to keep other white men away from the scenes of their exploitations gave pessimistic accounts. The fabled great American desert was a fiction which they originated. The Minnesota River, at that time known as the St. Peter's, had not been navigated by any explorer since Carver, whose account of its extensive valley is so full of exaggeration as to warrant the suspicion that his ascent of it was wholly imaginary.[42] Vague rumors of a region of great richness and promise drained by the Red River of the North had been brought by occasional emissaries from the Hudson's Bay Company's settlement near the national boundary. To extend and correct the map of these rivers and valleys would have justified the government in sending out another party of exploration. It is probable, however, that the decisive consideration was the complaints of interested American citizens that British subjects, concealed behind American licenses, were still getting the better part of the fur trade in the Red River country.

By a war department order of April 25, 1823, Major Stephen H. Long was authorized to conduct an expedition up the Minnesota and down the Red River to the forty-ninth degree of north latitude and thence eastward along the Canadian boundary, which had not yet been traced from the latter river to Lake Superior. Five days later the party left Philadelphia and, traveling by the then usual

[41] In his letter to Secretary Calhoun, November 18, 1820, Cass estimated that from $1,000 to $1,500 would be required to finance the expedition. The bill of expenditures actually totaled $6,318.02. *American State Papers: Indian Affairs*, 2: 284, 304, 305, 308, 313, 319.

[42] For example, he reports the stream as holding a width of one hundred yards for two hundred miles and as of great depth. See his *Travels*, 75. See also *ante*, p. 56.

conveyances, it reached Fort Snelling on July 2. On the staff were a zoölogist and antiquary and a landscape painter. Professor William H. Keating of the University of Pennsylvania was mineralogist and geologist. The narrative of this expedition, compiled and composed by Keating, is one of the most interesting contributions to our early history and is, in many respects, valuable.[43] The accounts of the Potawatomi, Sioux, and Chippewa Indians derived from persons residing among and familiar with them are among the best sources of our knowledge of these nations. With a guard of soldiers and with Joseph Renville, the French half-breed who had been a British captain in the late war, as guide and interpreter, the expedition set out from Fort Snelling on the ninth of July.[44] The main body moved in four canoes, the remainder marching along the south bank of the Minnesota. Beyond the Traverse des Sioux canoe navigation was abandoned on account of low water and obstructions in the channel.[45] Learning that the Sioux residing in the Minnesota Valley were absent hunting buffaloes on the plains of the West, Major Long sent back a part of his guard. With the explorers on horseback and the soldiers on foot, the party now proceeded by land. It struck across the country to the mouth of the Cottonwood, forded to the west bank of the Minnesota, and continued its course not far from that stream to the head of Big Stone Lake, where it crossed to the east bank. A short march brought it to the post of the Columbia Fur Company on the

[43] Keating's account was published first in Philadelphia in 1824 under the title *Narrative of an Expedition to the Source of St. Peter's River, Lake Winnepeek, Lake of the Woods, etc., Performed in the Year 1823.* A second edition was brought out in London in 1825. The present narrative follows the 1825 edition. The original field notes of Major Long, in three small books three by six inches in size, are in the possession of the Minnesota Historical Society.

[44] See Keating, *Narrative,* 1: 324, for an appreciation of Renville, who is to be met with later.

[45] Traverse des Sioux was the name of the ancient fording place of the Minnesota River on the trail between the villages of the upper and the lower Sioux. The town of great expectations laid out there in the early fifties was long ago abandoned, some of the houses being moved to the city of St. Peter. Edward D. Neill, *History of the Minnesota Valley, Including the Explorers and Pioneers of Minnesota,* 640 (Minneapolis, 1882).

east bank of Lake Traverse near its head. The geologist, on reaching the outcrop of primitive rock at Patterson's Rapids, recorded his satisfaction with having predicted such a discovery two or three marches in advance.[46] He did not fail to observe with interest the ambiguous divide between Lakes Big Stone and Traverse, whence the waters flow, those of the former southward to the Gulf of Mexico, those of the latter northward to Hudson Bay.

At this post Major Long learned that the furs collected by the British fur companies on the Red River and its tributaries in a former typical season and carried over the Canadian border amounted to 637 packs, worth 64,877 Spanish dollars at Montreal prices. One of the objects of the expedition was thus justified. The party proceeded northward down the Red River Valley and encamped at Pembina on August 5. But few Indians were encountered and game was plentiful. During a four days' rest the astronomer ascertained a point on the forty-ninth parallel of north latitude and there planted a substantial wooden post, properly inscribed, to mark the common boundary of the United States and Canada. All the sixty log houses of the Selkirk settlers at Pembina, with one exception, were found to be on American soil; with this discovery the 350 inhabitants were quite content. Major Long's orders directed him to proceed from Pembina along the international boundary toward Lake Superior; but he was advised, and properly, that such a route was impossible for a mounted party. He therefore decided to abandon it in favor of a canoe route and accordingly exchanged his mounts for canoes and needed supplies. The reader is referred to Keating's narrative for details of the homeward journey by way of the lower Red River, Lake Winnipeg and its tributary river of the same name flowing from the Lake of the Woods, the chain of lakes and streams along the northern border of Minnesota to Lac

[46] These rapids are in that part of the river bordering on section 29 in the northwestern corner of Delhi Township, Redwood County.

La Croix, the Kaministiquia River, the Great Lakes, and the Erie Canal. Major Long's modest official report in the same work should not be neglected.[47] If this expedition did not make large additions to existing knowledge, those it did make were reliable, and it dispelled a body of illusions in regard to the great valleys of the Minnesota and the Red River of the North, which are now the richest wheat lands of the continent. While modestly disclaiming to be a judge of prairie soil, Major Long declared the Red River Valley to be in places extremely fertile.

Major Long's expedition was accompanied from Fort Snelling to Pembina by an Italian gentleman, whose meteor-like passage over Minnesota soil is worthy of brief notice. Giacomo Constantino Beltrami, an Italian lawyer and linguist, at one time an officer in the Italian army and later a civil judge, left his country, probably as a political refugee, provided with considerable means. Long before this, as he claims, he had had dreams of being the discoverer of the true sources of the Mississippi. At any rate, he set his heart on this problem as soon as he reached America, near the end of February, 1823. He traveled immediately by way of the Ohio and the upper Mississippi to Fort Snelling, and was there when Long's expedition arrived. Upon his solicitation the commander permitted him to travel with the expedition. There is ground for the suspicion that he was not a congenial companion, but no serious falling-out is reported. At Pembina Beltrami took leave of Major Long's party on its departure for Lake Winnipeg, and, with a slender outfit, struck out into the wilderness to the southeast, where he believed the Mississippi to have its origin. After a few marches his guide was obliged to return; the two Chippewa who had been his companions, being fired upon by a party of Sioux, as he relates, deserted, and he was left alone somewhere on the Red Lake River. He could not paddle the canoe containing his belongings and was obliged to tow it

[47] Keating, *Narrative*, 2: 202–248.

upstream by the painter until he met with a Chippewa whom he induced to navigate it for him to Red Lake. Here he dispatched a letter to a certain *bois brûlé*, who later joined him and who not only rendered him faithful service but also expedited the object of his journey. This man Beltrami praises and afterwards endeavored to reward, but he suppresses his name. After a few days devoted to rest and to an excursion along the shores of Red Lake, he proceeded, under the guidance of his French half-breed, up a stream emptying on the south shore, which he was pleased to believe was an upper reach of the Red or Bloody River, and which is marked Mud Creek on modern maps. On August 31 he reported himself, in a letter written on the spot, as resting on the bank of a small, heart-shaped lake, three miles in circumference, in the middle of which the water was boiling up from a depth he was unable to sound, and which was without visible issue. To it he gave the name of Lake Julia, in honor of a lady not living, whose memory he wished to perpetuate. The water of the lakelet he conceived to filtrate through its banks both northward and southward, and he pronounced his Lake Julia to be at once the most southern source of the Red River and the most northern source of the Mississippi.[48]

Beltrami had now, he believed, accomplished the object of his adventure, and he was pleased to fancy himself surrounded, as he wrote, by the shades of Marco Polo, Columbus, the Cabots, and other great Italian discoverers. He

[48] Lake Julia lies in range 33 west in Turtle Lake and Durand townships of Beltrami County, its waters being divided by the northern line of township 148 north. Professor Newton H. Winchell, in his note on a map of the county prepared by James E. Todd in 1899, in Minnesota Geological and Natural History Survey, *Final Report*, 6: plate 64, says: "Some lakes, near the watershed, having no visible outlets, probably are drained both ways by entering the gravel beds of the drift. Lake Julia is described by Beltrami as one of that kind." Upham, however, in *Minnesota in Three Centuries*, 1: 374, calls attention to the fact that recent surveys show that Lake Julia has an outlet into Lake Puposky or Mud Lake and is, for this reason, definitely a part of the Red River basin. See the map of Beltrami County in *Plat Book of the State of Minnesota* (Rockford, Illinois, W. W. Hixson and Company, 1916). It is to be noted that Beltrami, having learned by hearsay of the existence of Lake La Biche, marked it down on his map as "Doe Lake" and characterized it as the western source of the Mississippi.

was no doubt entirely ignorant of the fact that David Thompson, geographer for the Northwest Company, had traversed the region in 1798, following the usual route of the Northwest Company's fur-traders.[49] Beltrami proceeded to Cass Lake, took the usual canoe route down the Mississippi, and on September 15 reached Fort Snelling, where he was cordially welcomed. In the following year, 1824, he published in New Orleans an account of his journey, entitled *La découverte des sources du Mississippi et de la rivière Sanglante; description du cours entier du Mississippi . . . ainsi que du cours entier de l'Ohio*. Four years later a translation, or rather a version, of this narrative was brought out in London, forming the second volume of a work entitled *A Pilgrimage in Europe and America Leading to the Discovery of the Sources of the Mississippi and Bloody River, with a Description of the Whole Course of the Former, and of the Ohio*.[50] It pleased the author to throw his matter into epistolary form, which gave him opportunity to display his classical learning and his fondness for grandiloquent expression. In spite of much exuberant rhetoric the writer impresses one as a high-minded gentleman, of romantic nature, not without much shrewd common sense.[51]

[49] David Thompson, surveyor and astronomer, entered the employ of the Northwest Company in the spring of 1797. He immediately set out from Grand Portage on a surveying expedition, which had for one of its objects the determination of the forty-ninth parallel of latitude. During 1797 Thompson explored the valleys of the Assiniboine and Saskatchewan rivers and visited the villages of the Mandan on the Missouri River. He returned by way of the Assiniboine and reached its junction with the Red River on March 7, 1798; thence he proceeded up the Red River to the Red Lake River, whence he made his way to Red Lake and Turtle Lake, which he assumed to be the northern source of the Mississippi. From this point he descended the latter river to Sandy Lake and at length reached Lake Superior by way of the Savanna portage and the St. Louis River. Thompson's account of his journey through this region may be found in his *Explorations in Western America, 1784-1812*, 245–286 (Champlain Society, *Publications*, no. 12—Toronto, 1916).

[50] Beltrami's account of his journey with Major Long's expedition and of his own subsequent exploration of the sources of the Mississippi, including the return trip to Fort Snelling, it contained in pages 301 to 482.

[51] An interesting sketch of Beltrami is that by Alfred J. Hill, in *Minnesota Historical Collections*, 2: 183–195. Major Taliaferro says of him that he was a man of talent and that he deserved credit for his information "as far as it goes." He mentions that he gave the Italian his "noble steed 'Cadmus' with full equipments and provisions for the journey overland." See *Minnesota Historical Collections*, 6: 241. The only reference to Beltrami which Taliaferro makes in his journal is the following entry on September 15, 1823: "Mr.

It has already been related that Henry R. Schoolcraft accompanied Governor Lewis Cass, as mineralogist, on his expedition to the upper Mississippi in 1820.[52] Ten years after this expedition Governor Cass, who was still in office and in charge of Indian affairs in the Northwest, by direction of the war department authorized Schoolcraft, then in the Indian service, to proceed into the Chippewa country and make an effort to persuade the Chippewa and the Sioux to cease their immemorial warfare. It was thought that it would not be necessary to go beyond the head of Lake Superior. When Governor Cass's letter of instruction, dated August 9, 1830, reached Schoolcraft, the season was too far advanced for the proposed expedition. In the following April Cass was in Washington and reopened the matter with the war department, with the result that Schoolcraft was ordered to proceed with his expedition "into Lake Superior and the Mississippi country" without further instructions than those contained in Cass's letter of the previous August.[53] Under this order Schoolcraft and his party spent seventy-two days in the summer of 1831 ranging in the "belt of country between Lake Superior and the Mississippi," traveling more than two thousand miles by canoe. Much good tobacco and eloquence were wasted in councils with the tribes. In his report to the office of Indian affairs Schoolcraft is admirably modest in estimating the effect of this expedition, but

---

Beltrami arrived this day from the Sources of the Mississippi in company with forty or Fifty Chippeways — Mr. B. accompanied Maj Long on his expedition as far as Pembina then left him and crossed over to Lake Superior." The noble steed did not return. Nicollet's opinion of Beltrami and of·the reliability of his narrative may be read in his *Report*, 59. See *post*, p. 123, n. 78.

[52] In 1822 Schoolcraft was appointed Indian agent to the Chippewa at Sault Ste. Marie, where he married a woman in part of Chippewa blood, the daughter of John Johnson. In 1832 the agencies of Sault Ste. Marie and Michilimackinac were consolidated, and Schoolcraft conducted the business of the joint agency with headquarters at Michilimackinac until 1841. From 1836 to 1841 he was also acting superintendent of Indian affairs for Michigan. Henry R. Schoolcraft, *Personal Memoirs of a Residence of Thirty Years with the Indian Tribes on the American Frontiers*, 87, 350–391, 404, 541 (Philadelphia, 1851); Neill, in *Minnesota Historical Collections*, 5:446–448; "Henry Rowe Schoolcraft," in the *International Magazine*, 3: 300–302 (June, 1851).

[53] Henry R. Schoolcraft, *Narrative of an Expedition through the Upper Mississippi to Itasca Lake*, iii–v (New York, 1834).

SCHOOLCRAFT DISCOVERING LAKE ITASCA, 1832

Water color by Seth Eastman, owned by the James Jerome Hill Reference Library, St. Paul

AMERICAN FUR COMPANY POST AT FORD DU LAC, 1826

he believed it to have been sufficiently productive of good results to warrant a similar one the next summer.[54] In a letter to the commissioner he suggests that a similar mission to the upper Mississippi would "result in effects equally useful" to the Indians and to the government. He adds that American citizens engaged in the Indian trade were needing the countenance and support of the government against the unlawful competition of the agents of the Hudson's Bay Company, who were not always careful to keep on their own side of "an imaginary territorial line." Their influence on the Indians, also, was not wholesome. The department was asked to authorize a second expedition, to travel in a single canoe, with a sufficient crew of *engagés* and a small escort of soldiers. If thought necessary, an engineer officer might be sent out to take latitudes and note down topography. For the purpose of "evangelical observation" Schoolcraft proposed to invite a clergyman, afterwards widely known in Minnesota, to join the expedition.[55]

Under date of May 3, 1832, the authority thus asked for was given by an order issuing from the office of Indian affairs of the war department. The general views set forth in Schoolcraft's letter were approved, and he was ordered to "proceed to the country upon the heads of the Mississippi, and visit as many of the Indians . . . as circumstances will permit." He was to establish permanent peace among them, look after the Indian trade, gather statistics, and do all manner of things except the one which was the actual object of the expedition. In particular, he was to have as many of the Indians vaccinated as might be convenient. For this purpose a surgeon was added at three dollars a day.[56]

[54] Schoolcraft's report of September 21, 1831, is found in his *Narrative of an Expedition*, 265–285; it is also published as 22 Congress, 1 session, *House Documents*, no. 152 (serial 219).

[55] *Narrative of an Expedition*, 258–260. There is an obscure suggestion that the proposed expedition might reach the "sources of the Mississippi."

[56] *Narrative of an Expedition*, 260. For the report of Dr. Douglass Houghton on the vaccination of the Chippewa Indians, submitted to Schoolcraft September 21, 1832, see the *Narrative of an Expedition*, 250–257.

The party left Sault Ste. Marie on June 7, 1832, reached
Fond du Lac on the twenty-third, and had penetrated by
way of the Savanna portage to Sandy Lake by July 3. A
week later it was at Cass Lake. On the outward journey,
at the mouth of the Brulé River, Schoolcraft encountered a
small company of Chippewa from Cass Lake under the lead
of one Ozawindib, the Yellow Head, bound for the Sault.
It was ascertained that this man would be a useful guide in
the Cass Lake region, and he was induced to return with the
expedition. This was an excellent piece of luck. On the
very day of their arrival at the Cass Lake village the Yellow
Head collected five small canoes, drew maps, and engaged
additional guides for the capital object of the expedition.
Early on the morning of the eleventh of July a select party
of sixteen persons lightly equipped set out for the true
sources of the Mississippi. Guided by Ozawindib, the flotilla
ascended to and traversed Lake Bemidji and, turning southward, commenced the ascent of an east fork of the Mississippi
now known as the Yellow Head or Schoolcraft River. The
extreme head of that river was reached after two days of
toilsome navigation. A portage of thirteen pauses, about six
miles, trending southwest over a succession of sand ridges,
brought the party suddenly in view of a "transparent body
of water. . . . It was Itasca Lake — the source of the
Mississippi."[57] The leader had not left the name of the lake
to be suddenly selected upon his arrival. As he was coasting
along the south shore of Lake Superior, he had asked his
clerical companion for some classical words signifying true
source, or head, of a river. The missionary was able to
remember only that the Latin for truth was "*veritas*" and
for head, "*caput*," and he obligingly wrote the two on a bit of

[57] *Narrative of an Expedition*, 16–56. For a map of this region, see the "Detailed
Hydrographic and Topographic Chart of the Itasca State Park at the Source of the Mississippi River, State of Minnesota," which was prepared in 1892 by Jacob V. Brower, commissioner of the Itasca State Park, and which appears as a frontispiece to his *Mississippi
River and Its Source* (*Minnesota Historical Collections*, vol. 7). The same chart, reduced and
corrected by "annotations in color," is in Brower, *Itasca State Park: An Illustrated History*,
xiii (*Minnesota Historical Collections*, vol. 11— St. Paul, 1894).

paper. Schoolcraft struck out the first syllable of "*veritas*" and the latter syllable of "*caput*" and, merging those remaining, declared, "I-tas-ca shall be the name."[58] And Itasca is and will ever be the name; Schoolcraft, as the first explorer to look upon its waters, had the right to give it. The fur-traders had called it Lac La Biche, or in English, Elk Lake. Lieutenant James Allen, commander of the military escort of Schoolcraft's party, ignores "Itasca" in his

[58] The clerical companion was the Reverend William T. Boutwell, who was appointed in 1831 by the American Board of Commissioners for Foreign Missions to aid in establishing missions among the Chippewa to the south and west of Lake Superior. Extracts of a journal kept by Boutwell are in *Minnesota Historical Collections*, 1: 153–176. On page 165 he speaks of reaching the lake to which the Indians had given the "name of Elk, in reference to its branching horns," but he makes no note of any new name assigned to it by Schoolcraft. The authority for this account of the origin of the name "Itasca," given in the text as first written, is Jacob V. Brower, who had it in substance from Boutwell himself a short time before the latter's death. See his *Mississippi River and Its Source*, 144, 148, n. 1. Schoolcraft, in his *Narrative of an Expedition*, makes no reference to Boutwell's part in forming the name and gives no account of its origin. In his *Summary Narrative*, 243, he says: "I inquired of Ozawindib the Indian name of this lake; he replied *Omushkös*, which is the Chippewa name of the Elk. Having previously got an inkling of some of their mythological and necromantic notions of the origin and mutations of the country, which permitted the use of a female name for it, I denominated it *Itasca*." Since this chapter was written, a letter from Boutwell to Alfred J. Hill, dated May 13, 1872, has been found in the *St. Paul Daily Pioneer* for June 16, 1872, which fully confirms Brower's report of his interview. "One morning we were coasting Lake Superior. Mr. S. said to me, 'I would like to give a name to Elk Lake that will be . . . expressive of the *head* or *true source* of the Mississippi. Can you give me any word in Latin or Greek that will convey the idea?' I replied . . . 'the nearest I can come to it is *Verum Caput*, or, if you prefer the noun *Veritas*.' In less than five minutes he replied: 'I have got the thing' . . . Itasca." Still the question remains — why did not Boutwell mention Itasca in his journal cited above?

Major Taliaferro in his journal, July 15, 1836, charges Schoolcraft with wiping out the name "Le Beasch" (La Biche) and, "to swell your own consequence," with giving the lake the new name "Ithaka or Itashkah . . . never known to hundreds before this worthy disciple made it known in July 1832." Three days earlier the following entry was made: "M. Nicollet on a visit to this Post on scientific researches, & at present in my family, — has shown me the late work of Henry R Schoolcraft on the discovery of the Source of the Mississippi (which claim is ridiculous in the extreme)." The reader should here be reminded that ever since the treaty of 1825 at Prairie du Chien Taliaferro had cherished a grudge against Schoolcraft, which was now to be aggravated by a passage in the book wherein Flat Mouth, the Pillager chief at Leech Lake, is made to "boldly accuse" traders and also persons holding office under the government on the upper Mississippi of inducing the Sioux to extend their hunting beyond the line of 1825 into Chippewa country. See the *Narrative of an Expedition*, 86. The Sioux agent could not believe that his friend Flat Mouth had uttered such an accusation and thought that Schoolcraft had falsified in order to weaken the prestige of Taliaferro in Washington and elsewhere. He therefore spares no pains (in the entry of July 15) in denouncing the egotism, the hypocrisy, and other infirmities of Schoolcraft, going so far as to observe that he had not "satisfactorily accounted for his traveling on Sunday." He notes also his "cruel desertion" of Lieutenant Allen at Fort Snelling. In a letter from Taliaferro to Governor Henry Dodge, December 26, 1836, Schoolcraft is accused of failing to learn the true condition of the Chippewa of the Mississippi, when "specially dispatched . . . in 1832 at a per diem alowance of five dollars for this object." Taliaferro Letter Book, B.

report and uses the French name.[59]   William Morrison, who traveled throughout this region from 1802 to 1826 in the service of the X Y, Northwest, and American fur companies, lays circumstantial claim to having passed Lake Itasca on trading journeys in 1804 and 1811. The claim may well be just, but the failure to make any report or record, and a silence of forty years or more, debars Morrison from credit as an exploring discoverer.[60]   Schoolcraft's confidence in the Yellow Head was so great that he did not think it worth while to tarry on Itasca.   He made a hasty tour along its shores in his canoe, broke out a little clearing on the island since known by his name, erected a flagstaff, and ran up the American colors.   The same night he encamped thirty-two miles below the lake on the west or main branch of the Mississippi.   He had fully succeeded in his worthy undertaking. He had reached and identified that considerable body of water whence he believed the Mississippi first to issue as a true river.   On returning to Cass Lake, July 15, he gave Oza-windib a flag and the president's medal, thus investing him with chieftainship.   Perhaps the Yellow Head has not received his full share of credit.[61]

The return journey began the next day, July 16.   Instead of floating down the Mississippi the expedition struck direct

[59] *American State Papers: Military Affairs,* 5: 332. Lieutenant Allen's official report to the war department is a much more detailed description of the topographical features of the country traversed than that of Schoolcraft and is accompanied by a map.

[60] Three versions of a letter or letters bearing the signature of William Morrison and setting forth his claims are in print. One, said to have been transmitted in February, 1856, by Allan Morrison, his brother, to whom it is addressed, to Alexander Ramsey, president of the Minnesota Historical Society, was published in *Materials for the Future History of Minnesota; Being a Report of the Minnesota Historical Society to the Legislative Assembly,* 104 (Minnesota Historical Society, *Annals,* 1856), reprinted in *Minnesota Historical Collections,* 1: 417–419 (St. Paul, 1872). Charles Hallock, in an article on "The Red River Trail," in *Harper's New Monthly Magazine,* 19: 53 (June, 1859), published a communication purporting to be a "correct copy of a letter transmitted to the Historical Society of Minnesota by Mr. Morrison," which, however, differs textually from that published by the society in 1856. Brower, in his *Mississippi River and Its Source,* 122–124, reproduces a letter which is declared to be "given in full" from the "original draft," and is dated Berthier, January 16, 1856. See Coues's critical analysis of the Morrison letters in Pike, *Expeditions,* 1: 326, n. 23; also a letter from A. J. Hill to Sibley, September 23, 1886, and Sibley's reply, September 24, 1886, in the Hill Papers. A county in Minnesota is named for the Morrison brothers.

[61] *Narrative of an Expedition,* 60–62, 67, 71, 236.

for Leech Lake, taking two portages of considerable length. From Leech Lake it followed a chain of small lakes stretching to the southwest and gained the headwaters of the Crow Wing River.[62]   This stream was rapidly descended to its mouth, whence a day's paddling brought the party to Fort Snelling.   The leader tarried but a day at this post and departed in haste for his home at the Sault, leaving Lieutenant Allen and his soldiers to follow as best they could without a guide or interpreter by way of the St. Croix route. In his official report to the Indian office, under date of December 3, 1832, Schoolcraft omits all details of the excursion from Cass Lake to Itasca, because they "afford none of the political information" required by his instructions.   The reader may form his own opinion of the pains taken to avoid avowal of the real object of the expedition.[63]

In 1834 Congress added a small appropriation to the river and harbor bill to be "applied to geological and mineralogical survey and researches" on public lands.   Under this authority the war department appointed George William Featherstonhaugh, an Englishman long resident in the United States, as United States geologist.[64]   In the course of the same year this scientist made an examination of the Ozark Mountain region, upon which he submitted a report.[65] In the following year, 1835, he made an extensive "geological reconnoissance" from Washington to the Coteau des Prairies, in southwestern Minnesota and northeastern South

[62] This chain of lakes lies in the southeastern part of Hubbard County.

[63] "It will be sufficient to remark that the object was successfully accomplished, under the guidance of Oza Windib.   I planted the American flag on an island in the lake, which is the true source of the Mississippi."   This is Schoolcraft's modest record.   See his *Narrative of an Expedition*, 236.   Schoolcraft's official report forms appendix 6 (pp. 228–250) of the *Narrative of an Expedition*.   It was also issued, under the title *Northwestern Indians*, as 22 Congress, 2 session, *House Documents*, no. 125 (serial 235).   See also the account in his *Personal Memoirs*, 405–421.

[64] *Statutes at Large*, 4: 703; 23 Congress, 2 session, *House Documents*, no. 2, pp. 182, 183 (serial 271); J. D. Featherstonhaugh, "Memoir of Mr. G. W. Featherstonhaugh," in the *American Geologist*, 3: 220 (April, 1889).

[65] *Geological Report of an Examination Made in 1834 of the Elevated Country between the Missouri and Red Rivers* (23 Congress, 2 session, *House Documents*, no. 151 — serial 274).

Dakota. Upon this excursion he also made a report,[66] the first ninety-four pages of which are devoted to a general elementary treatise on geology, which might "serve to soften the difficulties to those who are engaging for the first time with geological literature, and to assist in guiding observers." A "geological column" illustrates this part of the work. The last thirty-eight pages of the report cover the geologist's reconnoissance on Minnesota area. The excursion was too rapid to permit careful studies and yielded but a trifling contribution to knowledge. Because Major Long had not examined the neighborhood of Le Sueur's fort of 1700 and had left the existence of his copper mine in doubt, a careful examination was made, resulting in the conclusion that Le Sueur's "discoveries were fables invented to give him influence at the court of France."[67] Featherstonhaugh was accompanied on this journey by an officer of the United States Army, Lieutenant William W. Mather, a fact not revealed by his report. Not the slightest reference is made to Mather, nor is there any acknowledgment of his topographical sketch of the Minnesota Valley, which his chief appropriated. The report of Mather was not printed and has not been found.[68]

In 1847, twelve years after this reconnoissance, there appeared in London a two-volume work, beautifully printed and illustrated, written by "G. W. Featherstonhaugh, F.R.S., F.G.S.," and bearing the title *A Canoe Voyage up the Minnay Sotor*. This is a book of travel, in journal form, of no small interest, devoid of display of scientific knowledge. About one-fourth of the pages relate to Minnesota. The

[66] *Report of a Geological Reconnoissance Made in 1835, from the Seat of Government, by the Way of Green Bay and the Wisconsin Territory, to the Coteau de Prairie, an Elevated Ridge Dividing the Missouri from the St. Peter's River* (24 Congress, 1 session, *Senate Documents*, no. 333 — serial 282). Two maps accompany this report, one showing the boundaries of the alleged Carver grant.

[67] *Geological Reconnoissance*, 142–145.

[68] Mather to Charles K. Smith, secretary of the Minnesota Historical Society, February 22, 1851, in *Minnesota Historical Collections*, 1: 133; Sibley, in *Minnesota Historical Collections*, 1: 481; Taliaferro, in *Minnesota Historical Collections*, 6: 246; Neill, *Minnesota*, 416. See also C. H. Hitchcock, "Sketch of W. W. Mather," in the *American Geologist*, 19: 1–8 (January, 1897).

military companion figures no more in these volumes than in the report. Milor, the half-breed guide whom Sibley had selected for Featherstonhaugh, seems to have been his best friend, as he frequently mentions and praises him and at parting promised to put his name in his book. Although twelve years had elapsed, he remembers and records a number of disagreeable passages with military officers, traders, and missionaries, whose manners were not to his taste.[69]

The visit of George Catlin, the eminent painter of Indian scenery and personages, to Fort Snelling in the summer of 1835, described by himself with no little interest, would not warrant his enumeration among Minnesota explorers; but the excursion made by him in the following year from Fort Snelling to the red pipestone quarry near the southwestern corner of the state may justify such enrollment.[70] At Le Blanc's trading house at the Traverse des Sioux he and his

[69] The brief visit of another Englishman, the distinguished novelist, Captain Frederick Marryat, to Fort Snelling in 1837 hardly deserves mention under the head of explorations. His account of the visit may be found in his *Diary in America, with Remarks on Its Institutions*, first series, 2: 78–124 (London, 1839). The impression which this traveler made on Sibley, who was his host, and Taliaferro, the Indian agent, was not favorable. See *Minnesota Historical Collections*, 1: 482; 6: 240. The Englishman, however, records his appreciation of the intelligent and hospitable officers of Fort Snelling, socially the most agreeable he had met in America, and his regrets at parting from them and his "kind host, Mr. Sibley." *Diary in America*, 101, 125.

[70] Catlin's account of his wanderings among the Indian tribes of North America during the years from 1832 to 1839 appeared in a series of letters in the *New York Daily Commercial Advertiser*. These letters, together with additional material from his notebooks, he published in 1841 in London and New York as a two-volume work entitled *Letters and Notes on the Manners, Customs, and Condition of the North American Indians, Written during Eight Years' Travel among the Wildest Tribes of Indians in North America, 1832–1839*. Many editions followed. The one here cited is the third London edition of 1842. The narrative of the visit to Fort Snelling comprises pages 131 to 140 of volume 2. An exhaustive account of the career and writings of George Catlin is to be found in Thomas Donaldson, "The George Catlin Indian Gallery in the U. S. National Museum," in the Smithsonian Institution, *Annual Reports*, 1885, part 2, appendix. A proposal in 1852 to purchase the Catlin collection of Indian scenes and portraits was the occasion for a spirited debate in the United States Senate, Senators Seward and Cooper favoring the purchase, and Senators Clemens and Borland opposing it. The unfavorable opinion of Captain Seth Eastman as to the merit of the collection was quoted. See the *Congressional Globe*, 32 Congress, 1 session, p. 1845. For Sibley's pungent criticism of the Catlin letters, see *Minnesota Historical Collections*, 1:481. The Taliaferro Journal for 1835 contains several references to Catlin's visit. Under the date of June 24 his arrival is noted; on July 4 he attended a game of ball by Sioux players from the neighborhood for a study of poses and movements; on July 9 he witnessed a dance by forty-five visiting Chippewa, who were attired only in breechcloths; and on the twenty-seventh he took his departure.

companion, an English traveler named Wood, were surrounded by a "murky cloud of dark-visaged warriors and
braves," who, through twenty spokesmen, poured out invec-
tives and threats "nearly the whole afternoon," warning
them not to trespass on the "sacred fountain of the pipe."
Said one: "No white man has ever been to the Pipe Stone
Quarry, and our chiefs have often decided in council that no
white man shall ever go to it." Another, holding a red
pipe to the side of his naked arm, said: "You see . . . that
this pipe is a part of our flesh. The red men are a part of
the red stone." A third declared that the red pipestone
"was given to us by the Great Spirit, and no one need ask
the price of it, for it is *medicine*." Catlin assured the
Indians that he and his friends were not government officials
nor private agents sent to find out the location and value of
the quarry, but desired only to satisfy a reasonable curiosity
about so wonderful a work of nature. The warrior who
closed the interview said: "White men! your words are very
smooth . . . you have no good design, and the quicker you
turn back the better; there is no use of talking any more
about it — if you think best to go, try it; that's all I have to
say." The next morning the travelers, heedless of the
advice of Le Blanc, who told them these Sioux were the most
disorderly and treacherous of the whole nation, mounted
their horses and rode off unmolested. The conjecture is
ventured that the Indians decided to let them take their
journey in peace because Catlin's companion was an Englishman.[71]

[71] Catlin, *North American Indians*, 2: 166, 172–176. On page 173 Catlin relates
that when he told the Indians at Le Blanc's that his companion was a Saganosh (an Englishman), the whole party rose and shook hands with Wood, and many took out from under
their clothing British medals and showed them. Taliaferro, in his journal, September 6,
1836, remarks that the Sioux were very much incensed at the determination of Catlin and
Wood to visit and inspect the pipestone quarry, a thing which no white man excepting one
or two traders had been permitted to do. The journal records the arrival of the men at
Fort Snelling on August 17, their departure for the quarry on the twenty-first, and their
return on September 5. Under the date September 6, the agent attempts a description of
the quarry and its surroundings, based apparently on statements of Catlin or his companion. Le Blanc's real name was Louis Provençalle. The Sioux called him Skadan, which
in English would be Whitey.

At a point near the base of the Coteau des Prairies, some forty miles from the quarry, the two found a welcome at the comfortable trading house of Joseph Laframboise, who gave them his escort to the quarry.[72]   What the explorers saw was "a perpendicular wall of close-grained, compact quartz, of twenty-five and thirty feet in elevation, running nearly North and South with its face to the West, exhibiting a front of nearly two miles in length," disappearing under the more elevated prairie at both ends.   The wall on both its front and its horizontal surfaces was "highly polished or glazed, as if by ignition."   On the return journey from the quarry Catlin and his friend left their horses at the Traverse des Sioux and betook themselves to a canoe, so difficult to handle that Catlin suggests that it must have been dug out of the wrong side of the log.   At Fort Snelling they failed to find an expected steamer and continued their canoe voyage down to Prairie du Chien.   It occupied ten days, during which they "experimented on many things for the benefit of mankind."   For example, they added to their larder "clams, snails, frogs, and rattlesnakes; the latter of which, when properly dressed and broiled, we found to be the most delicious food of the land."[73]   A specimen of the red pipestone was sent by Catlin to a Boston chemist, who after analysis pronounced it to be a new mineral compound and gave it the name "catlinite."[74]

[72] The red pipestone quarry lies in the west central part of Pipestone County in a reservation one mile square covering parts of sections 1 and 2 of Sweet Township, set aside for the Yankton Sioux Indians by the treaty of April 19, 1858. See *Statutes at Large*, 11: 744. The geology of the quarry and the surrounding region is fully described by Newton H. Winchell in Minnesota Geological and Natural History Survey, *Final Report*, 1: 533–561. Comparative analyses therein cited (p. 542) seem to warrant the conclusion that the red pipestone "is not truly a mineral but an indurated clay," graduating into red shale. Winchell includes in his *Aborigines of Minnesota*, 563–565, a map of the quarry and also reproductions of pictographs and of the inscription made by a member of Nicollet's party in 1838.

[73] Catlin, *North American Indians*, 2: 176, 201–209.

[74] A slab of the red pipestone, procured by General Sibley and presented to the first territorial legislature in 1849, was forwarded to the national capital to be built into the Washington Monument. In a letter accompanying the slab, Sibley protested against the use of the name "catlinite" on the ground that the quarry was well known to white men before Catlin's visit. Minnesota Territory, *Council Journal*, 1849, p. 30.

The roll of our early explorers closes with one whose work left more definite and lasting impressions than that of his predecessors. A man of science, provided with proper instruments, he laid out a comprehensive program, followed it out to completion, and recorded the results in a report which will ever remain a classic. Joseph Nicolas Nicollet was born in 1790 in a small town in Savoy, now a province in the extreme northwest of Italy.[75] At the age of ten he was apprenticed to a watchmaker, with whom he served eight years.[76] A few years were spent in the capital of his province, where he supported himself by his trade while engaged in study. He won a mathematical prize of some importance. When he returned to his native village, he taught mathematics and studied Latin and other languages, English probably being one of them. Later we find the young craftsman in Paris, first a student in the École Normale and not long after an instructor in the Collège Louis-le-Grand. His first publication, which appeared in 1818, was on the mathematics of life insurance. It brought him into notice and opened the doors of society. He next turned his attention to astronomy, in which he soon distinguished himself; he was employed in important investigations, advanced to a professorship, and decorated with the medal of the Legion of Honor. About the year 1830 this career of prosperity and

[75] The sketch here given follows Henry H. Sibley, "Memoir of Jean N. Nicollet," in *Minnesota Historical Collections*, 1: 183–195. Sibley acknowledges the use of "copious extracts" from an account by Colonel John J. Abert, chief of the corps of topographical engineers, under whose supervision Nicollet pursued his explorations. See also the *American Geologist*, 8: 343–352 (December, 1891), for an appreciation by Newton H. Winchell, and *Minnesota Historical Collections*, 6: 242, for interesting particulars recorded by Major Taliaferro, the Indian agent at St. Peter's. *La grand encyclopédie* and Larousse, *Grand dictionnaire universel*, give the explorer's full name as Jean Nicolas Nicollet. *Appletons' Cyclopaedia of American Biography*, Sibley, Neill, Newton H. Winchell, and others follow these authorities. Horace V. Winchell, in the *American Geologist*, 13: 127 (February, 1894), asserts the true name to be Joseph Nicolas Nicollet, giving as authority Hoefer, *Nouvelle biographie générale* (Paris, 1863). As the *Nouveau Larousse illustré* (Paris, 1898–1904), concurs, Joseph is assumed to be the true name. In various United States publications the name appears as I. N. Nicollet.

[76] According to the French encyclopedias Nicollet did nothing but herd cows until he was twelve years old; he then learned to read, and was put to school to an ecclesiastic. These encyclopedias make no mention of his apprenticeship to watchmaking and give the date of his birth as 1786.

distinction was rudely checked. The slender biographical materials available barely indicate that Nicollet, who had been successful in a financial way and had saved up a little fortune, entered upon certain speculative enterprises in which he not only lost his all but involved his friends as well. The character of the man as revealed to his American acquaintances nullifies the suggestion that this disaster was due in the least degree to dishonesty. He was, however, bitterly reproached by those who had been his friends. Stung by their revilements, he suddenly abandoned all his engagements, turned his back on Parisian delights, and sailed for New Orleans in the year 1832.[77]

In 1833 Nicollet obtained from the war department letters to commanding officers and Indian agents on the upper Mississippi and the loan of some astronomical instruments to be used in a proposed exploration. Why the execution of his project was delayed for three years is not known. A part of that time was spent in scientific labor on the lower Mississippi. It was not until the summer of 1836 that he arrived at Fort Snelling, where his charming manners rendered him a welcome guest. On July 29 his canoe left the Falls of St. Anthony, upward bound.[78] Gaining the mouth of the Crow Wing, without delay he chose a little-used, but well-known, route through Gull Lake and River, White Fish Lake, the upper reaches of Pine River, and Little Boy Lake and River, over which he floated into Leech Lake. From here he proceeded under the guidance of Francis Brunet, an amiable

---

[77] "Ruiné par des spéculations de bourse en 1830, il se rendit aux Etats-Unis." *Nouveau Larousse illustré.*

[78] Nicollet's narrative, here followed, comprises pages 53 to 74 of his *Report Intended to Illustrate a Map of the Hydrographical Basin of the Upper Mississippi River* (26 Congress, 2 session, *Senate Documents*, no. 237 — serial 380; also printed as 28 Congress, 2 session, *House Documents*, no. 52 — serial 464). The report was not restricted to an account of the expedition to the upper Mississippi but included other explorations, chiefly on the Missouri, made in 1837 and 1838. The map accompanying the report, covering the area between the longitudes of Madison, Wisconsin, and Fort Pierre, North Dakota, and between the latitudes of St. Louis, Missouri, and Red Lake, Minnesota, and not only recording Nicollet's observations but also summarizing the work of previous explorers, was a contribution of the first importance to American geography. Being himself an expert astronomer, Nicollet determined the astronomical positions of many important points.

half-breed of gigantic size and a natural geographer, who resided on the lake. He took a Chippewa, Kegwedzissag (or Gaygwedosay), "Who-tries-to-walk," well acquainted with the upper country, and Desiré Fronchet, the Frenchman who had come up with him from Fort Snelling in the character of a servant with leave to do what trading he might by the way. His guides took him out of Leech Lake by way of the northwest arm and a chain of lakes and streams into Assawa or Pearl Lake at the head of the east fork of the Mississippi, the Yellow Head. Here he found marks of Schoolcraft's bivouac, and from it he made the same portage over the "Big Burning" and found himself on the shores of Lake Itasca.[79] He established himself on Schoolcraft Island and devoted three days and nights to examining the topography and to fixing the latitude, longitude, and height above sea level. He found in a morainic basin nearly surrounded by *hauteurs des terres* (heights of land) five creeks, "formed by innumerable streamlets oozing from the clay-beds at the bases of the hills," flowing into the lake. These waters he considered "to be the utmost sources of the Mississippi." Visiting the five creeks, he found one largest of all and its waters most abundant. "This creek," he says, "is truly the infant Mississippi." On August 29 he gave the valley of that tributary a careful examination, tracing the course of the stream three miles or more through two lakelets to a third, from which he found "the Mississippi flows with a breadth of a foot and a half, and a depth of a foot."

In his report Nicollet accords to Schoolcraft and Lieutenant Allen credit as first explorers and modestly claims merit only for having completed their labors. Schoolcraft

---

[79] Relating the hardships experienced in making this portage, Nicollet says: "I carried my sextant on my back, in a leather case, thrown over me as a knapsack; then my barometer slung over the left shoulder: my cloak, thrown over the same shoulder, confined the barometer closely against the sextant; a portfolio under the arm; a basket in hand, which contained my thermometer, chronometer, pocket compass, artificial horizon, tape line, &c., &c. On the right side, a spy-glass, powder-flask, and shot bag; and in my hand, a gun or an umbrella, according to circumstances." *Report*, 56.

was content to have rested his eyes on Lake Itasca; Lieutenant Allen, by means of his pocket compass, was able to
correct somewhat the rude, but still truthful, map drawn
by Ozawindib. Two hours sufficed those rapid travelers.
Nicollet was not so precipitate. From observations taken
on Schoolcraft Island he found the latitude to be 47° 13′ 35″
north and the longitude 95° 2′ west. By the barometer he
found the height above sea level to be 1,575 feet, a figure
which the better methods of later geographers have reduced
to 1,462 feet. What is more, he cast the eye of a trained
observer over the whole situation, divined the relation of
Itasca to the environing heights, and traced its principal
affluent to its ultimate visible source.[80] The narrative of
Schoolcraft, addressed to the general public, is an addition
to the literature of voyage and travel; Nicollet's much too
brief and modest report to the government is a contribution
to science. The splendid map of this and later explorations
in the Northwest, standing for years of travel, observation,
and delineation, will remain his sufficient monument. It
determined all the subsequent cartography of an immense
region.

Having completed his examination of the ultimate source
of the Mississippi, Nicollet returned to Fort Snelling on
September 27. A spell of cold weather came on which
threatened to put a stop to canoe navigation, and he decided
to pass the winter at that post. Major Taliaferro gave him
a lodging in a room of his office building and Sibley had him
for a delightful guest at Mendota.[81] He appears to have

[80] Warren Upham, *Altitudes between Lake Superior and the Rocky Mountains*, 148
(United States Geological Survey, *Bulletins*, no. 72). That portion of Nicollet's map
delineating the sources of the Mississippi is reproduced in Brower, *Mississippi River and
Its Source*, 161.

[81] *Report*, 67. See also letters written by Nicollet to Sibley at intervals during the
years from 1837 to 1840, which contain many allusions to his sojourn in the Sibley home and
bear witness to the warm friendship between the host and his guest. On November 27,
1837, he wrote (in French), "You have been so good to me, that my affection and gratitude
are yours forever, and always and everywhere it will be sweet to prove this to you, as it will
also be pleasant to me to learn that you still preserve a remembrance of me." The following is from a letter of April 26, 1840: "I need not tell you that all our regards and remem-
brances are perpetually turned toward the west — to St. Peters, and the dear Mississippi

divided the winter between studying the Sioux and Chippewa languages, working up his field notes, and arranging his collections. The expedition just described was made wholly at private cost. It is believed that the Chouteaus of St. Louis, who had become interested in and were to acquire the principal proprietorship of the American Fur Company, contributed liberally. Sibley was his banker.[82] Late in 1837 Nicollet went to Baltimore, Maryland, and established himself near St. Mary's College. Early in the following winter he was enabled to lay before the secretary of war, Joel R. Poinsett, his maps and journals. This intelligent and sympathetic official at once appreciated the importance of the work of Nicollet and had him employed by the government. He was charged particularly with the exploration of the vast region lying between the upper Mississippi and the Missouri. Lieutenant John C. Fremont was detailed as his assistant. Three successive seasons were passed in the field. The results of the surveys are embodied in the report and map already mentioned. The infirm health of Nicollet long delayed their completion. It was his hope and ambition to be enrolled among the members of the French Academy of Sciences. He was nominated, but a single adverse vote defeated him. It is believed that the disappointment hastened the end of his life, which came in September, 1843. Until very recently all efforts to discover and collect his numerous and extensive unpublished writings

from its Mouth in the Gulf to its sources. All our conversations are on the fields of our labor, the friends such as you that we have made there, and on the sincere regret of not being there with them. If we take a promenade our recollections haunt us — the sight of a fine hunting dog, a double-barrelled gun, the sound of the wild cry of the geese which emigrate from North to South, all this for us, seems to come from Sibley! When we drink a toast, it is to Sibley's health, the dearest, and most beloved of all our friends. Fremont says to me every now and then; 'Let us go and see Sibley. When will we go and see Sibley? We must go and see him; let us go.' And I answer; 'Yes, certainly; we will go and see him.'" These letters are in the Sibley Papers. The entries for July, 1836, in the Taliaferro Journal contain numerous references to Nicollet and his activities. See also the entries for September 27, October 1, 4, 24, and December 2, 1836, and September 22, 27, 28, 1839.

[82] Sibley, in *Minnesota Historical Collections*, 1: 187; Nicollet to Sibley, November 27, 1837, in *Minnesota Historical Collections*, 1: 195. The Sibley Day Book, September 17, 1838, contains the following entry: "To J N Nicollet's Dft on P. Choteau & Co . . . fav. H H Sibley Agent Am Fur Co $1899.33."

have been fruitless.[83] His name has been given to that affluent of Itasca which he called the infant Mississippi, to the lakelets through which it flows and the springs which feed it and them, to a large island above the Falls of St. Anthony, to a principal street in Minneapolis, to a town in Nicollet County, and to a Minnesota county.

Near half a century passed, and no one arose to question the correctness of Nicollet's designation of the true source of the great river. In 1881, however, an unconscionable adventurer, following the track of Schoolcraft and Nicollet, appeared on the shores of Itasca. The half day spent there was devoted to the ascent of an inlet, about one hundred feet in length, leading out of the west arm into a lakelet some hundred acres in area, which was doubtless in Nicollet's time an arm of Itasca. This body of water he pronounced the true source; and by means of a book widely heralded, in which Schoolcraft's narrative was shamelessly plagiarized, he claimed the right to have his name inscribed above those of his predecessors. So extensively and persistently was the claim urged that it became necessary for learned societies to entertain it, and finally for the legislature of Minnesota to forbid the use in the schools of the state of any textbook recognizing the claim of this pretended discoverer.[84] But this action was long delayed, and might not have been taken but for the interference of a citizen of Minnesota who cared for the truth of history. In the autumn of 1888 Jacob Vradenberg Brower spent thirty days in the Itasca basin and made a careful examination of its topography. He

[83] According to Colonel Abert, chief of the corps of topographical engineers, to whom Nicollet's report was submitted, his journals, from which he drew the material for the report, were to be deposited with the topographical bureau. See the *Report*, 5. J. Fletcher Williams, in an editorial note in *Minnesota Historical Collections*, 1 : 194, says that the "valuable and voluminous papers of Mr. Nicollet relating to this region, were lost after his death. The most persevering search by Gen. Sibley and others, who endeavored to secure them for this Society, were fruitless to discover their fate." During World War I the demand for room in the building occupied by the state, war, and navy departments in Washington led to the removal, for storage elsewhere, of certain archives, and in the process a chest containing Nicollet papers came to light. These papers, which include journals of explorations in Minnesota, were turned over to the Library of Congress in March, 1921.

[84] *Laws*, 1889, p. 182.

became convinced of the substantial correctness of Nicollet's statements and of the falsehood of this impudent claimant. On the presentation of Brower's sketches and observations to the Minnesota Historical Society, that body authorized him to proceed with a thorough topographic and hydrographic survey of the Itasca basin, mostly covered by township 143, range 36, west of the fifth principal meridian. With a sufficient party and an outfit provided with necessary instruments Brower spent fifty-eight days there in the summer of 1889.[85]

One result of this survey was the establishment by the Minnesota legislature of the Itasca State Park on thirty-five sections of land, granted by Congress and, for the most part, still public.[86] On May 4, 1891, Governor Merriam appointed Brower commissioner of the park. In the summer and fall of that year seventy-two days were devoted by Brower to a further examination of the Itasca basin. He fully confirmed Nicollet's general observation that the "waters supplied by the north flank of these heights of land . . . on the south side of Lake Itasca . . . are the utmost sources of the Mississippi," and that the Mississippi flows into as well as out of Lake Itasca. His careful and protracted survey revealed, however, that Nicollet's "infant Mississippi" is created by the seepage and overflow of a group of lakelets lying in an "ultimate bowl" in the upper part of the valley of Nicollet's creek. The remotest of the lakelets, called by Brower Hernando de Soto, is 101 feet above Itasca, and the height of land to the south of it is 300 feet.[87] The crowning

[85] An account of the exposure of the Glazier fraud and of the Brower explorations of 1888 and 1889 is given in Brower, *Mississippi River and Its Source*, 191–209, 225–231, and in his *Itasca State Park*, 74–76. See also James H. Baker, "The Sources of the Mississippi: Their Discoverers, Real and Pretended," in *Minnesota Historical Collections*, 6: 3–28 (St. Paul, 1894). Brower's work was materially expedited by the monuments established in the course of a survey made in 1875 by Edwin S. Hall under the direction of James H. Baker, surveyor-general for the district of Minnesota. *Mississippi River and Its Source*, 171–178; United States Commissioner of the General Land Office, *Annual Reports*, 1876, p. 200.

[86] *Statutes at Large*, 27: 347; Minnesota, *Laws*, 1891, pp. 137–139; 1893, p. 111; Brower, *Itasca State Park*, 58–71.

[87] Brower, *Mississippi River and Its Source*, 274–277; Nicollet, *Report*, 58.

labor of Brower, seconded by the Minnesota Historical Society, has forever put to rest the question of the source of the Mississippi, which had interested geographers for more than a century.[88]

The expedition led by Brevet Captain, afterwards Major General, John Pope for the exploration of the Red River Valley in the summer of 1849 may be mentioned here, but need not be described in detail. It was undertaken not as an original exploration but rather to gather for the guidance of settlers and the planners of state boundaries desirable information of a region already mapped.[89] In his very readable report Pope was "at a loss . . . to do justice to the beautiful country . . . which is perhaps the most remarkable in the world for its peculiar conformation and vast productiveness." He was not at all reluctant to give to Congress such recommendations as the following: (1) the purchase from the Indians of all lands west of the Mississippi as

---

[88] The two works of Brower cited, *Mississippi River and Its Source* and *Itasca State Park*, are largely devoted to the problem of the sources of the Mississippi. The latter volume contains a reduced facsimile of the map of the Itasca basin made under the direction of the Mississippi River Commission in 1900. The survey of the commission confirmed the important topographic and hydrographic features brought out by the Brower survey of 1891 (p. 161). A large part of the volume relates to the struggle to secure the establishment and maintenance of Itasca Park. An account of the devastations of squatters, the tools of lumbermen, is given on page 73. For a brief biography of Brower, see that by Josiah B. Chaney, in *Minnesota Historical Collections*, 12: 769-774.

[89] Pope's *Report of an Exploration of the Territory of Minnesota* (31 Congress, 1 session, Senate Executive Documents, no. 42 — serial 558) is accompanied by a map, founded on Nicollet's, showing the routes followed to and from the Red River Valley. The expedition left Fort Snelling on June 6, and proceeded up the Mississippi to the Sauk Rapids and thence across the territory to the great bend of the Red River; it crossed that river twice and pursued a route parallel with and distant about twenty miles from the Red River to Pembina. The latitudes and longitudes of the principal camps and the distances traversed were recorded, the figures for the latter being ascertained by means of an odometer actuated by a wagon wheel. Having sent his escort of dragoons back by land, Pope bought a thirty-three-foot birch-bark canoe, loaded it with a thirty-day supply of pemmican and dried buffalo meat, and hired eleven *bois brûlés* as navigators; thus equipped he ascended the Red River to Otter Tail Lake, portaged over to Leaf Lake and River, and followed the latter to the Crow Wing, whence a few days' paddling brought him down the Mississippi to Fort Snelling. The report was reprinted in the *Chronicle and Register*, January 13, 20, February 10, 1851. The expedition of Captain (afterwards Major General) Edwin V. Sumner from Fort Atkinson, Iowa Territory, in the summer of 1845 by way of the Traverse des Sioux and Big Stone Lake to Devil's Lake in North Dakota, while adding little to geographical knowledge, is interesting for its account of the upper Sioux, not yet annuity Indians, and of the half-breed hunters of the Selkirk colony, who were still trespassing on the American side of the international boundary. It was his opinion that they would soon move over. 29 Congress, 1 session, *Senate Documents*, no. 1, pp. 217-220 (serial 470).

far north as the Crow Wing River, and as far west as the
head of the Minnesota; (2) the abandonment of Fort Snelling
and the establishment of new military posts at the mouths
of the Bois des Sioux and Pembina rivers; (3) the grant of
alternate sections of public lands for the construction of
railroads from the head of navigation of the Red River to the
head of navigation of the St. Peter's (i.e., from Breckenridge to Mankato) and from the head of navigation of the
Red River, by way of the mouth of the Crow Wing, to the
western extremity of Lake Superior (i.e., from Breckenridge
by the way of Brainerd to Duluth).   More informally he
suggested that a new state of forty thousand square miles
should embrace the territory west of the Mississippi below
the head of navigation of the Red River, including the
valleys of the Minnesota and the James.

VI. THE WHITE MAN ARRIVES

A S ALREADY related the British gave up the North-west Territory with reluctance. During the conferences preceding the treaty of Ghent the British plenipotentiaries made the specific demand that all territory north and west of the Greenville line of 1795 — roughly a zigzag line from Cleveland to Cincinnati — should be set apart as a "permanent barrier" between the British dominions and those of the United States, both parties to be forbidden to purchase lands of the Indians in the region. The American commissioners, of course, promptly rejected the proposal.

After May, 1815, the British flag waved no more on the Mississippi, but British influence continued for a period to control the region from Prairie du Chien to the Lake of the Woods, and from Lake Superior indefinitely westward.[1] All Americans who knew anything about this vast region and its trade desired to see an end of the absorption of the profits of this trade by a powerful foreign corporation. The government sympathized with this desire, and an opportunity for its beneficent interference at length presented itself.

In the year 1783 a young German who had resided in London departed for Baltimore with a small adventure of merchandise. Storm-stayed in Chesapeake Bay, he made the acquaintance of a furrier, who good-naturedly communicated to him some of the lore of his craft. The knowledge thus gained changed the destination of the young merchant to New York. There he sold his merchandise, invested the proceeds in furs, and returned with them to London. Such was the beginning of John Jacob Astor's career in the fur trade.[2] On April 6, 1808, with the approval of

[1] See *ante*, p. 101.
[2] Irving, *Astoria*, ch. 2; Turner, in Wisconsin Historical Society, *Proceedings*, 1889, pp. 83–85. For good sketches of Astor see James Parton, *Life of John Jacob Astor* (New

the general government, he procured from the legislature of New York the charter of the American Fur Company.[3] The company was capitalized at one million dollars, all of which amount Astor supplied, the other stockholders being merely ornamental. In 1811 Astor and several partners of the Northwest Company who were operating at Mackinac under the name of the Montreal-Michilimackinac Company formed a merger known as the Southwest Company. An arrangement was made with the Northwest Company whereby the latter firm was to confine its trading operations to the Indians north of the boundary line, and the former to those within the limits of the United States.[4] The War of 1812 came on and the resulting disorganization of the fur trade led to the dissolution of the Southwest Company. No sooner was that contest closed than Astor proceeded to revive the American Fur Company and to seek active support from the general government. By adroitly arousing the pride and patriotism of leading men at Washington he secured the passage of the act of April 29, 1816, for the regulation of trade with the Indians. The first and cardinal section of the act provided that "licenses to trade with the Indians within the territorial limits of the United States shall not be granted to any but citizens of the United States, unless by the express direction of the President."[5] This provision was intended to exclude British

York, 1865), and *Appletons' Cyclopaedia of American Biography*, 1: 112. See also Anna Youngman, "The Fortune of John Jacob Astor," in the *Journal of Political Economy*, 16: 345–368, 436–441, 514–530 (June–July, October, 1908).

[3] New York, *Private Laws*, 1808, p. 160. Jefferson, writing to Astor, April 13, 1808, noted with satisfaction that associations of Americans were being formed to engage in the Indian trade, and assured him that "in order to get the whole of this business passed into the hands of our own citizens, and to oust foreign traders . . . every reasonable patronage and facility in the power of the Executive will be afforded." Three months later, in a letter to Lewis, Jefferson declared, "Nothing but the exclusive possession of the Indian commerce can secure us their peace." Jefferson, *Writings*, 12: 28, 100 (Monticello edition, Washington, 1903–05); James H. Lockwood, "Early Times and Events in Wisconsin," in *Wisconsin Historical Collections*, 2: 101, n. (Madison, 1856).

[4] Stevens, in Mississippi Valley Historical Association, *Proceedings*, 9: 289.

[5] *Statutes at Large*, 3: 332; Chittenden, *American Fur Trade*, 1: 310; Lockwood, in *Wisconsin Historical Collections*, 2: 102. The act declared forfeited all merchandise in the hands of foreigners in the Indian country and forbade foreigners to be in the Indian country without passports obtained from the governor of some state or territory, or from some other

trading companies from United States soil, and it precipitated their elimination, which had already been anticipated.
The American Fur Company secured not only the interests
of the Southwest Company but also all the posts and
outfits of the Northwest Company south of the Canadian
boundary, and established its headquarters at Mackinac. In the course of two years it was doing business
throughout the upper valley of the Mississippi. The
American company adopted the policy of retaining the
old *engagés* and *voyageurs* of the Northwest Company,
but replaced its clerks and agents by enterprising young
Americans, who easily adapted themselves to the situation and soon became efficient.[6] It must, however, be
noted and remembered that some of the former traders of
the Northwest Company speedily obtained naturalization
papers and, as American citizens, continued in the business.
Familiar names of such in the Minnesota trade are Rolette,
Renville, Faribault, Bailly, Provençalle, and Laframboise.[7]

The establishment of American citizens in the Indian
trade of the Northwest led to measures for the protection of
those thus lawfully engaged. The first step was the negotiation of a treaty with the Sioux at the Portage des Sioux, near
St. Louis, on July 19, 1815, by which these Indians agreed
to resume friendly relations with the United States and to

licensed person authorized to issue them. It did not forbid licensed American traders to
employ alien servants. Marcus L. Hansen, in his *Old Fort Snelling, 1819–1858*, 209, n. 44
(Iowa City, 1918), says that the law was not wholly satisfactory to Astor, and that entire
credit should not be given him for its passage. He quotes from a letter of William H. Put-
huff, Indian agent at Mackinac, in *Wisconsin Historical Collections*, 19: 423, as follows: "I
have seen a letter addressed by J. J. Astor to a Mr. Franks a British trader now at this
place in which Mr. Astor expresses surprise and regret at the passage of a law forbidding
British subjects from trading with Indians, within the American limits etc." Hansen
adds, without further citation of sources: "What Mr. Astor wanted was the prohibition
of trade by American private citizens as well as by British private citizens. If his American
Fur Company were given a monopoly as he desired, he also wanted to be free to employ
such persons — American or British — as he needed."

[6] Buck, *Illinois in 1818*, 23–25, 27–29.

[7] It is evident from numerous statements and innuendoes of Major Taliaferro that in
his judgment these men, although supplied with naturalization papers in due form, never
became Americanized. Note in particular his denunciation of "these Mississippi demi-
civilized Canadian mongrel English American citizens," in his Letter Book, A, p. 3 of the
article "Indian Trade Upper Mississippi," which precedes the index.

acknowledge the president as their only Great Father.[8] This treaty was followed in the summer of 1816 by the reoccupation of Prairie du Chien by a four-company detachment of United States infantry, which was at once employed in the erection of a new fort on the site of the old one. This was named Fort Crawford in honor of the secretary of the treasury.[9] But this post was not long to remain the extreme outpost in the Northwest. In 1817 Secretary of War John C. Calhoun announced that a "board of the most skilful officers in our service" had been delegated "to examine the whole line of our frontier, and to determine on the position and extent of works that may be necessary to the defence of the country."[10] The task of surveying the upper Mississippi, which included the making of plats of the fortifications already in existence and the designation of sites suitable for future military establishments, was intrusted to Major Stephen H. Long of the corps of topographical engineers. His journey of seventy-six days in a six-oared skiff from St. Louis to the Falls of St. Anthony was performed very comfortably in the summer of 1817. On July 17 and 18 the two sites which Lieutenant Pike had obtained by treaty with the Indians in 1805, the one at the junction of the Minnesota and Mississippi rivers, the other at the mouth of the St. Croix, were examined and recommended to the consideration of the war department.[11] The former site was regarded as the more satisfactory, and in a report to Con-

---

[8] *Statutes at Large*, 7:127. At the same time peace treaties in the same terms were made with other tribes of the Northwest, including those near the mouth of the Missouri River.

[9] Lockwood, in *Wisconsin Historical Collections*, 2:122, 127; John W. Johnson to Francis Bouthilier, June 23, 1816, in *Wisconsin Historical Collections*, 19:424; Thwaites, *Wisconsin*, 181. For Long's description of the fort and its situation, see *Minnesota Historical Collections*, 2:56.

[10] *American State Papers: Military Affairs*, 1:669. This board was instituted by President Madison. In an article on "A Larger View of the Yellowstone Expedition, 1819-1820," printed in the *Mississippi Valley Historical Review*, 4:303 (December, 1917), Cardinal Goodwin cites a letter from James Monroe to Andrew Jackson, December 14, 1816, outlining the work of the board.

[11] Major Long kept a journal of his trip from July 9, when he began the ascent of the Mississippi at Prairie du Chien, to August 15, the date of his return to St. Louis. His narrative was first published in 1860 by the Minnesota Historical Society under the title

gress, December 14, 1818, Calhoun stated that "our posts are now, or will be shortly, extended, for the protection of our trade and the preservation of the peace of the frontiers, to Green Bay, the mouths of the St. Peter's and the Yellow Stone river, Bellepoint, and Natchitoches."[12] It is probable that Calhoun was largely responsible for the adoption of these measures of defense. His writings show a hearty and intelligent interest in the welfare of the Indian tribes, then and long after in the care of the war department, and a clear appreciation of the needs of the expanding West.[13] Under his direction Major General Brown, commanding the division of the North, on February 10, 1819, issued an order for the concentration of the Fifth United States Infantry at Detroit, Michigan, and its preparation for a westward expedition under the command of Lieutenant Colonel Henry Leavenworth. This officer was directed to transport his force by the lakes to Fort Howard on Green Bay, and thence to proceed by the old Fox-Wisconsin route to Fort Crawford at Prairie du Chien. After detaching a sufficient garrison for that post and for Fort Armstrong at Rock Island, he was to ascend the Mississippi and establish a military post at the mouth of the St. Peter's.[14]

Voyage in a Six-oared Skiff to the Falls of Saint Anthony in 1817. It is also in *Minnesota Historical Collections,* 2: 7–88 (St. Paul, 1889). The original manuscript, consisting of twenty-nine pages of foolscap and containing maps not published, is in the possession of the Minnesota Historical Society. The journal is pleasant reading, but it did not contribute largely to existing information.

[12] *American State Papers: Military Affairs,* 1: 779.

[13] The reports of Calhoun and his letter to the Reverend Jedidiah Morse, February 7, 1820, in *American State Papers: Indian Affairs,* 2: 200, 273, 275, 284, are typical examples. See also Hermann E. von Holst, *John C. Calhoun,* 45–49 (*American Statesmen* series — Boston, 1895).

[14] Calhoun to Major General Jacob Brown, October 17, 1818, in J. Franklin Jameson, ed., "Correspondence of John C. Calhoun," printed in the American Historical Association, *Annual Reports,* 1899, vol. 2, p. 147. Letters transmitting the orders of Major General Brown and of Major General Macomb, commanding the department at Detroit, are in Schoolcraft, *Summary Narrative,* 35. In 1817 Leavenworth was appointed Indian agent for the northwestern territory with headquarters at Prairie du Chien. His wife and daughter are said to have been the first white women to travel through the wilderness to this region. He was promoted to the rank of lieutenant colonel and assigned to the Fifth Infantry on February 10, 1818. Sketches of Colonel Leavenworth may be found in *Missouri Historical Collections,* 3: 104, n. 35, and in Elias W. Leavenworth, *A Genealogy of the Leavenworth Family in the United States,* 150–154 (Syracuse, New York, 1873).

It now occurred to somebody that the Indians had never been paid the price fixed by the Senate for the tracts ceded by them in their treaty with Pike, and that it would be prudent for the government to pay before taking possession. Accordingly Major Thomas Forsyth, an experienced Indian agent at Rock Island, was directed to proceed to the neighborhood of the contemplated military post with two thousand dollars worth of goods to satisfy the bands concerned. From Prairie du Chien he traveled with the troops. He divided his goods among Wabasha, Red Wing, Little Crow, Shakopee, and two other chiefs, according to his judgment of their relative importance. He gave all the bands a little whisky and they went home contented. Major Forsyth seems not to have laid much stress on the consummation of a bargain in his interviews with the chiefs, but, after telling them that the Great Father had resolved to build a fort at the mouth of the St. Peter's, which would be a twofold benefit to them in the way of a blacksmith shop and a trading center, he reminded them that it would not be well for them to make any opposition, since the Great Father could get at one blow of his whistle as many soldiers as he wanted. The chiefs thus conciliated appear to have been satisfied with the bargain; but some years later a claim was made that no such large area had been ceded to Pike, and a demand was made for increased compensation, which was tardily granted.[15]

Leavenworth's advance party reached Prairie du Chien on June 30,[16] where it was held for more than a month awaiting

[15] Major Forsyth, who joined Colonel Leavenworth and his detachment of "98 rank and file" at Prairie du Chien, gives an account of the journey and of the location and building of the first cantonment, in his "Journal of a Voyage from St. Louis to the Falls of St. Anthony in 1819," in *Wisconsin Historical Collections*, 6: 188–219, reprinted in *Minnesota Historical Collections*, 3: 139–167. Interesting details of the journey and of the delivery of "presents" by Major Forsyth to the chiefs of the Sioux may be found in three letters written by him to Governor William Clark and dated St. Louis, May 3, September 23, and October 3, 1819. The letter of September is in *Minnesota Historical Collections*, 3: 163; copies of the others have been kindly furnished by the Missouri Historical Society. See also the Appendix, no. 2.

[16] This is the date given by Major Forsyth. See *Minnesota Historical Collections*, 3: 145. Scarcely an hour after the arrival of the detachment at Prairie du Chien its number

supplies. While thus detained, Leavenworth executed a civil commission with which he had been charged by Gover-nor Lewis Cass.[17] The expected supplies and ordnance arrived during the first week of August and the expedition set out on the morning of the eighth. It reached the mouth of the St. Peter's on the twenty-fourth.[18] Selecting a site on the right bank of that river near the present hamlet of Mendota, Colonel Leavenworth set his soldiers at work building the huts and other structures of a cantonment in which to pass the coming winter. Here the command, increased early in September by the arrival of a detachment of the regiment numbering 120, remained for the next two years, save when in summer camp near the well-known "cold spring" still flowing above the present fort.[19] During the first winter, 1819–20, scurvy in a malignant form broke out in the cantonment and raged to such an extent that there were barely men enough to care for the sick soldiers. Men who went to bed at night in apparent good health would be found dead the next morning; one man who had stretched himself on a bench in the guardroom after a tour of sentry duty was found lifeless four hours later. The cause of this sudden and violent outbreak of disease was attributed to the villainy of certain contractors or their agents, who drew the brine from the barrels of pork to lighten the loads on leaving St. Louis and refilled them with river water before delivery. Vinegar and other anti-

was increased by one by the birth of Charlotte Ouisconsin (Clark) Van Cleve, widely known through her interesting narrative of Fort Snelling entitled *"Three Score Years and Ten,"* *Life-long Memories of Fort Snelling, Minnesota, and Other Parts of the West* (Minneapolis, 1888). On page 13 of her narrative, Mrs. Van Cleve gives July 1 as the time of the arrival at Prairie du Chien.

[17] See *post*, p. 231.

[18] Forsyth, in *Minnesota Historical Collections*, 3: 149–154, 163. Mrs. Van Cleve in her *"Three Score Years and Ten,"* 17, gives the date of the arrival of the expedition as "sometime in September."

[19] Traces of the cantonment building were detected by the author on a visit to the site in April, 1908. The summer camp was called "Camp Coldwater," and the name was long retained for a small cluster of cabins about the trading house of Benjamin F. Baker located there. "The Rev. Mr. Bronson of the Methodist Church preached at 'Cold Water' also this day." Taliaferro Journal, June 17, 1838.

scorbutics were obtained from Prairie du Chien, and decoctions of "vegetable productions" were found remedial.[20]

Early in the summer of 1820 Colonel Leavenworth began preparations for the erection of the contemplated fort by gathering building materials and selecting a site on the right bank of the Mississippi where it terminates in the more ancient and principal valley of the Minnesota, about three hundred yards west of the present location. The timber was hewed from hardwood trees felled in the neighborhood; the lumber was sawed by hand from pine logs rafted down from the banks of Rum River.[21]

The monotonous routine of life at Camp Coldwater was interrupted on July 25 by the arrival of an exploring party detached from the Yellowstone expedition, which had been dispatched in 1819 from St. Louis to the Missouri River. The party had come across the country from Camp Missouri, later known as Fort Atkinson, near the present city of Omaha, with the object of finding a practicable overland route between the two frontier posts. It was "most kindly & hospitably received & entertained by Col. L. & his Lady," and on July 29 started down river for St. Louis.[22]

In August Colonel Leavenworth was relieved by Colonel Josiah Snelling, who had been promoted and assigned to the Fifth United States Infantry on June 1, 1819. The new commandant was at this time thirty-eight years of age, and had done gallant service in the War of 1812. The tradition is that he "infused system and energy among men and

---

[20] The number of fatalities is variously given. Mrs. Van Cleve estimates that forty succumbed; Sibley, that "nearly one-half the command perished"; Prescott, who arrived at the post late in the winter, says that "some fifty or sixty had died, and some ten men died after I arrived." Mrs. Van Cleve tells of the relief obtained by the use of "spignot root," doubtless spikenard (*aralia racemosa*), then and now abounding in the region. Prescott attributes the abatement of the malady to the "groceries" which he brought and a "quantity of spruce that Dr. Purcell had sent to the St. Croix for." See Van Cleve, "*Three Score Years and Ten*," 19; Sibley, in *Minnesota Historical Collections*, 1: 473 (St. Paul, 1872); and Philander Prescott, "Autobiography and Reminiscences," in *Minnesota Historical Collections*, 6: 478. Hugo W. von Ziemssen gives an account of land scurvy in his *Cyclopedia of the Practice of Medicine*, 17: 112 (New York, 1874–1881).

[21] Prescott, in *Minnesota Historical Collections*, 6: 478.

[22] Stephen W. Kearney, "Journal," in *Missouri Historical Collections*, 3: 104–110.

officers" of the garrison, over which he retained command for seven years. The plan for the new fortification was somewhat altered, and the location was changed to that of the present fort.[23] Perhaps no more picturesque site is to be found throughout the whole course of the great river. Although commanded by higher ground a half mile to the rear, it was obviously the proper one to be chosen, the sole danger of attack being from Indians destitute of artillery.[24] On September 10 the corner stone was laid with some ceremony.[25]

The discovery was soon made that the great quantity of lumber needed could not be sawed by hand. It was, therefore, decided to erect a sawmill to supersede the broadaxe and the whipsaw, on the neighboring Little Falls, now called Minnehaha, but the water in the stream in the summer of 1820 was so low that the more distant Falls of St. Anthony were preferred. A logging party of soldiers cut two thousand pine logs on the Rum River in the following winter

[23] Prescott, in *Minnesota Historical Collections*, 6:478. Compare, however, Mrs. Van Cleve's statement that Colonel Snelling "immediately began preparations for building the fort, the site of which had been selected by Colonel Leavenworth." "*Three Score Years and Ten*," 20.

[24] Of this location Joseph N. Nicollet says, "St. Peter's is, in my opinion, the finest site on the Mississippi river." In his *Report*, 67, 129, he gives its astronomical position as latitude 44° 52′ 46″ north and longitude 93° 4′ 54″ west. Major Long's opinion as to the suitableness of the site is in *Minnesota Historical Collections*, 2:41. There is a plan of Fort Snelling as it stood in 1839 on a map made by Lieutenant Thompson, entitled "Topographical Survey of the Military Reservation Embracing Fort Snelling." A map of "Fort Snelling and Vicinity," made by E. K. Smith in 1837, shows substantially the same plan on a smaller scale and includes a larger territory. Both maps show the locations of Camp Coldwater, the American Fur Company's establishment, the Indian agency, and the mission buildings at Lake Harriet. The Minnesota Historical Society has photostatic copies of these maps made from the originals on file in the war department. Hereafter they will be referred to as the Thompson Map and the Smith Map. See also chapters 8 and 16 and the map facing page 424, *post*. A plan of Fort Snelling, drawn in 1898, but showing the buildings of the fort and the inclosing wall as they were before the Civil War, is to be found in *Minnesota Historical Collections*, 8:430. The wooden buildings were not replaced by stone until 1830, and additions continued to be made until after the close of the Mexican War. The only remaining vestiges of the old Fort Snelling are in the round (Martello) tower at the gateway and the hexagonal tower on the bluff overlooking the river. An army quartermaster in 1904 had the Martello tower plastered over with cement which some beneficent authority has had removed. The layout of the new fort, with its barracks and stables facing the river fronts, is simply atrocious.

[25] Neill, in *Minnesota Historical Collections*, 2:105. In his *Minnesota*, 337–339, n., Neill quotes an article written by Taliaferro and published in the *Daily Pioneer and Democrat* (St. Paul) for July 11, 1856.

and rafted them down after the ice went out in the spring of 1821. The sawmill was not begun until late in the summer of that year and it was not completed until the spring of 1822. On October 1, 1821, Taliaferro made the following entry in his journal: "Visited the Falls of St. Anthony this forenoon to see the sawmill erecting under the direction of Lieut. McCabe. It certainly is not only better constructed but more substantial than any that ever came under my observation."[26] Although the fort was far from completion, it gave shelter to the troops during the winter of 1822–23.[27] Major General Winfield Scott, visiting the post in 1824, was so much impressed by the efficiency of Colonel Snelling that he recommended that the name be changed from Fort St. Anthony to Fort Snelling. The war department accepted the recommendation.[28]

The immediate objects of the establishment of the military post at the mouth of the Minnesota River were the protection of the fur trade, now in American hands, and the control of the aborigines. The supervision and regulation of that trade and the safeguarding of the interests and welfare of the Indians called for the installation of a civilian Indian agent. For this service President Monroe personally selected Law-

[26] Descriptions of the first buildings at the fort and an account of the erection of the sawmill are given by Prescott, in *Minnesota Historical Collections*, 6: 478, and in Elizabeth F. Ellet's sketch of Abigail Snelling in her *Pioneer Women of the West*, 326 (New York, 1852). In 1823 a flour mill, provided with a single pair of buhrs and the necessary bolting apparatus, was built adjacent to the sawmill. Edward A. Bromley, in an article entitled "The Old Government Mills at the Falls of St. Anthony," in *Minnesota Historical Collections*, 10: 635–643 (part 2), has clearly shown that there were separate saw and flour mills at the falls, which is contradictory to the recollections of many old settlers and the statements of numerous writers. See also Keating, *Narrative*, 1: 309, and Van Cleve, "*Three Score Years and Ten*," 37.

[27] Neill, in *Minnesota Historical Collections*, 2: 107. Prescott's statement is that "before the autumn of 1823 nearly all the soldiers had been got into quarters, and considerable work had been done on the officers' quarters." See *Minnesota Historical Collections*, 6: 479. Mrs. Van Cleve says, however, that the regiment moved into the fort in 1821, "although it was by no means completed. The outside wall was up on three sides only, and a heavy guard was stationed on the fourth." "*Three Score Years and Ten*," 32.

[28] War Department, General Orders, no. 1, January 7, 1825, quoted in a letter from Henry P. McCain, adjutant general of the war department, to Warren Upham, in the *Magazine of History*, 21: 39 (July, 1915). The same letter contains an extract from General Scott's report of November, 1824, recommending the change of name. See also Neill, in *Minnesota Historical Collections*, 2: 108.

MAJOR LAWRENCE TALIAFERRO, INDIAN AGENT
Oil by an unknown artist

GOVERNMENT MILLS AT THE FALLS OF ST. ANTHONY

rence Taliaferro, a first lieutenant in the Third United States Infantry, and commissioned him as Indian agent at St. Peter's, March 27, 1819. Taliaferro, then twenty-five years of age, belonged to an old Virginia family of Italian extraction. As a boy of eighteen he had volunteered for the War of 1812, and its close found him a lieutenant in the regular army. In the years following that war his activity in various widely scattered military operations was such as to attract the attention of the war department and to lead to this unsolicited appointment.[29] For seven years his jurisdiction embraced both the Sioux nation and the Chippewa of the upper Mississippi.[30] For twenty years "Major" Taliaferro (pronounced Tol'-li-ver) was the most important and influential civil official on the upper Mississippi.[31] He

[29] There is a sketch and a brief appreciation of Major Taliaferro in J. Fletcher Williams, *History of the City of Saint Paul*, 40 (*Minnesota Historical Collections*, vol. 4 — St. Paul, 1876). Neill, in *Minnesota Historical Collections*, 5: 465–510, quotes from Taliaferro's journal and makes interesting comments on his work among the Chippewa. An "Autobiography of Maj. Lawrence Taliaferro," written in 1864, is in *Minnesota Historical Collections*, 6: 189–246. A brief survey of his work written upon the occasion of his death appeared in the *St. Paul Pioneer* for February 26, 1871.

[30] In a letter to Major Taliaferro written March 26, 1827, General William Clark, superintendent at St. Louis, informed the agent that his dominion extended only to the Sioux-Chippewa line of 1825, and that beyond it lay the agency of Schoolcraft. Nevertheless, the Indians from the region north of the line continued to visit the former agency. In numerous talks with Major Taliaferro their chiefs complained of the labors and dangers of the long journey to Mackinac, comparing it with the easy trip down the Mississippi in their canoes. Taliaferro repeatedly and firmly urged the establishment of a subagency for these Chippewa on the upper Mississippi. He virtually served as their "father" from July, 1829, to September, 1836, "by *permission*, by *order*, & by assumption." Two appointments, and perhaps three, to this proposed subagency were made in 1835 and 1836, which, for reasons not clearly revealed, proved abortive. In the latter year Major Miles W. Vineyard accepted the position. In a letter to Governor Henry Dodge, Taliaferro criticized sharply Schoolcraft's neglect of the Chippewa of the Mississippi. Taliaferro Papers; Taliaferro Journal, June 30, August 6, 1836; Taliaferro Letter Book, B, December 26, 1836; Taliaferro, in *Minnesota Historical Collections*, 6: 209, 213.

[31] Abundant material for a story of Agent Taliaferro's official acts, and incidentally for an understanding of the man, can be found in his unpublished journals and letters, written and received, which are in the possession of the Minnesota Historical Society. In a letter published in the *Pioneer and Democrat* July 11, 1856, Major Taliaferro mentions "seventeen manuscript journals." Some of these, along with other papers, he presented to the society in 1863. A number of the journals are missing, and these may have been lost in the fire which destroyed the Taliaferro home in Bedford, Pennsylvania, in 1865, since the greater number of the journals and papers were presented to the society in 1867 and 1868. It is evident that Neill drew from these journals, without reference to or acknowledgment of them, the material for his "Occurrences in and around Fort Snelling, 1819 to 1840," which was first published by the Minnesota Historical Society in its *Collections for the Year 1864*, 21–56 (St. Paul, 1865) and was reprinted in 1889 in *Minnesota Historical*

had two eminent qualifications for dealing with red men: one, absolute truthfulness; the other, a tolerance of Indian fondness for gaudy apparel, ceremonial, and oratory. A vein of egotism, proceeding from pride of family and breeding, enabled him to impress the savage with a sense of his importance. It is to his credit that he was cordially hated by all who could neither bribe nor frighten him to connive at lawbreaking to the harm of Indians. In spite of the complaints and machinations of traders and politicians he held his place until 1839, when he voluntarily resigned after a sixth appointment — a fact as creditable to four presidents, their cabinets, and the Indian office as to the incorruptible and high-toned Virginian.[32]

Collections, 2: 102–142. In his *Saint Paul*, 40, n., Williams mentions a "minute diary" of Taliaferro in the possession of the historical society. In 1905 the writer was able to find only two unbound booklets, much damaged by fire, covering the second part of the year 1831 and the years 1833 and 1834, and a bound volume of letters received by Taliaferro. When the library of the historical society was moved from the Capitol in the winter of 1918 nine volumes of journals and two letter books turned up. On December 19, 1919, Mr. Edson S. Gaylord of Minneapolis found in a secondhand bookstore in St. Louis the journals covering the years 1827, 1828, and part of 1829, which he purchased and made available to the writer. The journals begin with 1821 and end with 1839, but those for 1822, 1824, and 1837 are still missing. Since the last named is for the treaty year, its loss is to be greatly lamented. The letter books cover the periods from 1820 to 1829 and from 1836 to 1839. A third book is evidently missing. The journals and letters alike are restricted to official matters with here and there a personal item. Much room is given to speeches of Indian chiefs and headmen and to replies by the agent, who never failed to descant on the power and magnificence of the Great Father and on his own solicitude for the welfare of his children of the forest and prairie. The historical society also possesses 362 letters received by Taliaferro. See Taliaferro to Neill, October 22, 1863, on the back cover of the Taliaferro Journal for 1832; Taliaferro to Neill, April 11, 1865, and Taliaferro to A. J. Hill, August 12, 1868, in the Taliaferro Papers. "Major" was at the time, and has ever since been, a courtesy title of Indian agents. Taliaferro was known to the Indians, so he states, as "Mahsabusca," or "Iron Cutter," which was a translation of his name into Dakota. According to Dr. Charles A. Eastman, however, "mazabaksa" is the correct Dakota form for iron cutter. Taliaferro, in *Minnesota Historical Collections*, 6: 219.

[32] Taliaferro himself, in his journal, October 21, 1836, summed up his merits as an Indian agent by compiling a catena of charges and complaints held against him by "the company" — the American Fur Company. On August 25, 1839, he made the following entry: "I leave the whole *nest* this fall Indians & traders. . . . I am disgusted with the *life* of an *agent* among such discordant materials & bad management on the part of Congress — the Indian Office &c &c." He had tendered his formal resignation July 15, on the ground of enfeebled health after twenty-seven years in the public service in a high latitude. In a letter written at the same time to T. Hartley Crawford, the commissioner of Indian affairs, he hinted, however, that he would be ready for further service in this or any other section of the Indian territory. He also offered some suggestions as to the qualifications to be desired in a successor and remarked on the distress of well-informed Indians at his determination to leave them. The real reasons for his resignation appeared a little later. In the first place, the Indian office had failed to enable him to fulfill treaty stipulations,

Agent Taliaferro's original order to join the expedition under Colonel Leavenworth was modified so as to send him to St. Louis to report to his immediate superior, General William Clark, superintendent of Indian affairs in the West. The time of his arrival at St. Peter's after a leisurely journey in a keel boat with an Indian escort has not been ascertained, but he was "in the quarters of the old cantonment" in the summer of 1820.[33] Here he embraced an early opportunity to display an element of his character. In what particular ways the veteran colonel of the Fifth Infantry intruded upon the domain of the youthful Indian agent is not now known, but his action was speedily resented. On July 30 Taliaferro began a letter to Colonel Leavenworth: "As it is now fairly understood that I am the agent for Indian affairs in this Country, I beg leave to suggest," et cetera.[34] Colonel

thereby discrediting him with the Indians. In the second place, he had been kept in the dark as to the views and intentions of that office, when the American Fur Company, or individuals connected with it, had been well informed in advance. Indeed, Taliaferro went so far as to hint at a "Judas" at the elbow of the commissioner. In the third place, he had not been so well provided for as other agents, having been obliged to furnish quarters for himself and his hired men and presents for the Indians. Finally, "from the fault" of the Indian office, he had been threatened with assassination. It is interesting to note that in October of that year he recalled his resignation on account of the brutal behavior of a deputy sheriff, who arrested the agent in a suit for damages brought by a whisky-seller. *Minnesota Historical Collections*, 6: 226; Taliaferro to Poinsett, July 16, 1839, to Crawford, July 15, 1839, in Taliaferro Journal; Taliaferro to Plympton, July 30, 1839, in Taliaferro Letter Book, B; Taliaferro Journal, October 5, 6, 7, 1839.

[33] Taliaferro, in *Minnesota Historical Collections*, 6: 197-199; Neill, *Minnesota*, 337, n. Major Taliaferro brought with him to St. Peter's a number of negro slaves, whose color and curling hair greatly amused the Indians, who called them "black Frenchmen." There are many references to his "servants" in his journals. On March 31, 1826, he "Let Col. Snelling have my . . . Boy William until the 1st of October next — for his *Victuals & Clothes.*" On May 29, 1826, he wrote: "Capt. Plymton wishes to purchase my servant girl Eliza. I informed him that it was my intention to give her her freedom after a limited time but that Mrs. P could keep her for two years and perhaps three." See also the entries for February 23 and September 22, 1831, August 30, 1834, and November 28, 1835. It is interesting to note that he literally gave his servant girl, Harriet Robinson, in marriage to Dred Scott, the plaintiff in the celebrated case, and that he himself performed the nuptial ceremony. Later he emancipated all his servants, at a time when, as he estimated, their money value would have been twenty-five or thirty thousand dollars. Taliaferro records an incident in the family of Subagent Langham which occurred on March 30, 1831, and which illustrates the amenities of slavery. A young daughter of Langham was missing and after a search she was found hidden under some stable litter. Three days later his colored servant girl confessed to mischievous assault. The master adjudged as her punishment an iron collar about her neck, handcuffs, and a ball and chain to her feet. It was the opinion of Taliaferro that murder was intended. *Minnesota Historical Collections*, 6: 235; Taliaferro Journal, March 30-April 3, 1831.

[34] Taliaferro to Leavenworth, July 30, 1820, in Letter Book, A.

Leavenworth, however, seems not to have shared Taliaferro's opinion concerning his position, for on August 9 we
find the commandant in council with some chiefs, warriors,
and headmen of the Sioux nation at his cantonment. He
made with them there a treaty by which they "granted,
conveyed, and confirmed" to Colonel Henry Leavenworth
for the use and benefit of the United States forever a large
tract of land on the southeastern side of the Minnesota and
Mississippi rivers, which for some miles have the same north-
easterly course. The consideration for the grant was the
"many acts of kindness received by said Indians from said
Leavenworth . . . and such other compensation (if any)
as the said Government may think proper to appropriate."
Three reservations were made from the tract: the first, of
one square mile fronting on the Minnesota River, including
the site later occupied by the American Fur Company's
establishment, for Duncan Campbell, "a friend and
brother"; the second, of the same area, lying below and
adjoining the former, for Campbell's sister Peggy; the third,
our well-known Pike's Island, for Pelagie Faribault, wife of
Jean Baptiste Faribault, and her heirs forever.[35] The parcels were not merely reserved from the grant to the United

[35] There has been a perennial misunderstanding in regard to the location of the land
which Colonel Leavenworth desired to acquire. In the opinion of Henry Hastings Sibley,
Colonel Leavenworth procured a "grant of land nine miles square at the junction" of the
rivers. In a letter written to John Bell, the secretary of war, at the time when the negotiations for the abortive treaty with the Sioux were in progress, James Duane Doty, on the
other hand, stated that "in the year 1819 Genl. Leavenworth arrived here with a detachment of troops, but before he took possession he entered into an agreement with the Indians
for a tract embracing that which was selected by Genl. Pike." A reading of the description
given in the Leavenworth treaty will show at once that the tract lay wholly on the southerly
side of the two rivers, with some overlapping of the cession of Pike. It reads: "Beginning
on the southerly bank of the river St. Pierre, and running at right angles with said river,
from the first bend below the village of the Black Dog . . . three miles . . . into the
prairie back from said river; thence, easterly, on a line parallel with the general course of
the rivers Mississippi and St. Pierre . . . to a place opposite to the Old Cave . . . thence,
up the Mississippi and St. Pierre rivers, including all islands, to the place of beginning."
Sibley, "Memoir of Jean Baptiste Faribault," in *Minnesota Historical Collections*, 3: 177;
Doty to Bell, August 12, 1841, in Sibley Papers; *Purchase of Island — Confluence of the St.
Peter's and Mississippi Rivers*, 5 (26 Congress, 1 session, *House Documents*, no. 82 — serial
365). See the Appendix, no. 1, *post*, for the story of the Faribault claim. The boundaries of
the "Leavenworth Grant" and of the Campbell reservations are indicated on the map
facing page 424, *post*.

States, but were in specific terms given, granted, and conveyed to the beneficiaries. A few days after this treaty was made, Colonel Leavenworth was succeeded in command of the fort by Colonel Snelling, with whom Taliaferro long lived in complete harmony.[36]

The ambitious young agent set before himself three principal tasks: (1) to establish and maintain peace between the warring Indian nations; (2) to protect the Indians from the white man's lust and greed, in particular from the traders and their satellites; (3) to induce the savages to cultivate the soil as the beginning of their civilization. His first undertaking was to make clearly known to the Indians of his district the fact that the president of the United States and not the king of England was their Great Father, with whom alone they could make treaties and to whom they must look for protection. Notwithstanding the War of 1812, the treaty of Ghent, and acts of Congress, the influence of the old British traders was still effective, and the cross of St. George was better known in the wilds of Minnesota than the flag of the American Union. In two years Major Taliaferro secured the surrender by the chiefs of thirty-six medals of George III, twenty-eight British flags, and eighteen gorgets.[37]

It was the complacent belief of Taliaferro, for a time, as well as of his immediate superior, Governor Cass, of the war department, and of good Americans generally, that the immemorial hatred between rival Indian nations could be dissipated by some fair speeches in council, a distribution of batches of Indian goods, and a final circle of the calumet. In the year following his appointment and arrival in Michigan Territory, Governor Cass, as already related, presided in person over a council of Sioux and Chippewa at Fort Snelling, and went through the motions of a conclusive treaty of peace.[38] Three years later Major Taliaferro

[36] Taliaferro, in *Minnesota Historical Collections*, 6: 199.
[37] Taliaferro, in *Minnesota Historical Collections*, 6: 190–198, 200, 235–239.
[38] There is an account of the treaty in Schoolcraft, *Narrative Journal*, 304–307.

repeated the performance, trusting that from this time his red children would never again dig up the bloodstained hatchet. Before the delegation had got off the government reserve, a detachment from the garrison had to be ordered out to prevent a bloody collision.[39] In 1824 the agent took a mixed party of the two nations to Washington in the hope that a peace might be concluded which the white man's power, thus revealed to the savages, might guarantee. The outcome was that it was agreed and ordered that in the following year there should be a grand conference or convocation of the northwestern tribes to compose their differences and to establish a permanent peace.[40]

The "grand conference" of 1825 was the most spectacular event not military which had yet taken place on the upper Mississippi. It was held at Fort Crawford, Prairie du Chien, on August 19. Agent Schoolcraft set out from Sault Ste. Marie with his 150 Saulteurs, escorted by 60 soldiers with their officers in a numerous flotilla, with music and banners. The expedition departed from the rendezvous at Mackinac on July 1, traveled by way of the Fox-Wisconsin route, and arrived at Prairie du Chien on the twenty-first. Agent Taliaferro had gathered at Fort Snelling a delegation of 385 Sioux and Chippewa of the Mississippi, including interpreters and assistants. The united tribesmen made their way down river and at length halted at the "Painted Rock" above Prairie du Chien. Here the savages dressed for a solemn entry with as much care as an ambassador and his suite would have taken at the court of the Grand Monarque. When all was ready, the boats, arranged in columns, swept down with flags flying, drums beating, and guns firing, and rounded up at the levee at Fort Crawford in imposing array. The commissioners for the United States government were Governor Lewis Cass of Michigan and Governor William Clark of Missouri, both superintendents of Indian affairs. The negotiations between the Sioux and the Chippewa, with which alone we are concerned, resulted in an agreement on a dividing line between their respective countries, which the Indians solemnly promised would never be crossed by either nation unless on peaceful missions. The boundary agreed on stretched in a general southeast direction from the junction of Goose Creek, a North Dakota streamlet, with the Red River of the North to a point on the St. Croix about eight miles below Osceola, Wisconsin. It passed east of Fergus Falls, west of Alexandria, and crossed the Mississippi between St. Cloud and Sauk Rapids. Prolonged into Wisconsin, it continued to a point on the Chippewa River just below Eau Claire, thence eastward to the Black River, which it followed to its junction with the Mississippi.[41] It was not till 1835, after repeated requests by the Indians, that any part of this line was run out, and then the savages pulled up the stakes as fast as they were driven. Its tardy establishment was without material effect.[42]

[41] Schoolcraft, *Personal Memoirs*, 213–217; Taliaferro, in *Minnesota Historical Collections*, 6: 206–208; *Statutes at Large*, 7: 272. For the location of the Sioux-Chippewa line, see the map facing page 80, *ante*. No entries for 1825 are found in the Taliaferro Journal until August 22, when the agent begins an account, which continues until September 20, of the return of his Indians, Sioux and Chippewa, from Prairie du Chien. On the way up many of them were taken violently ill and some died. The Indians attributed the disease to a mixture of sugar and whisky which had been given to them at the Prairie, and they were incensed at having been taken there. To comfort those who had lost relatives and to restore good feeling, the agent sent to their villages fifteen kegs of whisky and goods worth $250.

[42] Taliaferro to William Clark, September 2, 1835, in Taliaferro Papers; Neill, in *Minnesota Historical Collections*, 2: 126; William J. Snelling, "Running the Gantlet," in *Minnesota Historical Collections*, 1: 440. In the Taliaferro Journal for 1835 there are twenty-seven entries, beginning June 10 and ending September 23, relating to the survey of the "S & C Line" by Major John L. Bean, whom the Sioux called "Blue Cloud." Most of the entries are in regard to guides, interpreters, horses, oxen, provisions presents for Indians, and other details. Major Bean arrived at St. Peter's from Standing Cedar on the St. Croix on June 15. On June 18 he left for the Sauk River with an escort of soldiers and with Philander Prescott as guide. At the Otter Tail portage his escort left him to return to Fort Snelling. His Chippewa interpreter had already deserted him. On the night of July 19, a lurking party of Sioux killed a horse and a fine mule in his camp. The major returned to the agency on August 16, leaving his work half finished. While the survey was in progress both Sioux and Chippewa complained of the location. Taliaferro wrote to Major Bliss, the commandant at Fort Snelling, on August 30, 1835, that the Chippewa would not observe the landmarks, but on the contrary had been throwing them down and attempting to demolish many of them. He predicted occasional bloodshed for the reason that, since their country was "not at all adequate to the support of their population," the

By the address and influence of the agents the delegations of the rival nations were got away from the Prairie and to their homes without collision. But a year had not passed before Chippewa blood was spilled by Sioux warriors within a mile of Agent Taliaferro's office door.[43] In the year 1827 a more serious affair took place, also near the fort. A party of Sandy Lake Chippewa, twenty-four in number, arrived in May to confer with the agent. They were allowed to encamp in front of the agency near and under cover of Fort Snelling, and were assured of protection from any Sioux who might be lurking for scalps. In the course of the day they were visited by a party of nine Sioux warriors, who were hospitably received and feasted on commissary sugar and meat. The pipe of peace was smoked. At the close of the visit, which was prolonged until nine o'clock, the Sioux guests by way of a parting salute fired their guns on their unsuspecting hosts. Two were killed outright and many were wounded, among them a girl of seven who did not long survive, notwithstanding the kindly ministrations of the women and the surgeon of the post. Upon the demand of Colonel Snelling the assailants were delivered to him, and the principal offenders were turned over to the Chippewa to be dealt with according to savage law. They led the culprits out onto the plain, gave them thirty yards' start, and ordered them to run for their lives. The Chippewa guns soon cut short their race for life. Their scalps were snatched and their bodies were gashed with knives. The women tasted the oozing blood and danced with joy about

Chippewa would force themselves on the hunting grounds of the Sioux. He made no mention of the destruction of markers by the Sioux. Major Bean left the agency on August 22. In a conference held on June 15, 1829, between Little Crow and Agent Taliaferro, the chief blamed the agent for requiring his people to give up too much land to the Chippewa. The agent replied that if the Sioux were not so lazy and cowardly they could hunt right up to the Sauk River and the Chippewa would not molest them. On July 21, 1829, Taliaferro records a speech made on July 19, in which he told Red Wing that his "high hopes" for the treaty of 1825 were short lived and that he was fearful that the Sioux were blowing up embers which would create a flame to consume their nation. Taliaferro Journal.

[43] William J. Snelling, in *Minnesota Historical Collections*, 1: 441; Henry H. Snelling, in the *Pioneer and Democrat*, April 28, 1856.

the corpses.   The accounts of this execution as related by eyewitnesses and annalists vary greatly in details.[44]

Until the removal of the Sioux from the state after the outbreak of 1862, the immemorial warfare between them and the Chippewa went on.   Hardly a year passed without an encounter, and in some years conflicts were numerous.

[44] This narrative follows Neill, *Minnesota*, 391–394.   Four reminiscent accounts by eyewitnesses are extant: William J. Snelling, in *Minnesota Historical Collections*, 1: 442–456; letter of Henry H. Snelling, in the *Pioneer and Democrat*, April 28, 1856; Charlotte O. Van Cleve, "A Reminiscence of Fort Snelling," in *Minnesota Historical Collections*, 3: 76–81, reprinted in her "*Three Score Years and Ten*," 74–79; and Ann Adams, "Early Days at Red River Settlement, and Fort Snelling: Reminiscences, 1821–1829," in *Minnesota Historical Collections*, 6: 107.   Schoolcraft, in his *Personal Memoirs*, 618, gives Major Garland's recollections of the affair.   Neill has a somewhat different account in *Minnesota Historical Collections*, 5: 474–476.   It was Sibley's judgment "that Col. Snelling committed a grave error, in sacrificing four Dakota lives as an atonement for the wounding of two Chippewas, both of whom recovered."   See his annual address before the Minnesota Historical Society, February 1, 1856, in the *Pioneer and Democrat*, February 5, 1856, and in *Minnesota Historical Collections*, 1: 475.   It was in answer to what he considered to be Sibley's unjust criticism of his father's policy, as well as to correct what he believed to be misstatements of fact, that Henry H. Snelling wrote his letter on the subject.

A contemporary record of this affair is contained in the Taliaferro Journal for 1827, which was not available when the above was written. (See *ante*, p. 142, n. 31.) The agent's account of the murder and its sequel is brief and prosaic but, in general, not inconsistent with the sources cited, though it is devoid of their romantic embellishments.   He relates that on May 26, 1827, some of the Sandy Lake Chippewa with Strong Earth, Hole-in-the-Day, and Flat Mouth arrived at the post.   A council was held with these Indians the next day, in which nothing unfriendly to the Sioux transpired.   In the forenoon of May 28 the six Sioux chiefs near the post came to the council.   One of them "used some mysterious and unfriendly words towards the Chippewas."   The Sioux had in some unaccountable manner learned that the Chippewa would not visit the agency at St. Peter's again because a new agency had been established for them.   Taliaferro asserts that he "discovered a disposition on their part to have some difficulty with the Chippeways encamped near my house."   At nine o'clock the same night the agent heard the report of seven guns and soon learned that "9 Sioux . . . had fired on one of the Chippeway Lodges & wounded 8 of them 3 supposed mortal 4 very severely and one slightly."   One little girl, the daughter of Hole-in-the-Day, was among the severely wounded.   The wounded were all taken to the council house.   Early the next morning, May 29, the agent sent word to the Sioux that they must give satisfaction to the Chippewa.   They gave up one murderer and Colonel Snelling secured the arrest of seven others.   "The Chippeways however called for but two of this party and they received & dispatched them a short distance from the Fort."   On May 30 the Sioux "delivered up to the Chippeways two other Indians . . . who had been most forward in firing on them and requested that they might be executed in the same place where the others had been.   The Chippeways after a short speech received them as a Sacrifice, took them near the same place & shot them."   Entries relating to the Chippewa party and the dead and wounded are those for June 1, 2, 5, 12, 16, July 7, 10, 15, 18, 1827, and May 1, 3, 1828.   See also the account in Hansen, *Old Fort Snelling*, 120–124, which is based in part on documents in the files of the Indian office at Washington.

That traces of ancient barbarism still survived in that day even among Christian white men may be inferred from the following entry for June 23, 1827, in the Taliaferro Journal: "An affair of Honor settled this evening between Lieut I M Buxley and Capt L Leonard — Captain L. wounded severely in the head, Lieut B. in the hand.   *5 shots each* both remarkably firm, all the time."

They formed a continuous series of retaliations. Indian warfare, however, must not be too closely compared with that of civilized men. Without transportation facilities and organized commissariat an Indian campaign had to be brief. The white man's objectives — the enemy's capital, his lines of transportation, his bases of supplies, his fortified places, his armies in the field — all were lacking. The campaign was reduced to a mere raid, and was counted a success if scalps were taken. If but a single scalp, and that of a woman or a child, was gathered, the returning braves were welcomed as heroes, and the scalp dance went on for days. Indian campaigns generally were not public nor political. They were often the private ventures of warriors ambitious to qualify as braves by winning a first eagle feather, or by adding to the number of those already acquired. The forays were simply a kind of man-hunting. As the greatest secrecy was preserved and all possible precautions were taken to prevent surprise, the losses were usually very small. The red man practiced for ages that art which the white man has but lately learned — fighting under cover.[45]

There is no occasion here to follow the continual encounters between the Minnesota tribes. A single example, in a late period, of the give-and-take affairs resulting in engagements of rather unusual magnitude will suffice. Early in April, 1838, a party of Sioux residing on Lac qui Parle set out to hunt in the valley of the Chippewa, a tributary of the Minnesota River. After a few days the party divided, a detachment of three lodges consisting mostly of women and children being left in camp at the forks of the Chippewa near the site of the town of Benson, Swift County. Hole-in-the-Day, the Gull River Chippewa chief, with nine followers prowling in the same region came upon this little

<hr/>

[45] There are some very illuminating pages on "Wars" in Samuel W. Pond, "The Dakotas or Sioux in Minnesota as They Were in 1834," in *Minnesota Historical Collections*, 12: 439–453. See also Prescott, in *Minnesota Historical Collections*, 6: 485.

company, and, professing himself peaceful, was offered hospitality. He and his men were feasted on dog meat, the red man's daintiest food. At night all lay down to sleep. At an agreed signal the Chippewa arose, seized their guns, and killed all but three of the Sioux. The survivors were a woman, a wounded boy, and a girl whom the murderers took with them. The woman, whose children had been killed, escaped and made her way to the advance Sioux party, taking the wounded boy on a travois. Gideon H. Pond, who was accompanying this party in order to enlarge his knowledge of Indian life and language, returned with one of the hunters to bury the mutilated bodies.[46]

The counterstroke came promptly. Although Agent Taliaferro had warned the Chippewa to keep away from the agency and the fort, on August 2 of the same year, 1838, Hole-in-the-Day, accompanied by the White Fisher, two Ottawa Indians, and one woman, appeared at the falls. Two young Sioux related to the victims of the April slaughter at the forks of the Chippewa River heard of the arrival and, suspecting that the party would be likely to visit the Chippewa wife of Patrick Quinn, whose house was near the Baker trading house at Camp Coldwater, hid themselves in a convenient spot. As the Chippewa party passed late in the afternoon of the following day, the Sioux fired and Hole-in-the-Day, as supposed, fell. It was not he, but one of the Ottawa, with whom the chief had exchanged clothing or ornaments. The other Ottawa was wounded at the same fire. One of the Sioux rushed to tear off the scalp of his victim, but White Fisher shot and mortally wounded him. Taliaferro, who had been apprised by Samuel W. Pond that

[46] The number of Sioux killed is variously estimated. Pond believed that seven died; Neill, in his *Minnesota*, 455, gives the number as eleven, and in *Minnesota Historical Collections*, 2: 134, as thirteen. William A. Aitkin, the agent of the American Fur Company at Sandy Lake, reports that sixteen were killed; whereas Brunson, the Methodist missionary, says that fifteen were killed. Samuel W. Pond Jr., *Two Volunteer Missionaries among the Dakotas, or the Story of the Labors of Samuel W. and Gideon H. Pond*, 96–102 (Boston, c. 1893); W. A. Aitkin to Boutwell, April 23, 1838, and John Aitkin to Boutwell, April 25, 1838, in Sibley Papers; Brunson, *Western Pioneer*, 2: 96.

some Sioux had gone to Baker's to attack the Chippewa, arrived just as the first shots were fired. The assassins, of course, fled. The agent had the Chippewa, dead and alive, taken to the fort, and late in the evening he sent a Sioux to the guardhouse as a hostage. The corpse of the murdered Ottawa was buried in the graveyard at the fort, and the Sioux attempted the same night to disinter it. The commanding officer put Hole-in-the-Day across the Mississippi to make his way to his country as best he could; and a few days later he compelled the band to which the murderers belonged to make a most degrading expiation, not for the crime, but for the insult to the Great Father by assault and homicide on "sacred ground," under the guns of the fort.[47]

On the day following the murder, August 4, Taliaferro and Major Plympton were in council with the chiefs of three neighboring villages, who had come in without waiting for a summons. The agent records the speeches at length. All the chiefs regretted the misbehavior of the foolish young men but thought clemency was appropriate under the circumstances. Mazahota said that Hole-in-the-Day had "no more sense than a dog to do as he has done, and then come down here . . . I suppose I must comply with your request — but what is to be done with the Hole-in-the-Day." Major Plympton was firm and insisted that the guilty men be delivered to him. The agent, through his interpreter, told the Lake Calhoun Indians they must have them brought in. It was evening when the party sent out returned to the agency with the prisoners. The captives were accompanied by their mother, who with tears begged that the last of her seven sons might be spared to her. She presumed that they would be shot. The agent was much moved but none the less he marched the two sons of Toka to the gate of the fort and turned them over to Major Plympton, who, of course, sent them to the guardhouse.

---

[47] Taliaferro Journal, August 2, 3, 1838. See also the account in Brunson, *Western Pioneer*, 2: 104.

The two braves thus in durance belonged to the Red Wing band at Lake Pepin. Two days were passed in awaiting the coming of the chiefs of that band. On August 7 Iron Cloud and Wacouta came in and in council besought the agent to obtain the release of their foolish young men. Major Plympton was inexorable. He reminded the suppliants that their people had committed many outrages which had been pardoned, and declared that this last insult to the Great Father could not be condoned. But, said he, "if you can to my satisfaction punish your people I will release them."

The council broke up and the Indians were given a night to sleep over the matter. On the next day, August 8, there was another and final council attended by many headmen. Iron Cloud again besought clemency for his foolish young men who had only killed a Chippewa. Wacouta thought they deserved some kind of punishment. Little Crow voiced the friendly feelings of his band, but was noncommittal. The Good Road began a foolish harangue about what might have happened had Major Plympton undertaken to arrest the men with his soldiers, referring to a previous expression of the commandant. "Stop, stop," said the major. "Tell the Good Road I am not boasting nor have I boasted — therefore I shall not hear him do so." Turning to Iron Cloud, the major asked him if he thought he was strong enough to punish his people. "I am," was the reply, "& if you will bring them out I will . . . satisfy you I can do as I say."

In a short time the officer of the day at the fort brought the two sons of Toka to the agency, and on the suggestion of the chief led them outside the agency grounds so as not to "disgrace the House of my Father." The principal soldiers of the band then executed the Indian law. They first cut up the blankets of the culprits into small pieces, and next their leggings and breechcloths. They then cut their hair short, in itself a very humiliating penalty; and

last of all they flogged them with heavy gads.   The remarks
of Taliaferro are notable: "I never saw the ceremony
before — in fact it was new & novel & interesting (feelingly
so) to all present.   This unfortunate affair was thus amicably settled.   The Indians, relations & all satisfied it was no
worse.   And soon all dispersed, and all was again tranquil —
One Chippewa killed & One Sioux killed — *even*."[48]

The next act in the tragedy opened in the midsummer of
the following year.   In the third week in June, 1839, some
nine hundred Chippewa appeared at the St. Peter's agency
under the mistaken expectation that the annuities due them
under the treaty of 1837 would be distributed to them at
that place.   Hole-in-the-Day with five hundred of his
people, a hundred and more from the Crow Wing country,
and some hundred and fifty villagers from Leech Lake came
down the Mississippi in their canoes.   Those from the St.
Croix Valley also came by canoe, down that river and up
the Mississippi.   A body from Mille Lacs marched overland.
More than twelve hundred Sioux assembled at the same
time to receive their annuities under their separate treaty
of the same year.   The agent and the commandant both
explained to the Chippewa that they could not receive their
annuities there but must go to their own agency at La Pointe.
Still, they furnished some rations and grudgingly allowed
them to linger about the post for several days.   On that
neutral ground the two hostile parties willingly fraternized.
They feasted and danced together.   There were foot races
and horse races and a splendid ball game on the prairie at
Land's End in which eighty Sioux athletes contended
against an equal number of Chippewa.   There were two
mutual councils, in the latter of which the calumet went
round and each party pledged itself not to make war on

---

[48] Taliaferro Journal, August 3–8, 1838.   Neill's narrative in *Minnesota Historical
Collections*, 2: 134, is based on this journal.   The article on "Indian Warfare in Minnesota," in *Minnesota Historical Collections*, 3: 130, by Samuel W. Pond is based on a record,
kept by him for many years, "of the number of Dakotas killed by their enemies, and the
number of their enemies killed by them, so far as it could be ascertained."

the other for a year "and longer if practicable." Fortunately no whisky was obtainable till one of the last days,
when some drunkenness was obvious, but there was no
general debauch. The month ended before the reluctant
Chippewa, having eaten up their rations, could be started
for home by the routes over which they had come.[49]

Belonging to Hole-in-the-Day's band were two warriors
who were relatives of the Chippewa who had been shot at
Camp Coldwater in August of the year before. These men
did not depart with their band but, possibly with the knowledge of Hole-in-the-Day, remained to visit the grave of
their murdered kinsman at the fort and to weep over it
according to their savage religion. It may be assumed that
they felt themselves called upon by the spirit of the dead to
avenge his murder. In the night they made their way to
the neighborhood of a summer camp of the Lake Calhoun
band near Lake Harriet, and were in ambush there at daylight on July 2. At sunrise Nika, "a most respectable &
much esteemed" Dakota, was starting out to hunt. A shot
from the Chippewa in hiding laid him low in death. The
assassins were so eager to get his scalp that they did not
notice a small boy, Chief Cloudman's son, who ran to the
village with the alarm. Nika was a brother-in-law of the
chief and a nephew of Red Bird, a medicine man of renown,
who hurried to the spot where the body lay, knelt down,
kissed it, and swore to have revenge. The missionary,
Stevens, carried the news to Taliaferro; but the agent had
neither opportunity nor power to restrain the maddened
warriors. Runners had already been scudding to the

[49] Taliaferro Journal, June 21–July 3, 1839. In regard to the unwillingness of the
Chippewa of the Mississippi to resort to La Pointe to receive their annuities under the
treaty of 1837, see Taliaferro to Governor Henry Dodge, June 10, 17, 25, 26, to Governor
Robert Lucas, June 17, 24, 26, to Hole-in-the-Day, June 18, and to Major D. P. Bushnell,
the Chippewa agent at La Pointe, July 1, 1839. These letters are all in Taliaferro Letter
Book, B.
    An article by Gideon H. Pond in the *Chronicle and Register* for May 4, 1850, dis-
cusses the immemorial struggle between the two tribes: In February, 1838, peace was
made, Hole-in-the-Day dictating the terms himself; these were then translated into Dakota
by Wamdiyokiya; then followed the killing of the Sioux in April of the same year and
the revenge at Rum River. The account is dated at Oak Grove, April 22, 1850.

neighboring villages, and the braves were donning war paint and arming. Two expeditions were spontaneously formed. One of them consisted of about a hundred warriors, mostly from Little Crow's village at Kaposia a few miles south of St. Paul, where the St. Croix Chippewa had slept the night before. Little Crow was not present when the party left, but followed it in its march across country to the neighborhood of Stillwater. It was easily divined that the enemy would bivouac in the ravine where the old Minnesota state prison afterwards stood. At daylight the Sioux looked down from the bluffs to see the Chippewa still sleeping off the stupor of a drunken revel. All accounts agree that a certain trader after whom a Minnesota county has been named was in the company, as if that were a sufficient explanation of their condition. After waiting a little while for the trader and other white men to depart, the Kaposia Indians poured a murderous fire into the unsuspecting Chippewa. Little Crow told Taliaferro that "we might have killed every soul of the Chippewas, had there been no white people along." Surprised as they were, the Chippewa warriors made a gallant defense and drove the assailants to some distance. The Sioux, however, had not come to lose men. Their loss has not been precisely ascertained but it was small. The Chippewa had twenty-one killed and twenty-nine wounded.

The second expedition chose the pursuit of the Mille Lacs Chippewa. Red Bird's runners carried his summons also to the bands of Shakopee, Good Road, Black Dog, and others along the Minnesota, to rendezvous at the Falls of St. Anthony, the Mini-ihaha of the Sioux. As they arrived, they were ferried over the Mississippi in canoes above the head of Nicollet Island, and at sunset on July 3 they were in line on the east bank. Red Bird, in war paint and little else, sent the war pipe down the ranks and, himself following, laid his hands on the head of every warrior and swore him to smite without pity and to take no captives. Before leaving his village, Red Bird told Samuel W. Pond that he should follow the Mille Lacs Chippewa, although the slayers of his nephew were of Hole-in-the-Day's party. He admitted that it was unfortunate that the innocent should suffer, but argued that the laws of Indian warfare justified him in retaliating on any Chippewa he might most conveniently overtake. An all night's march brought his command to a point on the Rum River some miles above Anoka, where the Mille Lacs bands had passed the night. The Sioux waited until the Chippewa warriors had gone forward to hunt for the day's food and until the few remaining older men and the women had taken up their loads of baggage for the day's march; then they fired with deadly effect. In spite of the rude surprise, the Chippewa warriors nearest at hand rallied and made gallant resistance, covering the retreat of the women, children, and old men, making successive stands to return the enemy's fire. Seventy, mostly women and children, fell. Their assailants, however, did not escape unscathed. Red Bird fell, and a son beside him. The Chippewa hunters in front, recalled by the firing, arrived too late to retaliate on the departing foe. The seventy scalps were elevated on poles in the villages of the Sioux on Lake Calhoun and it was a month before the triumphant scalp dances were ended. The Sioux lost seventeen, all braves.[50] In this series of retaliatory frays we have

[50] Taliaferro Journal, July 2–6, 8, 14, 21, 1839; S. W. Pond, in *Minnesota Historical Collections*, 3: 131–133; Pond, *Two Volunteer Missionaries*, 139–146, an account given partly in the words of Gideon H. Pond; "Sketches of Indian Warfare," by Sibley and signed "Hal, a Dacotah," in the *Spirit of the Times* (New York), March 11, 1848; the same narrative from Sibley's original manuscript, with some omissions, in the *St. Paul Pioneer Press*, May 13, 1894; Neill, in *Minnesota Historical Collections*, 2: 138, 139; 5: 487–489; Neill, *Minnesota*, 456–458. A very graphic description of the two battles is that by Return I. Holcombe, in *Minnesota in Three Centuries*, 2: 163–169. Taliaferro gives the name of the murdered Sioux as "Neekah" or "the Badger." Neill following him gives it as "Meekah, the Badger," an evident misspelling. The Dakota dictionaries do not give the word "nika," and they translate "badger" by "hupa." Samuel J. Brown in a letter to the author says that he does not know of any Dakota word "nika." Gideon H. Pond, who reached the body of the victim about as soon as the Indians, states that the name is Hupachokamaza, which according to Brown is a common name meaning Iron-in-the-Middle-of-the-Wing. There is a good deal of variance in the statements of losses sustained on both sides. S. W. Pond estimates that the Sioux lost in all twenty-three; the Chippewa, about one hundred, mostly women and children. The trader who accompanied the St. Croix Chippewa was William A. Aitkin. See Aitkin to Sibley, October 12, 1839, in the Sibley Papers. Brunson,

a fair example of the wars which for generations had made the Minnesota region a dark and bloody ground. This outbreak, sudden as the lightning, much weakened Major Taliaferro's confidence in his ability to control his red children by fine words and fair treatment.

One of the young Dakota braves who took part in the Rum River battle had, while his people were encamped under Fort Snelling exchanging visits and feasts with their ancient foes, been smitten by the smiles and charms of a certain Chippewa maiden. There were stolen interviews, the immemorial dalliance of lovers, and a tearful parting. When the Sioux sprang forward after their first blasting fire on the unsuspecting Chippewa on Rum River, to gather the scalps of the fallen, this brave was in the lead. As if expecting him, the Chippewa girl sprang to meet him, crossing her wrists in token of surrender. He remembered Red Bird's oath. The warrior overmastered the lover. He touched her lightly with his spear and sprang on, leaving the warrior next in rear to cleave her head with his tomahawk. Sibley, who took this relation not long after from the brave himself, states that the Sioux was still broken with grief and wished that he might fall in some early battle. And this wish was gratified.[51]

A second conference of the northwestern tribes was held at Prairie du Chien in the summer of 1830, William Clark, superintendent of Indian affairs at St. Louis, and Colonel Willoughby Morgan, of the First United States Infantry, being commissioners for the United States. The delegations of the tribes were not full, but an important treaty was negotiated, containing provisions for the adherence of absentees. The inevitable half-breeds were present and secured the insertion of provisions permitting the Indian

in his *Western Pioneer*, 2: 106, says that Aitkin was reported to be slightly wounded. Note the following from the Taliaferro Journal, 1839: July 4, "Mr. Aitkin, & Francis Brunet, & a Frenchman were wounded Mr. A's tent — a linen one was shot to pieces." July 21, "Aitkin is said to be slightly wounded a scratch on the thigh — *supposed* by some to have happened in his *flight* a *scratch* from a *bush or stick*."

[51] Sibley in the *Pioneer Press*, May 13, 1894.

chiefs to bestow on them certain grants of land. The Sioux half-breeds thus obtained Indian title to that tract known as the Wabasha or Pepin Reservation, which will later demand our attention.[52] The traders were on this occasion less influential. Major Taliaferro claims to have defeated a scheme of the American Fur Company for collecting lost credits to Indians through the United States, and thereby to have gained the ill will of that powerful corporation.[53]

The tract acquired by Pike in 1805 at the confluence of the Minnesota and Mississippi rivers, being, in the terms of the treaty, "for the establishment of a military post," was not open to settlement. And there was practically no other white man's ground in Minnesota when Nicollet made his exploration in 1836. The reports of officials and narratives of explorers and tourists had by this time spread the rumor of a land of promise about the upper Mississippi and its tributaries. The great wave of migration which had been moving westward south of the Great Lakes had already curved northward and had spread over large parts of Wisconsin. The beauty and richness of these lands were taken as the warrant of others equally desirable lying beyond. Lumbermen under permits liberally construed were already cutting pine on the Chippewa and Black rivers to supply the market opened in the lead mines of Galena and Dubuque. The authorities of Wisconsin Territory, organized in 1836 with the Missouri River as its western boundary, were prompt to desire the extension of her area of settlement. On July 29, 1837, Governor Henry Dodge, acting as commissioner for the United States, negotiated at Fort Snelling a treaty of

---

[52] *Statutes at Large*, 7: 328; Taliaferro, in *Minnesota Historical Collections*, 6: 211. The lands ceded were in Iowa except for two small projections across the line, one of which was part of the "Neutral Ground" assigned to the Winnebago in 1832. See pages 322–325 and the map facing page 324, *post*.

[53] In a letter to the commissioner of Indian affairs, July 24, 1837, Taliaferro arraigns the American Fur Company. In a similar fashion one prominent factor of the company, Hercules L. Dousman, expresses his feeling toward Taliaferro in a letter to Sibley, written December 22, 1837: "I shall remember our friend T's good offices and if he does not get his pay at my hands, it is because I shall never set my eyes on him again." Taliaferro Letter Book, B; Sibley Papers.

cession with the Chippewa bands of the Mississippi. Precisely two months later the secretary of war, Poinsett, at the seat of government concluded a similar treaty with chiefs and braves of the Sioux, who had been conducted thither by Agent Taliaferro. These two treaties, when ratified by the Senate on June 15, 1838, made white man's country of the large delta between the St. Croix and the Mississippi, extending northward to include the south parts of Crow Wing and Aitkin counties and the north part of Pine County. The cession of the Chippewa lay to the north of the partition line of 1825; that of the Sioux, to the south. In both cases the considerations granted to the Indians were annuities in money, goods, and provisions; large allowances for "the relatives and friends of the chiefs and braves," that is to say the half-breeds, and for the payments of debts due to traders; and small annual grants for physicians, farmers, blacksmiths, and the materials of their respective callings. The money annuity of the Sioux was to be perpetual; that of the Chippewa, for twenty years. Taliaferro boasts that he made the better bargain for the Sioux. The Chippewa reserved the right to hunt, fish, and gather wild rice on the lands ceded by them. The Sioux made no such reservation, and the agent secured the removal of the few residing on the east side to the west of the Mississippi at an expense of less than five hundred dollars, pending the consideration by the Indian office of the offer of an enterprising citizen to accomplish the same for fifty thousand dollars. The commissioner of Indian affairs in his report of December 1, 1837, congratulates the country on having, by the treaties mentioned, secured "permanent boundaries" and a "more regular form" for the Union.[54]

<hr>

[54] *Statutes at Large*, 7: 536–540; report of the commissioner of Indian affairs for 1837, in 25 Congress, 2 session, *Senate Documents*, no. 1, p. 527 (serial 314). Taliaferro, in *Minnesota Historical Collections*, 6: 214–220, 250–252, describes the negotiations, setting forth in particular the allowances made to the traders among the Chippewa. He states that the practice of recognizing claims of traders for lost credits began during the superintendency of Governor Cass. See also Neill, in *Minnesota Historical Collections*, 2: 131–133, and Brunson, *Western Pioneer*, 2: 82–87. Brunson "attended this treaty" with the Chippewa Indians under his charge. See the map facing page 324, *post*.

The American Fur Company had not been able after its reorganization, as its founder had hoped, at once to engross the Indian trade of the upper Mississippi. Among the factors and clerks who had served the old Northwest Company were men of experience and enterprise who became naturalized and organized for competition. The Columbia Fur Company, legally the partnership of Tilton and Company, promoted by Joseph Renville in 1822, may serve as an example. The competing concerns, however, had but brief lives, and before the end of the decade beginning with the establishment of the post at Fort Snelling the American Fur Company had made its monopoly absolute. The so-called "desertion" of the old traders, who undertook a separate business, led the company to employ capable young men from the States in their places. Among these men were some of the most notable characters in the early history of the region. It was this policy which, becoming a settled one, brought in 1834 to the trading post at New Hope, later named Mendota, Henry Hastings Sibley, then a young man in his twenty-third year. He was the son of Judge Solomon Sibley of Detroit, Michigan, who had played a distinguished part in that state. By the time he was eighteen young Sibley had obtained a good education in the local academy and from private instruction, and had studied law for two years. But he had no stomach for the law or for scholastic or sedentary pursuits. His heart was in the wild West. Then and all through his life he was a master of the rifle, the fishing rod, and the canoe. Endowed with a splendid athletic figure, he developed such skill and strength in the manly art of self-defense that, in the traditional words of a contemporary, "there was but one man in the territory that dared stand up against him and that was 'Bully' [*James*] Wells," a member of the first territorial legislature. Still, he was a man of peace, and his calm, steady, imposing demeanor was quite sufficient to preserve the order of any company in which he might be.

Judge Solomon Sibley, who had been a pioneer and doubt-less sympathized with the passion of his boy, suffered him at the age mentioned to accept employment as a sutler's clerk at Sault Ste. Marie in 1828. A year later Robert Stuart, manager for the American Fur Company, took the youngster into his employ at Mackinac as clerk, in which capacity he served for the next five years. Mere clerical duty seems to have occupied but part of his time. He was dispatched to distant points on important errands. One of these, to Detroit, made in an eight-oared canoe, was full of romance. He performed the responsible duty of purchasing agent for the company at Cleveland, Ohio, for a considerable time. Governor Porter of Michigan made him a justice of the peace for the county of Michilimackinac before he was of age. This apprenticeship was sufficient to satisfy the officials of the American Fur Company that they had in young Sibley the very man they needed to manage for them on the upper Mississippi. He was able from his savings and other sources to invest enough money to secure the position of partner, as well as that of agent. On October 28, 1834, after a journey of nearly a fortnight, the young adventurer rode on horseback into the little group of log huts at Mendota, where his home was to be for nearly thirty years. From this day till that of his death in 1891, Henry Hastings Sibley is easily the most prominent figure in Minnesota history.[55]

[55] The account of Sibley's education and of his career up to the time of his arrival in Minnesota is derived from Nathaniel West, *The Ancestry, Life, and Times of Hon. Henry Hastings Sibley, LL.D.*, 1–55 (St. Paul, 1889). West in the preparation of his volume had access to a "manuscript autobiography" of Sibley, which, so far as known, is not now extant. It is unfortunate for Sibley's fame that his biographer, by extravagant laudation, carica-tured the great services performed for Minnesota by Sibley. Absurd as the production is, it has its uses for the historian. A portion of the edition was suppressed by the family. See also J. Fletcher Williams, "Henry Hastings Sibley: A Memoir," in *Minnesota Historical Collections*, 6: 257–265, 268, 271. Williams enjoyed an intimate acquaintance with and the friendship of General Sibley for more than twenty years, as did the author of the present volume. Sibley's certificate of membership in the Presbyterian Church, signed by Henry R. Schoolcraft, May 14, 1835, is in the Sibley Papers. The remark concerning "Bully" Wells was quoted by the Honorable John D. Ludden in an interview on August 5, 1904, notes of which are preserved. West gives the date of Sibley's arrival at Mendota as November 7, 1834 (pp. 54, 368). A letter from Sibley to Crooks, dated St. Peter's, Novem-

Upon the ratification of the treaties of 1837, so-called "independent" traders swarmed up and lined the east bank of the Mississippi from Prairie du Chien to the mouth of the Crow Wing. Having no license to trade with the Indians, they could not cross that stream, but there was no law which forbade or could prevent the Indians' crossing it to trade their peltries for goods and for the deadly fire water. Thus was the long monopoly of the American Fur Company broken. Because the fur-bearing animals were no longer so plentiful and the Indians, spoiled by cash annuities, no longer hunted with diligence, the fur business had much declined. In 1842 the company was forced to assign, and in the following year Pierre Chouteau Jr. and Company of St. Louis took over the business.[56] The concern, however, continued to be popularly known for many years by its old name of the American Fur Company.

Compared with modern operations the fur trade was a small business. The crop of many a single township far surpasses in value the annual fur output of Minnesota at any time. The total value of the furs and peltries from the Sioux outfit for the year 1835 was $59,298.92. The traders, whether independent of or subordinate to the American Fur Company, did not make great fortunes. If they exacted excessive prices from the Indians, they paid high prices for their outfits.[57] The trade had, however, the charms of the

ber 1, 1834, states, however, that Sibley "having been detained . . . did not arrive here [*St. Peter's*] until the 28 ult." See the Sibley Papers. In an interview on March 19, 1905, William L. Quinn furnished the account of Sibley's mastery of the art of self-defense. The notes of this interview are preserved. Copies of an unpublished doctoral thesis by Wilson P. Shortridge on "The Life of Henry Hastings Sibley" (1919) are in the libraries of the University of Minnesota and the Minnesota Historical Society. See also Shortridge, "Henry Hastings Sibley and the Minnesota Frontier," in the *Minnesota History Bulletin*, 3: 115–125 (August, 1919).

[56] Henry H. Sibley, "Memoir of Hercules L. Dousman," in *Minnesota Historical Collections*, 3: 196. News of the assignment was conveyed to Sibley in a letter from Dousman, October 20, 1842. Sibley Papers.

[57] A statement of furs and peltries received at Prairie du Chien, July 20, 1836, from the Sioux outfit for the previous year is in the Sibley Papers. In his journals Taliaferro refers at times to the excessive prices extorted by traders from the Indians. The best example of such a reference is in the entry for October 21, 1836, which presents the following table of prices as part of a protest against "Lost Credits in *Rats* by the Trade." See also the entries for August 25, October 5, and November 1, 1835. The table is quoted by Neill in *Minnesota Historical Collections*, 2: 131.

campaign and the seductions of wild life on the border. There were always plenty of romantic spirits eager to enter it, and rarely did any one leave it for a more prosaic vocation. The literature of the Indian trade abounds in wholesale denunciations of the craft. Such terms as "cutthroat," "bloodsucker," and "miscreant" are applied to the whole body of traders with indiscriminate emphasis.[58] Any such sweeping condemnation of men is unjust. Among the furtraders could have been found men of commanding ability

ST. LOUIS PRICES		SOLD TO INDIANS		NET GAIN
1.3 pt Blanket............	$3.25	60 Rats at 20 cts	$12.00	$8.75
1½ yds Stroud...........	2.37	60 " " 20 "	12.00	8.63
1. Gun N. W.............	6.50	100 "	20.00	13.50
1. lb. Lead..............	0.06	2 " " 20 cts	00.40	00.34
1. lb. Powder...........	0.28	10 " " 20	2.00	1.72
1. Tin Kettle............	2.50	60 " " 20	12.00	9.50
1. Knife................	0.20	4 " " 20	00.80	.60
1. lbs Tobacco...........	0.12	8 " " 20	1.60	1.48
1. Looking glass.........	0.04	4 " " 20	00.80	.76
1½ yd Scarlet Cloth......	3.0	60 " " 20	12.00	9.00
St. Louis Cost........	$17.32	358 at 20 cts	$71.60	$54.28

This table will serve to indicate the make-up of the stock in trade of the traders to the Sioux. The articles were sent up from St. Louis by boat and later by steamer year by year soon after the opening of the river and were stored in the great warehouse of the American Fur Company at Mendota. In the spring or early summer months after the streams were clear of ice the licensed traders came down from their respective posts with their packs of furs collected during the previous winter. Among them were the Faribaults from Shakopee and Cannon River, Provençalle from the Traverse des Sioux, Laframboise from the mouth of the Cottonwood, Renville and McLeod from Lac qui Parle, J. R. Brown from Lake Traverse, and Kittson from distant Pembina. The furs were assorted and repacked at Mendota for shipment below. Excessive as the profits apparently were, few of the traders became rich from trade alone, and some would have been bankrupt but for bonuses received through Indian treaties. Sibley's correspondence with the Chouteaus shows that about the time he withdrew from the trade he was barely even with the world. Still there must have been cases in which comfortable profits were made. Sibley states that in the year 1852 Kittson at Pembina made ten thousand dollars on a capital of twenty-five thousand dollars. See Sibley to Grant and Barton, February 10, 1854, in Sibley Letter Book, no. 4. Sibley evidently took no great pride in his fur-trading, for his biographer, writing under Sibley's eye, made but few references to it. On the customs of the Indian trade see the statements of James H. Lockwood, Robert Stuart, and John H. Kinzie, in *Execution of Treaty with the Winnebagoes*, 34-46 (25 Congress, 1 session, *House Documents*, no. 229 — serial 349).

[58] Taliaferro's opinion of the Indian traders, as expressed in his autobiography, was none too favorable. He seems, however, to have made an exception of Sibley. See *Minnesota Historical Collections*, 6: 203, 210, 222, 249, 250, 254, 266. In his journal, June 9, 1835, Taliaferro records one of his many expressions of confidence in Sibley. "Your word on honor Mr Sibley that the law shall not be violated by the introduction of prohibited articles and you may rest assured of never having a visit from me or by my authority . . . I shall rely on your word from my knowledge of your character." For Sibley's apology for the traders, see *Minnesota Historical Collections*, 1: 462. See also *post*, p. 173, n. 7.

Furs & Peltries rec'd from Sioux Outfit 1835

This is the A. L. H. Emigh & E. Estrayer mk 5 acct mg
Sen 2 t mg

S. B. Faribault' Lot

31.059	Rats	16c	4969 44
665	Kittens	2c	13 30
110	Otters	5	550 —
142	Fishers	1.50	213 —
319	Minks	30c	95 70
248	Martens	1.25	310 —
206	Coons	30c	61 80
34	Bear (20 very infr.)	1.50	51 —
37	Cubs	1.50	55 50
13	Wolves	50c	6 50
6	Foxes	75c	4 50
6	Badgers	25c	1 50
1301	Deer Skins	30	390 30
			6722 54

154,800	Rats	16c	24768 —
796	Kittens	2c	15 92
901	Coons	30	270 30
459	Otters	5	2295 —
294	Fishers	150	441 —
1167	Minks	30c	350 10
43	Bear	2.50	107 50
14	Cubs	1.50	21 —
1850	Beaver	4	740 —
131	Foxes	75	98 25
73	Swan Skins	1	73 —
16	Wolves	50c	8 —
3	Rabbits	12c	36
167	Martens	1.25	208 75
1660	Deer Skins	30c	498 —
1039	Buffalo Robes	4	4156 —
	Carid Forw'd		$40773 74

A FUR TRADE INVENTORY

[Facsimile of the first page of an original document in the Sibley Papers. The list is continued to a total of $59,298.92. The document is dated at "Prairie des Chiens," July 20, 1836.]

and irreproachable reputation; one such has just been named. Of the rank and file of the traders, clerks, and interpreters, it may be said that they did not fall much below the average standard of the mercantile class. Among them, however, were those who were not proof against the peculiar temptations which beset the whole body. They were dealing with persons almost devoid of any sense of the value of goods or money and ever ready to surrender their dearest possessions to gratify a momentary whim. There was no call for nice adjustment of price to cost. Minnesota prices for Indian goods and furs were commonly about fourfold those of St. Louis. But it must be remembered that most sales were upon credit. When the Indian, at the close of a hunting season, squandered his money in debauchery, he had then to obtain his outfit for the hunt of the coming season on credit. Sickness, death, and occasional dishonesty of Indians carried increasing sums to the wrong side of the trader's profit and loss account. In some cases the licensed trader in the Indian country had to consider the sums which from time to time he must, according to custom, render to the Indian agent to whom he owed his license.[59]

The worst count in the arraignment of the traders is that of selling intoxicating liquors to their savage customers. Here again discrimination is necessary. The American Fur Company respected the act of 1834 forbidding the introduction of liquor into the Indian country[60] and, so long as its monopoly continued, generally conformed to it. There were, however, individual traders in its employ who did not resist the temptation to attract business by surreptitiously offering spirits to the Indians. Such was the case with Sibley's immediate predecessor, Alexis Bailly, who was

---

[59] In his report to the secretary of the interior in 1865, Indian Commissioner Cooley proposed that a law be enacted making it a penal offense for any agent to be interested with traders as they "too often" were. He stated that applications for appointments to agencies were innumerable although the salary was but fifteen hundred dollars. Commissioner of Indian Affairs, *Annual Reports*, 1865, p. 2.

[60] *Statutes at Large*, 4: 732.

cashiered for the offense.[61]   At the northern posts remote from the agencies the traders deemed it necessary to furnish whisky; for, if they did not do so, whole bands of Indians would troop off with their furs to the border, where Canadian traders would gladly supply them.   The persistent endeavors of these traders to attract the Minnesota Indians were represented to Congress in a long series of agency reports.[62] No vigilance of the military, the Indian agent, or the chief factor of the American Fur Company could prevent the movement of whisky to the upper country.   As for the independent traders on white man's ground, there was no law human or divine which could check their greed.   So long as they did not "introduce liquors into Indian country" they were committing no offense against the United States. When years later the territorial legislature of Minnesota passed a law to punish white men for selling liquor to Indians,[63] it was a dead letter for the reason that among the border population, composed chiefly of traders and their satellites, no grand juries could be assembled which would indict, no unbiased trial juries could be impaneled, and no witnesses could be discovered who would reveal the illicit transactions.

The groggeries which were opened on the east side of the Mississippi after the treaties and before the lines of the military reservations were drawn became an intolerable nuisance to the military authorities of Fort Snelling, because of a passion for drink among American soldiers of the time,

[61] Taliaferro, in *Minnesota Historical Collections*, 6: 203.   In his journal, June 23, 1835, Taliaferro writes: "*Alexis Bailly* left this day this country with his family haveing by his own imprudence & folly thrown himself out of business. . . . Had I have permitted him to have done as he pleased with my office & thus have prostituted its powers & privileges to his will I should have been *a most noble* & very clever fellow.   *But no.*   I kept my ground, & secured enemies accordingly, *& I regret it not.*"   Bailly, pronounced Bä-yē, afterwards returned to the territory, engaged in trade, and became a member of the first territorial legislature.

[62] See especially the statement of Amos J. Bruce, Indian agent at St. Peter's, September 1, 1846, in 29 Congress, 2 session, *Senate Documents*, no. 1, p. 246 (serial 493), and that of Alexander Ramsey, superintendent of Indian affairs, Minnesota Territory, October 17, 1849, in 31 Congress, 1 session, *Senate Executive Documents*, no. 1 pp. 1033, 1036 (serial 550).

[63] *Laws*, 1849, p. 34.

fairly equal in intensity to that of the savages. On June 3, 1839, a party from the garrison resorted to an establishment across the Mississippi kept by Joseph R. Brown, a man who afterwards became deservedly prominent in Minnesota. The effect of the goods sold there was such that forty-seven of the men were in the durance of the guardhouse that same night.[64] On a previous occasion some soldiers desired a supply of liquor with which to celebrate the birthday of the Father of his Country. A well-known trader was discovered who supplied one gallon at a charge of eighty dollars, under a promise of absolute secrecy. When that costly jug was opened on the looked-for day, the contents were found to be diluted to such a degree that the indignant purchasers felt justified in reporting the outrage to the commandant.[65]

It was to be expected that the Indian trader would be influential with his Indian customer. He had preceded the military by a generation. To the savages he was the typical white man. In countless instances he and his *engagés* had intermarried and established social relations with Indian families and tribes. If he drove hard bargains and at times exacted the uttermost farthing, stripping a delinquent creditor to his very hide, he still gave credit, so that the Indian and his family could live, after squandering in a day the whole proceeds of a season's hunting. He had no reason for being unkind and often assumed a paternal attitude toward those so dependent on him. Few were the instances in which a trader's life was endangered or his property molested when it was so guarded as to indicate that it was not anybody's goods. Such associations necessarily gave the traders a powerful influence over the Indians,

---

[64] Taliaferro Journal, June 4, 1839. See also the report of Agent Bruce, St. Peter's, September 30, 1840, in 26 Congress, 2 session, *House Documents*, no. 2, p. 325 (serial 382).

[65] Taliaferro, in *Minnesota Historical Collections*, 6: 223. Since this incident occurred when Faribault "was on the island" — that is, in 1820 or 1821 — the story may have expanded somewhat by the time that Taliaferro wrote his autobiography in 1863. That there was foundation in fact need not be doubted, but no contemporary reference to it has been found in the agent's journal. In the entry for May 23, 1839, Taliaferro interlined "Old Faribault got $80 for one gallon [*of whisky*] paid by Sergt. Mann."

compared with which that of the government officials, civil or military, was relatively insignificant. Complaints of the control of tribes by traders are frequently reiterated in the reports of agents not confederated with traders.[66] The whole system of Indian trading was vicious, considering men as they are and circumstances as they were. There is reason to be thankful that its evils were no greater, its operation not more demoralizing to all concerned. With our American traditions of the "rights of man," it was politically impossible to establish over the Indian a régime of restraint. A beneficent servitude was what he needed. Our traditions forbade that in theory, and there was not virtue enough to put it into practice, could it have been tolerated. We left the savage free — free to copy the white man's vices — and suffered the white man to furnish him the means of indulgence. The government factory plan of supplying the Indians with essential white man's goods, begun in 1796, had in it the germ of a good system.[67] Jefferson in his message of January 18, 1803, commended the

[66] See especially the statement of Governor Lucas of Iowa Territory, October 23, 1839, in 26 Congress, 1 session, *Senate Documents*, no. 1, p. 491 (serial 354), and that of Governor Dodge of Wisconsin Territory, September 22, 1840, in 26 Congress, 2 session, *House Documents*, no. 2, p. 334 (serial 382).

[67] T. Hartley Crawford, commissioner of Indian affairs, in his report of 1841, after a recital of the evils of the existing system which he thought could be corrected only by radical changes, says: "The factory system is, *in principle*, it strikes me, the true plan of supplying the wants of the Indians. I do not mean *the* factory system as it was used . . . between 1816 and 1822, but *a* factory system properly arranged and guarded." See 27 Congress, 2 session, *House Documents*, no. 2, p. 239 (serial 401). See also a short chronology of the factory system by Crawford and the statement of Governor Dodge of Wisconsin Territory, in 26 Congress, 2 session, *House Documents*, no. 2, pp. 240, 334 (serial 382); the statement of John C. Spencer, secretary of war, and that of Crawford, in 27 Congress, 3 session, *House Documents*, no. 2, pp. 190, 375 (serial 418); and the statement of Crawford in 28 Congress, 2 session, *House Documents*, no. 2, p. 306 (serial 463). No study of the system can be complete without a perusal of Benton's speech in the Senate in *Annals of Congress*, 17 Congress, 1 session, vol. 1, pp. 317–331, 417–423.

Further information on government Indian trading houses or factories may be found by consulting, under Furs, Trade, Traders, and Trading houses, the index to *American State Papers: Indian Affairs*, vol. 2. See also Turner, in Wisconsin Historical Society, *Proceedings*, 1889, pp. 52–98; Neill, in Minnesota Historical Society, *Annals*, 1856, pp. 96–99; Buck, *Illinois in 1818*, 17–21; Chittenden, *American Fur Trade*, 12–16; Coman, *Economic Beginnings of the Far West*, 1: 289–375; and Taliaferro, in *Minnesota Historical Collections*, 6: 228. There is a brief but comprehensive account in Milo M. Quaife, *Chicago and the Old Northwest*, ch. 13 (Chicago, 1913). In Taliaferro Letter Book, A, is a paper dealing with the factory system, warmly commending it if well administered and if, in particular, Con-

government trading houses then existing, and urged Congress to continue the system to "undersell private traders . . . drive them from the competition, and . . . rid ourselves of a description of men who are constantly endeavoring to excite, in the Indian mind, suspicions, fears, and irritations, towards us."[68] But the factory system was killed by the Indian ring, and Ramsay Crooks, chief factor of the American Fur Company, rejoiced over the extinction in 1822 of "the pious monster."[69] Calhoun, while secretary of war, submitted to Congress a proposition to grant a monopoly of the Indian trade to a company, to be rigidly controlled by the government.[70] This plan also was impossible.

gress should allow the importation of certain English goods to which the Indians were accustomed. Taliaferro's denunciations of the extortions of the American Fur Company are notable. Frequent brief references to the factory system are made in his journals, always with implied approval. His most vigorous commendation of the system may be found in a letter to the commissioner of Indian affairs, July 24, 1837, which contains a most impassioned arraignment not only of the American Fur Company but also of the policy of paying Indian annuities in specie and of including in Indian treaties payment for "lost credits," a fraud on both the Indians and the treasury. See Taliaferro Letter Book, B.

[68] *American State Papers: Indian Affairs*, 1: 684.

[69] Chittenden, *American Fur Trade*, 1: 15.

[70] The same suggestion was made by Ninian Edwards, governor of Illinois Territory, to Secretary Crawford in 1815. See *American State Papers: Indian Affairs*, 2: 66, 184.

VII. EARLY INDIAN MISSIONS

THE Indian missions of the period beginning with the foundation of Fort Snelling and ending with the establishment of the territorial government in 1849 might easily fill a considerable volume with annals of thrilling interest. Since, however, those missionary labors, earnest and heroic as they were, left such slight effects, on either the red man or the white, we should not be warranted in delaying the progress of our narrative to gather up all their fascinating details.

The first attack of the missionary upon such heathen as the Minnesota savages was bound to be disappointing. The new religion had to supplant an old one ardently believed and interwoven with the traditions of ages. The Indian was intensely, even devoutly, religious. The medicine men exercised an influence over the tribe surpassing that of any body of ecclesiastics over civilized believers. The evil deities whom they could placate with charms and offerings would, according to their teachings, destroy the nation, should it abandon the ancient religion for a new one. The incantations of the medicine men secured success in the hunt and on the warpath. The feasts and dances led by them celebrated victory over the enemy and welcomed the returning braves laden with the fruits of the chase or flaunting the bloody scalps of the foe.[1] The missionary had before him, therefore, the double task of clearing the wilderness of an ancient and almost ineradicable superstition and sowing

[1] There are detailed accounts of the religion of the Sioux by Edward D. Neill, James W. Lynd, Gideon H. Pond, and Samuel W. Pond, in *Minnesota Historical Collections*, 1: 254–294; 2: 150–174, 215–255; 12: 401–429; also in Stephen R. Riggs, *Tah-koo Wah-kan; or, the Gospel among the Dakotas*, 54–103 (Boston, c. 1869), and Winchell, *Aborigines of Minnesota*, 506–508. A novel of Indian life of the period of the early advance in the great Northwest, having for its purpose the portrayal of the nature and effects of the Algonquian religion, is Joseph A. Gilfillan, *The Ojibway* (New York, 1904).

the good seed of Christianity in the soil thus cleared. The white man's example did not to any great extent illustrate and commend his religion. The greed and licentiousness of traders and still more of their satellites, the debauchery of Indian women by the military ("exceedingly common," says Riggs) the indifference of agents appointed in consideration of political services, and the brutality of agency employees — all these discouraged the missionary and discredited the religion he came to teach.[2] The Protestant missionary felt obliged to give the savage a book religion. He could not be content to communicate the faith by means of symbols, ritual, and oral tradition. As the wild man had no written language, years of time had to be devoted to making one for him, and to translating the Sacred Scriptures into it. The teaching of letters, therefore, chiefly occupied the time of the early missionary, for only or mainly through letters could the word of life be opened. The missionary was a puzzle to the Indian. He could understand the trader, whose business was to make gain; the military man, whose function was warfare; the agent and his assistants, who were paid for their services; but the missionary, who labored, asking nothing in return, he could not understand; and he suspected him accordingly. He was ready at any time to credit the insinuations of traders and whisky-sellers that the missionary was secretly rewarded.[3]

[2] Stephen R. Riggs, *Mary and I: Forty Years with the Sioux*, 46 (Chicago, 1880). An unanswerable argument by an Indian chief is found in Bishop Henry Whipple, "Civilization and Christianization of the Ojibways in Minnesota," in *Minnesota Historical Collections*, 9: 130. "A chief asked me if the Jesus of whom I spoke was the same Jesus that my white brother talked to when he was angry or drunk. . . . 'You have spoken strong words against fire-water and impurity; but, my friend, you have made a mistake. These are the words you should carry to your white brothers who bring us the fire-water and corrupt our daughters. They are the sinners, not we.' "
Taliaferro drew up a list of white pioneers most of whom "had the use of Indian women . . . and children were born to them." The agent might, however, have added his own name. See Taliaferro, in *Minnesota Historical Collections*, 6: 249; the Taliaferro Journal, December 9, 1836, September 19, 23, October 3, 28, 1838; and Taliaferro to S. W. Pond, January 1, 1846, and the S. W. Pond Narrative, 1: 47, in the Pond Papers. This collection came into the possession of the Minnesota Historical Society in 1919. It consists of photostatic copies of about two hundred letters of Samuel and Gideon Pond, a narrative written by the former in 1881, some Dakota dictionaries, and a few miscellaneous documents.

[3] Riggs, *Forty Years with the Sioux*, 79.

Practicing among themselves an almost absolute commu-
nism, the Indians distrusted the men who preached to them
the duty of love to all and yet persisted in keeping their
dwellings and furniture, their domestic animals, and the
produce of their gardens for their own use.[4]   Remembering
that the heart of the white man, whose civilization has been
established for centuries, is still, by nature and diabolical
influences, averse to the true religion, need one wonder that
those untutored savages were slow to give up their ancient
religion and accept in its place one so ill commended to them
by the hated paleface.[5]   The fact that missionaries came to
them commissioned by different religious bodies, separated
by shades of doctrine or practice much too fine for their
analysis, aroused the suspicions of the Indians.   If Christians could not agree as to the content of the true faith, how
could the Indian convert be sure that he was getting the
genuine?

The effort to evangelize the Chippewa people preceded
the missions to the Dakota by a short interval. By 1818
the American Fur Company had covered the whole Chippewa country within the United States with its outfits.
Mackinac Island presently became the convenient center of
its operations for the regions embracing the Michigan, Wisconsin, and Minnesota trade.[6]   Among its managing officials
were Ramsay Crooks and Robert Stuart, natives of Scot-
land, both men of ability, aware of the value of civilization
and religion. The latter became "an ardent Christian
worker." At the instance of these men, it may be conjectured, a mission school was begun at the post in 1823.
To this school were sent the mixed-blood children of traders

---

[4] Neill, *Minnesota*, 422, 437, citing the journal of the Reverend Sherman Hall.

[5] Charles E. Flandrau, in his memoir of "The Work of Bishop Whipple in Missions for the Indians," in *Minnesota Historical Collections*, 10: 694 (part 2), cites an example of the difficulty which a Christian convert, who had slain the murderer of a relative, had in sloughing his heathenism. The same story is graphically told by Return I. Holcombe, in *Minnesota in Three Centuries*, 2: 256. See also Riggs, *Forty Years with the Sioux*, 89-92, 153, and the report of Colonel Amos J. Bruce, Indian agent at St. Peter's, September 30, 1840, in 26 Congress, 2 session, *House Documents*, no. 2, p. 325 (serial 382).

[6] Warren, in *Minnesota Historical Collections*, 5: 382; Neill, *Minnesota*, 424.

from many quarters, including the posts on Lake Superior and the upper Mississippi.[7]

Another trader with the Chippewa, of American birth and a member of an evangelical church, was Lyman M. Warren, who became a partner of the American Fur Company and, in 1824, established his principal house at Madeline Island on Chequamegon Bay.[8] He, also, became desirous to have a school kept at this post, where a considerable population, partly resident, had centered. It was not till the summer of 1830, however, that he was able to make a beginning, when he induced a young American teacher in the Mackinac school to come to La Pointe. This was Frederick Ayer, a native of Massachusetts and the son of a Presbyterian minister, who had already devoted himself to mission work among the Indians. He kept his school at La Pointe during the winter of 1831, and in the summer of 1832 went back to Mackinac to pilot the Reverend Sherman Hall and his wife, sent out by the American Board of Commissioners for Foreign Missions, to La Pointe, where they were to establish a mission station opposite the site on the mainland abandoned by the Jesuits in 1671. Ayer

[7] Stephen R. Riggs, "Protestant Missions in the Northwest," in *Minnesota Historical Collections*, 6: 119; Warren, in *Minnesota Historical Collections*, 5: 386; Edward D. Neill, "Memoir of William T. Boutwell," in *Macalester College Contributions*, second series, no. 1, p. 4, and his *Minnesota*, 424. Interesting descriptions of this school are given by Bishop Jackson Kemper, in his "Journal of an Episcopalian Missionary's Tour to Green Bay, 1834," in *Wisconsin Historical Collections*, 14: 407, and by Thomas L. McKenny, in his *Sketches of a Tour to the Lakes*, 386–388 (Baltimore, 1877).

It may be but justice to offset the flood of denunciation of the fur-traders with the following extract from a letter of David Greene, secretary of the American Board of Commissioners for Foreign Missions, to Samuel W. Pond Jr., written on May 23, 1845. "It seems to me that the restraints which the providence and Spirit of God have laid upon the principal fur-traders among the Northwestern Indians, from the time when we first became acquainted with them through the Mackinaw mission in 1823, till the present time — the number of them who have become hopefully converted, or at least serious & moral, — who have been decidedly friendly to missionary operations & to the moral and social improvement of the Indians, is an indication of the favor of God toward the Indians in that quarter, of great importance, & which has not been sufficiently noticed. It has facilitated our entrance and residence among the Indians; removed many embarassments and greatly promoted the quiet and comfort of the mission families. If the traders had been of the opposite character, & exerted an opposing influence, it would have been nearly impossible to maintain our missionary stations in the Indian country." Pond Papers.

[8] Ramsay Crooks to William Morrison, quoted by Neill, in *Macalester College Contributions*, second series, no. 1, p. 9, n. 1; Warren, in *Minnesota Historical Collections*, 5: 9–12, 383, 384.

remained only during the following winter, when he yielded
to the urgent solicitations of the Scotch trader, William
Alexander Aitkin, in charge of the Fond du Lac department
of the American Fur Company, to push on to Sandy Lake,
then his most important interior post, and open a school for
the children of his *voyageurs*.   Here Ayer completed an
Ojibway spelling book, which he took to Utica, New York,
in the spring of 1833 to get it printed.   Before the close of
that year he had married and had put himself under the care
of the American Board.   The adventurous pioneer did not
resume work at either of his previous stations but journeyed
on to Yellow Lake in the northwestern part of Burnett
County, Wisconsin, where Dr. Charles William Wulff Borup,
later prominent in the financial affairs of St. Paul and of
Minnesota Territory, had a trading station.   That the
missionary and his wife were welcome there may be inferred
from the fact that they were taken into the Borup family.
When the local Chippewa saw, not long after, some log
houses and a school building erected, they were displeased,
and their speaker said to Ayer, "We don't want you to
stay; you must go."   The next day he changed his mind
and informed Ayer that he and his teachers might stay but
that no more might come.   The Indians feared the beginning
of a movement to take their land away.   "If we should sell
our land," they asked, "where would our children play?"
The work at Yellow Lake did not prosper, and in the spring
of 1836 the mission was moved to Lake Pokegama in the
southwestern part of Pine County, Minnesota.   In this
case the invitation seems to have come from the chief of
the Snake River Chippewa, whose village was on that lake.[9]

[9] Riggs, in *Minnesota Historical Collections*, 6: 119–122; "Frederick Ayer, Teacher
and Missionary to the Ojibway Indians, 1829 to 1850," probably written by Mrs. Elizabeth T. Ayer, in *Minnesota Historical Collections*, 6: 429–431. The locations of missions in
Minnesota are indicated on the map facing page 80, *ante*. Although Ayer was doubtless
the pioneer missionary to the Chippewa in Minnesota, mention may be made of an earlier
reconnoissance in the field.   On September 1, 1829, the Reverend Jedediah Stevens and
the Reverend Alvan Coe, recommended as missionaries of the "Presbyterian Congregational
Church," arrived from Prairie du Chien at St. Peter's on their way to Mille Lacs, where
they planned to establish a colony.   They remained a fortnight as guests of the Indian

For the present purpose it would not profit to name the considerable number of contemporaries of Ayer in the mission to the Chippewa, nor to follow their several movements.[10] Some of them, however, must be mentioned, particularly the Reverend William Thurston Boutwell, who accompanied Schoolcraft on his expedition to Lake Itasca in 1832 and rummaged the two Latin words from which his chief extracted the name. After graduation from Dartmouth College in 1828 at the age of twenty-five, Boutwell studied divinity at the Andover Theological Seminary. When he was near the close of his studies a fervid appeal was made to his class to furnish two men to go as missionaries to the Chippewa Indians on Lake Superior. In response, he and another, the Reverend Sherman Hall, after prayer unto tears, offered themselves. The two traveled together and reached Mackinac Island on August 30, 1831, where Boutwell at once began the study of the Chippewa language. In the autumn of the same year upon an invitation from Schoolcraft he repaired to Sault Ste. Marie, where he might pursue his study under favorable circumstances. The Schoolcraft party returning from the source of the Mississippi reached La Pointe on August 6, 1832. Here Boutwell detached himself and remained for the next year assisting his fellow missionary, Hall. On August 21, 1833, he took his journey thence for the field of labor selected by or for him, the Pillager band of Chippewa about Leech Lake. Things seen, or heard, when he was on Leech Lake the previous year may have persuaded him that there was a favorable place for converting and civilizing heathen Indians,

agent, Major Taliaferro, who consulted with them upon the subject of inducing the Indians to engage in agriculture. He apparently hoped to enlist them in his "agricultural establishment" which he had planned five years before and which was already in operation at Lake Calhoun. Stevens and Coe visited the Falls of St. Anthony with the object of finding thereabouts a suitable location for an agricultural school. The reconnoissance, however, seems to have been fruitless. Taliaferro Journal, September 1–14, 1829; Taliaferro to the Reverend Joshua T. Russell, September 8, 1829, in Taliaferro Letter Book, A.

[10] See Riggs's account of the Chippewa missions, in *Minnesota Historical Collections*, 6: 119–125. Riggs derived his information mainly from the *Missionary Herald*, vols. 29–42, *passim* (Boston, 1833–46).

where he would not be merely keeping school for half-breed children. If he was looking for a place which would challenge his industry, patience, and courage to the utmost, he could not have been more successful.

Here at Leech Lake Boutwell remained four years, but the dreary monotony of the period was broken by certain absences. The most notable of these, lasting through the summer, took place in 1834, the year after his arrival among the Pillagers. To obtain needed supplies he went down by canoe to Fort Snelling, and he was there on the sixth of May when the steamboat "Warrior" landed the Pond brothers, of whose mission labors among the Sioux we are to hear. The months of June and July Boutwell spent at Yellow Lake, assisting Ayer in the preparation of a Chippewa grammar and certain translations. These literary engagements did not so engross him as to prevent his enjoying the society of Miss Hester Crooks, mixed-blood daughter of Ramsay Crooks, who had joined Ayer as a teacher. The result was a ten days' journey by the Brulé River route to Fond du Lac. In descending that turbulent stream, Boutwell and his *voyageurs* had to wade a large part of the distance and he was in the water from noon till night for more than three days. The party reached Fond du Lac at two o'clock in the afternoon of September 10, and the wedding took place at eight in the evening. Tea and doughnuts served for the wedding feast. The next morning the married pair began their journey to Leech Lake by the six-mile Savanna portage, where the mud and water were half-leg deep. The journey lasted forty-three days. Boutwell at once built a log cabin to take the place of the bark lodge which had been his shelter.[11] The arrival of Nicollet on Leech Lake in the late summer of 1836 was an event which relieved the dullness of

[11] The account of Boutwell and his work among the Chippewa is based on Neill, in *Macalester College Contributions*, second series, no. 1. This work embodies extracts from the journal of Boutwell, to which Neill had access but which has not since been found. A copy of that part of the journal which was written from June 5, 1832, to August 28, 1837, is in the possession of the Minnesota Historical Society.

the situation. When the Pillagers were about to confiscate Nicollet's outfit and leave him in the wilderness without food, shelter, or arms, Boutwell was able to pacify them and make them friends to the explorer. Nicollet, in his report, made a grateful acknowledgment of this.[12] Early in the summer of 1837 Boutwell brought his family down to Fond du Lac and, leaving them there, journeyed on to St. Peter's to be present at the treaty of July 29 with the Chippewa, of which mention has been made.[13]

The outcome of this long experiment with the Pillagers was so disappointing that it was arranged that Boutwell should not return to Leech Lake, but should remain for a time at Fond du Lac. Sometime in the following year, 1838, he moved to Lake Pokegama to have principal charge of the mission.[14] At Pokegama he adopted a new policy with the Indians. In a letter to Sibley he says: "I resolved on adopting a new policy the present winter, & I have been astonished at the result. When Inds. came begging I gave them my axe & showed them my wood pile. . . . Seven winters that I have been in the country, I have fed the hungry, & they are none the wiser, none the more provident. Tis enough, I will feed you no longer, if you choose to smoke & sleep all summer, you may beg in winter & get nothing. I have planted, hoed & dug potatoes with my own hands, till I am tired, & if you will not raise them for yourselves you shant eat them hereafter. . . . The result is, those very fellows . . . have taken their axes & gone to work in good earnest."[15]

Another member of the mission to the Chippewa of Minnesota was Edmund F. Ely, from Massachusetts, who came out in time to travel with Boutwell on his way to Leech Lake

[12] Nicollet, *Report*, 55.
[13] See *ante*, p. 159.
[14] Boutwell to Sibley, July 2, 1838, Sibley Papers; American Board of Commissioners for Foreign Missions, *Reports*, 1837, p. 119; 1838, p. 130.
[15] Boutwell to Sibley, March 23, 1839, Sibley Papers; extracts quoted by Holcombe, in *Minnesota in Three Centuries*, 2: 226. A letter from Boutwell to S. W. Pond, December 22, 1838, in the Pond Papers, contains other points of his policy.

in 1833. Without delay Ely took up the school work at
Sandy Lake which Ayer had begun and inculcated gospel
doctrine and sentiment chiefly by singing, in which the
Indians greatly delighted. In August, 1834, upon the advice
of Aitkin, he removed to Fond du Lac, where he opened a
school in a house built by the local trader. Here he labored
with admirable zeal for the next five years, meeting with the
same discouragements which beset Boutwell at Leech Lake,
to which were added the indifference, not to say hostility, of
the French trader and his employees, who were Roman
Catholic Christians. One of his frequent absences took him
to La Pointe, whence he returned with a bride, to whom he
had been married in church by Boutwell on August 30,
1835.[16]

In a consultation of the principal members of the mission,
which was held at Fond du Lac on June 18, 1838, it was
decided that all other stations should be abandoned and the
workers concentrated at Pokegama Lake.[17] The early
effects were encouraging. A number of Indian families
settled near the mission, built houses, and cultivated gardens and fields. In 1839 the Indian bureau employed Jeremiah Russell, afterwards prominent in Minnesota affairs,
as farmer to the station, to teach the Indians how to clear
land and cultivate.[18] Many of them believed that the
object was not so much to educate them as to provide them
with food. A nucleus of a church was gathered, to which
the sacraments were administered by Boutwell. There was
reason for the expectations of the missionaries and their
supporters that substantial and permanent results would
follow the new policy and that many of the wild Indians

[16] Unpublished journal of Ely in the possession of Mrs. Henry S. Ely of Duluth, Minnesota; biographic sketch of Ely by his son, Henry S. Ely, in John R. Carey, "History of
Duluth and of St. Louis County to the Year 1870," in *Minnesota Historical Collections*, 9:
246–248; Neill, in *Macalester College Contributions*, second series, no. 1, pp. 19, 23, 37 n. 2.

[17] Ely Journal; Boutwell to Sibley, March 23, 1839, Sibley Papers; Neill, in *Macalester
College Contributions*, second series, no. 1, p. 44.

[18] United States, *Official Register*, 1839, p. 84; Ayer to the secretary of war, August 24,
1840, in 26 Congress, 2 session, *House Documents*, no. 2, p. 382 (serial 382). For a sketch
of Russell, see William H. C. Folsom, *Fifty Years in the Northwest*, 466 (St. Paul, 1888).

would become civilized and live blameless Christian lives.[19] These bright hopes were to be rudely blighted.

The immemorial warfare of the Sioux and Chippewa did not end with the ambuscades of Rum River and Stillwater in 1839. Early in the spring of 1841 a small party of Chippewa warriors stole down the Mississippi to a thicket near Camp Coldwater, within a mile of Fort Snelling, shot a Sioux chief, and made their escape.[20] This murder caused intense exasperation among the Sioux of the vicinity, and their leaders plotted an elaborate scheme of retaliation. The purpose was to destroy the settlement at Pokegama and secure a goodly harvest of Chippewa scalps. This might have been effected but for a mistake, of which the white man can furnish many examples: that of dividing the forces, marching on different roads, and failing to make the intended concentration for action. One party, collected at Kaposia, which moved up the St. Croix Valley, was accidentally discovered by two Chippewa warriors, who shot and killed two sons of Big Thunder (Little Crow IV), the Kaposia chief. As the opportunity for a surprise had been lost, this party returned home. A second party heard of the fortune which had overtaken the first and gave up the campaign. A third body, composed of warriors of the Lake Calhoun bands, took the Knife River road and made its way without discovery to the west side of Pokegama Lake, where it arrived in the evening of May 23. In the course of the night the main body moved around the south end of the lake and hid in the convenient forest, to deliver the main attack on the Chippewa in the morning, when they should be at work in their gardens. A small party was left to intercept any fugitives who should cross to the west shore in canoes. When three Chippewa runners, on their way to Mille Lacs to summon help, reached that shore, the lurking

[19] American Board, *Reports*, 1841, p. 189.
[20] S. W. Pond, in *Minnesota Historical Collections*, 3:133; Pond, *Two Volunteer Missionaries*, 152; Neill, *Minnesota*, 463; Williams, *Saint Paul*, 122.

Sioux could not restrain their ardor and fired upon them. All the warriors escaped into the forest unhurt, but two young girls who had been brought along to take the canoe back were killed and their bodies were literally hacked to pieces. This premature firing gave alarm to the Indians near the mission. They had already moved their women and children to an island, and the warriors at once collected in their log houses about the mission. The attack of the Sioux was abortive, and they returned to their own country disappointed.[21]

The Sioux had not long to wait for the inevitable counterstroke. In June of the following summer, 1842, a party of Chippewa, perhaps one hundred strong, recruited from various bands, passed unobserved from the head of Lake St. Croix to a point opposite Little Crow's village of Kaposia, which had been moved to the west side of the Mississippi. It was the probable expectation of the raiding party that, without revealing its position and numbers, it might gather some scalps from individual Sioux who, for one reason or another, should cross the river. But the premature murder of two women at work in a garden on the east side and an alarm carried by a half-breed, whose horse ran away with him at sight of a Chippewa warrior, brought on an open fight which lasted some hours and resulted in the repulse of the invaders. The affair has been called the battle of Kaposia and the battle of Pine Coulie.[22]

[21] The accounts of the battle of Pokegama vary much in details. The present narrative is based on the unpublished journal of Ely, who begins the entry as follows: "May 24th, 1841, Pokegama. While I now write, the noise of battle rages without." See also the description by Mrs. E. T. Ayer, a member of the mission at Pokegama at the time of the attack, in *Minnesota Historical Collections*, 6: 431–434, and Neill, "Battle of Lake Pokeguma as Narrated by an Eye Witness," in *Minnesota Historical Collections*, 1: 177–182 (St. Paul, 1872). The latter article was written from notes furnished the author by Ely, which are now in the possession of Macalester College, St. Paul. The same account is repeated substantially in Neill, *Minnesota*, 463–469.

[22] Williams, *Saint Paul*, 122–125; Auguste L. Larpenteur, "Recollections of the City and People of St. Paul, 1843–1898," in *Minnesota Historical Collections*, 9: 363–394; Boutwell to S. W. Pond, June 29, 1842, Pond Papers. All the authorities cited obtained their information from participants, or eyewitnesses, and their accounts furnish an example of the not infrequent discrepancies in the observations and reports of truthful persons upon the same series of events.

Although the losses of the Indian defenders of the Poke-gama mission and colony during the attack of 1841 were slight — two girls killed and three men wounded — the band decided that the place, though very convenient for the members of the mission, was much too near the danger line. Families began at once to depart, and not many months had passed before the whole band was scattered along the trails leading northward. Small bodies returned to Poke-gama from time to time, reviving the hopes of the missionaries, but the band as a whole never returned and its identity was at length lost. In 1847 the station at Pokegama was abandoned. The three leaders sought other locations and at length resigned from the mission service.[23]

Beginning in 1839, Methodist Episcopal missionaries established stations at Fond du Lac, Sandy Lake, and various other points in the Chippewa country, some of which flourished off and on during the next few years.[24]

A mission opened at Gull Lake in Crow Wing County in 1852 by the Reverend James Lloyd Breck, a clergyman of the Protestant Episcopal church, would furnish the subject of an interesting chapter in a history of Indian missions in

[23] Report of Ayer, September 1, 1841, in 27 Congress, 2 session, *House Documents*, no. 2, p. 295 (serial 401); report of Ely, August 6, 1842, in 27 Congress, 3 session, *House Documents*, no. 2, p. 477 (serial 418); reports of Russell, May 22, June 30, 1843, in 28 Congress, 1 session, *House Documents*, no. 2, pp. 446–448 (serial 439); American Board, *Reports*, 1842, p. 199; 1843, p. 175; 1844, p. 223; 1845, pp. 199, 200; Riggs, in *Minnesota Historical Collections*, 6: 143–151. Boutwell writing to S. W. Pond, January 27, 1847, says, "The Board instructed us last winter to call a council of the brethren at La P.[ointe] & advise with them on the expediency of discontinuing this station. We did so & the result was to abandon it on account of the drunkenness & indisposition of the Inds. to be benefited by the gospel." Pond Papers.

[24] Riggs, in *Minnesota Historical Collections*, 6: 135–143; Chauncey Hobart, *History of Methodism in Minnesota*, 12–33 (Red Wing, 1887). See also John H. Pitezel, *Lights and Shades of Missionary Life during Nine Years Spent in the Region of Lake Superior*, 181–374 (Cincinnati, 1883), and reports of the commissioner of Indian affairs from 1841 to 1851, containing communications from district superintendents or teachers in charge of the missions or from United States Indian agents within whose districts the stations were located. Unpublished letters, memoirs, and biographies dealing with this work of the Methodist church are in the collections of the Historical Society of the Minnesota Annual Conference of the Methodist Episcopal Church recently transferred from Hamline University to the Minnesota Historical Society. Especially valuable are the letters from Thomas M. Fullerton to Benjamin F. Hoyt, March 19 and 22, 1859, and from Joseph W. Hancock to Jabez Brooks, undated.

Minnesota, but its results were too inconsiderable to warrant description in this place. After four years of encouraging progress Breck transferred his labors to the more numerous community at Leech Lake, in November, 1856. The enterprise was a disappointment. The Pillagers were so drunken and disorderly that the missionary, his life endangered, gave up his apostleship to the Chippewa after an eight months' experiment. The station at Gull Lake was cared for by a successor, residing at Fort Ripley, till the outbreak of the Civil War. Connected with this mission was the Ottawa Indian, John Johnson Enmegahbowh, afterwards ordained to the ministry, whose devoted labors among the Chippewa did not end till 1897.[25]

Three of the seven tribes of the Sioux or Dakota nation, the Teton, the Yankton, and the Yanktonai, for an unknown time had had their homes and hunting grounds on the great plains to the west of the Minnesota border. With these the present narrative has little concern. The Minnesota Sioux, collectively called by the western tribesmen Isanti (knifemen), were separated into four tribes, each subdivided into bands commonly called after the names of their leading chiefs. The Mdewakanton tribe had its villages, up to 1853, about Winona, Red Wing, St. Paul, Shakopee, and Fort Snelling. It could muster some six hundred warriors. The Wahpekute had their chief seat near the city of

---

[25] Riggs, in *Minnesota Historical Collections*, 6: 161–166. See also George C. Tanner, *Fifty Years of Church Work in the Diocese of Minnesota, 1857–1907*, 52–88 (St. Paul, 1909); Charles Breck, *The Life of the Reverend James Lloyd Breck*, 181–333 (New York, 1883), a biography composed mainly of letters written by Breck himself; and Theodore I. Holcombe, *An Apostle of the Wilderness: James Lloyd Breck*, 69–136 (New York, 1903). The Oberlin mission to the Chippewa of Red Lake, opened in 1843 under the leadership of the Reverend Frederick Ayer, was not abandoned till 1859. Unfortunately, however, this is but another example of the ultimate failure of work begun with high hopes and prosecuted for a time with promising results. It had finally to be given up when the tide of white immigration following the Chippewa treaty of 1855 exposed the Indians to influences with which the missionaries were powerless to contend. The story of it is best told in a manuscript volume of reminiscences of the Reverend Sela G. Wright in the library of Oberlin College, a copy of which is in the possession of the Minnesota Historical Society. This devoted missionary remained till the end and later labored for the Chippewa as a government agent. The files of the *Missionary Herald* furnish but little information about the enterprise because it was only to a very limited extent, if at all, under the auspices of the American Board.

Faribault in Nicollet's Undine Region and could assemble some one hundred and fifty warriors. These two tribes on account of geographical and social affiliations were spoken of as the lower Sioux. The upper Sioux included the Wahpeton and Sisseton tribes, whose villages were on the Minnesota River from Carver to the foot of Lake Traverse. These tribes were themselves separated into "upper" and "lower" groups, somewhat sandwiched. The lower Wahpeton dwelt near the site of Belle Plaine, Scott County; the upper group, about Lac qui Parle. The lower Sisseton were at the Traverse des Sioux, Swan Lake, and the Cottonwood River; the upper, on Big Stone Lake and Lake Traverse. It will be convenient to remember these groupings. With the exception of the Wahpekute all these Indians were strung along the Mississippi and Minnesota rivers from Winona to Lake Traverse.[26] Indians never occupied the whole country after the white man's fashion. "We cannot dig wells like the white man; we must have our homes by the flowing rivers," said an Indian orator.

The missions of the American Board to the Sioux were anticipated by two young laymen who, in the spring of 1834, appeared at Fort Snelling without commission or license from any religious body, resolved to devote themselves to the civilization and conversion of those Indians. These were the brothers, Samuel William and Gideon Hollister Pond, then twenty-six and twenty-four years of age respectively. Reared in an obscure Connecticut town,

---

[26] S. W. Pond, in *Minnesota Historical Collections*, 12: 320–324; Henry H. Sibley, "Reminiscences of the Early Days of Minnesota," in *Minnesota Historical Collections*, 3: 250; Hodge, *Handbook of American Indians*, 1: 826; 2: 577, 580, 890, 891, 988. The present writer excludes from the Minnesota Sioux the Yankton, because they were Indians of the plains. They had, however, some connection with the Sisseton. Neill, in *Minnesota Historical Collections*, 1: 258, includes the Yankton with the Dakota of the Missouri or "Far West"; a catalogue of Dakota villages derived from the journal of Le Sueur may be found on page 257. A map showing the distribution of the Dakota in Minnesota, according to S. W. Pond, and a careful tabulation of the tribes in 1851 are in Winchell, *Aborigines of Minnesota*, 72, 552. See also the map facing page 80, *ante*. After the establishment of the reservations under the treaties of 1851 the lower Sisseton made their homes partly on the headwaters of the Yellow Medicine River in Lyon County and partly in Pipestone County.

they had had good elementary schooling, had worked on farms, and had learned trades. The older brother had taught school. In personal appearance they were prepossessing. Both were over six feet tall, stalwart and sinewy, alert and genial. Riggs, quoting from the Book of Judges, wrote of them, "they seemed the children of a king." Both were converted at a memorable revival and thereupon resolved to devote themselves to gospel work in the West. Against the wishes of friends, Samuel Pond set out with the money he had earned at teaching. He found himself, he hardly knew why, in Galena, Illinois, where he remained for about a year. One day he undertook to persuade a liquor-seller to choose another calling. The interview must have been amicable, for in later conversations the man described to him the country and the customs of the Sioux Indians, among whom he had been. Young Pond at once wrote to his brother that he had found a virgin field for mission work.[27] The result was that on May 6, 1834, the Pond brothers arrived at Fort Snelling on the steamboat "Warrior," to be welcomed by Boutwell, the Chippewa missionary, then on a visit to that post.[28] Although they had absolutely no license to enter the Indian country, both Agent Taliaferro and Major Bliss, commanding the post, waived all technicalities, provided them with lodging, and put them in the way of getting at the Sioux. Samuel Pond, at Major Bliss's request, at once went down

[27] The main facts in the account of the Pond brothers are taken from an unpublished narrative entitled "Pioneer Work among the Dakotas," by Samuel W. Pond, in the possession of Mrs. Frances Pond-Titus of Boisé, Idaho, the daughter of S. W. Pond Jr.; from numerous letters in the Pond Papers; and from *Two Volunteer Missionaries*. The author of the latter volume was the son of the older missionary and a pupil of the present writer. In the preparation of his story he had access to the narrative and papers mentioned. The letters of S. W. Pond to G. H. Pond, October 6 and December 3, 1833, in the Pond Papers, are especially valuable. In the letter of December 3 the fact that the main body of the Sioux were not in a position to obtain spirits is given as the reason for choosing to work among them rather than among the miserable remnant of the Potawatomi. A letter written by G. H. Pond to Neill in 1856, which gives an interesting account of the early experiences of the brothers in their mission work, is in Neill, *Minnesota*, 770, n.

[28] Boutwell's account of this meeting is quoted by Neill, in *Macalester College Contributions*, second series, no. 1, p. 24; S. W. Pond's account may be found in his *Narrative*, 1: 11.

to Kaposia and gave Big Thunder, father of Little Crow, a week's lessons in plowing.[29]

An interesting explanation of the welcome given the Pond brothers may be found in Taliaferro's journal. How early that excellent friend of the Indian had conceived a plan for inducing his wards, or some of them, to cease depending wholly on the chase for their living and to become cultivators of the soil, is not known. He found at length in Cloudman, chief of the Lake Calhoun band, a response to his hope. That chief, while lying under a snow bank waiting for the subsidence of a blizzard, had resolved that he would have his people plant corn and beans and store up the produce for winter food.[30] In a letter dated September 8, 1829, Taliaferro mentions his "present infant colony of agriculturists together with their implements of husbandry Horses, etc." To this colony he was pleased to give the name "Eatonville," after that member of President Jackson's cabinet whose marital and social relations in Washington were for a time a matter of national curiosity.[31] In his journal the agent frequently mentions, year after year, his agricultural establishment. On April 14, 1831, he consults with Cloudman about it. Four days later he orders hoes and plows repaired for the Eatonville agricultural establishment. On May 1 he goes out to find "most of them at work, cuting down trees, grubing out the roots &c. what was more encouraging, some few of the men were at this unusual kind of labour for them. They *laughed* when they saw me. I praised them in every agreeable way that could be conveyed to them in their language." On May 7 he notes that "M^r

[29] Letter of G. H. Pond, May 19, 1834, quoted in Neill, "A Memorial of the Brothers Pond, the First Resident Missionaries among the Dakotas," in *Macalester College Contributions*, second series, no. 8, p. 166; S. W. Pond to his sister and Herman Hine, May 25, 1834, Pond Papers; Pond, *Two Volunteer Missionaries*, 30–34; S. W. Pond Narrative, 1: 12–15.

[30] Pond, *Two Volunteer Missionaries*, 27.

[31] Taliaferro to the Reverend Joshua T. Russell, in Taliaferro Letter Book, A; John H. Stevens, *Personal Recollections of Minnesota and Its People and Early History of Minneapolis*, 396 (Minneapolis, 1890), quoting from an address by Neill in 1872; John B. McMaster, *A History of the People of the United States from the Revolution to the Civil War*, 6: 120–123 (New York, 1906).

Prescott [is] in charge"; adding, "I hire him to superintend at $10 per month."[32] On August 14, 1833, the journal records: "Much corn is being raised — from 800 to 1000 bushels — 3d year of this establishment — advanced for [*from*] 8 to 125 souls."

When the Pond brothers arrived at Fort Snelling, without definite plans, it must at once have occurred to Major Taliaferro that here were the very men, perhaps directed by Providence, to take charge of his agricultural establishment. He gave them free quarters in an agency building and allowed them the services of his interpreter, Scott Campbell. When he learned that they desired to build a cabin in or near an Indian village, he at once suggested a site near Cloudman's village. The spot on the east bank of Lake Calhoun, now covered by a private residence, has been marked by a bronze tablet. One of the brothers wrote that the selection was in fact made by Cloudman, who recommended the site because from it the loons could be seen on the lake. To expedite the work of building the agent furnished a yoke of oxen, a log chain, and certain tools. Thus provided, and much aided by Gideon's knowledge of carpentry, by midsummer the missionaries were able to report themselves as sheltered by "a good snug little house, delightfully situated . . . with a good yoke of oxen to use as we please, and possessed of the confidence of the Indians." The snug house was a two-room cabin of oak logs, twelve by sixteen

---

[32] Philander Prescott. For sketches of this interesting personage, see S. W. Pond, in *Minnesota Historical Collections*, 12: 337; Williams, in *Minnesota Historical Collections*, 3: 318, n.; and Neill, *Minnesota*, 737, n. Stevens, *Personal Recollections*, 43–46, contains passages concerning Prescott's domestic life, including an account of his marriage and a description of the wedding of his daughter and Eli Pettijohn, who died in Minneapolis, May 25, 1915. Prescott's writings are of no little historical value. He contributed three articles on the Sioux Indians to Schoolcraft, *Indian Tribes*, 2: 168–199; 3: 225–246; 4: 59–72. Schoolcraft evidently relied greatly on Prescott's statements. He described him as a man "whose judgment . . . is believed to be at once accurate, and perfectly candid and truthful" (4: 59). Prescott's "Autobiography and Reminiscences," written in 1861, is in *Minnesota Historical Collections*, 6: 475–491. A letter of S. W. Pond to John H. Stevens, March 6, 1891, in the Pond Papers, contains a criticism of the latter's "fiction" in regard to Prescott and also a remark on his life. The statement of Pond that Prescott, who lost his life in the Sioux Outbreak, might have escaped with the party of Other Day but for his own fault, indicates a lapse of memory. Other Day's party escaped from the upper agency.

feet and eight feet high, with a cellar beneath and a roof of
bark lashed to tamarack poles by strings of basswood bark.
Major Taliaferro gave a window, an inside door, and a lock,
and offered a stove, which was declined. The only cash
outlay was a "York shilling," twelve and a half cents, for
nails with which to batten the door. Four acres were
inclosed with a stout fence of logs.[33] The entries in Agent
Taliaferro's journal quite clearly record his expectation that
the Pond brothers would relieve him of concern about the
agricultural establishment. On July 7, 1834, after an interview with the elder Pond he wrote: "These young men are
to have charge of them [*the oxen*] for the winter. They will
plough some *this fall* and again in the spring for the Indians,
& go on thereafter to instruct them in the *arts* & *habits* of
civilised life. The Indians are pleased & authorise me to
aid him with the *loan* of *all the means* in *my possession*."
He added some words of high praise for their philanthropic
and Christian devotion: "[I] . . . thank *my God* for permit[ting me to know] them." On July 17 the agent, after
mentioning a loan of oxen and tools, added that the beneficiaries "are to instruct the Indians in the art of [agricul-
ture] & for the present on their own expenses." On July 24
he wrote that nothing but money was lacking to realize his
most sanguine expectations of the enterprise.

But the young zealots from Connecticut had not abandoned the comforts and employments of civilization to plow
ground for Indians and show them how to grow corn. They
came filled with the missionary ideal of the day, to evangelize heathen, enlighten their understandings, and save their
souls from impending perdition. Doubtless they more
than paid for all the indulgences and gratuities of Major

[33] S. W. Pond Narrative, 1: 12–17; S. W. Pond to Herman Hine, January 19, 1835,
Pond Papers. Pond, *Two Volunteer Missionaries*, 38–49, contains an account taken from
the above mentioned letter. See also Riggs, *Forty Years with the Sioux*, 329–338; Stevens,
Personal Recollections, 52; and the Taliaferro Journal, July 11, 17, 1834. The agent states
that he gave a gratuity of $3.50, which may have been the value of the door, window, and
nails furnished. The Dakota name for Lake Calhoun, Mde Medoza or Loon Lake, explains
the chief's pleasantry.

Taliaferro, but his naïve expectation that they would devote themselves chiefly to his agricultural establishment was never seriously entertained, although he evidently thought it was. Aware that a knowledge of the language of the Indians was indispensable to the proclamation of the Gospel, the brothers began learning it on their way to St. Peter's. Lieutenant Edmund A. Ogden of the Fort Snelling garrison, lately come to the post, had collected a small Dakota vocabulary, for which the agency interpreter had furnished doubtful definitions. The officer gave his manuscript to the Ponds, who, with the help of some Indians, gathered "a considerable number of words" that were new to them. Thus aided, they soon made progress in understanding and speaking Dakota. After their first year they had no difficulty in conversing with Indians. At the same time they undertook the task which at length gave the Dakota the Word of Life in their own tongue. By the time their cabin on the lake was completed, in July, 1834, they had devised the "Pond alphabet" of the Dakota language, so named by Neill. Fortunately the young men knew no language but their own English, and had no conception of the niceties of modern phonology. They soon discovered that the five vowel characters of the English were enough to represent the Dakota vowels. It was not so easy to frame the consonant system. The Dakota had two guttural sounds unknown in English, and had no *g*, *l*, nor *r*. By putting into service the superfluous letters *c*, *q*, and *x*, by using *g* and *r* for the two gutturals, and by making final *n* nasalize the preceding vowel, they had, before the summer was over, an alphabet which for all ordinary occasions was practically phonetic. For one sound there was one letter; for one letter, one sound. A Dakota could read as soon as he had learned his letters. One of them very soon learned not only to read but also to write letters which his teachers could understand.[34] A capital merit of the Pond alphabet was that it

[34] S. W. Pond Narrative, 1: 9–11, 18–21, 22–24. See also the Appendix, no. 3, *post*.

called for no new types and could be set up in any printing office.

The pious enthusiasts spent the fall of 1834 and the following winter in their comfortable though rude log cabin on Lake Calhoun, studying the Dakota and praying for success in opening the gospel of salvation to "a host of immortal spirits going swift to hell."[35] They were not to remain alone in their chosen field of labor. On May 16, 1835, there arrived at Fort Snelling a missionary band of five adults and three children, conducted by the Reverend Thomas Smith Williamson, M.D., a regular appointee of the American Board. His principal associate was Alexander G. Huggins, a lay appointee of the board, who was to instruct the Indians in the cultivation of the soil and in other arts of civilization. On the thirtieth of the same month there arrived a smaller group of missionaries, also under the auspices of the American Board; it consisted of the Reverend Jedediah D. Stevens, his wife, and a niece who came out to be a teacher.[36] As the Pond brothers were not ordained ministers and had no credentials from any board or association, Williamson and Stevens, duly commissioned, could recognize them only as mere private adventurers, at the same time appreciating their zeal and piety; but the newly arrived ministers had no scruples about entering into the labors of the two brothers. Williamson immediately planned to build near the Pond cabin and stored some of his baggage in it. "The farmer," wrote S. W. Pond on May 31, "expects to bring his family here." Gideon Pond at once promised to help as much as he could in building.[37] Stevens on his arrival let it be known that he had preëmptive right to the location because of his visit in 1829. It is not necessary to conjecture what

---

[35] S. W. Pond to Mrs. Sarah Pond, September 2, 1835, Pond Papers.

[36] Riggs, in *Minnesota Historical Collections*, 6: 126. See also Riggs, *Forty Years with the Sioux*, 347, for that author's curious testimony that Dr. Williamson and his wife hesitated about leaving their pleasant home in Ohio for the mission work among the Dakota because of their children till "God removed this obstacle in his own way — by taking the little ones home to himself."

[37] S. W. Pond to Mrs. Sarah Pond, May 31, 1835, Pond Papers.

amount of friction might have ensued between the claimants, because Williamson was diverted to another and distant field of labor.[38] In what way this was brought about the reader will better understand when he shall have returned from a necessary digression.

Mention has already been made of Joseph Renville as holding a British captaincy in the War of 1812. He was the son of a French trader and a woman of the Kaposia band of Sioux, whose home was in early days on the east bank of the Mississippi, some miles below St. Paul. He was born about the year 1779. While a young boy, he was sent by his father to Canada and was placed in the care of a priest, who taught him the French language and the elements of the Catholic faith. Later young Renville returned to his birthplace and became a *coureur de bois* and an interpreter to Colonel Robert Dickson, the chief factor of the old Northwest Company above the Falls of St. Anthony. He guided Pike in 1805 from Prairie du Chien to Mendota without pay, and was highly commended by that officer. After the War of 1812 he was in the service of the Hudson's Bay Company, trading posts of which still extended into the heart of Minnesota. He broke away at length from the British, and threw himself into American associations. In 1822 he organized the Columbia Fur Company, and he remained its leading spirit till it was absorbed by the American Fur Company in 1827. In 1823 he was interpreter and guide for Long's expedition and furnished the historian of the expedition with one of the best accounts of the Sioux Indians ever made. Remaining in the employ of Astor's company, he

---

[38] Riggs, *Forty Years with the Sioux*, 19. In the entry for June 24, 1836, in his journal, Taliaferro expresses dissatisfaction with the Stevens mission at Lake Harriet. "My views & arrangements as well as those of the Messers Pond in refference to the improvement in the condition of the Indians of this vicinity has been interrupted by the establishment of the Indian Mission at Lake Harriet. We had commenced a system of agriculture previous to opening a school for children which [it] was necessary to perfect in order [to] *civilize* – as *to civilize*, is to *Christianize*. . . . As for geting an *Interpreter* . . . to Expound the Bible to a set of ragged half starved indolent beings [it] is the heit of extravagance, and *folly*." Further views of Taliaferro on the missionaries in his jurisdiction may be found in his journal, September 16, 1836.

established himself in the Wahpeton country on the north side of the Minnesota River in sight of Lac qui Parle in Chippewa County. Here he built a stockaded inclosure, often called Fort Renville, and in it maintained a considerable bodyguard of old *voyageurs*, Indian relatives, and half-breeds, and lived in a baronial fashion. Such protection was not superfluous in that time and among such Indians. He taught the wild Indians about him to plant corn. He accumulated large herds of horses and cattle and a flock of sheep. To the end of his life he practiced an abounding hospitality. With the Indian and the half-breed his word was law.[39] This man of experience and sense and some education could not be content to see his numerous children grow up in the wilderness without letters.

In 1835, at the usual time of year, Renville went down to Mendota to bring his return of furs and to buy his outfit for the following year. On June 4, the day after his arrival, he appeared in council at the agency to meet Chief Hole-in-the-Day, who, with a party of Chippewa, had been awaiting his coming. Addressing Renville the chief boldly charged that some of his people had been murdered by the trader's relations. This was not denied by Renville, who admitted that some "people of his place" had killed three Chippewa, but in revenge for murders committed by that nation. He had never encouraged war between the nations. He had had Sioux shot and their guns broken for breaking the peace. His business would be ruined by war, and he had lost heavily by the late affairs. Agent Taliaferro warned the Sioux and the Chippewa present that if they did not keep the peace the Great Father would compel them to, and he severely blamed the Sioux for endangering the life of their good friend Renville.[40]

[39] Neill, "Sketch of Joseph Renville," in *Minnesota Historical Collections*, 1: 196–206. The same abridged but with some additions is in his *Minnesota*, 474–479, n. See the Taliaferro Journal, June 16, 1829, for an account of how Renville paid one Gibson, through the agent, $732 for fifty-eight head of cattle from a drove abandoned by the owner on the upper Minnesota.

[40] Taliaferro Journal, June 3–5, 1835.

Our story may best be continued by an extract from the agent's journal for June 6, 1835: "After the various difficulties which have & are still occurring on the Sioux & Chippeway line occasional Suspicions as to the part Mr Joseph Rainville [*Renville*] was acting & had been acting, I proposed to as we had no sub agent to Locate the Rev. Mr Williamson & his family & also Mr Huggins as agriculturist with his family at Lac qui parle. For this purpose I invited Mr Renville to dine with me, and after detailing to him the advantages which would result to him & his large family from having such a valuable acquisition as Doct Williamson & his family, he readily consented & he offered his protection, and every facility in his power if they would go." On June 23 Williamson and Huggins with their families, provided with passports by the Indian agent, departed in Renville's caravan for Lac qui Parle, where they had been "from motives of policy permitted to locate for *Missionary purposes* & agricultural for the benefit of the wild Indians of that place, & vicinity." The agent had "long felt the want of a correspondent in the region." It was by such human means that Providence sent Williamson to a station relatively as far away from Lake Calhoun as the Yukon River would be today.

Both groups of missionaries had been heartily welcomed by the commandant of Fort Snelling, Major Gustavus Loomis, an earnest and active Christian. With his aid and countenance religious meetings were held, and on June 11, before the departure of Williamson's band, the first Christian church within the present area of Minnesota was organized at Fort Snelling. One of the ruling elders was Henry H. Sibley, who had brought with him from Michilimackinac a certificate of church membership in the hand writing and with the signature of Henry R. Schoolcraft, clerk of session.[41]

---

[41] Westminster Presbyterian Church Minutes, in the possession of that church in Minneapolis; Pond, *Two Volunteer Missionaries*, 61, 63; Riggs, *Forty Years with the Sioux*, 30; Riggs, in *Minnesota Historical Collections*, 6: 128; Neill, in *Minnesota Historical Collections*, 2: 126. The church was known as the First Presbyterian Church at St. Peter's. A

Stevens lost no time in selecting as the site of his mission house a point on the northwestern limb of Lake Harriet very near the site of the present recreation pavilion of the Minneapolis Park Commission, a mile distant to the south of the Pond cabin.[42] He found in Gideon Pond an efficient skilled laborer on the mission house, which he occupied with his family on September 18. The genial missionary had found no difficulty in securing the willing aid of the brothers. In a letter to his mother, September 2, 1835, Samuel Pond, after expressing a fear he had indulged that the missionary and he might not think alike, wrote: "Mr Stevens is just such a man as we want He has not a liberal education & was bred a farmer. . . . He is a very intelligent man & a good minister He is the most agreeable companion that I have found since I left home. He works with his men and understands the common business of life which is much more essential to his usefulness here than a classical education would be He has been employed several years among Indians."[43] This generous appreciation presently underwent a diminution. While the younger brother labored gratuitously on the mission house the elder tended their three acres of corn and potatoes, studied Dakota in the Indian village, and prepared a spelling book. When this book, the first printed in the Dakota language, appeared from the press in 1836 it bore the title "Sioux Spelling Book . . . by Rev. J. D. Stevens." In the fall of 1835 it was suggested that the good cause would be promoted by a closer union of effort, to be secured by the brothers' taking up their lodging in the mission house. With reluctance they did so, and also turned over to the good minister their cow, bought with their own money, their corn, less a part sold to Sibley,

detailed account of the first services held in the church and the names of the first members are in Albert B. Marshall, *History of the First Presbyterian Church of Minneapolis, Minnesota, 1835–1910*, 11–26 (Minneapolis, 1910). Schoolcraft's certificate to Sibley, dated May 14, 1835, is in the Sibley Papers.

[42] Taliaferro Journal, July 6, 1835; Pond, *Two Volunteer Missionaries*, 63; Thompson Map. See the map facing page 424, *post*.

[43] Pond Papers.

and their potatoes, of which there was a large crop.[44] The consolidation lasted only through the ensuing winter. In the spring of 1836 Gideon Pond, weary of the manual labor heaped upon him "without measure," left to join the mission at Lac qui Parle, where we shall later find him. No sooner had he gone than the elder brother was informed that, as he was only a layman, he was expected to act in the capacity of interpreter and to perform necessary manual labor about the mission.

Samuel Pond had not come to the land of the Dakota to act as interpreter or to do the work of a common laborer for anybody.[45] He, therefore, took his departure for his native state to study theology with his old pastor. On March 4, 1837, he was ordained a minister of the Congregational church, and soon after he set out for the West with money enough, earned by teaching school, to pay his traveling expenses. In the summer of the same year he was appointed a missionary to the Sioux by the American Board. In his narrative Pond remarks that he thought a license to preach would not add anything to his authority or his ability to preach the gospel to the Dakota but it might relieve him from some embarrassment in his intercourse with his clerical associates. While awaiting his appointment he translated the story of Joseph, which was the first publication, with the exception of a few school books, in the Dakota language. In the fall he went on a three months' hunt with his Indians for the purpose of gathering, not pelts, but new Dakota words and phrases. By living with the Indians both brothers gained a mastery of the language not attained by any of their associates. A gift of mimicry aided the

[44] *Missionary Herald*, 32: 188 (May, 1836); S. W. Pond Narrative, 1: 24–26.

[45] G. H. Pond to Ruth Pond, March 16, 1836, Pond Papers; S. W. Pond Narrative, 1: 33, 35; Pond, *Two Volunteer Missionaries*, 107. In his journal, May 23, 1836, Taliaferro records his regret at the departure of the brothers. "I feared looseing these young men when it was decided to open a Mission at Lake Harriet under Mr. J. D. Stevens. The loss of the services of these two disinterested and worthy young men will be a serious loss to the Indians who are much and deservedly attached to them, and I shall loose two faithful & trustworthy assistants in improveing the condition of the Mdawakanton Sioux."

younger brother in understanding the spoken Dakota.[46] Through the years 1838 and 1839 Samuel Pond kept a residence at the Lake Harriet station, but he was absent for considerable periods. In his letters he makes no complaint of interference with his work or of offense to his clerical dignity. He prosecuted his studies in Dakota and near the close of the period finished a small grammar and a dictionary of three thousand words.[47]

Stevens continued in charge of the mission, obtaining, however, but slight influence over the Indians. He either could not or would not acquire the language. He preached frequently in English at the fort or at the mission. He opened two schools: one for Indian children, taught by his niece, who learned Dakota rapidly; the other a small boarding school for the mixed-blood daughters of traders, army officers, and the Indian agent. The rules and regulations of the latter school, elaborate enough for a populous female seminary, have been preserved. In July, 1839, Stevens was appointed farmer to Wabasha's band, which was then living on the site of Winona, and resigned from the Lake Harriet mission, of which Samuel Pond then took charge.[48] The retirement of Stevens was attended by disagreeable incidents, not fully revealed, and probably not worthy of the reader's attention. The secretary of the American Board wrote his successor that the resignation was a relief to the board and advised him to have no further dealings with Stevens either in business or in mission affairs. There is small ground for believing that any of the Calhoun Indians

[46] S. W. Pond Narrative, 1: 26–28, 36, 41–43, 89; Pond, *Two Volunteer Missionaries*, 67–69, 115–123.

[47] S. W. Pond to his sister, January 7, 1840, Pond Papers.

[48] S. W. Pond Narrative, 1: 29, 41. The rules of the school are in the Sibley Papers, under date of August 18, 1836. An account of a "commencement" at the school is in the Taliaferro Journal, December 30, 1836. The agent and Henry H. Sibley attended as "Visitors, Inspectors &c." Major Loomis, Lieutenant Ogden, and Dr. Emerson with their families were also present. They all "passed a pleasant as well as a highly satisfactory day." According to Riggs, *Forty Years with the Sioux*, 20, "of the girls in that first Dakota boarding-school, quite a good proportion became Christian women and the mothers of Christian families." The departure of Stevens is recorded in the Taliaferro Journal, July 11, 1839.

were saved by his ministrations from — the fate of uncon-
verted Indians.[49]

For two reasons the Dakota band on Lake Calhoun was
soon obliged to leave its fields and dwellings. The situation was too easily accessible to the Chippewa warriors who
would be sure to seek revenge for the slaughter on Rum
River on July 3, 1839. Moreover, Major Plympton had
decided that he would have no Indian village inside the
military reservation, which he was engaged in delimiting.[50]
The history of the Lake Harriet mission thereafter is so
meager that it may conveniently be disposed of while the
matter is in hand. As soon as they had gathered their crops
of corn and potatoes in the fall of 1839, the Indians moved
their stuff and encamped on the north side of the Minnesota
about six miles above Fort Snelling. They chose a convenient and beautiful spot long known, and to a few still
known, as Oak Grove.[51] More than four years now elapsed
during which the mission was virtually suspended. Some
time passed pending the negotiation of the Doty treaty, and
more pending the action of the Senate. Had the treaty been
confirmed all the lower Sioux would have been moved far to
the west; but it was not confirmed. Meanwhile the missionaries at the inland stations, without ascertaining the
views of the Ponds, advised the board that it would be a
sound policy to locate them at the Traverse des Sioux or at

[49] S. W. Pond Narrative, 1: 55; David Greene, secretary of the American Board, to
S. W. Pond, March —, August 14, October 12, 1839, February 18, April 29, 1840, Pond
Papers. This correspondence shows that Stevens entertained views with regard to the
disposition of the sum of five hundred dollars allowed by the Indian office in 1839 in which
the board did not fully concur. See also Pond, *Two Volunteer Missionaries*, 73.

[50] S. W. Pond Narrative, 1: 55; Taliaferro Journal, October 5, 1839. The sketch map
given by Major Taliaferro, which must have been made from a rough verbal statement, is
not of value. The lines do not correspond with those of the Thompson Map. There is
an account of a previous survey in Williams, *Saint Paul*, 38, 60, 77, 95, 99. The establishment of the lines of the military reservation had an effect upon the location of St. Paul.
See *post*, p. 223.

[51] Major Plympton and Colonel Bruce attempted to locate the Calhoun band and
their missionaries on the Credit River on the site of the village of Hamilton. Major
Plympton, however, was transferred to another post and Colonel Bruce became indifferent;
so both the band and the mission remained at Oak Grove. See the S. W. Pond Narrative,
1: 55–58. An interesting description of the site is in Pond, *Two Volunteer Missionaries*,
166.

‑ ‑ Divisions of time &c.

The Year will be divided into four terms or Quarters
of twelve weeks Each, with a vacation of the school
one week at the termination of Each Quarter — at
which time there will be an examination of the
School, and every thing pertaining to it. The Exam-
-ination will be in the presence of any who feel disposed to witness it.

5th ‑ ‑ Divisions of Each Day) (Sunday Excepted)

Eight and a half hours allowed for Sleep
Six hours for Study or School hours
Four hours for Labour ‑ ‑ ‑ ‑
Three hours occupied for meals, and family worship
Two and a half hours for recreation ‑ 24.h

th ‑ ‑ Order of Each day in respect to time

1st ‑ Hour for rising in the morning) 5 oclock
2 ‑ Half an hour for dressing and washing) ‑
" ‑ Half an hour for Labour ‑
" ‑ Half an hour for recreation or reading)
5th ‑ Breakfast at half past 6 oclock ‑ Breakfast and morning worship
6th ‑ One and a half hours labour immediately after breakfast
7th ‑ School goes in at 9 oclock ‑ Dismissed at 12. 3 hours in
8th ‑ Half an hour for recreation ‑
9th ‑ Dine at half past 12 oclock One hour allowed) ‑
" ‑ School recommences at half past 1 oclock — dismissed at ½ past 4 o
11th ‑ Two & a half hours Labour immediately after School ‑

RULES OF THE LAKE HARRIET MISSION SCHOOL

[Facsimile of the third page of an original document in the Sibley Papers. The document consists of four
pages and is dated August 18, 1836.]

Lake Traverse.   And the board seems to have approved the recommendation.   At the risk of being reproached for contumacy, the brothers flatly refused to take their families "among the desperadoes of that lawless region."   And the board did not insist.[52]   During the two years 1840 and 1841 the Pond families resided in the "Stone House" at Camp Coldwater, but Samuel was absent for the latter year supplying at Lac qui Parle for one of the missionaries there. In the summer of 1843 they all moved into the large log house which Gideon Pond had built near the Indian camp on the Minnesota, in the south part of what is now the township of Bloomington, Hennepin County.   Gideon Pond lived in it, and in the better one which replaced it, till the end of his life in 1878.   In 1848 he was ordained to the ministry, having prepared for it by private study during many years.[53]

In the year 1846 Samuel Pond, upon the suggestion of Oliver Faribault the trader, was invited by Shakopee to move to his village near the site of the present city on the

[52] S. W. Pond Narrative, 1:61; letters of Secretary Greene to S. W. Pond, April 2, June 15, 1841, February 12, 1842, December 23, 1843, Pond Papers.   An additional reason for the unwillingness of the Ponds to leave their Lake Calhoun Indians was the appointment of the younger brother as farmer for the band.   Taliaferro made the appointment, which carried with it a salary of six hundred dollars a year, under the treaty of 1837.   The elder brother held the place temporarily during the winter of 1838-39.   The liberal appropriation for farming enabled the agents to appoint a farmer for each of the several bands of lower Sioux.   According to the account of S. W. Pond, most of the appointees regarded the position as a sinecure, punctually drew the salary, hired the plowing done for the Indians, and used the animals, wagons, and implements for their own purposes.   Subagent Murphy, in his annual report for 1848, stated that the farmer at Wabasha's village, who was dismissed in August of that year, had never resided there.   It was the opinion of this agent that a single well-managed farm would have been more beneficial than all the scattered ones and that the government would have saved money by buying in the market an amount of produce equal to that raised on all the Indian farms.   Taliaferro took great interest in the Indian farms.   Perhaps it was on his suggestion that the liberal allowance for this work was made in the treaty.   It was ever his opinion that the Indians must be civilized before they could be converted.   In his report for 1838 he said, "I have endeavored to impress all missionaries with the true fact that Christianity must be preceded by civilization among the wild tribes . . . an Indian must be taught all the *temporal* benefits of this life first, before you ask him to seek for eternal happiness hereafter."   S. W. Pond Narrative, 1: 46, 51, 54; Murphy, in 30 Congress, 2 session, *House Executive Documents*, no. 1, p. 474 (serial 537); Taliaferro, in 25 Congress, 3 session, *House Documents*, no. 2, p. 495 (serial 344).

[53] S. W. Pond Narrative, 1: 56, 65, 68; G. H. Pond to S. W. Pond, November 11, 1842, January 2, 1843, Pond Papers.   These letters contain an account of the building of the mission house at Oak Grove.   The stone house was that built by Benjamin F. Baker, the trader.

Minnesota which bears the chief's name and to open a
school and a mission. Shakopee promised that his people
would send their children to the school and agreed to allow
fuel and pasturage for the mission. After some deliberation
Pond decided to accept the invitation and built a frame
house at Prairieville, as he named the place. In the fall of
1847 he occupied it with his family, and in it he kept his
home till his death in 1891.[54] Before their separation the
brothers working coöperatively, the elder performing the
clerical work, had completed a Dakota dictionary, which
was borrowed and copied at the inland stations. It contained as many words as that published five years later.[55] On
taking leave of the Pond brothers it ought to be remarked
that, although they had received in early life but elementary
schooling, they became learned in languages. They knew
and spoke Dakota better than any other white men. They
learned French, Latin, Greek, and Hebrew. Samuel
learned German also and made a small Hebrew-Dakota
dictionary. In his last years he made a comparative study
of the Vulgate and the Septuagint and wrote an article on
the chronology of the Septuagint, which was published the
week of his death.[56] So much more does the student himself avail than any apparatus of schools, colleges, and
libraries.

Williamson with his party reached Lac qui Parle on the
ninth of July, 1835. He was thirty-five years of age, a
graduate of Jefferson College, Pennsylvania, and of the
Yale Medical School. He had practiced medicine for nine
years near his family home in Adams County, Ohio, before

---

[54] S. W. Pond Narrative, 1: 70, 73.

[55] S. W. Pond Narrative, 1: 89. See also the Appendix, no. 3, *post.*

[56] Pond, *Two Volunteer Missionaries,* 251, 264; *Minnesota Historical Collections,* 3:
361, 366, 370. In the Pond Papers is a letter from S. W. Pond to his sister, Mrs. Rebecca
Hine, December 10, 1840, in which he says: "I have spent a little time lately in studying
Hebrew. I think I can learn to read the greatest part of the Bible in that language with-
out much difficulty. I have continued to read the Greek since I left home [*1837*] and can
understand most of the New Testament in Greek nearly as well as in English." The
Hebrew-Dakota dictionary is in the manuscript collection of the Minnesota Historical
Society.

devoting himself to the gospel ministry and in particular
to mission work among the Indians. On receiving his
license to preach from his local presbytery in the spring of
1834 he was sent by the American Board to visit the country
of the Sauk and Foxes and to gather what information he
could about the Sioux and other northwestern tribes. He
continued his journey up the Mississippi where he found the
Pond brothers beginning their work. It was doubtless on
the strength of his report that the American Board appointed
him a missionary to the Dakota after his ordination in
September. He was a man of intense but simple piety,
possessed of strong common sense and indefatigable industry, absolutely devoted to the missionary life. Discouragements and obstacles only roused him to new and stronger
effort.[57] Utterly ignorant of the Indian language, he and
his associates for many months made but slight impression
on the Wahpeton. He presently organized a church with
three members to which was soon added the Indian wife of
Renville, made so by Christian rite before the missionaries
came. Renville, although educated a Roman Catholic,
joined the church, became a ruling elder, and magnified his
office.[58] Aware of the value of such an assistant as Gideon
Pond, Williamson soon invited him to his station. As
we have already learned, Pond was more than content to
leave Lake Harriet. He arrived at Lac qui Parle in April,
1836, and at once set about building the big log mission house,
taking his part with the whipsaw on the needed boards.

As soon as the mission was housed Williamson set about
what was to become the principal work of his life, the translation of the Sacred Scriptures into Dakota. In Renville
and Gideon Pond he found efficient guides and helpers.
The work was carried on in the living room of Fort Renville,
with members of the bodyguard seated on the surrounding
benches smoking their pipes. Williamson read the French

    [57] Riggs, in *Minnesota Historical Collections*, 3: 372–374; 6: 126; Riggs, *Forty Years
with the Sioux*, 345–348.
    [58] Neill, in *Minnesota Historical Collections*, 1: 204, 205.

version from the great family Bible of his host. Renville, accustomed to rapid interpretation, promptly dictated the Dakota translation to Gideon Pond, who acted as scribe. In that winter, 1837-38, the Gospel of Mark and selected chapters from other books were translated. They were printed in Cincinnati in 1839 under the editorship of Williamson.[59] In the winter of 1838-39 a beginning was made in translating the Gospel of John, also from the French. Much was expected from the coöperation of the Reverend Daniel Gavin, who was one of the two Swiss Protestant missionaries lately established at Red Wing's village, and who had come up to Lac qui Parle to prosecute his study of the Dakota. It may easily be believed that his French was much more classical than that of the hospitable trader, but the latter had difficulty in appreciating the fact. By the time the seventh chapter was reached relations between the two had become so strained that the work was abandoned. From that time the missionaries translated from the original tongues. Renville afterwards furnished a translation of the Gospel of Luke and a number of hymns in Dakota, some of which are still sung by the Santee in Nebraska.[60]

The American Board was disposed to expend liberally on the Lac qui Parle mission. Because it was situated far from white settlements and from any military post, it was believed that the Indians, thus fortunately isolated, would be the more likely to accept the truth and live according to its principles. The first reënforcement was the Reverend Stephen Return Riggs, who arrived in September, 1837, after spending three months at Lake Harriet studying the Dakota language with Samuel Pond. He had just closed a year's study at a theological seminary after graduation at Jefferson College and was now twenty-five years of age and happily

[59] S. W. Pond Narrative, 1: 30–33. Stevens, *Personal Recollections*, 386, quoting from a lost diary of G. H. Pond, July 14, 17, 1837.
[60] S. W. Pond Narrative, 1: 33; Riggs, *Forty Years with the Sioux*, 52. The Minnesota Historical Society has a letter written in 1837 or 1838 by Alexander Huggins to his brother, in which he describes the way in which the first translation was made.

married. When he was still a boy his people moved to or near the village of Ripley, Ohio, the home of the Williamson family, where he attended a Latin school lately opened. He naturally heard much about the departure of Williamson to the Dakota field and his work there. He himself states that Williamson's "representations of the needs of these aborigines" attracted him to the same field.[61] Riggs possessed a native talent for language, and no little literary ability. His still youthful heart burned with zeal to aid in saving some souls from the penalty of original and individual sin and to lead them into the green pastures of the Christian life. It was natural for him to enter upon the work of translation and the preparation of much-needed textbooks for the mission schools. With the start given him by Samuel Pond he learned the Indian language rapidly and after some two years began to preach, but it was not till years later that he spoke with "joy and freedom."[62] Few of the missionaries ever attained such fluency. After five years of labor at Lac qui Parle, Riggs was detached by the American Board to establish a mission at the Traverse des Sioux among a band of lower Sisseton residing thereabout. Four years of labor and sorrow passed with disappointing results, and he was more than content to go back in 1846 to Lac qui Parle to take charge of the station made vacant by the departure of Williamson.

Some of the native converts, mostly women, at Lac qui Parle had made their way to the village of Little Crow at Kaposia and had reported the good work done by the missionaries. That chief, who was not without sense, was disposed to secure like advantages for his band, and through the Indian agent he invited Williamson to come and open a school and a mission.[63] Such is the explanation given by

[61] Riggs, *Forty Years with the Sioux*, 4–7. See *Minnesota Historical Collections*, 6: 187, for a brief biographical sketch of Riggs.

[62] S. W. Pond Narrative, 1: 40; Riggs, *Forty Years with the Sioux*, 19, 35–37.

[63] Riggs, *Forty Years with the Sioux*, 76–100; Riggs, in *Minnesota Historical Collections*, 6: 152; S. W. Pond Narrative, 1: 63–65; Holcombe, in *Minnesota in Three Centuries*, 2: 180.

Riggs of the transferal of Williamson from Lac qui Parle
to Kaposia; but a better one may, perhaps, be found in the
fact that for some years before 1845, the year in which his
father, Big Thunder, died and left him heir to the chieftainship of the Kaposia band, Little Crow had been living in
virtual banishment at Lac qui Parle, where he had married
three daughters of a Wahpeton chief.   They may have come
under missionary influences, and he must have observed the
effects of the mission on the Indians.   Little Crow may,
therefore, have resolved to signalize his accession to authority by securing the establishment of a mission, and he
doubtless selected Williamson because of his personal knowledge of the qualities and merits which the missionary
possessed.   Doubtless the missionary in accepting the invitation was influenced by a desire to place his growing family
nearer a civilized environment, but it may be surmised that
he was more than willing to escape with his family from the
barbarous Wahpeton, no longer restrained by the powerful
hand of Renville, who in March, 1846, had died the death of
the righteous.[64]   Desirable as had been the protection of the
mission by Renville, it had not been unattended by embar-
rassments.   Educated in the Roman Catholic religion, the
trader did not hold to such rigid standards of faith and
morals as did the Protestant missionaries of Calvinistic
persuasion.   As the chief personage of the place and a ruling
elder, he easily felt himself the head of the church and
insisted that persons converted and prepared by him should
be admitted to the church.   Under this tolerant dispensa-
tion in the course of seven years forty-nine persons, some of
doubtful qualifications, became communicants.   By 1846,
persecution by heathen Indians, deaths, removals, and
backsliding had reduced the number by more than one-half.[65]

    [64] Riggs, in *Minnesota Historical Collections*, 6:153.   The Methodist mission at
Kaposia had been moved to Red Rock.   For an account of the death of Renville, at the age
of sixty-seven, see Neill, in *Minnesota Historical Collections*, 1:205.
    [65] Pond, *Two Volunteer Missionaries*, 161; Riggs, *Forty Years with the Sioux*, 100;
S. W. Pond Narrative, 1:82–87.   Pond writes, "The fact is Mr Renvilles ideas of religion

LITTLE CROW'S VILLAGE

From Henry Lewis, Das illustrirte Mississippithal, 1848

SAMUEL W. POND'S MISSION HOUSE, SHAKOPEE

After his return to Lac qui Parle, Riggs gave much time to the completion of the Dakota dictionary, which had been slowly growing since the arrival of the missionaries, and to its preparation for the press. An effort to secure subscriptions for its publication ceased when it was learned that the Smithsonian Institution, after an examination by experts, would publish it. The work appeared in 1852 as a handsome quarto of 338 pages under the title "Grammar and Dictionary of the Dakota Language, collected by members of the Dakota Mission, edited by Rev. S. R. Riggs." It is a matter of regret that the reverend editor did not take occasion to give to the Ponds, especially to the elder brother, adequate credit for their contributions to the grammar and dictionary and for their ingenious adaptation of the Roman alphabet to the Dakota language. While Riggs was more than an editor, the Pond brothers were more than nameless collectors of words.[66]

Three other missions to the Dakota, hopefully begun, were too short lived and fruitless to warrant extended accounts in this work. In 1836 the Committee of Missions of Lausanne, Switzerland, sent two Protestant missionaries to aid in evangelizing the Dakota. After a brief but discouraging effort with Wabasha's band, then living on or near the site of Winona, they moved up to Red Wing's village at the head of Lake Pepin, hoping to have better success with the small band of Wahpekute there than they had had among the Indians below, who were too abundantly supplied with whisky from Prairie du Chien. The Reverend Daniel Gavin and the Reverend Samuel Dentan and their devoted American wives seem to have labored faithfully, but no record remains of noteworthy results. In 1845 Gavin was compelled by the impaired health of his wife to retire, and his colleague soon followed him. In 1848 the American

were derived chiefly from Catholics, and we could have had plenty of such converts as his at Lake Calhoun or Oak Grove if we had had a Mr. Renville to 'convert' and 'prepare' them."

[66] For a discussion of the authorship of this work, see the Appendix, no. 3.

Board sent the Reverend Joseph W. Hancock and the Reverend John F. Aiton to continue the work of Gavin and Dentan; this they did till the Indians were removed.[67]

The brief experiment by the Methodist Episcopal church toward the evangelization of the Dakota was originated by the Reverend Alfred Brunson, a preacher of the Pittsburgh conference.[68] Upon reading the report of Lieutenant Allen, commandant of Schoolcraft's military escort on his expedition to the source of the Mississippi in 1832, he was so much affected by the account of the wretched condition of the Indians of the regions traversed that he felt a strong desire to see a mission established among them. In 1835, at the age of forty-two years, he obtained a transfer to the Illinois conference and was assigned to the Galena district, extending from Rock Island to the Falls of St. Anthony. In the following summer he moved his family to Prairie du Chien and established it in a house built from materials brought by keel boat from his old home in Meadville, Pennsylvania. It was not till May, 1837, that he was able to set out for his mission on the upper Mississippi. He took with him David King as teacher, a farmer and his family, a hired man, and an interpreter. The last named was one James Thompson, a negro, whom he found at Prairie du Chien as the servant of an army officer. Thompson had been with his master at Fort Snelling, had married a Dakota woman, and had picked up some of her language. He professed to be pious and was devout. The missionary, already an abolitionist, saw here an opportunity to serve the good cause by setting

[67] S. W. Pond Narrative, 1: 38–40; Riggs, in *Minnesota Historical Collections*, 6: 134, 154; Pond, *Two Volunteer Missionaries*, 111, 176, 178. Writing on June 11, 1846, the Reverend C. A. Dupples, president of the Committee of Missions of Lausanne, asked Samuel Pond if Dentan could bear the burden after the departure of Gavin. Pond Papers.

[68] This account is derived mainly from Brunson, *Western Pioneer*, 2: chs. 3, 4, 5. See also Brunson to Benjamin F. Hoyt, March 28, 1859, in the Minnesota Methodist Historical Society Papers; Riggs, in *Minnesota Historical Collections*, 6: 135–143; and Holcombe, in *Minnesota in Three Centuries*, 2: 261–270. All these relations include brief statements of Elder Brunson's establishment of short-lived missions among the Chippewa of the Mississippi Valley. Brunson was a representative of St. Croix County in the Wisconsin territorial legislature in 1840 and was Chippewa agent at La Pointe from 1842 to 1843. His journal is in the manuscript collection of the State Historical Society of Wisconsin.

a bondman free.   The generous owner valued his property
at two thousand dollars but, to aid the cause of missions,
would sell him for twelve hundred dollars.   An appeal was
made through the *Western Christian Advocate* for means to
make the purchase, and "the money came in in showers";
the pious slave soon had his free papers.   It may as well be
said here that the investment was a disappointment.   The
happy freedman's piety did not long survive his emancipa-
tion, his morals were or became depraved, and he was of
slight account as an interpreter.   It is reported that soon
after his early dismissal he opened a whisky shop on the east
side of the Mississippi opposite Fort Snelling.   The mission
party, properly authorized by the secretary of war to enter
the Indian country for its purposes, was duly welcomed by
the commandant at Fort Snelling and by Major Taliaferro,
the Indian agent.   Upon the invitation of the Little Crow
of that day,[69] the village of Kaposia on the site of South
St. Paul was chosen as the scene of operation.   A log house
was at once built and a garden was dug up and planted.
King began immediately the study of the Dakota language,
but not to employ it, as the Presbyterian missionaries had
been doing, in translating the Scriptures for the Indians.
The leader decided that the Indian children and the adults
also so far as possible should be taught the English language.
The knowledge of this language would enable them to do
business with the whites and would open the whole range of
its literature including the Bible.   One may venture the
opinion that this policy, if long and patiently adhered to,
would have proved the better one.

In the summer of 1837 Elder Brunson made a hasty
journey to Prairie du Chien and found there three young
Canadian Chippewa, John Johnson,[70] George Copway, and
Peter Marksman, who had been sent to the States to be put
to school.   Before the summer was over he took them up

[69] His proper name in English was Big Thunder.

[70] John Johnson was the Indian, better known as Enmegahbowh, who afterwards
became a missionary of the Protestant Episcopal church.

to Kaposia, where they proved themselves expert axmen in the building of a log schoolhouse and a dwelling. The young Indian converts were taken to the fort at the time of the negotiation of the Chippewa treaty of that year. The commissioners, the officials, and the Presbyterian missionaries were pleased with these first fruits of mission planting. The converts gave some aid in interpreting. In the fall of the same year they were shown off at the Illinois conference as examples of Indian conversions. It was not till the spring of 1838 that the head of the mission was able to return to Kaposia, where he found the farming going on prosperously under King's direction. The school, however, was not flourishing, because of the irregularity of attendance. This was Brunson's last visit. A long illness detained him at his home till the following spring. In the meantime brethren of his conference, from motives not understood, suggested that the Dakota mission was costing too much for the apparent results, and some went so far as to insinuate that Brunson was making profit in land operations at Prairie du Chien. To these charges he replied through the conference organ with such vigor that they were heard of no more.[71] Nevertheless, the elder was constrained to resign from the mission and from active ministerial work in the fall of 1839. His successor, the Reverend B. T. Kavenaugh, found the mission depleted by resignations, the Indians unfriendly and even insolent. Little Crow had ordered the school closed because he did not want the boys spoiled as soldiers.[72] In 1841 the reduced mission was transferred across the Mississippi to a point near the well-known Red Rock of the Sioux, and a school was opened for the children of whites and mixed-bloods. From this station Methodism was radiated over Minnesota. So far as known no Indian converts were

[71] Brunson, *Western Pioneer*, 2:81, 127–135.
[72] Taliaferro Journal, August 10, 1838. The agent informed Brunson that the chief had decided not to send the children to school until he had received his annuities under the treaty of the previous year. On October 25, 1842, David King wrote to S. W. Pond, "Our missions and school have been all abandoned. The property is all for sale." Pond Papers.

made, but the conversion of one white man and his family was worth, in the estimation of Elder Brunson, the whole cost of the Kaposia mission. This man was one Jacob Falstrom, a Swede who had emigrated from the Selkirk settlement years before the building of Fort Snelling and had engaged in the service of the American Fur Company. He became a preacher and a missionary and at length a pioneer settler in Washington County. Samuel Pond's judgment of the Methodist experiment was summed up in the phrase, "so badly managed."[73]

An effort to establish a Roman Catholic mission to the Sioux was made by the Reverend Augustin Ravoux, a French cleric, who, in 1841 was commissioned by the bishop of Dubuque to visit the nation. In the fall of that year Ravoux visited the Traverse des Sioux and in the following winter he passed two or three months at Lac qui Parle. In 1842 another visit was made to the Traverse des Sioux and a mission was opened at Chaska, then called Little Rock. Father Ravoux acquired enough of the language to write in it a little book entitled *The Path to the House of God*, which was published. This much-respected priest lived till 1906, having long held the office of vicar-general of the diocese of St. Paul.[74]

The story of the Dakota missions is a melancholy one. It was uphill work all the way for the men and women who gave their years of toil and sacrifice to these barbarians. On a previous page were suggested the primary reasons for the Indian's rejection of the white man's religion: race hatred, attachment to his ancient superstitions, the influence of the medicine men, and the evil example of some white men.

[73] S. W. Pond *Narrative*, 80; Winchell, *Aborigines of Minnesota*, 508; Holcombe, in *Minnesota in Three Centuries*, 2: 268; *Minneapolis Journal*, March 29, 1914.

[74] Augustin Ravoux, *Reminiscences, Memoirs, and Lectures* (St. Paul, 1890), and *The Labors of Mgr. A. Ravoux among the Sioux or Dakota Indians* (pamphlet, St. Paul, 1897); Newson, *Pen Pictures*, 25–27; Stevens, *Personal Recollections*, 59; Sibley, in *Minnesota Historical Collections*, 3: 269; Williams, *Saint Paul*, 113–115; Ravoux to Sibley, December 15, 1866, Sibley Papers. *The Path to the House of God* was published in Dakota under the title of *Wakantanka ti ki canku* in 1843. A second edition appeared in 1863.

The missionaries frequently added to these the tireless industry of Satan, the enemy of souls. These considerations
were operative on all the Dakota Indians in Minnesota, but
there were others which rendered the lower bands at first
indifferent and later hostile to the missionaries. Chief of
these was the annuity system with its consequences. The
annuities granted to the Sioux by the treaty of Prairie du
Chien in 1830, amounting to little more than presents to
the chiefs and headmen, had but a slight demoralizing effect.
Sibley dates the decay of the Sioux from the treaty of 1837.
Up to that time they had lived in comfort — as comfort goes
with savages. The men had been industrious in hunting;
the women, in fishing and tending their corn and potato
patches. Respected chiefs maintained a good degree of
peace and order in their villages. Ignorant of the value of
money, they immensely exaggerated the promised benefits of
the treaty. They imagined that the annual payments would
so nearly give them a living that they would need to hunt
and fish only for pleasure. From that time the men would
not touch a plow. They preferred to stand in the shade of a
silk parasol and watch their women toil. The young men,
idle and reckless, came to despise the reasonable rule of the
chiefs and spent much time in gambling and sports. The
day of payment became the great day of the year. The
money received, after the traders were paid, went for useless
ornaments and trinkets. They gorged for a few days on the
provisions, which, if cared for and added to their game and
fish, might have lasted for months. No better illustration
of the iniquity of the annuity system is easily found.[75]

The intended and effectual purpose of the treaty of 1837
was to open to settlement all the Sioux land east of the

[75] S. W. Pond Narrative, 1: 52; Philander Prescott, in 31 Congress, 2 session, *House
Executive Documents*, no. 1, p. 119 (serial 595); Sibley, in *Minnesota Historical Collections*, 1:
461. "Ceasing gradually to rely," says Sibley, "upon their own efforts for support, they
looked forward with more and more anxiety to the pittance annually doled out to them in
money, goods and provisions. . . . Recourse to liquor, and other evil habits, are but the
natural consequences of that system which drives him [*the Indian*] from his home, interferes
with his habits of life, and regards him as an outcast from the land of his fathers, without
holding out to him any promise for the future."

Mississippi, or rather to enable the adventurous lumbermen to get at the pineries of the St. Croix and the upper Mississippi. An incidental effect was that the whisky trade was permitted to be opened anywhere along the left bank of the great river. The sellers lost no time in establishing their "groceries" opposite the Indian villages. They were not breaking the law forbidding the introduction of whisky into the Indian country. The Indian came over to the white man's country and bought the coveted fire water. Immediately after the first payment under the treaty in September, 1839, there began a carnival of intoxication which continued for years. No better description has been found than that by Gideon H. Pond in 1851 in his short-lived newspaper, the *Dakota Friend*.[76] "Twelve years ago they bade fair soon to die, all together, in one drunken jumble. They must be drunk — they could hardly live if they were not drunk. — Many of them seemed as uneasy when sober, as a fish does when on land. At some of the villages they were drunk months together. There was no end to it. They *would* have whisky. They would give guns, blankets, pork, lard, flour, corn, coffee, sugar, horses, furs, traps, any thing for whisky. It was made to drink — it was good — it was wakan. They drank it, — they bit off each other's noses, — broke each other's ribs and heads, they knifed each other. They killed one another with guns, knives, hatchets, clubs, fire-brands; they fell into the fire and water and were burned to death, and drowned; they froze to death, and committed suicide so frequently, that for a time, the death of an Indian in some of the ways mentioned was but little thought of by themselves or others." It is pleasant to record that their best men at length became alarmed and united in a reform

[76] "The Treaty with the Mdewakantonwan and Warpekute Bands of Dakotas," in the *Dakota Tawaxitku Kin, or the Dakota Friend*, 1: no. 11 (St. Paul, September, 1851). A file of the *Dakota Friend* is in the library of the Minnesota Historical Society. The first volume, begun in November, 1850, contains twelve numbers. Of the second volume, which was much enlarged, but eight numbers were issued. Half of the matter was in Dakota. See Riggs, *Forty Years with the Sioux*, 87–89. For the reports made by Agent Bruce and Riggs in 1846, see 29 Congress, 2 session, *House Documents*, no. 4, pp. 245–247, 314 (serial 497).

movement, which was seconded by the missionaries, the military officers, the agent, Sibley, and the respectable licensed traders in the Indian country. The result was a marked diminution in the consumption of liquor and a corresponding increase in the peace and comfort of the Indians.[77] Still an old Sisseton chief at the Traverse could not understand why white people should object to the Indians' enjoyment of good liquor, while they placed no limit on their own.

There was another ground for suspicion of and at length for active opposition to mission effort in school and church. The treaty of 1837 with the Mdewakanton contained, as part of the consideration for the land ceded to the United States, an ambiguous item granting an annual sum, which might amount to five thousand dollars, "to be applied in such manner as the President may direct." The understanding was that this money should constitute "an education fund," but the treaty did not so state in terms. In spite of executive directions, through influence now impossible to trace, this money was left for long to accumulate in the treasury. Those who hoped for a different destination of the money for years darkly hinted to the Indians that the missionaries were getting it, or were going to get it. The only ground for this suspicion was that in 1839, upon the recommendation of Agent Taliaferro approved by the Indian office, the sum of five hundred dollars was paid to Stevens and to each of the two Swiss missionaries toward the support of their schools. Years passed and, as the ambiguous fund accumulated, the clamor of the Sioux for cash distribution became every year louder. Moved by the suggestions of traders, whose strong boxes would not be the lighter by the disbursements of those thousands of silver and gold, the Indians became in the late forties even more distrustful of the missionaries and teachers.[78] When the lower

[77] Neill, *Minnesota*, 510; annual report of Subagent Murphy, 1849, in 31 Congress, 1 session, *Senate Executive Documents*, no. 1, p. 1053 (serial 550).

[78] Riggs, *Forty Years with the Sioux*, 56; Taliaferro's report for 1839, in 26 Congress, 1 session, *House Documents*, no. 2, p. 515 (serial 363). The final disposition of the accumulated fund in 1851 is discussed on pages 285-287, *post*.

Sioux were removed to their reservation on the upper Minnesota after the treaty of Mendota, in 1851 and 1852, all their mission stations — Red Wing, Kaposia, Oak Grove, and Prairieville — were abandoned. The clerical missionaries at these stations remained as pastors of local white congregations, with the exception of Williamson, who was transferred to a new station among the Wahpeton near the Yellow Medicine agency. Why the lower Sioux were left on their reservation without a missionary for seven years, from 1853 to 1860, remains a matter of conjecture. Did Williamson prefer resuming life among the wild Wahpeton to continuing his labor with the besotted lower Indians?[79]

The inland missions at the Traverse des Sioux and Lac qui Parle suffered less, but more than enough, from the evil effects of the treaty of 1837, to which their Indians were not parties. Whisky-sellers could not penetrate to their villages, but Indians themselves engaged in the ruinous traffic. Kegs of whisky bought of Indians below were easily transported by canoe to the Traverse, where they were packed on horses in quantities sufficient to cause a great deal of drunkenness, even after customary dilution.[80] Although the upper Sioux had no interest in the education fund, they joined in the suspicion that the missionaries were conspiring to absorb it and became indifferent and insulting. The killing of cattle and the destruction of mission property were even more extensive than at the stations below. The mission at the Traverse des Sioux was given up at the same time as those below, but that at Lac qui Parle, reduced in personnel, held on till 1854, when it was moved down to a point near Williamson's new station.[81] There it continued as long as the Sioux remained in Minnesota.

[79] Riggs, in *Minnesota Historical Collections*, 6: 171.
[80] For a typical example see the letter of Williamson to S. W. Pond, written at Lac qui Parle, July 21, 1846. He writes: "Most of the men and some of the women seem crazy after whiskey. [*A backslider convert*] brought up a large horse load from below. . . . The first night in a drunken spree [*an Indian named*] and his son killed two men." Pond Papers.
[81] Riggs, in *Minnesota Historical Collections*, 6: 172.

Numerically considered, the conversions of Dakota Indians to the true religion were pitifully few. Samuel Pond, looking back on his work, was constrained to say: "Before the outbreak of 1862 I saw very few Dakotas who seemed to give evidence of piety. A few at Oak Grove, a few at Lac Qui Parle, and that was all."[82]

[82] Pond, *Two Volunteer Missionaries*, 219; S. W. Pond Narrative, 1: 82.

VIII. FIRST SETTLEMENTS

UP TO the time of the ratification of the treaties of 1837 there were no lands in the area of Minnesota open to settlement. All was "Indian country." Pike's purchase was for military purposes only. Nevertheless, with the doubtful permission of the Indian agent and of the military commanders, a certain nucleus of white settlers had established themselves at Fort Snelling. The newcomers did not come from below in the wake of the military and the traders. They came down before the north wind from the Canadian border and beyond.

In 1811 the Scotch Earl of Selkirk, of philanthropic turn, having secured a controlling interest in the Hudson's Bay Company, acquired from that organization a tract of about 116,000 square miles of land west and south of Lake Winnipeg and the Winnipeg River, to be known as Assiniboia, and comprising roughly the province of Manitoba and the northern part of the states of North Dakota and Minnesota.[1] It was Selkirk's purpose to establish within the limits of his grant colonies of evicted Scotch peasants. On August 30, 1812, an advance body of Scotch with a few Irish emigrants arrived at the confluence of the Red and Assiniboine rivers. In 1813 and 1814 additional bands of colonists, for the most part Scotch Highlanders, numbering about two hundred, reached the new settlement. The Northwest Company regarded these colonists, ostensibly introduced by the Hudson's Bay Company, as intruders into territory which had been explored by Canadian adventurers and in which its trading posts had long been established. Various impediments were thrown in the way of the newcomers, and in the

---

[1] For the text of the grant, see Chester Martin, *Lord Selkirk's Work in Canada*, 201–215 (*Oxford Historical and Literary Studies*, vol. 7 — Oxford, 1916), or Neill, *Minnesota*, 302. It included portions of North Dakota, the valley of the Red River of the North, and the lands of northern Minnesota draining toward Hudson Bay.

summer of 1815 nearly half of them were induced by promises of land, provisions, money, and free transportation to desert the colony and remove to Upper Canada. Those remaining withdrew down the Red River and made their way to Lake Winnipeg. A few months later they returned and were reënforced by a considerable body of new emigrants. In the summer of 1816 the Northwest Company let loose upon the colony a band of *bois brûlés*, mounted and armed, who murdered Governor Semple and twenty men with him.[2] Again the colonists withdrew down the Red River, and the settlement at Fort Douglas was utterly destroyed. In the summer of 1817 Lord Selkirk appeared in person with a reënforcement of about one hundred men who had been discharged from two regiments composed of Swiss, Italians, and other mercenaries for the British Army sent over to aid in the War of 1812 and disbanded at Montreal and Kingston. With this force, which he had armed, he was able to rally and reëstablish his scattered colonists. The unhappy contest between the Hudson's Bay and Northwest Companies went on until their union on March 26, 1821, a year after the death of Lord Selkirk.[3]

[2] William J. Snelling, in his *Tales of the Northwest; or Sketches of Indian Life and Character*, 85 (Boston, 1830), describes the *bois brûlés* as "the offspring of intermarriages of the white traders and their subordinates with Indian women. Good boatmen, expert hunters, and inimitable horsemen . . . their number . . . probably . . . amounts to four or five thousands [*1830*]. . . . They are . . . as ignorant of Christianity as Hottentots. In manners and morals they are on a par with the Indians." Unrestrained by the government, they rejoiced in the title of "*gens libres*," and were called *bois brûlés*, "burnt wood," on account of their complexions. See also Alexander Ross, *The Red River Settlement; Its Rise, Progress, and Present State*, 84–86 (London, 1856); Pope, *Report* (serial 558); Beltrami, *Pilgrimage*, 2: 357; and Keating, *Narrative*, 2: 40.

[3] For the tragic history of the Selkirk settlement, see Martin, *Selkirk's Work in Canada*; Ross, *Red River Settlement*; Charles N. Bell, *The Selkirk Settlement and the Settlers* (Winnipeg, 1887); Bryce, *Hudson's Bay Company*, 202–267; Kingsford, *Canada*, 9: 109–155; the "MacLeod Manuscript," containing the diary of John MacLeod and other documents, in *North Dakota Historical Collections*, 2: 106–134; H. G. Gunn, "The Selkirk Settlement and Its Relation to North Dakota History," in *North Dakota Historical Collections*, 2: 78–106; and Davidson, *Northwest Company*, ch. 6. The controversy between the Hudson's Bay Company and the Northwest Company, which arose as a result of Lord Selkirk's colonizing projects, forms an interesting chapter in the history of the two organizations. The contentions of the former are set forth in *A Letter to the Earl of Liverpool from the Earl of Selkirk; Accompanied by a Correspondence with the Colonial Department (in the Years 1817, 1818, and 1819), on the Subject of the Red River Settlement in North America* (London, 1819), and in John Halkett, *Statement Respecting the Earl of Selkirk's Settlement upon the Red River in*

Before his death in France in 1820 Lord Selkirk had sent one or more agents to the continent to enlist recruits for his colony. One of them succeeded in gathering a company of Swiss mechanics and tradesmen to try their fortunes in a promised El Dorado.[4] After a toilsome journey they reached Fort Douglas late in the fall of 1821. All the marriageable young women of the party were at once bespoken by the disbanded soldiers, and many unions were the result. The Swiss found a condition of things far different from that pictured by the immigration agent in his glowing recitals and in an ingenious prospectus which told the truth and much more than the truth.[5] Five families immediately decided not to remain in the settlement but to proceed at once to the States. The road they took was not an unbroken one. The Hudson's Bay Company had long had its traders as far south as Lake Traverse, where its establishments met a chain of the American Fur Company's posts extending to the mouth of the Minnesota River. In the year 1820 Laidlaw, Lord Selkirk's superintendent of farming, in order to relieve an alarming scarcity of seed grain, had gone down to Prairie du Chien, where he had bought some three hundred bushels of wheat, oats, and peas. These he loaded into keel boats, which he navigated up to the mouth of the Minnesota and onward by way of that river into Big Stone Lake; from there he made a portage of one and one-half miles to Lake

North America (London, 1817); the Northwest Company's side of the question is presented in A Narrative of Occurrences in the Indian Countries of North America since the Connexion of the Right Hon. the Earl of Selkirk with the Hudson's Bay Company and His Attempt to Establish a Colony on the Red River (London, 1817). See also A. Amos, Report of Trials in the Courts of Canada Relative to the Destruction of the Earl of Selkirk's Settlement on the Red River (London, 1820), and Papers Relating to the Red River Settlement, 1815–1819 (printed by order of the House of Commons, July 12, 1819).

⁴According to the reminiscences of Mrs. Ann Adams, one of the emigrants, the party numbered 165. See Minnesota Historical Collections, 6: 79. Their names are given in George Bryce and Charles N. Bell, Original Letters and Other Documents Relating to the Selkirk Settlement, 7 (Historical and Scientific Society of Manitoba, Transactions, no. 33). Among them were "watch and clock makers, pastrycooks and musicians." See Ross, Red River Settlement, 57. General Augustus L. Chetlain, whose father, Louis Chetlain, was of the party, gives in his Red River Colony (Chicago, 1893) some valuable data on the later history of its various members.

⁵ For a copy of the "Prospectus of a Plan for Sending Settlers to the Colony of the Red River in North America," see Beltrami, Pilgrimage, 2: 360–366.

Traverse, reloaded his cargoes, and proceeded down the Bois
des Sioux and the Red to the settlement, where he arrived
on June 3, in time for seeding in that latitude.[6]　Early in
August, 1821, Alexis Bailly, Sibley's predecessor as agent of
the American Fur Company at Mendota, in fulfillment of a
contract with the governor of the Selkirk colony, drove a
herd of cattle down the Red River trail and sold them to the
colonists for one hundred dollars a head and more.　The
five Swiss families probably accompanied his party on its
return.　They were permitted to squat near Fort Snelling.[7]

Two years later, in 1823, thirteen other Swiss families,
discouraged by grasshoppers and rats — cats had not been
imported — left by the same route.　Some of these immediately, others after tarrying for a year or more at Fort
Snelling, went on down river to the French communities
below.　There was probably no year during a double decade
in which some disheartened Selkirk people did not dribble
over the border and take the Red River trail for warmer
climes.　In the summer of 1823 Beltrami relieved some of
them at Fort Snelling and met others at the "Lake of the
Rock" (Big Stone).　It must have been a considerable
migration which the Italian geographer encountered, and
some of them must have been possessed of means.　The
trader Baker complained to Indian Agent Taliaferro that
"these people that come from Red River have lodged about
a hundred head of Cattle in the Bottom where we had inclosed for our Stock and they are destroying the Pasture.
I wish you would direct them to move them over on the
opposite side of the Mississippi."[8]　A long succession of

<hr />

[6] The expedition cost Lord Selkirk six thousand dollars.　Sibley, in *Minnesota Historical Collections*, 1: 470; Ross, *Red River Settlement*, 50, 77.

[7] Sibley, in *Minnesota Historical Collections*, 1: 469; Neill, in *Minnesota Historical
Collections*, 2: 106, 107; Bryce and Bell, *Selkirk Settlement*, 5; Chetlain, *Red River Colony*,
20; Taliaferro Journal, January 12, 1822; Snelling to Taliaferro, November 7, 1821, Taliaferro Papers.

[8] Mrs. Adams, in *Minnesota Historical Collections*, 6: 89–95; George A. Belcourt,
"Department of Hudson's Bay," in *Minnesota Historical Collections*, 1: 220 (St. Paul,
1872); Chetlain, *Red River Colony*, 21–24; Beltrami, *Pilgrimage*, 2: 353; Baker to Taliaferro, July 16, 1823, Taliaferro Papers.

hardships, due to excessive cold, drought, grasshoppers, and mice, culminated in the spring of 1826 in a rise of the Red River which spread wide desolation. This roused many who had intended deserting to immediate action. On June 24 two hundred and forty-three, mostly Swiss, left Pembina in a body.[9] The number of refugees in following years is not chronicled. All these came to Fort Snelling, some under a delusion that the authorities were ready to give them land and farming outfits. Many, after resting, took their way down the Mississippi to settle at and about Galena and other points. A goodly number, however, remained and became the earliest settlers in the oldest towns of the state within a radius of twenty miles from Fort Snelling.[10] A number of farms were opened on the military tract in 1827 and were quietly cultivated until after the ratification of the treaty of 1837.

In the summer preceding the negotiation of that treaty, fearful of an enforced removal if the government were to set aside a definite tract for a military reservation, the squatters sent a memorial to the president praying to be remunerated for their improvements.[11] No attention appears, however, to have been given to the claims of the obscure petitioners. Major Joseph Plympton, who, on August 20, 1837, arrived to assume command at Fort Snelling, immediately interested himself in determining the territorial limits of the post under his jurisdiction and in ascertaining the status of the settlers

[9] Ross, *Red River Settlement*, 97–109; Chetlain, *Red River Colony*, 26. The Taliaferro Journal for the latter half of the year 1826 has not been found.

[10] Neill, in *Minnesota Historical Collections*, 2: 127, states that up to August 1, 1835, four hundred and eighty-nine persons had arrived at Fort Snelling from the Red River settlement. Holcombe estimates that by the year 1840 nearly two hundred more had found their way to the post; in his opinion about one half of the entire number of refugees remained in Minnesota permanently. See *Minnesota in Three Centuries*, 2: 76. In his journal, September 14, 1827, Taliaferro records that the "Red River Colony appears to be diminishing rapidly. . . . Since 1822 it appears that to the number of 330 Swiss, Canadian & Irish Settlers, men women & children have passed this post for the interior of the United States."

[11] The text of the memorial to President Van Buren, dated August 16, 1837, is in *Sale of Fort Snelling Reservation*, 14 (serial 1372). It was the contention of the memorialists that the land acquired by the United States through Pike's treaty was public domain and was therefore open to settlement under the same conditions as was other government land.

in its vicinity.[12]   Under his direction Lieutenant E. K. Smith
made a survey and a map of "Fort Snelling and Vicinity,"
and took a census of the white inhabitants, exclusive of the
garrison, but he did not attempt to set definite boundary
lines for the military reserve.[13]   In a letter transmitting the
map the commandant called the attention of the war department to the "sparseness of timber within the space supposed
to be embraced in Pike's treaty," which resulted in "much
labor and inconvenience to the garrison to obtain the
necessary fuel, and should this point be required for the
next 20 years for military purposes the difficulty will be
great, and very much increased, by these settlements in
obtaining the article of fuel."   Acting on these suggestions,
the war department, on November 17, 1837, issued instructions to Major Plympton "to mark over" what in his judgment should be reserved for military purposes.   Accordingly
Lieutenant Smith prepared a second map outlining such a
tract, "embracing a considerable quantity of land on the
east side of the Mississippi river."   This map was transmitted to the proper officials in Washington, and on July 26,
1838, the settlers were notified by the commandant that they
were residing on land under military jurisdiction and that
further cutting of timber or erection of buildings or other

[12] In a letter to the war department, September 11, 1837, Major Plympton says:
"I should before this have made a full report of the ground which I supposed from the payment made to the Indians in 1819 in my presence, & which at that time was understood by
the Indians to be for military purposes, agreeably to Gen! Pikes treaty, but my bad state
of health since my arrival has prevented.   So soon as my health will permit I shall forward
a statement of particulars.   I take the liberty to address you at this time, from a belief
that many persons will be applying at the War dept. for favors which will continue their
encroachments upon what I have always thot. to be a military reservation, thereby increasing an evil at this post which has at this time a strong commencement."   The original of
this letter is in the files of the Indian office at Washington; the Minnesota Historical Society
has a photostatic copy.
[13] "The white inhabitants in the vicinity of the fort, as near as I could ascertain, are:
82 in Baker's settlement, around old Camp Coldwater, and at Massey's landing.   On the
opposite side, 25 at the fur company's establishment, including Terrebault's [Faribault's]
and Le Clerc's [Le Claire's], 50.   Making a total of 157 souls in no way connected with the
military."   See Smith to Plympton, October 19, 1837, in Sale of Fort Snelling Reservation,
16.   The locations of the settlers and the business establishments are indicated on the Smith
Map of October, 1837.   The Minnesota Historical Society has a photostatic copy of this
map.

improvements was forbidden.[14]   This really amounted to a warning to leave, and a few of the settlers withdrew to the east side of the river, to a point below its confluence with the Minnesota, where they squatted on land which they believed to be outside the reservation.[15]

At every Indian trading post there was a collection of white and half-breed employees, besides some mere hangers-on.   At Mendota, Minnesota center of the American Fur Company, there had long been such a gathering, more numerous than those at minor stations.   Their number varied from season to season, and few were genuine residents.   Still, this hamlet of traders and *voyageurs* may be properly regarded as a settlement nearly contemporaneous with the arrival of the Red River people.   In July, 1839, Bishop Loras of Dubuque visited the station and found 185 Catholics, who welcomed him and with great joy received the sacraments of the church.[16]

Mention has already been made of a class of men disguised as independent traders, but in fact mere whisky-sellers, who planted themselves along the east bank of the Mississippi upon the opening to settlement of the triangle in 1837.   It was the fortune of one of these to be the first to stake a claim on the site of what became the capital city of the state. Pierre Parrant, a Canadian *voyageur*, who had been some

[14] Plympton to Jones, October 19, 1837; Major General Alexander Macomb to Plympton, November 17, 1837, in *Sale of Fort Snelling Reservation*, 16–18, 23, 29.   See also a drawing in a manuscript entitled "History of Fort Snelling, Minnesota," probably compiled from archives in the war department at Washington by Jasper W. Johnson at the suggestion of Alexander Ramsey.

[15] Williams says that assurance was given by the commandant that the boundary of the reserve intersected the Mississippi River at Fountain Cave and that they located therefore along the river beyond this point.   See his *Saint Paul*, 67.   That the line of the second Smith survey cut the river near the cave is confirmed by a statement of Samuel C. Stambaugh.   In a letter to the secretary of war, February 11, 1839, transmitting for a second time the memorial of the settlers residing on the reservation, he says: "It [*the boundary line*] commences some distance above the Falls of St. Anthony on the west side of the Mississippi, but instead of crossing immediately and traversing the country to strike the angle of the river below the fort, it runs along the west side about three miles below the falls, where it crosses the river, and thence strikes across the country to Carver's Cave [*Fountain Cave*], which is three miles below Fort Snelling by the course of the river." *Sale of Fort Snelling Reservation*, 25.

[16] Bishop Loras to his sister, July 26, 1839, in *Annals of the Propagation of the Faith*, 3: 339 (Dublin, September, 1840); reprinted in *Acta et Dicta*, 1: 14 (July, 1907).

years in the region and who had given Indian Agent Taliaferro no little vexation by his illegitimate practices, to make
sure of a first choice of location, began, about the first of
June, 1838, to build a lonely hovel in a secluded gorge at the
mouth of the creek which flowed out of Fountain Cave in
upper St. Paul. The historian of the capital city humorously
conjectures Parrant's motive to have been to make sure of
plenty of water for the navigation of canoes and for the
dilution of fluids intended for Indian consumption. Some of
the Red River refugees, so recently warned off the military
tract west of the Mississippi, took up claims below him.
The Indians complained of this premature occupation of
their land, ceded but not yet accepted nor paid for, but,
the news of the ratification being received, they did not
insist on evacuation.[17]

In the spring of 1839 Major Plympton again agitated the
question of having the reservation cleared of settlers on the
ground that several persons had established whisky shops on
the east side of the river, which were injurious to both the
Indians and the soldiers; at the same time, to afford further
protection to the garrison, he recommended an extension of
the limits previously laid down. A definite and final delimitation of the reserve was also necessary at this time in
order that the general land office might withdraw from sale
the tract required. Plympton's representations to the war
department were corroborated by the surgeon of the post
in a letter to the surgeon-general of the army, in which he
says: "Since the middle of winter we have been completely
inundated with ardent spirits, and consequently the most
beastly scenes of intoxication among the soldiers of this

---

[17] Williams, *Saint Paul*, 64–69. Late in the fall of 1839 Parrant lost his claim near
the cave and immediately thereafter he established himself on a tract farther down the
river extending approximately from the present Minnesota Street to Jackson Street in St.
Paul; at the foot of what is now Robert Street he built a hovel in which he continued to
conduct his liquor business. From his peculiar facial appearance, Parrant was known as
"Pig's Eye"— an appellation that for a time attached itself to the settlement which grew
up around him. See Williams, *Saint Paul*, 75, 84. The Taliaferro Journal, August 22, October 12, 1835, mentions Pierre Parrant under the name of "Peter Perron."

garrison and the Indians in its vicinity. . . . The whiskey is brought here by citizens who are pouring in upon us and settling themselves on the opposite shore of the Mississippi river, in defiance of our worthy commanding officer, Major J. Plympton, whose authority they set at naught. At this moment there is a citizen named Brown, once a soldier in the 5th infantry . . . actually building on the land marked out by the commanding officer as the reserve . . . a very extensive whiskey shop. . . . In my humble opinion the immediate action of the government is called for, to give us relief in pointing out the military reserve, which ought not to be less than 20 miles square, or to the mouth of the St. Croix river." General John E. Wool in an inspection report fully approved of these contentions, and declared that the government "should immediately adopt measures to drive off the public lands all white intruders within 20 miles of Fort Snelling."[18]

The war department accordingly issued directions for another survey, which was made by Lieutenant J. L. Thompson in October and November of 1839. According to Major Plympton the boundaries as fixed by Thompson conformed to those indicated on the Smith Map "with this slight difference, that in his [*Smith's*] survey the principal lines from river to river were necessarily (from the season and weather) left imaginary, which upon an actual survey will be found (to embrace the necessary woodland and to preserve the cardinal points) to cross the Mississippi a little further down than that imaginarily indicated on the map of Lieutenant Smith's survey."[19] "Slight" as was the difference in the two surveys, it was enough to bring within the forbidden limits the small settlement near Fountain Cave. From the settlers there was prompt and lively protest against the action of the military authorities. On the sixteenth of November a public meeting of those interested was held;

[18] *Sale of Fort Snelling Reservation*, 23, 26, 29.
[19] *Sale of Fort Snelling Reservation*, 31.

arrangements were made for the drafting of a petition to the legislature of Wisconsin Territory asking that body "to pass a resolution requesting our Delegate in Congress" to oppose the extension of the military reserve at Fort Snelling to the east side of the Mississippi; and Joseph R. Brown, one of the settlers, was appointed to take the petition to Madison and also "to use his endeavors to procure the passage of such laws as may be best adapted to the wants of this portion of the Territory." On December 16, 1839, the resolution petitioned for was passed by the legislature, and later it was forwarded to the territorial delegate, James D. Doty. In a letter to the secretary of war Doty suggested as a legal obstacle to the proposed extension that the United States had not the right to extend its military jurisdiction by a simple declaration.[20] Neither personal nor official protests were of any avail. The reserve as "marked out" by Lieutenant Thompson was established.

On October 21, 1839, the secretary of war directed the United States marshal of the Territory of Wisconsin to eject all intruders from the reserve and authorized him to call upon the officer commanding at Fort Snelling for such forces as might be deemed necessary. Through a misdirection of the order to Iowa Territory it was not received by the marshal until February 18, 1840. It was May before a deputy was able to reach the scene of action. The considerable population, a large proportion of which was made up of the Swiss who during the two preceding years had been obliged

[20] *Reservation at Fort Snelling; Resolutions of the Assembly of Wiskonsin*, 1–5 (26 Congress, 1 session, *House Documents*, no. 144 — serial 365). In his letter to Doty, Brown gives what the settlers believed to have been the reason for the extension of the reserve: "a company of speculators . . . which included the commanding and other officers of Fort Snelling," desirous of removing all obstacles to the monopoly of the trade of the Mississippi pine region, were using every possible means to obviate the possibility of interference on the part of the settlers. The resolution of the Wisconsin legislature was introduced by Doty in the House of Representatives on March 16, 1840, and was referred to the committee on the judiciary. See 26 Congress, 1 session, *House Journal*, 629, 630 (serial 362). The Minnesota Historical Society has a photostatic copy of the Thompson Map. See the map facing page 424, *post*. There is an entry, accompanied by a drawing, in the Taliaferro Journal, October 5, 1839, noting the laying out of the lines which were to bound the reservation.

to remove from their homes adjacent to the fort on the west side, paid slight attention to his notice to move. On the sixth of May a detachment from the garrison proceeded to remove the people and their goods and to destroy their log cabins. Complaint was made in later years to Congress, and memorials praying indemnity for furniture damaged, cattle killed, and women insulted were submitted, only to find their way into the pigeonholes of committees.[21] The unlucky squatters at once moved in a body and planted themselves beyond the now ascertained line of the reserve on ground that forms the heart of the present city of St. Paul. Among their names are the well-known ones of Abraham Perry, Benjamin Gervais, the purchaser of Parrant's claim, his brother, Pierre Gervais, Joseph Rondo, and Pierre Bottineau. Their scattered shanties formed the nucleus of a nameless settlement on a site selected almost by accident.[22]

Father Lucien Galtier, who had been ministering to the little flock at Mendota for a year, now extended his care over the colony which so suddenly gathered on the broken hillside nearly opposite. On land given by two of the farmers he built in the month of October, 1841, a rude log chapel, which on the first day of November he blessed and "dedicated to Saint Paul, the apostle of nations." As he was residing at

[21] *Wiskonsan Territory — Settlers on the Military Reservation near Fort Snelling* (27 Congress, 2 session, *House Reports*, no. 853 — serial 410); *Sale of Fort Snelling Reservation*, 36. On January 4, 1841, Doty presented in the House of Representatives a petition of "Peter Miller and others, citizens of St. Croix county, in the Territory of Wiskonsin, praying compensation for losses sustained by them in their removal from their settlements on the public lands, by order of the Department of War." The petition was referred to the committee on public lands, which, on June 10, 1842, brought in an adverse report, which was laid on the table. See 26 Congress, 2 session, *House Journal*, 131, 132 (serial 381), and 27 Congress, 2 session, *House Journal*, 942 (serial 400). For the report, see 27 Congress, 2 session, *House Reports*, no. 853 (serial 410). A similar memorial of "Bartholomew Baldin, James R. Clewett, Abner Powel, and Pierre, Benjamin and Julian Gervais, of the Territory of Wisconsin," was introduced in the House by Sibley on January 25, 1849, and was referred to the committee on claims; it was presented a second time by Sibley on January 16, 1852, and was referred to the same committee. 30 Congress, 2 session, *House Journal*, 313 (serial 536); 32 Congress, 1 session, *House Journal*, 222 (serial 632); Williams, *Saint Paul*, 94–100.

[22] For an account of a small and temporary settlement of Canadian *voyageurs* in the employ of the American Fur Company at the Grand Marais on the alluvial bottoms of the river some two miles below the site of the Union Depot in St. Paul, see Williams, *Saint Paul*, 86. Thither in 1844 went Parrant, after disposing of his holdings on the levee above. His sobriquet, "Pig's Eye," by which the lower settlement was at once known, still attaches to the locality. Williams, *Saint Paul*, 85, 101, 146; Neill, *Minnesota*, 475–479.

St. Peter's (Mendota), it was natural that the name "Paul" should be thought of, especially as gentiles in the persons of Indians still abounded in the neighborhood. There being no geographic feature or historic incident to suggest another name, the settlement was soon known as St. Paul's Landing or St. Paul's and later on as St. Paul.[23] Father Galtier expected this and used the name in his official notices. Still, the enterprising priest did not think proper to take up his residence in the new town but remained in the more considerable Mendota until he was called to other duty in 1844. St. Paul did not become an independent parish until the arrival in 1851 of the Right Reverend Joseph Cretin, the first bishop of St. Paul.[24] There were only thirty families or thereabouts in the settlement at the beginning of the year 1845, and the French language was spoken in all but three or four. American names largely predominated, however, in the list of settlers of the next two years, as recorded by the city's historian; St. Paul thus suddenly became American. The accession of newcomers from below was of course not very great, but their enterprise and enthusiasm were phenomenal.[25] A post office was established April 7,

[23] On January 1, 1850, the *Minnesota Pioneer* issued a New Year's greeting to its patrons in the form of a humorous and poetic account of the transformation of "Pig's Eye" to "St. Paul." The poem was reprinted in the issue of January 2, and it is quoted in part in Williams, *Saint Paul*, 113, 247.

[24] The Most Reverend John Ireland, "Memoir of Rev. Lucian Galtier: The First Catholic Priest of Saint Paul," in *Minnesota Historical Collections*, 3: 222–230. On pages 224 to 229 are extracts from a letter of Father Galtier to the Right Reverend Thomas L. Grace, bishop of St. Paul, January 14, 1864, giving an account of his mission in Minnesota. The letter is given in full in *Acta et Dicta*, 1: 184–190 (July, 1908). See also the Reverend Ambrose McNulty, "The Chapel of St. Paul and the Beginnings of the Catholic Church in Minnesota," in *Minnesota Historical Collections*, 10: 233–245 (part 1); on page 238 may be found the relation of Isaac La Bissonniere, one of the builders of the chapel. The author of the present work had substantially the same account from Mr. La Bissonniere on November 6, 1909. Captain Edward W. Durant, in his article, "Lumbering and Steamboating on the St. Croix River," in *Minnesota Historical Collections*, 10: 650 (part 2), gives an account of how the pine slabs used for the roof and floor were obtained from the first sawmill in the St. Croix Valley, at Marine. The Reverend Augustin Ravoux succeeded Father Galtier in 1844; the history of his ministry in Minnesota from 1844 to 1851 may be found in his *Reminiscences*, 59–64.

[25] Williams, *Saint Paul*, 149–163. See also page 198, where Williams gives a "complete and accurate list of all the pre-territorial settlers and residents in Saint Paul, with the years in which they came." An article on the "Rise and Progress of St. Paul" appeared in the *Minnesota Democrat* (St. Paul) for November 1, 1854.

THE CHAPEL OF ST. PAUL, 1852

Oil by Robert O. Sweeny

RED RIVER CARTS AND BOIS BRÛLÉS FROM PEMBINA, 1858

1846. Stillwater had obtained its post office the preceding January, Point Douglas in 1840, and there had been a post office at Fort Snelling since 1828.[26]

At the opening of the river in 1847 a regular line of steamboats was put in service between St. Paul and down-river points. Hitherto boats had come and gone as they could obtain cargoes.[27] In this year also the general land office extended its surveys west of the St. Croix and about the Falls of St. Anthony from the fourth principal meridian in Wisconsin. The squatters of St. Paul, taking the hint, proceeded in an informal, coöperative way to have some ninety acres, embracing the principal business places and dwellings, surveyed and platted. It was not until the summer of 1848, however, that the government was ready to offer the land for sale at the St. Croix Falls land office. The St. Paul proprietors-to-be attended in a body, having previously arranged to have Sibley bid for all, as the sections or fractions were offered. In after years Sibley was pleased to relate how he performed this duty and how he observed at the time of the bidding that he was closely surrounded by men from the future capital city, each provided with a big stick. It was his surmise that something unpleasant might have happened to any bystander who had inadvertently injected a counter bid. None was offered, however, and Sibley conveyed to each person in interest his proper area. In the cases of some of his old Canadian clients it was only after long delay and much persuasion that he could induce them to take their deeds. Ignorant of American ways, they felt that their homes would be more secure in the hands of Monsieur Sibley, their ancient patron, than in their own.[28]

[26] Williams, *Saint Paul*, 154.

[27] Williams, *Saint Paul*, 43, 173; Blakeley, in *Minnesota Historical Collections*, 8: 380; George B. Merrick, *Old Times on the Upper Mississippi: The Recollections of a Steamboat Pilot from 1854 to 1863*, 259 (Cleveland, 1909). A claim that Captain R. S. Harris, brother of the better known Daniel S. Harris, ran the first regular boat, the "Otter," from Galena to St. Paul, beginning in 1845, has not been verified. Clipping in Minnesota Historical Society Scrapbooks, 2: 81, quoting the *Dubuque Times*.

[28] Report of the commissioner of the general land office, 1847, in 30 Congress, 1 session, *Senate Executive Documents*, no. 2, pp. 82–87, 94–97 (serial 504); 1848, in 30 Con-

It does not need to be added that the colony, being American, immediately provided itself with schools, churches, hotels, banks, and all the apparatus of civilization.

The growing trade of St. Paul was not all down-river business. The people of the Red River settlements found that the road to the States taken by so many of their discouraged fellow colonists was a shorter one to market than that by way of Lake Winnipeg to Hudson Bay or the Dawson route. From small beginnings the Red River trade increased after 1847 to a surprising magnitude. The means of transportation was the Red River cart, two wheeled, built wholly of wood, with the exception of a little shaganappy or rawhide. It was drawn by a single ox and carried a load of near half a ton. As no axle grease was used, the creaking of the wheels could be heard for miles. The Red River caravan, often composed of hundreds of these loaded carts, would leave the settlements as soon as the grass was high enough to furnish good feed and, by marching fifteen miles a day, would reach St. Paul in July. The downward loads consisted almost wholly of furs; on the return trip the loads were made up of merchandise as miscellaneous as the stock of a country store. The arrival, sojourn, and departure of a Red River train were for many years the most interesting events of the summer, and the camp of the *bois brûlés* in their semibarbaric costumes was the delight of multiplying tourists. In later years the old Red River trail by way of the Traverse des Sioux was abandoned for the Sauk River route, which early became the principal stage road to the Northwest. On its line the Great Northern Railroad was afterwards located.[29]

gress, 2 session, *Senate Executive Documents*, no. 2, p. 75 (serial 530); 1849, in 31 Congress, 1 session, *Senate Executive Documents*, no. 1, pp. 38, 44 (serial 550); Williams, *Saint Paul*, 170–172, 183–185; Nathan Butler, "Boundaries and Public Land Surveys of Minnesota," in *Minnesota Historical Collections*, 12:656; Sibley, in *Minnesota Historical Collections*, 3:244. The present writer more than once heard from the lips of General Sibley the account of the purchase of the town site of St. Paul.

[29] Williams, *Saint Paul*, 48, 160, 304–308; Bryce, *Hudson's Bay Company*, 361–364; *Report from the Select Committee on the Hudson's Bay Company; together with the Proceedings of the Committee, Minutes of Evidence, Appendix, and Index*, 1857, index, pp. 524, 526. The

The St. Croix River forms part of an old canoe route from the Mississippi to the head of Lake Superior. Du Luth came down it in 1680; Schoolcraft went up it in 1832. Without doubt many white men had, between these dates, navigated this beautiful stream. None could have failed to note the magnificence of the pine forests which bordered its upper reaches. To bring these forests, along with those of the wide-branching tributaries of the Chippewa River, into market was the main object of the treaties of 1837. There is a tradition, without doubt authentic, that on the day of the negotiation of the treaty with the Chippewa at Fort Snelling, July 29, 1837, a party of gentlemen set out in a birch-bark canoe manned by eight men and, without losing time by the way, reached the falls of the St. Croix at noon of the next day. The claim then and there made, on the Wisconsin side, while controlling a large water power, was not otherwise well suited to lumber manufacture. Two years later the first sawmill on the St. Croix was put in operation at Marine some twenty miles below these falls.[30] Five years later, in 1844, lumber manufacture was begun at Stillwater. Through this industry the town gained such a lead that its enthusiastic founders believed it would become and remain the chief city of the region. Many enterprising persons established themselves there, and afterwards

three well-known routes used at different periods by traders to and from the Red River country are traced on the map accompanying Pope's *Report*. See also the map facing page 80, *ante*. Pope's expedition followed the Sauk River route both going and coming; Pope himself, accompanied by a small party, returned by way of the Crow Wing River. See *ante*, p. 129, n. 89. A Red River cart is preserved in the museum of the Minnesota Historical Society.

[30] Report of the commissioner of Indian affairs, 1837, in 25 Congress, 2 session, *Senate Documents*, no. 1, p. 526 (serial 314); Edward D. Neill, "The Beginning of Organized Society in the Saint Croix Valley, Minnesota," in *Macalester College Contributions*, first series, no. 3, p. 55, quoting an account of the trip to St. Croix Falls by Jeremiah Russell, one of the party; William H. C. Folsom, "History of Lumbering in the St. Croix Valley, with Biographic Sketches," in *Minnesota Historical Collections*, 9: 293, quoting a statement by Franklin Steele, who was also of the party. Steele says, however, that the journey was undertaken in September. In the spring of 1838 Steele organized in St. Louis a corporation known as the St. Croix Falls Lumber Company to operate in the St. Croix Valley. At the site selected work was begun on a mill, a dam, and a mill race, which were completed in 1840. At that time the settlement numbered twenty. George E. Warner and Charles M. Foote, eds., *History of Washington County and the St. Croix Valley*, 191–193 (Minneapolis, 1881); Folsom, *Fifty Years in the Northwest*, 92.

migrated to other points of promise. For nearness to pine forests, convenience in the handling of logs, and access to down-river markets it had a decided advantage for many years.

With the forests of pine, believed to be inexhaustible at the prevailing rate of consumption, only forty miles away, and with a water power of great magnitude easily improvable, the Falls of St. Anthony were soon to offer a splendid example of those "natural opportunities" which it has been the traditional policy of the United States to give away to the first lucky finders or occupants.[31] We have already noted the pains taken to run the line of the military reservation in such a way as to exclude the left bank of the Mississippi to a point well below the Falls of St. Anthony.[32] Efforts were made by various persons to establish claims to the land abutting on the falls before the ratification of the treaty. The reconciliation of the conflicting traditions may be left to the local annalist. One of these persons, Franklin Steele, by dint of characteristic activity succeeded, on the day after the receipt of official notice of the ratification of the treaties of 1837, in locating a claim on the east side immediately abreast of the cataract with a frontage sufficient to command the water power to mid-channel — a claim not thereafter successfully disputed. Other claims were made

[31] Neill, in *Macalester College Contributions*, first series, no. 3, p. 65; Durant, in *Minnesota Historical Collections*, 10: 650–652 (part 2); Folsom, in *Minnesota Historical Collections*, 9: 301–305, 321–323; Daniel Stanchfield, "History of Pioneer Lumbering on the Upper Mississippi and its Tributaries, with Biographic Sketches," in *Minnesota Historical Collections*, 9: 329, 331, 339, 344. Folsom estimates the amount of pine timber cut in the St. Croix basin from 1837 to 1898 at over fourteen billions of feet, board measure, and its stumpage value at approximately forty-two million dollars. Stanchfield states that: "From the upper Mississippi region, above the falls of St. Anthony, it [*the pine timber*] has yielded twelve billion feet of lumber, having a value, at the places where it was sawn, of not less than $75,000,000."

It should be noted that the primitive lumbermen did not wait for government surveys, but cut as they pleased of the best pine accessible to water. Of this custom, Folsom says: "The government subsequently sent timber agents to investigate and report, regarding the cutting of timber on these uncared-for lands. It was generally conceded to be a benefit to the government; it being occupancy under an endowed right, as citizens inheriting an interest in the government. In many instances where the government demanded payment, the demand was promptly met by purchasing the denuded lands, or by paying a fair compensation for the timber cut." *Minnesota Historical Collections*, 9: 296.

[32] See *ante*, p. 219, n. 15.

above and below, all of which by the year 1845 had fallen into the hands of this original claimant and one other. There was some jumping of claims, which resulted in expected cash redemptions, but the legal demands of continued occupancy were kept up by resident tenants and otherwise, so that when, after the government survey, the first public land sale took place in 1848 at St. Croix Falls, the claimants became legitimate proprietors by the payment of one dollar and a quarter per acre. Soon after the sale it appeared that Steele had become the sole owner of all lands abutting on and adjacent to the falls, lands sufficient for effective control of all the water power east of the middle of the main channel of the Mississippi. In 1847 he built a dam across the east channel and erected a sawmill which went into operation the next year. The erection of this mill occasioned the first permanent settlement at the falls and a very rapid increase of inhabitants thereafter.[33] The first town plat was made in 1849 by William R. Marshall, afterwards a governor of the state.[34] There was a considerable migration of lumbermen from Stillwater, and some exchange of residents between St. Paul and the newer St. Anthony.

As we reach 1849, the close of the period under present observation, we find the major part of the white population on Minnesota soil in the villages of St. Paul, Stillwater, and St. Anthony — the first, a commercial river port, the other two, lumbering towns. Other aggregations, mostly of transient persons, there were at minor points on the St. Croix, at Fort Snelling and Fort Gaines, at Mendota and other trading posts. To these must be added the *bois*

[33] For an account of the Steele preëmption at the falls see the Appendix, no. 4. See also *Statutes at Large*, 7: 536. For a memoir of Franklin Steele by Neill, see Warner and Foote, *Hennepin County*, 635–638. This paper Neill read at a meeting of the American history department of the Minnesota Historical Society in September, 1880. The present writer was at that meeting and shared in the admiration of the "fine presence and manly form" of its chairman, Franklin Steele.

[34] This map of "Saint Anthony Falls," after having been lost for more than fifty years, was purchased for $13.50 by the Minnesota Historical Society from Littlefield's bookstore in Boston, November, 1911. It is in an excellent state of preservation.

brûlés at Pembina, resident more or less permanently on the American side of the international line.   Of rural settlement there was but a bare beginning, on the beautiful prairie lands abutting on Lake St. Croix in Washington County. With the exception of the trifling amount of produce from these farms and a few gardens and of wild game, the whole subsistence of the white population was brought up from below by steamboats.   Whole cargoes of pork and flour were discharged at St. Paul and Mendota for distribution. Even forage for animals was thus imported.[35]

[35] Warner and Foote, *Washington County and the St. Croix Valley*, 194.   Sibley, in *Minnesota Historical Collections*, 1: 478, refers to Joseph Haskell and James S. Norris as the first farmers of Minnesota "who demonstrated that our lands are equal to any other in the West for the production of the cereals, a fact which was denied not only by men not resident in the territory, but by individuals among us."   These men opened up farms near Afton and Cottage Grove, respectively, about 1839.   The newspapers of the early territorial period are filled with notices of the arrival of the steamers plying between points on the lower Mississippi and St. Paul or Mendota and bringing cargoes which they discharged at these ports.

IX. THE TERRITORY ORGANIZED

BY A SECTION of the Illinois enabling act, approved on April 18, 1818, the residue of the old Northwest Territory north of that state was attached to and made part of the Territory of Michigan. A proclamation by Governor Cass on October 16 of the same year established as the County of Crawford approximately all the area lying west of a meridian drawn through the middle of the Fox-Wisconsin portage, and south of a line dividing the rivers flowing south from those emptying into Lake Superior.[1] Colonel Henry Leavenworth, conducting a detachment of the Fifth Infantry from Detroit to the site of Fort Snelling in the following summer,[2] had been intrusted by the governor of Michigan with blank commissions for the officers of the new county. Prairie du Chien was made, and long remained, the county seat. That part of Minnesota east of the Mississippi then came under civil authority, and was, in theory, represented in the Michigan legislature for seventeen years. In 1836 Wisconsin Territory was created, and Crawford County, Michigan, became, with some change of eastern and southern boundaries, Crawford County, Wisconsin.[3]

One of the Minnesota counties bears the name "Brown," and was so named in honor of Joseph Renshaw Brown, who is entitled without controversy to the distinction of being called pioneer Minnesotan. He was born on January 5, 1805, in Harford County, Maryland, the son of the Reverend Samuel Brown, a local preacher of the Methodist Episcopal church, who presently moved with his family to Lancaster, Pennsylvania. He was a precocious youth

[1] *Statutes at Large*, 3: 428.
[2] See *ante*, p. 135.
[3] *Statutes at Large*, 5: 10.

and must have had some good elementary schooling. At about the age of thirteen he was apprenticed to the art and mystery of printing. Within a year he ran away from an uncongenial master, made his way to Pittsburgh, where he enlisted as a drummer in the Fifth Infantry, and was sent with other recruits to Fort Snelling with Colonel Leavenworth's expedition. He reënlisted as a private in 1822, was soon promoted, and at the end of his term in 1825 was the first sergeant of his company, although only a boy of twenty.[4] This ingenuous youth was a star pupil in the first Sunday school in all the Northwest, that kept by Mrs. Snelling and Mrs. Clark, the mother of Charlotte Ouisconsin Van Cleve.[5] On an excursion made in 1822, as a companion of "Joe" (William Joseph) Snelling, the gifted son of Colonel Snelling, he aided in tracing Minnehaha Creek from the falls to its source in Lake Minnetonka.[6] Not long after leaving the military service, Brown embarked in the Indian trade, which he followed intermittently till late in life. But his activities extended, as we shall see, to other pursuits. He is said to have broken up a piece of prairie near Minnehaha Falls and to have raised a crop

[4] Holcombe, in *Minnesota in Three Centuries*, 2:91. This author derived his information largely from Samuel J. Brown, of Brown's Valley, Minnesota, son of Joseph R. Brown. An unpublished letter of Samuel J. Brown to Judge A. Goodrich, April 21, 1871, and another of Andrew Henderson, of Frederick, Maryland, to S. J. Brown, January 19, 1871, indicate that young Brown enlisted as a soldier and was not a drummer but played the fife; and in the former it is noted that he was a member of the regimental band at Fort Snelling. It is probable that the young man was proficient on both instruments. Both letters are in the Brown Papers. This collection, containing papers of both Joseph R. and Samuel J. Brown, was presented to the Minnesota Historical Society by the latter in November, 1917. It contains approximately ten thousand letters, nine account books, and numerous miscellaneous books, maps, and plats. It is of especial value for a study of Indian affairs in Minnesota. The village of Henderson was laid out by Joseph in 1854 and was named for a cousin, Andrew Henderson. See S. J. Brown to the author, October 4, 1920, in the Folwell Papers. Further biographical material on Joseph R. Brown will be found in volume 3, *post*.

[5] Van Cleve, "*Three Score Years and Ten*," 38; Neill, *Minnesota*, 895.

[6] Neill, *Minnesota*, 331. These falls were known in an early day as Brown's Falls, and by some are believed to have been so named in honor of Joseph R. Brown. Major Lawrence Taliaferro, however, in a reminiscent letter in the *Pioneer and Democrat*, July 11, 1856, reprinted in Neill, *Minnesota*, 338, n., states that the falls were named in honor of Major General Jacob Brown, who was then in command of the United States Army. This is more probable than that the military would have complimented an enlisted man, not yet eighteen years old, who doubtless was merely a companion or an orderly to the son of Colonel Snelling on the expedition.

in 1829. He has, therefore, been given credit for being our pioneer farmer.[7] There was no one who more keenly appreciated the effects, commercial and political, which the treaties of 1837 were to have than this experienced pioneer. The leader of the party already mentioned, which in the summer of 1837 had made haste to reach the falls of the St. Croix in order to stake out an original claim, relates: "I found the veritable Joe Brown on the west side cutting timber and trading with the Indians, where now stands the town of Taylor's Falls."[8] Brown's rafts of logs were the first to be floated down the St. Croix; this gave him the place of pioneer lumberman of Minnesota. In 1838 he was appointed by the authorities of Wisconsin Territory justice of the peace for Crawford County.[9]

On January 9, 1840, the county of St. Croix was established, embracing all that part of Crawford County lying west and north of a line beginning at the mouth of the Porcupine River, and running thence east of north to Lac Court Oreille; thence northeast to the west fork of the Montreal River; thence down that river to Lake Superior; and thence north to the Canadian boundary. It included ten of the present counties of Wisconsin and fractions of some others.[10] In the same year Brown was elected a member of the Wisconsin territorial assembly, and as such he served in the sessions of 1840–41 and 1841–42.[11] During his two terms in that legislature he added largely to his

[7] It is more probable that this credit belongs to some of the Selkirk refugees. Cass and Schoolcraft found a crop of vegetables at Fort Snelling in 1820. Schoolcraft, *Narrative Journal*, 294.

[8] Folsom, in *Minnesota Historical Collections*, 9: 293, quoting a statement of Franklin Steele. The same statement, with a slight variation in the wording, is in Folsom, *Fifty Years in the Northwest*, 83. See also *ante*, p. 227.

[9] *Minnesota Historical Collections*, 3: 202; 9: 299. An example of Justice Brown's style of procedure and method of disposing of suits may be found in Williams, *Saint Paul*, 147; Sibley, in *Minnesota Historical Collections*, 3: 267; and Henry S. Fairchild, "Sketches of the Early History of Real Estate in St. Paul," in *Minnesota Historical Collections*, 10: 437 (part 1). Another example is given by Holcombe, in *Minnesota in Three Centuries*, 2: 141.

[10] Wisconsin Territory, *Laws*, 1839–40, no. 20, p. 25.

[11] Moses M. Strong, *History of the Territory of Wisconsin, from 1836 to 1848*, 325 (Madison, 1885).

knowledge of public affairs and parliamentary procedure and developed his remarkable gift for winning men. In accordance with the act creating the new county, a proper organization was at once made, and the county seat was located on "Joe Brown's claim" at the head of Lake St. Croix. It was given the name "Dakotah."[12] When only a few settlers arrived, however, Brown turned to other enterprises, and years later his projected village of Dakotah became an addition to Stillwater. In the very year of the organization of the new county of St. Croix, 1840, Judge David Irwin of Madison, Wisconsin, was assigned to hold court there. He reached the county seat by way of the Fox-Wisconsin portage and Fort Snelling. On his arrival he found a sheriff in attendance, but Clerk Brown was absent, there were no jurors, and, so far as known, no cases awaiting trial. After passing a night on the floor of an unfinished log cabin, and faring on venison and fish seasoned with the salt he had brought in his pocket, the judge departed on the morrow never to return. Years passed before there was any further effort at nisi prius in Minnesota.[13]

The population of Wisconsin, which had become a territory in 1836, swelled rapidly and the middle of the next decade had hardly passed before there were movings toward a state organization. It was not expected that the new state would cover the whole region embraced by the territory, which reached from Lake Michigan to the Mississippi River. In anticipation of the admission of a state of reduced area, the delegate from Wisconsin Territory, Morgan L. Martin, who was one of the most distinguished pioneers of that territory,[14] acting probably on the suggestion of a personage

[12] Folsom, *Fifty Years in the Northwest*, 35.

[13] Henry L. Moss, "Last Days of Wisconsin Territory and Early Days of Minnesota Territory," in *Minnesota Historical Collections*, 8: 73; Charles E. Flandrau, "Minnesota Territorial Lawyers and Courts," in *Minnesota Historical Collections*, 8: 91; Holcombe, in *Minnesota in Three Centuries*, 2: 107; Folsom, *Fifty Years in the Northwest*, 35. These accounts vary much in details. The surmise may be risked that Brown dreamed not only of a county seat but also of a territorial capital at Dakotah.

[14] For information about Martin, see Reuben G. Thwaites, "Sketch of Morgan L. Martin," and a "Narrative of Morgan L. Martin, in an Interview with the Editor," in

not now necessary to name, introduced into the national House of Representatives on December 23, 1846, a bill to organize the Territory of "Minasota." The bill was referred to the committee on territories, which took it up seriously, and through the chairman, the Honorable Stephen A. Douglas, returned on January 20, 1847, a favorable report, but changed the proposed name to "Itaska." In a debate which preceded the passage of the bill a month later, February 17, 1847, various names were proposed, but the House restored that used in the original bill, spelled, however, "Minnesota." The bill passed to the Senate, and when called up on March 3, the last day but one of the session, was laid on the table upon a suggestion that the population of the region was altogether too sparse to warrant the creation of a new territory and that the object of the bill was in fact to create some new offices. So ended a project which, if successful, would have made Sibley a territorial governor and given Joseph R. Brown whatever he wanted.[15]

By this time the leading men of the "Minnesota Country," as Joseph R. Brown was pleased to call it, became much in earnest in their efforts to secure the establishment of a new

Wisconsin Historical Collections, 11: 380–384, 385–415. It has been claimed that Martin County, Minnesota, was named in his honor. See Warren Upham, *Minnesota Geographic Names, Their Origin and Historic Significance*, 332 (*Minnesota Historical Collections*, vol. 17 — St. Paul, 1920).

[15] 29 Congress, 2 session, *House Journal*, 88, 194, 371 (serial 496); *Congressional Globe*, 441, 445, 572. At the time of the final consideration of the bill, Senator Ashley said that the population was estimated at six thousand. Woodbridge of Michigan was understood to say that it was not one-tenth of that number. During the discussion of the bill the names "Chippewa," "Jackson," and "Washington" were proposed with considerable oratory. The name "Minnesota" was spelled in various ways in the bills for the organization of the territory presented in the Senate and the House, but the present spelling was sanctioned at the Stillwater convention on August 26, 1848, by the adoption of the following resolution on the motion of Joseph R. Brown: "Resolved that our delegate be requested to cause the orthography of *Minnesota* . . . to be according to that used in this resolution." Henry M. Rice, in a letter to Hercules L. Dousman, January 8, 1850, gives Dousman credit for first suggesting the name "Minnesota" for the territory and states that he (Rice) had so written in the preface to a map about to be published. "This," he adds, "will make Sibley squirm, but it is true." The letter is one of the Dousman Papers belonging to the Wisconsin Historical Society. The map referred to is the *Map of the Organized Counties of Minnesota*, published by Thomas Cowperthwait and Company (Philadelphia, 1850). See the "Accompaniment" to this map, page 2. For a discussion of the meaning of the name, see the Appendix, no. 5, *post*. D. G. Fenton of Prairie du Chien wrote Sibley on April 13, 1847, that Martin had arranged that he, Fenton, should be secretary of the new territory and that Sibley could have the governorship for the asking. Sibley Papers.

territory. A prolonged and heated controversy over the location of the western boundary of the projected state of Wisconsin, of which some notice may be taken further on in this narrative, had made the idea familiar, and even the name of the desired territory had been broached. Again, in 1848, Congress was invoked. On February 3, Senator Stephen A. Douglas introduced "a bill to establish the Territory of Minesota." It had the usual reference, came up for consideration, and was recommitted. After long delay Douglas on August 8 reported the bill with amendments. Congress adjourned six days later without having taken action. Thus the effort to secure the establishment of the territory by Congress according to the ordinary procedure had once more failed.[16]

When Wisconsin was admitted as a state on May 29, 1848, a new situation was presented. A large part of St. Croix County had been excluded from the new state and had been left, apparently, a no-man's land without law or government, and its people, without corporate existence. It was thought that no sanction remained for the determination of rights, the punishment of crimes, the solemnization of marriages, the devolution of estates, and the collection of debts. This idea was somewhat industriously bruited. The demand for a territorial government, up to this time confined to a few public men having personal interests, now became general, and the proposition was talked about in all the settlements. The agitation resulted in a public meeting in Stillwater on August 4. The attendance was not large, and those present decided to issue a call for a "convention" to be held at the same place on the twenty-sixth.[17] The

---

[16] 30 Congress, 1 session, *Senate Journal*, 187 (serial 502); *Congressional Globe*, 136, 656, 772, 1052. On the controversy over the western boundary of Wisconsin, see the Appendix, no. 12, *post*.

[17] *Minnesota Historical Collections*, 1:53. A variant account of the calling of the Stillwater convention, not necessarily incorrect, is given by Moss, in *Minnesota Historical Collections*, 8:72, 75. A preliminary meeting of citizens of St. Paul had been held in the month previous at Henry Jackson's store. See Neill, *Minnesota*, 490, and Holcombe, in *Minnesota in Three Centuries*, 2:361. This store, or "caravansary," as J. Fletcher Williams

phraseology of the call is noteworthy: "We the undersigned citizens of Minnesota Territory [*sic*] . . . respectfully recommend that the people of the several settlements in the proposed Territory appoint delegates to meet in convention at Stillwater on the 26th day of August inst. to adopt the necessary steps for that purpose." There were eighteen signatures.[18]

The "convention" assembled accordingly, and there was no scrutiny of credentials, nor inquiry as to the manner of appointments. Joseph R. Brown made the motion for the temporary organization and followed it with another for the appointment of a committee to nominate permanent officers. The men recommended were unanimously elected. Joseph R. Brown then offered a resolution for the appointment of a committee "to draft a memorial to Congress for the early organization of the Territory of Minnesota." This was adopted and Joseph R. Brown was appointed chairman of the committee. The committee reported such a memorial to Congress and also another to the president, together with appropriate resolutions and a preamble. All were unanimously adopted. The principal resolution provided for the appointment by the convention of a delegate to visit Washington and represent the interests of the proposed territory, with full power to act. Henry H. Sibley received a majority of the votes for this position and, on the motion of Joseph R. Brown, was declared unanimously elected by the convention. Upon the motion of Morton S. Wilkinson a certificate signed by the officers of the convention was issued to Sibley as a duly elected delegate of the convention. The memorials of the convention were then signed by all the delegates,

calls it in his *Saint Paul*, 153, was also the post office and the general rendezvous for the citizens of the community. A brief sketch of its proprietor is included in Henry L. Moss, "Biographic Notes of Old Settlers," in *Minnesota Historical Collections*, 9: 144–146.

[18] The call is prefixed to the manuscript copy of the proceedings of the convention in the possession of the Minnesota Historical Society. This copy is in the handwriting of and is signed by David Lambert, one of the two secretaries. The document is printed, but not *verbatim et literatim*, in the account of the "Organization of Minnesota Territory," in *Minnesota Historical Collections*, 1: 55–59.

sixty-one in number, who, after extending a vote of thanks to
their officers, adjourned.[19]

According to its records the Stillwater convention had in
view no object other than to obtain the establishment of the
proposed Territory of Minnesota by the usual procedure. So
hopeful were the delegates that they, or some of them, had
already called themselves "citizens of Minnesota." Whether
there was any foreshadowing of a scheme to effect that purpose by an ingenious indirection is not known. What mind
concocted that scheme is also unknown. The fertile intellect
of Joseph R. Brown was quite capable of the feat, but no
record of his initiative has been discovered.[20] The first
formulation of the plan, so far as is known, is found in a letter
of the Honorable John Catlin, who had been secretary of
the Territory of Wisconsin, to William Holcombe, one of the
secretaries of the convention.[21] The printed record of the
preliminary meeting of August 4 states that this letter was
then and there read, but, as the letter is dated August 22,
that was impossible.[22] If it was received in time and was
read at the Stillwater convention of August 26, it did not
make a sufficient impression to be noted in the minutes. The
scheme fathered by Catlin was the benign fiction that the
Territory of Wisconsin continued to exist in the area excluded from the state and that the rights of the people and
their government were perpetuated in accordance with the
organic act of that territory, which Congress had not repealed. The governorship having become vacant, Catlin had
become acting governor according to law.[23] The late delegate from Wisconsin Territory would, Catlin suggested,

[19] Manuscript copy of the proceedings; *Minnesota Historical Collections,* 1: 55–61.

[20] For the opinion of a member of the convention, see Moss, in *Minnesota Historical
Collections,* 8: 79.

[21] *Minnesota Historical Collections,* 1: 53. An opinion of James Buchanan, secretary of
state in the Polk administration, follows on page 54. In substance it is that the laws
of Wisconsin Territory remained in force and local officers might continue to exercise their
functions, but as to "general officers, such as Governor, Secretary, and Judges," he expressed
no opinion. The Catlin letter is also in Neill, *Minnesota,* 491, n. 2.

[22] *Minnesota Historical Collections,* 1: 53.

[23] Henry S. Dodge, who had been governor of Wisconsin Territory, had been elected
United States senator from the state immediately after its admission to the Union.

resign his office, and thereupon the acting governor could lawfully call an election to fill the vacancy. It was the opinion of Judge Catlin that "if a delegate was elected by color of law, Congress never would inquire into the legality of the election."

The scheme was carried out precisely as outlined. On September 18 the Honorable John H. Tweedy resigned his office as delegate from Wisconsin Territory. Catlin presently established a constructive residence at Stillwater, as if it were a capital city, and on October 9 he issued his proclamation under the seal of the Territory of Wisconsin for an election to be held on the thirtieth of the same month to fill the vacancy.[24] He directed that polling places be opened at Stillwater, Marine, St. Paul's, Prescott, Sauk Rapids, Crow Wing, and Pokegama. Under the circumstances Sibley was the logical candidate. As he had been for many years the big man of the Minnesota country, the general expectation naturally was that he would meet with no opposition. Those who indulged that expectation did not anticipate the intrusion of a newcomer of talent and ambition, who for many years was to be the most prominent of Minnesota's public men.

This was Henry Mower Rice, a native of Vermont, who was born in 1816.[25] At the age of eighteen, with an academy education supplemented by some study of the law, he emigrated to Michigan, where he was employed on a survey for the location of a canal at the Sault de Ste. Marie. After two years spent in some mercantile employment at Kalamazoo, the enterprising young Vermonter made his way to St. Louis, performing part of the journey on foot. Here he engaged with Kenneth McKenzie, one of the well-known

²⁴ Tweedy's letter of resignation and Catlin's proclamation are printed in *Henry H. Sibley, Delegate from Wisconsin Territory*, 7 (30 Congress, 2 session, *House Reports*, no. 10—serial 545).

²⁵ The best biographical sketch of Rice is that by William R. Marshall, in *Minnesota Historical Collections*, 9: 654–658. See also Newson, *Pen Pictures*, 128–138; Williams, *Saint Paul*, 185–190; Neill, *Minnesota*, 498–500; and Charles D. Gilfillan, "The Early Political History of Minnesota," in *Minnesota Historical Collections*, 9: 180.

traders of the time, to attend to his sutler's store at Fort Snelling. He reached that post on November 5, 1839. In the following summer a large detachment of the garrison was sent to the Winnebago reservation in northwestern Iowa, where Fort Atkinson was then under construction. Rice accompanied the troops and soon became sutler at the new post. In 1842 he relinquished that employment and connected himself with Hercules L. Dousman and other traders at Prairie du Chien.[26] The Winnebago trade was assigned to him, and was conducted in such a manner as to gain the good will of those Indians to a remarkable degree. The relations between Rice and the Winnebago continued for many years, and will engage the attention of the reader hereafter.[27] In 1847 he joined the American Fur Company[28] as a partner, took up a residence at Mendota, and conducted the trade with the Winnebago at Long Prairie and with the Chippewa of the Mississippi. As copartners in the American Fur Company, Sibley and Rice had certain common interests, although each had his separate territory and was expected not to meddle with the affairs of the other.[29]

It was this alert, ambitious, and already experienced man who aspired to the delegacy in opposition to Sibley. The campaign was brief but spirited. Rice, by engaging to keep the land office at Stillwater, which Sibley, it was assumed,

[26] For an appreciation of Dousman, see Sibley's "Memoir," in *Minnesota Historical Collections*, 3: 192–200.

[27] See *post*, pp. 310–317.

[28] The American Fur Company "suspended or *busted* about the 10" Sept." See Dousman to Sibley, October 20, 1842, in the Sibley Papers. The assets and good will of the company were soon after taken over by the firm of Pierre Chouteau Jr. and Company of St. Louis. The old name, however, clung to the concern until it went out of business in the early sixties.

[29] In a letter to Sibley, July, 1841, printed in the *St. Paul Daily News* for January 18, 1894, Rice says: "I hope to arrange to return to St. Peters [*Mendota*], and make that region my future home." That the business relations between the two men soon became strained is evident from extant correspondence. Sibley's side of the case may be found in Sibley to Chouteau, June 20, 25, September 5, 11, 12, 27, 28, October 10, 1849; Sibley to Borup, September 15, 28, 1849; and Sibley to Lowry, October 9, 10, 1849, in Sibley Letter Book, no. 4. It is unfortunate that no papers of Henry M. Rice have been discovered. Mrs. Rice, in an interview with the author on October 18, 1904, charged Sibley with treachery toward her husband. See also Chouteau *et al. v.* H. M. Rice, *et al.*, 1 *Minnesota*, 106–119.

would move to St. Paul, gained a number of votes. He had a large clientele in the Crow Wing precinct, in which his expectations were disappointed. The strength of Rice lay in the belief shared by many that he would be able, with his tact and address and his acquaintance at Washington, to secure more good things for the territory than could Sibley with his dignity and grand manner.[30] The election went to Sibley, however, much to his relief.[31]

Upon the opening of the second session of the Thirtieth Congress on December 4, 1848, Sibley's certificate of election as delegate from Wisconsin Territory was laid before the House of Representatives and was given the usual reference to the committee on elections.[32] On the twenty-second he was heard by the committee, and delivered a speech warranting the surmise that he made a mistake when he chose the Indian trade instead of the profession of law, for which he had studied.[33] He argued tersely that Congress could not have intended to disfranchise and outlaw some thousands of citizens, whose petitions were before that body asking not to be included in the state of Wisconsin but to remain under the existing territorial government. They surely did not ask to be left without the protection or denied the benefits of law. Objections made by members of the committee were met with tactful ingenuity. The result was a favorable report, which came up for consideration on January 15. It embodied a resolution that Henry H. Sibley be admitted to a seat on the floor of the House of Representatives as a

[30] A letter of D. G. Fenton, October 4, 1848, giving that as the opinion of Dousman, although the latter thought Sibley entitled to the delegacy, is in the Sibley Papers.

[31] With the exception of the St. Anthony precinct, where Sibley had twelve votes and Rice thirty, the record of this vote has not been found. Daniel S. B. Johnston, "Minnesota Journalism in the Territorial Period," in *Minnesota Historical Collections*, 10: 296 (part 1).

[32] The certificate of the Stillwater convention seems not to have been presented, or if presented it was altogether ignored. The only reference to the Stillwater certificate by Sibley's biographer is in the clause: "also bearing a memorial . . . from the citizens of the portion excluded from the State of Wisconsin." See West, *Sibley*, 105. Evidently Sibley did not seek admission as a delegate from the proposed Territory of Minnesota.

[33] This speech is quoted in full in *Minnesota Historical Collections*, 1: 69–76. A convenient summary is given in West, *Sibley*, 109. Sibley was admitted to the bar of the supreme court of Minnesota on July 13, 1858. The certificate is in the Sibley Papers.

delegate from the Territory of Wisconsin.[34]   The previous question having been ordered, the resolution was carried by a vote of 124 to 63, such members as Giddings, Lincoln, Horace Mann, and Alexander H. Stephens voting in the affirmative, and such as Cobb, Greeley, Johnson, and Toombs, in the negative.[35]   "Governor" Catlin in his correspondence had prophesied aright that a delegate elected by color of law would be admitted by Congress without inquiry into the regularity of election.   Since it was understood that the Territory of Minnesota would soon be created the House was disinclined to be technical.   The delegate, a young man of thirty-seven, of engaging presence and courtly manners, dressed, not as some expected, in strouds, buckskin, beaded belt, and moccasins, but in the height of fashion, had made a very pleasing impression.[36]   Some affirmative votes were given with the statement that they were accorded out of courtesy.   Members were willing to give Sibley the best opportunity for prosecuting his real business in the Capital.   Nobody seems to have been concerned in bringing out the fact that the delegate elect, residing in Mendota west of the Mississippi River, had not been a citizen of Wisconsin Territory since 1838, but held some unascertained political status in that residue of Iowa Territory which had been relegated to the Indian country, without name, when Iowa was admitted to the Union in 1846.[37]   Nobody was more surprised at the action of the House than the Minnesota delegate himself.   He has recorded that he regarded his admission as "extremely uncertain, in fact absolutely improbable."

[34] *Henry H. Sibley, Delegate from Wisconsin Territory*, 1–8; a minority report, strongly adverse to the seating of Sibley, signed by two representatives, follows (pp. 11–16).

[35] Upon the motion to reconsider the vote and to lay the motion to reconsider upon the table, the usual method of removing a matter from further consideration, the vote was 110 to 82.   30 Congress, 2 session, *House Journal*, 245 (serial 536).

[36] See Sibley's own account, with a note by Judge Aaron Goodrich, in *Minnesota Historical Collections*, 3: 270.

[37] The same was true of Rice.   On September 4, 1848, James Duane Doty, formerly governor of Wisconsin Territory, wrote to Sibley: "I . . . am confident if you will establish your residence on the East Side . . . you can be elected the Delegate.   Let me urge you to do so, as nothing would please me more than your election."   On October 15, Doty advised Sibley that the organic act of Wisconsin Territory did not require that the

The extent to which courtesy and good will had influenced the voting may be judged from a debate which sprang up in the House on January 18. A representative who had signed the minority report moved that as an amendment to the pending civil appropriation bill an item of $10,500 for the officers of the Territory of Wisconsin be added. The motion precipitated a discussion of the question, already practically decided by the admission of Sibley, on its merits. Thirteen members took the floor. Thompson of Indiana, chairman of the committee which had reported favorably on Sibley's application for admission, and one other insisted that the Territory of Wisconsin was not a fiction but a reality, and as such was entitled to representation in Congress by delegate. Eleven other members held that when the state of Wisconsin was admitted to the Union the Territory of Wisconsin ceased to exist. Upon a suggestion by one of the debaters that the joke had been carried far enough, the House by a vote of 76 to 35 refused to order the appropriation. The member who made the motion took no part in the debate, content apparently to enjoy the muddle into which the majority had thrown the House against his counsel.[38]

But Sibley was *persona grata*, and no objection was made to his holding his seat, drawing his per diem, and enjoying all the privileges belonging to a territorial delegate. From this place of advantage he at once proceeded to the business intrusted to him.

On the opening day of the session Senator Douglas gave notice of his intention to introduce a bill for the creation of the "Territory of Minesota." This, however, he did not do, but on December 20 he secured consideration by the Senate of his bill for the same purpose which was pending when the first session of the same Congress closed.[39] In this

governor, delegate, or other officers should be either citizens or residents of the territory. Sibley Papers.

[38] *Congressional Globe*, 30 Congress, 2 session, 295. Holcombe, in *Minnesota in Three Centuries*, 2: 375–415, describes at length the debates over the seating of Sibley and the establishment of the Territory of Minnesota.

[39] *Congressional Globe*, 30 Congress, 2 session, 1, 68.

bill Senator Douglas had made Mendota the capital of the new territory. It was with reluctance that he yielded to Sibley's preference to have St. Paul designated. Whatever may have been the considerations which governed Sibley's action it is evident that he did not allow his business interests to control. In the ordinary course of things the location of the capital at Mendota, his home, would have insured him a considerable fortune. He was capable of such disinterestedness.[40]

Sibley was careful to see that a precedent very lately set in the case of Oregon Territory was followed, by which two sections, instead of one, of public land in every township were set apart for public schools. This was the more readily conceded because of the prevailing belief that, on account of the desert soil and the hyperborean climate of the region, the lands of Minnesota would have but little value.[41]

In the brief debate on the bill on January 19, the only question raised was whether there was a sufficient population in the area of the proposed territory to warrant the creation of a government. Senator Douglas in reply to inquiries gave it as his impression "that there are now somewhere between eight and ten thousand people . . . aggregated into compact settlements." Thus informed, the Senate passed the bill without division.[42]

The slender Whig majority of the House would have been content to leave the Minnesota bill to the same fate as that which overtook the Martin bill of 1847. It was not till February 8 that the bill was reported from the committee on territories, which had tacked on a dozen amendments, all but

[40] West, *Sibley*, 122; Sibley to J. Fletcher Williams, February 3, 1873, Williams Papers. The Minnesota Historical Society has a copy of a letter from Sibley to John H. Thurston, dated December 23, 1878, in which Sibley says that the committee yielded to his "entreaties." Sibley moved his family to St. Paul in December, 1862.

[41] West, *Sibley*, 122. Sibley has often been mistakenly given credit for originating the double school grant.

[42] *Congressional Globe*, 30 Congress, 2 session, 298. One of the senators stated that in a conversation with the Minnesota delegate he had learned that there were about six thousand people located in an area of one hundred square miles. A letter written by Sibley to a relative, June 16, 1849, shows that he was at that date of the same opinion. Sibley Letter Book, no. 4.

one of small importance.   Sibley had evidently assured himself of votes enough to pass the bill if not delayed in debate. On February 22 he secured the consideration of the bill by moving in succession (1) the suspension of the rules, (2) the discharge of the committee of the whole from further action, and (3) the previous question on the proposed amendments. The first two were agreed to without opposition, but the third was carried by the close vote of 102 to 99.[43] The amendments of the committee were thereupon taken up in order and disposed of to the satisfaction of the friends of the measure.   Of one of these amendments, the first reported, particular mention needs to be made. As received from the Senate the bill contained the usual paragraph, "This act shall take effect upon its passage." The House committee recommended that the last three words be struck out and replaced by the words, "the tenth day of March, eighteen hundred and forty-nine." This the House disagreed to by a vote of 97 to 101. When the committee amendments had been disposed of a member moved from the floor a thirteenth amendment of precisely the same tenor. Thereupon another representative inquired of the chair whether the palpable object of the proposed amendment was not to deprive President Polk of the right to appoint the territorial officers and give it to his successor to be inaugurated on March 4. Speaker Winthrop dryly remarked that he had not been furnished with any information on the point. The vote stood: yeas, 99, all Whigs; nays, 95, every one a Democrat.[44] The Whigs thus expressed their intention to defeat the bill unless they could secure the offices.

On February 28 Sibley obtained the passage of the bill as amended, content to lose the offices if only the main purpose was effected.   On March 1 the Senate, by a strict party

[43] 30 Congress, 2 session, *House Journal*, 396, 420, 502 (serial 536).   Sibley made an abortive effort to secure consideration on February 12.

[44] 30 Congress, 2 session, *House Journal*, 505–507; *Congressional Globe*, 582, 583. The figures for the vote on the thirteenth amendment in the *Globe* differ from those in the *House Journal*.

vote, refused to concur in the insolent proposition of the Whig majority in the House.[45]　To all appearances the Minnesota bill had been put to sleep.　It had, however, a speedy and effectual awakening.　There was then pending in the Senate a bill to establish a "Home Department" in the executive branch of the government to be called the department of the interior, and this bill carried with it many desirable offices and opportunities for honors and profits, all to be at the disposal of the Whig president soon to be inaugurated.[46]　The Senate was indifferent, if not opposed, to the bill.　After conferring with colleagues Senator Douglas authorized Sibley to say to opponents of the Senate bill for organizing Minnesota Territory that unless they receded from their obnoxious amendment thereto the House bill to create the department of the interior would be in great jeopardy.[47]　The "bluff" was effective.　At an early hour on the last day of the session Delegate Sibley was accorded the floor to move that the House recede from the obnoxious amendment, that the rules be suspended, and that the previous question be ordered; to all of which the House agreed, without debate, by a vote of 107 to 70.[48]　On April 9, 1849, the first steamer from "below" brought to the levee at St. Paul the good news that the ghost of Wisconsin Territory had been laid and a new body politic, real and living, had been created, the Territory of Minnesota.[49]

The civil appropriation bill already passed carried with it no sum for the expenses of the Territory of Minnesota, either because of an oversight or because the committee had no expectation that the territory would come into being.　At the last moment an amendment, appropriating $19,300 for

---

[45] 30 Congress, 2 session, *House Journal*, 558 (serial 536); *Senate Journal*, 288 (serial 528); *Congressional Globe*, 617, 666.

[46] *Home Department* (30 Congress, 2 session, *House Reports*, no. 66 — serial 545) shows the need for such a department.

[47] As related to the author by General Sibley.　There are slightly different accounts in *Minnesota Historical Collections*, 1: 62, n., and in West, *Sibley*, 128–130.

[48] 30 Congress, 2 session, *House Journal*, 620; *Congressional Globe*, 693.

[49] Neill, *Minnesota*, 494; *Minnesota Pioneer*, April 28, 1849.

salaries, legislative expenses, and contingencies, was added
to a pending private bill for the relief of Dr. James Norris of
New Hampshire, a navy surgeon's mate in the War of 1812,
who was to be put on the roll of pensioners. The bill with
this irrelevant amendment was duly passed and approved.[50]

The organic act of Minnesota was framed in the form
already traditional. It prescribed the boundaries of the new
territory, directed that the principal executive and judicial

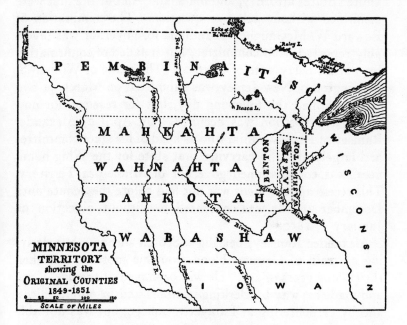

MINNESOTA
TERRITORY
showing the
ORIGINAL COUNTIES
1849-1851

SCALE OF MILES

officials be appointed by the president, provided for an elective legislature of two houses, and opened the suffrage for the
first election to all resident free white male inhabitants.[51]
The boundaries were so drawn as to include not only the
present state of Minnesota but also all of North and South

[50] The bill, H. R. 779, was passed by the House early in the evening session of March 3.
It was amended by the Senate very soon after, and the House concurred about midnight.
Congressional Globe, 30 Congress, 2 session, 681, 694, 697; *Statutes at Large*, 9: 416, 787.

[51] *Statutes at Large*, 9: 403–409. The organic act may also be found in any issue of the
Legislative Manual of Minnesota. On the boundaries see the Appendix, no. 12, *post*.

Dakota east of the Missouri and White Earth rivers. There was no precedent compelling the appointing authority to select the officials from pioneer residents; rather was it expected that the places would be handed out to nonresidents who had rendered good service in the late political campaign. President Taylor did not leave the principal offices of the territory long vacant. On March 15, he sent to the Senate nominations for governor, secretary, three justices, United States attorney, and marshal. All but the first were confirmed without delay or question. The nomination of Edward W. McGaughey of Indiana for governor was favorably reported from committee, but it failed of confirmation by a strict party vote of 22 to 25. The name of William S. Pennington of New Jersey was submitted on March 21 and was confirmed the following day, but for reasons not now known the position was declined. On April 2, Alexander Ramsey of Pennsylvania, who as head of his state committee had largely aided in carrying that state for the Whig nominees, was commissioned governor of Minnesota Territory. This recess appointment was not laid before the Senate until December 21. It was consented to without objection on January 9, 1850.[52]

Alexander Ramsey, bearing a Scotch surname but deriving a strain of German blood from his mother, was then thirty-four years of age. He was orphaned at the age of ten and made his way by clerking in stores and in public offices, and by carpentering at Lafayette College, but was not able to complete a college course. At twenty-two he began the study of law and two years later was admitted to the bar. In 1841 he was made chief clerk of the Pennsylvania assembly. From 1843 to 1847 he was a member of the Twenty-eighth and Twenty-ninth Congresses. It is related that, sitting next

---

[52] *Senate Executive Proceedings*, 8: 84, 85, 88, 89, 90, 93, 98, 104, 117. Alexander Ramsey was chairman of the state central committee of the Pennsylvania Whigs and contributed largely to the election of Taylor. See James H. Baker, "Alexander Ramsey," in *Minnesota Historical Collections*, 10: 726 (part 2). Ramsey's commission is in the possession of the Minnesota Historical Society.

to David Wilmot, he wrote out on his own desk for the use of his colleague that "proviso" which has fixed Wilmot's name in the annals of our national legislation.[53] Ramsey brought to his new task a practical education and much experience in public affairs. Throughout his long life he was ardently devoted to public interests and earned all the honors which his fellow citizens were pleased to bestow upon him. From the moment of his appointment Governor Ramsey gave his whole mind to the affairs of his new field and completely identified himself with the people of Minnesota. He was eminently a man of practical sense, who wasted no effort on fanciful projects. It was fortunate that so skillful, judicious, and broad-minded a man was sent to be the governor of the new territory. A popular tradition runs that so little was known east of the Alleghenies of the whereabouts of the region to which he was bound that while Ramsey was preparing for his journey his neighbors inquired whether he could reach it by way of the Isthmus of Panama, or whether he would have to sail around the Horn. The new governor arrived on May 27, 1849, and, according to previous invitation, became Sibley's guest at Mendota.[54] This generous hospitality established a friendship between the two men which adverse political interests never disturbed and which showed its effects on certain public issues. On the twenty-fifth of June, Ramsey and his family were transported in a birch-bark canoe to the residence in St. Paul which had been prepared for their occupancy. It is a notable coincidence that on the same day Henry M.

[53] Baker, in *Minnesota Historical Collections*, 10: 726; Baker, *Lives of the Governors of Minnesota*, 8 (*Minnesota Historical Collections*, vol. 13 — St. Paul, 1908). Other biographic sketches of Ramsey may be found in Neill, *Minnesota*, 496; *Legislative Manual*, 1903, pp. 651–653; Newson, *Pen Pictures*, 123–128; Williams, *Saint Paul*, 216–219; and Warren Upham and Rose B. Dunlap, *Minnesota Biographies, 1655–1912*, 624 (*Minnesota Historical Collections*, vol. 14 — St. Paul, 1912). The incident in connection with the Wilmot Proviso is thus described in a letter of Baker to the writer, November 16, 1907: "Ex-speaker Grant told me of it, and I think Colfax was another who referred to it. Wilmot and Ramsey sat side by side on the House floor and talked the matter over and Wilmot said 'Ramsey you write it out and I will offer it' that is the way I heard it."

[54] Sibley's letter of invitation, dated May 24, 1849, is among the Ramsey Papers.

Rice took up his residence in the capital city.[55] Both
these men were to have a large part in the sudden and
undreamed-of development of that city, a favorite theme
with local historians.

When Governor Ramsey arrived, he found the only white
man's country in Minnesota to be the delta between the St.
Croix and the Mississippi up to the latitude of the mouth of
the Crow Wing, and that part of Pike's purchase west of
the Mississippi. As he came up the river he passed a very
small hamlet at the mouth of the St. Croix and mission
houses at Red Wing, Red Rock, and Kaposia, now South St.
Paul. "A dozen framed houses, not all completed, and some
eight or ten small log buildings with bark roofs, constituted
the capital of the new territory." As told by Neill, St. Paul
was then "just emerging from a collection of Indian whiskey
shops, and birch-roofed cabins of half-breed voyageurs" and
"the population had increased to two hundred and fifty or
three hundred inhabitants," the increase being due to rumors
that the place might become the capital of the territory. It
was the expectation of opportunities which such a location
would open that had started and was to swell a tide of immigration to St. Paul. All accounts agree that it was phenomenal. It was not a wave, but the sea itself, says Williams,
quoting Whittier.[56] The *Minnesota Pioneer* for May 26
records an estimate of seventy buildings erected in the previous three weeks. An enterprising tourist relates that on
June 13 he counted one hundred and forty-two buildings,

[55] Sibley to Chouteau, June 25, 1849, in Sibley Letter Book, no. 4; Neill, *Minnesota*,
494.
[56] Accounts of the growth of St. Paul may be found in Williams, *Saint Paul*, chs. 16
and 17; Henry A. Castle, *History of St. Paul and Vicinity: A Chronicle of Progress and a
Narrative Account of the Industries, Institutions and People of the City and Its Tributary
Territory*, 1: ch. 6 (Chicago, 1912); and J. Wesley Bond, *Minnesota and Its Resources*, ch. 7
(New York, 1853). There is a very graphic description of St. Paul as seen by James M.
Goodhue on his arrival on April 18, 1849, in the *Minnesota Pioneer* of April 15, 1852, and the
message of Governor Ramsey to the legislature of 1853, in *Council Journal*, 1853, p. 35,
contains a comparison of the city in 1849 and 1852. The quotation mentioned is in Wil-
liams *Saint Paul*, 208:
　　　"The first low wash of waves, where soon
　　　Should roll a human sea."

including those in every stage of erection, and shanties.[57]
The lumber for the frame buildings was hauled from Stillwater and St. Anthony by ox teams.   As for these settlements, Stillwater had a larger population than St. Paul, but
the population of St. Anthony, where settlement had begun
only two years before, was smaller.[58]

As might be expected, the establishment of a new territory with a capital aroused the attention of newspaper men
as well as that of land speculators and merchants.   James
Madison Goodhue, a native of New Hampshire, a graduate of
Amherst College, and a lawyer by profession, had become by
an accident the editor of a newspaper in a Wisconsin village.
He found the work agreeable to his taste and, on learning of
the establishment of a new territory, he resolved to be, if
possible, its pioneer journalist.   Accordingly he bought a
newspaper outfit and shipped it to St. Paul by one of the
first boats in the spring of 1849.   He arrived there on the
eighteenth day of April, "a raw and cloudy day."   Ten days
later he issued the first number of the *Minnesota Pioneer*.   To
the day of his death, August 25, 1852, he was the foremost
figure in his profession in the territory.   He foresaw a great
future for the town and the territory and painted it in the
most glowing colors.   In that day of personal journalism, the
day of Bennett, Greeley, and Weed, Goodhue poured out
vials of wrath on political opponents and on men whose influence he believed mischievous.   His ancestry and training
had been Puritan; he stood for order and virtue, a foe to all
kinds of iniquity.[59]   The *Pioneer*, under the title *St. Paul
Pioneer Press*, still remains one of the leading newspapers of
Minnesota, while scores of others have come and gone.

[57] E. S. Seymour, *Sketches of Minnesota, the New England of the West; with Incidents
of Travel in that Territory during the Summer of 1849*, 99 (New York, 1850).
[58] Folsom, *Fifty Years in the Northwest*, 51.
[59] *Minnesota Pioneer*, April 15, 1852; Neill, *Minnesota*, 574–577; Williams, *Saint Paul*,
210; Johnston, in *Minnesota Historical Collections*, 10: 247–253.   In particular see Neill,
"Obituary of James M. Goodhue," in *Minnesota Historical Collections*, 1: 245–249, followed
by a reprint from the *Minnesota Pioneer* for April 15, 1852, of Goodhue, "The First Days
of the Town of Saint Paul."   An editorial appreciation of Goodhue by Joseph R. Brown

Governor Ramsey was not tardy in assuming the duties of his office. On June 1 he issued his proclamation announcing the passage of the organic act of the territory and giving the names of the officers whom the president had appointed; he declared the territorial government to be established, and enjoined all persons to respect and obey the laws thereof.[60] On June 11 he followed this proclamation with another dividing the territory into three judicial districts. As later defined these were St. Croix County, embracing the area between the St. Croix and the Mississippi rivers, with its county seat at Stillwater; La Pointe County, west of the Mississippi and north of the Minnesota and of a line running due west from its headwaters to the Missouri River, with its county seat at the Falls of St. Anthony; and Dakota County, covering all the land west of the Mississippi and south of the Minnesota, with its county seat at Mendota.[61] One of the three territorial judges was assigned to each district and courts were held by them in the course of the summer.[62]

On July 7 Governor Ramsey issued a proclamation declaring a provisional division of the territory into legislative districts and ordered an election on August 1 for the choice of nine territorial councilors and eighteen representatives as authorized in the organic act, and also of one delegate to represent the territory in the national House of Represent-

appeared in the *Minnesota Pioneer* for September 1, 1853. The press which Goodhue brought to Minnesota in 1849 is now in the museum of the Minnesota Historical Society.

[60] Minnesota Territory, *House Journal*, 1849, p. 187. The territorial officers were: Alexander Ramsey of Pennsylvania, governor; Charles Kilgore Smith of Ohio, secretary; Alexander M. Mitchell of Ohio, marshal; Henry L. Moss of Minnesota, attorney; Aaron Goodrich of Tennessee, chief justice; David Cooper of Pennsylvania and Bradley B. Meeker of Kentucky, associate justices. The three judges sitting together formed the territorial supreme court. Biographical sketches of these first territorial officers may be found in Newson, *Pen Pictures*, by index; Williams, *Saint Paul*, 216–222; and Holcombe, in *Minnesota in Three Centuries*, 2: 425–428. The circumstances under which the proclamation was drawn up are described in Newson, *Pen Pictures*, 107.

[61] *House Journal*, 1849, p. 194.

[62] Judge Aaron Goodrich, "Early Courts in Minnesota," in *Minnesota Historical Collections*, 1: 77–80. Sibley, who was foreman of the grand jury at Mendota, was fond of relating how Judge Cooper was gratified with the close attention of the members to his learned and eloquent instructions, to be later chagrined when informed that not more than three of them understood a word of English.

ST. PAUL IN 1848

From Henry Lewis, Das illustrirte Mississippithal, 1848

THE CENTRAL HOUSE, ST. PAUL, IN 1852

atives.[63] The election was held accordingly. The count showed that Sibley had received all the votes cast, 682, for delegate to succeed himself.[64] There was no lack of men who would have been very willing to relieve Sibley of his duties and responsibilities, but there was none who, in the absence of organized party machinery, thought it worth while to come out as a candidate against one so popular and so much respected for private and public services. His success at Washington in the previous winter rendered any contest hopeless.

The first legislative assembly of Minnesota convened on September 3, 1849, in St. Paul, the place designated in the organic act. The houses were easily accommodated in rooms of the Central House, a hotel then and long afterwards standing on Bench Street, at the corner of Minnesota Street. Having organized in the morning, the houses met in joint session in the dining room in the afternoon of September 4 to listen to the message of the governor. Prayer was offered by the Reverend Edward D. Neill, the well-known historian of Minnesota, then a young Presbyterian missionary in the embryo capital city.[65]

The four messages of Governor Ramsey are thoroughly interesting and will remain so. While generally confining himself to a rather prosaic, businesslike style, he does not disdain to throw in a dash of rhetoric when occasion may warrant. In this first message[66] he cannot help reminding the legislators that they are about to make laws for an area of 166,000 square miles, with the Father of Waters flowing through its center, with a fertile soil and a salubrious climate, and with no malaria to sap the vigor of the settler.

[63] *House Journal*, 1849, p. 215. The legislature of 1849 established nine counties roughly corresponding to the provisional districts named by Governor Ramsey. See *Laws*, 1849, pp. 7–9; also the map on page 247, *ante*.

[64] Neill, *Minnesota*, 508; *House Journal*, 1849, p. 219.

[65] *Minnesota Pioneer*, September 6, 1849. Names of the members of both houses are given in Neill, *Minnesota*, 511, n. 1, 512, n. 1. For biographical sketches of Neill, see Williams, *Saint Paul*, 212, and Newson, *Pen Pictures*, 120–123. He arrived in St. Paul in April, 1849.

[66] *House Journal*, 1849, pp. 6–18.

With much earnestness he urges conservatism in legislation and economy in appropriations. Estimating the number of Indians in the territory to be twenty-five thousand, he suggests that the general government must be looked to for protection from Indian wars and, in particular, that a great military road be built from Fort Snelling to the Missouri River, over which a respectable military force be marched at least once a year, in order to give the wild Sioux a proper sense of the military power of the whites. Speaking from observations made on a visit to Long Prairie in July, he urges the legislature to enact "prompt, decided, severe, and almost summary" laws to repress the "abominable" liquor traffic with the Indians. He inveighs against land speculation and desires to see some check placed on the use of military bounty land warrants for that purpose. The extension of preëmption right to unsurveyed land is given his cordial approval. He ventures the opinion that a mail only once a week from Prairie du Chien is quite inadequate to the business and dignity of the territory. The legislature is advised to give due attention to the opening of roads, to provide for a code of laws, and to preserve at the Capitol a copy of every newspaper published in the territory. The adoption of an official territorial seal for the authentication of documents and signatures is suggested.[67]

There was, however, one matter which Governor Ramsey knew to be of supreme interest to the whole people and that was the opening to settlement of the lands west of the Mississippi River. Without this the creation of the territory would have been farcical. The legislature is therefore strongly pressed to memorialize Congress for the purchase of the whole Sioux country from the Iowa line to the Watab River; which "extensive, rich and salubrious region . . . equal, in soil, to any portion of the valley of the Mississippi; and in healthfulness, is probably superior to any part of the

[67] The subject of a seal received serious consideration from the legislature, the results of which are set forth in the Appendix, no. 7, *post*.

American Continent. It is known to be rich in minerals as in soil; is sufficiently timbered . . . watered by some of the finest rivers . . . and is be-spangled with beautiful lakes in every direction . . . an agreeable mingling of high rolling prairies and gentle slopes; wooded hill-tops, luxuriant natural meadows, and abundance of the purest water."[68] In the concluding paragraph of this first message Governor Ramsey says, "I trust to be believed when I say, that I brought with me only the sincere determination to do right, to do justice, to live in harmony with all, and to use whatever power I incidentally possess, entirely for the true and abiding weal of Minnesota." When more than half a century later he closed his long career as a citizen of Minnesota, he might have made the same declaration, with none to challenge it.

In his message of 1851 Governor Ramsey makes a noteworthy recommendation — that of a compulsory arbitration law to lessen litigation and to bring unavoidable controversies to a speedy determination. He proposes that either party might rule the other to hearing before a board of arbitrators which should have all the functions of a court. The award of this board should have the effect of a judgment, to be followed, when necessary, by execution. A right of appeal to the district court should be allowed within a limited time. There were lawyers enough in that legislature to ignore a proposition which promised so little profit to their profession.[69]

Prophecy is always risky, especially if the seer descends into details. Governor Ramsey, however, may have been content when in later years he recalled his prognostications of 1852 in regard to the principal villages of the territory. St. Paul was to become "the great Capital of the Northwest"; St. Anthony, "the seat of learning in the valley of the

---

[68] The legislature so inspired lost no time in agreeing to the proposed memorial. *House Journal*, 1849, p. 63; *Laws*, 1849, p. 165.

[69] *House Journal*, 1851, p. 17. Among the laws of Wisconsin Territory which remained in force under the organic act of Minnesota was one for voluntary arbitration. *Laws*, 1849, p. 126.

Mississippi"; and Stillwater, "the central mart of the opulent valley of the St. Croix."[70]

The labors of the first legislature were greatly lightened by the fact that under the organic act the laws of the Territory of Wisconsin, which had remained in operation in the residue of Wisconsin recognized by Congress by the seating of Delegate Sibley, were made operative throughout the whole Territory of Minnesota. The routine of business was much expedited by the expert services of the secretary of the Council, Joseph R. Brown, who had learned the ropes in the Wisconsin territorial legislature. The larger number of the acts of this session were necessary administrative measures. A very stringent Sabbath law testifies to the orthodoxy of these pioneer lawmakers. Two important liquor laws were enacted: one forbidding the sale or gift of liquor to Indians throughout the territory, under penalty of fine and imprisonment; the other establishing a license system.[71]

By far the most important measure adopted was the "Act to establish and maintain Common Schools." The opening section of this act announced the provision of a fund "for the education of all the children and youth of the Territory." A state tax was authorized of one-fourth of one per cent, which might be supplemented when necessary by a tax to be voted in each school district; and the common schools were opened to all persons between the ages of four and twenty-one years, *free*.[72] The author of this bill was Martin McLeod, Canadian born, of Scotch parents who had come into the territory from the Red River settlement in

---

[70] *House Journal*, 1852, p. 28. A favorite project advocated in 1853 was that of connecting the head of Lake Superior with the upper Mississippi by a hundred miles of rail, thus bringing St. Paul as near to New York as was Galena. For the construction of such a railroad Governor Ramsey advised a memorial to Congress for a grant of public lands. *Council Journal,* 1853, p. 30.

[71] *Laws*, 1849, pp. 43, 45, 84. The licensing act was entitled "An Act regulating Grocery Licenses," but it provided that "a grocery shall be deemed to include any house or place where spirituous, vinous or intoxicating liquors are retailed in less quantities than one quart."

[72] *Laws*, 1849, p. 41. See also *Council Journal*, 1849, pp. 68–70, for the report of Martin McLeod of the committee on schools; and McLeod to Sibley, February 10, 1851, in the Sibley Papers, which refers probably to an amending bill.

1837. He entered into the fur trade at Lac qui Parle in connection with the American Fur Company, in which business he continued for some twenty years. From that distant post he ordered through Sibley such books as Alison's *History of Europe*, Prescott's works, and Lamartine's *Histoire des Girondins*. A contemporary described him as "a man of noble form, commanding presence, cultured intellect . . . dignified, eloquent, persuasive, charming." McLeod served in the first four legislatures, and one of the counties of the state takes its name from him.[73] With the name of this enlightened legislator who laid the foundation of a comprehensive school system must be associated that of the Reverend Edward D. Neill, already mentioned, who was doubtless his adviser.

Upon the initiative of Charles K. Smith, the secretary of the territory, the Minnesota Historical Society was incorporated on October 20, 1849. In the rich collections of this body may be found those files of Minnesota newspapers the preservation of which was recommended by Governor Ramsey in his message.[74]

There was no session of the territorial legislature in 1850, and the year passed without incident of first importance. A steamboat excursion on the "Yankee" up the Minnesota River as far as the mouth of the Cottonwood was thought to be of moment as demonstrating the navigability of that stream much farther than had previously been attempted.[75]

A more notable event was the council of Indians, Sioux and Chippewa, held at Fort Snelling on June 11. At day-

[73] Stevens, *Personal Recollections*, 266; McLeod's journal of his journey from Pembina to Lake Traverse on his way to Fort Snelling in the winter of 1837, in which he tells of his narrow escape from death, may be found on pages 345 to 353. The Minnesota Historical Society possesses a manuscript copy of this journal, made by J. Fletcher Williams from the original; this manuscript includes also McLeod's earlier narrative of the trip from La Pointe to "Red River Colony." Numerous letters by him are among the Sibley Papers.

[74] *Laws*, 1849, p. 106; *Chronicle and Register*, January 5, 1850. On the controversy and litigation in regard to this act, see Minnesota Historical Society, *Annual Reports*, 1878, p. 15. On the origin of the society and its progress to 1892, see Minnesota Historical Society, *Seventh Biennial Report* (Minneapolis, 1892).

[75] Dr. Neill, who was one of the party, describes his impressions of the trip in a graphic style in his *Minnesota*, 534–541.

break on April 2 a party of Sioux from Red Wing and Kaposia, seeking an adventure, attacked a sugar camp of Chippewa on the Apple River in Wisconsin some twenty miles from Stillwater. Stupefied with sleep and whisky, the Chippewa could make no resistance and the whole party of fifteen was inhumanly butchered, with the exception of one boy, who was made a prisoner. The Sioux murderers paraded the bloody scalps in Stillwater the next day.[76] Governor Ramsey, as superintendent of Indian affairs in the territory, decided that some action was called for and caused the arrest of thirteen Sioux warriors, who were sent for confinement to Fort Snelling. About a month later Chief Hole-in-the-Day with one or two companions came down from the Chippewa country and hid in the gorge of Fountain Cave in the upper part of St. Paul. On May 15 they crossed the river, fell upon an unsuspecting group of Sioux, killed one man, and, in spite of lively pursuit, escaped with his scalp.[77]   Governor Ramsey thereupon decided not to proceed further against the Apple River miscreants, but to summon the chiefs of both the Sioux and the Chippewa to a council for the purpose of arranging a peace. On June 9 a hundred Chippewa led by Hole-in-the-Day arrived at Fort Snelling. Late on the following morning three hundred mounted Sioux swept in grand array on to the treaty ground, dismounted, and formed a line to salute the Chippewa, who had lined up for the ceremony. Governor Ramsey and his interpreters with other white personages took their seats in a marquee and the chiefs ranged themselves on the sides. The proceedings began with a speech both tactful and forcible from the governor. He reminded the Indians that the Great Father had ten thousand villages "each larger than all the villages together of either of your tribes." The Great Father was not only mighty but he was good, and desired the welfare of his red children. But he was determined to put a stop to their fighting and in

[76] *Minnesota Pioneer*, April 10, 1850.
[77] *Minnesota Pioneer*, May 16, 1850; Williams, *Saint Paul*, 261.

particular to the slaughter of women and children. A white man who would kill a woman or a child was considered lower than a dog. A treaty made by and between the Sioux and Chippewa nations in 1843, in which they agreed to keep peace and in case of unauthorized homicide by individuals to have the damages paid out of the annuities of the tribe, was then read and interpreted. Thereupon William W. Warren, later to be the Chippewa historian, read a long statement of the assassinations committed by the Sioux; and Bad Hail, the Sioux spokesman, made a corresponding arraignment of the Chippewa. Upon the suggestion of Governor Ramsey four white men were appointed, with the acquiescence of the Indians, to ascertain what new agreement, if any, could be made. At an adjourned council late in the day the conferees reported that the parties cared for no new stipulations but were disposed to leave it to the governor to enforce the existing treaty according to his discretion. On the following morning the proceedings were concluded with a love feast by the hostile chiefs, much to the pleasure of the governor, who gave each party an ox. At an early stage of the proceedings the Sioux chiefs suddenly rose and left the council. They had been scandalized by the presence of some white women who were of the governor's party. Hole-in-the-Day had the address to rise and offer the ladies seats on his side of the tent, where they would be heartily welcome. They thought it best, however, to retire. When the disgruntled Sioux returned they were sharply rebuked by Governor Ramsey for their discourtesy. As an indication of the effect of the council toward establishing friendship may be mentioned the fact that neither party would leave the council ground till hostages had been exchanged to secure the safe return of the delegations.[78]

[78] A long communication by William W. Warren, declaring that the Chippewa would have their revenge for the Apple River murders, is in the *Chronicle and Register* for June 10, 1850. Accounts of the treaty and reports of the proceedings occur in the *Chronicle and Register* for June 10, 17, 1850, and in the *Minnesota Pioneer* for June 13, 1850. The latter account is quoted in Neill, *Minnesota*, 528–534. See also the *Minnesota Pioneer* for April 10

The second session of the territorial legislature opened on January 1, 1851. A very spirited contest over the election of officers resulted in the triumph of Sibley's friends, supported by Whigs, over the adherents of Henry M. Rice, who had become a political factor to be reckoned with.[79] The territorial printing went to James M. Goodhue, editor and publisher of the *Minnesota Pioneer*, but the Whigs were able to exact a moiety of the profits, which was devoted to the establishment of the *Minnesotian* as their organ.[80] The exciting event of the session was the contest over the location of the capitol and the prison. This had already been the subject of much private and some public discussion. That the capitol temporarily established in St. Paul by the organic act should remain there was almost a foregone conclusion. But that was settled only after lively parliamentary battles in both houses. A bill to place the capitol at St. Paul and the prison at Stillwater naturally united the delegations of those towns, and they succeeded in overcoming a similar combination between the St. Anthony and upper Mississippi members by splitting the votes from remaining precincts. In the Council the vote, reached after interminable filibustering, stood 5 to 4, one councilor having been excused from voting; in the House it stood 10 to 8.[81]

Apparently St. Anthony, rapidly passing to second place among the settlements, was getting no share of the good things. Her principal citizens had notified the opposition in the capitol contest that St. Anthony did not want the prison. Apparently, also, the studied indifference of her

and May 16, 1850. For information concerning Warren, see the memoir by J. Fletcher Williams, in *Minnesota Historical Collections*, 5: 9–20; Truman A. Warren to H. M. Rice, January 3, 1884, and Rice to Williams, January 7, 1884, in the correspondence files of the Minnesota Historical Society; and a manuscript sketch by his sister, Mary Warren English. Rice says, "He was the most Eloquent & fluent speaker I ever heard. The Indians said he understood their language better than themselves."

[79] *Council Journal*, 1851, pp. 4–7; *House Journal*, 1851, pp. 5–11.

[80] *Council Journal*, 1851, p. 37; *House Journal*, 1851, p. 41; Ramsey to Sibley, January 14, 1851, and Dr. Potts to Sibley, same date, Sibley Papers.

[81] *Laws*, 1851, pp. 5–9; *Council Journal*, 1851, pp. 54–57; *House Journal*, 1851, pp. 59–62. See also J. R. Brown to Sibley, January 24, 1851, Forbes to Sibley, January 28, 1851, and McLeod to Sibley, February 4, 1851, in the Sibley Papers.

delegation had for its object to obtain something in the way of consolation which would be worth acquiring. That was the university, for which Governor Ramsey had bespoken action. A few days after the passage of the capitol and prison bill, the House committee on schools, headed by John W. North of St. Anthony, submitted a report on the university item of Ramsey's message, which had been referred to it. The committee suggested that it was none too soon to provide for "liberal, scientific and classical education." The New England colleges were almost coeval with the settlements. Harvard, for instance, was established only eight years after the founding of the Massachussetts Bay colony and only eighteen years after the landing of the Pilgrims at Plymouth. "There were at that time, only about half as many inhabitants in all New England, as are now residing in the Territory of Minnesota." The committee was aware that the proposed institution could not mature for many years, but it was careful to point out that "it may now receive an endowment in lands," a sufficient reason for providing for a university before the common schools had secured a firm footing. The bill to incorporate the University of Minnesota was passed without serious opposition, there being but two negative votes in the House and none in the Council. After the passage of the bill in the Council, Martin McLeod moved to amend the title by adding the words "at the Falls of St. Anthony," which was agreed to.[82] North's committee was not mistaken in its opinion that years would pass before the project could mature. It was eighteen years before collegiate work was begun. It may be remarked that there is

[82] *Council Journal*, 1851, pp. 15, 84; *House Journal*, 1851, pp. 69–71. In his message of January 7, 1851, Governor Ramsey suggested that "as the endowment of a University will also naturally . . . attract your attention, it might be proper farther to memorialize Congress for a grant of one hundred thousand acres of land . . . for this most desirable object." The House committee on schools pointed out that, pending the maturity of the university, "its preparatory department may serve as an Academic Institution for the entire youth of the Territory." McLeod, writing to Sibley on February 4, 1851, said he thought St. Anthony the proper place for the prison, but "Mr. Steele and others . . . declared . . . they *did not* want the prison while they admitted that they could not get the capitol." Sibley Papers.

a tradition, still widely current, that as early as the Still-water convention of 1848 a tripartite agreement was made to assign the establishments mentioned, the capitol to St. Paul, the prison to Stillwater, and the university to St. Anthony. There was no such formal agreement, and memories differ as to any informal understanding. It may perhaps be considered that at different times the location of the institutions was the subject of remark and suggestion, but there is no evidence that the representative men of the three towns ever "got together" on the proposition.[83] St. Anthony lost nothing in the deal. The legislature memorialized Congress for a grant of one hundred thousand acres of public land for the endowment of the institution for which it had wisely provided.[84]

A matter before the legislature of 1851 quite as interesting, if not so exciting, as the location of public buildings was the framing of a complete code of laws for the territory. The laws of Wisconsin Territory in effect under the organic act had been enacted during ten successive legislative sessions and had to be sought for in as many separate volumes, some of which it was almost impossible to procure. Upon the recommendation of the governor, the legislature promptly undertook the task of selecting, arranging, and completing this imported body of municipal law. After much maneuvering the two houses on January 21 made a resolution uniting the judiciary committees into a joint committee for revising and consolidating the general statutes of the territory, and authorizing them to call to their aid three persons learned in the law. The men selected were Morton

---

[83] Neill, in a letter to the author, in the Folwell Papers, pronounces the story of the tripartite agreement a "myth." Murray, in *Minnesota Historical Collections*, 12: 116, declares that "there is not a word of truth" in it. See also Moss, in *Minnesota Historical Collections*, 8: 77. In a letter to J. Fletcher Williams, February 3, 1873, in the Williams Papers, Sibley states that at the time when he persuaded Douglas to substitute St. Paul for Mendota as the capital in his bill for the formation of Minnesota Territory, he, Sibley, "felt it to be my duty to carry out the wishes of my Constituents, in placing the Capital at St. Paul, the State prison at Stillwater, and the University at St. Anthony."

[84] Murray, in *Minnesota Historical Collections*, 12: 117; *Laws, 1851*, p. 41.

S. Wilkinson, Lorenzo A. Babcock, and William Holcombe.[85]
The revisers went resolutely to work and in about a fortnight began furnishing a series of chapters for the consideration of the two houses. We now have the unusual spectacle
of a legislature, composed in large measure of fur-traders and
lumbermen, seriously engaged in the work of revising a code
of laws. It was not a mere formal performance. They
struck out and inserted, they added new sections, they improved phraseology. There were good lawyers enough to
prevent any ridiculous errors. On March 31 the final consolidated bill was passed and approved by the governor.
Thus was enacted what was for a long time known as the
"Code of 1851."[86] It was not superseded by an authorized
revision till 1866, but in pursuance of a joint resolution of
March 5, 1853, there was published a work entitled *Collated
Statutes of the Territory of Minnesota*.[87] A sufficient explanation of this publication may lie in the circumstance that
Joseph R. Brown was territorial printer. There is a tradition, needing confirmation, that this enterprising person
had a way of preparing elaborate bills which his friends
introduced and which were ordered printed at one dollar per
thousand ems, no further action being desired or expected.
Bills to charter plank road companies appear at this period
with suspicious frequency, but never a plank road was built
in the territory.

Some Minnesota lawyers will be interested to learn that,
while the Code of 1851 abolished all distinctions between
the forms of actions at law and merged all the old common
law actions into one "to be called a civil action," that code
did not go the full length of the New York code of procedure

[85] *Council Journal*, 1851, pp. 12, 30, 31, 39–43, 62; *House Journal*, 1851, pp. 42, 44, 48,
50; *Revised Statutes*, 1851, p. vii. Holcombe did not participate in the work until after it
had been under way for several weeks.

[86] The progress of the code, which was Council File no. 13, may be traced by means of the
indexes of the journals. It was published under the supervision of Wilkinson with the
title *The Revised Statutes of the Territory of Minnesota Passed at the Second Session of the
Legislative Assembly* (St. Paul, 1851. xvi, 734 pp.).

[87] St. Paul, 1853. 198, 96 pp. The second pagination is that of decisions of the supreme
court.

and also merge suits in equity with civil actions. The organic act had simply provided that the supreme and district courts of the territory should possess chancery as well as common law jurisdiction. It was by an act of the legislature of March 5, 1853, that the chancery jurisdiction was required to be exercised "by the like process, pleadings, trial, and proceedings as in civil actions."[88]

The legislature of 1852 passed on the sixth of March, in response to numerous petitions, an exceedingly stringent "Maine" liquor law. It forbade under penalty of fine and imprisonment the manufacture or sale of spirituous or intoxicating liquors by any person not appointed as a public agent by county commissioners. The bill passed by precisely a three-fourths vote in the Council and a two-thirds vote in the House.[89] Mahlon Black offered at the proper stage an amendment that the only penalty for violation of the act should be death. But two colleagues supported him with their votes. Another amendment, which was agreed to, became the unexpected means of defeating the well-intentioned measure. It provided that the act should be submitted to the voters at a special election.[90] At the election held in April of that year the vote stood: for, 853; against, 662.[91] One Andrew Cloutier, a few months later, defied the will of the people and, being fined twenty-five dollars, took an appeal to the territorial supreme court, which held the act to be no law for the reason that, the legislative powers of the territory being completely vested by Congress in the two houses, they could not delegate it. The popular vote could therefore have no effect.[92]

[88] Revised Statutes, 1851, p. 330; Collated Statutes, 1853, p. 19.

[89] Collated Statutes, 1853, pp. 7–13; Council Journal, 1852, p. 95; House Journal, 1852, p. 133.

[90] House Journal, 1852, p. 122. See page 126 for the refusal of Chief Justice Fuller to furnish the House with an extrajudicial opinion on its power to pass a prohibiting law, of which no draft had been furnished him.

[91] Neill, Minnesota, 572, n.

[92] Minnesota Democrat (St. Paul), December 1, 1852. The decision of Judge Henry Z. Hayner is in the Weekly Minnesotian (St. Paul) for February 26, 1853. See St. Paul newspapers for accounts of numerous public meetings to agitate for the reënactment of the "Maine law." See also Murray, in Minnesota Historical Collections, 12: 121.

Anyone inspecting the statutes of the first three legislatures even casually will notice the frequent appearance of special enactments establishing new towns and counties, opening roads, and chartering ferries, dams, and boom companies. As there was a government appropriation for territorial roads, there was no lack of propositions for its rapid expenditure. No small fraction of the money lodged in the pockets of commissioners, surveyors, and contractors.[93] The idea of general corporation laws was still novel, but the Code of 1851 provided for the organization of nearly every kind of company but railroad companies. Still, there being no limitations in the organic act on granting special charters the legislature continued to hand them out with great liberality. In the first two sessions a number of divorces were granted, but so great were the vexations attending the necessary investigations into cases that the legislature of 1850 ignored all applications and but few were afterwards granted by legislation.[94]

[93] "Wonder if J. R. B[rown] wants any more road charters. Oh, Lord!" said McLeod, writing to Sibley on March 31, 1853. Sibley Papers.

[94] *Laws*, 1851, pp. 39, 40.

X. THE "SULAND" ACQUIRED

FROM the May day of 1849 on which Ramsey arrived in Minnesota and became the guest of Sibley in his famous stone house at Mendota there was not a day in which, whether in season or out of season, he was not reminded that the one predominant and absorbing interest of the white people of the territory was the acquisition of the lands occupied by the Sioux Indians, lying west of the Mississippi River. The little delta of territory between this river and the St. Croix acquired by the treaties of 1837 was a trifling fraction of the immense domain embraced within the boundaries of Minnesota by her organic act.[1] To have restricted the white settlements to this fraction would have run counter to that policy of expansion which had spread population and improvement from the Alleghenies and the Great Lakes to the Mississippi. For a long period the national authorities had complacently assumed that the great river would forever mark the extreme verge of white settlement.[2] But the wave of migration had already swept over it, and whole states had been created bounded on the east by its mid-channel. Ramsey did not have to put his ear to the ground to catch distant vibrations of a coming tempest of public urgency for the opening of the "Suland," as the

[1] Governor Ramsey in his message of 1849 estimated this area at 166,000 square miles. *Council Journal*, 1849, p. 8.

[2] The government had indeed acted on this presumption in a previous year. On July 31, 1841, at the Traverse des Sioux in what was then Iowa Territory, James Duane Doty, governor of Wisconsin Territory, acting as a special Indian commissioner, negotiated a treaty with the "Seeseeahto, Wafpato, and Wofpakoota" bands of Sioux Indians for the cession by them of some thirty million acres, lying north of the present boundary between Iowa and Minnesota and west of the Mississippi River, to be used as a permanent Indian territory. On August 11 he signed a supplementary treaty with the "Minda Waukanton" band of Sioux for a cession of some two million acres lying to the north of the principal cession, the eastern, Mississippi River, boundary of which ran up nearly to the mouth of the Crow River. From that river the tract extended westward in quadrilateral shape so as to embrace the area mentioned. The two grants formed part of one system. A further account of the Doty treaties of 1841, which were not ratified, is given in the Appendix, no. 6, *post*.

newspapers soon began to call it. It was in the air. It was the talk in the hotels, on the levee, in the social circle, and in the village post office. There survives a curious and interesting expression of this passion in the great seal of the state. The first territorial legislature, after an effort in committee at designing a seal, left the problem to Governor Ramsey and Sibley, then territorial delegate. With the assistance of experts in Washington a design was worked out which gave expression to the dominant Minnesota sentiment of the hour: a white man at his plow on the east bank of the Mississippi at the Falls of St. Anthony and a mounted Indian starting out at full speed toward the setting sun. The trifling error of the artist or draftsman, who placed the Indian also on the east side of the river and pictured him riding eastward to the setting sun, dulled not the keen message of the seal. It spoke the burning sentiment of the infant territory, in no uncertain language. "The white man is here with his plow; the Indian must go."[3] And the Latin motto, borrowed from a Scottish earldom, spoke the white man's reason for thus bidding the red man march. It was to be *Quae sursum volo videre*, "I fain would see what lies beyond." Here again someone blundered. *Quo* was used for *quae*, and *velo* for *volo*, and the result was nonsense. The main device still remains on the great seal of the state with the meaningless change of motto; but both the white man and the red man have been placed on the west bank of the Mississippi, the latter riding to the west.[4]

[3] The white wife of Captain Seth Eastman interpreted the seal in a poem of eight stanzas which begins:

> "Give way, give way, young warrior,
>   Thou and thy steed give way—
> Rest not, though lingers on the hills
>   The red sun's parting ray.
> The rocky bluff and prairie land
>   The white man claims them now,
> The symbols of his course are here,
>   The rifle, axe, and plough."

The whole poem is given in Neill, *Minnesota*, 517.

[4] The matter of the territorial seal is discussed at length in the Appendix, no 7 *post*.

There was one powerful concentrated interest which was now desirous of a cession of Indian lands. This was the fur trade. The successors of the American Fur Company, old traders still affiliated with them, and independent dealers, some newly come to the country, saw that their occupation must soon be gone. Game and fur animals were already scarce on the old hunting grounds of the lower Minnesota and the Undine Region of Nicollet, and the buffaloes had been driven to the Coteau des Prairies toward the Missouri. The paying stations were on the Cannon River, on Lakes Traverse and Big Stone, at Lac qui Parle, and at distant Pembina. Many of the old traders would gladly have seen the white man's plow stop at the bank of the Mississippi, and the Indians left to hunt and fish about their ancient homes. This they saw would be impossible and therefore with one consent they joined in the clamor for a treaty. Owing to a long-existing custom, an Indian treaty meant much to an Indian trader. Mention has already been made of the habitual sale of goods to Indians upon credit, to be paid for by the furs and skins brought in at the close of the hunting season. There were inevitable losses on these credits, some through dishonesty, more through ill fortune and accident, some through death. Although these losses were pleaded in justification of high prices to the Indians, still they stood on the traders' books and accumulated and swelled into prodigious unpaid debts. While these were originally obligations of individual Indians, it was not difficult to persuade the red man with his communistic ideas and customs to regard them as tribal obligations. There were ways of convincing Indian chiefs making treaties for their tribes that such debts should be paid out of moneys coming from the United States to the tribes. The sums thus allowed and paid in liquidation of the debts of traders were, as stated by a commissioner of Indian affairs, "an addition to the consideration which would otherwise content the Indians," by which the treasury of the United States had been heavily taxed.[5] The effect on the Indians was to encourage the more reckless and dissolute in extravagant expenditure. But the practice of liquidating Indian "credits" had become traditional, and whenever an Indian treaty was appointed the traders swarmed to the gathering place with their claims, big and little.[6] More important than the claims themselves or the amount of them was the long existence of an unwritten law that unless some proportion of claims was allowed and provided for there would be no treaty. The reasons why the influence of traders was so great as to enable them to bring the Indians to a treaty rendezvous or to keep them away at their pleasure have already been given. On this occasion the traders with the Sioux desired a treaty and a cession of lands, provided some liberal sums should be diverted to their hands.[7]

There was another body of persons more numerous, possessing perhaps less influence with the Indians, but still far too influential to be neglected. These were the half-breeds

[5] T. Hartley Crawford in his report for 1840, in 26 Congress, 2 session, *House Documents*, no. 2, p. 239 (serial 382).

[6] For a typical example see Taliaferro, in *Minnesota Historical Collections*, 6: 215, where an account is given of the negotiation of the treaty of 1837 with the Chippewa. On page 250 Taliaferro states that the precedent —"most fatal and dishonest" —of recognizing traders' claims for lost credits was established in the superintendency of General Cass. Unfortunately the Taliaferro Journal for 1837 has been lost. See also a letter, probably from Ramsay Crooks, to Aitkin, May 18, 1838, and one from Gabriel Franchere to Aitkin, August 17, 1838, in the Sibley Papers.

[7] Sibley to Ramsey, March 21, 1851, Ramsey Papers. "I do not know of a single man, who is not anxious that the Govt. shall succeed in making these treaties . . . in which the traders . . . are particularly interested." That the anxiety of the Sioux traders and of Sibley in particular was justifiable may be inferred from such information as that derived from the testimony of Joseph Sire, partner of the Chouteaus. Sibley's outfit had shown a loss since 1842 of at least ten thousand dollars a year, amounting to as much as thirty thousand dollars in some years. On September 3, 1849, Sibley wrote to missionaries of the American Board: "It is notorious that not a single man who has been engaged in the trade for any length of time, is not reduced to utter poverty or overwhelmed with debt, because none have been paid their dues by the Indians." Again writing on August 24, 1851, to C. C. Trowbridge, he said: "The amount allowed us . . . will suffice, if the treaties are ratified . . . to set me on my feet, and pay all my heavy liabilities for losses." There are other interesting comments in Sibley to Sire, September 7, and to McKenny, September 28, 1851, in Sibley Letter Book, no. 4. See also 33 Congress, 1 session, *Senate Executive Documents*, no. 61, p. 324 (serial 699). This document consists of the "Report of the Commissioners Appointed by the President of the United States to Investigate the Official Conduct of Alexander H. Ramsey, Late Governor of Minnesota Territory, with the Testimony Taken in the Case by Them, Transmitted to the Senate with the Message of the President of the United States, January 10, 1854." Hereafter it will be cited simply as the *Ramsey Investigation Report*.

or mixed-bloods, among whom were some men and women of intelligence, education, and gentle breeding. To secure the influence of an element which might prevent the negotiation of a treaty, or at least of a favorable one, it was necessary and it had become customary to provide a donation to the "breeds." In this case the Sioux half-breeds were quite willing to lend their aid to a treaty; the more so, as they had a long-standing claim which they greatly desired to have adjusted. Reference is here made to the grant of 1830 to Sioux half-breeds, known as the Wabasha Reservation, the advantage of which they had for twenty years failed to enjoy. The half-breed influence was reënforced by that of white men who had become fathers to numerous progeny by Indian women, all of whom would count to the paternal advantage when it came to a division of money or a grant of lands to half-breeds.[8]

A third group, small but very influential, to be found at and about the seat of government, had to be considered whenever Indian treaties were to be negotiated and ratified. These men possessed the art of drafting feasible bills, of interesting and steering committees, of moving departmental officials to action, and of advising them as to the action most beneficial to the interests which could afford the luxury of their services. They belonged in part to that third house so well known in our legislative history. To secure an appropriation for the expenses of an Indian treaty, the necessary administrative action, and at length its ratification by the Senate without the intervention of the lobby would have been possible, but only after interminable delays and vexations.[9]

As for the Sioux, who had already been sounded by both the traders and the half-breeds, they had in the year 1849

[8] An extant list of the beneficiaries of the Sioux half-breed scrip legislation reveals a notable fecundity in half-breed families. See the Appendix, no. 11, n. 38, *post*.

[9] The services of subordinate officials in the interior department were desirable, for Ramsey advised Sibley on August 18, 1850, to "have some confidential friend (a whig) who can be about the Indian bureau — and can have influence there." Sibley Papers.

little desire for a treaty and less for any alienation of their lands. The lower Sioux, who in 1837 had had a taste of the good things commonly plentiful on a treaty ground, and who had been in receipt of considerable annuities thereafter, were not averse to a repetition of that good time, though they were loath to entertain the idea of leaving their beautiful country.

Such were the conditions under which Governor Ramsey, in his message to the first territorial legislature on September 4, 1849, strongly urged that body to memorialize Congress to provide for a treaty of cession with the Sioux.[10] Both Governor Ramsey and the legislature had been anticipated by Delegate Sibley, who in the winter of 1848–49 had labored without success to secure appropriations for various Indian objects, among them the expenses of a treaty with the Sioux. The delegate was more successful with the commissioner of Indian affairs, the Honorable Orlando Brown. In June of 1849 that official addressed a letter to the Honorable Thomas Ewing, secretary of the interior, recommending the negotiation of a treaty of cession with the Sioux, "in order to make room for the emigrants now going in large numbers to the new Territory of Minnesota." The expenses, he wrote, could be met out of his small current appropriation.[11] The secretary approved this recommendation and promptly appointed as commissioners to conduct the negotiations Alexander Ramsey, governor of Minnesota and ex officio superintendent of Indian affairs in the territory, and John Chambers of Iowa, former governor of that state, who had had much experience in Indian affairs. On the twenty-fifth of August, 1849, the commissioner

---

[10] He proposed a cession of the land between the Mississippi and a meridian line drawn through the lake at the head of the Long Prairie River (probably Lake Carlos near Alexandria, in township 129, range 37). Later, in a letter to Commissioner Lea, he wrote of the popular demand for a treaty, and continued, "I soon imbibed this feeling, and lent myself with all my energies to bring about a purchase of the country in question." *Council Journal*, 1849, p. 15; *Ramsey Investigation Report*, 324 (serial 699).

[11] 31 Congress, 1 session, *House Executive Documents*, no. 5, part 2, pp. 978, 985 (serial 570).

transmitted to these men a document of instructions for their guidance. It is important that some passages of this paper be noted. As for the amount of territory to be acquired from the Indians, the ancient maxim of the frontiersman, "when you are gittin', git a plenty," was adopted, clothed, of course, in formal official phrasing. The northern boundary was to be the Sioux-Chippewa line of 1825. The Mississippi was, of course, to be the eastern boundary. The southern line was to be so drawn as to include in the cession all lands claimed by the Sioux, or any of their bands, in Iowa. On the west a line joining the headwaters of the Big Sioux and the Wild Rice was to be the utmost bound. If the treaty commissioners could not get all, then let them take what they could get. As for the price, it was the opinion of the Indian office that two or two and one-half cents per acre would be ample. Any increase upon that price must be on evidence and information which would satisfy the president and Congress. As for payment, the Sioux were to be persuaded to waive demands for large sums of money whether in hand or in annuities. Experience had shown that Indians receiving the largest cash annuities were invariably the most dissolute and degraded. It was, therefore, recommended that the Indians be offered liberal remuneration in useful goods, in provisions, in implements of agriculture, in domestic animals, and in furniture. All annuities, whether in money or in kind, should be terminable and adjustable to the numbers of the tribe.

The most notable item, however, in this catena of instructions is that "No reservations of lands can be allowed, and no stipulations be inserted in the treaty for the payment of the Indians' debts — both being expressly prohibited by a resolution of the Senate passed on the 3d of March, 1843, and which, it is known, that body has refused to rescind." An act of Congress of March 3, 1847, had reiterated the prohibition by providing that all annuities and other moneys and all goods under treaties be divided and paid to heads of families or individuals entitled, instead of to chiefs or their assignees; but the insertion of the phrase "at the discretion of the president" transformed the prohibition into a mere piece of advice. It is not hard to guess what great interest had had its attorney on hand at the proper moment. It was expressly stated that it was very desirable that there should be but one treaty with all the bands and that their varying interests should be adjusted by graduating the cash payments. A departure from the instructions was allowed the commissioners if deemed advantageous in the settlement of the half-breed claim to the Wabasha Reservation. The strictest economy was enjoined, because the expense of the treaty would have to be met out of current appropriations of a general character. Not more than six thousand dollars could be spared for presents to the Indians. The commissioner ventured the opinion that, while some of the land to be acquired might be of excellent quality, a great part of it could never be more than of trifling, if any, value to the government.[12]

On the very day of the receipt of these instructions Governor Ramsey wrote to Sibley at Mendota requesting him to send out runners to notify the chiefs of the Sioux bands to meet in council at Mendota on an early day in October, and to file his bill for the expense of the embassy.[13] On repairing to the rendezvous the commissioners found no general assemblage of the chiefs. The few who attended listened languidly to the propositions of the government and suggested postponement until a fuller concourse could be brought together. The Sioux chiefs had no disposition to leave their villages or hunting grounds and make the long march to Mendota upon the bare invitation of two unknown government officials, however attractive and costly the

[12] 31 Congress, 1 session, *House Executive Documents*, no. 5, part 2, p. 980 (serial 570); *Statutes at Large*, 9: 203. A manuscript thesis by Ruth Thompson, entitled "The Sioux Treaties at Traverse des Sioux and Mendota in 1851 and Their Outcome," contains a good general account of the negotiations. Copies of this thesis are in the libraries of the University of Minnesota and the Minnesota Historical Society.

[13] September 21, 1849, Sibley Papers.

presents they might be opening in the council house. The commissioner of Indian affairs quietly reported to Congress that the failure to effect a treaty of cession with the Sioux was due to the fact that "most of the Indians had left for their fall hunt, and to other causes of difficulty."[14] A sufficient number of half-breeds, however, attended and the commissioners came to an agreement with them by which for a consideration of two hundred thousand dollars they were to relinquish their claims upon the tract on Lake Pepin granted them by the treaty of 1830. This side dish of a treaty, however, was not ratified by the Senate, and need not at present further occupy attention.[15] Among extant letters relating to the abortive effort of 1849 are two deserving mention. One from Sibley to Ramsey, dated September 15, 1849, expresses Sibley's belief that all influences combined could not accomplish the making of a treaty with the Sioux unless the price of the land were enhanced, and adds, "Then there are the claims, for the payment of which as well as the half-breeds, due provision must be made, and which I am convinced the Ex-Governor [*Chambers*] will oppose." The other letter is that of Henry M. Rice, dated December 1, 1849, expressing the hope that no treaty would be made with the Sioux for two years. If it were made prematurely the east side (St. Paul) would stand still and Mendota would get the start. He speaks of a plan to make St. Peter's a great town, of which Sibley would be "the man."[16] Governor Ramsey now understood what any old frontiersman could have told

[14] 31 Congress, 1 session, *House Executive Documents*, no. 5, part 2, p. 945 (serial 570).

[15] Governor Doty had negotiated an abortive treaty in 1841 for the cession of the Wabasha Reservation for two hundred thousand dollars. See *post*, p. 323. Commissioner Lea in his instructions to Ramsey and Chambers in 1849 stated that he thought this consideration far more than the half-breed title was worth. Nevertheless they allowed the full amount by treaty, and the commissioner reported to the secretary of the interior late in November that a cession had been arranged "on reasonable terms." A draft of the half-breed treaty, dated July 31, 1841 bearing the indorsement in pencil, "in Doty's writing," is in the Sibley Papers. See also 31 Congress, 1 session, *House Executive Documents*, no. 5, part 2, pp. 945, 982, 983, 1018 (serial 570). Sibley as attorney for the half-breeds of the lower Indians negotiated the abortive treaty of 1849 and lodged a memorial with the Senate for its ratification. See *Senate Executive Proceedings*, 8: 174, 396. A copy of this treaty, dated October 9, 1849, is in the Sibley Papers.

[16] Ramsey Papers.

him, that Indian treaties were made not at times and seasons appointed by government agents but according to the pleasure of Indian traders, half-breeds, and squaw men, and that their advice and consent could be obtained only by allowances for traders' claims and bonuses to half-breeds.[17]

Upon the assemblage of the Thirty-first Congress in December, 1849, no time was lost in putting matters in train for a treaty in the following summer. Delegate Sibley's expectation was that a treaty with the Sioux might be made about the fifteenth or the twentieth of September, immediately after one at Pembina.[18] But Congress was not greatly interested in projects so remote and advocated chiefly by a few officials, Indian traders, and aspirants to appointments. The only step taken at this session was the setting apart by a section of the general Indian appropriation bill, approved on September 30, of fifteen thousand dollars for the expenses of a treaty with the Mississippi and St. Peter's Sioux for the extinguishment of their title to lands in Minnesota Territory.[19] Although it was late in the season, negotiations might have been entered upon, had the president been disposed to appoint the treaty commissioners without delay. Those appointments were long postponed. Accordingly all proceedings in regard to treaties with the Minnesota Sioux and Chippewa went over to the following year and the next session of Congress, when agitation was actively resumed.[20]

Of first importance was the make-up of the treaty commission. There was a general consent that Governor Ramsey should be one member. Indeed, to have left him off while he was holding the office of superintendent of Indian affairs in the territory would have been an indignity. But he was a

[17] Sibley to Ramsey, September 15, 1849, February 9, March 21, 1851, Ramsey Papers.
[18] Sibley to Ramsey, May 30, June 1, 1850, Ramsey Papers; F. B. Sibley to Chouteau and Company, August 21, 1850, in Sibley Letter Book, no. 1.
[19] *Statutes at Large*, 9: 556.
[20] Sibley to Chouteau and Company, October 21, 1850, to Laframboise, October 25, 1850. In a letter to Chouteau and Company, November 3, 1850, Sibley says: " The Indians are all prepared to make a treaty when we tell them to do so, and such an one as I may dictate." Sibley Letter Book, no. 1.

favorite with all, respected for his dignity and fair-mindedness. He was already the close and trusted friend of one of the most respectable and influential of the traders, in spite of opposed political affiliations.[21] Evidence of his standing at Washington is the fact that when Congress, by an act approved on February 27, 1851, separated the offices of superintendents of Indian affairs from the governorships of territories, a particular exception by name was made of Governor Ramsey, who was to continue to hold both offices until the president should otherwise direct.[22] The choice of an associate was the subject of extensive correspondence and numerous conferences. One of the men proposed was thought to be too old for efficient service, another was an "old tinker" altogether undesirable. At one time Ramsey was led to believe that Hugh Tyler of Pennsylvania, who will appear later in this chapter, was to be his associate, an appointment which would have been very agreeable to him.[23] But Tyler made the mistake of being too willing to serve, and there is good ground for believing that he was regarded by the appointing power as too friendly to a certain body of traders. He was much too impetuous in repelling the insinuation. His influence, however, was at one time great enough to enable him to obtain permission from the Indian office to furnish a draft of the instructions to be given the treaty commissioners, whosoever they might be. In the composition of this draft he availed himself of the skill and experience of Sibley.[24] When the Indian appropriation bill, approved on February 27, 1851, appeared in its

---

[21] William H. Forbes wrote to Sibley on July 11, 1850, "I do not believe you have a warmer or more sincere friend than he [*Ramsey*] is." Likewise Dr. Thomas Foster informed Ramsey, on August 13, 1850, that "Sibley is I believe really, truely, and without *much* selfishness, your warm friend. . . . I think we have got Sibley in the proper place; and that we can use him in the future, quite effectually. He is at any rate the best man here [*at Washington*] for the Territorial, and yours and my, interests! !" Sibley Papers; Ramsey Papers.

[22] *Statutes at Large*, 9: 586.

[23] Ramsey to Sibley, July 10, 24, August 6, 1850, Sibley Papers; Sibley to Ramsey, August 28, 1850, Ramsey Papers.

[24] Sibley to Ramsey, May 27, 30, June 1, 20, 26, July 26, September 5, December 4, 1850, Foster to Ramsey, September 24, 1850, Ramsey Papers. Tyler played an important part in the consummation of the Sioux treaties, as will appear.

final shape, it was found to contain a provision that thereafter all Indian treaties should be negotiated by officials selected from the Indian service, who should act without additional compensation. There is no known record of the authorship of this provision, but there can be no doubt that it was altogether satisfactory to the Sioux traders.[25] Early in the summer of 1851, it was announced that the Honorable Luke Lea of Mississippi, commissioner of Indian affairs, had been designated by the president as treaty commissioner, with Governor Ramsey as his associate.[26]

[25] *Statutes at Large*, 9: 586. John H. Stevens wrote exultingly to Ramsey on February 25, 1851, just after the passage of the Indian bill: "Sibley has and can beat them on every corner. . . . Everything here is safe thanks to Mr. Sibley." See also his letters of February 16, 22, 1851. In a letter to Ramsey, January 23, 1851, Sibley wrote: "I am now striving to get his [*Lea's*] consent to allow himself to be appointed third on the Sioux commission and think I shall be able to bring it about." Ramsey Papers.

[26] An explanation of the contest, lasting many months, over the appointment of the second treaty commissioner may be found in the rivalry of the two great trading companies, the American Fur Company and the firm of W. G. and G. W. Ewing, of Fort Wayne, Indiana, which also had a body of claims against the Sioux Indians. The favored candidate of the former concern was Hugh Tyler of Pennsylvania; the Ewings championed Richard W. Thompson of Indiana, then and later a prominent figure in the public affairs of his state. At one time or another each of the interests believed that it had secured the appointment. With a degree of confidence not justified by the event, Sibley wrote to Ramsey from Washington on May 18, 1850, "Tyler has worked manfully with me to break up that *clique*. . . . I intend to have him appointed him [*sic*] Comr. jointly with yourself for the Sioux, and I think it can be managed." On February 7, 1851, Thompson wrote Ramsey asking him to make the arrangements for the Sioux treaty and to get the council house ready. He suggested a division of the money appropriated for supplies and of the patronage, commissions, messengers, expresses, and other perquisites. Each commissioner he thought should have a good saddle horse. He had bought himself a rifle for fifty-five dollars, a shotgun for sixty-five dollars, and a pair of pistols for sixty dollars. He would be pleased to buy any comforts that Governor Ramsey might desire. The designation of Commissioner Lea was of course very satisfactory to Sibley, for it eliminated Thompson. Indeed, he wrote a private letter to Lea to express his pleasure that he (Lea) was to serve on the treaty commission and assured him of his "hearty co-operation." "I am to meet them [*the Sioux*] in Council next week, when I shall endeavor to prepare them to meet you with a favorable impression." Dr. Thomas Foster, who aspired to be, and finally became, the secretary of the commission, was not so well satisfied. In a letter to Ramsey from Philadelphia, November 1, 1850, at a time when the *New York Tribune* announced the selection of Thompson, he remarked, "Damn the whole thing. Since Tyler was defeated, I have several times wished the whole thing was postponed *sine die*." Sibley to Ramsey, May 18, 1850, Foster to Ramsey, November 1, 1850, Richard Thompson to Ramsey, February 7, 1851, J. H. Stevens to Ramsey, February 16, Ramsey Papers; Sibley to Luke Lea, April 27, 1851, in Sibley Letter Book, no. 4.

Further information in regard to the importance attached to the selection of the treaty commissioners and the efforts of the American Fur Company to secure appointees favorably disposed to its interests may be gathered from the following correspondence: letters to Sibley from Ramsey, July 10, 24, August 6, 18, 1850, from Forbes, July 11, 1850, from Brown, November 29, 1850, from Sellors, December 1, 1850, from Foster, December 3, 1850, from McLeod, January 27, 1851, in the Sibley Papers; letters from Sibley to Lea, April 27,

There were those who favored taking a delegation of chiefs to Washington and making the treaty there. Alexander Faribault, an influential half-breed trader, wrote Sibley on January 21, 1850, recommending Washington, "w[h]ere we could fight a few chief not the hole tribe, & all the missionarys, that are stronger than all the Indians put together." Old Wabasha was reported as preferring Washington, where it would be easier to allow traders' claims, which he favored, but to which his young men were objecting.[27] This preference seems not to have been entertained in the Indian office, and it was decided beforehand to hold separate councils with the upper and the lower Sioux. The controlling reason for this was that a successful effort with the upper Sioux would induce the lower bands, less disposed to treat on favorable terms, to waive their well-known reluctance. There were, indeed, influential personages in both divisions opposed to any treaty, especially to one which should provide for payment of traders' claims.[28]

At half past five o'clock on the morning of June 29, 1851, the treaty commissioners with a considerable party of interested persons left Fort Snelling on board the steamboat "Excelsior" for the Traverse des Sioux, where they arrived in the forenoon of the next day.[29] The commissioners found no Indians awaiting them except the resident Sisseton. On July 4, one hundred and fifty came in from the Minnesota Valley; on the ninth, fifty more appeared; on the twelfth, a considerable body of Wahpeton from Lac qui Parle came

1851, to Ramsey, June 25, 1851, in Sibley Letter Book, no. 4; and letters to Ramsey from Sibley, May 13, June 1, 20, 26, July 15, August 6, 25, 28, September 6, 19, December 4, 5, 1850, February 9, 19, March 21, 1851, from Cooper, December 3, 1850, from Thompson, February 7, 1851, from Stevens, February 25, 1851, in the Ramsey Papers.

[27] Sibley Papers.

[28] McLeod informed Sibley that the "lower fellows" could be brought to terms only by first treating with the upper Indians, "who are friendly to us." Letters of September 16, 24, 1850, Sibley Papers.

[29] See the issues of the *Minnesota Democrat* and the *Weekly Minnesotian* for August 4, 1852. There is an interesting letter from G. H. Pond, dated July 8, 1851, in which he remarks upon the very early hour at which the "Excelsior" started up the Minnesota and the class of persons on board. These things begot in him "painful suspicions." Query: Were the services of Mr. Pond not desired? Ramsey Papers.

into camp; and so they dribbled in from day to day. Well fed on the pork, beef, and flour distributed by the commissary of the commission, Alexis Bailly, the Indians were in no haste. From day to day they amused themselves and the white people with medicine dances, ball games, horse and foot races, and mimic battles, sometimes giving splendid spectacular effects.[30]

On the eighteenth of July the commissioners, considering that the Indians were sufficiently represented, opened the council in an ample bough house, which had been erected for the occasion on the high ground back of the wide river bottom. Both of them made elaborate speeches expressing the desire of the Great Father to acquire of the Indians lands already useless to them and his willingness to pay a just price. An ample home would be provided for his red children, where farms and houses and schools would be opened, and where physicians, blacksmiths, and other artisans would teach the white man's arts. Indian fashion, Sleepy Eyes, the leading chief present, asked for an opportunity to sleep on the proposition, a request immediately granted. The morrow found the Indians in council in no happy frame of mind. Some did not want to treat; some proposed impossible terms; others begged for delay until the arrival of the Indians from

---

[30] These dates and figures are from Governor Ramsey's diary of the excursion, in the possession of his daughter, Mrs. Marion R. Furness, of St. Paul. The classical account of the treaty is that by James M. Goodhue, the editor of the *Minnesota Pioneer*, who was present from June 30 to July 21; it appears as "Editorial Correspondence" in the *Pioneer* between July 3, and August 7, 1851. The articles of the last two dates are unsigned and may be the work of another hand. This journal, with the exception of the entries for the last three days, is substantially reprinted in the *Minnesota Year Book* for 1852, compiled by William G. le Duc. According to the unfriendly *Minnesota Democrat*, July 29, 1851, "Messrs. Sibley & Co., were the real parties to the Treaty. The Indians were like potters' clay in the hands of those who trade among them." Commissioner Lea, however, should not be placed "in the same category with Messrs. Ramsey and Sibley, who are grandiloquent specimens of the Ephraim Smooth school of tacticians." Thomas Hughes, "The Treaty of Traverse des Sioux in 1851, under Governor Alexander Ramsey, with Notes of the Former Treaty There, in 1841, under Governor James D. Doty, of Wisconsin," in *Minnesota Historical Collections*, 10: 101–129 (part 1), is largely drawn from Goodhue's report, supported by Mr. Hughes's own studies on the treaty ground. On June 17, 1914, the large bowlder on which presents for the Indians were displayed was placed on the treaty site, and a brass plate with an appropriate inscription was affixed to it. See the *St. Peter Herald* for June 19, 1914. The large painting by Francis D. Millet in the governor's reception room in the state Capitol finely illustrates the scene of the treaty.

Lake Traverse. This the commissioners refused. Thereupon Sleepy Eyes and other Sisseton chiefs left the council. The commissioners gave notice that no further issues of provisions would be made and that they would take their leave in the morning. The same evening a deputation of chiefs came to say that Sleepy Eyes had acted without authority and to ask for another council.[31] When the council reopened on the twenty-first, after an intervening Sunday, the chiefs were more disposed to negotiate. The older and wiser heads understood that sooner or later the white man would sweep them off their hereditary lands and would dictate the kind and the amount of recompense he might please to pay, no matter with what solemnity he might go through the farce of a treaty. Their counsel was to make the best terms possible. Some extremists, who had learned to read, proposed six million dollars as an ultimatum.[32] The negotiations, formal and informal, now went on for two days. Provisions were issued with a liberal hand. The traders and half-breeds had their influential men present to work on the weak side of Indian nature. Mrs. Nancy McClure Huggan, who was present, in her narrative drops the remark: "I have always wondered how so much champagne got so far out on the frontier!"[33] Martin McLeod, in a letter of December 20, 1851, says that "there was mismanagement with the Indians at the Traverse Making them large offers of blankets &c was bad policy, and led to suspicion. It looked like bribery — and the Indians and enemies of M. Sibley and his friends will make great *capital* out of it."[34] As the commissioners report, the Indians were "induced" to agree to the terms which had been proposed to them and on Wednesday,

[31] Ramsey Diary.
[32] Report of the treaty commissioners, in 32 Congress, 1 session, *Senate Executive Documents*, no. 1, p. 279 (serial 613). Sibley in his correspondence had repeatedly suggested ten cents an acre as a fair price.
[33] "The Story of Nancy McClure," in *Minnesota Historical Collections*, 6: 446. The beverage was opened at her wedding feast, but she, "a stout Presbyterian . . . and a teetotaler . . . would not take even the smallest sip." Mrs. Huggan is still living (December, 1919) at the Sisseton agency in South Dakota.
[34] Letter to F. B. Sibley, Sibley Papers.

THE TREATY OF TRAVERSE DES SIOUX, 1851

Oil by Frank B. Mayer

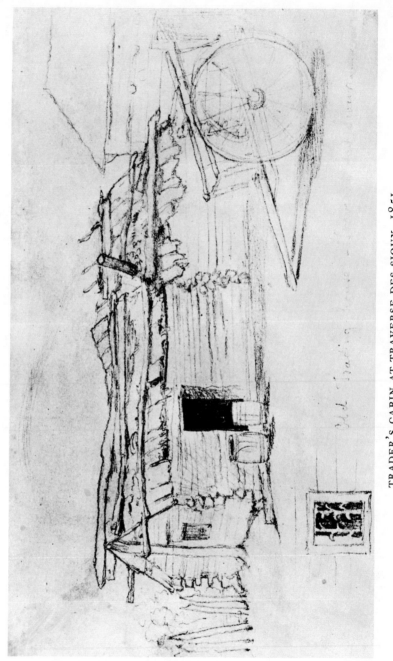

TRADER'S CABIN AT TRAVERSE DES SIOUX. 1851

July 23, the treaty was signed by thirty-five chiefs and thirteen witnesses.[35]

By this treaty the Sisseton and Wahpeton bands of the Sioux sold to the United States all their lands in Iowa and Minnesota east of the Red River–Lake Traverse–Big Sioux line, reserving for their use and occupation, to be held as Indian lands are held, a tract stretching from Lake Traverse down the Minnesota River to the Yellow Medicine and extending ten miles on each side of the former stream. The consideration was fixed at $1,665,000, but the government did not agree to pay that sum on the spot. It was stipulated that the principal amount of $1,360,000 should draw annual interest at five per cent for fifty years, after which the obligation for payment of principal as well as interest should cease and determine. It was further particularly stipulated that the annual interest payment of $68,000 should be divided as follows: for a civilization fund, $12,000; for an education fund, $6,000; for goods and provisions, $10,000; for cash annuity, $40,000. It is remarkable that the commissioners, in the face of former instructions, of law, and of the experience and testimony of those best qualified to judge, consented to so large a cash annuity. They gave as their main reason the convenience of the Indians in "procuring such things as they desire," naïvely adding, "while extortion is prevented by the competition of their numerous traders." Cash annuities they should have known and did know passed almost immediately into the hands of traders quite irrespective of value received. But this item was merely another concession to the parties who alone could induce the Indians to sign a treaty.

There remained a balance of $305,000 of purchase money. Of this sum $30,000 were to be presently expended, under the direction of the president, on farms, schools, mills,

[35] 32 Congress, 1 session, *Senate Executive Documents*, no. 1, pp. 279–282 (serial 613); *Statutes at Large*, 10: 949–953. The original treaty, which is in the handwriting of Dr. Thomas Foster, the secretary of the commission, may be seen in the files of the Indian office.

blacksmith shops, and other beneficial objects. This deduction made, there remained $275,000. It was stipulated that this sum was to be paid "to the Chiefs of said bands, to enable them to comply with their present just engagements" — a well-known euphemism for the payment of traders' and half-breeds' claims — and to defray the expenses of the removal of the Indians to the reservation and of one year's subsistence while they were establishing themselves thereon. A proviso expressly stated that this money should be "paid to the chiefs in such manner, as they, hereafter, in open council, shall request." It will be observed that, as this treaty provision would when ratified have the force of law, it would set aside, for this transaction, the act of 1847 requiring all moneys due Indians to be paid to heads of families or individuals as entitled.

As each chief signed the treaty and stepped aside he was "pulled by the blanket" and directed to a place a few feet distant where on the head of a barrel or on a piece of board on the barrel lay another document to be signed. Joseph R. Brown held the pen and all the chiefs signed but two.[36] This document, which later became notorious under the name of the "traders' paper," stripped of formal verbiage, contained: (1) an acknowledgment by the chiefs, signing as the authorized representatives of their bands, of sums of money justly due to their traders and half-breeds; (2) a request "hereby, in open council" that the sums below specified should be paid to the persons designated; (3) a solemn pledge by themselves and their nation to make such payment. The paper had not been read nor explained to the Indians in open council at any time, but it was later

[36] Two of the chiefs, Limping Devil and Sounding Moccasin, testified in the investigation that the Reverend Stephen R. Riggs had pulled them by the blanket to the barrel where Joseph R. Brown held the pen for the signing of the second paper, and Riggs admitted that he had done so in several instances. The missionaries, indeed, received eight hundred dollars by that agreement, in payment, as he explained, for some cattle which had been killed at the mission by the Indians. Other witnesses told of various circumstances connected with the signing of the "traders' paper." Testimony of Williamson, the Orphan, Limping Devil, Sounding Moccasin, Riggs, and Foster, in *Ramsey Investigation Report*, 9, 117, 120, 123, 291, 293 (serial 699).

contended by and in behalf of the traders and the half-breeds that the arrangement was fully understood by the chiefs and braves, that it was consented to by them, and that they were not deceived. Dr. Thomas S. Williamson thought when he signed the paper that it was a third copy of the treaty. At the time of signing, the schedule of payees with sums of money assigned to each was not annexed to the paper. In the afternoon a committee of the traders — McLeod, Brown, and Robert — scaled down and tabulated the traders' claims so as to bring them within the amount limited in the treaty. In the evening the chiefs announced the amounts they desired to be paid to the half-breed families and individuals, and Sibley took down the names and the amounts by candlelight. The combined schedule was attached to the paper by Martin McLeod the following morning.[37] Nathaniel McLean, the Sioux agent, writing a year later, said that he saw nothing of the traders' paper until the Indians were called over to the side table to sign it. He requested the person having it in charge to have it read and explained but his request was refused because "it would make a disturbance" and the Indians understood it anyway. It was the agent's opinion that had the paper

[37] The essential words of this document, which was the occasion of controversy for many years, are: "We, the undersigned, chiefs, soldiers, and braves . . . having this day concluded a treaty . . . and being desirous to pay to our traders and half-breeds the sum of money which we acknowledge to be justly due to them, do hereby obligate and bind ourselves, as the authorized representatives of the aforesaid bands, to pay to the individuals hereafter [not "hereinafter"] designated the sum of money set opposite to their respective names . . . and as it is specified that said sum shall be paid in such manner as requested by the chiefs in open council thereafter [after ratification], we do hereby in open council request and desire that the said sums below specified shall be paid to the persons designated . . . and for this payment . . . we hereby solemnly pledge ourselves and the faith of our nation." The paper was signed by thirty-three Indians and was witnessed by nine whites. A schedule of the amounts to be paid to designated individuals follows the signatures. Twenty-three traders, two missionaries (Riggs and Williamson), and fifty half-breeds with their families are named as beneficiaries. The traders' claims, according to accounts filed under oath with Governor Ramsey, totaled $431,735.78, but this sum was scaled down to $210,000. Some notable examples of this reduction are: Bailly and Dousman, from $43,122 to $15,000; Sibley as agent of the American Fur Company, from $144,984.40 to $66,459; J. B. Faribault, from $33,000 to $22,500; Alexander Faribault, from $18000, to $13,500; and McKenzie as assignee of the Ewings, from $57,175 to $5,500. The total amount designated for the half-breeds was $40,000. *Ramsey Investigation Report*, 9–12, 15, 20 (serial 699); 32 Congress, 2 session, *Senate Executive Documents*, no. 29, part 2, pp. 22–25, 27, 31 (serial 660).

been read and explained at that time the Indians would not have signed it. Some of the accounts which were presented and allowed would not, wrote Agent McLean, bear the light of the disinterested investigation which ought to be made.[38]

The commissioners, having concluded the negotiations, returned to St. Paul. A fortnight later, on August 5, they secured at Mendota the signatures of the chiefs and headmen of the lower bands to a treaty differing in its essential provisions from that of Traverse des Sioux only in the amounts of money named.[39] The allowance for "settling affairs" was ninety thousand dollars for each of two tribes. A "traders' paper" was signed by seven chiefs, soldiers, and braves of the Wahpekute band.[40] As there were no claims against the Mdewakanton antedating 1837, a separate procedure was adopted for them. The reserve set aside for the lower bands was also in the Minnesota Valley, from the Yellow Medicine about sixty miles down to the Little Rock, an insignificant stream, and extending ten miles on either side of the river. The treaty of Mendota contained also an article providing for the surrender of the Wabasha Reservation by the half-breeds for the sum of one hundred and fifty thousand dollars. The commissioners should cer-

---

[38] 32 Congress, 2 session, *Senate Executive Documents*, no. 1, p. 351 (serial 658). Witness after witness testified in the investigation that the traders' paper was not read nor explained to the Indians and that the schedule of traders' claims was not attached at the time of signing, but a number stated that the great majority of the chiefs and braves knew what they were to sign. Brown, Dousman, and Riggs told of councils which were held between the Indians and the traders for the purpose of discussing and arranging a settlement of their accounts. See the *Ramsey Investigation Report*, 109, 154, 198, 203, 211, 219, 227, 233, 237, 245, 269, 282, 291; also a letter by Williamson, quoted in the *Minnesota Democrat* for December 29, 1852, and one by Henry Jackson in the same paper for January 5, 1853. Interesting side lights, especially on Williamson's understanding of the traders' paper, appear in letters to the author from Judson Jones, July 30, 1904, from A. M. Williamson, August 4, November 4, 1904, and from A. R. Riggs, November 18, 1904, in the Folwell Papers. The Jones letter contains obvious errors.

[39] 32 Congress, 1 session, *Senate Executive Documents*, no. 1, p. 279 (serial 613); *Statutes at Large*, 10: 954–959. The lower Sioux simply ceded all their lands in Minnesota and Iowa without description.

[40] The traders' paper signed by the Wahpekute chiefs promised the money to the "individuals hereinafter designated" instead of to the "individuals hereafter designated," as was the case with the Sisseton and Wahpeton traders' paper. 32 Congress, 2 session, *Senate Executive Documents*, no. 29, part 2, pp. 22, 32 (serial 660).

tainly have known that the half-breeds were not and could not be competent parties to a treaty, and that the article would be inoperative. For this reason, doubtless, it was stipulated that the rejection of this article by the Senate should not invalidate the others. But the half-breeds were placated and lent their influence to the closing of the principal bargain.

The agreement was not reached without difficulties, however. At the first council, on July 29, Wabasha in an opening address spoke of funds lying back in the hands of the Great Father and added, "These you see here around, are anxious to get that which is due them, before they do anything." The treaty of 1837 provided for a perpetual annuity of fifteen thousand dollars in specie, except a portion not to exceed one-third of that amount which should be applied in such manner as the president should direct. There was an understanding that this reserved third would be used for the enlightenment of the Indians, and it came to be spoken of as the "education fund." The retention of the greater portion of this fund in the treasury for twelve years is not easily explainable, but the suggestion is ventured that it could not be placed in the hands of missionaries of different denominations, in those days less tolerant of competition in the good work of salvation. At the council on the second day the Indians were not prepared to negotiate. At that on the third day, July 31, Little Crow, not head chief of the tribe but chief of the Kaposia band and the most influential orator of all the bands, splendidly dressed for the occasion, addressed the commissioners. Referring to money due under the old treaty he said, "We do not want to talk on the subject of a new treaty, until it is all paid." Commissioner Ramsey, interrupting, suggested an immediate cash payment equal to the usual cash annuities for three years. The money, he said, was on hand in boxes and they might go on with the treaty while it was being counted and divided up for the bands. Little Crow replied, "We will talk of nothing else but that money, if it is until next spring."

The council broke up at this point, and four days passed with but one brief session in which no progress was made. Consultations went on with individual chiefs and modifications were made in the text of the treaty which it was believed would satisfy the Indians. On Monday, August 5, the commissioners met them in council expecting to obtain their signatures without delay. They were disappointed. Wabasha was a man used to the woods and he wanted no home on the prairies. He wanted no money paid for farmers, schools, physicians, traders, and half-breeds. The Indians had had all these things in the old treaty and had got no good from them. Little Crow was of the same mind as Wabasha about the proposed reservation but would be content if it were to be brought down as far as the Traverse des Sioux. Shakopee's brother said it ought to come down to Lake Minnetonka. Wacouta preferred the Cannon River country where his band was then living; otherwise he was pleased with the treaty but protested that no changes should be made in it after it was taken to Washington. After other propositions of trivial character had been made, Ramsey asked the Indians to name the chief who should sign first. Little Crow was named. He rose and renewed his request that the reservation should come down to the Traverse des Sioux. The commissioners at once declined, and Colonel Lea added that a man "may often get hungry by too long talk." Little Crow then wrote his own name, Taoyateduta (His Red People). Wabasha signed next and was followed by sixty-three chiefs and braves of the seven lower bands. In this final session nothing was said about the money due under the old treaty — the education fund. That obstacle had been removed by the insertion of an article providing that the whole fifteen thousand dollars annuity should thereafter be paid in cash and that the sum of thirty thousand dollars should also be immediately paid on account of the education fund.[41] It was probably no accident that the American Fur Company had that amount of specie on hand and at once advanced it to the Indian agent, who paid it out the next day. Not many days passed before substantially the whole amount was in the hands of the traders and the merchants of St. Paul. A large proportion of it went for whisky and for horses. "The Indians," wrote Sibley, "are horse-mad." Few of those animals were alive when winter came. Although greatly in need of provisions, the Indians would not buy any considerable quantities, and in three weeks they were begging for food.[42]

The commissioners in their report, drafted by Dr. Thomas Foster, their secretary, congratulated themselves and the country on the consummation of these important negotiations, by which an area computed at thirty-five million acres, including the splendid region described by Nicollet as the garden spot of the Mississippi Valley, had been acquired.[43] Assuming that the lands would annually yield the interest on the price paid, they suggested that the cost of the "magnificent purchase is only the sum paid in hand." They advised a prompt ratification of these treaties, for otherwise the government would be compelled to eject by

[41] *Statutes at Large*, 10: 954; *Minnesota Pioneer*, August 14, 1851; *Minnesota Year Book*, 1852, pp. 74–87; Holcombe, in *Minnesota in Three Centuries*, 2: 308; Sibley to Chouteau and Company, July 11, August 8, 1851, in Sibley Letter Book, no. 1. Letters from Sibley to the Chouteaus, June 26, 1850, July 24, August 23, 25, 1851, illustrate his interest and assistance in the treaties.

[42] " I send down Buisson to purchase all the cheap horses he can find about St. Paul or Little Canada. I want twenty at least." Sibley to Borup, August 8, 10, 1851, to Chouteau and Company, August 8, 1851, to Dousman, August 17, 1851, in Sibley Letter Book, no. 1; Neill, *Minnesota*, 560; Indian Agent McLean and Philander Prescott, in 32 Congress, 1 session, *Senate Executive Documents*, no. 1, pp. 434, 436 (serial 613); *Minnesota Pioneer*, August 14, 1851; *Dakota Friend*, September, 1851. This issue of the *Dakota Friend* contains a translation of the treaty of Mendota into the Dakota language.

[43] Nicollet, *Report*, 17. The area of the cession has, so far as known, never been accurately computed. According to the estimate of Thomas Hughes it comprised "over 19,000,000 acres in Minnesota, nearly 3,000,000 acres in Iowa, and over 1,750,000 acres in South Dakota, making in all nearly 24,000,000 acres of the choicest land on the globe." See *Minnesota Historical Collections*, 10: 112 (part 1). The part of the cession in Minnesota is indicated on the map facing page 324, *post*. A map of the territory ceded in Iowa is in "Public Surveys in Iowa, 1851," in 32 Congress, 1 session, *Senate Executive Documents*, no. 1, p. 582 (serial 613).

force thousands of citizens who were already streaming over the border.[44]

A few days after the completion of the Sioux treaties Governor Ramsey, acting under instructions of May 16 of the same year, with Hugh Tyler as special agent and acting commissary and Dr. Thomas Foster as secretary to the commission, set out for Pembina to negotiate a treaty with the Chippewa residing thereabout. From Sauk Rapids he had an escort of dragoons, and the march occupied three weeks. Of the region passed over, Governor Ramsey reports that "no finer country exists anywhere in the Union, and few capable of subsisting a denser population." On September 20 a treaty of cession was signed, conveying the Indian right over some five million acres in the Red River Valley for the very reasonable sum of $230,000. The odd $30,000, to be paid in hand, was a *douceur* to half-breeds. The principal sum was not itself to be paid; the Indians were to receive only the annual interest, at five per cent, for twenty years.[45]

Not many weeks had passed after the treaty of Traverse des Sioux had been signed when there appeared at the St. Peter's agency at Fort Snelling, and later at the Traverse, a man named Madison Sweetser, who opened at the latter

[44] 32 Congress, 1 session, *Senate Executive Documents*, no. 1, pp. 279, 281, 284, 413–420.

[45] Sibley seems to have suggested the territory to be acquired, a strip about sixty miles wide from Goose Creek to the Canadian border, with the Red River running through the middle of it. The demand for a cession of Chippewa lands in that remote region came from white people of the Selkirk settlements who had mistaken the boundary and had settled on American soil. The federal census of 1850 shows 1,134 people enumerated in Pembina County. The territorial census of the previous year, however, listed only 643 in the Pembina and Red River district. No explanation of the discrepancy is given, but it may be largely due to a difference in the area reporting. These people had frequently appealed to Governor Ramsey by petitions and by committees to obtain for them the right to own property and to have justice administered; for until a cession was arranged their status was that of trespassers on Indian lands. The probable destination of the thirty thousand dollars which were to be paid to the half-breeds may be inferred from a letter of Sibley to Chouteau and Company, dated November 1, 1851. "K[ittson] will of course stand the best chance to secure the largest portion of the $30,000 when paid." See also a letter of Sibley to Kittson, August 17, 1851. Both are in Sibley Letter Book, no. 1. An interesting and graphic account of the journey to Pembina is given under the title "Camp-Fire Sketches," in Bond, *Minnesota and Its Resources*, 253–358. See also the report of Governor Ramsey, in 32 Congress, 1 session, *Senate Executive Documents*, no. 1, pp. 284–288 (serial 613), and Kittson to Sibley, September 23, 1851, in the Sibley Papers.

place a trading house under a proper license. Whether his business in Minnesota was merely that of carrying on a legitimate commerce with the Indians, or whether he had an ulterior motive as intimated in many places, are questions not capable of proof from material now known. There is abundant evidence, however, that he did concern himself with other matters.[46]

On December 6, 1851, twenty-one chiefs and braves of the upper bands of the Sioux, some of whom had traveled 250 miles, arrived at Fort Snelling and held a council with Nathaniel McLean, their agent. Their spokesman, as McLean reports, again and again asserted that the signatures of the chiefs and braves to the traders' paper at the Traverse des Sioux on July 23 were obtained by fraud and deceit, that that paper was not explained to them at the time, or at any other time, and that they thought it was a part of the treaty. They declared that they owed no such sums to the traders but professed themselves willing to pay all such debts as should appear to be justly due, after a proper investigation of the accounts. They submitted a written protest against paying out their money in bulk to the individuals named in the said instrument, to the exclusion of all other creditors. Fifteen of the signers were among those who had signed at the Traverse des Sioux. On the eighth of December the same delegation waited on Governor Ramsey and when he opened council they repeated the statements relating to the traders' paper. The governor explained to them the provisions of the treaty relating to the payment of the $275,000. This money was to be paid to the chiefs and braves in such manner as they in open council should

[46] McLeod wrote to F. B. Sibley from the Traverse des Sioux on November 15, 1851, that "Mr. Sweetzer (who appears to be respectable, and is certainly a very plausible man, and probably is possessed of means, as he says he is)," intends "to establish himself here." On November 30, Duncan R. Kennedy notified F. B. Sibley that "Mr. Sweetzer is intrigueing with the indians to keep the Traders from getting indemnified for the losses they sustained in the Trade." These letters are in the Sibley Papers. On September 3, 1851, H. H. Sibley wrote a letter to the Chouteaus in which he suggested that the Ewings be allowed one-fourth of the town plat of Traverse des Sioux if they would not interfere in the Sioux trade before the treaty was ratified. Sibley Letter Book, no. 1.

determine. The traders' paper was no part of the treaty. The payment of traders' debts was a "matter entirely between themselves, over which the commissioners would exercise no control."[47]

In the character of attorney for the upper chiefs, Sweetser presently forwarded that protest, doubtless prepared by himself, to the Indian office, with an ingenious letter of advice, dated December 15, 1851. In this and in a later communication he insisted that the chiefs and braves at the Traverse des Sioux did not know the nature of the traders' paper. He hoped that the government would "interfere and prevent the payment of claims as provided by the contract" and that it would not allow ten or twelve men to execute "so stupendous a fraud."[48] Agent McLean, on December 13, 1851, through his superior officer, Governor Ramsey, reported the transactions of the councils or talks of December 6 and 8 to the commissioner of Indian affairs.[49]

The Thirty-second Congress met on December 1, 1851, but it was not till February 13 that the president laid the three Minnesota Indian treaties before the Senate.[50] Two months passed before the Senate committee on Indian affairs took them up for consideration. A vigorous opposition at once appeared, covering with various pretexts its real ground. Southern senators did not desire to see an enlargement of the area of settlement in a new northern territory, which would soon be knocking at the door for admission as a state. Bell of Tennessee led this opposition, but he overdid it so much as to make a few friends for the treaties. The advocates of the treaties in Congress and out exerted themselves with their utmost energy and tact. Finally on June 23, 1852, a ratification was secured by a

[47] 32 Congress, 2 session, *Senate Executive Documents*, no. 29, part 1, pp. 20, 22, 23, 25 (serial 660).

[48] 32 Congress, 2 session, *Senate Executive Documents*, no. 29, part 1, pp. 14, 24.

[49] 32 Congress, 2 session, *Senate Executive Documents*, no. 29, part 1, p. 20.

[50] James D. Richardson, *A Compilation of the Messages and Papers of the Presidents, 1789–1891*, 5: 145 (Washington, 1897); *Senate Executive Proceedings*, 8: 368.

narrow margin. Delegate Sibley wrote to Governor Ramsey: "The long agony is over. . . . Never did any measures have a tighter squeeze through. The Pembina treaty went by the board. . . . It had to be offered up as a conciliatory sacrifice by the friends of the other treaties."[51] The two Sioux treaties, however, passed with amendments. One cut the half-breed provision out of the treaty of Mendota; the others canceled the two reservations on the Minnesota River, authorized the president to select for the Sioux suitable homes outside the ceded territory, and gave him large discretion in making such selection. The reservation lands were to be taken over by the government at ten cents per acre and the value was to be added to the trust funds. An addition of eight thousand dollars, it was estimated, would thus be made to the cash annuities.[52] It would appear that the opponents of ratification, failing to muster votes enough to defeat the treaties, comforted themselves with the reflection that they had succeeded in amending them to death and that they would be heard of no more. The Sweetser and other documents had been presented and were before the Senate, but they seem not to have received the least attention at the time. Sibley wrote to Ramsey some days before the ratification: "I have had more

[51] During the contest the Senate, with the Sweetser documents before it, discussed the whole affair of the treaties, the connection of Sibley and his group therewith, and the question of the debts. No amendments relating to these matters were adopted, however, but "the half-breed clause was stricken out, because," wrote Sibley on June 26, "the treaty could not pass with it. . . . Dodge of Iowa was my main reliance in the Senate, and he acted a firm & noble part throughout, as did Cass, Clemens, Douglas, Hale, Mangum, & others." In May Sibley wrote a remarkable letter to Senator Dodge, in which he exhibited a high degree of unselfishness and magnanimity. After stating that the Indians had voluntarily arranged to pay their debts, and that he himself after seventeen years in the Sioux trade was thirty or forty thousand dollars worse off than when he began, he continues: "But if this contemplated arrangement, or any feature of the treaties stands in the way of their ratification private considerations however important must give place to the general good. The treaties must be ratified, and we who are interested must submit to the sacrifice however ruinous to us." According to his judgment, moreover, failure to ratify would mean a fierce Indian war. Letter of May 3, 1852, Sibley Papers, and published in the *Minnesota Pioneer*, March 30, 1854; Sibley to Ramsey, January 28, February 4, March 23, April 11, May 3, 10, June 10, 26, 1852, Ramsey Papers.

[52] *Senate Executive Proceedings*, 8: 368, 380 (Sweetser documents presented), 382, 384, 396 (memorial by Sibley presented), 401, 404. The treaty of Traverse des Sioux was ratified by a vote of 25 to 12 and that of Mendota by a vote of 31 to 13.

vexation & hard labor, mingled with no little mortification
this past winter & spring, in pushing forward these treaties,
than any consideration would induce me to undergo again.
. . . Tyler has rendered good service."[53] It may be noted
here that Sibley's biographer, who is never remiss in adding
to the catalogue of his subject's public services, makes not
the slightest reference to the matter of these Indian treaties.

The Indian appropriation bill approved on August 30,
1852, embraced an appropriation of $690,050 for carrying
out the Sioux treaties. This was attended by two provisos:
one, that no payment should be made till after the assent
of the Indians to the treaty amendments should have been
obtained; the other, that the moneys appropriated for
Indians should not be paid to any attorney or agent but
directly to the Indians, "unless the imperious interest of
the Indian or Indians, or some treaty stipulation, shall require the payment to be made otherwise, under the direction of the President." This superfluous recognition of the
act of March 3, 1847, naturally met with no opposition
from friends of the Sioux treaties, which specifically
provided for payment to the chiefs.[54] Hugh Tyler with a
ready eye to business at once proposed to the commissioner of Indian affairs that he designate Governor Ramsey
to disburse these moneys, and in a letter of June 27, 1852,
he stated that that official "thought he would do [so], and
thus head off Sweetser and Co."[55]

[53] May 10, 1852, Ramsey Papers. An editorial in the *Minnesotian* for July 10, 1852,
entitled "Hugh Tyler, Esq." represents him as a person "of a fine address and suavity of
manner, well calculated to win the esteem and confidence of every one he meets . . . at the
same time, one of the most modest and unassuming of men." Tyler, according to the
writer, had worked harder and had accomplished more toward the ratification of the Sioux
treaties than any person outside of Congress, and he had done this without any personal
interest or hope of reward. Six months later, December 25, the same paper informed its
readers that "At the time of the treaty, the traders and half-breeds engaged his services to
press the ratification of their treaty, with the understanding that if the treaties were ratified
and their claims eventually paid, he was to receive a per centage as compensation. There
is certainly nothing very novel or unusual in this — lawyers work for contingent fees every
day." See also Sibley to Ramsey, June 26, 1852, in the Ramsey Papers.

[54] *Statutes at Large*, 10: 51, 56.

[55] Ramsey Papers.

The opposition in the Senate, which hoped that it had at least fatally amended the two Sioux treaties, was to be disappointed, but not without a vigorous effort on the part of those interested in their consummation. They immediately understood that it would be necessary to obtain the consent of the Indians to the Senate amendments to the treaties. The upper chiefs, especially, were averse to "signing any more papers" and would have to be placated. It was thought necessary also to explain the situation to the missionaries and to secure their very desirable influence with some of the Indians.[56] Early in August Sweetser was reported to be feeding and clothing Indians at the Traverse des Sioux and making extravagant promises. Some halfbreeds were found to be unreliable.[57] When on the third of August the commissioner of Indian affairs authorized Governor Ramsey to obtain the assent of the Sioux,[58] the opposing influences were so great that traders such as Sibley, Brown, McLeod, Robert, and Kittson, who had long enjoyed the confidence of the Dakota chiefs, found themselves powerless. The season was passing. The assent of the Indians must, if possible, be obtained before their departure for the fall hunt. In this emergency the intervention of a man well known in the territory and experienced in all Indian business was invoked. It had been supposed that Henry M. Rice was a sympathizer at least with the supporters of Sweetser.[59] If so, they were now to lose his countenance of their proceedings. For a promised consideration of ten thousand dollars and all expenses necessary

[56] Sibley at first hoped that it would not be necessary to lay the amendments before the Indians, but he later wrote that the changes must be submitted to them *pro forma*. He advised Ramsey, also, that if he "were to see the missionaries or write to them in explanation of the amendt. they would at once see the propriety & necessity of laboring for and not against it." Sibley to Ramsey, June 26, July 25, August 13, 1852, Ramsey Papers; McLeod to F. B. Sibley, July 28, 1852, Sibley Papers.

[57] Rice to Borup, August 2, 1852, Sibley Papers.

[58] Copy of a letter from Lea to Ramsey, August 3, 1852, Sibley Papers; Ramsey to Lea, March 2, 1853, in *Ramsey Investigation Report*, 324 (serial 699).

[59] Sibley to Dousman, October 16, Sibley to Chouteau and Company, November 1, F. B. Sibley to Laframboise, November 23, 1851, in Sibley Letter Book, no. 1; Sibley to Ramsey, December 26, 1851, Ramsey Papers.

and proper, Rice undertook to secure the assent of the Indians to the treaty amendments and the signatures of chiefs to a paper which should constitute Governor Ramsey their attorney to receive and disburse their moneys. Rice had never traded with the Sioux of Minnesota, but he knew Indians and the ways to gain their confidence. Early in August, 1852, he was at the Traverse, where he found matters discouraging, but he did not despair.[60] Of the "operations" at the Traverse and at Mendota there is no record. Whatever they may have been, the result was gratifying to all desiring the consummation of the treaties.

It was considered that general councils of the tribes were not legally essential for ratifying the Senate amendments, but that signatures of chiefs would suffice. Governor Ramsey was urged not to permit any Sioux delegations to go to Washington.[61] On September 4, 1852, forty-five chiefs and headmen signed at St. Paul, on behalf of the lower bands, the formula of assent. Four days later twenty-seven chiefs and headmen of the upper bands took at St. Paul the same action,[62] but not till after another document

[60] The difficulty was casually mentioned in the presence of Rice, who "in a braggadocio spirit" offered for a bonus of ten thousand dollars to get the assent of the Indians. Dousman accepted the offer on behalf of the traders, but F. B. Sibley wrote to Laframboise on July 21, 1852, "I do not think he was anxious to undertake it, nor do I think he imagines now that he has the least chance of success, unless *we and those connected with us* assist him." See Sibley Letter Book, no. 2. By authority of Governor Ramsey as superintendent, Rice expended the sum of $5,713 for supplies, presents, and subsistence necessary to procure the approval by the Indians of the amendments of the Senate. The amount was charged against the fund reserved for removal and subsistence, in pursuance of instructions issued by Commissioner Lea on October 4, 1852. Ramsey's use of this subsistence fund was criticized by Governor Gorman in his report as superintendent of Indian affairs for 1853. Dousman, when testifying as a witness before the investigating commission, refused to answer a direct question regarding the contract with Rice. See 32 Congress, 2 session, *Senate Executive Documents*, no. 29, part 2, pp. 5, 11, and 17 (serial 660); *Ramsey Investigation Report*, 4, 288 (serial 699); Gorman, in 33 Congress, 1 session, *Senate Executive Documents*, no. 1, p. 296 (serial 690); and Rice to Borup, August 2, 1852, McLeod to F. B. Sibley, July 28, 29, 30, August 12, 24, 1852, in the Sibley Papers. When it came to payment, Dousman brought out a note for five thousand dollars, then past due, which Rice had made as his subscription to the building of the steamboat "Nominee." A lively correspondence and a suspension of friendly relations followed. See the Dousman Papers in the possession of the State Historical Society of Wisconsin: Dousman to Rice, January 1, 1853, Letter Book 1,000; January 8, 1853, MS. 18c106; January 24, 1853, Letter Book 1,000. With these may be found other letters of the two men relating to the treaty of Traverse des Sioux.

[61] Sibley to Ramsey, June 10, 26, July 25, 1852, Ramsey Papers.

[62] *Statutes at Large*, 10: 949-959.

had been prepared for execution at the same time. That other document was a power of attorney authorizing Alexander Ramsey to receive from the United States the $275,000 promised in article four of the treaty of Traverse des Sioux for the expense of removing the Indians to their reservations, their subsistence for one year, and the "settling of their affairs"; and to appropriate that money "in accordance with and for the purpose of carrying out the equitable and true intent" of the treaty. All former and other powers of attorney given in the matter were revoked and annulled.[63] This document was read and explained to the chiefs at Rice's store in St. Paul. Assured that it "broke all former papers," the chiefs believed that it would set aside not only their former power of attorney to Sweetser, but also the traders' paper signed at the Traverse on July 23, 1851. Thus believing, they proceeded to the office of the superintendent and there signed the two papers.[64] They then set out for their distant homes and hunting grounds in high spirits, to await the longed-for pay day.

On the fifth day of October the treasury department issued, on the requisition of the commissioner of Indian affairs, its draft for $593,050 on the assistant treasurer at New York to Alexander Ramsey for disbursement under the fourth articles of the treaties of Traverse des Sioux and Mendota. The proceeds of this draft, paid in gold coin, were deposited in the Merchant's Bank of New York on October 11, less ten thousand dollars reserved for immediate use. One hundred thousand dollars in gold coin and the

---

[63] 32 Congress, 2 session, *Senate Executive Documents*, no. 29, part 2, p. 25 (serial 660); *Ramsey Investigation Report*, 205 (serial 699).

[64] It was later argued on behalf of Ramsey that the traders' paper was not a power of attorney and hence could not be annulled by the words, "We do hereby revoke and annul all former and other powers of attorney executed or given by us with reference to the receipt or collection of the said sum of money, or any part thereof," in the document signed on September 8, 1852. The revocation would apply, therefore, only to the powers of attorney which had been executed in behalf of Sweetser and Sibley. McLean and Prescott, however. testified that the Indians understood this Ramsey paper to annul all earlier papers. 32 Congress, 2 session, *Senate Executive Documents*, no. 29, part 2, p. 26 (serial 660); *Ramsey Investigation Report*, 191, 204, 382 (serial 699); interview with William L. Quinn, May 19, 1905.

same amount in bank notes were drawn out later. The remainder was paid out in drafts, mostly in favor of Hugh Tyler.[65] It is notable that Ramsey had not seen the traders' paper executed at the Traverse des Sioux until he arrived in Washington near the end of September to draw the money he was to disburse under the treaties; nor had he understood its exact purport. That paper was there laid before him by Tyler. Ramsey had previously known only that the Indians had executed some kind of paper at the Traverse by which they had secured to their creditors the amounts stipulated in the treaty. Now, upon examining the document, he "discovered that while not a power of attorney, it was a most *solemn acknowledgment*, made by the chiefs in open council, of their indebtedness to certain individuals, 'pledging the faith of their tribe' for payment, and requesting, in the words of the treaty, that the United States would pay the individuals named the sums acknowledged to be respectively due them." Commissioner Lea, who had acted with Ramsey in making the treaty, advised him that the Indians "should be required to abide by the agreement between them and their traders, provided it was fairly and understandingly made." Ramsey at no time contemplated any other procedure. He construed the traders' paper as an irrevocable order to pay to the persons named, or to their assigns, the designated sums.[66]

When Ramsey, accompanied by Tyler, reached St. Paul late in October, he found the lower Sioux assembling at the agency near Fort Snelling. After several meetings had been held at the agency the councils were transferred, at the request of the Indians, to Mendota, and the sessions were continued in the warehouse of the fur company, where the negotiations for the treaty had been begun the previous year. The Wahpekute bands of the Cannon River country seem not to have been "operated" upon by adverse interests.

[65] *Ramsey Investigation Report*, 3, 301–303.
[66] *Ramsey Investigation Report*, 308, 324.

Under the influence of Alexander Faribault they had been willing all along to pay their traders. In November four of the seven chiefs signed a receipt for ninety thousand dollars and authorized Ramsey to pay the amount to their licensed traders, according to the schedule attached to their traders' paper of August 5, 1851. Two days later the claimants authorized Sibley to collect their money, and on the following day he gave Ramsey a receipt for ninety thousand dollars. This closed the transaction with the Wahpekute.[67]

The Mdewakanton were less disposed to follow the procedure thus marked out. In council Wabasha, speaking for all the bands, demanded payment of the "hand money," cash to be paid in hand, then and there, to the chiefs in open council. Other chiefs seconded this demand. They had not, they claimed, at any time assigned their dues under the treaty. Ramsey exhorted the chiefs to be honest and pay the just debts of their people as they had agreed to do. If they would not do so, he would carry the money back to the Great Father at Washington. "Take it back," said Wabasha, "we will take back our land."[68] To bring the seven chiefs to a right frame of mind was a difficult problem. It was solved, however. In the first place, cold weather was coming on and the Indians were greatly in need of provisions.[69] There were still due the bands $45,600 of interest on their trust funds under the treaty of 1837. As to this there was no question. The annuities of the Mdewakanton under the treaty of 1837 were also due, and Agent McLean had brought the money from St. Louis.[70] Both of these payments were delayed for "two or three weeks" while

---

[67] 32 Congress, 2 session, *Senate Executive Documents*, no. 29, part 2, pp. 16, 32, 33 (serial 660); *Ramsey Investigation Report*, 23, 25, 325–327.

[68] Testimony of Little Crow, Grey Iron, Shakopee, the Star, Cloudman, McLean, and Prescott, in *Ramsey Investigation Report*, 170, 174, 176–179, 181, 189, 208.

[69] *Ramsey Investigation Report*, 59.

[70] 32 Congress, 2 session, *Senate Executive Documents*, no. 29, part 2, p. 3 (serial 660); *Ramsey Investigation Report*, 194.

negotiations were progressing.[71]   There is no evidence that
the Indians were told by any white man in authority that
these moneys would not be paid unless the "new papers"
were signed, but there can be no doubt that many of them
so believed.   The most effective means, however, used to
induce compliance on the part of the chiefs was the division of twenty thousand dollars among seven principal
chiefs in equal proportions.   Ostensibly this money was intended for distribution by these chiefs among certain half-
breeds of their bands who had not been able to secure from
the treaty commissioners an acknowledgment of their demands.[72]   In two cases this intention was hardly literally
complied with.   Wabasha and Wacouta, the two oldest and
most influential chiefs, were encamped with their bands
on the east side of the Mississippi.   On the evening of November 8, Governor Ramsey met them at Findley's house on
the road from Fort Snelling to St. Paul.   At a late hour
the two chiefs signed a receipt for ninety thousand dollars
and in the same instrument requested the superintendent
to pay seventy thousand dollars to the licensed traders.
Thereupon Ramsey placed a bag of gold before each chief.
Jack Frazer, nephew of Wacouta, pushed the bags over to
the sutler of Fort Snelling, who carried them away.   The
chiefs testified that they did not see the contents of those
bags then or later, and Franklin Steele swore that he
paid out the whole amount to Frazer.[73]   The example of

[71] The lower chiefs said they waited two months, but they doubtless included the time
after their premature arrival.   McLean admitted that there was some little delay.   *Ramsey
Investigation Report*, 204.

[72] Testimony of Alexis Bailly, various Indian chiefs, and Sibley, in *Ramsey Investigation
Report*, 157, 170, 175, 180, 182, 218; F. B. Sibley to Chouteau and Company, November 16,
1852, in Sibley Letter Book, no. 2.

[73] Sibley to Ramsey, October 31, 1852, in Sibley Letter Book, no. 4; *Ramsey Investigation
Report*, 25, 82, 167–170, 260, 267; interview with William L. Quinn, May 19, 1905.   Sibley
suggested such a meeting to Ramsey in a private letter dated October 11, 1852, in the
Ramsey Papers.   Steele testified that the two chiefs requested to be paid on the east side
of the river and that Wacouta had alleged that his poor health would prevent his crossing.
An account of the career of Jack Frazer, written by Walker-in-the-Pines (Henry H. Sibley),
was published weekly in sixteen chapters in the *St. Paul Pioneer* beginning December 2,
1866.   Clippings of the articles are in Sibley's scrap book for 1866–70.   Franklin Steele's
ledger shows that Frazer drew out from time to time after this payment sums amounting

these chiefs had such an effect that on the following day five others signed the same receipt and received each a bag of gold. The reasons given by them for the bestowal of these gifts were various and all different from the true one.[74] On the eleventh the seven chiefs signed a voucher acknowledging each the receipt of $2,857.14$\frac{2}{7}$. As in the case of the Wahpekute, the money was not, as it might have been, paid directly to the traders as listed, but it was turned over to Hugh Tyler, whom they on December 11 made their agent and attorney for the purpose. Two days later he gave his receipt for seventy thousand dollars to be distributed among the licensed traders.[75] At the time of the payment at Mendota there were five young Sioux braves confined in Fort Snelling for the murder of Chippewa Indians. Some of these were related to the Mdewakanton chiefs. In one of the councils, Governor Ramsey was asked to order them released. His reply was that they would be freed if the chiefs would take proper action in regard to the payments. The prisoners were liberated about the time the receipts were signed.[76]

A settlement had still to be made with the Sisseton and Wahpeton bands assembled in considerable numbers at the Traverse des Sioux. To that place Governor Ramsey, Agent McLean, Hugh Tyler, and others proceeded on or about the fourteenth of November. Madison Sweetser was either of the party or, more probably, already on the ground. As Ramsey afterwards remarked, he was already sufficiently authorized to pay to the traders and the half-breeds the gross sums stipulated in the traders' paper; but

to those paid to the two chiefs; but it may be supposed that he acted as their agent and did not appropriate the money.

[74] "Wa-ba-shaw and Wah-coo-ta fixed it," said Little Crow. *Ramsey Investigation Report*, 170, 171, 175, 178, 181, 182.

[75] It will be noted that payment was deferred for a month after the date of the receipt given by the chiefs, until Ramsey's return from the Traverse des Sioux. The delay may have been for the purpose of adjusting Tyler's commission. *Ramsey Investigation Report*, 26–28, 337.

[76] Testimony of Alexis Bailly, the various Indian chiefs, and Sibley, in *Ramsey Investigation Report*, 163, 166, 172, 176, 178, 215.

with characteristic caution he deemed it prudent to secure "cumulative evidence" of those disbursements by obtaining from the chiefs a witnessed receipt. He found a "very evil and turbulent spirit" in the camps.[77] A few of the chiefs were in favor of signing the desired receipt; the majority, however, and those the older and more influential chiefs, believing that the paper signed at St. Paul on September 8 "broke" the traders' paper, refused to sign and persisted in demanding that the "hand money" be paid to them in open council, according to their interpretation of the treaty. The governor replied that these demands could not be granted because the chiefs who had signed the traders' paper and his power of attorney had irrevocably disposed of that money. They had devoted it to the payment of their just debts and had authorized him so to apply it.[78]

Inspired, doubtless, by a certain individual, the Indians were not disposed to acquiesce, and a party led by Chief Red Iron now undertook a revolutionary proceeding. According to Indian law it was the right of the soldiers of a band to build a "soldiers' lodge" and under its shelter to organize an armed force to exercise martial law over all persons and things within the territory claimed by the particular band.[79] By means of a soldiers' lodge Red Iron undertook to prevent intercourse between the government agents and all chiefs present and thus to prevent the transaction of business. A summons from Governor Ramsey to come before him he treated with contempt. By this time the Indians had become much excited and indulged in yelling and firing their guns. Ramsey saw that at least a show of force would be necessary to obtain order and the com-

---

[77] *Ramsey Investigation Report*, 220, 328, 333. See page 239 for the testimony of Joseph R. Brown.

[78] Testimony of A. J. Campbell, William B. Dodd, Alexis Bailly, Sibley, and Alexander Faribault, in *Ramsey Investigation Report*, 129, 150, 156, 216, 276.

[79] Testimony of Sibley and Joseph R. Brown, in *Ramsey Investigation Report*, 213, 239. Brown's testimony is generally trustworthy.

pletion of his task. A message to the commanding officer at Fort Snelling brought a detachment of infantry and dragoons on the nineteenth of November. They were at once so disposed as to protect the council house and to control the approaches to it. Red Iron and his leading braves, "forty to fifty in number, came down from the house of Mr. Sweetser" in war attire, and made a demonstration as if to break the line, but withdrew when satisfied that the troops were ready to open fire. A summons carried by an officer in uniform to "his majesty," as Red Iron was at the time ironically called, resulted in a promise that the chief would attend Governor Ramsey at a certain hour. This promise not being kept, a guard of soldiers went to his lodge and marched him to the council house. After a proper statement of his acts of misconduct, Governor Ramsey deposed Red Iron from his chieftainship and ordered him into confinement. The result was the immediate dissolution of the soldiers' lodge, the consent of the chiefs to listen to reason, and freedom for all to attend the councils.[80]

Still the parol demands of the Indians, or some of them, were renewed in a formal paper drawn up by an educated Dakota and presented to Governor Ramsey by a party of Indians under the influence of Sweetser, a day or two after the dispersion of the soldiers' lodge. Its notable propositions were to increase the award of hand money to the half-breeds from $40,000 to $60,000 and to reduce the allowance to traders from $210,000 to $70,000. The list of favored traders contained ten names. Sibley as the

[80] *Ramsey Investigation Report*, 94, 212, 256, 266, 279–282, 329, 370. It would appear that the military force had been summoned in advance and was near by. The *Minnesota Democrat* for December 22, 1852, gives a romantic account of the passage between Ramsey and Red Iron, which the writer states was derived from the stories of several persons who were present. Isaac V. D. Heard repeats substantially the same account and says he received it from an eyewitness. Red Iron, however, had no reputation as an orator, and it may be assumed that the kernel of fact in the story received liberal embellishment from the reporter. No contemporary account of the trouble at the Traverse has been found in the *Minnesota Pioneer*. Heard, *History of the Sioux War and Massacre in 1862 and 1863*, 35–40 (New York, 1864).

chief creditor was to receive $20,000. The name of Madison Sweetser followed with $10,000 set against it. Sibley had traded with the Sioux nearly twenty years; Sweetser, about as many months. One need not wonder that the governor instantly refused "attention to a document which was such a manifest concoction of fraud and roguery."[81]

The policy of obtaining signatures by delaying payment of the current annuities was again resorted to. The winter had set in and the people were impatient to return to their villages.[82] At length eleven chiefs and braves were found willing to cease opposition, and on the twenty-ninth of November they signed a receipt to Governor Ramsey for $210,000 for the traders and $40,000 for the half-breeds. Of these signers only two were old and recognized chiefs and but one had signed the treaty of 1851.[83] The payment of the annuities due under the treaty was now begun by the Indian agent and in the course of a few days the camps were empty of Indians. Governor Ramsey, now doubly fortified by the power of attorney and the receipt obtained at the Traverse, returned to St. Paul, prepared to disburse the "hand money" "according to the true intent of the treaties."

The manner of disbursement, however, was such as to occasion comment at the time and severe criticism later. Instead of paying directly to the beneficiaries, Ramsey preferred to make Hugh Tyler his convenient intermediary. The traders to the upper Sioux had at the Traverse on December 1 appointed Tyler their agent and attorney to receive and receipt for the moneys due them. A week later Tyler gave to Ramsey a receipt for $209,200, and a few days after, one for the $800 allowed the missionaries to the upper Sioux as recompense for cattle killed and property destroyed. On December 11 the half-breed claimants of the

[81] *Ramsey Investigation Report*, 97, 130, 139, 192, 331.
[82] Testimony of McLean and William B. Dodd, in *Ramsey Investigation Report*, 55, 152, 203.
[83] *Ramsey Investigation Report*, 53, 101, 133.

upper Sioux made Tyler their attorney and on the same day he signed a receipt for the $40,000 due them.[84]   The payments to the larger beneficiaries were made, at their request, in drafts on the Merchants' Bank of New York City, where Governor Ramsey had deposited the gross sum intrusted to him for the consummation of the treaties.   Other payments were made in New York bank notes or in gold, according to preferences of payees.[85]

Governor Ramsey had now disbursed all the so-called "hand money" appropriated for carrying into effect the treaties of Mendota and Traverse des Sioux.   He had paid in person to Mdewakanton chiefs $20,000, to Sibley as attorney for the Wahpekute, $90,000, and to Hugh Tyler, $320,000.   The moneys, however, did not reach the beneficiaries without discount.   According to an agreement or understanding, Tyler retained fifteen per cent, $37,500, of the several amounts awarded to the traders and the half-breeds under the treaty of Traverse des Sioux, and of those awarded to the claimants under the treaty of Mendota, twelve and one-half per cent, $8,750.   Sibley deducted ten per cent, $9,000, from the Wahpekute fund and turned that sum over to Tyler.   The ultimate distribution of this relatively large fraction of the "hand money," $55,250, has not been disclosed and probably will not be.   The evidence shows that, at a meeting of claimants after the conclusion of the treaty of Traverse des Sioux, it was suggested that some expense would be incurred in securing the rights of the claimants, and Sibley was intrusted with authority to act for the whole body, so far as those rights were involved.[86]   Aware from his experience as delegate in

---

[84] The *Weekly Minnesotian* for December 25, 1852, explains that the claimants made Tyler their attorney for the collection of the money because Ramsey was so occupied with arrears of official business that he could not at once pay them individually, and also that Ramsey paid Tyler nothing for his trouble.   The *Minnesota Democrat* for December 29, however, suggests that Dr. Foster, private secretary to Ramsey, who had recently become coeditor of the administration paper, was the author of the article defending the governor's actions.   *Ramsey Investigation Report*, 17, 19, 20, 21, 27, 28.

[85] *Ramsey Investigation Report*, 223, 266, 355.

[86] *Ramsey Investigation Report*, 66, 221, 222, 243, 356.

Congress that obstacles might be thrown in the way of the ratification of the treaties, he employed Tyler to aid him in removing such obstacles. It is known to the reader that ratification came only after a long and lively struggle, and then with amendments which some senators hoped would never be agreed to by the Indians. "Tyler has rendered good service," was Sibley's comment at the time. Sibley originally suggested to Tyler that two and one-half per cent of the claims to be paid would be a suitable compensation, which the claimants would not object to paying. When Tyler arrived in Minnesota in October, 1852, to assist in the payments, it was given out that eight per cent more must be added for "expenses he had been at."[87] And when, a month later, "the amount of expenses incurred for the payment of agents and attorneys was aggregated," it was found necessary to increase the percentages to those named. It was Sibley's judgment that the sum paid Tyler did not exceed the value of his services, under the circumstances.[88] With the submission to the treasury of Governor Ramsey's accounts for the last quarter ending December 31, 1852, the treaties of Mendota and Traverse des Sioux might have passed into history but for the renewed activity of Madison Sweetser.[89] Said Interpreter William L. Quinn to the author: "They were as fair as any Indian treaties."

[87] *Ramsey Investigation Report*, 158, 162, 222.

[88] The traders grumbled somewhat about paying the percentage. See the *Ramsey Investigation Report*, 161, 192, 209, 231, 243, 267, 356. In the Sibley Papers is a receipt given by Charles D. Fillmore, brother of President Fillmore, to Franklin Steele on December 13, 1852, for $2,000 for services in securing claims. Fillmore told the Sioux that the Great Father would be gratified if they would agree to the amendments to the treaty. See also 32 Congress, 2 session, *Senate Executive Documents*, no. 29, part 2, pp. 3, 4, 15 (serial 660).

[89] For an account of the investigation of Governor Ramsey's conduct in the negotiation of these treaties and the distribution of these funds, see the Appendix, no. 8, *post*.

XI. CHIPPEWA AND OTHER INDIAN AFFAIRS

THE acquisition of the "Suland" by the treaties of 1851 left much more than half the area of Minnesota in Indian hands. The Chippewa, roughly classed geographically as the Lake Superior, the Mississippi, and the Red Lake and Pembina bands,[1] held a right of occupancy over all the land to the north of the Sioux-Chippewa partition line of 1825 except the small cession of 1837 and the two tracts northwest of St. Cloud, acquired from them in 1847 for the Winnebago and the Menominee.[2] It was not to be expected that a tribe of savages numbering not more than ten thousand souls would hold indefinitely fifty thousand square miles of land against the pressure of advancing civilization and the lumber interest. An account has already been given of the effort to acquire some five million acres in the extreme northwest of the territory by the abortive treaty negotiated by Governor Ramsey in the summer of 1851.[3] The Senate deemed it unwise to acquire so distant and isolated an area.

Before that time, however, a break had been made into the Chippewa country, though not to extinguish the Indian title. The emissaries of Champlain had seen specimens of native copper brought from the shores of Lake Superior and had heard from the natives reports of great deposits of that metal on its tributary waters.[4] The tradition survived when white men came into the region to trade and

---

[1] Warren, in *Minnesota Historical Collections*, 5: 31–34, gives a more detailed classification. The Pillager and Winnebagoshish bands were but loosely connected with the Chippewa of the Mississippi and were sometimes dealt with in separate treaties or in special articles in the same treaty. Page 257 contains a version of the tradition that the Pillagers obtained that name from having robbed a trader in 1781 on the Crow Wing River a few miles above its junction with the Mississippi. "Ojibway" is doubtless the better term to apply to these Indians but "Chippewa" is so extensively employed in government publications that it seems advisable to use it here.

[2] See *post*, pp. 310, 320.

[3] See *ante*, p. 288.

[4] See *ante*, p. 4.

settle. It was this, doubtless, which served as the convenient pretext for moving the government at length to action. In 1826 Lewis Cass, then governor of Michigan, and a colleague concluded a treaty at Fond du Lac, Minnesota, with the Chippewa nation, by which that nation ceded "the right to search for, and carry away, any metals or minerals from any part of their country."[5] Although no developments worthy of note followed, the belief persisted that to the north of Lake Superior immense deposits of copper awaited the miner. There was not the least suspicion of the wealth of iron ores which have been unearthed in that region.[6]

On September 30, 1854, a treaty was negotiated at La Pointe, Wisconsin, with the Chippewa of Lake Superior, by which those bands ceded to the United States the "triangle" north of Lake Superior having its apex at Pigeon River and its base on the line of the Vermilion, East Swan, and St. Louis rivers, with a southwestern arm reaching down to the northern boundary of the cession of 1837. Five months later there was negotiated at Washington a second treaty with the chiefs of the Chippewa of the Mississippi and other bands, by which they surrendered an immense area in northern Minnesota, stretching west from the base of the "triangle" to the Red River of the North, and from the latitude of the mouth of the Crow Wing River to that of Turtle Lake, plus a considerable triangle west of the Big Fork River with a narrow apex on the Rainy River.[7] The total area of this cession was more than half that of the "Suland." Just as the acquisition of 1854 was a

---

[5] *Statutes at Large*, 7: 291. The numerous grants of land to mixed-bloods on the St. Mary's River indicate the "interest" which secured the negotiation of this treaty.

[6] The geological survey made by David D. Owen and his associates beginning in 1848 furnishes no information tending to confirm the tradition as to copper or the possibility of the existence of iron ores. Owen, *Report of a Geological Survey of Wisconsin, Iowa, and Minnesota*, 145 (Philadelphia, 1852).

[7] *Statutes at Large*, 10: 1109, 1165. For the location and extent of these and other acquisitions, see the map facing page 324, *post*; also Royce, *Indian Land Cessions*, 794 and maps 33, 34. The "other bands" were the Pillager and Winnebagoshish Indians, who were partly dealt with in separate articles.

miners' proposition, so that of 1855 was a lumbermen's. About the included headwaters of the Mississippi and the Crow Wing were the best stands of pine timber in the territory. The two treaties were indeed parts of one scheme. Both provided for annuity payments in money and goods and liberal presents of guns, ammunition, and clothing; for payment of traders' claims; for preëmption of quarter sections of land by missionaries, teachers, and other legal residents; and for eighty-acre grants of land to mixed-bloods. They also forbade the making, sale, and use of spirituous liquors on the lands ceded. This prohibition in the earlier treaty was to continue until revoked by the president; in the later treaty, until revoked by Congress.[8] In both, reservations were made for the residences of the Indians, the most considerable being those about Leech, Cass, and Winnebagoshish lakes. After these acquisitions there remained in the hands of the Red Lake and Pembina bands a large region, roughly quadrilateral, in the extreme northwest part of the territory; and in the hands of the Bois Fort band, an area of about one hundred townships between the Vermilion and the Big Fork, north of the cession of 1855.[9]

The Chippewa treaty of 1855 has been spoken of as having been made in the interests of lumbermen. It opened for legitimate purchase great pine regions about the headwaters of the Mississippi as fast as surveys could be extended; and meantime it gave opportunity for those irregular harvests of timber which have already been noted. An interesting example of this is also found in the operation of a provision in the treaty of 1854 making small grants of land to mixed-bloods, the consequences of which extended beyond the territorial period, and traces of which have

---

[8] The enforcement of the prohibition clauses became difficult after the spread of settlements in the regions. The earlier one was revoked by President Taft, but all efforts to induce Congress to take similar action with reference to the treaty of 1855 have been futile.

[9] About half of the first and all of the second of these areas, less reservations for the Indians, were acquired by the treaties of October 2, 1863, and April 12, 1864, and the Bois Fort treaty of April 7, 1866. *Statutes at Large*, 13: 667, 689; 14: 765.

lingered almost to the present. It well illustrates the manner in which the Indian office and the general land office have been played against each other by operators in timber lands, and how clear provisions of law have been evaded by ingenious devices of conveyancing not forbidden by law or judicial decisions. It also shows how expectations of large profits may tempt persons of easy conscience to commit actual fraud, and how citizens of prominence fully capable of distinguishing between legitimate and illegitimate business enterprises may become the beneficiaries of fraud.[10]

There were two other early Indian cessions of land. These, however, were obscured by the acquisitions of the immense areas ceded directly by the Chippewa and the Sioux. Because of their inferior importance and a certain subordination to the other transactions, they may be treated out of chronological order. Both were cessions of territory originally obtained from the Chippewa — the larger area for the Winnebago, the smaller for the Menominee Indians.

At the time they come under our observation the Winnebago Indians were a virile and prosperous tribe claiming a large area in middle and southwestern Wisconsin.[11] At the grand conference of the western nations at Prairie du Chien in 1825 they agreed to accept boundaries stipulated in the treaty. Four years later they ceded a large wedge-shaped tract extending from the Wisconsin River southward into Illinois and embracing the lead mines of that region; and in 1832 they gave up all their land south and east of the Fox and Wisconsin rivers and agreed to move to and occupy a portion of a tract known as the "Neutral Ground," located mainly in northeastern Iowa but embracing a small triangle in southeastern Minnesota. In 1837 they sur-

[10] The story of the Chippewa half-breed scrip is told in the Appendix, no. 9, *post.*

[11] Further information regarding this tribe may be found in *Execution of Treaty with the Winnebagoes* (25 Congress, 1 session, *House Documents*, no. 229 — serial 349); Schoolcraft, *Indian Tribes*, 3: 277–288; 4: 227–243; Governor Ramsey's report for 1849, in 31 Congress, 1 session, *House Executive Documents*, no. 5, pp. 1005–1036 (serial 570); and Hodge, *Handbook of American Indians*, 2: 961 (bibliography).

rendered the small remnant of their Wisconsin lands and again agreed to move to the Neutral Ground.[12] They were so reluctant and tardy, and the government officials were so indulgent, that it was not till 1842 that they were established there. Even then they were discontented and turbulent and indisposed to permanent settlement. Although they rendezvoused at their agency at Fort Atkinson when the annual payments were made, a large proportion of them were wanderers, some on their old hunting grounds in Wisconsin, others among the neighboring tribes with which they mingled.[13]

Under the three treaties of cession just named, the Winnebago had received large amounts of money and goods and were drawing liberal annuities in cash, provisions, and beneficial aid. These annuities were their undoing. Relieved from the necessity of work, they became idlers; they almost abandoned hunting. Their money went immediately into the hands of their traders to pay debts, and many of these debts were for whisky.[14] Never did traders have fatter picking than did those among the Winnebago. The treaty of 1837 gave them two hundred thousand dollars for "lost credits," the half-breeds received one hundred thousand dollars, and fifty thousand dollars were given the Indians in hand for horses and goods. But the Winnebago were not content. There were strong influences at work to foment their dissatisfaction. Their white neighbors, who were multiplying, were none too hospitable; the Indians themselves thought of the feasts of good things on treaty grounds and the pomp and circumstance of sitting in council with the agents of the Great

---

[12] *Statutes at Large*, 7: 272, 320, 370, 544; Royce, *Indian Land Cessions*, pp. 710, 712, 724, 768, and maps.

[13] Schoolcraft, *Indian Tribes*, 2: 534–537; 3: 280–283; report of the commissioner of Indian affairs for 1849, in 31 Congress, 1 session, *House Executive Documents*, no. 5, pp. 1027–1030 (serial 570). Fort Atkinson was in Winneshiek County, Iowa, on the Turkey River.

[14] Report of the commissioner of Indian affairs for 1843, in 28 Congress, 1 session, *House Executive Documents*, no. 2, p. 364 (serial 439); for 1844, in 28 Congress, 2 session, *House Documents*, no. 2, p. 421 (serial 463).

Father. The accumulation of unpaid credits naturally made the traders hope for another adjustment.[15]

To relieve the whites in Iowa of the presence of the troublesome Winnebago and at the same time to gratify the passion of those Indians for wandering, a plan was conceived of transplanting them to the north and placing them as a buffer tribe between the Sioux and the Chippewa, in the hope of thus keeping peace between those immemorial enemies. To effect this purpose another treaty was concluded on October 23, 1846, at Washington, a place very convenient for negotiation with a few selected chiefs. The Winnebago ceded their lands in the Neutral Ground and agreed to accept a tract of not less than eight hundred thousand acres north of the Minnesota River and west of the Mississippi, to be selected by themselves. In the diplomatic language of Indian treaties they were allowed one hundred and ninety thousand dollars "to settle their affairs, and for other purposes." A remarkable instance of the influence which white men have acquired among red men is found in the fact that the Winnebago delegated the selection of their new home to Henry M. Rice, then residing at Prairie du Chien, who formerly had traded among them. It was believed that the Sioux of Minnesota would be pleased to have the Winnebago for neighbors and would surrender a portion of territory for their occupation. This expectation proved to be unfounded. Rice, for reasons best known to himself, pitched upon that fertile and diversified region west of the Mississippi lying between the Watab and Crow Wing rivers and extending sufficiently westward. This land was still Chippewa country. By a treaty concluded on August 2, 1847, with the Mississippi and Lake Superior bands of the Chippewa, the area selected was acquired for the Winnebago.[16]

[15] Henry Dodge to T. Hartley Crawford, July 1, 1845, in 29 Congress, 1 session, *House Executive Documents*, no. 2, p. 461 (serial 480).

[16] *Statutes at Large*, 9: 878–880, 904–907; report of the commissioner of Indian affairs for 1847, in 30 Congress, 1 session, *House Executive Documents*, no. 8, p. 739 (serial 515); for 1849, in 31 Congress, 1 session, *House Executive Documents*, no. 5, p. 944 (serial 570).

The treaty of 1846 having been ratified and their new country found, the time for the removal of the Winnebago was set for the early summer of 1848. As the time approached they showed an unexpected reluctance to leave their Iowa settlements for new lands in the far north. On the day set for the march they refused to budge and took their goods out of the wagons on which they had been loaded. A detachment of troops from Fort Atkinson did not scare them into compliance with the agent's demands. After a "big feed" on the following day, a small party was persuaded to be good and consented to start. Presently others complied and in a few days nearly the whole tribe was concentrated at Wabasha Prairie, the site of Winona. Here there was a delay of a week or more. For three days not a soul of the Winnebago was in sight, all having stampeded over into Wisconsin with their dogs and ponies. The powerful attractions of the commissary's beef and flour put an end, however, to this wild break for liberty, and they returned to Wabasha Prairie in a flotilla of decorated canoes. Wabasha, the Sioux chief, proposed that they go no farther but settle on a bit of land he would sell them. It took the dragoons from Fort Atkinson, a company of infantry from Fort Snelling, and a body of Wisconsin volunteers, reënforced by the tact and address of Rice, to break up this arrangement and get a segregated band on board a steamboat headed for Fort Snelling. It was near the end of June when the main body was gathered at that post, and another month passed before it reached its destination, Long Prairie in Todd County, Minnesota.[17] About

[17] Neill, *Minnesota*, 483–487; J. E. Fletcher to Thomas Harvey, October 4, 1848, in 30 Congress, 2 session, *House Executive Documents*, no. 1, p. 459 (serial 537). A graphic account of the demonstrations on Wabasha Prairie is that by Russell Blakeley, in *Minnesota Historical Collections*, 8: 382–386. J. Fletcher Williams credits David Olmsted with the management of the reluctant Winnebago at Wabasha Prairie. See *Minnesota Historical Collections*, 3: 234. W. E. Alexander has included an account of the reluctance with which the Winnebago left Iowa in his *History of Winneshiek and Allamakee Counties, Iowa*, 146 (Sioux City, 1882).

Holcombe, in *Minnesota in Three Centuries*, 2: 211, states that all would have gone well with the original removal of the Winnebago to Long Prairie in 1848 "but for a malicious

half of the tribe fell out by the way. The agent reported
that in the course of the fall the majority would come into
the new agency. More of them came up, but instead of
joining the nucleus at Long Prairie, they strung themselves
along the Mississippi from Sauk Rapids up. Here the white
traders on the east shore of the Mississippi had an opportunity, which they did not hesitate to use, for illicit commerce beyond the reach of law.[18]

At no time during the residence of the tribe at Long
Prairie were all its members collected there, and some who
came strayed away. Many built huts along the upper
Mississippi, some lingered about their ancient Wisconsin
homes, others returned to the Neutral Ground in Iowa, and
a few strolled as far as the Missouri River. In the winter of
1850 the governor of Wisconsin, moved by petitions of
citizens, called on Governor Ramsey to gather in his scattered Winnebago and made complaint to the Indian department of nuisances and depredations committed by them.
In the spring the commissioner of Indian affairs took
vigorous hold of the matter, and his prompt decision was

and very harmful interference on the part of certain Minnesota traders." He charges in
particular that Dr. Charles W. Borup of St. Paul, a partner in the American Fur Company,
sent among the Winnebago agents who demoralized and scattered one-half of the tribe.
It is to be regretted that the evidence to sustain such serious charges is not cited. The
author apparently confuses the original removal of 1848 with that of 1850 under the Rice
contract. On May 16, 1850, Borup made a shipment of goods to La Crosse. One affidavit
taken at the time the House inquired into the Rice contract asserts that these goods were
intended for free shipment to the Winnebago, another that they were to be sold to them.
The amount of the shipment — ten bags of shot, five barrels of flour, two kegs of powder,
one package of cloth, and a few papers of vermilion — is too trifling to be considered as a
means of corrupting several hundred Indians. The advice of Borup to the consignee,
however, rather indicates his willingness to embarrass Rice: "Do the best you can with
it . . . we will duly appreciate all you can do." Sibley would not have tolerated such
interference. See *Removal of the Winnebagoes*, 49, 52, 57, 61–64 (31 Congress, 1 session, *House
Reports*, no. 501—serial 585). This document of sixty-four pages contains the report of the
committee on Indian affairs respecting the Rice contract, to which is appended the text of
the contract, Sibley's protest, and the reply of the commissioner of Indian affairs. See also
Dr. Thomas R. Potts to Sibley, May 29, 1850, in the Sibley Papers, and Sibley to Ramsey,
June 20, 1850, in the Ramsey Papers.

[18] Fletcher to Harvey, October 4, 1848, in 30 Congress, 2 session, *House Executive
Documents*, no. 1, p. 459 (serial 537). The agent attributed the reluctance of the tribes to
move to the north to their fear of the Sioux and the Chippewa. A census taken in 1848
numbers the Winnebago at 2,531. Schoolcraft, *Indian Tribes*, 1: 498; Ramsey to Luke
Lea, October 21, 1850, Fletcher to Ramsey, September 30, 1850, in 31 Congress, 2 session,
House Executive Documents, no. 1, pp. 81, 96–98 (serial 595).

not to call upon the military to collect and remove the
Indians. Previous experience had shown such means to
be costly and not fully effective. A display of force would,
he believed, only scatter the wanderers more widely. He
was convinced that there was one man, and but one, who
could accomplish this task without force and arms, and that
man was the Honorable Henry M. Rice, then residing in
St. Paul. With the approval of the secretary of the interior,
the commissioner, accordingly, entered into a contract with
that experienced gentleman in which it was agreed that the
government would pay seventy dollars per head for the
assemblage and transportation of such Winnebago as either
had not been on the new reserve at all or, having been there,
had strayed away intending not to return. Mere temporary absentees from the agency were not included.
This contract was executed on April 13, 1850, and in
accordance with Rice's request it was kept a secret during its pendency, for the reason that, should his proposition be made public, there were "many persons who would
take every means in their power to scatter the Indians
through the swamps of Wisconsin, and then it would be
next to impossible to find them."[19]

The commissioner, the Honorable Orlando Brown of
Kentucky, little dreamed of the tempest of protest and
denunciation which was thus postponed, but not averted.
Five days later, Delegate Sibley delivered into Brown's
office an "official protest" of some fifteen hundred words
about the purport of which there was not the slightest
obscurity. It contained five counts: (1) When Rice represented that there would not be over four hundred Indians
to be removed, he knew that there were "fully 1,000 or
1,200." (2) Seventy dollars a head for transporting Indians
four hundred miles at most was "at least three times what

[19] *Removal of the Winnebagoes*, 4–6, 11, 12–19, 30, 34 (serial 585); Rice to Ramsey,
March 19, 1850, Sibley to Ramsey, March 22, 1850, Ramsey Papers. The *Chronicle and
Register* for April 13, June 10, and July 8, 1850, contains an extended account of the removal
of the Winnebago and a defense of the action of the government.

it should cost." (3) The contract thus made involved an imputation on other officials connected with the Winnebago and in particular on Governor Ramsey, their superintendent. This gentleman of character and dignity would not be content to act as a subordinate to a private citizen of his neighborhood, especially to one regarded by him as well as by the writer as "wholly irresponsible and unreliable." (4) Governor Ramsey, who was much more influential than Rice with these Indians, could secure their removal by a bonus of twenty dollars to each individual Indian, though a military force would be necessary to hold them on the reservation. (5) Although the writer of the protest was present in the Indian office on the day the contract was signed and while this matter was under discussion, no revelation of the pending contract was made to him. Such "studied concealment" the delegate deemed "a just subject of complaint."[20]

On the day following, April 19, the commissioner, apparently anticipating a cold wave from the Northwest, wrote apologetically to Ramsey that he had not consulted him in regard to the Rice contract for two reasons: (1) lack of time, and (2) the fact that Governor Ramsey had his hands so full of Chippewa business that "it was not deemed just or proper" to burden him with the rounding up of the vagabond Winnebago. These fine words could not have been altogether consolatory. Before the middle of March Ramsey had notified the office that he was sending the Winnebago agent down to induce those Indians to return, and within a fortnight after the signing of the Rice contract Agent Fletcher had notified the commissioner that he had made arrangements for the removal and subsistence of the Indians, but was permitting them to wait till the grass would be sufficient to feed their horses. The commissioner's apology did not reach St. Paul till May 2, on which date Ramsey

[20] Sibley to Brown, April 18, 1850, Ramsey Papers; Sibley to Stevens, May 15, 1850, Stevens Papers; *Removal of the Winnebagoes*, 6–9.

replied that the agent had made good progress; that several hundred Winnebago were ready to move; that it would, however, be useless for him to make further effort, it being known that a private citizen had a large sum of money to be disbursed; that the Honorable David Olmsted, "a gentleman who possesses probably as much influence over the Winnebagoes as any other man in the country . . . says that he would gladly have taken the contract at $30 per head, with the expectation of making a large profit at that price"; and that "from my knowledge of the country, I am satisfied it could be done for less." On April 25 the Indian commissioner replied suavely to Delegate Sibley. He did not imagine that the Minnesota delegate could have the least concern in relieving the people in Wisconsin and Iowa of the presence of marauding savages. Governor Ramsey, he was sure, would take no offense. The price agreed upon was not excessive, when it was understood that the contractor was to furnish blankets, shoes, tents, and cooking utensils and was to put in and cultivate a full crop in readiness for the Indians to harvest after their arrival. Captain Eastman, Senator Jones of Iowa, and Colonel Mitchell, the marshal of Minnesota, had commended Rice so unconditionally that the office was fully warranted in contracting with him. He made no suggestion of reopening the matter.[21]

Rice did not wait for the possible effects of official or other protests. Immediately upon the signing of the contract he telegraphed to the West for men, teams, and supplies and presently took his journey in that direction. On May 3, 1850, he wrote to the commissioner from Prairie La Crosse, Wisconsin, that Agent Fletcher had succeeded in removing three Indians; that he interpreted his contract to include all Winnebago found below St. Paul; and that he had twenty teams engaged at that place. As for Sibley's estimate of numbers, his (Rice's) opinion was that it was worth no more in this case than it had been in that of

[21] *Removal of the Winnebagoes*, 9–12, 18, 23, 40–42.

the admission of the territory. On that occasion, he asserted, the delegate had estimated the population to be twenty-five thousand, but the census when taken in 1849 had shown a total of less than five thousand. Early in June Rice reported that 323 Indians had been transported to the reserve; also, that he had discovered a band of some two hundred who had expatriated themselves and had gone to live west of the Missouri.[22] The Indian commissioner stood by his contract. On May 6 the House of Representatives adopted a resolution instructing the committee on Indian affairs to investigate the Rice contract and report what action, if any, ought to be taken to cancel it. The committee was not precipitate in beginning its work. Not till June 19 did Delegate Sibley secure a hearing. His statement of that date addressed to a subcommittee recapitulated the allegations of his letter of April 18 to the commissioner, with additional piquant detail. He quoted from a letter of David Olmsted relating to "Rice's infamous contract" in which Olmsted estimated the number of Winnebago off the reserve at eighteen hundred and declared that Rice would clear one hundred thousand dollars. Judge Cooper of the territorial supreme court had written to his brother in the Senate that the contract could have been let to a reliable and responsible individual for ten dollars a head, or even less. The secrecy enjoined by Rice was, the delegate averred, for the purpose of excluding protest and competition. The committee took time for deliberation. Meantime Rice, having fulfilled in part his contract, sublet the remainder and turned to other pursuits. It was September 17 when the report of the House committee was submitted. For a cleaner bill of health Commissioner Brown could not have wished. "The measures which the Commissioner adopted . . . were provident, humane and effective, and meet the entire approbation of the com-

[22] In a letter to the commissioner, written June 18, 1850, Rice stated that it cost the government over one hundred thousand dollars to move about thirteen hundred Winnebago from the Turkey River to Long Prairie. *Removal of the Winnebagoes*, 45, 46–48.

mittee." Nor was the least censure cast on Rice. The only comfort Sibley got was a compliment from the chairman of the committee, who assured him that his communication to the committee was "a d——d elegant piece of diplomatic skill, for which he would vote to send me as minister to St. Petersburg."[23]

The experienced reader will have surmised already that it was not any ardor of compassion for the suffering Winnebago which moved the hearts of the parties to this controversy. The burning question was: Who was the great man from Minnesota whose influence was dominant at the national capital; who could best wake the sleepers in the circumlocution offices there, get the ear of congressional committees, and secure the largest disbursements of public money in the territory? If a private citizen lately come to Minnesota could walk all around both the territorial delegate and the governor, a change of situation would soon be in order. The manner in which Rice followed up the advantage he had thus gained in an unsuccessful endeavor

[23] *Removal of the Winnebagoes*, 1, 58–61; Sibley to Ramsey, June 26, 1850, Ramsey Papers. The correspondence of the time between Ramsey and Sibley abounds in incidents relative to the Rice contract. See Sibley to Ramsey, March 22, April 14, 20, 23, May 5, 15, 22, 27, June 1, 20, 22, 1850, Rice to Ramsey, March 19, 1850, Ramsey to Sibley, April 10, 1850, in the Ramsey Papers; and Ramsey to Sibley, April 10, June 3, July 24, August 18, September 9, 1850, in the Sibley Papers. A letter from Nicholas Boilvin to Sibley, May 9, 1850, in the Sibley Papers, contains a vigorous denunciation of Rice and the contract.

There was a sequel to the Rice contract of some interest. Rice's returning parties of Winnebago reached Long Prairie in June, August, and November, 1850. The agent, Jonathan E. Fletcher, refused to certify to the correctness of the several rolls and to take the Indians off Rice's hands. As a result they were not formally taken over until May, 1851, when Fletcher was succeeded by Abram M. Fridley, whose appointment was, doubtless, recommended by Rice himself. The considerable cost of maintaining the 672 Indians for varying periods fell on Rice, and affidavits of persons acquainted with the circumstances show that, had he not provided for their subsistence, the majority of them at least would have returned to their old home. Rice's claim for remuneration came before Congress in 1853. On February 17, the Senate committee made a report recommending that an appropriation be made to pay it. See 32 Congress, 2 session, *Senate Reports*, no. 419 (serial 671). Congress did not then nor at any other time make the appropriation. It was passed up by the accounting officers of the treasury. Rice was a member of the Senate during the Buchanan administration and "from motives and feelings of delicacy was unwilling . . . to have the claim prosecuted before that body." In December, 1860, assignees of Rice brought the claim before the Indian office. The commissioner found it just and ordered its payment out of the accumulated balance of appropriations on hand. On February 20, 1861, the assignees received the sum of $24,327.46. *Claim of Hon. H. M. Rice* (36 Congress, 2 session, *House Executive Documents*, no. 75—serial 1101).

to prevent Sibley's reëlection as delegate will be reported in a later chapter.[24] The reëlection of Sibley gave much satisfaction to members of both parties at Washington, and the president offered his personal congratulations. The Rice contract left its most noticeable effects on the commissioner of Indian affairs. His part in it discredited him so much with the administration that he resigned.

The Winnebago were induced to maintain a constructive residence at Long Prairie because their annuities were paid there, but many individuals and small bands remained wanderers. The more the government, the agent, the farmers, the blacksmiths, the physicians, and the missionaries did for them, the less grateful and contented they became. They were not good hunters and game had become scarce in the region. Their souls were disquieted by a fear, probably not unfounded, of hostile raids from both Sioux and Chippewa, between whom they were sandwiched. Although the reservation at Long Prairie had been selected for them by an agent of their own choosing, those of the Winnebago who were brought to it were dissatisfied with it from the beginning. Accustomed to prairie life, they did not like a wooded country, especially one so remote from the Mississippi, where it was convenient to meet with dealers in fire water.[25] Governor Ramsey in 1852 recommended that the government assign to them a more congenial home, and his successor, Governor Gorman, assisted by the agent, in the following year negotiated a treaty by which the Indians were to be established on a tract fronting on the Mississippi, between the Crow and the Clearwater rivers.[26]

[24] See *post*, pp. 367–372.
[25] Ramsey to the Indian office, September 14, 1850, Agent Fletcher to Ramsey, September 25, 1850, in 31 Congress, 2 session, *House Executive Documents*, no. 1, part 1, pp. 84, 98–100 (serial 595); Agent Fridley to Ramsey, September 9, 1852, in 32 Congress, 2 session, *House Executive Documents*, no. 1, p. 346 (serial 673); Gorman to the Indian office, September 14, 1853, in 33 Congress, 1 session, *House Executive Documents*, no. 1, p. 296 (serial 710); Fletcher to Gorman, September 13, 1855, in 34 Congress, 1 session, *House Executive Documents*, no. 1, p. 376 (serial 840).
[26] See the Appendix, no. 10, *post*, for an account of this treaty.

The Indians did not wait for ratification by the Senate, but at once encamped on the lands. When the Senate on July 21, 1854, tardily acted, it struck out the description of the reservation and inserted a paragraph authorizing the president to designate a reservation for the Winnebago west of the Missouri or elsewhere. On January 24, 1855, Governor Gorman advised the Indian office that the Indians had refused to agree to the amendment. A month later, on February 27, a new treaty was framed at Washington with a delegation of Winnebago brought there by Agent Jonathan E. Fletcher. Under its terms the Long Prairie Reservation of 893,700 acres was exchanged for seventy thousand dollars and a tract of land on the Blue Earth River equal to eighteen miles square, to be selected by the agent and a delegation of Winnebago. The Senate on March 3, 1855, ratified this so-called agreement and convention. Why this body of statesmen, which a month before had been so keen to banish the vagrant and besotted Winnebago to some far-away region where they would trouble the white man no more nor be troubled by him, was now pleased to set apart a home for them in the very garden spot of Minnesota, in which greedy settlers were already staking claims, the present writer cannot offer even a guess. Before the season of 1855 was far advanced Agent Fletcher had moved a large majority of the vagrants to the Blue Earth River at very small expense.[27]

On the small reservation of two hundred thousand acres the maintenance of life by hunting and fishing was impossible, and the annuities provided by early treaties and not rescinded were insufficient for the support of the tribe. Fletcher applied himself vigorously and not without success to lead it toward civilized life. He induced many of the

---

[27] *Statutes at Large*, 10: 1172; report of the commissioner of Indian affairs for 1855, in 34 Congress, 1 session, *House Executive Documents*, no. 1, pp. 323, 368, 376–378 (serial 840). See the map facing page 324, *post*. The tract selected consisted of townships 106 and 107, in ranges 24, 25, 26, and 27, plus a strip one mile wide along the north and east sides to make up the equivalent of eighteen miles square, i.e., nine townships.

Indians to plant crops, to build houses, and to wear white men's clothes; he persuaded some to have their children in school; but he did not succeed in getting any considerable number converted to the white man's religion, chiefly because that was so ill commended to them by the white man's example. The neighboring country, the beautiful Undine Region of Nicollet, was already filling up with white men who had no love for "Injuns." Soon there was pressure for the reduction of the reservation, and at the end of four years the Indians surrendered the west half for an addition to their annuities. After this there was even better progress among them. They improved their farming, gambled less, and many of them abandoned whisky. They framed and adopted a code of laws for their government. There is reason to believe that, could they have been allowed to remain on this reserve, within a lifetime they would have become nearly if not quite as civilized as the Indians of New York and New England.[28] But the storm of wild rage which rose among the whites after the Sioux Outbreak of 1862 so terrified the Winnebago that they consented with eagerness to a proposal for their removal to some new home beyond the Missouri. Thus they pass beyond our horizon.[29]

Although the Menominee never had a residence in the area of Minnesota, there is a reason for mentioning them in this chapter. This tribe of Indians of Algonquian stock was found by Jean Nicolet in 1634 not far from the head of Green Bay, and it has never been "removed" to any great

[28] The progress of the Winnebago on the Blue Earth Reservation may be followed in the reports of the northern division superintendent to the Indian office and of the Winnebago agent to the superintendent, in 34 Congress, 3 session, *House Executive Documents*, no. 1, pp. 590, 602 (serial 893); 35 Congress, 1 session, *House Executive Documents*, no. 2, pp. 335, 403 (serial 942); 36 Congress, 1 session, *Senate Executive Documents*, no. 2, pp. 422, 476–479 (serial 1023); 36 Congress, 2 session, *Senate Executive Documents*, no. 1, pp. 269, 297–300 (serial 1078); 37 Congress, 2 session, *Senate Executive Documents*, no. 1, p. 680 (serial 1117); 37 Congress, 3 session, *House Executive Documents*, no. 1, pp. 202, 236–240 (serial 1157).

[29] *Statutes at Large*, 12:658. There is an account of the removal in Commissioner of Indian Affairs, *Annual Reports*, 1863, pp. 303–313, 317–322, also printed in 38 Congress, 1 session, *House Executive Documents*, no. 1, pp. 417–428, 437–442 (serial 1182).

distance. A scheme, much discussed and generally favored in the early forties, to establish all the wild Indians on reservations west of the Mississippi included the Menominee. In anticipation of their removal the United States acquired of the Pillager band of Chippewa, by a treaty concluded on August 21, 1847, a large tract of land lying to the west of and adjoining the reservation of the Winnebago at Long Prairie. Because the purpose of the cession was the establishment of a friendly tribe between their country and that of the hated Sioux, the Chippewa band was willing to accept a very small compensation for its rights.[30] The Menominee, in a treaty made with them on October 18, 1848, agreed to cede all their lands in Wisconsin in exchange for the Minnesota reservation. They very soon repented of this agreement and declined to move. Upon various pretexts they obtained from the government successive postponements of removal and at length a revocation of the agreement. In 1854 they gave up all claim to the lands in Minnesota in exchange for the sum of $242,686 and a small reservation on Wolf River, in Wisconsin, where they have since resided.[31] The Pillagers, who had parted with their lands, not for money, but for protection from the Sioux, at once declared that they had been defrauded, and in later years they voiced loud protest. At the close of the century we shall find this ancient grudge alive. But for that the transaction might be passed without record.

Reference has been made to the Wabasha Reservation, called also the Half-Breed Tract on Lake Pepin, which was

---

[30] *Statutes at Large*, 9: 908. See the map facing 324, *post*. The consideration was a five-year annuity of 400 blankets, 790 yards of cloth, 1,800 yards of prints, 275 pounds of twine, 25 pounds of linen thread, 200 combs, 5,000 needles, 150 "medal [*sic*] looking-glasses," 10 pounds of vermilion, 30 nests of tin kettles, 500 pounds of tobacco, and 5 barrels of salt. At the first payment the Indians were to receive, in addition and "as a present," 200 beaver traps and 75 guns. The tract was equivalent to thirty townships. All claim of the Mississippi and Lake Superior bands to this tract had been surrendered by the treaty of August 2, by which they had ceded the land for the Winnebago Reservation. *Statutes at Large*, 9: 904.

[31] *Statutes at Large*, 9: 952; 10: 1064–1068. On April 23, 1851, Luke Lea, the commissioner of Indian affairs, wrote to the secretary of the interior recommending that the Menominee be paid $221,840 to satisfy them for a fraud practiced on them in the treaty of 1848. See 32 Congress, 1 session, *House Executive Documents*, no. 2, pp. 290–300 (serial 636).

still Indian country. Although of relatively inconsiderable area, it lay in the way of settlement and shut off much back territory from the river landings. Its liberation was, therefore, much desired for public reasons, and there were private interests not unconcerned. For the convenience of the reader it may be well to recall the origin of this reservation. At the grand conference of 1830 at Prairie du Chien, where the traders in general failed to extort any concessions of money or lands, certain of them related by marriage to the Sioux were more successful. In consideration of their aid in securing the attendance of the Indians and their consent to a treaty, the commissioners inserted the following articles:[32]

ARTICLE IX. The Sioux Bands in Council having earnestly solicited that they might have permission to bestow upon the half breeds of their Nation, the tract of land within the following limits, to wit: Beginning at a place called the barn, below and near the village of the Red Wing Chief, and running back fifteen miles; thence in a parallel line with Lake Pepin and the Mississippi, about thirty-two miles to a point opposite Beef or O-Boeuf River; thence fifteen miles to the Grand Encampment opposite the River aforesaid; The United States agree to suffer said half Breeds to occupy said tract of country; they holding by the same title, and in the same manner that other Indian Titles are held.

ARTICLE X. . . . but the President of the United States may hereafter assign to any of the said half-breeds, to be held by him or them in fee simple, any portion of said tract not exceeding a section, of six hundred and forty acres to each individual.

The Senate had no sooner ratified the treaty than applications were presented to the president for patents to individuals. There is good reason to believe that he was dissuaded from issuing individual patents by representations made by Major Taliaferro, the incorruptible agent at St. Peter's, who had been resident there for ten years. In a later year Taliaferro boasted that he had prevented the allowance of traders' claims at that treaty. The half-breeds as a body had no desire to separate themselves from their white or Indian relatives and settle down to live by tilling land. It

[32] *Statutes at Large*, 7: 328. See the map facing page 324, *post*.

was the expectation of the movers in this operation that most of the half-breeds, could they be given patents in fee simple, would at once alienate the land for nominal considerations.[33] Major Taliaferro blocked this game effectually. Neither Jackson nor Van Buren would issue patents to individual Sioux half-breeds. The scheme was, therefore, a failure. The half-breeds did not occupy the reservation. A few whites, willing to take chances on Indian deeds, were the only settlers.

For many years no other plan was thought of for ousting the half-breeds than by means of a treaty, notwithstanding the obvious fact that they could not be recognized as a treaty power. Nevertheless, the abortive Doty treaties of 1841 were accompanied by a separate treaty with the Sioux half-breeds, in which it was stipulated that they should relinquish their interest in the lands reserved for them in 1830 for the sum of two hundred thousand dollars. The Senate refused to ratify this treaty. The situation remained unchanged till 1849 when, as already related, Governor Ramsey and his colleague effected a second treaty which was to extinguish the half-breed interest for the same amount.[34] If there was a trading interest opposed to the ratification of this treaty, it was not that of the American Fur Company and its clients. Delegate Sibley exerted himself in vain to counteract the "malignant influences brought to bear upon it from the Territory." Governor Ramsey naturally desired the consummation of his effort. Writing to Sibley in Washington, on July 10, 1850, he inquired in the plain language he knew how to use, "How the devil is it that there should be so much difficulty about the Half Breed treaty?" On August 29, he wrote again, "If you secure the ratification of the Half Breed Treaty it will be the greatest triumph you can effect over your enemies — do it by all means." William H. Forbes, an old business

[33] Taliaferro, in *Minnesota Historical Collections*, 6: 211.
[34] See *ante*, p. 266, n. 2, and p. 274.

associate of Sibley's, advised the delegate on July 11, 1850, to "stick to the half breed treaty I tell you the country wants that money." The Minnesota legislature agreed to a joint resolution asking the Senate for early ratification. But neither this nor the tact and diligence of the delegate could neutralize the "malignant influences" and the Senate, by a vote of 28 to 17, refused to ratify.[35] As previously related, the treaty of Mendota of August 5, 1851, contained an article providing for the payment of one hundred and fifty thousand dollars to the half-breeds of the Sioux nation for the Wabasha Reservation, as it had come to be popularly called; but the Senate expunged the article.[36]

So long as all of Minnesota west of the Mississippi was Indian land, the existence of the Sioux half-breed reserve caused little inconvenience; but, when the river counties were filling up after the treaties of 1851, this tract abutting on Lake Pepin was much coveted. There is no finer body of farming lands in the region. The Senate, it was now understood, would never ratify a treaty with or in behalf of the half-breeds; nor would the president ever issue patents to individual half-breeds. A new procedure was now conceived and adopted. On July 17, 1854, the president approved a bill which had been introduced into the House by Henry M. Rice, the delegate from Minnesota, and which provided, according to its title, for the survey of the tract "and for other purposes." The meat of the act was in the first section, which authorized the president to issue to the half-breeds, in exchange for their claims to the tract, "certificates or scrip for the same amount of land to which each individual would be entitled in case of a division of the said grant or reservation *pro rata* among the claimants." This scrip might be located upon any of the lands on the reservation itself when not already lawfully occupied, "or upon any other unoccupied lands subject to preemption

[35] Sibley Papers; *Laws*, 1849, p. 162; *Senate Executive Proceedings*, 8: 174, 229, 248.
[36] *Statutes at Large*, 10: 954–960; see also *ante*, pp. 284, 291.

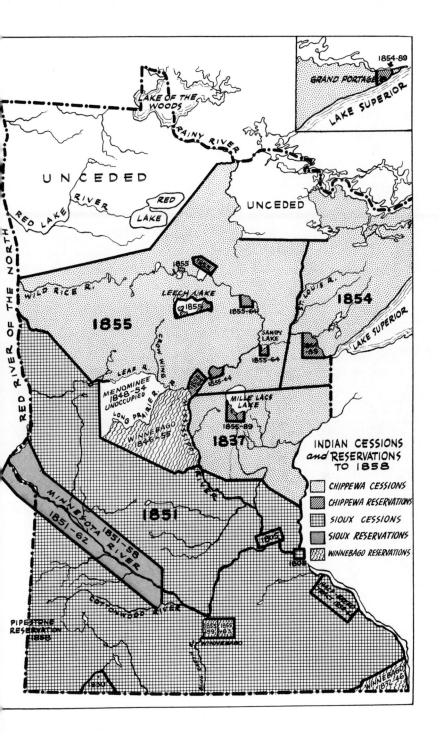

LAKE OF THE WOODS

RAINY RIVER

GRAND PORTAGE

1854-89

LAKE SUPERIOR

U N C E D E D

UNCEDED

RED LAKE RIVER

RED LAKE

RED RIVER OF THE NORTH

WILD RICE R.

1855

1855

LEECH LAKE

1855

1855-64

ST. LOUIS R.

1854

LAKE SUPERIOR

SANDY LAKE

1855-64

LEAF R.

CROW WING R.

MENOMINEE
1848-54
UNOCCUPIED

1855-64

LONG PRAIRIE

MILLE LACS LAKE

1855-89

1837

WINNEBAGO
1846-55

MISSISSIPPI RIVER

INDIAN CESSIONS
and RESERVATIONS
TO 1858

CHIPPEWA CESSIONS
CHIPPEWA RESERVATIONS
SIOUX CESSIONS
SIOUX RESERVATIONS
WINNEBAGO RESERVATIONS

1851

MINNESOTA 1851-58

1851-62

1858

COTTONWOOD RIVER

PIPESTONE
RESERVATION
1858

1855
859

1855
783

WINNEBAGO

1850

WINNEBAGO
1857-46

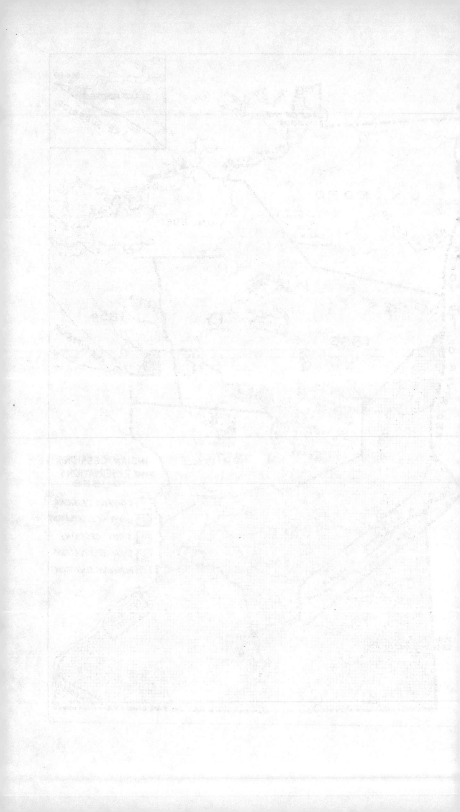

or private sale, or upon any other unsurveyed lands, not reserved by Government, upon which they have respectively made improvements." The provision that "no transfer or conveyance of any of said certificates or scrip shall be valid" was easily circumvented, and they proved to be convenient vehicles for the transfer of valuable lands from government to private ownership, in advance of surveys.[37]

During the territorial period the two great Indian nations were so far removed from the white settlements, for the most part, that no attacks or depredations were suffered till the last year, when one murderous assault was delivered by a band of Sioux, and one trifling disturbance was caused by a handful of Chippewa. The slaughter of a whole settlement of whites in Jackson County, after that of fifteen or more in the neighboring county of Dickinson in Iowa in March, 1857, by a band of outlawed Sioux led by Inkpaduta is so intimately related to the great Sioux Outbreak of 1862 that further account of it may be advantageously deferred for consideration in connection with the causes of that outbreak.[38]

Late in August, 1857, word was brought to Governor Medary that a party of Chippewa warriors was hovering about the Sunrise settlement on a small stream of that name in Chisago County. They had committed some thefts, had caused great alarm by insolent behavior, and were too numerous and too well armed to be dealt with by the local authorities. Governor Medary promptly ordered out the new St. Paul Light Cavalry Company commanded by Captain James Starkey. The command, "arrayed in red coats and white pants" and armed with heavy swords and army pistols, took the road on Monday, the twenty-fifth,

[37] *Statutes at Large*, 10: 304. The legislature of 1854 memorialized Congress to pass the bill. In a letter to Sibley written on January 7, 1854, Rice said: "I have drawn up a Bill giving to claimants of the Half-breed reservation land warrants for the amount of land that they would each be entitled to. The Warrants they can locate upon said tract or any other Govt land, or sell." See *Laws*, 1854, pp. 156–158, and the Sibley Papers. The "other purposes" of the act are discussed in the Appendix, no. 11, *post*.

[38] See *post*, volume 2, Appendix, no. 10.

and advanced by way of Cambridge, Isanti County. It was not till late on Friday, the twenty-eighth, that the enemy was discovered in full retreat across the prairie in the valley of the north branch of the Sunrise River. An advance guard of two troopers was sent forward, which soon overtook, halted, and marched back to where the company was awaiting them the whole Chippewa army of six hunters. Their leader evidently took in the situation and gave a signal. Instantly the savages dropped their blankets and sprang over a neighboring board fence into a field of standing corn. Beyond it lay a piece of woodland, toward which the flight was directed. Captain Starkey at once ordered the fence broken down in two places and led his company forward through the gaps. After a gallop of some four hundred yards the advance came up with the fugitives. Trooper Frank Donnelly was in the lead shouting and flourishing his pistol. One of the Chippewa, Shagoba by name, turned, leveled his gun, and shot Donnelly through the arm and the body. He died in a few minutes. Then there was firing from both sides and one Indian was killed and another was wounded. Escape now being impossible, the survivors of the battle surrendered. Late in the afternoon of the next day they were lodged in the Ramsey County jail. On September 3 they were brought into the United States district court on a writ of habeas corpus, sued out by Indian Agent William J. Cullen. After a full hearing Judge R. R. Nelson discharged all but Shagoba, whom he committed for trial for homicide in Chisago County. He was turned over to the sheriff of that county. For lack of a jail the sheriff undertook to keep the prisoner in his own house, and did so for about a week. Choosing a favorable moment, Shagoba broke jail, swam the St. Croix, and disappeared in the tall timber of Wisconsin. So ended the "Cornstalk War." The action of the court seems to have met with public approval.[39]

[39] *Pioneer and Democrat*, August 25, September 1, 3, 4, 13, 1857; Williams, *Saint Paul*, 377; Newson, *Pen Pictures*, 667. See also Captain Starkey's account in *Glimpses of the Nation's Struggle*, a series of papers read before the Minnesota Commandery of the Military Order of the Loyal Legion of the United States, third series, 265–279 (New York, 1893).

XII. TERRITORIAL RAILROAD MISCARRIAGE

THE adventurous pioneers who in the early fifties were laying the foundation of a new commonwealth were not indifferent to their need of railways, both to connect the territory with the states to the south and the east and to extend the area of settlement within its borders. They were fully conscious of their remoteness and isolation. At the same time they did not in the first years of territorial life dare hope for early relief. Of capital at home there was none to be spared for railway building, and there was little which could be expected from abroad. They were disposed to await with patience the slow but sure progress of events, which must eventually bring the railroad to their doors. Governor Ramsey in his first three messages made no suggestion on the subject. In his fourth and last, in January, 1853, he modestly recommended early railroad connections between Lake Superior and the Mississippi and between that river and the Red. Near the close of that message, however, in the course of a glowing prophecy of the coming magnificence of Minnesota, he pictured the "great New Orleans and Minnesota Railroad," carrying furs and merchandise of the polar land to be exchanged for the products of the sunny South.[1]

Meantime an unexpected resource, a basis of credit which would, it was believed, invite abundant capital and enterprise, was revealed. After a disastrous experiment in state railroad building, the state of Illinois, on March 6, 1843, chartered the Great Western Railway Company to build a road from Chicago to Cairo. On behalf of this corporation Senator Sidney Breese introduced into Congress a memorial praying for the privilege of entering all lands on both sides of the proposed road for a given distance at one dollar

[1] *Council Journal*, 1853, p. 36.

and a quarter an acre. It was not until four years later, however, that a bill based on the memorial received serious consideration in the Senate. Fortunately Stephen A. Douglas appeared in the Senate at this time. Although he supported Breese in his contention that the general government should aid in the construction of a railroad through central Illinois, he advocated a grant of land to the state and not to a private corporation. He therefore introduced an alternative bill to grant to the state of Illinois the alternate sections and at the same time to double the price of those retained by the government. This bill carried in the Senate but, on August 12, 1848, was defeated in the House. Five months later the Great Western Railway Company, the charter of which had been repealed in 1845, was reorganized. The new charter contained an amendment which provided that all lands granted by Congress to the state of Illinois for aiding railroad construction should be vested in that one corporation, without placing any restrictions on their use. The senator denounced the transaction in a public address, and later, by threatening a change of the southern terminal, where the promoters had made large investments, forced the corporation to release its charter. The way was now open for a grant to the state, provided Congress could be propitiated. The story of the struggle for the bill need not be related here. Senator Douglas devoted two entire years to it and at length, as he declares, it "went through without a dollar, pure, uncorrupt." It became a law on September 21, 1850, to be the precedent for a long line of railroad land grants. In the following year the state of Missouri obtained a similar grant.[2]

[1] Thomas Donaldson, *The Public Domain*, 262–264 (46 Congress, 3 session, *House Executive Documents*, no. 47, part 4 — serial 1975); *Statutes at Large*, 9: 466; 10: 8; Illinois, *Laws*, 1842–43, p. 199, *Private Laws*, 1849, p. 89; *Congressional Globe*, 30 Congress, 1 session, 723, 1071; 28 Congress, 1 session, *Senate Journal*, 47 (serial 430); 31 Congress, 1 session, *Senate Journal*, 659 (serial 548); John B. Sanborn, *Congressional Grants of Land in Aid of Railways*, 287–289 (University of Wisconsin, *Bulletin*, no. 30, *Economics, Political Science, and History Series*, vol. 2, no. 3 — Madison, 1899); Theodore C. Pease, *The Frontier State*, 216–235 (*Centennial History of Illinois*, vol. 2 — Springfield, 1918); Howard G. Brownson, *History of the Illinois Central Railroad to 1870*, 20 (University of Illinois, *Studies in the Social Sciences*, vol. 4, nos. 3 and 4 — Urbana, 1915).

The men of enterprise in Minnesota were by no means indifferent to these movements, but they were in doubt as to whether Congress would make a grant of land to a territory. In the hope that the objections to such a donation might be obviated, and to test the question, they asked and obtained from the territorial legislature of 1853 five railroad charters, similar in their provisions and wording. The names of Sibley, Rice, and Steele were prominent among those of the incorporators. Among the eastern capitalists willing to encourage the enterprises were Robert J. Walker, Abbott Lawrence, and Simeon Draper. The most ambitious of the chartered companies was the Lake Superior, Puget's Sound, and Pacific Railroad Company with an authorized capital of fifty million dollars.[3] In his first message to the legislature, delivered on January 11, 1854, Governor Gorman said, with reference to railroads: "To get out from here, during the winter . . . is far above and beyond any other consideration to the people of Minnesota. To accomplish this, in my judgment, you must concentrate all the energies of the people to one or two roads, AND NO MORE, for the present. I have but little doubt that Congress will grant us land sufficient to unlock our ice-bound home, if we confine our request to one point."[4] The legislators appear to have been moved by this advice, and chartered but two more companies during the session.

The story of one of these companies, which terminated abortively, forms an episode of no little interest in the territorial history, complicated as it is with the politics of the time. Joseph R. Brown introduced into the Council a bill to incorporate the Minnesota and Northwestern Railroad Company. This bill was probably drafted in New York by attorneys for persons connected with the Illinois Central Railroad and doing business in Wall Street. It was brought to St. Paul by their western attorneys, who desired

[3] *Laws*, 1853, pp. 15, 27, 35, 47, 50.
[4] *Council Journal*, 1854, p. 29.

the utmost dispatch and suggested that a failure to enact the measure promptly into law would result in the defeat of the land grant bill in Washington.[5] The action of the Minnesota Council was rapid enough, and the bill was passed by a vote of 5 to 3 with one member absent. The favorable report of a select committee on the bill is notable as expressing the airy hopefulness of the majority. The amount of land to be donated by Congress, said the committee, "will exceed but a trifle, if any, over a million of acres, which are worth nominally one million two hundred and fifty thousand dollars . . . but the rapid influx of population, capital, increase of agricultural and all other industrial pursuits, which the building of this railway will draw along with it, will increase the prosperity of the Territory to a degree, in comparison with which the emoluments of the company will be but a mere trifle." The committee proposed that the company be allowed five years in which to build, and recommended that the name of Alexander Ramsey be added to the list of directors. The bill did not reach the lower house till late on the second of March. Here a stubborn minority fought vigorously but vainly for its defeat. Among the amendments proposed was one to incorporate a bill to prevent traffic in intoxicating liquors. Another, which occupies nine closely printed pages of the *House Journal*, was for the establishment of a bank to be known as the "Bank of Minnesota." All the minority effected by this protracted filibustering was to delay the passage of the bill. On the final vote it numbered but six against a solid majority vote of eleven. Governor Gorman

[5] *Council Journal*, 1854, p. 177. See the testimony of Isaac Van Etten, a member of the Council, in *Alteration of the Text of House Bill No. 342*, 40 (33 Congress, 1 session, *House Reports*, no. 352 — serial 744). A contributor to the *Minnesota Democrat* for March 8, 1854, characterizes the measure as a "villainously concocted Wall street brokers' railroad bill, recently brought to St. Paul, and insultingly presented to our Legislature." An editorial in the issue of July 19, 1854, asserts that, "Under this charter, with its present fraudulent features our Territory is as firmly sold to the Wall street sharpers for all time to come, as Legislative action can effect it." The same issue announces the defalcation of Robert Schuyler, railroad king and head of the Minnesota and Northwestern corporation, who is said to have drafted the charter of the company. See also the *St. Anthony Express* for July 15, 1854.

announced his approval in a special message to the Council near midnight on March 4. Because the act had been presented to him but one hour and five minutes before the time of final adjournment of the House, he had not been able to examine the details. Unable, therefore, to formulate his objections, he decided not to withhold his signature but to "leave the responsibility upon those who passed the bill."[6] How the governor of the territory, aware of the pendency of a measure of such importance, which was the subject of general remark and conversation about the Capitol and the city, could have been kept for a fortnight in such deep ignorance of its provisions, is a question worthy of the attention of some curious investigator. His name was on the list of incorporators.

The bill had been drawn with dexterity.[7] The following items need be kept in mind if the reader desires to pursue the story of this corporation:

(1) At the first meeting of the incorporators, to be held in New York City within sixty days after the passage of the act, they were to determine whether or not they would accept the charter, and if they did accept they were to give immediate notice to that effect by mail to the governor of Minnesota.

(2) The northern terminus was designated with conspicuous particularity as "a point on the North-West shore of Lake superior in Minnesota Territory, north of the St. Louis River, opposite the entrance of the Left Hand River into Lake Superior; and near the mouth of the St. Louis River, Minnesota, on Lake Superior."

(3) The southern terminus was to be the city of Dubuque, but the land grant was confined to Minnesota. The designation of Dubuque implied an extension of the Illinois Central Railroad system. For reasons easily surmised the route was derisively called by opponents "The Ramshorn Road."

---

⁶ *Council Journal*, 1854, pp. 221, 256, 301; *House Journal*, 1854, pp. 294-304, 306; *Weekly Minnesotian*, March 15, 1854.

⁷ *Laws*, 1854, pp. 121-129.

(4) The kernel of the measure was comfortably tucked into the middle of a long section, in these words: " . . . it is further enacted that any lands that may be granted to the said Territory to aid in the construction of the said railroad shall be and the same are hereby granted in fee simple, absolute, without any further act or deed," to the said company.[8]

(5) Another provision, which, contrary to expectation, contributed to the undoing of the company, was that the act should be void unless the board of directors should be constituted and organized on or before the first day of July, 1854.

All was well at the St. Paul end of the enterprise. At Washington it did not advance so smoothly. Delegate Rice on December 19, 1853, gave notice of a bill to grant public lands in aid of railroad construction in Minnesota, and on February 6, 1854, he presented a "petition of himself" for a land grant in aid of a railroad from Lake Superior via St. Paul to connect with the Illinois Central.[9]   On February 7, a bill to grant land to Minnesota Territory in aid of railroad construction, which had been introduced into the Senate by Shields of Illinois, was passed without debate or division.   Precisely one month passed before it came up for consideration in committee of the whole of the House of Representatives.   The bill carried a grant to the territory and future state of Minnesota of alternate sections of public lands for six miles on both sides of the proposed railroad, as described in the pending Minnesota charter.   The chairman of the House committee on territories in explaining the bill stated that the distance from St. Paul to the head of Lake Superior was only about one hundred and twenty miles and that the land was mostly

---

[8] Section 8.   A proviso required that when the net earnings of the road should exceed twenty per cent of the capital actually expended, the corporation should pay seven per cent of the "said net earnings" into the treasury of the territory or of the future state. The probable revenue may be conjectured.

[9] 33 Congress, 1 session, *House Journal*, 321 (serial 709).

tamarack swamp of no value. The government would really gain by giving half of it to anybody who would penetrate the region with a railroad. A letter from Jefferson Davis, then secretary of war, recommended the bill to Congress as one of great importance to the government, much in need of a railroad to transport troops, munitions of war, and mails from the head of Lake Superior inland.[10]

An effort to pass the bill without discussion was futile. The railroad land grant policy was still novel. Precedents were few. This grant of a million acres, more or less, aroused attention and suspicion. Upon inquiry whether there was not a corporation ready to gobble the whole grant the moment it was made, the delegate from Minnesota was able to reply truthfully that, although a number of railroad charters had been legally granted in his territory, he knew of none for the object mentioned.[11] The mails in those days were slow. To an inquiry whether gentlemen in Washington and some of them about the Capitol had acquired for speculation some thousands of acres of land at and about the northern terminus of the projected road, Rice with equal truth replied that no such purchase could have taken place in Minnesota for the simple reason that the lands had not been surveyed and opened to market.[12] No

---

[10] 33 Congress, 1 session, *Senate Journal*, 106, 165 (serial 689), *Congressional Globe*, 564, 566; *Weekly Minnesotian*, January 28, 1854.

[11] "There is no charter which covers this grant." *Congressional Globe*, 33 Congress, 1 session, 565.

[12] While the Minnesota charter and the pending bill located the northern terminus with much emphasis in Minnesota, an uncontradicted rumor spread that an alternate and, in fact, the principal terminus would be Superior City, Wisconsin. Failure to distinguish between these points led to misunderstandings, followed by explanations. When Mr. Lane, a representative, stated on the floor of the House that he was informed that six thousand acres of land about "the terminus" had been claimed, and that one-fourth of the amount had been sold for twenty-eight thousand dollars, he evidently had the Wisconsin location in mind. In reply to an interrogation, Delegate Rice replied that he owned no land about the terminus and knew of no men who did own such claims — all of which was perfectly true of the Minnesota terminus described in the bill. The statement of the delegate could not apply so well to the unadvertised terminus at Superior. On July 4, 1854, he wrote to Governor Ramsey, "Now in Confidence if you can buy a few lots in 'Superior' you had better do it, I had to sell all of my interest for influence." See the Ramsey Papers. W. W. Corcoran, a Washington banker, held shares in the town-site claim for Senators Douglas, Bright, and Hunter, for Representatives Richardson and Breckinridge, and for Forney, clerk of the House. Before the catastrophe of 1857 wiped out the ambitious city,

statement was called out as to the condition of lands not in
Minnesota though near the head of the lake.   An objection evoking discussion was that the whole grant would
vest instantly in a company, which might take an indefinite
time within which to build.   To this it was effectively replied that the whole grant was necessary as a basis of credit.
Fault was found with the covert conveyance of a right of
way in Iowa, although the grant was confined to Minnesota.
Gerritt Smith of New York, the great abolitionist, opposed
the grant on the ground that Congress had no right to give
the lands to a corporation — they belonged to the landless
people of the world.   The opposition, although stout and
determined, was uncertain as to the result of a direct vote,
and therefore it resorted to the policy of smothering the
bill by amendment.   Various amendments were proposed
and mostly voted down.   Finally a proposition to divide
the proceeds of the sales of the reserved sections among
the states which enjoyed no land grants prevailed.   Whereupon a motion to table the bill gave it an immediate quietus.[13]
Against this disposition of the Minnesota land grant bill
there was a prompt reaction.   The delegations from the
South and the West were not disposed to see a railroad land
grant policy, so full of promise for their sections, thus put
in abeyance.   Sympathy for a remote territory straining
for a market and a road to the States and the seat of government found earnest expression.   Indications of a readiness on the part of Congress to make a liberal grant of
public lands to the Territory of Minnesota, provided that no
particular set or clique of promoters should be the beneficiaries, multiplied.

A new bill, following in the main the terms of the defeated measure, was drawn up and introduced into the

the twenty-seven shares were valued at six million dollars and one share was sold for one
hundred and sixty thousand dollars in cash. Lots were sold at from fifteen hundred to
two thousand dollars each. Superior, Wisconsin, *Report of the City Statistician for 1892*,
7–11.

    [13] *Congressional Globe*, 33 Congress, 1 session, 564–568, 573–576, 582–590, 601, contains
the details of this notable debate.

House on May 6. The route of the proposed railroad, however, beginning on the northern boundary of Iowa, between certain ranges, was to be northward through St. Paul in the direction of Lake Superior, and no reference was made to any particular terminus there. To prevent the benefits of the act from inuring to any particular corporation, a new section was framed providing that the contemplated grant of land should be "at the disposal of any future legislature of the Territory or state of Minnesota" and should not vest "in any company constituted or organized before the passage of the act." An objection to the introduction of the bill on the ground that it was "the same old bill" which the House had laid on the table, was quieted by assurances that it contained new and desirable provisions. It was the twentieth of June before it could be taken up again. By this time it had gained friends and they were so well organized that they secured an easy triumph and passed the measure by a handsome vote. It passed the Senate in the usual course and was approved by the president on June 29.[14] The satisfaction of the western congressmen was great. An Illinois member wrote to Ramsey: "Dear Gov. The Minnesota Bill has this moment passed the Senate. 'In gloria excelsis.' "[15]

An act of so much financial importance as this would naturally be carefully scrutinized at the earliest moment after becoming law. The original friends of the bill were astounded to discover two changes in its wording, which, however trifling they might appear, were of great import. In the new third section so carefully drawn by Sibley they found these two alterations: (1) the word "future" before "legislature" was omitted, and (2) the word "or" was replaced by "and" between the words "constituted" and

---

[14] 33 Congress, 1 session, *House Journal*, 720, 1025 (serial 709), *Congressional Globe*, 1120–1122. Sibley is usually credited with the drafting of the bill. See Eastman to Sibley, June 20, 1854, in the Sibley Papers, and *Alteration of the Text of House Bill No. 342*, 38, 49 (serial 744).

[15] Washburne to Ramsey, June 28, 1854, Ramsey Papers.

"organized."[16] As thus changed it was possible so to construe the paragraph as to place the land grant at the disposal of the Minnesota territorial legislature lately adjourned and to allow it to vest in a corporation already created by that legislature, but not yet organized. The corporators of the Minnesota and Northwestern Railroad Company promptly gave it that construction. Claiming to have been merely "constituted" by the Minnesota legislature, they met in New York City on July 1, on one day's notice, and "organized" by the election of a board of directors, who proceeded to choose the usual officers of a corporation. The corporators at a previous meeting, held on April 4, had accepted the Minnesota charter. As this charter required that three directors be citizens of Minnesota, Edmund Rice, Lyman Dayton, and Alexander Ramsey were chosen. Necessary provisions for surveys and finances were attended to. It was the expectation of the promoters of the corporation that all opposition to it would disappear with the assurance of the land grant and the promise of a railroad. They were to be disappointed.[17]

The friends of the new bill were paralyzed with amazement at the pretensions of the Minnesota and Northwestern Company in appropriating the granted lands under an act carefully drawn to prevent it from so doing. By what persons and by what process their intentions had been reversed they could not at once ascertain. About a fortnight after the passage, the secretary of Minnesota Territory, Joseph T. Rosser, appeared in Washington and, at the request of Governor Gorman, proceeded to examine and compare the original and engrossed copies of the bill. He discovered that the word "future" had been struck out of the original,

---

[16] This section read originally as follows: "*And be it further enacted*, That the said lands hereby granted to the said Territory shall be subject to the disposal of any future legislature thereof for the purpose aforesaid, and no other; nor shall they inure to the benefit of any company heretofore constituted or organized." See *Alteration of the Text of House Bill No. 342*, 2 (serial 744). The act as passed is in *Statutes at Large*, 10: 302.

[17] *Council Journal*, 1855, pp. 32–36; *House Journal*, 1855, p. 82; Billings to Ramsey, July 5, 1854, Rice to Ramsey, July 4, 1854, Ramsey Papers.

and was accordingly omitted in the engrossed copy. In the former the word "or" stood, but the engrossed bill showed the word "and" written over an evident erasure. On July 24 it was "*quite* hot in *the House*." Washburne of Illinois, rising to a question of privilege, charged that this alteration of "or" to "and" in the third section of the Minnesota land bill had been made after its passage by the House and moved the appointment of a select committee to inquire into so gross an offense. Representative Stevens of Michigan, of the public lands committee, at once rose and frankly assumed the responsibility for the changes. While the bill was still in committee and in his hands, he had been convinced by gentlemen interested that the word "future" ought not to remain and that "or" should give place to "and." He had so explained to the committee and had been directed to report the bill thus altered. With his own hand he had struck out "future," and supposed he had written "and" for "or." After the passage he was informed that the word "or" was still there. He applied to the engrossing clerk of the House to make the change, believing at the same time that he had himself made it in the reported bill. This official was not willing to act unless by the direction of the chief clerk of the House. To that officer the two proceeded, accompanied by the engrossing clerk of the Senate. The chief clerk of the House, after hearing the explanation made, said that the change "had better be made." The representative had no knowledge of the design of the gentlemen in desiring the changes, had no personal interest in the measure, and intended no wrong.[18] This explanation, however, did not satisfy the House.

A select committee of investigation was ordered, which began on the same day, July 24, to take testimony. The

[18] *Alteration of the Text of House Bill No. 342* (serial 744); *Congressional Globe*, 33 Congress, 1 session, pp. 1887–1891; Rice to Ramsey, July 24, 1854, Ramsey Papers; Eastman to Sibley, July 25, 1854, Sibley Papers. In an affidavit dated December 1, 1854, Robert W. Lowber, acting president of the Minnesota and Northwestern Railroad Company, places the blame for the changes on George W. Billings, one of the promoters of the company. *Minnesota Democrat*, January 3, 1855.

statements of fact of the Michigan member were repeated to the committee and were corroborated. A large part of the time during eight sessions was taken up with ineffective efforts to discover the persons or interests who were so desirous of securing "purely verbal alterations" of the bill. Witnesses had not informed themselves, or their memories were at fault. An official of the railroad company refused to divulge the names of his associates in office. The houses had fixed August 4 as the day of final adjournment. On the day preceding, the committee submitted its report exonerating members and officers of the House from all blame, and recommending the passage of a new bill in the precise terms of that which had been unlawfully changed. The minority of the committee also submitted a report, alleging that a culpable error deserving severe censure had been committed, by which members were made to appear as voting for a bill which they would have opposed. They recommended withholding the evidence from publication and the continuation of the investigation.[19]

The House was in no mood to temporize and promptly substituted for the committee's bill one to repeal the act of June 29, passed it without division, and sent it to the Senate. When the bill was taken up there the same day, a Michigan senator objected to its second reading. This objection, delaying under the rules further action for a day, was fatal. There was at the moment among other House bills pending in the Senate one to raise the pension of one Thomas Bronough from four to eight dollars a month. To this Pearce of Maryland moved an amendment to repeal the Minnesota land grant bill and thus rub out a "stain on legislation." Douglas made a vain effort to save the grant to the territory by moving to substitute the

[19] *Alteration of the Text of House Bill No. 342.* The testimony of G. W. Billings (p. 42) and of Hugh Tyler (p. 38) in which each charged the other with suggesting surreptitious changes in the bill seems to prove that such action had been in mind. The testimony of Delegate Rice (p. 19), when compared with his letters to Governor Ramsey, leaves much to be desired in point of candor. Rice to Ramsey, July 4, 15, 24, 1854, Ramsey Papers; see also Rice to Olmsted, August 3, 1854, in Neill, *Minnesota*, 610, n.

original bill word for word, "future" and all. Benjamin reminded him that the passage of the bill would certainly vest the lands in a company "now" organized. Seward voiced the mind of the majority in proposing that the House be allowed to vindicate itself in its own way. The amended private bill with title properly changed was therefore passed, and the concurrence of the House was requested. Under the operation of suspended rules and the previous question, the House instantly concurred. Nevertheless the act of June 29, called the "Minnesota Land Grant Bill," still stands in the *Statutes at Large*.[20] A resolution to dismiss the clerk of the House, Colonel Forney, obtained but eighteen affirmative votes.

Although the special committee of the House had failed to obtain direct evidence, there was good ground for the belief that the tinkering with the engrossed bill after its passage was, in the words of a senator, "a deliberate and intended error." The circle of persons who conceived and undertook to carry out the insertion of the secret changes in the bill was doubtless a small one. Alexander Ramsey was not taken into their confidence, but he regarded the repeal as a misfortune for the territory.[21] A letter from one of the eastern promoters to him gives evidence that the incorporators were willing to go beyond mere moral suasion in securing votes. "Since the passage of the Nebraska bill," his correspondent wrote, "there are many *lame Ducks* who want assistance in the coming elections & *they or their friends*

[20] 33 Congress, 1 session, *House Journal*, 1272, 1302 (serial 709), *Senate Journal*, 647 (serial 689), *Congressional Globe*, 2100, 2172–2178; *Statutes at Large*, 10: 302. A marginal note in the latter states that the act was "Repealed by act of 1854, ch. 246." The *Minnesota Democrat* for August 16, 1854, calls the repeal "this stunning blow upon the interests of our territory." Certain newspapers of the territory charged Rice with being at least cognizant of the plan to alter the bill, and not altogether zealous to defeat the repeal, but the *Democrat* defended him. See the issues of August 23, September 27, and October 4, 11, 25, in which letters from senators and representatives are quoted. Rice's view of the matter is set forth in a letter to Ramsey, dated July 31, 1854, in the Ramsey Papers.

[21] The testimony of Stevens, Billings, Tyler, and Washburne indicates that the scheme for procuring alterations in the bill was not suddenly extemporized but had been the subject of consultation. See *Alteration of the Text of House Bill No. 342* (serial 744), and also Tyler to Sibley, August 1, 1854, in the Sibley Papers.

come here to *obtain relief*. We are making their wants inure to our benefit."[22]

The reader may not regret it if he follows further the schemes of the Minnesota and Northwestern Railroad Company. It had invited large real estate transactions in which men of speculative turn suffered some losses and much disappointment. Governor Gorman was advised on August 26 by a member of Congress that the president would remove him from office because of his advocacy of the repeal of the land grant, it being alleged that men high in the confidence of the president had "lost pecuniarily thereby." Among those who had coöperated to secure the land grant and turn it over to this corporation, as a basis of credit, were some who charged their opponents with being enemies of the territory, working to secure to themselves political advantages and to divert the grant to other persons. The delegate from Minnesota, Henry M. Rice, was of this number. He was of the opinion that the act of June 29 worked an irrevocable donation to the territory, which by anticipation had conveyed it to the railroad company duly begotten if not then born. The difference between "or" and "and," wrote Rice, was immaterial. In this opinion he was supported by distinguished lawyers of the counsel for the company. Advised by them that they had a good case, the directors early resolved to make vigorous efforts to gain possession of the lands. The first step was to secure the election of a legislature in Minnesota which would be favorably disposed to the company and its claims. On August 7 Rice wrote Ramsey, "The Legislature *must be right*," and a week later he followed this up with a plan of campaign. "The prospects are," he said, "that the company will *go ahead* — the people of the territory should do all in their power to aid — and not to thwart. . . . The Democrat will be right — the Minnesotian should appeal to the people — show the contrast between having five

[22] Billings to Ramsey, May 27, 1854, Ramsey Papers.

thousand men at work on the road, and ten thousand dollars paid out daily, or having no public works going on — in the former case, farmers could get cash and a high price for all their products, mechanics merchants & laborers would find money abundant, land now worth 5 s. per acre would go up to 25 $. . . . The people should with one voice sustain those who are willing to fight for the grant."[23] While the two political parties did not divide on this railroad question, it had its effect in the choice of candidates of both and was the occasion of much ticket-splitting at the polls. The now chronic conflict between the friends of Sibley and those of Rice was continued upon a new issue and lost none of its bitterness. It was a novelty, however, to see Ramsey coöperating with Rice against Sibley and Gorman. Confident that, if supported by the legislature, the company would secure the land grant and would promptly build the road, many voters were willing to condone any alleged irregularities of procedure, so eager they were for communication with the States. The vote on October 10 was not so adverse as to discourage the company from further effort. The election of Sibley to the lower house of the legislature was, however, a very discouraging circumstance.[24]

The next step was toward obtaining judicial decisions favorable to the company's claim. On October 23, 1854, John E. Warren, United States district attorney, filed in the district court of Goodhue County the complaint of the United States of America against the Minnesota and Northwestern Railroad Company, alleging that that corporation had "felled, cut down, prostrated, and killed" five hundred oaks and five hundred other trees on a certain parcel of land, "to the damage of the plaintiff of ten hundred and ten dollars." The company, through its attorneys, for answer set up the act of the Minnesota legislature of March and that of Congress of June and pleaded that being thereby

[23] Rice to Ramsey, July 15, 24, 31, August 3, 4, 7, 14, 1854, Ramsey Papers.
[24] West, *Sibley*, 211–216.

lawfully seized of the said parcel of land, it had by such
felling of trees done only what it lawfully might do. The
government rejoined, setting up the repealing act of Congress of August 4. To this the defendant company de-
murred, declaring the said act to be void and of no effect.
These pleadings were filed and issue was joined on October
23. Within a fortnight testimony was heard and, on November 4, Chief Justice Welch, holding the district court,
sustained the demurrer and ordered judgment for the defendant company.[25] Notice of appeal to the territorial
supreme court was given on November 20. An extra term
of that tribunal was called, a hearing was had, and on December 8 a decision was rendered affirming the finding of
the district court and the contention of the defending company that the repealing act of Congress of August 3, 1854,
was repugnant to the Constitution of the United States and
to great and fundamental principles of the common law.

The decision gave great satisfaction to the partisans of the
railroad company, who naturally gave it all possible pub-
licity. The zealous district attorney promptly appealed his
suit to the Supreme Court of the United States. On December 28, the solicitor of the treasury notified the attorney-
general that information had "reached him informally and
unofficially" of the suit of the United States against the
Minnesota and Northwestern Railroad Company, of the
decisions of the Minnesota courts adverse to the government, and of the appeal therefrom already docketed for
hearing at the then present term of the United States
Supreme Court. Two days later the attorney-general,
Caleb Cushing, wrote Attorney Warren expressing the surprise of the president at his presumption in commencing the
suit without any orders whatever, at his prosecution of it
without giving notice to any superior authority, and at his

[25] *Suit against the Minnesota and Northwestern Railroad Company*, 9–24 (33 Congress,
2 session, *House Executive Documents*, no. 35 — serial 783). "Adjudged that the United
States of America, the plaintiff, take nothing by this action, and that the Minnesota and
Northwestern Railroad Company, the defendants, go thereof without day."

failure to transmit the appeal papers to the law offices of the United States; all of which acts or omissions were in direct violation of explicit standing instructions. The letter concluded with notice to the officious attorney that his official service would terminate with the receipt of the communication. The attorney-general, in justice to Warren, included among the documents relating to this case transmitted to the House a letter of Warren's printed in the *Minnesota Democrat*, December 20, 1854, in which he repelled the insinuation that he had brought the suit for the express purpose of benefiting the railroad company. He included also a letter from John B. Brisbin, the attorney who acted for Warren in the proceedings, which had appeared in the *Democrat* for December 4, in reply to Goodrich of the *Minnesota Pioneer*, who had descanted on Brisbin's "unaccountable stupidity, or still more unaccountable corruption."[26] Thus ended the first phase of a long litigation.

The territorial legislature convened on January 3, 1855. Governor Gorman in his message recited at length the history of the Minnesota and Northwestern Railroad Company and of its abortive efforts to obtain possession of a congressional land grant by the "or-and" jugglery of the bill of June 29, 1854. He expressed the hope that Congress might be persuaded to undo its repealing act of August 4 and to reënact the land grant, believing that that body would be unwilling to punish a whole population for the transgression of a clique of speculators. The portion of the executive message relating to railroads was referred to the judiciary committee of the House of Representatives. A few days later the committee reported, through its chairman, Henry H. Sibley, some additional facts, and showed that the company

[26] The *Minnesota Democrat* for October 25, 1854, discusses the relation of Rice and Sibley to the railroad controversy. The issue of December 20 contains a history of the case and a statement of its status at that time. Warren's explanation of his conduct is in the issue of January 17, 1855. See also *Suit against the Minnesota and Northwestern Railroad Company*, 26, 36–40 (serial 783), and the *Daily Minnesota Pioneer* for December 2, 1854.

had done nothing toward construction and that the most prominent incorporator was a fugitive from justice. The committee had been utterly unable to learn even the names of the men to whose hands the direction had been transferred. All the proceedings of the company were shrouded in mystery. The committee advised, as the best way out of an uncertain and dangerous situation, that the legislature present to Congress a memorial praying for (1) the disapproval by that body of the charter granted by the Minnesota legislature to the Minnesota and Northwestern Railroad Company, as permitted by the organic act of the territory; and (2) the restoration of the grant of land to the territory according to the original bill of June, 1854. The minority of the committee also submitted a report. It is not known that this paper was prepared by the attorneys of the railroad company, but they could hardly have drawn a better one for their purposes. The alterations in the land grant bill were "merely verbal" and did not change the meaning. The land grant was therefore irrevocable. The company, having complied with the stipulations of its charter, had become completely vested with the title to the lands. If such a contract was not valid, "whose property or liberty is secure?" The courts of the territory held the attempt of Congress to recall the grant made to the territory to be unconstitutional. No obstacle should be placed in the way of the corporation and its enterprises. The temper of the House may be inferred from the fact that it refused by a decisive vote a third reading of the memorial proposed by the judiciary committee.[27]

Congress, however, without waiting for a memorial, had taken up the matter, and on January 29, 1855, the House passed a joint resolution disapproving and annulling the charter of the railroad company. This action was not agreeable to the Minnesota delegate, but he had the satisfaction of finding his influence at the other end of the Capitol

[27] *Council Journal*, 1855, pp. 32–36; *House Journal*, 1855, pp. 70–81, 89–93, 105–113.

sufficient to secure the nonconcurrence of the Senate.[28] The refusal of Congress to annul the railroad charter gave satisfaction to the company and to its friends in the territory. When the tidings reached St. Paul on March 24, there was a general illumination throughout the village.[29]

But the railroad company was in need of positive action by the Minnesota legislature. So much time had been lost that an extension of the period within which it was bound to complete a twenty-mile section of road was indispensable. It desired, also, to have certain irregularities in organization remedied. A bill was therefore introduced into the lower house to reënact the charter with amendments, the principal one of which was that extending the time. Petitions from citizens praying for such extension began to come in. One from St. Paul and Little Canada was signed by 729 persons in a district which had polled 833 votes at the late election. These petitions were referred to the committee on internal improvements, which presently submitted a report recommending that the prayers of the petitioners be granted. The committee found that the railroad company had acted in good faith; that the repeal of the land grant was caused by "a meddlesome and factious interference" by citizens of Minnesota, for which the company was not responsible; and that the company had asserted its legal rights in the courts "with the indomitable spirit of perseverance, worthy the conductors of a great enterprise." The committee would grant the company the extension of time desired, and

<hr>

[28] *Congressional Globe*, 33 Congress, 2 session, 450, 960. The Senate committee on territories, after presenting a somewhat elaborate history of the matter, reported that the Minnesota and Northwestern charter was a proper subject for Minnesota legislation, that Congress ought not to have postponed the question of disapproval for nearly twelve months, and that the supervisory power of Congress over territorial legislation had become obsolete. The committee, therefore, recommended the adoption of an amendment to strike out all the joint resolution after the word "resolved" and to insert a paragraph repealing that provision of the organic act of Minnesota which required the submission of all acts of its legislature to Congress and which authorized Congress to disapprove and amend. The Senate ordered the report printed, and adjourned four days later without taking further action. See 33 Congress, 2 session, *Senate Reports*, no. 547 (serial 775). The repeal of this provision was requested by both territorial houses. *House Journal*, 1855, p. 243; *Council Journal*, 1855, p. 103.

[29] *Minnesota Democrat*, March 28, 1855; *Weekly Minnesotian*, March 24, 1855.

would encourage it "to make the priceless improvements, specified in its charter" to the end that the "great valley at the head of which we stand, may be opened to the lakes of the North, the markets of the South and East, and have poured into it daily the productions of our possessions on the Pacific, and the treasure of Asia!" The reënacting bill was rapidly put through the successive stages, and on January 31, 1855, it passed by a vote of 10 to 8. Two days later the Council took it up and promptly passed it by a vote of 5 to 2.[30]

On February 8 Governor Gorman returned the bill to the House with a veto message embodying the sternest arraignment of the railroad company yet pronounced. While modeled on the charter of the Illinois Central Railroad Company, by which the land grant to the state of Illinois had been conferred upon that company, the charter of the Minnesota company left out nearly all, if not quite all, "the guards and securities" of the Illinois act. Illinois required a cash payment of twenty per cent of stock; Minnesota was to be content with ten per cent and no evidence of the payment of that. Illinois required a deposit of three hundred thousand dollars in securities; Minnesota, none. Illinois, when deeding her land to the company, took back a first mortgage and exacted seven per cent of the gross receipts of the road; Minnesota exacted the same proportion of the net proceeds only. Minnesota thus virtually lent the company six million dollars for three years without security and, moreover, exempted its stock from taxation by declaring it to be personal property. The message closes with a suggestion that the "Money King of our country has already more than a just share of influence among all the affairs of men." What justification in fact there may have been for this insinuation is not likely to be known, but it is not necessary to conclude that the legislative action

---

[30] *House Journal*, 1855, pp. 53, 57, 97–99, 103–105, 122–129; *Council Journal*, 1855, pp. 81–83.

which preceded or followed the veto was secured by the corrupt use of money. There was a great prize at stake, some millions of dollars, which the people of the territory and their representatives were assured with great confidence and emphasis could be won by supporting the claim of the railroad company. The territorial courts had pronounced in its favor and no superior tribunal had yet reversed their decisions. Congress, they were told, having dramatically stigmatized the trifling offense committed by irresponsible strangers, would presently relent and restore the land grant. The need of railroad communication to the north and to the south was keenly felt by all classes. This was the one company which, they felt assured, could soonest establish that communication, and a company which had suffered so much, it was pathetically declared, ought to have the support of the legislative body.[31]

It may not be forgotten that a political element was involved in the contest. Which were in greater strength, the friends of Sibley or those of Rice, and which of those leaders should receive an indorsement from the people of the territory entitling him to the confidence of the administration at Washington and to the control of the government patronage — these were the questions in issue. Within a week both houses passed the reënacting bill over the veto.[32] The defeated minority was obliged to be content with submitting to Congress a memorial drawn up by Sibley. His biographer speaks of this memorial as "a document the parallel to which for fearless and burning exposure of perfidy and wrong,— is perhaps unknown in the annals of any territory or state. . . . It has in it the tone and the tread of a lash-bearing Ajax. . . . It speaks the truth, shames the devil, and dares contradiction." To the reader of a half century later the

---

[31] *House Journal*, 1855, pp. 176–184; *Council Journal*, 1855, pp. 121–129; *Minnesota Pioneer Weekly*, February 15, 1855; *Weekly Minnesotian*, February 17, 24, 1855; *Minnesota Democrat*, March 21, 1855.

[32] *House Journal*, 1855, p. 241; *Council Journal*, 1855, p. 133; *Laws*, 1855, pp. 148–151. For supplementary acts, see *Laws*, 1855, pp. 66, 139.

memorial seems to be cast in no such heroic phrase. In moderate tones it charges that three representatives in the legislature from St. Paul had been corrupted by the company or its agents; that the whole course of the company had been characterized by fraud and had thus brought disgrace and shame upon the territory. The memorialists, therefore, pray Congress to annul the charter and then to restore to the territory the needed land grant. The friends of Rice up to this point had triumphed in the legislature as well as in the courts of the territory.[33]

The struggle for life and perpetuation was renewed by the Minnesota and Northwestern Railroad Company in the legislature of 1856. A bill granting an extension of time to the corporation, introduced early in the session, was passed through both houses by decided majorities. On the fifteenth of February, Governor Gorman returned it to the lower house disapproved, with a message stating his objections. Transmitting a copy of his veto message of the previous year on the same matter, he reaffirmed all the statements and arguments contained in it. The company, he urged, had done nothing to warrant this further expression of confidence. It would do nothing until possessed of the coveted land grant. The Congress in session would not renew that. Further extension of time to this company would be futile.[34] The company's friends could not rally votes enough to pass their bill over the executive veto. Cast down but not destroyed, they resolved on another trial. A new bill, sufficiently differentiated from that just defeated but fully rehabilitating the defaulting company, was introduced on the last day but two of the session, was passed by a strong vote in the House, and escaped defeat in the Council by a single voice. Governor Gorman approved this bill and so notified the lower house by a message in the nature of an apology. Although the bill did not provide such guards as

---

[33] West, *Sibley*, 217–219.

[34] *House Journal*, 1856, pp. 124, 212–220; *Council Journal*, 1856, p. 148. The vote was 22 to 10 in the House and 11 to 4 in the Council.

ought to surround so important an interest, and the means used by the company to accomplish its ends he did not approve and trusted he never would, still the measure provided for a payment to the territory of two per cent of the gross income of the road, which amount would be sufficient in a few years to pay all state expenses. As three successive legislatures had sustained the company, the executive was disposed to yield his objections. With feeble confidence in the professions of the company, he would await the future.[35] Both houses adopted a joint resolution declaring the removal from office of John E. Warren, as above related, "an act of injustice, at once to a high-minded and honorable man, an estimable and respected citizen, and an accomplished, faithful and incorruptible public officer."[36]

The railroad company, advised by eminent lawyers,[37] was already preparing an action at law, which it was hoped the national Supreme Court would, upon appeal, decide favorably. Edmund Rice, one of the directors of the company, having bought of the United States a piece of land in Dakota County on the line of the proposed road, on November 1, 1856, brought a personal action of trespass against the Minnesota and Northwestern Railroad Company, alleging unlawful destruction of trees growing on the land. The sole question put in issue was the repealability of the land grant. The United States was not made a party to the suit. The Minnesota district court found for the plaintiff, holding that the railroad company, having no title to the land, was a trespasser. The territorial supreme court reversed this decision on appeal. The case was carried on a writ of error to the United States Supreme Court, before which it was argued in January, 1862. The final decision was fatal to

[35] *House Journal*, 1856, pp. 260, 285–289, 332; *Council Journal*, 1856, p. 224; *Laws*, 1856, p. 76. See also Minnesota Constitutional Convention (Democratic), *Debates and Proceedings*, 300 (St. Paul, 1857) for another statement by Gorman of his reasons for approving the act.

[36] *Council Journal*, 1856, p. 122; *House Journal*, 1856, pp. 148, 172.

[37] West, *Sibley*, 220, gives the names of the counsel and their opinion in favor of the company's contention.

the contentions of the company. The act of Congress of June 29, 1854, did not vest the territory with ownership but devolved upon it "a mere naked trust or power to dispose of the lands" for a purpose and under conditions. Congress had the right to rescind the trust and to withdraw the power. The repealing act of August 4 was therefore "a valid law."[38] The controversy thus tardily closed had long ceased to interest anybody but the lawyers concerned and perhaps a few of the stockholders who held to the belief that the court of last resort might affirm the repeated decisions of those below. Congress never reinstated this particular land grant but it dealt liberally with the territory and the state. In expectation of such liberality, and believing that the Minnesota and Northwestern would cease from troubling, the Minnesota legislatures of 1856 and 1857 granted some twenty railroad charters. It being impossible to tell what ones would prosper, all had their platters ready, should it rain pudding. The curious student may find these elaborate charters in the territorial statutes of the years named.

[38] Minnesota and Northwestern Railroad Company *v*. Edmund Rice, 1 *Minnesota*, 358; Rice *v*. Railroad Company, 1 *Black*, 381. Four judges concurred in the opinion, two dissented, and one did not sit when this case came up before the United States Supreme Court.

XIII. PEOPLING THE TERRITORY

UP TO the ratification of the treaties of 1837, which occurred in the following year, there had been no white man's land in Minnesota.[1] As already explained, those treaties opened the delta between the St. Croix and the Mississippi. The census of 1840 gives the population of the west division of St. Croix County, Wisconsin Territory, as 351.[2] The whole number of whites, and half-breeds living apart from the Indians, on the area of Minnesota in that year could not have been more than double that number, counting in the garrison at Fort Snelling, the missionaries, and the people about the trading stations.

In the summer of 1849, John Morgan, sheriff of St. Croix County, was directed to take a census of the population of the territory, as provided in the organic act. After what had been stated to Congress when it was deliberating on the bill to establish the territory, it was very desirable that a full count should be made, and no pains were spared to enumerate all the white and mixed-blood inhabitants. Probably none escaped. All the *engagés* and *voyageurs* of the trading posts at Crow Wing, Long Prairie, Lake Traverse, Mendota, and many minor stations were carefully included. The main enumeration, submitted by the sheriff on July 4, 1849, before the returns from the Pembina and Missouri River districts had been received, recorded 3,814 inhabitants "without the Soldiers." This figure may be taken as approximately correct for the bona fide resident population in 1849 in the region which later became the state of Minnesota. The addition of 200 members of the garrison at Fort Snelling and 117 at Fort Gaines brought the number

---

[1] Squatters on the military reservation at Fort Snelling, although tolerated for some time, were at length expelled. Pages 217–223, *ante*, deal with this problem in detail.

[2] *United States Census*, 1840, *Enumeration of Inhabitants*, 461.

up to 4,131. St. Paul was credited with 910, Stillwater with 609, Little Canada with 322, and St. Anthony with 248. The enumerator at Pembina, Norman W. Kittson, was able to discover no fewer than 637 inhabitants on the American side of the international boundary, and 84 were listed by Edmund Brissett as "residing on the Missouri River within the limits of Minnesota." These supplementary returns increase the total to 4,852, but the deduction of the garrisons leaves 4,535 as the actual resident population in the territory as bounded by the organic act — a figure much below the generous estimates furnished to Congress.[3] But it was sufficient. The decennial census of 1850 gave the population of the nine counties of Minnesota Territory as 6,077; in the two counties of Ramsey and Washington, 3,283 were enumerated.[4]

No sooner was the signing of the treaties with the Sioux in 1851 noised abroad than enterprising white men began to

[3] June 11, 1849, was fixed in Governor Ramsey's order to the sheriff as "the date to which your enumeration and return will have reference." The official enumeration, certified by Sheriff Morgan, together with the supplementary returns from Pembina and the Missouri River, was discovered recently in a gunny sack of old papers which had been transferred from the basement of the Capitol to the Historical Building in pursuance of a law of 1919 authorizing the Minnesota Historical Society to act as custodian of state and local archives. Morgan's total, exclusive of the garrisons, is 3,816. The discrepancy of two between this figure and that given in the text is the result of the correction of an error of addition. The first volume of the Executive Journal, which has been transferred from the governor's office to the custody of the historical society, contains a transcript of the returns, and they are printed in the Council Journal, 1849, pp. 165–184. Both of these versions contain numerous errors of transcription and of addition, and those of the Council Journal have been widely copied. An incomplete collection of what appears to be original rolls or drafts from which the sheriff compiled his certified returns is also in the possession of the historical society, having been "presented by Charles H. Mix through H. H. Sibley." A table of the population arranged under the counties as later organized and totaling exactly 5,000, which purports to be based on "additional and revised census returns" received up to the time of the election on August 1, 1849, is given by Holcombe, in Minnesota in Three Centuries, 2: 436. This is obviously the same, with corrections in the totals, as the table in Neill, Minnesota, 507, n. 3, where it bears the date June 30, 1849, and is called an exhibit of "the result of the first census." Neill makes no reference to additional or revised returns, and it is not likely that there were any such of an official character.

[4] United States Census, 1850, Statistics, 993. The population is given by counties as follows:

Benton	418	Ramsey	2,227
Dakotah	584	Wabashaw	243
Itasco	97	Wahnahta	160
Mankahta	158	Washington	1,056
Pembina	1,134		
		Total	6,077

cross the Mississippi and invade the "Suland." They made their claims, opened roads, cut timber, and built houses and even mills.[5] They naturally followed up the valleys of the streams flowing into the Mississippi, that of the St. Peter's[6] being best known through traders and missionaries. There is a tradition that some impatient immigrants actually staked out their claims to cover the garden patches of the Indians. The Indian agent exerted himself in vain to prevent this unlawful occupancy of the Indian country, for the military at Fort Snelling refused to coöperate. In his report, dated September 1, 1852, Nathaniel McLean states that there could not have been less than five thousand white intruders resolved to occupy the country, treaty or no treaty.[7]

As already related, the treaties were not concluded till the fall of 1852, when the Indians consented to the Senate amendments; and they were not in full operation till February 24, 1853, when they were proclaimed by the president. The lower Sioux were loath to leave their beautiful homes for new ones on a reservation on the upper Minnesota which might not belong to them for more than five years. It was not till September, 1853, that the Mdewakanton could be collected at Little Crow's village, whence they moved on leisurely, some in canoes and some on foot, to the Redwood agency located by the agent near Fort Ridgely. The Wahpekute were equally tardy, and one small band was never induced to leave its old habitat about Faribault. The bands of the upper Sioux on Lac qui Parle, Big Stone Lake, and Lake Traverse were already on or near their reserve. The bands which had lived about the Traverse des Sioux and Little Rapids, now Carver, moved reluctantly to their designated places on the lower margin of the upper

---

[5] Governor Ramsey's message of 1853, in *Council Journal*, 1853, p. 36.
[6] By joint resolution, on June 19, 1852, Congress ordered that the St. Peter's River be designated in public records as the Minnesota River. *Statutes at Large*, 10: 147.
[7] 32 Congress, 2 session, *Senate Executive Documents*, no. 1, p. 349 (serial 658).

reservation, where the agent the following year located the upper agency at the mouth of the Yellow Medicine River.[8]

By the close of the year 1853 the "Suland" was nearly empty of Indians, but it was not till the late summer of the following year that it was legally open to settlement. The homestead act was still a dream, and the preëmption laws, codified in 1841, permitted occupation of surveyed lands only. The surveys of the public lands of the territory west of the Mississippi were not begun till the season of 1853, and it was not till 1855 that the first installment of lands, 1,178,003 acres in the extreme southeastern corner of the state, was offered for sale. The pioneers of the day, however, had no troublesome scruples, and they continued to swarm over the thirteen counties west of the Mississippi River in the region of the lower Minnesota. If there were twenty thousand people in the territory in the spring of 1852, as estimated by Bond, they were, with inconsiderable exceptions, trespassers with no justification but the ethics of the border.[9]

Relief from this situation came tardily. In his message to the territorial legislature of 1849, Governor Ramsey suggested as a matter of first importance the extension of the preëmption privilege to settlers on unsurveyed lands. He thought this modification of existing law was due the hardy and enterprising half million people who were making mere temporary locations on new areas, remaining only "until another wave of hardy adventurers, a little less restless in spirit, arrive to purchase their places and their

[8] Report of the Indian agent at St. Peter's, in 33 Congress, 1 session, *Senate Executive Documents*, no. 1, p. 314 (serial 690); 33 Congress, 2 session, *Senate Executive Documents*, no. 1, p. 271 (serial 746). The bands last mentioned were also upper Sioux. Because there was not sufficient time for finding a suitable permanent location for the Sioux as stipulated in one of the treaty amendments (see *ante*, page 291), the president had allotted to these Indians for a period of five years the reservation which was to have been theirs according to the original treaty. In 1854 Congress authorized the president to make this a permanent reservation for the Sioux. *Statutes at Large*, 10: 326.

[9] *Minnesota Democrat*, November 16, December 7, 1853; *Statutes at Large*, 5: 543; report of the commissioner of the general land office, 1855, in 34 Congress, 1 session, *House Executive Documents*, no. 1, p. 155 (serial 840); Bond, *Minnesota and Its Resources*, 22.

improvements, while they resume their never-ceasing journey towards the setting sun." The legislature responded with a memorial to Congress asking for the proposed extension, suggesting that it would benefit the territory, without loss to the United States, by encouraging sales to settlers.[10] To this appeal Congress gave no heed. In his second message, that of 1851, Governor Ramsey expressed his regret that Congress had taken no action in regard to this matter and renewed his recommendation in impassioned phrase. After remarking that all Minnesota settlers on unsurveyed lands were trespassers liable to prosecution, that the whole history of the West was witness that the pioneer had ever preceded the surveyor, and that settlements had always anticipated sales, he proceeded: "These hardy pioneers, who at the sacrifice of many of the comforts of life, have passed the frontiers of the Union . . . constitute the rank and file of that great army of peaceful progress, which has shed brighter lustre on our name, than all the fields, red with carnage, that have witnessed the triumph of our flag. They bring with them to the wilderness, which they embellish and advance, maxims of civil liberty, not engrossed on parchments, but inscribed in their hearts — not as barren abstractions, but as living principles and practical rules of conduct. They cost the Government neither monthly pay, nor rations — they solicit no bounty — they expect no hospital privileges — but they make the country, its history, and its glory. Extension to them of the preemption privilege would be an act of peace and repose. It would quiet titles, avoid excitement, perplexity and inconvenience, give a substantial character to frontier improvements, and secure to the enterprising settler the undisturbed possession and safe ownership of his home."[11]

Whether Governor Ramsey's was the first and original demand on behalf of a territory for the extension of

[10] *Council Journal*, 1849, p. 14; *Laws*, 1849, p. 173.

[11] *Council Journal*, 1851, p. 18. There is a tradition that the grandiloquent passages in Governor Ramsey's messages flowed from the facile pen of Dr. Thomas Foster.

preëmption privilege to settlers on unsurveyed lands is not known. It had little immediate effect, notwithstanding the eloquence of its diction. By an act of Congress approved on March 3, 1853, that privilege was granted to California for one year, and a supplementary act of March 1, 1854, extended its operation two years. By acts of 1854 preëmption was granted to settlers on unsurveyed lands in the territories of Kansas and Nebraska and of Washington and Oregon without limit of time. With these precedents, Delegate Rice had no difficulty, later in the session, in securing the passage of the act of August 4, 1854, granting the same privilege to squatters in Minnesota.[12] The "adjustments" of the boundaries of claims staked out at random required no little ingenuity and forbearance, but it was seldom that neighbors did not make them amicably. They were sometimes arbitrated by local "claims associations."

The farmers who took up claims on the arable lands west of the Mississippi after the treaties of 1851 were not the first to trespass on public lands in Minnesota. They had been anticipated by pioneer lumbermen on the St. Croix and later by those operating on the upper Mississippi. The beginnings of lumber manufacture at Marine in 1839 and at Stillwater five years later have been referred to already. It was not till September, 1848, that the first lumber for commercial purposes was sawed at the Falls of St. Anthony.[13] The log supply for these mills and others, which multiplied rapidly, came from distant upstream pineries. Preëmptions were illegal till 1854, and the government could offer no

---

[12] *Statutes at Large*, 10: 246, 268, 305, 310, 576. James Shields, afterwards prominent in Minnesota affairs, while commissioner of the general land office in Polk's administration had recommended in his report of November 29, 1845, the extension of preëmption privileges to settlers on unsurveyed lands. See 29 Congress, 1 session, *Senate Documents*, no. 16, p. 8 (serial 472). Sibley's biographer states that on January 18, 1850, the delegate introduced a bill into the House of Representatives for extending preëmption on unsurveyed lands. West, *Sibley*, 143.

[13] Frank R. Holmes, in *Minnesota in Three Centuries*, 4: 411; Stanchfield, in *Minnesota Historical Collections*, 9: 340. The lumber situation in Minnesota at this time is discussed on pages 227–229, *ante*.

lands for sale till after surveys had been completed. These were not ordered west of the St. Croix and east of the Mississippi till 1846, and even then they proceeded slowly. By the close of 1850 the boundary lines of one hundred and forty-four townships had been run and thirty-four had been subdivided into sections, but these did not cover much of the pine region. In the following year contracts were let for subdividing thirty-eight townships in the pine-bearing regions, but the season was so extremely wet that little was accomplished. Contracts for subdivision were let in succeeding years, the number in 1855 being sixty-five.[14]

Under the circumstances the lumbermen, according to their custom, sent their logging crews into the woods from winter to winter to cut the best timber they could discover in desired quantities; as no returns were exacted, it is impossible to estimate the amount of timber thus "abstracted," but it ran into millions of feet. The few seizures made by United States marshals had "anything but a desirable effect." One surveyor-general declared that the only remedy for the trespasses was the speedy survey and sale of the lands, so that private owners might preserve what the government could not. A well-informed historian, familiar with the transactions and the sentiment of the time, has remarked that the pioneer lumberman cut timber for a livelihood and not for speculation, and opened the country for settlement and cultivation, as the vanguard of civilization. The cutting of timber on uncared-for lands was continual, "generally conceded to be a benefit to the government; it being occupancy under an endowed right, as citizens inheriting an interest in the government."[15]

[14] Reports of the commissioner of the general land office, 1850, in 31 Congress, 2 session, *Senate Executive Documents*, no. 2, pp. 45, 59 (serial 588); 1851, in 32 Congress, 1 session, *House Executive Documents*, no. 2, pp. 13, 70 (serial 636); 1855, in 34 Congress, 1 session, *Senate Executive Documents*, no. 1, p. 198 (serial 810).

[15] Report of George B. Sargent, the surveyor-general of Wisconsin, Iowa, and Minnesota, for 1851, in 32 Congress, 1 session, *House Executive Documents*, no. 2, p. 71 (serial 676); Folsom, in *Minnesota Historical Collections*, 9: 296. The *Minnesota Pioneer* for January 15, 1852, prints a letter of Sibley to the secretary of the interior, which states that lumbermen since 1837 had been convinced they would not be considered willful trespassers and

The opening by the Chippewa treaties of 1854 and 1855 of the great pine forests about the headwaters of the Mississippi and St. Louis rivers to lumbermen, legitimate and other, did not so much extend the area of settlement as it occasioned large accessions to the population of the seats of lumber manufactures. St. Anthony received the most notable increase.

The year 1854 is known to old "Territorians" as that of "The Great Railroad Excursion." Early in the summer the track of the Chicago and Rock Island Railroad was built in to Rock Island, Illinois, on the east bank of the Mississippi. That event the contractors deemed worthy of a celebration. They accordingly invited a company of many hundreds to join an excursion over the road and up the Mississippi. Many persons of distinction in public affairs, literature, and divinity accepted. The party embarked at the river terminus on five large steamers and proceeded upstream. On reaching Lake Pepin the steamers were lashed abeam, after which they swept on through the lake while the people passed sociably from boat to boat. The party arrived at St. Paul on June 8 at an early hour, and the day was spent in an excursion to the Falls of St. Anthony and Fort Snelling. In the evening a banquet was served in the House chamber of the Capitol. Sibley gave the address of welcome. Speeches were made by ex-President Fillmore, George Bancroft, Governor Gorman, and others. The dancing program was cut short by the arrival of the midnight hour, which had been fixed for the departure of the excursionists. This demonstration meant much to Minnesota. It was notice that she was a part of the great outside world. It meant, in the warm season, the daily mail, Chicago within thirty hours, and the national

that government agents had permitted settlers to cut timber on unsurveyed lands. Non-residents, however, should be prosecuted for cutting. The editor remarks that the government knew very well that its acquiescence in permitting pine logs to be cut had peopled the territory and that villages had sprung up which were dependent solely on the business of lumbering.

capital in four days and nights. It meant also a shorter and an easier journey for the thousands of people who had despaired of ever reaching the beautiful territory in the Northwest.[16]

There was a notable access of settlers that season. It was not, however, till the spring of 1855 that a flood of immigration, perhaps without precedent, poured into Minnesota. Navigation opened on April 17 with the arrival of the "War Eagle," bringing 814 passengers. The packet company brought thirty thousand that season, clearing one hundred thousand dollars. The "War Eagle," which cost twenty thousand dollars, cleared forty-four thousand dollars. The hotels of St. Paul were so overcrowded that people had to encamp in the streets.[17] If we may trust to the political arithmetic of Minnesota's first and very capable statistician, Joseph A. Wheelock, there must have been forty thousand people in the territory by the close of 1855. A census taken in the early fall of 1857, in pursuance of the enabling act of that year, gave a total of 150,037 inhabitants. The reader who is a little tolerant of statistics may gather from the

---

[16] *Daily Minnesotian*, June 9, 1854. Extracts from this article are quoted by Blakeley, in *Minnesota Historical Collections*, 8: 395–401. The number of the tourists is given as "about twelve hundred" and the printed list of the more distinguished contains the names of thirty-eight editors of leading eastern newspapers. Captain Blakeley adds: "The success of this visit and the character of the people, especially the editors of the daily press of the country, did more than the best laid plan for advertising the country that has ever been made since. It cost nothing, but the great papers of the day and the magazines of the country were all full of the most laudatory literature in relation to the country. . . . Good results came back to us in a thousand ways and for many years, as immigration commenced to turn its attention to Minnesota." Neill's account of the excursion in his *Minnesota*, 595, is followed by extracts from a sermon which he delivered on the Sunday after the departure of the boats. His theme was "Railroads in the higher and religious aspects." It was his opinion that railroads would prove an antidote to bigotry, which prevailed in remote and sparse settlements. Transported by railroads, an eloquent preacher might discourse on a certain Sunday in an Atlantic city, on the next in the Mississippi Valley, on the third on the mountain tops of Oregon, and on the fourth on the Pacific coast. "A Pacific Railroad would be a voice in the wilderness, saying, 'Prepare ye the way of the Lord.' " The peroration was worthy of the day: "My hearers! some of you have tickets that will lead you to hell. The car of death is hastening on . . . we urge you to change that ticket. Christ is always in his office. . . . Hasten before it is too late." For other accounts of the excursion, the reader is referred to Newson, *Pen Pictures*, 428; the *Minnesota Democrat*, June 14, 1854; the *Weekly Minnesotian*, June 10, 13, 1854; and the *Daily Minnesota Pioneer*, June 15, 1854.

[17] Williams, *Saint Paul*, 357–360.

following table converging evidence of the remarkable development during the years included.[18]

Years	Number of counties	Popula- tion	Number of votes cast	Number of counties assessed	Tax valu- ations	Acres of public land sold
1854	23	32,000	.....	13	$ 3,508,518	314,715
1855	36	40,000	7,944	18	10,424,157	1,132,672
1856	42	100,000	.....	24	24,394,395	2,334,298
1857	63	150,037	35,340	31	49,336,673	1,468,434

The table indicates among other things that most of the immigrants of 1855 and 1856 immediately established themselves widely on the land and went to work. They formed a solid nucleus of industrious, reputable citizens, around which later accessions were to crystallize. They came in largest numbers from the middle states, New York in the lead; next from the northwestern states; then from New England. The slave states added but a trace to the mixture.[19] Numerous colonies like those at Rolling Stone, Zumbrota, Garden City, and Excelsior, having moved and settled as communities, resumed their accustomed relations and industries, briefly interrupted by their journeys. In every neighborhood schoolhouses were built, often of logs or sods, and in them the neighbors gathered for their gospel meetings until churches were erected. Within a few years the churches in the cities and towns were self-supporting, and not long after they were contributing not only to weaker societies in the territory but also to foreign missions. Literary and library associations sprang up in every town, and agricultural societies in every organized county. The ablest and most famous lecturers of the day were in many

[18] Joseph A. Wheelock, *Minnesota: Its Place among the States*, 125, 126, 144 (Minnesota, Bureau of Statistics, *First Annual Report* — Hartford, 1860).

[19] Wheelock, *Minnesota: Its Progress and Capabilities*, 109 (Minnesota, Bureau of Statistics, *Second Annual Report* — St. Paul, 1862).

instances secured. The Minnesota Territorial Agricultural Society was tentatively organized in the winter of 1854. As settlements multiplied the delegate at Washington was flooded with applications for new post offices, which he diligently secured. Beginning with the *Minnesota Pioneer*, established by the erratic but exceedingly able James M. Goodhue in 1849, newspapers increased rapidly at the Capital, in the cities, and at the county seats.[20] The moneys appropriated by Congress for road-building were distributed by the legislature as impelled by existing interests, and the highways thus opened served to unite the scattered settlements and to expedite a primitive commerce. Military roads constructed by the general government, such as those from Point Douglas to Fond du Lac, from Point Douglas to Fort Ripley and thence to the Red River of the North, from Mendota to Wabasha, and from Mendota to the Big Sioux River, invited settlement away from the river fronts into the interior.[21] In the short period now under consideration the Minnesota River became the scene of a lively navigation. In 1855 there were 119 steamboat arrivals at St. Paul from that river; in 1857 there were 292.[22]

There was another stratum of population thinly overlying the main rural deposit generally, but much thickened and congested in the towns, particularly in and about those aspiring to city organization. The speculator class had been represented from the beginnings of settlement, varying in all shades from the professional gambler up to the thrifty citizen willing and desirous to pocket successive profits on

[20] Darwin S. Hall and Return I. Holcombe, *History of the Minnesota State Agricultural Society*, 19 (St. Paul, 1910); Johnston, in *Minnesota Historical Collections*, 10: 248–351 (part 1).

[21] There is an estimate of the expenditures on military roads in Minnesota from 1850 to 1857 in Wheelock, *Minnesota: Its Place among the States*, 169. The total was $304,710.93. It should be noted that the open prairies without wood for fuel or building were comparatively late in coming into settlement. Edward V. Robinson, *Early Economic Conditions and the Development of Agriculture in Minnesota*, 404 (University of Minnesota, *Studies in the Social Sciences*, no. 3 — Minneapolis, 1915).

[22] Wheelock, *Minnesota: Its Place among the States*, 108; Thomas Hughes, "Steamboating on the Minnesota River," in *Minnesota Historical Collections*, 10: 142, 145 (part 1). The former gives the number of arrivals in 1855 as 119; the latter, as 109.

upward turns of the real estate market. These, however, were in small proportion as compared with the men who came to work and build up homes, to gather into communities, and to form a state. Along with the swelling tide of the latter floated in increasing numbers of men who came to profit by their labors without laboring themselves. No form of speculation was more alluring, and for a time more profitable, than operations in town sites.[23] Wherever along the rivers there was found a possible steamboat landing, there some enterprising operator, having secured a preëmption or established other inchoate title, laid out a town, of which he had a tasteful map drawn and multiplied by lithography. Inland by lakesides and at important road crossings towns were surveyed and platted. It is safe to say that in the three years from 1855 to 1857, inclusive, at least seven hundred towns were platted into more than three hundred thousand lots — enough for one and a half million people.[24] In the legislative session of 1857 a member is said to have submitted a resolution that one-third of the land of the territory be reserved for agricultural purposes, the remainder being sufficient for roads and town sites. The diversion of interest from agriculture to town-building and speculation in real estate is well illustrated in our foregoing table, which shows a falling off of nearly one-half in sales of land from 1856 to the following year, while the tax value of the territory doubled.

Such a tide of immigration as flowed in during 1855 and 1856, to say nothing of a high birth rate, could not fail to have its effect on business. There was little need, if any, of an export demand for produce salable at the gate of the farm or at the door of the shop. Furs, ginseng, and cranberries seem to have been the principal commodities as yet

[23] Williams, *Saint Paul*, 379. The well-known correspondent, Dr. Thomas T. Mann, writing on March 1, 1853, says: "Every eligible site for a town on the Mississippi from the Iowa line to St. Anthony, is claimed, and improvements in rapid progress." *Minnesota Democrat*, March 9, 1853.

[24] Based on estimates in Wheelock, *Minnesota: Its Place among the States*, 148.

A CLAIM SHANTY NEAR GLENCOE, 1856
Water color by Edwin Whitefield

THE SIBLEY HOUSE, MENDOTA
Water color by Mrs. I. H. Armstrong

THE ST. PAUL LEVEE ABOUT 1858

shipped down river.[25]   Money, in the shape of Indiana wild-
cat bills and the like, was none too plentiful, and the demand
for it was so great as to carry interest up to three per cent a
month and to five where notes were not paid at maturity.
One conservative Pennsylvanian who had come to St. Paul
refused at first to lend at that rate, believing that no honest
business could stand it.   He finally ventured a small loan
to a real estate dealer, who bought land of the government at
$1.25 per acre and sold it at $2.50 to another, who in turn
disposed of it at $15.00, all within a brief time.   The boom
of 1856–57 in Minnesota had its parallel in all our western
states, but it may be doubted whether its violence and rate
were elsewhere quite equaled.   The whole urban population
was more or less infected with the virus of speculation.
Fortunes seemed to be dropping from the skies, and those
who would not reach and gather them were but stupids
and sluggards.   Every man who had credit or could obtain
it invested in property which ever continued to rise in value.
At the existing interest rate, every man who had money to
spare would be slow to refuse a loan.   Debt became universal.   The boom was at no time greater than in the spring
and summer of 1857.   People were pouring in, hotels were
overflowing, merchants could hardly keep their stocks filled
up, the town-site speculators thronged the curbstones, there
was prospect of a good harvest — all signs pointed to
continued and increasing prosperity.[26]

On the twenty-fourth of August the Ohio Life Insurance
and Trust Company of New York failed; its immediate
creditors were forced to default, as were those next in order.
Before sundown there were suspensions and failures in
every considerable town in the whole country.   The panic
struck Minnesota with extreme violence.   The eastern
banks and other creditors called their loans.   What money

[25] James J. Hill, "History of Agriculture in Minnesota," in *Minnesota Historical Collections*, 8: 275.
[26] Williams, *Saint Paul*, 358, 379; Newson, *Pen Pictures*, 666, 672. The Pennsylvanian
referred to was the Honorable Pennock Pusey.

could be reached was shipped to them. There were no consignments of produce or merchandise to draw against, and there were no credits in favor of Minnesota. Eastern exchange rose to ten per cent. Everybody was in debt, and the territory was literally emptied of money. Business ceased, banks closed their doors, merchants suspended or assigned. Holders of property desiring to realize dropped their prices. City lots became virtually valueless. Thousands who had believed themselves wealthy soon found themselves in actual bodily need. The lawyers were busy with foreclosures, the sheriffs with attachments and executions. The floating population of speculators began to look for other scenes of operation and left the cities and towns none the worse for a numerous exodus. The historian of St. Paul, J. Fletcher Williams, then resident, is authority for the statement that the population of that city fell off almost fifty per cent.[27]

[27] Williams, *Saint Paul*, 380; Newson, *Pen Pictures*, 675; Holcombe, in *Minnesota in Three Centuries*, 2: 509.

XIV. TERRITORIAL POLITICS

A S ALREADY narrated, Henry H. Sibley was complimented with a unanimous election as first delegate from
the newly erected Territory of Minnesota.[1] As such delegate
once reëlected he sat in both sessions of the Thirty-first
and Thirty-second Congresses. In all he was much employed in the introduction of the numerous petitions and
memorials of the territorial legislature and of individuals.
His elegance of manner and dignity of demeanor insured
him the attention of committees and, upon occasion, of the
House. He took care to avoid taking sides with the factions
already forming within the Democratic party over the
slavery question.[2] Personally he was closely attached to
Senator Douglas, who had been his guest at Mendota and
had championed the establishment of his territory in the
previous Congress. The vigorous way in which the delegate
from the unknown Northwest took hold of general business
called out from two southern members a suggestion that
territorial delegates had no right to speak or act except
on business strictly pertaining to their respective territories.
Sibley replied in so clear and so forceful a way that the
House at once dropped the matter. A territory, he argued,
is a part of the nation and is interested in all national legislation; it is, therefore, entitled to be heard, all the more
because it has no vote.[3] The question has probably never
since been raised. The delegate was successful in obtaining
appropriations, fairly liberal, for the expenses of the territorial government, for public buildings, and for roads.[4] In

[1] See *ante*, p. 253.
[2] West, *Sibley*, 143, 158, 178, 201.
[3] *Congressional Globe*, 31 Congress, 1 session, 1505; Eugene V. Smalley, *History of the
Republican Party*, 146 (St. Paul, 1896).
[4] West, *Sibley*, 202. In the course of the five sessions in which he sat he secured appropriations for his territory amounting to $285,673.43 "against prejudices at times wellnigh
insuperable." See also the volumes of the *Congressional Globe* for this period.

1851, against some opposition, he secured the passage of the bill reserving two townships of land for a university in Minnesota Territory.[5] Another bill of Sibley's was framed to reduce the Fort Snelling Military Reservation to one square mile and to recognize preëmptions on the land excluded.[6]

On February 6, 1850, the Minnesota delegate introduced still another bill of much merit. It provided for the punishment of crimes and offenses by Indians. When the Indian appropriation bill came up for consideration on August 2, he addressed the House in a speech which occupies eight columns of the *Congressional Globe*. He denounced the habitual breaking of treaties by the government. Treaty commissioners made promises which they knew could not possibly be kept and then plumed themselves on having made good bargains for the government. As a consequence not one treaty in ten had been kept. He ridiculed the policy of making treaties with Indians as with really independent powers and advocated the use of reasonable force in dealing with them, under the law of the land. It was more than twenty years before Congress decided to stop making treaties with Indians and adopted the plan of making "agreements" which could be broken with somewhat less infamy. He gave two additional reasons why the Indians west of the Mississippi had generally become enemies of the whites. One was the introduction among them of "a horde of worthless vagabonds, reeking with the vices, but possessed of none of the virtues of the whites, to breed moral pestilence." The other was the manner in which removals of tribes had been conducted, the Indians having been "herded together like cattle . . . and threatened at every step." He saw in the policy which was pushing the Indian west from the Mississippi, east from the Pacific coast, and north from the overland trail a concentration of the tribes which must sooner or

---

[5] *Statutes at Large*, 9:568.
[6] *Congressional Globe*, 31 Congress, 2 session, 432. See also *post*, p. 425.

later bring on deadly conflicts between them and with the ever-advancing whites. Eleven years later his prophecy was fulfilled in his own state. No man in Congress was better qualified than Sibley, and very few so well as he, to speak on this question. For fifteen years he had been in daily contact with the red man, he spoke his language to some extent, he shared in his sports and festivals. Like all men who have known the Indian well, he had a high opinion of his capacity, while he was aware of his weaknesses and besetting sins. He believed that the Indian could be civilized and he therefore advocated permanent settlements, inalienable allotments of land, and schools, especially those of manual labor. In particular he wished to extend over the Indian the law of the land, as the great civilizer and schoolmaster. The House doubtless listened willingly to the earnest yet dignified appeal of the friend of the Indian, but gave his bill no hospitality. A Virginia member in reply said that of the three races of human animals, the white alone was capable of civilization; there was no hope of equality for the black or the red.[7]

Sibley had been elected delegate to the Thirty-first Congress without open opposition. It was not his fortune to be returned to the Thirty-second Congress without a great effort on the part of his friends. Mention has already been made of the opposition of Henry M. Rice to the election of Sibley as delegate from the Wisconsin rump in the fall of 1848. The prominent part played by Rice in Minnesota business and politics requires more extended reference. After the unpleasant termination of his connection with the American Fur Company, having married, he changed his residence from Mendota to St. Paul in June, 1849. In the previous year he had made a beginning toward the development of the city of St. Paul by purchasing a tract of land adjacent to the original town plat. On November 3, 1849,

---

[7] *Congressional Globe*, 31 Congress, 1 session, 295, 1506–1508; West, *Sibley*, 151–158. There is a printed copy of this speech in the Sibley Papers.

the original plat and Rice's and Irvine's addition were incorporated as the "Town of St. Paul" by a special act of the legislature. Rice set about the development of the property with his natural energy and foresight. He built stores, warehouses, and a large hotel. To stimulate settlement he gave the town the block of lots which still form Rice Park. He gave also for schools and churches without discrimination and even to some individuals. The mere fact of Rice's interest in the town gave it a new influence and attracted enterprise and capital. For many years he continued to be a large and successful operator in city property, town sites, railroads, Indian contracts, and other ventures.[8]

This young New Englander, fairly well educated, graceful in person, engaging in manner, did not establish himself in the future capital city of Minnesota at the age of thirty-three merely to immerse himself in private business and adventure. He aspired to a place among those engaged in great public affairs and, taking a long look ahead, planned for a political career.[9] At this point it is in order to relate that Rice had followed Delegate Sibley from Wisconsin Territory to Washington in the winter of 1849 and had remained there some weeks at his own expense lobbying for the Minnesota bill. His large knowledge of northwestern affairs and his wide acquaintance with public men gave him an effective influence. It is known that he was consulted about the wording of the bill and in particular about the boundaries of the proposed territory. It may well be surmised that but for his activity the slender majority of five votes in the House might not have been obtained. His friends naturally believed him entitled to no small share of credit for the creation of the territory.[10] No sooner had that

---

[8] Williams, *Saint Paul*, 186–188, 241; *Laws*, 1849, p. 99; Fairchild, in *Minnesota Historical Collections*, 10: 422, 424 (part 1); Bond, *Minnesota*, 119; Newson, *Pen Pictures*, 129–133. See also *ante*, pp. 239–241. There is a tradition, doubtless needing verification but so characteristic of the men that no historian of St. Paul has had the heart to suppress it, that when Rice had given Attorney William B. Phillips a town lot, the latter collected from the giver the sum of five dollars for making out the deed. Williams, *Saint Paul*, 191.

[9] Newson, *Pen Pictures*, 137.

[10] Williams, *Saint Paul*, 188; Holcombe, in *Minnesota in Three Centuries*, 2: 412.

taken place than the question arose as to its representation in Congress. Rice was too prudent to oppose himself to Sibley, whose forceful yet discreet behavior on the floor of the House had inspired confidence and had gained for him many friends. He therefore, as already related, acquiesced in the unanimous choice of Sibley for the delegacy at the election which took place on August 1.[11] None the less he was looking forward to a proper opportunity for shifting the honors and emoluments of that position from his successful rival to himself. In the previous autumn he had taken up the task of consolidating the support which had been given him in a desultory way. To this end he invited to his house in St. Paul a number of Democrats from several legislative districts for a consultation. These men organized as a caucus and issued a call for a Democratic mass convention, which was held in St. Paul on October 20, 1849. Officers were chosen, a platform was adopted, and the *Minnesota Pioneer* was declared the organ of the party. This was the beginning of party organization in Minnesota and of "Rice's machine."[12]

A year later, in the summer of 1850, the question of the delegacy in the Thirty-second Congress was before the people of the territory. Sibley might properly have openly declared his desire for a reëlection but he followed the fashion of reluctantly yielding to the importunity of friends and admirers. In an "Address to the People of Minnesota Territory," issued from Washington on July 29, 1850, he gave two reasons for consenting to go before the people again as a candidate for reëlection. The first reason was that friends irrespective of party had urged him so to do. The second reason was his "entire conviction, that one or more of those

11 West, *Sibley*, 138; Neill, *Minnesota*, 507; *Minnesota Pioneer*, August 2, 1849.

12 *Minnesota Pioneer*, October 25, 1849. That newspaper remained friendly to Sibley. The printed proceedings of the convention include a letter from Sibley excusing himself from attendance. He declared himself a Jefferson Democrat, but, elected as he had been by a united vote, he deemed it his duty to remain neutral in territorial politics. This letter is known as Sibley's "American House letter." The convention met in the American House, built by Rice.

who have been announced as probable candidates . . . seek to be elected, not for the advancement of the territory and its interests, but to subserve private ends and selfish purposes."[13] No second sight was needed to identify the one thus stigmatized. Under the circumstances Sibley did not receive, nor did he desire or expect to receive, a nomination from the Democratic party as organized. Accordingly on August 8 he announced himself through the *Minnesota Pioneer* as a "People's or Territorial" candidate for the office of delegate at the coming election on September 2. The same issue of the *Pioneer* contained the proceedings of an anti-Sibley convention held in St. Paul on July 31, composed mostly of Whigs as yet unorganized. This convention nominated for the delegacy Colonel Alexander M. Mitchell, already known to the reader as the lately appointed marshal of the territory. Mitchell was a graduate of the United States Military Academy and had served with credit in the Florida and Mexican wars.[14] Through influences set at work by him in Washington he had aided Rice in obtaining from the Indian office a contract for collecting stray Winnebago Indians and returning them to their reservation at Long Prairie. For this service Colonel Mitchell asked the delegacy from Minnesota, which he probably believed Rice would be able to deliver. Being a Whig in politics it was desirable that he should be nominated by Whigs and Rice's numerous friends in that party were disposed to further his desires.[15]

The Democrats were tardy in naming a candidate. Goodhue of the *Pioneer* on August 5 threatened that if they did not presently name their champion he would propose one

[13] West, *Sibley*, 177 n., 450–457.

[14] *Minnesota Pioneer*, August 8, 1850; Newson, *Pen Pictures*, 113. See also *ante*, p. 252, n. 60.

[15] Letters to Sibley from Ewing, May 6, 1850, from Foster, February 4, July 25, 1850, from Potts, January 15, April 17, 1850, from Brown, January 30, May 8, 1850, from Ramsey, August 18, 29, 1850, from Stevens, November 29, 1850, Sibley Papers; Sibley to Chouteau and Company, August 3, 13, September 9, 1850, in Sibley Letter Book, no. 1; letters to Ramsey from Foster, June 1, August 13, 1850, from Sibley, May 22, 30, June 26, July 26, August 6, 15, 25, 1850, Ramsey Papers.

for them. Rice was much too sagacious to take the chances of running against one who had so well deserved the unanimous election given him for the Thirty-first Congress. The Democrats met in a "Territorial Convention" on August 10 and selected as their candidate David Olmsted, an able and aspiring young man who had come into the country from Iowa along with Rice. Without sincere support from leading Democrats Olmsted's campaign was futile, and less than a week before the election he withdrew. The field was thus left to Sibley without organized support and to Colonel Mitchell backed by a strong coalition.[16]

Sibley's neutrality was turned by his opponents to their capital advantage. Rice had no pleasant recollections of his connection with the American Fur Company, of which Sibley was still the local head, nor of the intense and determined, though unsuccessful, efforts of Sibley and other leading spirits of the fur company to secure the revocation of his contract with the Indian office for chasing up some hundreds of straggling Winnebago and getting them back to their reservation at Long Prairie.[17] This meddling with the personal affairs of Rice gave him and his friends a cue for an attack on the fur company and its principal agent in the territory. On the stump and in the newspaper opposed to Sibley the American Fur Company was denounced as an ancient, shameless, grinding monopoly, engrossing trade, stifling competition in business, meddling in politics, and hindering the progress of the territory.[18] So adroitly and effectively was this diversion made that Sibley and his friends soon found themselves on the defensive. The distinction between "Whig" and "Democrat" was supplanted by that between "Fur" and "Anti-fur" and the campaign

---

[16] *Minnesota Pioneer*, August 29, 1850; *Chronicle and Register*, August 12, 19, 26, 1850. In an article entitled "Postscript" the *Pioneer* asserts that, after a champagne and oyster supper, Olmsted consented to the appointment of a joint committee to decide whether he or Colonel Mitchell should withdraw. The editor adds, "David walked right straight into the trap. . . . OH! FOOL, OR WORSE!" There is a sketch of Olmsted by Richard Chute in the Chute Papers, in the possession of the Minnesota Historical Society.

[17] See *ante*, pp. 313–317.

[18] *Chronicle and Register*, August 12, 19, 26, 1850.

degenerated into a rancorous squabble. Goodhue in the *Pioneer* of September 5 said he had never witnessed so hot a campaign. "Hope, fear, avarice, ambition, personal obligations, money, whiskey, oysters, patronage, contracts, champagne, loans, the promise of favors, jealousy, personal prejudice, envy, every thing that could be tortured into a motive, has been pressed into the canvass." Sibley, who had remained at his post in Washington, was reëlected, but by a majority of 90 only in a total vote of 1,208. St. Paul went against him by two votes, but he got all but three of the votes of Mendota. In the "up-river precincts" of Sauk Rapids, Swan River, and Crow Wing, where Rice had traded, his favored candidate received 164 votes out of 197. The fact that twenty-seven soldiers at Fort Gaines were allowed to vote evoked complaints from friends of Sibley, who seem to have taken it for granted that the votes of these soldiers were cast against him. Sibley's success was due mainly to the fidelity of "the French," the old settlers along the St. Croix, and the missionaries at Lac qui Parle.[19]

Sibley's honorable career in the Thirty-second Congress, as well as in the previous one, has been sufficiently described. At its close in March, 1853, he was content to return to his home and to give his attention to his private business, which had been necessarily neglected. He accepted, however, a nomination for member of the territorial House of Representatives, and his election enabled him to render an important

[19] The following table is based on one in Neill, *Minnesota*, 543, and such of the original returns as can be found in the secretary of state's archives in the custody of the Minnesota Historical Society.

	Sibley	Mitchell		Sibley	Mitchell
St. Paul	151	153	Sauk Rapids	3	60
St. Anthony	64	110	Swan River	22	56
Little Canada	44	8	Crow Wing	8	48
Stillwater	117	59	Elk River	16	8
Marine	17	4	Nokaseppi	36	26
Falls St. Croix	17	0	Lac qui Parle	12	0
Snake River	10	0	Mendota	78	3
Lake St. Croix	54	24			
				649	559

A printed broadside, dated April 1, 1850, and entitled "Address of the Hon. Hal Squibble," in the Sibley Papers, is an interesting example of the amenities of the campaign.

service in connection with the Minnesota land grant bill in aid of railroad construction.[20]   Henry M. Rice, widely known throughout the territory as the leading man of affairs in St. Paul and the guiding spirit of the organized Democracy, now came out as a candidate for delegate. The Whigs nominated Captain Alexander Wilkin, who had been United States marshal under Fillmore after the retirement of Colonel Mitchell.[21]   At the election in October, 1853, Rice was chosen by a very decisive majority, a triumph fairly earned by extraordinary activity in furthering the interests of the territory.[22]

Rice's service in the Thirty-third Congress was so marked by tireless industry in advancing the interests of the territory and of individual constituents that he had a right to aspire to a reëlection in 1855. That was accorded to him, but not without lively opposition. By this time a new alignment of political parties was taking place in Minnesota as elsewhere. The annexation of Texas and the Mexican War had added many thousands of square miles to the area of the United States. It will not now be disputed that it was the hope of the slaveholding interests of the southern states that the territory so acquired would be parceled out into states to be admitted to the Union, and that, being to the south of the line 36° 30″, these states would come into the Union as slave states without opposition. The "Wilmot Proviso," moved in the House of Representatives on August 12, 1846, was the first formal notice of protest. The Free-soil party, organized in 1848, cast a popular vote of 291,263. The Compromise of 1850, which conceded the Fugitive Slave Law to the South and attempted to placate the North by the admission

---

[20] West, *Sibley*, 211. See *ante*, pp. 343, 347.

[21] Gilfillan, in *Minnesota Historical Collections*, 9: 170.   There is a biographical sketch of Wilkin in Newson, *Pen Pictures*, 176.   The Whig party was never effectively organized in the territory.

[22] The official returns are given by counties in Neill, *Minnesota*, 591.   The totals are: Rice, 2,149; Wilkin, 696.   The legislature in March, 1852, had changed the elections of the delegate from the even to the odd years. Rice, accordingly, took his seat in the House in the December following his election. *Laws*, 1852, p. 37.

of California as a free state, was believed to have settled
this controversy for an indefinite period. As the presidential campaign of 1852 proceeded, it became evident that the
Democratic party was on safe ground, while the Whigs,
irresolute on the only issue which was of vital interest at the
time, drifting to sea, and yielding to adverse tides and currents, were disintegrating. The electoral vote was 42 for
Scott and 254 for Pierce. The Whig party was thereafter a
negligible faction. The Free-soil vote had shrunk to near
one-half of that of 1848.[23]

Had the slaveholders been content to maintain their peculiar institution in the existing slave states, it is more than
probable that it might have continued to exist for generations. Regarding the election of 1852 as a triumph for its
cause, the slave oligarchy at once renewed the claim that
slave property was legitimate in all the territories of the
United States and ought to be protected in them by the
national power.[24] To this proposition the great body of the
northern people were steadfastly opposed. Here was a
situation suggesting another compromise. It came two years
later in the Kansas-Nebraska Act, drafted and introduced
by Douglas of Illinois, doubtless with the expectation that
it would land him in the White House, an ambition he had
a right to entertain. The bill was passed on May 30, 1854.
Because it annulled the Missouri Compromise of 1820, regarded by the northern people for a generation as irrevocable,
there was an outburst of protest and indignation such as the
country had never before heard. The long-smoldering antislavery sentiment in the North was fanned into flame by
Harriet Beecher Stowe's novel, which appeared in book

---

[23] H. von Holst, *Constitutional and Political History of the United States*, 3: 286 (Chicago, 1877–85); Henry Wilson, *History of the Rise and Fall of the Slave Power in America*, 2: 16 (Boston, 1874–77); Edward Stanwood, *A History of the Presidency*, 243, 257 (Boston, 1900); James F. Rhodes, *History of the United States from the Compromise of 1850*, 1: ch. 2 (New York, 1893–1919).

[24] A simple and clear assertion of the claim may be found in the speech of John C. Calhoun in the Senate on February 14, 1847, in the *Congressional Globe*, 29 Congress, 2 session, 453.

form early in 1852. The book at once had an immense sale. Multitudes of people who had never read a novel devoured *Uncle Tom's Cabin* with tears for the slave and curses for the institution. It was dramatized and drew to the theater other multitudes who had been taught to regard the theater as a pathway to perdition. In the years following, millions of copies were printed in twenty languages. The historian Rhodes is safe in asserting that it was "the most successful novel ever written." It fired northern hearts to resist the extension of African slavery.[25]

The time was ripe for the appearance of a political party opposed to the extension of negro slavery. In 1854, the same year in which the Kansas-Nebraska Act was passed, sporadic nuclei were formed. One of these, at Jackson, Michigan, took the name "Republican," said to have been proposed by Horace Greeley.[26] It was a year later when the opponents of slavery extension got together in Minnesota. On March 29, 1855, a mass meeting was held in St. Anthony and was attended by some two hundred men. An address was issued, and a call for a territorial convention resulted. It met on July 25 in St. Paul. The platform adopted denounced the repeal of the Missouri Compromise, protested against the extension of African slavery, and demanded the repeal of the Fugitive Slave Law. It pronounced itself in favor of river and harbor improvements and of the prohibition of the manufacture and sale of intoxicating liquors. It was the year for the election of a delegate to Congress. The leading spirit in the movement was William Rainey Marshall of St. Paul, of the Kentucky family of that name, but reared in Missouri and resident in Minnesota since 1847. Minnesota had no citizen who more ardently loved justice and freedom. His education was sufficient for all the demands of business and citizenship,

---

[25] *Congressional Globe*, 33 Congress, 1 session, 221; Rhodes, *United States*, 1: 278–285.
[26] Francis Curtis, *The Republican Party*, 1: 184–192 (New York, 1904); Smalley, *Republican Party*, 20. The first local gathering to adopt the name "Republican" was held in the spring of 1854.

and he had already given good proof of capacity for public duties. We are to meet him more than once in the course of our story. As the organizing mind he was the logical candidate for the delegacy, but such was Ramsey's prestige that the convention gave him a large vote in spite of his previous refusal to be a candidate. He had been loath to leave the old Whig party, after having stood in its ranks for so many years and having worn its favors. It is said that the editor of the *Minnesotian*, regarded as Ramsey's organ, "sat up with the corpse." The nomination, however, went to Marshall and the election might have been his, it has been frequently claimed, but for the prohibition plank in the platform, which cost the party the German vote.[27]

Rice had also to encounter opposition in the ranks of his own party. Sibley and his friends had never been cordial in supporting him. Moreover, they were followers of Senator Douglas in his gospel of squatter sovereignty. The Democratic state convention, which met in St. Paul on July 25, was a riotous one. Resolutions to indorse the Baltimore platform and the administration of Franklin Pierce were received with derision and voted down. When it came to nominations for the delegacy and Rice was proposed, a large minority of members left the hall. They proceeded to the Capitol, where they organized a bolting convention and, after hearing speeches from Sibley and others, nominated David Olmsted, whose retirement from a previous contest could not have been a pleasant memory. Resolutions indorsing "the doctrine of popular sovereignty in the Territories" and denouncing the regular convention as

[27] *St. Anthony Express*, March 31, 1855; *Daily Minnesotian*, July 27, 1855; Baker, *Governors of Minnesota*, 147–165; Williams, *Saint Paul*, 238–241; Newson, *Pen Pictures*, 261; Smalley, *Republican Party*, 148–153; Gilfillan, in *Minnesota Historical Collections*, 9: 171. The proceedings of the St. Anthony convention, the resolutions adopted, and the "Circular Address of the Territorial Republican Convention, to the People of Minnesota," are printed in the *Minnesota Republican* (St. Anthony), April 5, 1855. The last two were doubtless written by the Reverend Charles G. Ames. The call for the St. Paul convention, presumably also the work of Ames, appeared first in the *Daily Minnesotian*, May 22, 1855. It was reprinted, with a letter appended, as a circular for mailing to prospective members of the party. A copy of this circular in the Sibley Papers is reproduced, with notes and an introduction, in the *Minnesota History Bulletin*, 2: 24–30 (February, 1917).

"not an assemblage of democrats" were adopted. In the triangular contest which followed Rice was returned by a large plurality.[28] In the Thirty-fourth Congress he displayed the same activity and fidelity as in the previous two sessions. He secured the extension of the right of preëmption on unsurveyed lands, the establishment of post offices and land offices, and the extension of territorial roads. Probably no representative from Minnesota has obtained so much desired legislation from Congress and so many favorable administrative arrangements for his constituents as Henry M. Rice.[29]

The election of Franklin Pierce to the presidency in the fall of 1852 was notice to Governor Ramsey and other federal appointees of the Whig persuasion in Minnesota that their services would presently be dispensed with. Sibley desired the governorship and was recommended to the president by a large body of friends, mostly fellow members of the House of Representatives whom he had attached to himself. He was opposed, however, by a powerful influence in his own party at home, and the administration decided that it would be the better politics to appoint a man from without the state.[30] On the thirteenth of May, 1853, Willis A. Gorman of Indiana succeeded to the office. Colonel Gorman was born in Kentucky on January 12, 1816. He was admitted to the bar at the age of twenty and established himself at Bloomington, Indiana. At the age of twenty-three he

[28] Gilfillan, in *Minnesota Historical Collections*, 9: 172. Accounts of the nominations and of the progress of the campaign may be found in the different papers. The *St. Anthony Express*, October 13, 1855, announced "The Result! Glorious Victory! The Democracy Triumphant! The Abolitionists Defeated!" Newson regarded Marshall's defeat as the result of "the pig-headedness of the anti-Nebraska wing of the Democratic party." He states that it had been agreed that "in case there was no show for Olmsted . . . his supporters should go to Marshall." Gorman, who had made the bargain, violated it, however, and thereby brought about the defeat of Marshall. *Pen Pictures*, 261, 503.

[29] There are appreciations of Rice's services as delegate by Neill, in his *Minnesota*, 499, and by Gilfillan, in *Minnesota Historical Collections*, 9: 180.

[30] The petition of Sibley's friends to the president was inclosed in a letter written by Dodge to Pierce on March 16, 1853, a copy of which is in the Sibley Papers. The petition was dated February 21 and was signed by fifty-eight members of the House. See also Sibley to Ramsey, March 14, April 1, 1853, in the Ramsey Papers, and Dodge to Sibley, April 1, 1853, in the Sibley Papers.

was elected to the state legislature, in which he served several successive terms. At the outbreak of the Mexican War he raised a battalion of riflemen, which he commanded with the rank of major. When the battalion was mustered out he raised the Fourth Indiana Infantry Regiment, which he led as colonel in the later operations. Having returned to private life, he was chosen in 1849 to represent his district in Congress and was reëlected in 1851. He possessed remarkable gifts as a public speaker and was welcome in all assemblages as a genial personage.[31] Other appointments made at the same time, of concern in this narrative, were those of Joseph T. Rosser of Virginia as secretary, and Moses Sherburne of Maine, Andrew G. Chatfield of Wisconsin, and William H. Welch of Minnesota as territorial judges, the last named as chief justice.[32]

The four legislatures in session during the period of Governor Gorman's term, 1854-57, if judged by their daily journals, were busy ones; but a review of their enactments discloses but few of exceptional importance. Private and special acts abounded, as there was no constitutional prohibition of them. Twenty-two railroad franchises were granted, which, added to five previous charters, raised the number enacted in the territorial period to twenty-seven.[33] Not a mile of railroad was built till the state was four years old. The story of the unhappy fortune of one company, the Minnesota and Northwestern, has already been told at a length that would have been disproportionate but for its

---

[31] Williams, *Saint Paul*, 338, n.; Newson, *Pen Pictures*, 376; *Minnesota Historical Collections*, 3: 314-332; Baker, *Governors of Minnesota*, 49-63.

[32] The secretary and the three justices are sketched in Newson, *Pen Pictures*, 384, 386. An account, by Henry L. Moss, of the changes in the office of chief justice during Fillmore's administration may be found in *Minnesota Historical Collections*, 8: 85-87. Aaron Goodrich was removed in 1851 and Jerome Fuller was appointed in his place, but the appointment was not confirmed by the Senate. Henry Z. Hayner served for a short time before new appointments were made by President Pierce. Letters of Goodrich, January 16, 21, February 11, 1851, and of Hayner, January 14, 1853, relative to their removals, may be found in the Sibley Papers.

[33] A convenient table of railroad charters granted in the territorial period, with citations of session laws, is in Rasmus S. Saby, "Railroad Legislation in Minnesota, 1849 to 1875," in *Minnesota Historical Collections*, 15: 11.

political complications.[34] Academies, colleges, and universities were established on paper with a liberality which would indicate an appreciation of the value of higher education, were it not known that many founders of new cities were ambitious to have announcements of such institutions on their advertising prospectuses. Ferry charters and franchises for lumbering and manufacturing companies were numerous, as were also divorce acts. In a special message to the legislature of 1856 Governor Gorman warned the members against too great liberality in the chartering of corporations and censured them for failing to exact additional contributions to the revenue of the territory. Many new counties were established and organized and towns and cities incorporated. St. Paul and Stillwater were incorporated in 1854, St. Anthony and Henderson in the year following. It is notable that the same legislature, that of 1855, which incorporated Henderson provided for the survey of nine roads radiating from that favored place to as many points of the compass. As Joseph R. Brown was the principal proprietor of the town it may be assumed that he looked after the legislation.[35] Upon the recommendation of Governor Gorman the legislature of 1856 raised the salaries of the auditor, the treasurer, and the superintendent of schools each from one hundred to five hundred dollars a year. Not these nor any of the territorial offices were fat jobs, with the exception of that of public printing. In 1854 this office was divided between David Olmsted and Joseph R. Brown representing the Rice and Sibley factions of the majority in power. In 1856 it fell wholly to Brown, who in the legislatures of 1854 and 1855 had been a member of the Council.[36]

The increase in the population and number of counties soon called for a corresponding augmentation of the membership of the legislative bodies and a new apportionment of

[34] See *ante*, ch. 12.

[35] *Laws*, 1855, p. 49; *Council Journal*, 1856, p. 90. Martin McLeod wrote to John H. Stevens on January 1, 1857, "If Paris is France, Henderson will soon be Minnesota." Stevens Papers.

[36] *Laws*, 1856, p. 9; *Council Journal*, 1854, p. 35; *House Journal*, 1856, p. 17.

the constituencies. The legislature of 1855 accordingly passed an act for a census to be taken by the sheriffs of counties, increased the number of councilors to fifteen and that of representatives to thirty-eight, and created a joint committee to make the new apportionment. The committee was required to meet in St. Paul on the first Monday in August, but by some oversight the census returns were not to be filed till the fifteenth of that month. The committee, however, with Joseph R. Brown at its head, went on with the apportionment on the basis of election returns and other information and made out schedules which, acquiesced in by all parties, proved that excellent judgment and impartiality had been exercised.[37]

One piece of legislation deserves notice because it brought about the tardy abolition of the ancient and absurd legalized custom of imprisonment for unpaid debts, which had survived in the territory. The legislature of 1849 enacted an elaborate statute providing for courts of justices of the peace. In an article on the execution of judgments it was enacted that "if the execution be issued against a male person . . . it [*the court*] shall command the sheriff or constable that if no goods or chattels can be found, or not sufficient to satisfy such execution, then to take the body of the person . . . and convey him to the common jail . . . there to remain until such execution shall be satisfied." According to the letter of this law an unfortunate or fraudu-

---

[37] *Laws*, 1855, pp. 36–39, 53–55. When the joint committee met on August 8 to make the required apportionment, the secretary of the territory was able to furnish it with returns from nineteen of the thirty-five counties, of which the aggregate population was found to be 34,210. In the cases of ten counties the committee took over "the returns made to conventions for nominating candidates for delegates to Congress," and found a total of 15,390. The population of six counties was ignored. For its purpose the committee assumed the number 49,600 to represent the whole population of the territory and proceeded to make the apportionment. A current estimate of the population of the six counties ignored at 4,000 brought the grand total to 53,600, the figure frequently quoted. Governor Gorman's generous estimate of "fully seventy-five thousand" was founded on this imperfect census and "other reliable sources." The failure of the counties to take the census may have been due to the fact that the small per capita compensation allowed the sheriffs was to be paid out of the county funds. *Minnesota Pioneer*, August 10, 1855; *Daily Minnesotian*, August 8, 9, 10, 1855; *Council Journal*, 1856, appendix, p. 2.

lent male debtor might remain "in durance vile" to the end of his days. To mitigate this possible severity the Code of 1851 provided for a hearing before two justices, the administration of a poor debtor's oath, and the discharge of the prisoner thereupon. There were, it is reported, some incarcerations and one case of death during imprisonment under the act of 1849. There was, however, so far as known, no loud clamor for the repeal of the act till 1854, when a bill was introduced into the House of Representatives for that purpose. A select committee made a report of great length, replete with historical precedents and legal citations, which was printed. In committee of the whole an amendment repealing a great part of the civil code was adopted. The House amiably agreed to the amendment and indefinitely postponed the bill. Some days after, a motion prevailed to expunge the report of the select committee because it was slanderous to the judiciary. Nevertheless the document of five pages was reprinted in the *House Journal*. In the following year, 1855, a bill introduced by Sibley and passed without opposition provided that "no person in this Territory shall be subject to imprisonment for debt or arrest . . . on account of any debt, judgement, pecuniary liability, or demand." Creditors desiring to charge fraud were required to do so in pleadings clear and distinct, to which the defendant might reply. So ended imprisonment for debt in Minnesota.[38]

The legislature of 1856 passed an act, along with others of the kind, to incorporate the St. Peter Company, which was to have power to erect buildings in Le Sueur and Nicollet counties.[39] The measure went through without suspicion being aroused that a plot of revolutionary proportions lay

[38] *Laws*, 1849, p. 20; 1855, p. 125; *Revised Statutes*, 1851, pp. 362, 450; *House Journal*, 1854, pp. 242-2,47 259, 269-274; 1855, p. 351; Murray, in *Minnesota Historical Collections*, 12:127. The preparation of the bill and the report is attributed by Murray to the able and erratic Chief Justice Aaron Goodrich. On January 15, 1856, several prominent lawyers presented a petition to the Council for the repeal of the act of 1855 on the ground that it was improperly entitled and enacted. *Council Journal*, 1856, pp. 63-67.

[39] *Laws*, 1856, p. 73.

concealed in it. The organic act of the territory had provided that the legislative assembly should hold its first session at St. Paul, that the governor and the assembly should at that session locate a temporary seat of government, and that at such time as they might deem proper they should prescribe the manner of locating the permanent seat of government by a vote of the people. As already related, the legislature of 1851 had determined that the capitol building should be erected at a central point in the town of St. Paul, and this had been done. All parties had acquiesced and for years no serious proposition had been made for a change.

On February 6, 1857, near the middle of what was understood to be the last session of the territorial legislature, a bill was introduced in the Council for the removal of the capital to the town of St. Peter in Nicollet County, a new municipality established on the southern verge of the old settlement and town of Traverse des Sioux. The terrain was the property of the St. Peter Company, specially chartered in the previous year. The bill embraced a contract with that company binding it to donate a site for the capitol and to contribute the sum of one hundred thousand dollars for its erection. A test vote taken on the ninth showed a majority in favor of the measure. Three days later it passed by the odd vote of the fifteen councilors present. On the sixteenth it came up for consideration in the House, where it was slated to go through without the least modification. The minority vainly resorted to every known parliamentary device to secure amendment or at least delay. It succeeded only in securing the passage of a resolution calling on the attorney-general of the territory, Lafayette Emmett, for an opinion upon the competency of the legislature to move the capital by act. The essence of his opinion was that by establishing the capital at St. Paul the legislature had exhausted all its powers except that of submitting the question to popular vote. Not a vote was changed. On the eighteenth the bill passed the House by a vote of 20 to 17, the same as that

MINNESOTA'S FIRST CAPITOL, BUILT IN 1853

ST. PAUL IN 1857

Looking north toward the Capitol, Fifth Street in the foreground

MINNEAPOLIS IN 1857

Looking north from Second Avenue toward the Suspension Bridge

ST. ANTHONY IN 1857

Looking southeast along Second Street toward the university campus

which had been recorded in the preliminary contests. One
of the amendments proposed in the House was to strike out
"St. Peter" and insert "Nicollet Island." This was lost by
a vote of 18 to 19. Four of the seven members from St.
Anthony and Minneapolis were in the negative; the five
representatives from St. Paul, in the affirmative.[40] One of
the legislators who took part in this affair, the Honorable
William Pitt Murray, assured the writer that these votes of
himself and his colleagues from Ramsey were in good faith
and that it was solely the stupidity or the distrust of the
members from Hennepin that prevented the establishment
of the capital of Minnesota on the beautiful wooded island
in the Mississippi a few hundred feet above the Falls of St.
Anthony. Little love as she might have for the town up river,
St. Paul would have preferred Nicollet Island to St. Peter.[41]

The newspapers of the capital city did not fail to de-
nounce the "atrocious scoundrelism" and "audacious im-
pudence" of the "transparent scheme of speculators."
Money and shares in St. Peter lots were, they asserted, the
"great motive power" behind the bill.[42] There can be little
doubt, if any, that the scheme was concocted in secret and
that votes enough to carry it were pledged before the bill was
sprung upon the chambers and an unsuspecting public. It
was well understood that the governor, who had a large
interest in the St. Peter Company, would approve the bill
should it reach him for signature.[43] There was not much

----

[40] *Council Journal*, 1857, pp. 98, 104–107, 119–121; *House Journal*, 1857, pp. 147, 153–155,
159, 162–168, 171–175. The opinion of the attorney-general is in the *Pioneer and Democrat*,
February 18, 1857. While the House was considering the bill in committee of the whole on
February 17, Joseph R. Brown offered an amendment, which was promptly voted down by
a majority of one. Under other circumstances his proposition might well have been entertained. It was to create a board of commissioners, of members elected one in each county,
with power to receive proposals from individuals or municipal authorities and to select a permanent seat of government on lands to be donated or on government land as near the geographical center of the state as the "general interest" should appear to demand.

[41] See Murray, in *Minnesota Historical Collections*, 12: 116, and the *Pioneer and Democrat*,
February 20, 1857.

[42] *Pioneer and Democrat*, February 21–24, 1857.

[43] "Gorman was the father of the scheme to move the capital to St. Peter," said William
P. Murray, in an interview with the author on March 21, 1905. Governor Gorman had been
president of the St. Peter Company from 1854 to 1856. Gresham, *Nicollet and Le Sueur
Counties*, 1: 192.

party politics in the scheme, although one newspaper correspondent declared that it was the work of "black Republicans" and two or three "pumpkincider Democrats," whatever that may have meant.[44] The bill went back to the Council to be enrolled and submitted to the governor.

Friends of St. Paul were assured that she need not fear; the courts following the counsel of the attorney-general would protect her. Still the minority schemed to contrive, if possible, some plan which might defeat the bill before it finally left the Council. For many days it lay in the hands of the chairman of the committee on enrolled bills, a majority of which was opposed to it. On February 28 a councilor of the impatient majority moved that the committee report the bill that day and demanded the previous question. An opponent promptly moved a call of the Council, which the unsuspecting majority did not oppose. The call was ordered and it showed one councilor, Joseph Rolette of Pembina, absent. The usual motion to dispense with further proceedings under the call was made and the yeas and nays stood 9 to 5. The rules provided that a two-thirds vote should be necessary to suspend a call of the Council. In vain did Councilor Balcombe argue that nine was two-thirds of fourteen. The chair ruled otherwise and refused to entertain an appeal. The majority did not wish an adjournment and it could not muster a two-thirds vote to suspend the rules so as to admit of other motions. This was on the morning of Saturday. In the afternoon of the following Thursday the parties agreed on a short truce for the transaction of indispensable business. The Council had remained in continuous session for 123 hours. Cots had been provided and meals had been ordered in, and the time had been passed in rather good-humored patience. But that quotient in vulgar fractions was unalterable.

Friday and Saturday passed quietly, the call of the Council still pending. In the evening of Saturday there was

44 *Pioneer and Democrat*, February 20, 1857.

another short truce near midnight, during which a member of the committee on enrolled bills stated that the committee had been unable to report the removal bill on account of the absence of the chairman, who had it in his possession, and that numerous errors existed in a copy furnished by the secretary of the Council, as compared with the engrossed copy. The committee, therefore, withheld the copy, subject to the order of the Council. But the call of the Council was thereupon renewed as agreed. The organic act of Minnesota provided "that no one session shall exceed the term of sixty days." That term in this case would expire at midnight of this Saturday, March 7. It is said that as the Council clock was striking that hour the Honorable Joseph Rolette stepped into the chamber and to his seat. "Mr. President," he began. Down came President Brisbin's gavel with a resounding whack. "The Council is adjourned, the councilor is too late."[45]

The question, where was "Joe" Rolette during this week of absence, was one which at the time could have been answered only by members of a limited circle and which remained a puzzle to annalists for many years. It is now well known, by the revelations of one of the limited circle, that on February 29 Rolette had deposited the enrolled copy of the removal bill in the safe of Truman M. Smith, a banker of St. Paul, and, having taken into his confidence the landlord of the Fuller House, had been comfortably lodged in a rear room on the top floor of that hostelry. There he had remained till the moment of his dramatic reappearance. It is not believed that he lacked any of the comforts of life, nor that he pined in absolute solitude. Meantime the sergeant at arms of the Council was ranging the town in search

[45] Council Journal, 1857, pp. 48, 177–184; Neill, Minnesota, 619–621; Williams, Saint Paul, 370–372; Dean, in Minnesota Historical Collections, 12: 9–15; Moss, in Minnesota Historical Collections, 9: 155; Holcombe, in Minnesota in Three Centuries, 2: 494–498; interviews on December 3, 1905, with the Honorable John D. Ludden, a member of the Council, and on March 31, 1905, with the Honorable William P. Murray, a member of the House; Harlan P. Hall, Observations: Being More or Less a History of Political Contests in Minnesota 32 (St. Paul, 1904).

of the absentee, in a manner so ostentatious that no complaint could be made of any lack of zeal in duty. It was commonly reported that "Joe" had harnessed up his dog train and had gone off to his home in Pembina. It must not be inferred that Rolette was a personage of trifling importance. He was a mixed-blood son of Sibley's old colleague in the fur trade. Having removed from Prairie du Chien to Pembina, he became a principal trader at that distant post and exercised a wide influence. He represented his district in six successive legislatures. To attend this session of 1857 he walked the whole distance, about four hundred miles, as the snow was too light to permit riding in his dog sled. Of a romantic and jovial disposition, he was not at all averse to playing the part assigned him in this little drama.[46]

The failure of the Council to pass upon the correctness of the enrolled bill did not finally dispose of the removal project. The speaker of the House signed what purported to be a copy of the original bill prepared by order of the House. To this the president of the Council refused his signature for seven alleged points of irregularity. Governor Gorman signed and approved the document as if it had been passed in due course. The act so approved still stands as chapter 1 of the *Laws* of 1857.[47] The St. Peter Company, believing the legislation valid or hoping, at least, that its validity might be upheld by the judiciary, proceeded to fulfill its contract. The promised site was set aside and a capitol building was erected, which remained a monument to the enterprise of the company and the liberality of the people of St. Peter for many years.[48] As the territorial

[46] Holcombe, in *Minnesota in Three Centuries*, 2: 499; Williams, *Saint Paul*, 370. There is an unsigned article in the *St. Paul Dispatch* for February 10, 1894, probably written by Holcombe, which contains interesting comments on the life of "Jolly Joe Rolette."

[47] A statement of Gorman's reason for signing the bill appeared in the *Pioneer and Democrat* for June 1, 1857.

[48] The building was of wood and was expected to accommodate the constitutional convention. The cost was five thousand dollars. It became the courthouse of Nicollet County when the county seat was moved from Traverse des Sioux to St. Peter in the winter of 1858–59, and remained in use till 1881. Gresham, *Nicollet and Le Sueur Counties*, 1: 89, 197.

officers did not remove their offices to St. Peter by May 1, the limit set in the removal bill, suit was brought on behalf of the company in the court of the second district for a mandamus. On July 12, after a hearing, Judge Rensselaer R. Nelson refused that remedy on two grounds: first, that the legislature had exhausted its power of location when it placed the capital at St. Paul; second, that no law had been duly passed for removal.[49]

[49] United States Ex-relator Alfred F. Howes *v.* Samuel Medary, governor, and others, in the *Pioneer and Democrat*, July 14, 1857, and in Hiram F. Stevens, ed., *History of the Bench and Bar of Minnesota*, 1: 59–64 (Minneapolis and St. Paul, 1904). There are appreciations of Judge Nelson in Newson, *Pen Pictures*, 218; Williams, *Saint Paul*, 344, n.; and the *St. Paul Dispatch*, February 7, 1894. The proceedings at St. Peter are described in Gresham, *Nicollet and Le Sueur Counties*, 1: 196. Later abortive efforts to remove the capitol are discussed by Dean, in *Minnesota Historical Collections*, 12: 17–42.

XV. PREPARATION FOR STATEHOOD

NOTWITHSTANDING extraordinary additions to population, growth of towns, and wide extension of cultivation in the middle of the fifties, Minnesotans were not unduly eager for statehood. Such was the liberality of the general government that territorial taxes were very light. Jefferson Davis said of Delegate Rice, "Rice is always wanting something for Minnesota and he almost always gets it."[1] In his message of 1856 Governor Gorman hardly more than hinted at the subject of admission to the Union. His moderation is notable when one reads his estimate of population. Deducing from the census of 1855 an increase of 114 per cent in one year, he easily computed a population of 343,000 after two years and 735,000 after three years. Nevertheless, he favored Minnesota's "remaining a Territory for a few years, without manifesting too much eagerness to assume the mantle of State sovereignty." The year passed without the display of such eagerness, silence on the subject being broken, so far as discovered, only by four articles in the *Pioneer and Democrat* by John Esaias Warren, who argued with no little force for the assumption of statehood.[2]

In the course of the year Governor Gorman changed his mind, and in his message to the legislature of 1857 he pronounced vigorously for statehood. He referred to the usual grants of land to new states and expressed the belief that no grants of land for railroads could be expected so long as Minnesota remained a territory. Furthermore, a territory had no credit; a state could borrow money. His crowning argument, however, was the importance of repre-

[1] Interview of the author with Mrs. Henry M. Rice, October 18, 1904.

[2] *Council Journal*, 1856, appendix, 2; *Pioneer and Democrat*, August 6, 16, October 2, December 22, 1856. See *Council Journal*, 1853, p. 36, for Governor Ramsey's prophecy: "In ten years a State — in ten years more half a million of people."

sentation in Congress, which should be influential in securing the building of a railroad to the Pacific Ocean through Minnesota. "There is no great interest," he said, "in which Minnesota has so heavy a stake to be won or lost, as in the Pacific Railroad. It may be constructed so as to make us one of the wealthiest States in the Union. . . . A Pacific Railroad will be a road to India. It will bring us in contact with six hundred millions of people. . . . The millions of wealth that has for ages doubled Cape Horn, will pass through the centre of the continent." The governor pointed out further that this would be not only the American but also the European channel of trade between the two oceans. It is notable that when fifty years later three or four railroads to the Pacific were running through Minnesota they had not made her excessively wealthy. The governor estimated the population of the territory to be easily 180,000 and assured the legislature that the number would swell to 200,000 or 250,000 before admission to the Union could be obtained in the usual course. He therefore urged the legislature not to wait for the action of Congress but to proceed of its own motion without delay to call a convention for the formation of a state constitution. He even furnished the outline of a bill for the purpose. The legislative bodies seem to have been much aroused by the gubernatorial rhetoric. A bill to provide for a census of population and for a constitutional convention was introduced into the Council on January 23, was favorably reported from committee five days later, and was passed on February 3. On March 4 the bill, much amended, was passed by the House, but the Council, deadlocked by the capital removal scheme, of which the reader was informed at the close of the foregoing chapter, took no action on the House amendments and the bill did not become a law.[3]

This, however, was not the beginning of the actual procedure which advanced Minnesota to statehood. On Decem-

---

[3] *Council Journal,* 1857, pp. 57, 65, 84; *House Journal,* 1857, pp. 43–47, 228, 230; *Pioneer and Democrat,* January 15, 21, February 6, 1857.

ber 24, 1856, Delegate Rice had introduced into the national House of Representatives a bill to authorize the people of the territory to frame a state constitution to be submitted to Congress.[4] Rice was too alert and able a politician to leave such initiative to other hands, especially to those of an opposing faction of his party. In his effort to secure home initiative, Governor Gorman, confident of legislative support, may have been actuated by a willingness to get the start of the delegate and win a triumph over him; but a more substantial reason for his action can be found in the expectation that a convention called by the Minnesota legislature of 1857 would be likely to provide for that division of the territory implied in the pending bill to remove the capital from St. Paul to St. Peter. That Rice's bill was pending and that it provided for a division of the territory by a north and south line presently became known in St. Paul and engaged the attention of the large majority of the legislative bodies, who favored the division of the territory by a parallel of latitude. To give expression to their desires a memorial to Congress was drawn praying for the submission of the question of the boundaries of the state to a vote of the people. This memorial was adopted in the Council by a vote of 11 to 4 and in the House by a vote of 25 to 10. The four nays in the Council, those of President Brisbin, Setzer, Ludden, and Freeborn, were cast by members who had voted against the bill to call a convention. Although approved by the governor on January 27, the memorial was not printed with the session laws.[5]

In his haste to be beforehand, Rice did not wait to perfect his bill, and for that reason the committee on territories reported on the last day of January a substitute embodying omitted details. There was no debate. A Missouri member indulged in a moment's pleasantry over the violation of the Ordinance of 1787, which provided that five states only

[4] 34 Congress, 3 session, *House Journal*, 163 (serial 892).
[5] *Council Journal*, 1857, pp. 52–54; *House Journal*, 1857, pp. 70, 89.

should be cut out of the Northwest Territory; here were northern members proposing a sixth or part of a sixth. The bill was passed on the same day by a vote of 97 to 75, which did not indicate a very hearty welcome for the expected addition to the national family.[6] On February 18, Senator Douglas reported the bill without amendments to the Senate from his committee on territories. Three days later it was taken up. There was, as will presently appear, a lurking opposition of no little strength. Because it was unorganized, and therefore unready, it found immediate expression in an amendment proposed by a senator from North Carolina, providing that only citizens of the United States should have the privilege of voting under the operation of the proposed act. A languid debate followed, the amendment was agreed to, and the bill thus modified was passed with but one dissenting vote. The members of the opposition could afford to be generous, aware that under ordinary circumstances a bill thus amended and requiring concurrence of the other house so near the close of an expiring Congress had small chance of survival.

The opposition was not, however, to rest in this comfortable delusion. Believing themselves sufficiently strong in the Senate, the friends of the measure resolved to make another trial there rather than to remit the amended bill, which the House might not reach before its final adjournment. On the twenty-fourth, therefore, a reconsideration was moved. Then set in a debate which occupies sixteen pages of the *Congressional Globe*. Most of the time was taken up by senators from the South, and it must be recorded that their speeches show a singular lack of candor. They grieved over the proposed admission of aliens to the suffrage when the making of a constitution was in hand. Such generosity to foreigners would make half a million "Know-Nothings." They did not favor a "hot-bed policy" of premature statehood for a remote and sparsely settled territory. There was,

[6] 34 Congress, 3 session, *House Journal*, 328; *Congressional Globe*, 517–519.

however, one of their number, John B. Thompson of Kentucky, who spoke his mind and theirs without reserve. He began by quoting a letter of Gouverneur Morris, dated December 4, 1803, giving the opinion that Congress could not admit as a new state territory which did not belong to the United States when the Constitution was made. He was, therefore, opposed to the admission of new states. He regretted that Iowa and Wisconsin had been admitted. He would rule the people of a territory "as Great Britain rules Affghanistan, Hindostan, and all through the Punjaub, making them work for you as you would work a negro on a cotton or sugar plantation." Territories should be governed by proconsuls, and should be "made to know their place, and constrained to keep it." He did not want "Sclaves, and Germans, and Swiss . . . to swarm up in these northern latitudes, and eventually come down upon the South." He did not welcome a new state to beg for land and all manner of appropriations imaginable. In particular, he was not desirous to see senators from the new state, "arrogant, assuming, pretentious, Free-Soilish, and Democratic," coming in to destroy the equilibrium of the Senate. Douglas replied to the attacks of the opposition with dignity and discretion and disarmed them by showing that the proposed enabling act followed exactly the suffrage provisions of the organic act of Minnesota Territory. The vote to reconsider stood 35 to 21, but before final action could be taken enough of the opponents had absented themselves to leave the Senate without a quorum. On the twenty-fifth the bill was passed as it came from the House, by a vote of 31 to 22, every one of the negative votes coming from south of Mason and Dixon's line.[7]

The Minnesota enabling act, approved on February 26, followed so closely the form that had become traditional that the chairman of the House committee on territories assured the House that it might have been taken from a

[7] *Congressional Globe*, 34 Congress, 3 session, 734, 808–814, 849–865, 872–877.

"form-book," with appropriate insertions for the particular case. The customary grants of public lands for schools, a university, public buildings, and salt springs, and the usual donation of five per cent of the proceeds of land sales were carefully embodied. As was proper and customary, the act began with an article prescribing the boundaries of the proposed state. In all countries in which the law of the land prevails, boundaries are obviously of prime importance. The western boundary of Minnesota was the only one which remained within the power of Congress to prescribe, the others having been determined by previous legislation or by treaties. The delimitation of that border begins at the northwest corner of the state, where the forty-ninth parallel of north latitude crosses the center of the main channel of the Red River of the North. From that point the western boundary proceeds up the main channel of that river and that of the Bois des Sioux, passes on through Lakes Traverse and Big Stone to the outlet of the latter, whence it takes a due south direction to the north line of the state of Iowa. Rice's original bill provided for a Red River, Bois des Sioux, and Big Sioux line, which the House committee on territories changed for reasons not recorded. It may be conjectured that it pleased the committee to give the new state a boundary closely following a meridian. South Dakota thus gained parts of seven counties.[8]

It is necessary to note and in some measure to explain the attitude of Minnesotans of this period toward the question of statehood. The new Republican party rapidly drew into its ranks many "good people" from the other parties. A great humanitarian principle was at issue; it was a time for

---

[8] *Statutes at Large*, 11: 285; *Congressional Globe*, 34 Congress, 3 session, 517–519; Henry Gannett, *Boundaries of the United States and of the Several States and Territories with an Outline of the History of All Important Changes of Territory*, 125 (United States Geological Survey, *Bulletins*, no. 226 — third edition, Washington, 1904). The definition of the boundaries in the Minnesota Constitution, article 2, section 1, was copied from the enabling act. Both of these documents may be found in any issue of the *Legislative Manual*. See the Appendix, no. 12, *post*, for an account of the transactions which settled the southern, eastern, and northern boundaries.

searching of hearts in politics. Although the territory could give no vote for president in 1856, there was a hot campaign, but the Democrats generally elected their candidates for the legislature and for the municipal offices. In this year Ignatius Donnelly, a Democrat, came to the territory and began to devote his singularly effective eloquence to the cause of free soil.[9] That members of opposing political parties should regard each other with distrust, even contempt, was not new, but in this period that spirit blazed out with unwonted violence. The newspapers reviled each other with fury. The Republican editors called their Democratic contemporaries "dough faces" and "boot-licks," and the latter retorted by characterizing their opponents as "Black Republicans" who were willing that their daughters should marry "niggers."[10] It was in this frame of mind that the two parties were as the time for the constitutional convention drew on. The partisan heat was so intense, indeed, that the grave duty of making a constitution was regarded for a time with comparative indifference.

Governor Gorman, who had previously been much in haste, proceeded but leisurely in the matter, and it was not until April 7 that the proclamation for an extra session of the legislature to make the necessary preparations for the constitutional convention was published. With Rice intrenched at Washington, Governor Gorman was well aware that it would be impossible for him to succeed himself in office when the Buchanan administration came to apportion the territorial offices to the faithful. He accordingly calmly awaited the appointment of his successor, Samuel Medary of Ohio, a man of reputable character and a very able journalist, who

[9] Newson, *Pen Pictures*, 627–630. Further biographical data concerning Donnelly will appear in the next volume. An interesting account of "The Early Political Career of Ignatius Donnelly, 1857–1863," may be found in a manuscript thesis by Franklin F. Holbrook (University of Minnesota, 1916). Copies of this thesis are in the libraries of the university and the Minnesota Historical Society.

[10] Minnesota Constitutional Convention (Democratic), *Debates and Proceedings*, 54 (St. Paul, 1857). See also the *Pioneer and Democrat*, May 17, 1857, and other partisan newspapers of the time.

had rendered long and loyal service to his party without seeking office. It is said that Medary accepted the governorship of the territory to oblige the administration. He qualified as governor of Minnesota on April 23, having arrived the day before by lumber wagon from Red Wing, where his steamer had been obliged to tie up on account of an accident.[11] In a brief message Governor Medary announced to the legislature, convened in extra session on April 27, the two objects of its assemblage: one, legislation called for by the enabling act; the other, the disposition of the public lands lately granted by Congress for railroads. It is convenient to postpone account of the action under the latter head, but it may be said that it interested that legislature so much more than prospective statehood that it was not till the last working day but one of the session, May 23, that the act providing for the expenses of the constitutional convention was passed.[12]

This measure needlessly appointed the first Monday in June for the election of delegates; that day had already been designated by the enabling act. It contained further a provision, not included in the enabling act, that delegates should have the same qualifications as had representatives in the legislative assembly of the territory. In regard to the number of delegates a notable departure was made. The enabling act provided that the legal voters in each representative district of the proposed state should elect two delegates to the

[11] *Appletons' Cyclopaedia of American Biography*, 4: 284; *Pioneer and Democrat*, March 23, April 7, 23, 24, 1857. Governor Gorman's proclamation was signed on March 16 but was not made public until April 7.

[12] *Council Journal*, 1857, extra session, 5–11; *House Journal*, 6–13, 80. At the opening of the session doubts as to the legality of an extra session were expressed in both houses, on the grounds that the organic act did not provide for such a procedure and Congress had made no provision for the expenses of such a session. Select committees were appointed in both houses to consider the matter. The House committee, with Joseph R. Brown at its head, submitted a carefully prepared report, in which the question was recognized as debatable but the opinion was expressed that the session was legal. Congress, the committee argued, could not have intended that the legislative powers of government could be exercised only in regular session regardless of emergencies. No report of the Council committee has been found. To provide for the expenses of the extra session, the legislature authorized the issue of territorial bonds to the amount of eight thousand dollars bearing interest at twenty per cent. *Council Journal*, 3; *House Journal*, 5, 19–22; *Laws*, 132.

convention for each representative in the legislature. This
provision was liberally construed to mean representatives
taken in a general sense so as to include councilors, and, accordingly, it was enacted that every council district should
elect two delegates for every councilor and every representative district, two delegates for every representative, as
respectively entitled. This absurd arrangement, as will be
seen, brought on unexpected complications. Thirty thousand dollars were appropriated for the payment of salaries
and expenses, and members, officers, and secretaries of the
convention were allowed the same mileage and per diem as
members of the legislative assembly. These amounts were
to be paid out of the territorial treasury on vouchers furnished by the secretary of the convention.[13]

Since the enabling act had fixed the day for the election of
delegates and had prescribed that it should be held according to the existing election laws of the territory, there was no
need for legislative action in that regard nor for an executive
proclamation. The voters had taken notice and caucuses
had already been held in the several districts. The alignment of parties was almost wholly on the slavery question.
The *Pioneer and Democrat*, then controlled by Rice, announced the issue to be "White Supremacy against Negro
Equality!" The Republicans, that organ declared, desired
a constitution which would permit "niggers" to vote and be
elected judges and legislators. Gorman, with lurid eloquence,
pictured the negro on the witness stand and in the jury box,
side by side with the Anglo-Saxon.[14] The contest, though
brief, was spirited. Both parties desired to control the

---

[13] *Laws*, 1857, extra session, 342. The *Minnesotian* for May 16, 1857, contains a table of
districts and the number of delegates assigned to each. For the apportionment of councilors
and representatives in the territorial legislature, see *Laws*, 1855, p. 36. There is an interesting interpretation of the clause on the size of the convention in the *Pioneer and Democrat*
for March 15. David Secombe considered the proper construction of the language of the
enabling act to be "the legal voters in each representative district . . . are hereby authorized to elect two delegates for each representative to which said district may be entitled."
Minnesota Constitutional Convention (Republican), *Debates and Proceedings*, 211–214
(St. Paul, 1858); *Statutes at Large*, 11: 166.

[14] *Pioneer and Democrat*, June 1, 1857; *Debates and Proceedings* (Democratic), 54.

convention in order to determine the character of the constitution and to arrange the voting districts in a way to secure the state and national offices under the charter. Whether the old party, which had had its own way in the territory, should represent the state in Washington or should give way to the insolent upstarts of Republicanism became a burning question. The Republican managers at large so much desired the assurance of a Republican delegation from the new state, which might be a deciding factor in Congress, that they sent some of their most persuasive orators to recruit the ranks of the party; Schuyler Colfax of Indiana, Lyman Trumbull and Owen Lovejoy of Illinois, Galusha A. Grow of Pennsylvania, John P. Hale of New Hampshire, and others were heard on the stump, and large sums of money, it is said, were expended in the campaign.

The vote at the election was unexpectedly light, and the result was not clearly decisive, both parties claiming a majority of delegates. In the interval of forty days between the election and the day set for the assemblage of the convention there was much concern about the organization of the latter. Democratic officials of the territory would under ordinary circumstances have the right to take the initiative in the proceedings. Inspired by the conviction that they represented the major part of the people, and those the good people full of zeal for virtue and humanity, the Republicans considered how in case of necessity they might be able to prevent the wicked Democrats from gaining any undue advantage.[15]

Toward the close of the week preceding the day set for assemblage, Monday, July 13, 1857, the delegates elected

[15] Gilfillan, in *Minnesota Historical Collections*, 9: 173; *Debates and Proceedings* (Democratic), 29; *Minnesotian*, May 21, 22, 23, 25, 26, 1857; *Pioneer and Democrat*, May 20, 22, 24. On June 30 the *Minnesotian* advised the Republican delegates to be in St. Paul by the tenth, "to thwart any rascality . . . planned by the Border Ruffian party." The *Pioneer and Democrat* answered the next day. After citing this exhortation of the *Minnesotian*, it called upon the Democratic delegates to assemble in time for consultation. "The game of the Republicans is to organize the Convention, on a Republican basis, with the aid of the bogus delegates from St. Anthony. This attempt must be defeated *at all hazards*." There are further statements in the *Minnesotian*, July 2, 3, 4, 8, 10, 11, 1857.

were arriving in St. Paul from their distant homes by conveyances of all sorts but railway. The usual consultations began. In the course of these it was discovered that the enabling act fixed no hour for the assemblage. Under ordinary circumstances this omission would have been remedied by an informal understanding among the delegates. In this case the mutual distrust was too intense for so reasonable a procedure. On Saturday evening the Republicans went into caucus behind closed doors and decided to meet in the Capitol at midnight of Sunday and then, in the language of one prominent among them, "watch for and pray over our Democratic brethren." A committee was appointed, however, to take any desirable action in the interim. Later on Sunday evening there was a meeting of Democratic leaders. That it amounted to a caucus on the Holy Sabbath day was disclaimed. The Republican committee, at Gorman's instigation, submitted to them a formal signed proposition that the hour of assemblage should be twelve, noon, expecting the concurrence of the Democrats. Instead of concurring, however, the Democrats returned the evasive written statement that they would "be governed as to time and place of meeting by the usual rules governing the assemblage of parliamentary bodies in the United States." This did not allay Republican suspicion, and an hour later the delegates of that persuasion began assembling in the Capitol. They made no attempt at organization. When workmen came in the morning to complete the preparation of the representatives' hall, the appointed place, the delegates trooped in and made themselves comfortable. Between nine and ten o'clock on Monday the Democrats held a caucus in the secretary's office and there adopted a resolution confirming the action of the previous evening concurring in the proposition to meet at twelve o'clock, noon. The Republicans were in no state of mind to trust to the Greeks. Their suspicions were further exasperated by the circumstance that presently a person, easily believed to be under Democratic instructions, came in and with much show of pains adjusted the clock behind the speaker's desk and set it going according to Democratic time.[16]

The Republicans in possession had agreed upon a line of procedure and had signed a request that Delegate John W. North should call the convention to order at the noon hour and should nominate a temporary chairman. About a quarter of an hour before twelve — precisely seventeen minutes by the Democratic time is the statement of one delegate — the quiet watch of the Republicans was suddenly broken by the irruption in a body of the Democratic delegates headed by Charles L. Chase, the secretary of the territory. Without a moment's pause the secretary mounted the platform and began calling the convention to order. Instantly North sprang to his side and, according to arrangement, also attempted to call it to order. All accounts agree that the convention did not come to order, but without pause, while members were still on their feet, Governor Gorman moved an adjournment till the next day at twelve o'clock, noon. Chase put the question; ayes were shouted by the Democratic members; and they claimed that Republicans were heard to shout, "No," thus recognizing Chase's call to order. The motion was declared to be carried and the Democrats at once hurried out of the hall. Their journal relates that "the Convention adjourned." This the Republicans stoutly denied, claiming that there was nothing to adjourn; a number of delegates elect prematurely and uncivilly absented themselves, that was all. The absentees claimed that they had merely exercised the highest privilege of parliamentary bodies, that of resting from labor at pleasure. This contention has never been judicially settled. The same uncertainty surrounds the question as to which one of the two personages had the right to call the convention to order. Precedents were quoted in behalf of both. The Democrats laid stress upon the fact that under the election law of the territory the

[16] *Debates and Proceedings* (Republican), 30–32, 303; (Democratic), 29–33.

secretary of the territory had received the election returns and was the legal custodian of them. If there had been no misunderstanding doubtless it would have been deemed appropriate that the secretary should call to order.[17]

The meteoric disappearance of the Democrats did not disturb the program of the Republicans. They proceeded at once to form their permanent organization. The committee on credentials reported fifty-six delegates present with certificates of election in proper form. The Republican body continued its sessions in the hall of representatives from day to day. On Tuesday, the second day, the Democratic delegates assembled at noon about the door of the hall in which the Republicans were in session. They were then informed by Secretary Chase that the hall was occupied by citizens, who refused to give place to the convention. An adjournment was taken to the Council chamber, where the territorial secretary called the convention to order. It was appropriate that Joseph R. Brown should offer the first motion, and that, the nomination of Henry H. Sibley as chairman. For the first week this body did little but adjourn from day to day. On the eighth day there were no chairs in the chamber. On the ninth day the committee on credentials reported. Forty-nine delegates, less than a majority of the number fixed for the convention, held proper certificates of election.[18]

The silly and extravagant action of the territorial legislature in raising the number of delegates from sixty-eight to one hundred and eight, by confusing councilors with representatives, now presented a mathematical problem which

[17] On July 14, 1857, the *Pioneer and Democrat* gave a report of the proceedings on July 13 of the Democratic body and of "the Black-Republican Mob." After this date only occasional flings at the "Republican meeting" or "Camp Meeting" are found in that paper. See also the *Minnesotian*, July 14, 1857. Various members of the two conventions commented upon the tactics of the opposition party. The speech of Thomas Foster may be found in the *Pioneer and Democrat*, July 14, 1857, and in *Debates and Proceedings* (Republican), 30–33; speeches of Amos Coggswell, St. A. D. Balcombe, and John W. North, on pages 74–78, 115–127, 303–307 of the same volume. The remarks of ex-Governor Willis A. Gorman, Charles E. Flandrau, Henry N. Setzer, and Henry H. Sibley are printed in *Debates and Proceedings* (Democratic), 8–10, 17–25, 27–38, 63–66, 92–96. There are no material disagreements as to the facts.

[18] *Debates and Proceedings* (Republican), 9–28; (Democratic), 3–13.

the two factions solved each according to its interest. The third council district, St. Anthony Falls, had no subdivisions and was, therefore, under the ruling, entitled to elect six delegates, two for its one councilor and four for its two representatives. The Democrats ignored the distinction and voted for six delegates at large. The Republicans had their tickets printed to designate two of their candidates for the council district and four for the representative district. The returns having been made, as required by law, to the register of deeds of Hennepin County, the Reverend Charles G. Ames, that official issued certificates of election to the six Republican candidates, although four of them had fewer votes than the same number of Democrats. Complaint of malfeasance was at once made to Governor Medary, who cited the accused register to appear. After a sufficient hearing, the governor, acting under existing law, removed him from office. The commissioners of Hennepin County, also acting under law, reinstated him the same day.[19]

The Republican section of delegates accepted these six St. Anthony certificates, and no persons appeared to contest. The holders sat unchallenged to the end. The Democratic section, being short of members, admitted four Democrats from that district on the strength of certificates from the judges of election that they had received the highest number of votes. By the same resolution a contestant from Houston County was seated, upon the recommendation of the committee on credentials, which found that he had received forty-nine more votes on a general ticket than his Republican opponent, to whom a certificate had been granted, had received on a representative ticket. On the twenty-fifth day of the session a contestant from Mower County was seated upon his petition, supported by affidavits showing that if

[19] There is an abstract of the vote in the third council district in *Debates and Proceedings* (Republican), 215–217. The board of canvassers ruled that "the votes cast for delegates to said convention, without designation of either Council or Representative District, could not legally be counted by them." Governor Medary's letter of dismissal to Ames, dated July 17, 1857, is published in *Debates and Proceedings* (Democratic), 39, and also, in connection with a long editorial, in the *Minnesotian*, August 22, 1857.

thirty-nine illegal votes were deducted his opponent had
been defeated. Six delegates from Pembina County had
been seated without question. In an undivided convention
the Republicans would have contested the right of some or
all of them to seats on the ground that they had been elected
by the votes of persons residing west of the Red River and
therefore outside the limits of the proposed state.[20] These
accessions raised the number on the Democratic roll to fifty-
five, a majority of the whole number of delegates authorized.
A doubt about the legality of their action had its effect on
the minds of the Democrats, however, as the sequel will
show. The Republicans were less solicitous for additional
delegates. They had fifty-six delegates holding certificates
on the opening day and no seats were contested. Two other
members presented certificates on the second and third days
and were accepted. On the fourth day a seat was allowed to
the Reverend Charles B. Sheldon of Hennepin County in
the eleventh council district on an application showing that
Roswell P. Russell, to whom a certificate had been allowed,
had refused to accept it and hence, since Sheldon had received the next highest number of votes, he was entitled to
fill the vacancy.[21] The Republican body now had on its roll
fifty-nine members, fifty-three of whom actually signed the

[20] *Debates and Proceedings* (Republican), 9, 213–219; (Democratic), 13–16, 20–25, 47–51,
69–71, 96, 398. Gorman defended the legitimacy of the Pembina delegation, and Joseph
R. Brown asserted that "no votes were cast except at the legally established election pre-
cincts, east of the proposed State line." The statement was doubtless correct. If tradition
runs true, the Pembina election was easily managed without much annoyance to electors.
Charles E. Flandrau, in his *History of Minnesota and Tales of the Frontier*, 300–302 (St.
Paul, 1900), presents an amusing account of how the election returns were brought from
Pembina in the fall of 1857.

[21] Russell, "when tendered a certificate of election, honorably declined," owing, perhaps, to the fact that as a United States official, receiver of the local land office, he would
probably have been rejected by a full convention. Gorman suggested that the Republicans,
by issuing a certificate to Russell, expected to unseat Charles E. Flandrau, at the time Sioux
Indian agent. North tabulated an analysis of the delegates and commented at length on the
irregularities of the Democratic procedure. See *Debates and Proceedings* (Republican), 10,
27, 33, 46, 52, 296; (Democratic), 46; and the *Pioneer and Democrat*, July 17, 25, 1857. The
issue of the latter for July 18, 1857, gives the Democratic list. From the issue of July 25,
it would appear that the Democrats claimed the correct figures to be as follows: Democrats
with certificates, 49; Democrats without certificates, but in fact elected, 6; total, 55; Republicans with certificates, 59; Republicans with false certificates, 6; leaving 53 legitimately
elected. This would make a Democratic majority o f2.

Constitution. One hundred and fourteen persons held seats in the two sections.

There was a marked contrast in the personnel of the two sections. Nearly one-half of the members of the Democratic body were or had been federal or territorial officials or members of the legislature. Sibley's long experience in the public affairs of the territory, his parliamentary training in the national House of Representatives, and his personal grace and dignity fitted him for the office of president, to which he had been unanimously elected. Of legal talent there was an abundance; the most eminent in that regard were easily Moses Sherburne and Lafayette Emmett. The adroit Rolette was on the roll, as was "the veritable Joe Brown," most skillful of all in the usages of conventions and legislatures. The Republicans had a much smaller proportion of pioneers and ex-officials; they were younger men, less experienced in the affairs of the territory. Of the eight lawyers in the body the most able and prominent were Charles McClure, John W. North, Amos Coggswell, and Thomas Wilson. Nearly three-fourths of the members of the two bodies were men of ephemeral prominence afterwards unknown in public affairs. Wilson, Thomas J. Galbraith, and Coggswell were afterwards reconciled to the Democratic party. Party politics kept many of the ablest men of the territory at home, among them Alexander Ramsey and William R. Marshall.

While the committees were at work for some days preparing the drafts of the usual articles, the orators of the two sections had opportunity to defend in elaborate speeches the legitimacy of their respective organizations. The speeches, as reported in the journals, are well worth reading as a recreation by the student of Minnesota history. There was much show of dignity and moderation, but occasionally some strong language escaped. Gorman in a heated moment exclaimed, "But where shall these details of outrages end? MR. PRESIDENT, give this Republican party the *prestige* of power in Minnesota, and they will flood your Territory with the minions of their Emigrant Aid Societies, armed with SHARP's rifles . . . to overturn your Democratic institutions, and will inaugurate scenes of violence and bloodshed, as they have in Kansas." A Republican delegate, Amos Coggswell, resenting an injurious imputation, said, "Sir, the Republican party acknowledges fealty—first, to the God of Heaven, and second, to the Federal Constitution; and I hurl back the charge which has been made against us as Republicans, of desiring to trample under foot the provisions of that sacred instrument, as totally, knowingly, and wickedly false."[22]

It was the twelfth day of their session before the Democrats were permanently organized and on that day Sibley was the unanimous choice for the presidency. During the next three days the standing committees were announced and the rules were adopted. Although the Republicans had the start of a week, they had made no material progress in the business. In the course of a fortnight, however, both bodies were working regularly. The reports of the committees as they came in were so fully discussed and amended in committee of the whole as to leave little for the houses to do but give the articles as reported their final passages. The framing of a constitution for a new western state was not a formidable task even in that day. The precedents of the states carved out of the old Northwest Territory left little to be devised anew. Iowa was revising her constitution that year. The Republican drafts were in the main quite close copies of the Wisconsin constitution of 1848. In a few instances Ohio, Michigan, and Iowa examples were used. The Democrats, while drawing from the same sources, were more catholic. Their bill of rights appears to be a compound of those of New York and New Jersey.[23]

[22] *Debates and Proceedings* (Democratic), 56; (Republican), 78.

[23] *Debates and Proceedings* (Democratic), 99–119. The constitutions of the states referred to can be found in Thorpe, *Constitutions*, or in Franklin B. Hough, ed., *American Constitutions* (Albany, 1872). A detailed study and comparison of the drafts is contained in an excellent *History of the Constitution of Minnesota*, by William Anderson, recently published by the University of Minnesota (Minneapolis, 1921).

It is quite unnecessary to trace the routine of either of the two sections, but some reference may be made to discussions of special interest which diversified the debates. No question aroused livelier controversy than that as to whether the proposed state should have the boundaries prescribed by the enabling act or should take a new configuration by the location of the northern boundary on the latitude of Little Falls or thereabout and the retention of the territorial western border on the Missouri River. Long before the date set for the convention the newspapers had been engaged in advocating, some the "north and south line" of the enabling act, others an "east and west line" from the St. Croix to the Red River or to the Missouri. Indeed, the question was deeply involved in that of the removal of the capital from St. Paul to St. Peter, for which majorities in both houses of the legislature of 1857 had voted, as the reader will easily remember, but which was defeated by an extraordinary and unparliamentary proceeding. The question came up in the Republican body at its first session. The enabling act having been read, a resolution was at once offered declaring it to be the wish of the inhabitants residing within the limits described in that act to be admitted to the Union in pursuance of the said act. Indeed, that act in express terms required the convention to determine this question first. There were motions to amend and to submit to a select committee. Delegates were cautious about declaring themselves prematurely on a question tacitly involved in the resolution. Thomas Foster said, "This is an important crisis! and we must move carefully, cautiously, and at the same time decisively." Upon his suggestion the convention went into committee of the whole for the consideration of the resolution. The discussion had not proceeded far when it was revealed by the mover of the resolution, Galbraith, that it contemplated the acceptance of the prescribed boundaries. The desire of the people of many southern counties for separation from the wilderness of the

northern part of the territory had already found expression
in various ways. This desire now broke out in the Republican convention. Thomas Wilson, delegate from Winona
County, afterwards a justice of the state supreme court, led
the opposition in support of a substitute resolution which
simply declared it to be the wish of the people to be admitted
to the Union, without reference to the requirements of the
enabling act as to boundaries. The merits of the question of
excluding the northern part of the territory from the proposed state were briefly but hotly debated, but the opinion
prevailed that the admission of the new state would be
jeopardized by an apparent rejection of the terms of the
enabling act. The Wilson substitute was, therefore, rejected,
and a substitute proposed by North that the people of the
proposed state desired to be admitted to the Union in
accordance with the enabling act was adopted by a vote of
41 to 15.[24]

When the select committee appointed to frame a scheme
of standing committees reported, it did not propose a standing committee on boundaries on the ground that the convention had already disposed of the subject. The dissent
from this opinion was so strong that the convention ordered
the appointment of such a committee. That committee
reported in favor of accepting the boundaries of the enabling
act without change. When the report came up for consideration in committee of the whole, Delegate Wilson offered a
substitute to make the forty-sixth parallel of north latitude
the northern boundary of the proposed state. The advocates of the east and west line had the debate mostly to
themselves. This line, they argued, would give Minnesota
a "square and compact" area of fertile land, including a
large part of the rich Missouri Valley. It would exclude an
immense region of vast forests never to be permanently
settled, but to be roamed over by "a sort of *omnium-*

[24] *Debates and Proceedings* (Republican), 11–26. On the project for the removal of the capital, see *ante*, pp. 381–387. An article in the *Pioneer and Democrat*, June 1, 1859, charges Gorman with hypocrisy in the matter of the removal.

gatherum" of trappers, miners, hunters, and lumbermen, from whom no taxes could be exacted. Almost the entire population of southern Minnesota, the convention was assured, desired the east and west line, and the belief was expressed that a majority of the whole people of the territory were in favor of it. The suggestion was made that in the square and compact state proposed it would be impossible for St. Paul to hold the balance of power. The Wilson substitute was rejected without division. Delegate Coggswell thereupon moved another substitute to make the forty-sixth parallel the north boundary and the ninety-seventh meridian the west line. The mover, aware that the committee of the whole intended to kill his amendment by an overwhelming majority, insisted on expressing his views and those of his constituency. His speech was tolerated but his proposition was quietly ignored by the committee. In convention Wilson renewed his substitute, demanded a roll call, and had it defeated by a vote of 37 to 15. The report was thereupon referred to the standing committee on arrangement and phraseology.[25]

Ten days later, August 10, an advocate of the east and west line offered a resolution to provide for submitting that proposition to the people. The delegate represented to the convention that in his section of the territory, Nicollet County, there was intense feeling and excitement upon the boundary question. An article from the *St. Peter Free Press* of July 29, read by him, contained the expression, "if a north and south line boundary be incorporated into the Constitution, *we will fight it to the death.* . . . As a Republican paper . . . we tell our Republican delegates . . . that if you attempt to force upon us this line contrary to our known and expressed wishes, *we will not submit to it.* . . . If, gentlemen, you desire to ruin yourselves and our party for the present, adopt a north and south line." Resolutions adopted by a meeting of citizens of St. Peter demanding an

[25] *Debates and Proceedings* (Republican), 37-39, 88, 221–229. For the proposed boundaries see the map on page 487, *post.*

east and west line or a submission of the question to the people were read. From these expressions the reader will at once infer that there was a political element in the controversy. The record of the debate on the proposition of an alternative northern boundary occupies nearly fifty pages of the printed proceedings. Wide scope was given for argument on the main question and for abounding innuendo. Advocates of the north and south line were taunted with distrust of the people. Wilson informed the convention that he was in Washington when the enabling act was pending and became aware of "immense pressure" to have the north and south line established. Balcombe gave to Rice the credit for having that line inserted in the enabling act. Davis of Traverse des Sioux declared that the location of the capital did not enter into the matter. The citizens of his district, he said, did "at one time, expect the Capitol to be located at St. Peter; but since ex-Governor Gorman, the father of the project, and the man who procured the passage of the bill, deserted them . . . they have not expected to get the seat of government there." The question was raised whether the alternative proposition would be submitted to the voters of the whole existing territory, or only to those in the area designated in the enabling act, who alone were represented in the convention. Little interest was taken in that question, however, and it was left undecided.

After the debate had proceeded at some length, delegates who favored submission to the people made the discovery that the pending resolution contemplated the east and west line as a part of the constitution if a majority of votes should be cast in its favor and Congress should ratify the vote. They had supposed that they were advocating a mere proviso or memorial to serve as a request to Congress to entertain the matter. The mover of the resolution stated that such was his intention; therefore the resolution was referred back to him for amendment. When reported again, the essential part of it read, "and if the same [*proposition*] shall receive a majority of all the votes cast for and against it, then the same shall be certified to the Congress of the United States, as the wish and request of the people to change the boundary line of said proposed State accordingly." Coggswell at once moved to restore the phraseology of the original resolution. Thereupon followed more debate, not in the best of temper, and some wrangling over parliamentary procedure. A variety of futile propositions were made, which were either ignored or voted down. The Coggswell amendment, rejected in committee of the whole, was renewed in convention to be defeated by a vote of 28 to 29. The Davis resolution with its memorial element was then adopted by a vote of 30 to 28. Later in the same session a member of the majority, to appease the "great feeling" of opponents who, under the operation of the previous question, had not been able to express their views, moved a reconsideration of the question of submitting the boundary to the people. This was carried by a vote of 32 to 21. But there was no delegate who cared for further debate, and the question was taken. The vote for submission stood: yeas 26, nays 31; and this was the end of the east and west line in the Republican convention.[26]

While the Republican delegates were at odds over the boundary question, the Democrats found it put up to them. On August 6 the standing committee on name and boundary reported an article in the precise language of the enabling act. The delegate from Nicollet County, Charles E. Flandrau, moved as an amendment an alternative proposition which was the same as that proposed by Wilson in the Republican assembly. The mover stated the now familiar considerations in favor of the "east and west line." Governor Gorman used the opportunity to explain his change of

[26] *Debates and Proceedings* (Republican), 408–410, 412–437, 439, 441–449, 452–454, 466–470. Just before the final vote was taken, Secombe informed the convention that "some gentlemen are so much aggrieved with the passage of the resolution that they are threatening to go off and leave us."

attitude. He had been favorable to the east and west line until his late visit to Washington, when he had found to his surprise that Congress was making a vast grant of land for railroads in the northern part of the territory. The east and west line would deprive Minnesota of from thirty to fifty millions of dollars. Now a wiser man, he changed his position. The Flandrau resolution, lost in committee of the whole, was renewed by its mover in convention, and was defeated by a vote of 6 to 36. Successive propositions to make the north line 45° 30′, 45° 15′, and 45° 10′ were promptly defeated. The report of the standing committee recommending the boundaries specified in the enabling act was concurred in by a vote of 32 to 9.

The advocates of the east and west line and the "square and compact state" in the Democratic wing were no more disposed to cease from troubling than those in the Republican camp. On August 19 Judge Flandrau came forward with a proposition that the question of a north line on the latitude of 45° 30′ be submitted to the people as a separate issue and that, if a majority of votes should be cast in its favor, a certificate of the votes be transmitted to Congress as a petition of the people of the state for a change of boundaries accordingly. In the long debate which followed great emphasis was laid upon the propriety of allowing the people to express their wishes. George L. Becker of St. Paul declared that the people had already done so, the question having been agitated and made an issue throughout the territory. A large majority of the delegates had been sent to the convention because of their known opposition to an east and west line. The question had been settled by the people, and it was an insult to ask them to vote upon it again. Lafayette Emmett concurred in this view and averred that the proposition for an east and west line had been "signally defeated" at the election; "except in St. Paul, and perhaps a few other places . . . almost every member of the Convention was elected upon that issue."

Flandrau admitted that the boundary question had been an issue in some localities but denied that it had been a general issue. Gentlemen would find out what the sentiments of the people were by allowing them to vote on a separate proposition. Other members concurred in this view. For the purpose of having the whole matter maturely considered, Flandrau moved that it be referred to a select committee. This was agreed to and he was made chairman of the committee. On August 21, by which date the business of the convention was substantially completed, he reported his resolution without amendment or suggestion. Joseph R. Brown desired to offer one or two amendments and to give his reasons for his vote, but because time was lacking he moved to lay the resolution on the table. The motion was agreed to and this was the end of the east and west line in the Democratic wing.[27]

It would be idle to speculate upon the probable results of such a division of the territory. No expressions of regret on the part of the advocates of the east and west line have been found. It is not difficult to conjecture that the north and south line was settled upon in Washington and partly, at least, on political considerations. There was lively opposition, as has been seen, to the admission of a new state in the Northwest; the addition of a Republican state would very probably have been impossible. The inclusion of the northern part of the Territory of Minnesota would, it was confidently believed, insure a Democratic majority in the new state. No one could have been more desirous of such an outcome than Delegate Rice, who — and there was no secret about it — was expecting to be one of the first United States senators from Minnesota. His influence, therefore,

[27] *Debates and Proceedings* (Democratic), 295–306, 525–539, 558. The Democratic convention avoided a premature discussion of the east and west boundary line in an interesting manner. See pp. 100–109. While the enabling act was pending in the Senate, Jones of Tennessee moved an amendment to submit to the people of the territory a choice between the boundaries set forth in the bill and an east and west line on the forty-sixth degree of north latitude. It was lost without division. 34 Congress, 3 session, *Senate Journal*, 237 (serial 873).

was thrown in favor of the north and south line, and the land grant of 1857 for railroads was distributed so as to favor that proposition and annul the opposition of Governor Gorman and other influential persons to it.

It was not to be expected that the Democratic delegates would make innovations upon the conditions of suffrage. President Sibley, however, ventured a proposal to strike out the word "white" where it occurred before "citizens of the United States," for the reason that in the Dred Scott case the national Supreme Court had taken the position that there were no citizens of the United States but whites. There was no second. The numerous delegates whose relations with Indians and half-breeds had been both extensive and intimate were able to persuade their colleagues to open the suffrage to them on conditions not over rigorous.[28] The hospitality manifested toward foreigners was conspicuous. The Democrats of that day had no sympathy with "Know-Nothingism." The draft provided that foreigners who had declared their intention to become naturalized might vote after a residence of six months in the state. The attorney-general of the territory, Lafayette Emmett, proposed to shorten the period to four months and remarked that he would prefer two months. In the course of the debate opinions were expressed that "the actual, *bona fide* resident" should be allowed to vote the next day after he arrived, and that no distinction should be made between white men from whatever part of the world they might have come. One delegate expressly stated that a foreigner direct from his native country was as competent to vote in Minnesota as a settler just arriving from Massachusetts.[29]   It was to be

[28] Sibley's understanding of the effect of the Dred Scott Decision was questioned, but Emmett supported him. In the interesting debate on the question of giving Indians the suffrage the views of Joseph R. Brown prevailed. Indeed, the paragraphs on Indian and mixed-blood suffrage were framed by him. Brown had reasons for advocating liberality toward mixed-bloods. Twelve half-blood Wahpeton Sioux petitioned for admission to suffrage. *Debates and Proceedings* (Democratic), 427–430.

[29] *Debates and Proceedings* (Democratic), 267, 426, 607–613. One delegate favored as low as four months' or even two months' probation so that settlers arriving by the early boats in April, May, and June might vote at the fall elections.

expected that among the Republicans there would be those who would not fail to advocate opening the suffrage without distinction of race and color. Much respectable eloquence was wasted on that theme. The able address of John W. North covers ten pages of the *Debates*. The wiser heads warned these enthusiasts that the people were not ready for negro suffrage and that they would certainly reject any constitution providing for it. The proposition to strike out the word "white" was lost by a two-thirds vote.[30]

Both branches debated upon banks as if the only banking function were the issue of circulating notes. Some Democrats were opposed to banks altogether, and a section making stockholders individually liable for all debts was actually approved. A similar proposition in the Republican assembly was lost by a two-thirds vote. After the experience of the preceding eight years with special charters of incorporation, there was no need of argument in either body in favor of a provision for general incorporation laws. Ex-Governor Gorman, speaking on a draft of a section to permit incorporation only under general laws and subject to legislative control and to make stockholders individually liable for the amount of their stock, delivered an address which would furnish a denouncer of "combines" in this day with striking arguments and many a piquant phrase. Brown favored general laws because under them corporations could be easily multiplied to develop the country. His colleagues seemed to be of the opinion that general laws would rather restrain the organization of corporations.[31]

In both assemblies elaborate articles were submitted providing for the organization of the militia. The Democratic draft excepted negroes and mulattoes in precise terms; the Republican article effected the same purpose by declaring

---

[30] *Debates and Proceedings* (Republican), 337–367. The vote was 17 to 34. The editor of the *Pioneer and Democrat* stated on September 2, 1857, that the Republican party greatly desired the extension of the suffrage to negroes in Minnesota as a protest against the Dred Scott Decision but that they got a rump convention of their own and then basely betrayed the negro by refusing him suffrage.

[31] *Debates and Proceedings* (Democratic), 124–148, 399–417; (Republican), 307–327.

the militia to be composed of all able-bodied white male citizens of military age. To this North objected because it excluded the half-breed men of Pembina, "the best cavalry in the world." After lively controversy both bodies substituted brief articles authorizing the legislature to pass necessary laws for the organization, discipline, and service of the militia. The article finally adopted is in the exact language proposed by Joseph R. Brown.[32]

Among other provisions bruited in one section or the other but not adopted by either were the following: a referendum of any act to the electors; the right of electors to vote anywhere in the state or district for candidates for state or district offices; the disfranchisement of any citizen concerned in a duel; the submission of negro suffrage to the electors; the concurrence of the Senate in pardons; the power of a number of jurors less than twelve to render a verdict in civil cases; the power of juries to act as judges of both law and fact in libel and slander cases; the exemption of ministers of the gospel who make the calling of their Master their sole profession and who refuse to hold civil offices from taxes on real and personal property to the amount of twenty-five hundred dollars; the election of regents of the university; the appointment of judges of the supreme court; the abolition of the death penalty; the abolition of the right of the legislature to license the traffic in intoxicating liquors; and the registration of voters.[33]

Doubtless from the beginning the steadier heads of the two assemblies appreciated the ridiculousness of the situation and were waiting for a happy moment for compromise. After the orators had let off their steam and the period of ebullition had given way to the steady grind of work, the sentiment grew and spread that in some way the chasm between the assemblies must be bridged. The hope of merging the two, if seriously entertained, was soon aban-

[32] *Debates and Proceedings* (Democratic), 122, 148–184; (Republican), 417, 454–462.
[33] *Debates and Proceedings* (Republican), 80, 86, 88, 153, 158, 190, 204, 337, 367, 386, 440, 538, 541, 546–551; (Democratic), 379, 391, 489, 493–509.

doned as impossible. The young men would never, never sacrifice principle. The plan of having both bodies continue in session and finally agree upon identical constitutions became, however, the subject of informal conferences of individual delegates before the first week of steady work was ended. When, on the eighth of August, Judge Moses Sherburne introduced a preamble and a resolution to that end in the Democratic section, after declaring that he had consulted not a single human being beforehand, he was much surprised to hear a colleague declare that he knew before that such a resolution was coming. Both statements were, no doubt, correct. The preamble, after reciting that the delegates duly elected, disagreeing upon some immaterial questions, had formed separate conventions, declared that the extraordinary proceedings would injure the reputation of Minnesota, would weaken confidence in her, and would put her in a false position before the world. The resolution called for the appointment of a committee of five to coöperate with a similar committee from the other body in forming a plan by which the two might unite on a single constitution. It was the opinion of the mover that the genuine constitutional convention could with propriety magnanimously take the initiative and hold out the olive branch to the seceders. Such, however, was not the opinion of the greater number present, who, after a brisk debate, postponed the olive branch indefinitely.[34]

There is good reason for believing that the Republican delegates were ready and desirous to meet any reasonable overtures which might come from the other end of the Capitol. They had not been many days in attendance before they discovered that George W. Armstrong, the

[34] *Debates and Proceedings* (Democratic), 350–361. The idea of having each convention submit its draft constitution to a vote of the electors seems to have been entertained and seriously discussed. See the *Pioneer and Democrat* for August 18, 21, 22. The statement of Holcombe, in *Minnesota in Three Centuries*, 3:48, that the proposition to have both bodies adopt an identical constitution was first voiced by Joseph R. Brown and that he drew up an agreement in writing to that effect has not been traced to any authentic source but is likely enough to be true.

territorial treasurer, being of the Democratic faith, naturally regarded the Democratic assembly as the only legal one. He therefore promptly accepted the pay warrants of the Democratic delegates and firmly refused to recognize those of the Republicans. This was an inconvenience and in some cases a hardship. Persistence in separate actions would, they saw, be likely to deprive them of all claim to remuneration or would at least force them to costly and tedious litigation. Not to be outdone in magnanimity, the Republican body on Monday the tenth of August unanimously adopted a preamble and resolution practically identical with that defeated by the Democrats two days before and on the next day ordered it transmitted to the delegates assembled in the Council chamber. It was so transmitted and was referred to a select committee, which on the fourteenth concluded a tedious report with a resolution that no communications which called in question the "legal character of this Convention" could be received. The resolution was unanimously adopted. Dignity was vindicated. Fortunately no personal asperities had soured the tempers of the opposing forces. Had they met in one assembly there would have been abundant reviling and the sergeant at arms might have needed to exercise his office to compel order. As the delegates sat at the same tables in the hotels and met at the same social functions there was opportunity for dispassionate interchange of views. Doubtless in pursuance of a common understanding among the leaders of the parties action toward compromise at length became practicable. On the morning of the eighteenth, a communication from the president of the Republican body announcing the appointment of the committee provided for in the resolution adopted on the tenth and requesting the appointment of a similar committee by the Democrats was formally laid before the convention sitting in the Council chamber. After a recess of half an hour a resolution to authorize President Sibley to appoint conferees was passed by a vote of 33 to 7, under the operation of the previous question moved by Gorman. Two Democratic delegates declared that by this action the "constitutional convention" had abdicated and took their departure without resigning, because, so they alleged, there was no body in existence to entertain a resignation. One of them when brought into the assembly as an absentee under a call of the House made no resistance and resumed his duties.[35]

The delegates from the two bodies who were to compose the "compromise committee" met for organization before the close of the day.[36] No minutes of the proceedings have been found. The discussions were no doubt animated, but, under the moderating guidance of Judge Sherburne, the chairman, they were orderly, with a single unfortunate exception. On the afternoon of August 25, Delegate Wilson made a remark which ex-Governor Gorman construed to be an impeachment of his veracity and a personal insult. Without demanding apology or explanation he rose to his feet and with his loaded cane struck Wilson, who was seated, a blow on the head violent enough to break the cane. The latter seized his own cane and started for his assailant, but bystanders prevented further conflict. In the absence of impartial testimony it is difficult to apportion the blame for the unseemly occurrence. It may be suggested that Wilson was blameworthy for using language capable of hostile interpretation, calculated to exasperate, and uncalled for by the occasion. For Gorman's sudden and brutal assault without warning there was no sufficient justification.[37]

By this time both bodies had gone over all the necessary articles so that they were ready for the harmonizing offices of

---

[35] *Pioneer and Democrat*, September 4, 1857; *Minnesotian*, September 8, 1857; *Debates and Proceedings* (Republican), 410, 441, 496, 525, 590–595; (Democratic), 421, 480, 521–523, 525, 556. The two were Baker and Setzer; the latter returned.

[36] The Republican conferees were Galbraith, McClure, Stannard, Aldrich, and Wilson. The Democratic members were Gorman, Brown, Holcombe, Sherburne, and Kingsbury. *Debates and Proceedings* (Republican), 411; (Democratic), 523.

[37] Gorman's written statements and explanatory remarks may be found in *Debates and Proceedings* (Democratic), 587–589, and in the *Pioneer and Democrat*, August 27, 1857. Wilson's defiant speech is published in *Debates and Proceedings* (Republican), 560–565, and

the conferees. This task was not one of great difficulty, since the two branches of the convention had drawn their material from the same or similar sources. Still, there were certain discrepancies to be composed and this took time. Probably the most troublesome part of this duty was that of subdividing the territory into judicial, senatorial, and representative districts. Both parties were keen to retain every possible advantage. The census required by the enabling act had not yet been taken, and the conferees were obliged to estimate the population of the counties. It was no easy problem to distribute the generously estimated aggregate of 247,500 among the widespread counties. But it was solved, as the old arithmetics used to say, "by inspection." Two United States senatorships and two or three seats in the House of Representatives hung on the solution. One illustration of the adjustments made by the conferees is worthy of particular notice. The Republicans desired to secure liberal conditions of suffrage. The Democrats resisted this but were ready to consent to a relaxation of their rigorous section on the amendment of the constitution. Both bodies had adopted articles providing for the proposal of amendments by any legislature and a seconding by the next legislature before submission to popular vote. When the conferees reached the subject of negro suffrage, a Republican, Judge McClure, submitted a proposition to empower the legislature to pass a law at any time for extending the right of suffrage, with a referendum attachment. A Democrat, Joseph R. Brown, at once declared that "that did seem democratic and that there could be no objection to it." In the end there was a ready agreement to the article still

in the *Minnesotian*, August 27. There is an account from the Republican point of view in two letters of Messer to Stevens, August 20, 26, 1857, in the Stevens Papers. The affair was ignored in both conventions. The traditional story that Democratic colleagues of Gorman presented him with another gold-headed cane in token of their recognition of valuable services to the party is told by Holcombe, in *Minnesota in Three Centuries*, 3:54, evidently adapted from Harlan P. Hall, *Observations: Being More or Less a History of Political Contests in Minnesota*, 22 (St. Paul, 1904). No other written or printed document confirming it has been found nor can any surviving relative furnish information on the subject. Pat Keeghan, in an interview with the author, said, "There was no cane presented to Gorman."

standing in the constitution, by which a majority of both houses of the legislature may propose amendments for submission to the people. In the last day's discussion a Republican delegate, who engineered this substitution, congratulated his colleagues on having secured a way presently to enlarge the suffrage. But the word "white" stood in the elective franchise article till 1868.[38]

Late in the afternoon of Thursday, August 27, Judge Sherburne brought into the Democratic convention a partial report of the conference committee. Motions to lay on the table and print, to amend, to adjourn, and the like were offered. A modification of the rules, made a week before, possibly in anticipation of this emergency, gave the chair large discretion in the suppression of dilatory proceedings, which President Sibley exercised with firmness. Flandrau deprecated the "desire manifested here to kick over everything looking to an agreement," and trusted "that gentlemen will act . . . a little like men of sense and not like school boys." Sherburne sugared the pill by assuring the members that the Republicans had magnanimously adopted the Democratic articles "almost altogether." A test vote, upon an appeal from the chair, showed more than a three-fourths vote for the report, but the minority were not pressed to final action that day. On the twenty-eighth, after much oratory, the previous question having been ordered, the report was agreed to by a vote of 38 to 13.[39]

The report did not reach the Republican convention till the morning of the twenty-eighth. The majority were ready for immediate action but, when some opposition developed, consented to grant dissentients time to free their minds and put themselves right with constituents. When all had been

---

[38] *Debates and Proceedings* (Democratic), 453, 605; (Republican), 390, 574–577, 578.

[39] A study of the proceedings seems to justify Sherburne's claim. The Republican schedule, however, was followed rather closely. The *Pioneer and Democrat* for August 28 said that "an occasional slight amendment" had been added to the Democratic document. Remarking upon the constitution, Coggswell, a Republican, said, "No democratic Constitution could be more anti-republican." *Debates and Proceedings* (Democratic), 595, 597, 599, 600, 602–614, 617, 632; (Republican), 573.

heard, a motion was adopted to suspend the rules so far as to allow the report to be read a third time. Coggswell, who had just spoken against the report, remarked, "This is a dose that has got to go down, and we might as well shut our eyes and open our mouth and take it." The final vote stood 42 to 8. Before the close of the day the presidents of the two bodies notified one another of the adoption of the report without amendment. On the following day the conference committees reported to the two bodies that they had enrolled the one constitution and had submitted to each a copy carefully prepared for ratification. The ratifications took place immediately, without debate or division.[40]

In the last days three propositions were generously submitted in the Democratic convention to provide for the payment of the Republican delegates, at least of those whose election could not be disputed; none met with acceptance. An argument offered by Joseph R. Brown in favor of such payment ought, it would seem, to have prevailed. The separation into two sections had been an economical arrangement. He ventured to say that "if both parties had remained in the same Convention, there would not have been two Articles of the Constitution adopted by the first of January next, and the expense would have been double that of both Conventions now."[41] In 1858 the legislature of the new state appropriated fifty-five thousand dollars for the payment of the members, officers, and incidental expenses of both branches of the constitutional convention and further sums for the printing and publication of the debates and journals of the two bodies. The latter fill two respectable octavos.[42] To maintain consistency,

[40] *Debates and Proceedings* (Republican), 565, 567, 569, 581, 582, 585, 588; (Democratic). 616, 628. Holcombe attributes to Joseph R. Brown the plan of using duplicate copies, *Minnesota in Three Centuries*, 3: 53.

[41] *Debates and Proceedings* (Democratic), 617–623, 625–627; (Republican), 449–451, 454, 584, 590–595. Treasurer Armstrong declared that the Republicans were as well off as the Democrats, for there was no money for either. *Pioneer and Democrat*, September 4, 1857.

[42] *General Laws*, 1858, p. 53. The proceedings of the Democratic wing were reported from day to day in the *Pioneer and Democrat*; those of the Republican, in the *Minnesotian*. The journal of the Democratic wing was published under the title, *Journal of the Constitutional*

each of the two bodies had its constitution enrolled, authen-
ticated by its officers, and signed generally by its members.
Both have been preserved in the state archives.   By a
provision of the schedule the governor of the territory
was required to transmit a certified copy of the constitution,
should it be ratified by the electors, to the president of the
United States to be laid before Congress.   Governor Medary,
in the discharge of that duty, transmitted an "official copy"
of the Democratic instrument.[43]   Both parties were content
with the outcome: the Democrats, because of what they
had preserved; the Republicans, because of good hopes of
future advantages.   The *Pioneer and Democrat* pronounced
the new constitution a "States Right National Democratic
Constitution," free from any "fanatical dogmas of the
Black Republican party," and consigned that dangerous,
wretched faction to "dens of obscurity."[44]

Convention of the Territory of Minnesota (St. Paul, 1857).   So far as is known, the journal of
the Republican body was not published.

[43] The document laid before the United States Senate on January 11, 1858, was beyond
doubt this copy of the Democratic constitution.   On the date mentioned it was referred to
the Senate committee on territories and was ordered to be printed.   See 35 Congress, 1
session, *Senate Executive Documents*, no. 14 (serial 918).   On January 26, 1858, the committee
submitted a report with a bill for the admission of Minnesota to the Union.   See 35 Congress,
1 session, *Senate Reports*, no. 21 (serial 938).   This report contains the text of the Republican
constitution including signatures (pp. 8–30).   Then comes a remark, in brackets, that the
same constitution had been adopted by the Democratic convention, and this is followed by
the signatures of the Democratic delegates.   The rest of the report is an exact copy of the
document, number 14, mentioned above.   In a previous work, *Minnesota, the North Star
State*, 151, the author expressed the opinion that the Democratic version of the constitution
was sent to the president.   The statement was made because he had been shown only the
Republican version by the secretary of state in St. Paul.   He therefore hastily inferred that
the Democratic text must have been sent to Washington.   On reaching the close of the
present chapter it occurred to the author that a search of the files of the United States Senate
might reveal the supposedly lost document.   Senator Knute Nelson kindly undertook to have
this search made.   It resulted in the discovery of a proper "official copy" of the Democratic
version, signatures and all.   See Knute Nelson to the author, January 13, 1920, in the
Folwell Papers.   Later it developed that the original Democratic constitution had been
preserved in the governor's office, whence it has recently been transferred to the archives
of the secretary of state.   An independent investigation of the Senate files, carried on unknown to the author by the Minnesota Historical Society, upon the suggestion of William
Anderson of the University of Minnesota, revealed the information that the Republican
text of the constitution given in the Senate report was reprinted from a printer's folio copy
printed in St. Paul by Owens and Moore and filed with the report.   This copy was furnished
to the committee by Delegate William W. Kingsbury and was vouched for by the Senators
and Representatives elect from Minnesota.   The Republican constitution also appears in the
Minnesotian, the paper published by Owens and Moore, for August 31, 1857.

[44] *Pioneer and Democrat*, August 16, 22, 30, 1857.

XVI. THE FORT SNELLING RESERVATION

FROM the time of the arrival of Colonel Leavenworth with a battalion of infantry in the late summer of 1819 to the establishment of the territory thirty years later, Fort Snelling was the principal point of interest on the upper Mississippi above Prairie du Chien. The American Fur Company had its chief trading post under the guns of the fort. The Indian agent had his residence and council house a short walk from the main gateway of the inclosure. There travelers and traders found their journey's end or their point of departure for further excursions. Above all, the garrison of the fort, though always small in number, was the only physical guaranty of peace and order over an immense area. Although its importance diminished after the establishment of the territorial government, events followed which may warrant the inclusion of the chapter here begun. Some reference has already been made to the delimitation in 1839 of the military reservation proper about Fort Snelling. On July 29 of that year the commissioner of the general land office notified the war department that the land would be reserved from sale. The land thus indicated was a tract roughly marked on a map transmitted by Major Joseph Plympton on March 26, 1838, in response to an order of the war department of November 17, 1837. The lines were run out in the fall of 1839 and a complete map was forwarded on November 27.[1] It may safely be assumed that when Major Plympton in March, 1838, sketched the boundaries of the tract deemed by him necessary for military purposes he found it convenient so to locate the easterly line as to leave

---

[1] *Sale of Fort Snelling Reservation*, 16, 17, 23, 29, 31, 33 (40 Congress, 3 session, *House Executive Documents*, no. 9 — serial 1372). This document contains 107 pages of reports, records, and papers furnished to the House committee on military affairs on December 10, 1868, by the secretary of war. See also *ante*, pp. 139 n. 24, 217–222. The maps referred to are the Smith and Thompson maps. See also the map facing page 424, *post*.

the land abutting on the Mississippi at the Falls of St. Anthony outside of the reservation and thus subject to preëmption when surveyed. Note has been taken of the acquisition by Franklin Steele in the summer of 1838 of an inchoate title to the water power east of the mid-channel of the Mississippi. The desirability of a similar lodgment to command the water power of the west portion of the river must have occurred to more than one enterprising citizen. It did occur to Henry H. Sibley, who with two others applied for a lease of the mill property on the west bank. In an extant letter, dated January 18, 1839, the secretary of war refused his consent.[2]

The main body of the reserve as defined by the Thompson survey lay in the fork of the Mississippi and Minnesota rivers, extending up the former to a point about half a mile above the falls. It included Lakes Calhoun and Harriet on the west and reached up the Minnesota about six miles above the fort. A much smaller area lay east of the rivers, and it was from this area that the squatters who formed the nucleus of St. Paul were ejected in 1840. The northeast corner was about where the "Seven Corners" of that city are today. A narrow strip lay southeast of the rivers.[3] After the expulsion of the unlucky Selkirk refugees from the reservation there were no further serious attempts to secure footings thereon till about the time of the establishment of the territory, on March 3, 1849. A few individuals, however, were specially licensed for short periods by the officers commanding at the fort to raise crops of grain and to cut hay, and Joseph R. Brown opened a small farm on Minnehaha Creek.[4] While Sibley, as delegate from the rump of Wisconsin Territory, was busied in the winter of 1849 with securing the passage of the act creating the Territory of Minnesota, one Robert Smith, a member of Congress who resided at Alton, Illinois,

[2] Stewart to Sibley, November 28, 1838, April 10, 1839, Mackenzie to Sibley, November 7, 1838, Poinsett, secretary of war, to Harrison, January 18, 1839, to Miller, January 18, 1839, Sibley Papers. See also *ante*, p. 228.

[3] Williams, *Saint Paul*, 93; Thompson Map. See also *ante*, pp. 221–223.

[4] Isaac Atwater and John H. Stevens, eds., *History of Minneapolis and Hennepin County, Minnesota*, 2: 1249 (New York, 1895).

was planning for an investment in that land of promise. On February 15 he sent to the secretary of war a letter of application for a five-year lease of the government house and the old mills at the Falls of St. Anthony. He stated that he intended to move into the territory after the adjournment of Congress and that he desired the house for his family and the gristmill to grind corn and other grain. On the last day of the session, March 3, 1849, the secretary of war gave his consent and on the same date the quartermaster-general notified the commanding officer of the concession. Such an indulgence granted to a stranger who had never lived in the territory could not have given much pleasure to Sibley, whose earlier application had met with a curt refusal. The commandant at Fort Snelling, Brevet Major Samuel Woods, on April 12 replied to the quartermaster-general that he would turn over the mill property with the condition that the lessee should grind all the corn needed by the animals of the garrison and pay a reasonable rental. He concluded his letter with the statement, "I doubt much if his [Smith's] aim, in wishing to settle there, is not in the expectation that the reserve will be taken off." In the fall of the same year Smith obtained from the war department permission to cultivate the land around the mills.[5] It is sufficient to say that, although the farseeing statesman never came to live in the territory, his venture was converted into a preëmption from which was derived the enormously valuable holdings of the Minneapolis Water Company.

The appointment of Governor Ramsey and a colleague in 1849 as commissioners to negotiate a treaty with the Sioux Indians for a cession of land was naturally taken to imply that those Indians would presently be moved to some distant home, that Fort Snelling would be abandoned, and that the reservation of some forty thousand acres would be opened, in part at least, for settlement. Adjacent residents were not

[5] *Sale of Fort Snelling Reservation*, 36–39. The government house and the mills may be seen in the drawing of the Falls of St. Anthony by Captain Eastman which is reproduced facing page 30, *ante.*

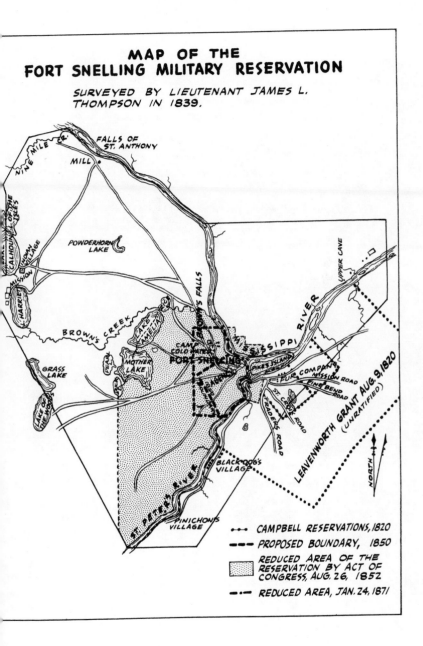

MAP OF THE
FORT SNELLING MILITARY RESERVATION

SURVEYED BY LIEUTENANT JAMES L. THOMPSON IN 1839.

FALLS OF ST. ANTHONY

NINE MILE CR.

MILL

LAKE OF THE ISLES

CALHOUN VILLAGE

LAKE CALHOUN

MISSION VILLAGE

HARRIET

POWDERHORN LAKE

BROWN'S CREEK

GRASS LAKE

LAKE OF THE WOODS

LAKE AMELIA

PEAK

MOTHER LAKE

CAMP COLD WATER

FORT SNELLING

BROWN'S FALLS

PIKE'S ISLAND

MISSISSIPPI RIVER

UPPER CAVE

FUR COMPANY

MISSION ROAD

PINE BEND ROAD

ST. CROIX ROAD

TRADER'S ROAD

LEAVENWORTH GRANT AUG. 9, 1820
(UNRATIFIED)

NORTH

BLACK DOG'S VILLAGE

ST. PETER'S RIVER

PINICHON'S VILLAGE

•••• CAMPBELL RESERVATIONS, 1820

‑ ‑ ‑ PROPOSED BOUNDARY, 1850

░░ REDUCED AREA OF THE RESERVATION BY ACT OF CONGRESS, AUG. 26, 1852

‑·‑ REDUCED AREA, JAN. 24, 1871

slow to perceive the opportunity for profits in timely claims. The territorial legislature on November 1, 1849, passed a joint resolution introduced by Martin McLeod calling upon Delegate Sibley to use his influence at Washington to have the reserve confined to the region between the Mississippi and Minnesota rivers and to secure preëmptions for the bona fide settlers who had been driven off by the military. A preamble contained the information that the reservation was no longer necessary for military purposes and that "the Government [would] reap a speedy income from the sale thereof."[6] Sibley drafted a bill to reduce the reserve to one square mile between the rivers and to provide for the desired preëmptions, which his friend, Senator Douglas, introduced on March 1, 1850. It was referred first to the committee on territories and later to the committee on public lands, which on August 23 reported it with amendments.[7] The first session of the Thirty-first Congress closed without further action on the bill.

Meantime there was great excitement in the settlements adjacent to the reservation. Enterprising citizens, equally as confident as they were desirous that the delegate would find little or no difficulty in obtaining a reduction, if not abandonment, of the reservation, lost no time in staking out preëmption claims on the land. "The whole country on both sides of the river has been marked off," wrote one correspondent. "He [Goodhue] and some others went over it and marked their names on trees stuck up bits of board in the snow," wrote another. Philander Prescott desired Sibley to inform his old friends in good time of any relinquishment.[8]

[6] Laws, 1849, p. 161.

[7] 31 Congress, 1 session, Senate Journal, 189, 305, 418, 556 (serial 548). On March 4, 1851, the Minnesota Democrat printed the text of the bill. The proposed boundary of the reservation indicated on the map facing page 424, ante, is taken from a manuscript map of the "Military Reserve embracing Fort Snelling," in the possession of the Minnesota Historical Society.

[8] Letters to Sibley from Prescott, January 22, from Steele, March 12, from Lambert, March 18, from Brown, November 25, from Le Duc, December 9, 1850, from Stevens, January 6, 1851, Sibley Papers; Military Reserve on the St. Peter's River, 4 (31 Congress, 2 session, House Reports, no. 99 — serial 606); Chronicle and Register, March 9, 1850. "Log

The bill came up in the Senate in the following session of the same Congress, 1850–51, and was passed without serious consideration and without division. On February 5 it came before the House from the committee on public lands. Sibley explained the bill but was careful to state that it had been much changed from his original draft. Lively objections being interposed because the bill had not been referred to the committee on military affairs, Sibley was content that it be so referred. On March 3 there came in a report so sharply adverse that the bill was never heard of more. Although Sibley had made fair show of argument in its favor, he was not pleased with the amendments which struck out preëmptions for the ejected bona fide settlers.[9] A further reason for his indifference to its fate may perhaps be inferred from a certain letter he had written to Governor Ramsey, in which he said that he found himself awkwardly situated with reference to the reserve bill. The provision for the protection of all settlers would give the mill at the falls and the property there to Smith, Mitchell, and Rice.[10] Obviously the slaughter of his bill by the committee on military affairs caused him no chagrin, while the introduction of it set him right with the ardent claimstakers at home.

The negotiation of the treaties of Traverse des Sioux and Mendota in the midsummer of 1851, by which the Indians were to surrender their right of occupancy over many millions of acres in the territory, naturally aroused anew the expectation that Fort Snelling would become useless and that the abandoned reservation would soon be opened for settlement. Colonel Francis Lee, then in command at the fort, was so much concerned and so fearful that some extreme step might be taken that on August 21, without waiting to be called upon for an opinion, he addressed a document of

pens and shanties of all descriptions have rushed up in the twinkling of an axe handle." *Minnesota Democrat*, March 4, 1851.

[9] 31 Congress, 2 session, *Senate Journal*, 83, 89 (serial 586); *House Journal*, 235 (serial 594); *Congressional Globe*, 433; *Military Reserve on the St. Peter's River*, 1; West, *Sibley*, 160–163.

[10] Sibley to Ramsey, May 22, 1850, Ramsey Papers.

three thousand words on the subject to the adjutant general. Assuming that the post would remain an important one as a depot for other advanced posts, he pictured the absurdity of restricting the reservation to one square mile. It was his opinion, however, that a considerable reduction might be made without injurious results. He suggested a new boundary which would include all the land necessary for the uses of the post. The easterly line would be the Mississippi River; the northerly, Minnehaha Creek, Rice Lake, and Lake Amelia; and the westerly, a course mostly due south to the Minnesota River, which stream would form the southerly line. He would abandon all the lands east of the Mississippi and south of the Minnesota except a quarter section contiguous to each of the two ferries abreast of the post.[11]

On June 22, 1852, the House passed a bill to reduce and define the military reservation at Fort Snelling and to "secure the rights of actual settlers thereon." On motion of Sibley the title was amended by striking out the latter clause, for the reason that the section relating to settlers' rights had been struck out in committee of the whole. The bill was passed by the Senate without division after Senator Douglas, in reply to an inquiry, had assured that body that it contained no preëmption provision. The act established for the diminished reserve precisely the boundaries recommended by Colonel Francis Lee and approved by the war department. Sibley was consoled by an appended section which delayed the sale of 320 acres at Mendota for one year and permitted the "proper authorities" to enter the same as a town site under the existing law of May, 1844. The original

[11] *Sale of Fort Snelling Reservation*, 42–46. Following page 107 of this document is a "Plan of the Military Reserve at Fort Snelling," made under the direction of Lieutenant James J. Abert in 1853, which indicates the outlines of the reserve as suggested by Colonel Lee. The same lines are shown on the map facing page 424, *ante*. From a "Map of the Military Reservation of Fort Snelling, Minnesota, Surveyed by S. Eastman . . . 1857," in the archives of the war department, it appears that the lines of the reserved "quarter section" south of the Minnesota River, as finally drawn, were somewhat different from those shown on the Abert map. The Minnesota Historical Society has a blueprint copy of a tracing of the Eastman map.

section providing for preëmptions by settlers was replaced by one requiring the immediate survey of the excluded parts of the reservation and their sale at public auction.[12]   Two years now elapsed while the surveys were being made from the Wisconsin base and meridian and the routine proceedings of the general land office were being completed.   The excluded area east of the Mississippi was offered for sale at the Stillwater land office on September 11, 1854. According to tradition and the ethics of the border a sufficient number of squatters were present at the public sale to prevent the approach and interference of undesired competitors.   As each parcel was offered a bid of $1.25 was promptly made, and in each case it was the highest bid.   In this manner 4,523.47 acres, all now included in the city of St. Paul, were sold for $5,654.28.[13]

When Robert Smith obtained a lease of the government mills at the Falls of St. Anthony, Franklin Steele, who had extended his business as sutler at the fort into other lines, doubtless became conscious that he had been outgeneraled. As he was already holding down a claim about the fort, he could not personally establish another at the falls; but he might have done what he soon afterwards did with regard to land lying above Smith's claim.   On June 10, 1849, he took his clerk, John Harrington Stevens, to the falls to see the lay of the land and dropped a timely hint that if Stevens so desired he would have no difficulty in obtaining from the war department a permit to occupy a quarter section on the west bank of the river.   The permit was granted on condition

---

[12] *Congressional Globe*, 32 Congress, 1 session, 1594, 2271; *Statutes at Large*, 10: 36.

[13] *Fort Snelling Investigation*, 433 (35 Congress, 1 session, *House Reports*, no. 351 — serial 965). The *Minnesota Democrat* of July 12, 1854, mentions a meeting of the Military Reserve Claim Association at which a resolution was passed to "repair to the land sale *en masse*, to protect our houses from the bids of wealthy and sordid speculators" and to appoint Marshall as "public bidder."   The issue of September 13 contains an account of the sale. The *St. Anthony Express* for January 6, 1855, contains a letter written by T. M. Fullerton, register, and W. Holcombe, receiver at Stillwater, describing the sale as follows: "The utmost harmony prevailed. . . . We neither saw nor heard of the presence of any deadly weapons or threats to use them, but for some half dozen more or less of cudgels or canes, left on the ground after the people had dispersed, we should not have inferred that any violent measures had been anticipated."

that a ferry, established by Steele in 1847 for government teams and troops going to and returning from Fort Gaines, be maintained free from tolls. In the fall of the same year Colonel Stevens built near the ferry a modest dwelling, which is still in existence in one of the parks of Minneapolis, and in the following summer he established his family in it. He had for a neighbor the tenant of the mills.[14]

The location of squatters' claims while the defeated bill of 1850–51 was before Congress has been noted. The claimants on the large northern portion of the reserve were almost wholly citizens of St. Anthony Falls, who would probably have made things unpleasant for any residents of "Pig's Eye" who should have ventured on the terrain. There is a tradition that officers of the garrison made some profit by supporting favored claimants against troublesome claim-jumpers and that some of them were virtual partners in lawless claims. If such cases there were, little or no recorded evidence of weight has been found, and the verdict of "not proven" may be charitably entered.

The pendency and passage of the reduction act of 1852 gave the claimants courage to hold on to their lots, but not enough to warrant them in building and improving on a large scale. As a result not more than twelve dwellings were erected in 1852, but claim shanties were plentiful. It should be noted that numerous squatters from distant parts of the country had made claims on Indian land outside of but adjacent to the reservation area, upon which they built houses and began cultivation. These settlers and the few resident claimants on the reserve now formed a community in the interest of which the legislature of 1852 established the new county of Hennepin. At an election held on October 10 a board of county commissioners was chosen. At its first meeting ten days later the board located the county seat at the Falls of St. Anthony on the west side of the Mississippi

---

[14] Stevens, *Personal Recollections*, 28, 84, 86; Atwater and Stevens, *Minneapolis and Hennepin County*, 1: 33; Warner and Foote, *Hennepin County*, 341.

and gave it the name of "Albion." The villagers were not pleased with the colorless title. In a communication to the *St. Anthony Express* of November 5, one of the preëmptors proposed the name "Minnehapolis." In the next issue of the paper the editor, George D. Bowman, gave his approval, but suggested the omission of the letter *h*. The name met with general approval and the county commissioners not long after formally adopted it. On December 3, 1852, the first common school was opened in a district established by the county commissioners. So many difficulties arose from the overlapping of claims made in good faith and so much annoyance came from unconscionable claim-jumpers that immediately after the passage of the reduction act there was organized the "Equal Right and Impartial Protection Claim Association of Hennepin County, M. T." A board of arbiters settled disputes, sometimes assessing money payments to equalize rights. A single instance of corporal admonition on the bare back of a dishonest intruder ended claim-jumping.[15]

The unascertained increase in the village in 1853 must have been considerable, for we find the *St. Anthony Express* of August 6, 1853, congratulating the west side on the possession of a church, a school, a county court, a masonic lodge, an agricultural society, a sawmill, and a gristmill and predicting the early establishment of a store. The editor was merely amused at a suggestion he had heard that a rivalry could ever spring up between the smart settlement on the west side and queenly St. Anthony with her big sawmill.[16]

As the time approached for the public sale in the early fall of 1854, there was much anxiety and searching of hearts among the claimants. They had in their claim association the machinery for much the same procedure which was

[15] Stevens, *Personal Recollections*, 128, 136, 171, 177, 180, 184–188; Warner and Foote, *Hennepin County*, 173, 183, 341; *Laws*, 1852, p. 51. "All Saints" and "Hennepin" were proposed as names for the county seat. The county seat was established by an act of the legislature on February 21, 1854. *Laws*, 1854, p. 86. In the *Minneapolis Journal* for January 7, 1917, there is a discussion of the question "Who Named Minneapolis?" by the Honorable John B. Gilfillan, confirming the statement in the text.

[16] Stevens dates the prosperity of the infant city of Minneapolis from this year and remarks on the marvelous number of marriages. *Personal Recollections*, 189.

adopted by St. Paul claimants on the land adjacent to their
town, but as American-born citizens, many seriously religious, they did not take kindly to a plan which involved mis-
demeanor if not crime. After numerous consultations, it was
decided to approach a benevolent Congress with a petition
that they be allowed the same preëmption rights as belonged
to settlers on public lands in general. On February 2, 1854,
the territorial legislature sent a memorial to Congress praying that the pioneers who had made the wilderness blossom
as the rose should have the benefit of the preëmption laws
and should not be "exposed to the merciless cupidity of
avaricious speculators." The commissioner of the general
land office, the Honorable John Wilson, took a sympathetic
view of the situation, postponed the public sale, and drew a
bill to grant the prayer of the humble petitioners, which was
introduced into the House late in January, 1855. In a
letter read in the House he stated that but for the improvements made by the settlers the land would be worth no more
than the mass of the public domain — an opinion which the
settlers themselves would hardly have dared to offer. When
the bill came up for consideration in the House, Eastman of
Wisconsin said that preëmption on reserved lands was wrong.
It gave influential men, "by the strong arm of money," the
right to make claims personally, or through employees; poor
men had no chance. Delegate Rice was surprised that a
western man could allow speculators to put in sealed bids
against these hardy pioneers and turn them out of house and
home. "This surely," he said, "is not the treatment which
this Government should give these men whom the goddess
of liberty sent into the great West to enlarge the area of freedom." He held up a petition signed by five hundred men,
women, and children, and declared that the improvements
they had made were worth $1,246,000. They did not ask
for a land grant; they asked only for a right to buy. It was
urged that there never was a more just proposition presented
for consideration by the House. When the bill came to the

third reading, Eastman said that after conversation with gentlemen from Minnesota he was satisfied it ought to pass; and pass it did, without division. It became a law on March 2, 1855.[17]

A section of the act required that the claimants should prove up and make their payments within three months from the passage. By the middle of May they had complied, and for the sum of $24,668.37, less costs of survey, they obtained certificates of title to 19,773.87 acres of land. Upon these acres a large part of the city of Minneapolis has been built. It is safe to say that, although some profits were made in the transaction, hardly a single great fortune resulted. After a short term of years Colonel Stevens turned over his interests to Steele and began anew as a pioneer of Glencoe, McLeod County.[18]

The Fort Snelling reserve retained the limits fixed by the act of June 22, 1852, til long after the close of the Civil and Indian wars; but there was a period of three years during which possession was in the hands of a private citizen to whom the government had sold and conveyed the reservation. The buyer was Franklin Steele, already known to the reader. The sale was made under a blanket amendment to the military appropriation bill of 1857 authorizing the secretary of war to sell any military reservations not needed for military purposes. The considerations which moved Floyd, Buchanan's secretary of war, to select for sale the reservation at Fort Snelling are a matter of conjecture. An insinua-

[17] *Laws*, 1854, p. 162. *Congressional Globe*, 33 Congress, 2 session, 449, 487–489, 504; *Statutes at Large*, 10: 627. Writing to Stevens on February 4, 1855, Rice said that Sibley's right-hand man, Benjamin C. Eastman, was the only man in the House who opposed the bill. "It is supposed here that Sibley looks upon Minneapolis as a rival to Mendota — hence his opposition. . . . No one here doubts but Sibley has secretly opposed the interests of the settlers upon the reservation. He is a double dealing hypocrite." Stevens Papers.

[18] Stevens, in *Minnesota Historical Collections*, 10: 265 (part 1). Light on the business relations of Steele and Stevens may be found in the letters of Steele to Stevens, March 10, 17, 1856, in the Stevens Papers; Stevens to Steele, November 22, 1858, September 16, 1861, in the Steele Papers; and E. C. Gale to Folwell, January 13, 1914, in the Folwell Papers. There is a statement of the "number of acres, the quantity sold, purchasers, and price of the land separated" in *Fort Snelling Investigation*, 423–433. A list of the original patentees and a map showing the location of the sections may be found in Atwater and Stevens. *Minneapolis and Hennepin County*, 1: 36, 37.

tion that he expected to share in the profits of a big land speculation can not be entertained in the absence of any proper evidence. Another suggestion that the sale was part of a scheme to weaken the North in an expected war between the states is absurd, because the war which did follow was four years away and was regarded at the time, even by extremists, as but a remote possibility. It is sufficient to say that Floyd believed the reserve to be of little value and no longer needed for military purposes, and therefore he was easily persuaded by friends whom he liked to please to order the sale.

The same considerations which moved Floyd to order the sale doubtless prompted him to depart from the customary usage of public sale and enter into a clandestine contract with an individual citizen. The whole tract of over seven thousand acres was sold to Franklin Steele on July 2, 1857, for ninety thousand dollars, of which one-third was presently paid. A few weeks later the appalling financial panic of 1857 spread over the country and Steele and his associates were unable to pay the second installment of the purchase money. Nevertheless, the accommodating secretary allowed the contract to run and in the following spring ordered out the little garrison guarding quartermaster's stores at the fort and gave Steele full possession. He remained in undisturbed possession till the outbreak of the rebellion in the southern states. Whether Governor Ramsey obtained any formal permission to occupy the old fort and the adjacent building and lands is not known, but Steele made not the least objection to occupation by such responsible tenants as the state of Minnesota and the United States. Governor Ramsey designated Fort Snelling as the place of rendezvous for the First Minnesota in April, 1861. From that time till the last squad of soldiers was mustered out late in 1866 the fort and the whole reservation remained in possession of the United States, except that Steele retained the valuable ferry privilege over the Mississippi River. Early in 1868 Steele filed with the war department a bill for eighty-one months' rent at two thousand dollars a month, which amounted to one hundred and sixty-two thousand dollars, and proposed that the sixty thousand dollars due on the contract of 1857 together with the interest thereon, be allowed as an offset. The claim remained in question for two years, when a settlement was reached, which resulted, in January, 1871, in a final reduction of the reserve. Upon the assumption that Steele's title had been completely vacated, the government conveyed to him by deed some 6,400 acres and retained 1,520 acres for military uses. Fort Snelling has ever since remained an important interior army post.[19]

The reader does not need to be told that the object of the purchase of Fort Snelling was to make a profit on the sales of the land. One of the first operations was the sale of an undivided twenty-seventh part of the tract to three of the most expert and enterprising of the dealers in Minnesota lands at a price that indicates a valuation of double the original purchase price. A town site had been laid out and surveyed into lots and a street had been graded when the panic of 1857 put an end to operations. What visions, if any, were indulged in of a great metropolitan city of the Northwest, with St. Paul, St. Anthony, and Minneapolis as prosperous contributing suburbs, have not been revealed.[20]

[19] The notorious "Sale of Fort Snelling" is more fully treated in the Appendix, no. 13, *post*. See the map facing page 424 for the boundary established in 1871.

[20] The reader may be interested in the notable prophecy of Elisée Reclus, in his great work, *The Earth and Its Inhabitants*, in nineteen volumes, *North America*, 3: 315 (New York, 1893); " The original intention was to group the metropolis of the upper Mississippi basin round about this station [*Fort Snelling*] . . . spontaneous effect will . . . ultimately be given to this intention, for with the continual growth of these urban groups [*St. Paul and Minneapolis*] the fort must become the natural centre of the whole aggregate."

APPENDIX

1. THE FARIBAULT CLAIM[1]

JEAN BAPTISTE FARIBAULT was a notable figure among the early Indian traders of the Northwest. He was the son of a French lawyer who came to Canada as military secretary of Montcalm's army and remained there after the conquest. He left school at the age of sixteen to pass six years in mercantile employments. With such education, at the age of twenty-four he entered in 1798 the service of the Northwest Company. For ten years he carried on trade at various western posts, the last five years at the Little Rapids of the Minnesota River, two and a half miles south of the village of Carver, where a band of Wahpeton Sioux then lived. While there he married a mixed-blood woman and gave up expectations of returning to Canada. In 1809 he established himself as an independent trader at Prairie du Chien. During the War of 1812 he remained loyal to the American cause and was imprisoned and stripped of his possessions by the British. He had to some extent recovered his losses when Colonel Leavenworth in 1819 arrived with his troops on his way to the upper Mississippi. Leavenworth was so much impressed with Faribault's intelligence and his knowledge of the Dakota language and customs that he urged him to move his business to the neighborhood of the new fort soon to be established. In the spring of 1820 Faribault accordingly appeared at Leavenworth's cantonment and was permitted to locate his cabin and storehouse on Pike's Island.[2]

The motives of Colonel Leavenworth for acquiring Indian lands additional to those purchased by Pike remain a matter of conjecture. No evidence has been found to justify Taliaferro's insinuation that he had a view to private gain.[3] His admiration for Faribault and his gratitude for his aid in gaining the consent of the Indians to the cession sufficiently account for his embodiment in the treaty of the grant of Pike's Island to the trader's wife. The grantee was not to remain long in possession of her estate. The watchful Indian agent was, or became, opposed

---

[1] See *ante*, p. 144.

[2] Sibley, in *Minnesota Historical Collections*, 3: 168–179. See also Franklyn Curtiss-Wedge, ed., *History of Rice and Steele Counties*, 1: 80–85 (Chicago, 1910), which contains an interesting paper on the Faribaults by Stephen Jewett, and J. A. Kiester, *History of Faribault County*, 35–37 (Minneapolis, 1896).

[3] Taliaferro to Plympton, July 10, 1839, in *Purchase of Island — Confluence of the St. Peter's and Mississippi Rivers*, 15 (26 Congress, 1 session, *House Documents*, no. 82 — serial 365). The outlines of the "Leavenworth Grant" are indicated on the map facing page 424, *ante*.

to the transaction. Before a year had passed he wrote to Calhoun, then secretary of war, on June 30, 1821, calling his attention to the obvious inconvenience of such a cession, and recommending that Faribault be ousted with pay for his improvements. To this the secretary replied, on August 14, that, as Colonel Leavenworth's treaty had not been laid before the Senate, the grants of land contained in it had no validity, and he directed the agent so to inform the individuals concerned. The duty was, of course, performed. Within a few months Faribault removed his effects, household and mercantile, and he never afterwards occupied the island or any part of it. In 1826, or a little later, he established himself at New Hope, afterwards Mendota, where he later built a substantial stone dwelling which is still standing.[4]

So far as is known, no claim of ownership was made by Mrs. Faribault or in her behalf for sixteen years. When the Sioux treaty of 1837 was being negotiated in Washington, Alexis Bailly, a son-in-law of Mrs. Faribault, and Samuel C. Stambaugh, a citizen of Pennsylvania, who was about that time the sutler at Fort Snelling, produced the unratified Leavenworth treaty and asked that the grant of Pike's Island to Mrs. Faribault contained therein be recognized and confirmed. The secretary of war, acting for the government, declined to have any provision on the subject inserted in the new treaty. He apprehended difficulty or delay, likely to impair the treaty, but he was willing to leave the claim to be considered by itself as if no treaty had been made. This concession was evidently construed as an invitation to prosecute the claim. On January 17, 1838, before the treaty of the previous September had been ratified, Stambaugh, the principal attorney in the case, wrote a letter to the secretary, in which he assumed as beyond controversy Mrs. Faribault's ownership; but, instead of asking that she be given possession of the land, he proposed a sale to the government for military purposes. He concurred in the opinion of all interested that the island ought to belong to the United States, so long as a military post was maintained adjacent to it. Ignoring the purchase by Pike, he suggested that if the land "would become part of the public domain otherwise than for military purposes" it would be settled by citizens as the most prominent town site at the head of navigation, whence whisky would be introduced to the troops and the Indians. Although it would sell for ten times the price if put upon the market, Faribault would be content with twelve thousand dollars.[5]

    [4] *Purchase of Island*, 7, 12, 16. In *Minnesota Historical Collections*, 3: 177, Sibley gives 1822 as the date of Faribault's removal from the island, but, in a letter in the Sibley Papers, written on March 15, 1852, to John C. Spencer, secretary of war, he states that Colonel Snelling ordered the Faribaults off the island in 1821. The dates 1822 and 1826 are given in Curtiss-Wedge, *Rice and Steele Counties* 1: 83.
    [5] *Purchase of Island*, 1–3, 18–20.

The matter came before Congress early in the winter of 1838–39, and a resolution was passed with little or no debate authorizing the secretary of war to enter into contract with the Faribaults for the purchase of the island, but requiring him to report his action for approval or rejection.[6] Within a few days after the passage of the act Stambaugh addressed a letter to the secretary of war reminding him that Congress had authorized by law the purchase of the island from the proprietors and announcing his readiness to convey the title. He renewed the offer to sell for twelve thousand dollars. The commissioner of Indian affairs, the Honorable T. Hartley Crawford, wrote Poinsett about the same time recommending the purchase and an appropriation. "This case," he said, "occupies a position of its own." On general principles the government could not recognize such grants; but the island was wanted and to avoid delay and difficulty — no particulars were suggested — it would be judicious to make the purchase. The resolution of Congress, although nominally conferring authority, seemed to him to carry an injunction. It may be presumed that the action of the secretary was expected to be sympathetic. He did regard the act as mandatory, and on the early date of March 12 he signed an instrument in which he agreed to pay for the Faribault title the sum of twelve thousand dollars, provided that Congress should ratify the agreement and make an appropriation of money to carry it out. He would recommend and ask for the appropriation.[7] Had the secretary waited for the unsolicited advice of Agent Taliaferro, furnished in a letter of April 19, 1839, he probably would have been less precipitate in obeying the implied injunction. In this letter the agent protested against the recognition of a purely "fictitious claim." The land was the property of the United States by virtue of the treaties of 1805 and 1837. The Leavenworth treaty was a nullity because it had never been submitted to the Senate for confirmation. He had, as directed by Secretary Calhoun, notified the claimants that no grants had been made to them.[8] This volunteer counsel had sufficient influence to move the secretary to look for further information. Under his direction the commissioner of Indian affairs wrote to Major Joseph Plympton, commanding at Fort Snelling, and suggested an interview with Agent Taliaferro. In a letter of July 10 to Plympton the agent did not mince matters. He denounced the fraud practiced on the Senate and expressed the hope "that *cupidity* may be defeated and the designing knaves unmasked." Two days later Plympton and Taliaferro interrogated two Sioux chiefs and some headmen, who denied that their nation had ever given the island to anybody.

---

[6] *Statutes at Large*, 5: 365. The resolution was approved on February 13, 1839.
[7] *Purchase of Island*, 3–5, 8–10.
[8] Taliaferro Letter Book, B.

Thus fortified, Plympton on July 18 wrote to the commissioner at length, giving the now familiar history of the claim and assuring him that Pike's Island had been in the continuous possession of the United States since 1819. A letter by the same officer to the adjutant general of the army, dated September 12, repeated the statements.[9] With such papers before him Secretary Poinsett drew up a report, which was laid before the Senate on January 7, 1840. His conclusion was that the island was the undoubted property of the United States, for two principal reasons: (1) the operation of the treaties of 1805 and 1837; (2) the total invalidity of the spurious Leavenworth treaty. There was no recommendation of an appropriation.[10] No serious attempt was made to secure the passage of a separate act to ratify the contract and to appropriate the necessary money. The less risky plan of obtaining the insertion of an item in the army appropriation bill was adopted. As usual, this bill lingered long in its passage. Meantime the attorneys and others were occupied in efforts to insure success. They were doubtless much encouraged by the comforting though ambiguous statement of Secretary Poinsett to the Senate military committee in July that in his opinion the island was "necessary to the police discipline and security of the post on the Upper Mississippi" and that he considered the value to be not less than ten thousand dollars nor more than twelve thousand dollars.[11]

Extant documents, found among the Sibley Papers and not heretofore published, show that the American Fur Company or some of its prominent officials took no little interest in the Faribault claim. They had two grounds of concern, as will appear. Seventeen days after the contract of March 12, 1839, Ramsay Crooks, president of the company, wrote to Sibley, the resident partner at Mendota, that the Faribault title had been recognized and that the island had been purchased for twelve thousand dollars. It was apparently his assumption that so solemn an agreement could not fail of ratification by Congress. In a second letter to Sibley, dated May 6, 1839, Crooks observed that the sale of the island would enable the company to obtain a fair price for its property at New Hope. The sale of New Hope was again mentioned in a letter from Crooks to Sibley, dated April 7, 1840, evidently in expectation that the desired appropriation would be made by the Congress then in session. The writer was willing to sell New Hope for a reasonable price. "No doubt it is admirably calculated," he wrote, "for the Indian Agency." He asked Sibley to send him the original title to the property

[9] *Purchase of Island*, 11–14, 16–18; Taliaferro Journal, July 11, 12, 1839.

[10] *Purchase of Island*, 1–3.

[11] Report of the committee on military affairs, in 34 Congress, 1 session, *Senate Reports*, no. 193, p. 2 (serial 836).

with a diagram and to give his opinion of its value. It is difficult to surmise what other title to New Hope the company could have had than one derived from Duncan Campbell, one of the intended beneficiaries of the Leavenworth treaty. Another ground for concern in the claim was the desire to collect from Stambaugh money due by him to the company or to members of it. It could not have been a large amount. Dousman, writing to Sibley on March 31, 1840, said, "Stambaugh is the only man who can manage it to advantage, and as we must get our pay out of him we must not let this opportunity slip." The officials of the fur company were not opposed to the urgent pressure of the attorney for a larger compensation for his labors than the three thousand dollars originally bargained for with Faribault. Dousman, in the letter cited, said that Stambaugh "ought to get at least $4000, if not the $5000 which he asks."[12] To prevent any mischance, Faribault was pleased to give a power of attorney to President Ramsay Crooks to receive the expected money from the treasury and to distribute it properly.[13]

When the army appropriation bill, which had come from the House, was under consideration by the Senate on July 17, an amendment was proposed providing for the purchase of Pike's Island for twelve thousand dollars. The matter was debated by Senators Benton, Buchanan, Calhoun, and others, and the proposition was agreed to by a vote of 16 to 13. Three days later the House refused to concur by a vote of 99 to 49.[14] Instead of exercising his power of attorney, Crooks was obliged to inform Sibley on August 22 that the item had been struck out of the appropriation bill, at the instigation, as he had heard, of a member from Virginia, a relative of the late Indian agent.[15] He probably made too generous an estimate of the influence of the retired official. Nevertheless, Secretary Poinsett sent to the attorney for the claimants, on August 13, 1840, a letter of condolence and encouragement. He remembered perfectly that during the negotiations of 1837 he had given him assurance that the rights of Mrs. Pelagie Faribault should not be prejudiced by not being

[12] Sibley Papers.
[13] Stambaugh to Dousman, March 6, 1840, Sibley Papers. Writing on December 4, 1839, to Dousman, Stambaugh expressed his confidence that the claim would be allowed and the appropriation made, provided Faribault and his wife sent their deed to Washington promptly, either to Buchanan or to Doty. "Mr. Sibley will understand how to draw it up." He also asked that Faribault direct the "purchase money to be paid to Ramsay Crooks, or to his order in any of the Banks — that is *eight thousand dollars*, & the balance four thousand to my order in Washington." His interest was to be one-fourth, and he charged one thousand dollars for expenses. He characterized the island as a "windfall for Mr. Faribault, which he should not neglect." Sibley Papers.
[14] 26 Congress, 1 session, *Senate Journal*, 520 (serial 353); *House Journal*, 1334 (serial 362); *Congressional Globe*, 535, 544. Millard Fillmore voted for the amendment, J. Q. Adams against it. In a letter in the Sibley Papers, written on April 7, 1840, to Sibley, Crooks acknowledges the "powerful aid" of Buchanan. The debates are not reported in the *Globe*.
[15] Sibley Papers.

inserted in the treaty. He regarded the contract as existing and advised the attorney to await the further action of Congress.[16] The indefatigable attorney was discouraged, but not disheartened. In anticipation of a renewed effort in the following winter he placed before Sibley in a letter of November 4, 1840, his plan of campaign. The secretary of war seemed disposed to support the claim and it was probable that the new administration, Harrison's, would not be so careful of public funds. He desired to be furnished with a "strong paper" signed by Sioux chiefs in council in the presence of the Indian agent to counteract the influence of Taliaferro and Plympton. The chiefs, he said, should declare that they had never recognized Pike's treaty and had never received money or goods in pursuance of it. They were also to assert that they would never have signed the treaty of 1837 had they not been solemnly assured at the time that the grant to Mrs. Faribault in 1820 would be protected. It was also suggested that Scott Campbell, the old interpreter, be spoken to and advised that "if Ferribault's claim succeeds it will secure a confirmation of all the claims *under Leavenworth's Treaty!* and would greatly benefit him." The attorney did not forget to drop a hint in regard to his compensation. All he could expect to receive would not compensate him for his time, trouble, expense, and vexation. He thought Faribault ought to be content with six thousand dollars. Then followed this enigmatical sentence: "He will not only make this handsome sum by my interference, but it will as I said before, secure him & those claiming under him, the possession of all the land on the St. Peters & Mississippi conveyed by the same grant."[17]

The short session of Congress in 1841 passed without action on the Faribault claim, but hope did not vanish. On April 23 Crooks wrote Sibley that Stambaugh had exerted himself with wonderful perseverence and would have succeeded if Poinsett had kept his promise. "In the face of his own written assurance, he chose to forget it." Crooks had declined a proposal of a committee to accept ten thousand dollars. He had conversed with the new secretary of war and had no doubt of eventual success. He desired to learn from his correspondent whether Faribault would accept a sum less than twelve thousand dollars and how much he, Crooks, might allow Colonel Stambaugh for his extraordinary exertions and expenses. Crooks also stated that he expected to ascertain the views of Secretary Bell with regard to the purchase of New Hope and that he had requested General Wool to look at the property on his next visit. "Be so good as [to] see the General on the subject: for if he recommends

---

[16] Report of the committee on military affairs, in 34 Congress, 1 session, *Senate Reports*, no. 193, p. 1 (serial 836).

[17] Sibley Papers.

it, the Secretary of War will probably buy it. What ought the price to be? or rather, what sum had we better accept?"[18]

The failure of 1841 did not, therefore, deter the attorneys and friends of the long-suffering Faribaults from renewed efforts to obtain partial if not full justice from the Congress of 1842. The officials of the fur company again interposed their coöperation. On March 7 Crooks asked Sibley for an extension of his power of attorney so that he might bargain for a sum less than twelve thousand dollars and might settle upon the compensation of Stambaugh. On March 21 he wrote again that, whatever might be the value of the island, the government was bound to fulfill the Poinsett contract and could not honorably annul it. Meantime Sibley had opened the subject on his own motion to the Honorable John C. Spencer, secretary of war, in a letter dated March 15, 1842. He recited the history of the Faribault claim as he understood it. "In 1819," he wrote, "this island was given by the Dacotah or Sioux Indians to Mrs. Pelagie Faribault, a half breed woman of their nation." Colonel Snelling had driven the family off in 1821 and the government had ever since held possession. The valuable island still belonged to Mrs. Faribault, who relied on the justice of the government. The important element in the letter was an appeal to the secretary that, if the purchase should not be concluded, Mrs. Faribault be allowed "to take and retain possession of it." "I trust, sir," he wrote, "that you will issue an order to the Commanding Officer at Fort Snelling requiring him to place her in immediate possession of her own property." The writer could not have expected an early compliance with his request, for on April 18 he framed, as their attorney, a new petition for Mr. and Mrs. Faribault for relief by Congress. But the session of 1842 wore on without action on the claim. Robert Stuart, the well-known head of the company's establishment at Mackinac Island, on August 1 wrote to Sibley from Washington: "Mr. Stanley promises me every 2 or 3 days, that a bill giving the Isl[d] to Farribault, shall be reported, '*but non appearance is the case as yet.*' . . . Stambaugh is working for it, but I fear he will do it more harm than good." His despair was justified, but as late as July 7 Crooks had written to Sibley that they would have had the money in hand but "for the interference of the military in your country."[19]

The industrious Stambaugh and the sympathetic officials of the American Fur Company now resigned their expectations of securing from Congress justice for their injured clients and some incidental advantages to themselves. That a ray of hope long continued to shine may be inferred from the fact that on August 30, 1848, Jean Faribault executed a

[18] Sibley Papers.
[19] Sibley Papers.

warranty deed of Pike's Island to Henry H. Sibley in consideration of
twelve thousand dollars, the receipt of which was acknowledged. This deed
was acknowledged before Joseph R. Brown, clerk of courts at Stillwater,
on October 23, 1848. Mrs. Faribault had died on June 19, 1847, and her
surviving husband was apparently assumed to be her heir or successor.
It may be doubted whether Faribault received payment in cash or things
of value and whether the grantee ever took possession.[20]

So far as is known the claim did not again appear in Congress till the
winter of 1855, when on January 23 Senator Bell of Tennessee laid before
the Senate the memorial of J. B. and Pelagie Faribault asking payment
for their island according to the contract of March 13, 1839. The Senate
committee on military affairs thereupon submitted a report reciting the
contract and the recommendation of Secretary Bell dated September 2,
1842, that payment be made. The report concluded with the astonishing
information that "upon this island Fort Snelling now stands." When
the Indian appropriation bill for the year came from the House, Senator
George W. Jones of Tennessee offered an amendment providing for the
payment of the Faribault claim in the sum of twelve thousand dollars
with interest from March 23, 1839. He explained to the Senate that in
1832 [sic] Colonel Leavenworth had made a treaty with the Sioux tribe
in which the island at the junction of the Mississippi and Minnesota rivers
had been reserved to the claimants; that Congress had authorized a
contract to be framed for the payment but had neglected to make the
necessary appropriation. The government had held possession of the
land and had built Fort Snelling on it. "It seems to me," he said, "that
not a man on earth can object to it." The Senate did not object and the
amendment passed without a roll call. It came up in the House on
February 27. Breckinridge of Kentucky championed it, on the strength
of information derived, as he stated, from Senator Bell. The island
had been set apart by a solemn treaty, which gave the claimants an
indisputable title. But the government had built a fort on it. This
statement he repeated in the course of the debate. The report of the
Senate committee was then read. A member suggested a doubt about the
location of Fort Snelling on the island, whereupon the reading clerk discovered an interlineation which had been overlooked stating that the
island was merely "a part of the military reservation of Fort Snelling."
Eastman of Wisconsin said his recollection agreed with that. The Senate
amendment was lost; but the Senate conferees succeeded in securing
the submission of a substitute providing for the payment of twelve
thousand dollars (interest not mentioned) in case the secretary of war

[20] Sibley Papers.

should be satisfied of the validity of the title and the conveyance to the United States. This substitute was agreed to by both houses.[21]

It would appear that the secretary of the interior was not satisfied with the title and conveyance, since he authorized no payment. On May 20, 1856, Senator Jones of Tennessee presented additional papers in the case, and on June 23 a report from the military committee recommended that long-delayed justice be done the Faribaults by the passage of a bill for the payment of twelve thousand dollars with interest from the date of contract.[22] No action was taken in that session of Congress, but on February 7, 1857, Senator Jones had the satisfaction of having his bill taken up for consideration by the Senate. He informed the Senate that the government had ordered the purchase of the island, that the purchase had accordingly been made, and that a fort had been built on the land. If Secretary Davis had doubts about the validity of the title, the military committee had none. Senator Bell, also of Tennessee, insisted that Secretary Poinsett's action at the time of the negotiation of the Sioux treaty of 1837 amounted to a recognition of the claim. The government took the island subject to a condition and "perhaps" built a fort on it. Senator Weller said, "You . . . established your military post there, and . . . will not allow them to have the money . . . nor will you give them back the land!" A motion by Senator Clay to pay the claim, if the attorney-general should be satisfied with the right of the parties to convey, was lost without division. The Senate seems to have accepted the theory that a legal conveyance was not important. The government had needed the island and had agreed to pay the parties in possession for a surrender. The bill passed by a vote of 31 to 7. When reported to the House a few days later, the bill was referred to its committee on military affairs.[23] No further proceedings have yet been discovered.

[21] Report of the committee on military affairs, in 33 Congress, 2 session, *Senate Reports*, no. 482 (serial 775); *Senate Journal*, 151, 202, 360 (serial 745); *House Journal*, 518 (serial 776); *Congressional Globe*, 728, 978. It may be remarked that Delegate Rice did not enlighten the House in regard to a matter on which he must have had knowledge.

[22] Report of the committee on military affairs, in 34 Congress, 1 session, *Senate Reports*, no. 193 (serial 836). The document shows the earmarks of a claimant's attorney.

[23] 34 Congress, 3 session, *Senate Journal*, 177 (serial 873); *House Journal*, 385, 421 (serial 892); *Congressional Globe*, 620.

As this appendix goes to print a letter signed "A. Faribault, per Richard," dated Faribault, February 8, 1868, which probably belongs in the Sibley Papers, is discovered. In this letter the following statement is made: "Perhaps you remember that Pike's Island was sold for $12000 out of which, my father paid Col. Stambeau one half. Mr Crooks of New York $1000, and McCallan [*McClelland?*] of Washington $1000. for collection. The balance was devided amongst six families, Fredrick and David Faribault, Mrs. Fowler, Mrs. Bailey, Mrs O. Faribault and myself." The statement cannot possibly be true. There was no sale of Pike's Island to be remembered. Alexander Faribault confusedly recalled the claim for an appropriation by Congress of twelve thousand dollars and a proposed division of the money,

2. THE REPURCHASE OF THE FORT SNELLING RESERVATION[24]

When Major Thomas Forsyth in the late summer of 1819 distributed goods to the value of two thousand dollars to the Mdewakanton chiefs, Little Crow was the only one of them who distinctly acknowledged that the money was paid in compensation for the Indian right to the land bargained for by Lieutenant Pike fourteen years before.[25] It was generally understood that a cession had been made, but there was no clear understanding among the Indians about the area of it. For many years while woodland was plentiful in the neighborhood of the fort, no complaints were made about the cutting of firewood for the use of the garrison; but doubts lingered in the minds of the Indians about the amount of land they had ceded. On September 7, 1830, a prominent chief called on the agent at St. Peter's and the commanding officer at Fort Snelling to learn the exact bounds of the reservation about the fort. He said that "*his people* wished to be *immediately* informed." The agent, with the text of Pike's treaty before him, rehearsed the now familiar description: from below the fort up the Mississippi to include the Falls of St. Anthony, extending back nine miles on each side of the river. He added that Colonel Leavenworth, by including in his treaty "4½ miles less than Pike," had led the Indians "into an error which has since given us much trouble," inducing them "to aver that they only gave Pike a *mile* around the present scite [*sic*] of Fort Snelling, or as they say just as far as can be seen around the Fort without *elevateing the eyes* — which would be at the rate of two miles in some places one mile in others."[26]

On June 18, 1836, the Sioux of three neighboring villages assembled at the agency to hold a council with the agent and the commanding officer of the post. Their spokesmen complained specifically that two hundred dollars promised for eighteen hundred cords of wood cut in 1831 had not been paid. They also renewed the allegation that they had never been paid for the reservation, which they understood to be two miles square. Again Taliaferro attributes the "idle sentiments" of the Indians to Colonel Leavenworth, who, adopting the ideas of the Indians, had bargained for "less by more than half of Pikes Cession." The text of the treaty of September 29, 1837, makes no allusion to the subject, but it may be

but the desired appropriation was never made. Pike's Island remained government property till January 4, 1871, when it was patented to Franklin Steele. George J. Ries to the author, April 29, 1921, Folwell Papers, in which is cited Book of Deeds 61, p. 255, in the office of the register of deeds of Ramsey County.

[24] See *ante*, p. 136.

[25] Forsyth to General William Clark, September 23, 1819, in *Minnesota Historical Collections*, 3: 165.

[26] Taliaferro Journal. See *ante*, p. 93.

suspected that parol inducements were made at the time of the negotiation at Washington to obtain the signatures of the Sioux delegates.[27]

On June 22, 1838, a local chief went to Taliaferro and demanded
payment for some wood which had been cut near his village without his
consent. The agent explained the position of the government and its
right to the whole "nine miles square" about the post, but said that
because of doubts in regard to the extent of the reservation, the "President had directed $4,000 more to be paid." On October 15 of the same
year, Taliaferro recorded the fact that he had that day paid to the five
neighboring Sioux bands the sum of four thousand dollars and added the
following statement: "This sum settles all difficulties in future to the
Land and the use of fire wood & timber destroyed by the Troops and
even the Traders. The Indians of course have now no just cause of
complaint against the United States on this Score."[28] Still, on March 11,
1850, Prescott wrote to Sibley, "The Indians talk a great deal and say
they have never sold the Reserve to the Govt. &c. &c."[29]

3. THE DAKOTA DICTIONARY AND GRAMMAR[30]

An early and possibly the first version of the Pond alphabet appears
in a Dakota grammar, unhappily fragmentary, in the handwriting of
Samuel W. Pond, which belongs to the Minnesota Historical Society:

A a	pronounced ah, has the sound		N n	Nee	n, in not
	of a as in bar		O o	O	o, in no
B b	Bee	b, in bite		P p	Pee	p, in pin
C c	Chee	ch, in chin		Q q		
D d	Dee	d, in dog		R r		
E e	A	a, in late		S s	See	s, in so
G g				T t	Tee	as t in tin
H h	Hee	h, in hand		U u	oo	oo in moon
I i	E	e, in me		W w	Wee	w in wise
J j	Zhee	as in French		X x	Shee	sh in show
K k	Kee	k, in king		Y y	Ye	y in yet
M m	Mee	m, in me		Z z	Zee	z in zebra

[27] Taliaferro Journal. Unfortunately the Journal for 1837 has not been found. Agent
Taliaferro, along with others, made the mistake of assuming that the cession bargained for
by Colonel Leavenworth was a reduced portion of the grant made to Pike.

[28] Taliaferro Journal. The payments were as follows: to Big Thunder's band, $850;
to Black Dog's band, $600; to Penetion's band, $700; to the Lake Calhoun band, $800; to
Six's village, $1,050; total, $4,000. The agent had taken the precaution on the same day,
before making the payment, to obtain in writing the relinquishment of any claim to this
money by the chiefs and headmen of the Wabasha and Red Wing bands, and to record the
same in his journal. It has not been learned from what fund the four thousand dollars were
paid; there is no such item in the Indian or army appropriation bills of 1838. Fort Snelling
had been located on public land to which the Indian right had been extinguished, but there
was no military reserve proper until it was marked out in the fall of 1839. See ante, p. 221.

[29] Sibley Papers.

[30] See ante, p. 203.

S. W. Pond Jr. omits the names of the letters and characterizes the *g* as low guttural, the *r* as high guttural, and the *q* as indescribable.[31] It is noteworthy that Taliaferro had long used *rh* for the high guttural, resembling the German *ch* as in *ach*.[32] This alphabet of five vowels and eighteen consonants was used in all Dakota printing until the publication of the grammar and dictionary in 1852. When Riggs went to Washington to attend to the printing of that work, he was induced by the experts of the Smithsonian Institution to modify the consonant system of the Pond alphabet. Its *j* and *x* were replaced by accented *z* and *s;* the *g* representing the sonant guttural was replaced by *g* with a superscript dot; the *r* representing the surd guttural was replaced by *h* with a superscript dot; for greater certainty, the *c* representing the English *ch* sound was given an accent mark; nasalized *n* at the ends of syllables was given a new type, an *n* with the second stroke prolonged downward. New types were made for accented *c*, *k*, *p*, and *t* to represent their sounds, modified in a few cases by so-called "clicks"; *l* was added for use in spelling Teton words in which the corresponding sound is used instead of that of *d*, as, for instance, "Lakota" instead of "Dakota."[33] When it is noted that these changes affected less than a thousand words, it may be questioned whether they were worth while. In the edition of the grammar prepared by Riggs shortly before his death in 1883 and edited by James Owen Dorsey, no further changes were made in the alphabet. In John P. Williamson's dictionary published in 1902, *z* and *s* received superscript dots instead of the accent marks and the accent over the *c* was dropped.[34]

Materials now available throw light upon, if they do not fully illuminate, the moot question of the authorship of the Dakota grammar and dictionary. In regard to the grammar, Riggs says in the preface of the work: "A manuscript Grammar of the language, written by the Rev. S. W. Pond, was kindly furnished to aid in the preparation of this work; but as it was not received in New York until mid-winter, it has been used only in the latter part. Since my arrival in this city [*Washington*], the Grammar has been entirely remodelled and rewritten." Samuel W. Pond, in his unprinted narrative, says: "My grammar was finished about the same time as the dictionary [*1848*] but I was not very well satisfied with either of them for I knew they were full of imperfections   Dr. W[illiamson]

[31] Pond, *Two Volunteer Missionaries*, 52.

[32] Taliaferro Journal, *passim*.

[33] Stephen R. Riggs, ed., *Grammar and Dictionary of the Dakota Language*, 3 (Smithsonian Institution, *Contributions to Knowledge*, vol. 4 — Washington, 1852). A second and enlarged edition of the dictionary was published under the title, *A Dakota-English Dictionary* (United States Geographical and Geological Survey of the Rocky Mountain Region, *Contributions to North American Ethnology*, vol. 7 — Washington, 1890).

[34] Riggs, *Dakota Grammar, Texts, and Ethnography* (*Contributions to North American Ethnology*, vol. 9 — Washington, 1893); John P. Williamson, ed., *An English-Dakota Dictionary* (New York, 1902).

borrowed my grammar and after examining it said to me. 'I thought once that if any one prepared a Dakota grammar it would be me but after a thorough trial I am convinced it is a work I cannot do and Mr. Rigg's grammar is not worth so [*words apparently omitted*]   I wish to have your grammar published with the dictionary' I did not however venture to offer Mr. Riggs my grammar . . . but while Mr Riggs was editing his grammar he wrote to me from New York saying 'I wish you would send me your grammar, immediately for Professor Turner has pulled mine all to pieces' I hesitated about sending my grammar until he wrote to me the second time for it, and I wish I had not sent it, for when it reached them they had printed a part of Mr. Rigg's grammar The syntax is mine but somewhat altered to adapt it to what was already in type. So the grammar is a patchwork — neither his nor mine but he may claim it, for I certainly disown it." Neill states that Dr. Turner was especially pleased with the grammar prepared by Samuel Pond.[35]

As regards the authorship of the Dakota dictionary, there is a regrettable variance of claims. Riggs placed his name on the title-page of the work simply as editor. In his preface he attributes the collection of words and definitions to the missionaries generally, himself included, and takes credit for the labor of a year and more in preparing the work for the press. When writing his *Mary and I, or Forty Years with the Sioux*, published in 1880, he employed terms which permitted the reader to infer that the Dakota dictionary as published "grew up" in his hands from small beginnings made by others; that he revised and rewrote it more times than he could remember; that although his colleagues, especially Samuel W. Pond, contributed to it, it was essentially his work.[36] In 1881 Samuel W. Pond wrote his narrative, in which appear the following passages: "We [*the Pond brothers*] began as soon as we came here to collect materials for a dictionary and grammar and prosecuted the work steadily from year to year with little help from others till it was completed . . . in 1848. . . . When our dictionary was finished it contained as many words as were published four years afterwards and was borrowed and copied at other stations up the river. . . . Doubtless we learned much from our associates . . . but no two or three persons could justly claim the authorship of the Dakota Dictionary It was the joint work of many men and women each contributing to it some more and some less according to his or her ability or opportunity And there is but *one* Dakota dictionary. I have it in manuscript and Mr Riggs had a copy of

[35] Riggs, *Grammar and Dictionary of the Dakota Language*, v; S. W. Pond Narrative, 1: 89–91; Neill, in *Macalester College Contributions*, second series, no. 8, p. 190.

[36] Riggs, *Forty Years with the Sioux*, 117–119.

it but it is the same work and though it cost me years of labor I should be ashamed to claim the authorship of it."[37] The reader will have noted the apparent discrepancy between the claim that the brothers wrought on the dictionary steadily from year to year, with little help from others, till it was completed, and the later statement that the dictionary was the work of many men and women each contributing more or less. Still, it appears that the writer intended to claim for himself and his brother only the actual record and arrangement of the collected materials in a completed manuscript work, a copy of which the editor of the dictionary had in his possession.

Whether the industrious editor in preparing the Dakota dictionary for the press used his own last revision or the Pond manuscript remains a question to be considered by the reader. The following additional notations may aid him in reaching a conclusion.

Neill makes this brief statement: "Samuel Pond enlarged his manuscript dictionary from year to year, and was accustomed to take it to the different mission stations for inspection, and additions from colleagues. At a meeting of the missionaries held in 1850, it was decided to attempt to publish the result of their labors, a Dakota-English dictionary of about 15,000 words. . . . Rev. S. R. Riggs was appointed to superintend the printing of the work."[38] On December 28, 1839, Riggs wrote to the Pond brothers: "Doct. Williamson is about to finish copying my vocabulary. He has been adding all the words he could get, and thus I presume will have the largest one in the Sioux language unless you have a better one." On January 7, 1840, Samuel Pond wrote to a sister: "I have lately finished a Dictionary containing about three thousand words. I have also written a small Grammar." On April 1, 1840, Riggs wrote Samuel Pond, "Was glad to learn that you had made a Dictionary and Grammar." On December 10 of the same year Samuel Pond wrote to another sister: "We have lately collected a great many new words & Gideon is making a new Dictionary."[39] On January 24, 1841, Riggs wrote from Lac qui Parle to the *Missionary Herald* that he had spent five weeks of the previous summer copying the Sioux vocabulary collected at that station, and that thereafter he and Williamson had increased the number of words from about fifty-five hundred to six thousand.[40] "I intend," he added, "to prosecute this work to perfection." The Minnesota Historical Society possesses a Dakota-English lexicon in octavo form in the handwriting of Riggs. On the last page is this note: "Commenced in Nov 1843, and finished March 22, 1844." Its 505 pages contain 8,047 words. Writing

[37] S. W. Pond Narrative, 1: 88–90.
[38] Neill, in *Macalester College Contributions*, second series, no. 8, p. 189.
[39] Pond Papers.
[40] *Missionary Herald*, 37: 271.

on April 4, 1845, Williamson said to Samuel Pond: "I would cheerfully send you my vocabulary if I thought it would be of any use to you, but I think you would find it a waste of time and labour to look at it after M^r. Riggs'. " The writer desired to have some questions answered before copying Pond's lexicon. On July 21 of the following year Williamson wrote again to Pond: "I have supposed in your last copy the definitions are more correct and complete than in any other which has been made . . . on the whole it is decidedly superior to mine." On March 22, 1850, Riggs wrote to Pond: "I am making some progress in my Lexicon."[41] Riggs's employment of the phrase "my Dakota Grammar and Dictionary" in his preface to *Mary and I, or Forty Years with the Sioux*, published in 1880, indicates that at that time he felt justified in claiming an exclusive authorship. On a flyleaf of the second volume of a Dakota-English dictionary, in two folio volumes, in the handwriting of Samuel W. Pond, presented by him to the Minnesota Historical Society, is the following signed statement, dated June 7, 1890: "This Dictionary was finished about forty years ago   It is almost exclusively the work of my brother G. H. Pond and myself. That we did our work thoroughly is proved by the fact that it contains almost every word now in use among the Dakotas by those who write the Dakota language."

The latest reference to the matter has been found in a letter from Samuel Pond to John H. Stevens, dated March 6, 1891: "Respecting what is called Mr Riggs' Dakota Dictionary it probably would not have been published if he had not been here, but it would have been completed as soon and as well if he had never seen the Dakotas, for I had it in manuscript and it was carried to the different mission stations and copied before he thought of publishing it, and in collecting words for it my brother and I received much more aid from Mr Gavin than we did from Mr. Riggs. I do not think that Mr. Riggs at first thought of claiming the authorship of the work, but when others ascribed it to him, it was perhaps natural that he should take no special pains to correct the error and after a while he began to call it his dictionary.   While Mr Riggs was living my brother and I told him plainly what we thought of his not rendering credit to whom credit was due, but I am not disposed to say anything to the public affecting his reputation, for I believe he was a good man and he is dead.   But so is Dr Williamson dead and Mr Gavin is dead and my brother is dead, and I shall soon be dead, and is it quite fair to our memory to have it understood that we were all here so many years waiting for him to come and reduce the language to writing and prepare a dictionary for us, when in fact he only followed where others led and prepared the way

---

[41] Pond Papers.

for him by doing a work for which he was incompetent and without which he could have accomplished so little?"[42]

A comparison of the text of the Dakota dictionary as printed and the manuscripts of Samuel Pond by one ignorant of the language leaves the question of authorship undetermined. The printed work contains about six per cent more words than Pond's, but the additions are mostly reduplications or other variants on root words. The definitions are the same or similar except where the editor has refined on or elaborated them. In the published work all words are syllabified and accented, which is not the case in the manuscripts. The talented editor, knowing the language, could have produced the work from the Pond manuscript without great labor; he could have produced it also from his own collections and records.

4. STEELE'S PREËMPTION AT THE FALLS OF ST. ANTHONY[43]

In the absence of documentary evidence the tradition regarding Franklin Steele's preëmption at the Falls of St. Anthony has undergone much transformation. The most probable hypothesis is that Major Joseph Plympton, commanding the post at Fort Snelling in 1838, was the competitor for the primary occupancy of the land fronting on the falls, the possession of which under existing law would carry the ownership of all the water power between the east bank and the mid-channel of the river. The suggestion has already been made that Plympton had an eye on this valuable location when, in his recommendation to the war department of proper bounds for the military reservation, he proposed a line which would leave the land mentioned outside the reserve and therefore open to occupancy.[44] It is also significant that the claim at the falls was known for some years — until 1842 or 1843, it is said — as the Plympton claim. The elementary tradition is that both Plympton and Steele received official notice of the ratification of the Indian treaties of 1837 by the same mail late in the day. Steele with one or more assistants and with such outfit as could easily be carried immediately started along the east bank of the river for the falls. Plympton was content to wait till morning, when he took his way along the west bank, forded the river above the

---

[42] Pond Papers. The Minnesota Historical Society possesses three manuscript copies of the Dakota lexicon, in addition to the two mentioned in the text. One, presented by Mr. and Mrs. Edward Pond, is evidently the work of the Pond brothers. About a quarter of this volume is missing. Another was made in 1851 by the Reverend Joseph W. Hancock, a missionary at Red Wing. The third probably was made by the Methodist Episcopal missionaries at Kaposia or Red Rock. It was found in a garret of an old house at Kaposia. The society possesses also a Sioux dictionary compiled by H. N. Dillon, a relative of Taliaferro, dated May 30 to August 9, 1835. The spelling antedates the Pond alphabet. The work contains some thirteen hundred words.

[43] See *ante*, p. 228.

[44] See *ante*, p. 422.

falls, and turning downstream a short distance found Steele at breakfast in a sufficient shack, and, according to one account, with a crop of corn planted; but July 16 is rather late for corn-planting.

Colonel John H. Stevens gives an account substantially the same except that the name of Captain Martin Scott, the famous marksman and hunter who had previously been in command at Fort Snelling, replaces that of Plympton.[45] Warner and Foote state that in 1836 Plympton made a claim at the Falls of St. Anthony and built a log house. On the same page they state that on June 18, 1838, a passenger arriving from below brought the rumor that the treaties had been ratified. Thereupon both Steele and Scott set out posthaste for the falls. Scott took the west bank of the river, but on his arrival "was unable to cross." Steele went up on the east side, built a shanty, and was ready to entertain the disappointed competitor on his arrival after a detour.[46] Atwater repeats the story of a claim by Plympton in 1836 and the building of a cabin, but he makes no reference to a competing adventurer.[47] Hudson also repeats the story of Plympton's claim of 1836, but does not name him as a competitor in the preëmption of 1838.[48] Holcombe relates that in 1836 Major Plympton, Captain Scott, and another officer made a claim at the falls and built a log cabin, and that Steele jumped the claim about July 16, 1838, and put up a tent which was soon replaced by a cabin. Scott arrived too late to make effective protest.[49] Two Minneapolis directories, those of 1873–74 and 1880–81, expand the story of Scott's effort at preëmption. Most of the foregoing variants are probably founded on the recollections of John H. Stevens. As Stevens was at first an employee and for some time a kind of business partner of Steele's he had sufficient opportunity to ascertain Steele's view of the matter; and his veracity is not to be questioned.

Two other variants of the story deserve attention. Henry T. Welles, a distinguished citizen of Minneapolis, who for some years had charge of Steele's affairs in that city and was otherwise intimately associated with him, was wont to relate that Scott, in expectation of notice of the ratification of the treaties, went up early in the season of 1838 and observed the situation. He also planted potatoes in a clearing which he found or made. He was so confident that he had made a lawful claim that it was

[45] Stevens, *Personal Recollections*, 14.

[46] Warner and Foote, *Hennepin County*, 358. In the Minneapolis *Directory* for 1883–84, p. 58, there is a variant of this story. Mention is there made that Joseph R. Brown had selected an eligible site, but failed to assume possession.

[47] Atwater, *Minneapolis and Hennepin County*, 29.

[48] Horace B. Hudson, ed., *A Half Century of Minneapolis*, 26 (Minneapolis, 1908).

[49] Return I. Holcombe, *Compendium of History and Biography of Minneapolis and Hennepin County, Minnesota*, 60 (Chicago, 1914).

not till some days after Steele's coup d'état that he went up to look after it. On his arrival he found Steele established in a shanty and exclaimed, "What can this mean, Mr. Steele?" "It means," was the reply, "that I am in possession of this land by preemption right." The captain could only acquiesce and accept an invitation to luncheon, at which he partook of potatoes of his own planting.[50] Major General Richard W. Johnson was the brother-in-law of Steele and the executor of his estate. It would be hard to find another more likely to receive from Steele an absolutely authentic account of a passage in his life of so great moment. The general relates that about 1840 the land on the east side of the Mississippi opposite the Falls of St. Anthony was thrown open to settlement, and that Major Plympton received by mail late one evening in winter the official notice. He sent at once for Captain Martin Scott and arranged with him to go early on the following morning to make a preëmption claim at the falls. Steele received the information at the same time and decided to take no chances. He immediately had a wagon loaded with boards, straw, and potatoes and other edibles and, accompanied by Norman W. Kittson, set out along the west bank of the river for the falls. Having reached the falls they crossed on the ice and arrived on the ground about midnight. They arranged their boards so as to look something like a shack or shanty, made some holes in the snow in which they planted potatoes, and then lay down to rest on their bed of straw. At an early hour the next morning their slumbers were disturbed by an alarm at their door — made by Plympton and Scott. The military men were obliged to confess themselves outgeneraled and partook with what grace they could of the breakfast "Commodore" Kittson got ready.[51] The participation of Captain Martin Scott in the competition for the preëmption at the Falls of St. Anthony in 1838 is rendered doubtful, to say the least, by the recorded fact that he was absent on leave from Fort Snelling from June 27 to September 30, 1838. The claim of Major Joseph Plympton of 1836 may be questioned in view of the fact that he did not take command at the fort until August 20, 1837.[52] It is of course quite possible that at some time the actual truth of the celebrated preëmption may be ascertained, but no research is necessary to reveal the colossal absurdity of our American policy of virtually making a gift of mines, deposits, and water powers to their lucky discoverers. Some day the American people will assert their common rights to such properties, and at prodigious expense they will recover possession of them.

[50] Colonel William E. Steele to the author, September 4, 1920, Folwell Papers.

[51] Johnson, "Fort Snelling from its Foundation to the Present Time," in *Minnesota Historical Collections*, 8: 437.

[52] Adjutant General, United States Army, to the author, September 17, 1920, Folwell Papers; *Minnesota Historical Collections*, 8: 430.

5. THE MEANING OF "MINNESOTA"[53]

The correct spelling of the word which designates our state is, according to the Pond alphabet, "Minisota." It is a matter of regret that this spelling was not retained, although it is liable to mispronunciation. The meaning given by Riggs to the word *sota* as a verb is "*to clear off*, as timber by cutting with an axe, and *to clear away*, as clouds, or *to be clear*, as the sky . . [hence] *unobstructed* or *clear*."[54] The compounds *bosota*, *kasota, kisota, nasota, yasota,* and *yusota* all mean "to clear off " or "away," or "to use up," in the particular manner indicated by the prefixes. *Kasota*, for instance, means "to clear off, as the sky," or "to use up by striking"; *nasota*, "to use up; to destroy with the feet"; *yasota*, "to use up with the mouth," that is, "to eat all up."[55] Samuel W. Pond gives for *sota* the single meaning "invisible."[56] There can be little doubt about the simple radical meaning of the word.

The early explorers and missionaries when explaining the word "Minisota" as the name of the river seem to have assumed that it was necessary to give *sota* a meaning descriptive of the water (*mini*) as they severally saw it. Schoolcraft said in 1820, "Its waters are transparent, and present a light blue tint on looking upon the stream. Hence the Indian name of Wate-paw-mené-Sauta, or Clear-water-river."[57] Three years later, in 1823, Keating, the naturalist of Long's expedition, said: "The river is called in the Dacota language Watapan Menesota, which means 'the river of turbid water.'" He adds, "The name given to the St. Peter is derived from its turbid appearance, which distinguishes it from the Mississippi, whose waters are very clear at the confluence. It has been erroneously stated by some authors to signify clear water." This interpretation was probably given by Joseph Renville.[58] Featherstonhaugh wrote in 1834, "The Indian name of the St. Peter's is '*Minnay Sotor*,' or '*Turbid Water*'; the water, in fact, looking as if whitish clay had been dissolved in it."[59] Samuel W. Pond, after defining *sota* as "invisible," enters in the next line, "Minisota, *turbid water*, water no[t] clear in which objects cannot be discerned, not transparent." In 1847

[53] See *ante*, p. 235.
[54] *Minnesota Pioneer*, July 28, 1853. In the same article Riggs insists that the adjective *sota* means "whitish."
[55] Riggs, *Grammar and Dictionary of the Dakota Language.*
[56] Pond, Dakota-English Lexicon, 350.
[57] Schoolcraft, *Narrative Journal*, 302. In "A Memoir on the History and Physical Geography of Minnesota," the same observer says that "Minnesota" is a "compound Dakota or Sioux word, describing the characteristic bluish green water of the St. Peters River." *Minnesota Historical Collections*, 1: 110.
[58] Keating, *Narrative*, 1: 328. Beltrami mentions the *Watpá-menisothé*, but does not give its derivation. *Pilgrimage*, 2: 305.
[59] Featherstonhaugh, *Canoe Voyage*, 1: 286.

Williamson wrote: "Some would render ["Minnesota"] 'clear water,' though it rightly signifies slightly turbid or whitish water."[60] School-craft makes no reference to the name in his *Narrative* of 1832, but in his *Summary Narrative* he states that "whenever the Mississippi is in flood . . . it backs up into the mouth of the St. Peter's, producing that addled aspect of the water . . . termed *sota*."[61] Nicollet, in 1836, selected the English word "blear" to characterize the water of the river, and explained it by the French *brouillé*, meaning "mingled," or "obscure."[62] Gideon H. Pond, by reputation the most expert Dakota linguist among the missionaries, is reported by Neill as stating that the Dakota applied the word *sota* "to the variegated or whitish blue appearance of the clouds." Neill uses *minisota* as meaning "water tinted like the sky, bluish rather than whitish." In another place Neill reports that Pond regarded *sota* as signifying "neither white nor blue, but the peculiar appearance of the sky on certain days," and that he gave "sky-tinted water" as the correct translation of "Minnesota."[63] Dr. Warren Upham adopts Gideon Pond's definition, "sky-tinted water," and states as a fact that the river in stage of flood becomes whitishly turbid. He adds the interesting state-ment that he was told by the widow of the Reverend Moses N. Adams, one of the later missionaries to the Dakota, that Indian women explained *sota* to her by dropping a little milk into water and calling the whitishly clouded water *sota*.[64] The Dakota dictionary published in 1852, which is supposed to summarize the opinions of numerous contributors, defines *sota* as "*clear*, but not perfectly so; *slightly clouded*, but not turbid; *of a milky whitish appearance; sky-colored:* Wakpa minisota, *the Minnesota River*; Mde minisota, *Clear Lake: used up.*" "Minisota" in its alphabeti-cal place is said to mean "whitish water."[65]

The writers just cited have attempted to find a meaning for *sota* descriptive of the water of the river as seen or described. The results, how-ever, are mostly quite at variance with the simple radical meaning of the

---

[60] Neill, *Minnesota*, 481, n.

[61] Schoolcraft, *Summary Narrative*, 156. Schoolcraft's other revelation, "Minnesota, from minne, colored water, and sota, a river," is, of course, a joke. *Indian Tribes*, 4: 384.

[62] Nicollet, *Report*, 68.

[63] Neill, in *Minnesota Historical Collections*, 1: 197, and in his *Minnesota*, li. Thomas Foster agrees with this interpretation. *Minnesota Pioneer*, May 16, 1850; *Chronicle and Register*, May 11, 1850.

[64] Upham, in *Minnesota in Three Centuries*, 1: 118.

[65] Riggs, *Grammar and Dictionary of the Dakota Language*, 140, 187. In the *Minnesota Pioneer* for July 28, 1853, Riggs remarks that the clear sky of Minnesota is often whitish rather than bluish. Hence the true idea of *sota* is "sky-colored," "sky-tinted," or "whit-ish." On page 2 of the "Accompaniment" to Cowperthwait, *Map of the Organized Counties of Minnesota*, the translation "grey water" is offered. The translation of "Minnesota" as "smoky water" comes from mistaking *shota*, meaning "smoky," for *sota*. In the Dakota alphabet the *sh* sound is indicated by an accented *s*.

word. Without presuming to challenge the high authorities, the writer ventures to raise the question whether in fact the water of the Minnesota was or is any more clear, or imperfectly clear, or slightly turbid, or non-transparent, or whitish, or bluish, or sky-tinted, or sky-colored, or whitishly clouded than that of the Mississippi or of other streams in the Northwest. His conclusion from observations and inquiries is that there is little or no difference. Since a doubt may be entertained whether the Dakota named the river from any distinctive hue or aspect of its water, there is room for one or two alternatives. The suggestion that the Minnesota was so named as the river of clear water in contrast with the muddy Missouri (in Dakota, *Minishoshay*) has sufficient plausibility to warrant mention, although no historical relation has been discovered.[66] An ingenious theory has been advanced to the author by Samuel J. Brown, an educated mixed-blood who learned Dakota in childhood and had long experience as an interpreter. He suggests that when the Dakota were driven from Mille Lacs and thereabout by the Chippewa and began to pitch their lodges about the junction of the two rivers, they observed that one of them, the smaller, disappeared, ended, was used up by the larger, and gave the name "Minisota" to the invisible or the lost water. Keating remarks that because the discharge of the Minnesota was concealed by Pike's Island it was, as suggested by Carver, unseen by Hennepin. Featherstonhaugh made a similar observation.[67] It is safe to assume, however, that Gideon Pond's poetic "sky-tinted water," already widely diffused in literature, will hold its place in spite of criticism.

6. THE ABORTIVE "DOTY" TREATIES[68]

The principal treaty which had been negotiated by Governor James D. Doty of Wisconsin with the Sioux Indians in 1841 was laid before the Senate on September 3, 1841, together with a communication from the secretary of war explaining the system upon which it was based. The project originated in an endeavor to find a suitable home for the Winnebago Indians, who at that time had a temporary abiding place on the so-called "Neutral Ground" in northeastern Iowa. The Sioux, it was believed, would readily yield a portion of their immense domain to the homeless tribe. It was presently observed, however, that there were reasons of importance for "emigrating" the Sauk and Foxes and the Potawatomi to some new region. Certain Chippewa and Ottawa of northern Michigan were under treaty obligations to move, and it was the desire of the secretary to transfer them to the southwest, if for no other

[66] Neill, *Minnesota*, li.
[67] Keating, *Narrative*, 1: 328; Featherstonhaugh, *Canoe Voyage*, 1: 258.
[68] See *ante*, p. 266, n. 2.

reason than to put them out of the reach of the perpetual British influences. It was also believed that the New York Indians might, with safety to themselves and benefit to the people of that state, be removed to the West. In short, the department proposed to convert the whole Sioux country, including some small reservations for the Sioux themselves, into a permanent Indian territory. The white man, it was assumed, would never push his settlements beyond the Mississippi.[69]

After a purely formal consideration, this treaty was ordered to lie on the table by a vote of 27 to 2. On March 10 of the following year, 1842, the petition of Joseph R. Brown and other citizens of Wisconsin Territory for the ratification of this treaty was laid before the Senate. On April 28 the president transmitted to the Senate a supplementary treaty which had been negotiated with the Mdewakanton Sioux shortly after the principal agreement was made, together with a report from the secretary of war which explained that the ratification of this secondary treaty would be ineffectual without that of the main one. Accordingly, the Senate referred both documents to the committee on Indian affairs. At length the main treaty was reported out without amendment or recommendation, and the Senate rejected it on August 29 by a vote of 2 to 26. Two days later the supplementary treaty was reported out and ordered to lie on the table.[70] A vote so close to unanimity seems to discredit the statements of contemporaries and of historians that this was a party issue, that the Democratic majority of the Senate did not desire to ratify treaties made under a Whig administration and so add to its prestige. It seems more likely that the Senate did not sympathize with the war department and the Indian office in their ambition to create a great northern Indian territory into which should be gathered many tribes, to be "hemmed in by the laws of the United States, and guarded by virtuous

[69] *Senate Executive Proceedings*, 5: 426–430. The original principal (unratified) treaty may be found in the files of the Indian office in Washington. It is accompanied by a long letter from Doty to the secretary of war, which explains its provisions and describes the country. The area to be acquired for an Indian territory, lying between the latitudes of 43° 30′ and 46°, contained about thirty millions of acres, and the cost of the cession would be a little less than one million dollars. The reservations for the several bands along the upper Minnesota River, some five hundred thousand acres in all, were to be protected against the incursions of whisky-sellers, a class distinct from the licensed traders. Traders' debts were allowed to an amount not exceeding fifty thousand dollars. Mixed-bloods were to be given a permanent home and were not to be allowed to float between civilized and savage lives. A rough pencil sketch of the proposed cessions, as drawn by Featherstonhaugh or Lieutenant Mather, is also preserved in the Indian office (tube 141). For a sketch of Governor Doty, see Albert G. Ellis, "Life and Services of J. D. Doty," in *Wisconsin Historical Collections*, 5: 369–377.

[70] *Senate Executive Proceedings*, 5: 431, 439; 6: 38, 58–60, 61, 105, 141, 147. On July 12, "Mr. Benton presented a communication from Law. Taliaferro in reply to certain interrogatories respecting the late treaty with the Sioux Indians," which was also referred to the committee on Indian affairs.

agents, where abstinence from vice, and the practice of good morals, should find fit abodes in comfortable dwellings and cleared farms."[71]

In the communication of the secretary of war accompanying the principal treaty, the Senate was informed that it had been found impossible to negotiate the treaty without providing for the payment of debts due from the Indians to the traders, but that very judicious guards had been introduced to exclude that interest in all future time. Governor Doty wrote a letter to Secretary Bell on August 12, 1841, in which he acknowledged the services of Sibley, J. B. Faribault, and the latter's son Alexander, and stated that "without their aid I do not think that it would have been possible to have obtained the assent of the Indians to them [the treaties]."[72]

The traders, naturally, were deeply interested in the success of the treaties, for Indian cessions meant the liquidation of outstanding debts. Correspondingly bitter, therefore, was their disappointment when the Senate in the summer of 1842 definitely rejected the Doty agreements. On September 23, 1842, Dousman wrote to Sibley: "Here is death to the great *Panacea* which was to cure all the lame *Ducks*, and give the wherewith to so many to be joyful. . . . It is no use to cry we have to swallow it as bitter a Pill as it may be — we shall have to work harder & spend less."[73]

7. THE TERRITORIAL SEAL[74]

The origin of the territorial seal was not known, or at least not widely known, till after the papers of General Sibley came into the possession of the Minnesota Historical Society in 1893. Governor Ramsey in his first message to the territorial legislature on September 3, 1849, informed that body that he had been using a seal of simple design for the authentication of executive acts. It may be described as follows: In the center there was a rude representation of a sunburst, about which, in a circle, were the words, "Liberty, Law, Religion, and Education"; in an outer circle were the words, "The Great Seal of the Territory of Minnesota, U. S. A."[75] The governor at the same time submitted, for approval or rejection, a design which he did not describe. The legislature

[71] Report of the United States commissioner of Indian affairs for 1840, in 26 Congress, 2 session, *House Documents*, no. 2, p. 233 (serial 382); Hughes, in *Minnesota Historical Collections*, 10: 119 (part 1); Holcombe, in *Minnesota in Three Centuries*, 2: 288.

[72] Richardson, *Messages and Papers of the Presidents*, 4: 62; Sibley Papers.

[73] Sibley Papers.

[74] See *ante*, p. 267.

[75] *Council Journal*, 1849, p. 14; an impression of this temporary seal may be seen on page 5 of the Executive Journal for 1849–53, in the custody of the Minnesota Historical Society. See also Holcombe, in *Minnesota in Three Centuries*, 3: 473.

evidently did not take the matter very seriously for it was not till the last day of the session that an act was passed providing for a great seal, of which the emblems and motto were to be selected by the governor and the delegate to Congress. For the correction of an erroneous statement, many times repeated in successive editions of the *Legislative Manual*, it is important to state that on the day preceding adjournment the Council approved by resolution of a design submitted by a committee. It depicted an Indian family with a lodge, a canoe, and accessories, receiving a white visitor accepting the calumet or pipe of peace. The idea was to symbolize "the eternal friendship of the two races." The resolution reached the House on the next and last day of the session and was rejected by it.[76] It may not be an unreasonable conjecture that the design was that proposed by Governor Ramsey and that it was executed by the chairman of the Council, James McClellan Boal, who had some skill in drafting.

The action taken by the two commissioners on the seal may best be apprehended by three letters, which seem to presume previous conference or correspondence. The first is one from Delegate Sibley, dated at Washington, December 23, 1849, to Governor Ramsey, who at the time was in Philadelphia on his own business. It reads: "My dear Sir, I only recd the designs of the Territorial Seal on Friday. Col. Abert sent me four, only one of which was at all appropriate, consisting of an Indian on horseback, lance in hand, with a man ploughing, cabin & haystack, the stump of a tree with an axe sticking in it, by way of contrast. I have turned it over to my friend Capt Eastman, who has just arrived, and whose talents as an artist are well known to you. He promised to *paint* the design and include if possible a view of the Falls, so that I could send it to you tonight or tomorrow morning." Another letter of the same date followed: "Sunday evening. My Dear Sir, I have just recd the devices from Capt Eastman, which I send you together with the one from Capt. Abert described in my letter of today, and which I think is the most appropriate. Those of Capt. E. contain a sketch of the Falls. Please choose & let me know." To these letters Governor Ramsey replied on the twenty-eighth as follows: "Upon a more careful examination of the designs & mottoes for our seal, I come to these conclusions viz: that in the drawing by Capt. Abert Civilization in the number & prominence of the objects predominates too much over the Indian state which at least for the present is our more distinctive characteristic. In Capt. Eastmans design the equilibrium is better preserved; his is also more bold grand & striking — if you think

---

[76] *Laws*, 1849, p. 50; *Council Journal*, 1849, pp. 122, 124, 128, 138, 145, 153, 155; *House Journal*, 1849, pp. 147, 161, 173, 176; *Chronicle and Register*, December 1, 1849. The *Legislative Manual*, 1921, p. 14, for example, contains the statement that the design submitted by the committee "was authorized by law but never used."

it better to adopt Aberts design would it not be well to take out some of the improvement ideas say the stump & axe and in some appropriate part locate a 'teepee' this would make the Indian life in the seal more striking & attractive."[77]

No record of further conferences has been found, but it is evident from an inspection of the seal that the Abert design, as redrawn by Eastman, was used with some modification. There is the Indian on horseback, lance in hand, a man plowing, and the stump of a tree with an ax sticking in it — and the Falls of St. Anthony suggested by Sibley. The cabin and

[From the face of the original seal in the museum of the Minnesota Historical Society.]

the haystack were omitted and Ramsey surrendered his desired "teepee." A rifle with a powderhorn slung to it leans against the stump. The setting sun appears to have been an afterthought. Sibley attended to the execution of the seal and press, for which he paid $150.[78]

Along with the designs for the seal sent by mail to Governor Ramsey, Sibley furnished a list of mottoes selected from Burke's *Peerage*, which

[77] Ramsey Papers; Sibley Papers. Colonel Abert's four pencil sketches, his letters to Sibley transmitting them, and Captain Eastman's design are in the Sibley Papers.
[78] Sibley to Ramsey, April 14, 1850, Ramsey Papers.

he said he had overhauled from one end to the other. He indicated his preference for the following: "*Ascendam! per vias rectas*"; "*Libertas in legibus*"; or "*Virtus sola nobilitas.*" In his reply Ramsey expressed his preference for "something characteristic in an eminent degree of American goaheadativeness — something suggestive of enterprise — courage — tireless industry." He would prefer English mottoes and in the following order: "'Forward without fear' 'Deeds show — Forward!' 'Advance with Courage.'" If the general taste, however, required French or Latin he would defer to Sibley, but would prefer one of the following: "'*Droit et Avant*' '*Ascendam! per vias rectas*' '*Quod potui perfeci*' '*Nec timide, nec timere.*'"[79] Why the two commissioners were unable to choose from so excellent a collection, and chose the Latin motto "*Quae sursum volo videre*" of the Scottish Earl of Dunraven, has not been ascertained.[80] The exact translation of the motto is, of course, "I wish to see what is above," but the less exact rendering, "I wish to see what is beyond," soon became and has remained current. It was this sentiment which the pioneer plowman was supposed to feel. The misquotation as "*Quo sursum velo videre*" is attributed by Neill to the engraver. A list of seventeen proposed Latin mottoes in Sibley's handwriting, however, shows "*Quo sursum velo videre*" with the translation, "I am resolved to look upward."[81]

8. THE RAMSEY INVESTIGATION[82]

From the time when Madison Sweetser first appeared with a stock of Indian goods at the Traverse in October, 1851, the traders attached to the American Fur Company, naturally resenting his intrusion, cherished the belief that not only was he actuated by purely mercenary motives but that he was the tool or confederate of one or more hostile interests.[83]

[79] The list of mottoes which accompanied Sibley's letter of December 23, 1849, and several other lists are in the Sibley Papers.

[80] Bernard Burke, *Dictionary of the Peerage and Baronetage*, 429 (London, 1881).

[81] Neill, *Minnesota*, 516; Sibley Papers. The *St. Paul Dispatch* for January 20, 1894, contains an illustrated article by R. I. Holcombe upon the question of the seals. The present author, drawing from the same sources, has found it proper to differ in details.

[82] See *ante*, ch. 10.

[83] The Ewings of Fort Wayne, Indiana, were said to be behind Sweetser in his opposition to the American Fur Company. Ramsay Crooks wrote to Sibley, "Notwithstanding the disclaimer of the Messrs. Ewing, I am hardly so 'green' as to believe that Mr. Sweetzer would ever of his own individual will, alone, have conceived the gigantic project." Rice, also, was supposed to be concerned in the operations, but he was willing to accept an offer from Dousman to arrange the matter of the amendments in the fall of 1852. The *Minnesota Pioneer* of February 17, 1853, gives a résumé of the treaty provisions for the relief of the traders and the half-breeds and expresses an opinion as to the motives which inspired the attack upon Governor Ramsey and, through him, upon Sibley. The editorial writer, Joseph R. Brown, gives to a partner of the Ewings who was present at the treaty of Traverse des Sioux the credit for divining means whereby the moneys intended for the traders and the half-breeds might be diverted to the coffers of his company. He boasted in St. Paul, says the writer, that he "would prevent the old traders from obtaining the money

If he was such an instrument, the relation has been so successfully concealed that no conclusive evidence has been found to sustain the insinuation. He compromised no other persons. As for being mercenary, that was no crime. It was his right to transfer his operations as an Indian trader to a new field, where Indians would presently have a large amount of money to expend for goods, and profits seemed to be in sight. It was an ordinary mercantile policy to ingratiate himself with those Indians and draw them to his trading house. The old traders cherished another belief which, if well grounded, would have justified their distrust and indignation. It was that Sweetser's principal object in coming to the country at the time was to force the beneficiaries of a treaty or treaties to divide with him — in plain English, to levy blackmail on them. In the correspondence of the time there are dark hints of overtures to such an end; but if made, they were barren of results.[84]

Up to the time when the payments of 1852 were completed, Sweetser had received nothing for all the trouble to which he had put himself, if pecuniary reward was his desire. He then assumed the rôle of a disinterested friend of Indians who had been plundered by a gang of conspirators, whom he resolved to prosecute to exposure and conviction; and he therefore prepared to transfer his activities to the national capital. At the close of Governor Ramsey's visit to the Traverse, Sweetser induced the chiefs, or some of them, to agree to two new "papers," doubtless with a

assigned them by the Indians." No confirmation of this allegation has been found. The Ewings had no claims against the upper Sioux. F. B. Sibley to Laframboise, November 23, to McLeod, November 24, 1851, in Sibley Letter Book, no. 1; Sibley to Ramsey, December 26, 1851, January 28, 1853, Hugh Tyler to Ramsey, June 27, 1852, Ramsey Papers; Crooks to Sibley, February 19, 1852, Sibley Papers.

[84] Several of the fur company traders sounded Sweetser and found him easily approachable. Sibley desired that some sort of arrangement should be made between them and accordingly it was suggested that Dousman should travel down to Galena on the same boat with Sweetser, to talk things over. Dousman, according to instructions, met the "Nominee" at Prairie du Chien prepared to make an agreement, but Sweetser did not come down as expected. In an affidavit, dated February 28, 1853, however, Dousman swore that "in the month of August or September last Madison Sweetzer of Indiana being then at St. Paul in the Territory of Minnesota, proposed to this deponent, that if the Traders who were claimants under the provisions of the Treaty made at Traverse des Sioux in the Summer of A. D. 1851 with the Sisseton & Wakpaton Bands of Sioux Indians, would pay to him the said Madison Sweetzer, the sum of Thirty Thousand Dollars, that he would desist from any further attempts to interfere with said Bands of Indians and that the money could be paid out as already agreed on between said Indians and Traders — this deponent thereupon told him that it was more than the claimants could afford to pay even to avoid the trouble & expense he could put them to, and said Sweetzer remarked in reply, that he was not alone in this matter & had to share with others in whatever he got, which was his reason for asking so much in the proposition which he made to this deponent." Dr. Borup also testified under oath that Sweetser had offered to withdraw his opposition upon the payment of thirty thousand dollars. Sweetser, of course, denied any such offer. F. B. Sibley to Chouteau and Company, May 19, June 27, to Laframboise, June 14, to Dousman, June 22, 1852, in Sibley Letter Book, no. 2; Dousman to F. B. Sibley, June 25, 1852, affidavit of H. L. Dousman, February 28, 1853, Sibley Papers; *Ramsey Investigation Report*, 315, 353.

view to their serviceability in Washington. On the night of December 2, 1852, a council was held in Sweetser's trading house. A paper was read by Agent McLean, interpreted to the Indians, and approved by them. It is uncertain whether the paper was signed; if so, the signatures have not been found. The document contained a protest against the traders' paper, a demand that traders' claims should be submitted to Nathaniel McLean, Thomas S. Williamson, and Madison Sweetser for examination and adjustment, and a request for larger allowances to half-breeds and smaller ones to traders.[85] As Governor Ramsey was getting into his sleigh the following morning Red Iron handed him the paper. At the same council a protest addressed to the president was agreed to. It was dated December 3, 1852, and was a new repudiation by the Indians of the traders' paper and a demand for a scrutiny of the claims.[86] As these papers were drawn up after the necessary receipts were obtained from the chiefs and payment according to the traders' papers was absolutely assured, it may be inferred that Sweetser was laying the foundation for a new line of operation. He could not hope to recover for his Indian clients any of the moneys already appropriated. In contemporary correspondence he and his alleged associates were charged with the intention of procuring from a benevolent Congress new appropriations to reimburse the poor Indians for the sums of which, as he expected to prove, they had been robbed by a gang of conspirators. From such a benefaction he might hope to be rewarded for his services. It was suggested that he would be aided by a brother who was a member of the House of Representatives.[87]

Sweetser appeared in Washington soon after the opening of the second session of the Thirty-second Congress and began operations with the Indian office, where he seems to have made but little impression. On January 4, 1853, Delegate Sibley, without waiting for a hostile movement, offered in the House a resolution to investigate the conduct of Governor Ramsey in the Sioux payments. The House was disinclined to take up the matter, and on the tenth the delegate had the resolution adopted by the Senate and referred to its committee on Indian affairs.[88] Up to this time there was nothing to be investigated except loose charges

[85] *Ramsey Investigation Report*, 151.

[86] 32 Congress, 2 session, *Senate Executive Documents*, no. 29, pp. 2–4 (serial 660).

[87] Sibley to Eastman, May 30, July 22, September 25, to Robert McClelland, October 17, to Dousman, October 22, to Lewis Cass, December 22, 1853, in Sibley Letter Book, no. 4.

[88] *Congressional Globe*, 32 Congress, 2 session, 208, 246; F. B. Sibley to Laframboise, February 8, 1853, in Sibley Letter Book, no. 2; Ramsey to Sibley, January 8, 1853, Sibley Papers. The Sibley Papers contain an unpublished manuscript of eleven pages in Sibley's handwriting, which was written in the winter of 1852–53 evidently for the eyes of senators, and which gives his views of the negotiation of the treaties and of the attempt of Madison Sweetser to have them annulled. The document deserves careful consideration.

and insinuations which had appeared in December in the *Minnesota Democrat*, copies of which had been mailed to each senator and representative and to various officials.[89] The committee was not disposed seriously to consider these newspaper aspersions, in spite of Sibley's importunity. At length, on February 26, Sweetser filed with the chairman his formal charges and specifications. It is evident that Sweetser either drew these up himself or employed a very unskillful lawyer to do it. Out of the confused statements these points may be collected: Governor Ramsey was charged (1) with having refused to pay the Indians their moneys directly but with having paid them to claimants, traders, and half-breeds through Hugh Tyler, their attorney; (2) with "confederating with Henry H. Sibley, Hercules L. Dousman, Hugh Tyler, Franklin Steele, and others, to absorb the whole fund named [the 'hand money'], to favorites, to the exclusion of meritorious creditors"; (3) with having used improper means and cruel measures to compel the Indians to sign receipts and assignments; (4) with holding councils and making payments in a private trading house rather than at the agency, and with conniving at keeping the chiefs drunk, or at least permitting it; (5) with not reserving sufficient funds for removal and subsistence, thus increasing the funds to be distributed among traders and half-breeds; (6) with depositing the gold received from the treasury in banks and paying by means of drafts and bank notes — all these in violation of law and treaties. Two days before the filing of these charges, President Fillmore had proclaimed the treaties of Traverse des Sioux and Mendota ratified and confirmed. On March 19 Daniel A. Robertson, editor of the *Minnesota Democrat*, submitted a shorter but similar catena of charges, verified before the clerk of the Senate committee.[90]

Meantime, on March 14, the Senate committee on Indian affairs began an investigation. At four successive sessions, ending on April 6, the

[89] See the article "Minnesota Galphinism," which occupies the entire second page of the *Minnesota Democrat* for December 15, 1852. The meaning of "Galphinism" is explained in the *Minnesota Pioneer* for May 9, 1850. The term originated in the Galphin case. George W. Crawford, secretary of war, was accused of using his position as a cabinet officer to obtain the decision in this case, which carried with it certain pecuniary advantage to him. He immediately demanded an investigation by Congress. Other attacks upon the treaties and their makers were published in the *Democrat* for December 22 and 29, 1852.

[90] *Ramsey Investigation Report*, 4–7, 37, 313, 317, 361. It is probable that Sweetser was encouraged in his attack by a provision in the Indian appropriation act of 1852, which forbade the payment of any of the moneys appropriated to agents or attorneys "unless the imperious interest of the Indian or Indians, or some treaty stipulations" required the payment to be made otherwise, although he seems not to have made specific reference to the statute. As soon as Robertson of the *Democrat* began the attack on Governor Ramsey, the *Minnesotian* sprang to the defense, and the two newspapers maintained for many weeks a battledore and shuttlecock engagement, which the curious reader if so disposed may follow for an example of the journalistic dialectics of the time. He will find, however, few if any facts not elsewhere better recorded. A desultory firing was kept up until Robertson retired from

committee examined as many witnesses, including Sweetser and Tyler. By this time it was apparent that no full investigation of the charges, which on their face seemed of grave import, could be made at so great a distance from the scene of events. After refusing to authorize a sub-committee to proceed to Minnesota, the Senate, on April 5, resolved to request the president "to cause to be investigated the charges of fraud and misconduct in office alleged against Alexander Ramsey . . . and to report the results of such investigation to the Senate at the next session of Congress."[91] In pursuance of the request President Pierce appointed, sometime in June, two commissioners. One was the Honorable Willis A. Gorman, who had succeeded Alexander Ramsey as governor of Minnesota Territory on May 15. This appointment called out some popular criticism, but it may be remarked that Gorman took no active part in the proceedings and did not sign the report.[92] The other appointee was Richard M. Young, who had been chief clerk of the House of Representatives and was as yet unknown in the territory. He was spoken of as "the agent" or "the special commissioner."[93] The government was represented by the Honorable Lafayette Emmett, attorney-general of the territory; Governor Ramsey, by David Cooper and Isaac Van Etten. The investigation began at St. Paul on July 6 and closed on October 7, 1853.

The government called forty-seven witnesses, among them sixteen Indians and about the same number of half-breeds and squaw men. The nature of the charges and specifications furnished latitude for inquiry and every possible opening for evidence was explored. If objections were interposed for the defense, they seem not to have been entertained.[94] The leading witness of the ten examined on the part of Governor Ramsey was, of course, Sibley, whose averments were generally confirmed by the testimony of such associates as McLeod, Brown, Forbes, Steele, Dousman,

the editorship of the *Democrat* at the end of June, 1853. From that time the *Democrat* made no mention of the Ramsey investigation. Robertson and his correspondents laid great stress on Ramsey's alleged criminality in not having brought to the territory the gold drawn from the treasury and literally paid it out to the chiefs in open council. The gold, they asserted, would have diffused itself and given life and buoyancy to industry. *Statutes at Large*, 10: 951.

[91] *Ramsey Investigation Report*, 315, 350–357; 32 Congress, 2 session, *Senate Journal*, 82, 347, 358 (serial 657).

[92] In a note appended to the report, Commissioner Young states that it is his "confident belief that Governor Gorman would have signed it [*the report*], if he had been here [*in Washington*]." *Ramsey Investigation Report*, 74.

[93] The secretary of the interior, in his letter of transmittal to the president dated January 9, 1854, speaks of the "report of . . . the agent." *Ramsey Investigation Report*, 1.

[94] Governor Ramsey's counsel complained that they were held to the strictest rules of evidence while the government was bound by no rules at all, that the protracting of the inquiry beyond all reasonable limits wasted Ramsey's time and subjected him to expense, and that peremptory refusal was given to their demands that their exceptions be noted. *Ramsey Investigation Report*, 360.

and Alexander Faribault. There was little dispute about the facts, most of which might have been stipulated at the outset. It was conceded that the Indians knew that they were in debt to the traders and that they were willing to have their debts paid. Efforts to ascertain the uses to which were put the percentages retained by Hugh Tyler and the compensation paid Rice for obtaining the approval of the Indians to the amendments were fruitless. Repeated efforts to trace a share of Tyler's commission to the hands of Ramsey were utter failures. Madison Sweetser would without doubt have been a willing witness, but for reasons which must be left to conjecture the government did not please to call him. Henry M. Rice could have disclosed information regarding the manner in which he had obtained the Indians' power of attorney for Ramsey and their understanding of the true purport of it, but he was not summoned. Hugh Tyler, if intelligently interrogated, could have thrown light on the whole progress of the Sioux treaties and in particular on his distribution of the mysterious percentages. The revelation of those disbursements might have spared many injurious insinuations, not to say open charges of graft. Tyler was in St. Paul in July, but not being called to the stand, he departed about his own affairs, after leaving his *ex parte* deposition of August 1. The salient points of this affidavit were: (1) that at an interview between Commissioner Lea and Governor Ramsey, at which he was present, Tyler heard the commissioner direct Governor Ramsey to pay according to the terms of the traders' papers; (2) that Governor Ramsey had not profited to the amount of one cent in handling the Sioux moneys; and (3) that the Sioux understood and acknowledged their debts to the traders before and at the signing of the treaties.[95] The deposition of the Honorable Luke Lea, commissioner of Indian affairs, was taken in Washington on December 1, 1853, and was added to the testimony. Lea averred that the "traders exercised a controlling influence over the Indians, and it was quite evident that no treaty could be made without their concurrence and active co-operation"; that the Indians were anxious that liberal provision should be made for paying the just claims of their traders; and that when the money for the payment was turned over to Ramsey in October, 1852, he, the commissioner, advised him not to allow the Indians to repudiate their just engagements but to require them "to abide by the agreement between them and their traders, provided it was fairly and understandingly made."[96]

Governor Ramsey's personal reply to the Sweetser and Robertson charges had been made long before this investigation began. On March 2,

[95] Ramsey to Sibley, March 8, 1853, Sibley Papers; *Ramsey Investigation Report*, 427, 430.

[96] *Ramsey Investigation Report*, 308.

1853, he addressed the Indian office giving a history of all the transactions concerning the treaties and the payments. In particular he declared his conviction that the traders' papers were most solemn acknowledgments of Indian debts and that he had made his payments accordingly, in spite of all efforts of interested parties to prevent that just disposition. "Without the assistance of the traders," he said, "no treaty could have been effected at all." It was, therefore, necessary to permit the Indians "to set apart in the treaty a certain sum for clearing off their 'engagements.'" He freely expressed his opinion of Madison Sweetser "and his fellow conspirators." In concluding, Ramsey said, "I cannot observe that in any particular I would change my action, if the whole affair was to be gone over again."[97]

The report upon the investigation, dated December 20, 1853, was filed with the office of Indian affairs on the thirtieth. On January 5 it reached the secretary of the interior, who transmitted it to the president on the ninth. On the same date it was communicated to the Senate, where on the day following it was read and referred to the committee on Indian affairs. Before its submission a friend of Sibley's was allowed to read the report to be assured that it contained nothing injurious to Sibley's fair standing, as Judge Young had repeatedly promised. The findings leave much to be desired in point of clearness and simplicity. It was conceded that Indian testimony must be taken with many grains of allowance; that, before or at the time of the treaties, the Indians had acknowledged their indebtedness in much larger amounts than the treaties allowed; that after the treaties they were stirred up by "adverse influences" to repudiate their obligations; and that had the money been paid in hand to the chiefs, they would have squandered it in foolish ways, or they would have been robbed of it as in the cases of Wabasha and Wacouta. It was affirmed, however, that some upper chiefs had been left in ignorance of the intent of the traders' paper and had been allowed on two separate occasions to believe that it had been annulled; that payment according to the terms of the traders' paper was not payment according to the treaty; that oppressive measures had been used to compel acquiescence in such payment; and that the sum retained by Hugh Tyler, by way of discount and percentage . . . could not have been necessary for any reasonable or legitimate purpose," and was exacted in such a way as to indicate that, unless it was consented to, there would have been no payments to traders. Commissioner Young was of the opinion that the government was bound by the treaty to pay the "hand money" to the chiefs as requested by them in open council, no matter if they should

[97] *Ramsey Investigation Report*, 8, 322–329; 32 Congress, 2 session, *Senate Executive Documents*, no. 29, part 2, pp. 2–21 (serial 660).

squander the whole sum in a fortnight. The government in making treaties with Indians presumed that they knew what to do with the moneys paid for lands.[98]

Ramsey's counsel submitted an elaborate argument setting up a general traverse and refining on many points of slight importance.[99] His own clear and vigorous explanation already referred to was better calculated to secure a favorable verdict. The Senate committee had barely time to examine the large number of papers in the case, when a new face was put upon the matter by the appearance of a letter from Robertson, one of the complainants, dated January 24, 1854, withdrawing his charges and assuring Ramsey that the testimony taken in the late investigation had fully acquitted him of corrupt or fraudulent design and had left no stain on his character. He, Robertson, had never made charges of pecuniary or personal considerations, but only of technical violation of law in administering the trust. Sweetser and his remaining associates were naturally discouraged by the withdrawal of one whose standing and reputation had given weight and countenance to their attack. They seem to have abandoned the field.[1] On February 24 the Senate committee on Indian affairs submitted its report. The committee reached the conclusion, after having "carefully examined all the testimony . . . that the conduct of Governor Ramsey was not only free from blame, but highly commendable and meritorious." Not one of the charges had been sustained. The report was considered by the Senate and agreed to on the same day, and the committee was discharged from further consideration of the subject.[2]

It is no duty of the writer to harmonize the discrepancies in the findings of the commissioners and the verdict of the Senate. If in the former there was a dash of political venom, the latter sounded a note of triumph over a vindictive and defeated prosecution. A member of the House much interested in the outcome wrote to Sibley a breezy note of congratulation.[3]

---

[98] *Ramsey Investigation Report*, 1–3, 71–73; Eastman to Sibley, January 11, 21, February 9, 20, 1854, Gorman to Sibley, February 15, 1854, Sibley Papers; Sibley to Eastman, February 1, to Dodge, February 1, to Ramsey, February 1, 1854, in Sibley Letter Book, no. 4. In a letter to Sibley, January 8, 1854, Ramsey expressed his opinion of Young's report. Sibley Papers.

[99] *Ramsey Investigation Report*, 358–426.

[1] Robertson was an aspirant for the governorship of the territory. His action may reasonably be attributed to a desire to have Sibley, "the biggest log in the jam," out of his way, rather than to a deliberate attempt to injure Ramsey. Both the *Minnesota Pioneer* and the *Minnesotian* assert that the whole investigation was the result of a political fight directed against Sibley. *Minnesota Pioneer*, June 16, 1853, February 2, 1854; *Minnesotian*, August 27, 1853; Robertson to Ramsey, January 24, 1854, Ramsey Papers, reprinted in *Ramsey Investigation Report*, 428; Eastman to Sibley, February 9, 1854, Sibley Papers.

[2] 33 Congress, 1 session, *Senate Reports*, no. 131 (serial 706); 33 Congress, 1 session, *Senate Journal*, 14–17, 211 (serial 689).

[3] "The MUS is born! Amen. The Com. on Indian Affairs in Senate this day reported in the RAMSAY Case and ask to be discharged!! *Bah! !* Ramsey feels *bon. Il bon com ça.*

The Senate evidently took the view that Governor Ramsey acted the part of a statesman and, to carry out a great national measure, ignored technicalities and errors in procedure, permitted individuals to deceive themselves, and stood like a rock against the assaults of an opposition which had no other motive than to extort a share of the funds pledged to those beneficiaries whose interference was absolutely indispensable to the great end. Exeunt Hugh Tyler and Madison Sweetser.

9. CHIPPEWA HALF-BREED SCRIP[4]

As usual in Indian treaties of the period, a gratification was provided in the Chippewa treaty of 1854 for the mixed-bloods of the bands, to secure their desirable assistance in gaining the consent of the Indians to the treaty, or at least to prevent their possible opposition. The provision in this treaty was in the following clause of the second article: "Each head of a family or single person over twenty-one years of age at the present time of the mixed bloods, belonging to the Chippewas of Lake Superior, shall be entitled to eighty acres of land, to be selected by them under the direction of the President, and which shall be secured to them by patent in the usual form."[5] The treaty was proclaimed on January 29, 1855. Early in that year Henry C. Gilbert, the agent of the Lake Superior band, was instructed to report the number of persons entitled to claim land under it. On November 21, he reported 278 names and stated that the number could not be "very materially increased." In a letter of February 17, 1856, Agent Gilbert offered a suggestion that "certificates" be issued to the persons entitled, for their convenience in locating the lands. This suggestion met with the approval of the Indian office, but the commissioner of the general land office filed an emphatic objection. Patents, he held, "should issue to the reservees themselves, and not to assignees." The secretary of the interior put a brief indorsement on the letter of Commissioner Hendricks suggesting that "memorandums be given Indians" with a clause forbidding "transfer, mortgage &c.," and declaring that patents should be issued to Indians only, so that no benefit could inure to any other persons. The commissioner of Indian affairs at once interpreted this indorsement as authorizing what he pre-

All right. Dodge is a Captain. Write and tell him so." See Eastman to Sibley, February 24, 1854, in the Sibley Papers. In a letter to Dousman, written on May 28, 1854, Sibley stated that Governor Ramsey's defense had cost that gentleman five thousand dollars. Sibley expressed his willingness to subscribe five hundred dollars to reimburse him "if the rest of you including the House are also disposed to do something." Sibley Letter Book, no. 4.

[4] See *ante*, p. 307. The reader may find further details about the Chippewa scrip in Matthias N. Orfield, *Federal Land Grants to the States with Special Reference to Minnesota*, 189–206 (University of Minnesota, *Studies in the Social Sciences*, no. 2 — Minneapolis, 1915). This account was written before Mr. Orfield's valuable work appeared.

[5] *Statutes at Large*, 10: 1109.

ferred to call "certificates" and accordingly he submitted a form for the secretary's sanction. This was given. The form contained a clause declaring that no certificate nor any right under it could be sold, transferred, mortgaged, assigned, or pledged; and that a patent would be issued directly to the person named. By the close of the year 1856 Agent Gilbert, instructed to act with liberality, reported that he had issued certificates to substantially all the beneficiaries, in number 312. It would naturally be supposed that this part of the treaty was fulfilled.[6]

Eight years later there were issued two pieces of scrip to members of the well-known Borup family of St. Paul, who, though connected with the Chippewa of Lake Superior, had not resided among them either at the time of the treaty of La Pointe or thereafter. These claims had been filed on September 3, 1857, by Henry M. Rice and had been rejected by both the Indian office and the department of the interior. On March 19, 1863, Rice renewed the applications before a new commissioner of Indian affairs, of an accommodating temper, who ruled that it was a forced construction which required residence on the ceded land. The secretary of the interior sustained this ruling and the Borup scrip was issued on January 29, 1864.[7]

Immediately there was a remarkable access of persons proud and happy to be known as mixed-bloods of the Chippewa of Lake Superior. The practice of the Indian office operated to swell the number of applicants. On the ground that all Chippewa were related, it was held that all were Chippewa of Lake Superior and that all half-breed Chippewa were proper beneficiaries of the treaty. At once there was great industry in discovering widely scattered Chippewa half-breeds and in making known to them their good fortune. A "factory" was established by the United States Indian agent at La Pointe, Wisconsin, aided by willing or subsidized confederates, at which over two hundred applications, some of them sheer forgeries, were manufactured. On the basis of these applications, 199 pieces of scrip were issued. A coöperative mill in St. Paul ground out 756 applications, of which apparently some 261 were approved. But the search for mixed-bloods "entitled" was not confined to Wisconsin and

---

[6] *Chippewa Half-Breeds of Lake Superior*, 2–4, 33–38 (42 Congress, 2 session, *House Executive Documents*, no. 193 — serial 1513). In the original issues of the scrip, the clause designed to protect the poor Indians against the speculators read as follows: "It is expressly understood and declared that any sale, transfer, mortgage, assignment, or pledge of this certificate, or of any rights accruing under it, will not be recognized as valid by the United States; and that the patent for lands located by virtue thereof shall be issued directly to the above-named reservee, or his heirs, and shall in nowise inure to the benefit of any other person or persons."

[7] *Chippewa Half-Breeds of Lake Superior*, 4, 38, 40. Rice's argument was that, as the Indians concerned had had no reservations and consequently no homes from 1842 to 1854, mixed-bloods could not reside with them.

Minnesota. In the spring of 1865 an enterprising notary in the employ of the best-known trader at Pembina, after exhausting the vicinity, traveled down the Red River as far as Fort Garry, now Winnipeg. His diligence was rewarded with about 415 applications, part or all of which were sent to Washington, and on them the commissioner of Indian affairs issued 105 pieces of scrip. Probably not one of those whose names were signed to these applications had any real right under the treaty.[8]

At this point it is in order to explain the remarkable activity displayed in the search for mixed-bloods of the Chippewa of Lake Superior, who were heads of families or persons twenty-one years old or more in 1854. By the time of the issue of the Borup scrip in 1864, the certificates had become a desirable vehicle for the location of pine timber lands in unsurveyed districts. A standard procedure was soon developed. Notwithstanding the plain declaration on the face of each certificate that it could not be sold, transferred, mortgaged, assigned, or pledged, astute attorneys soon devised a scheme to circumvent the benevolent safeguards of the government. A mixed-blood having been discovered or imagined, he was induced, for a trifling consideration paid or promised, to sign an "application" to the Indian office for scrip. At the same time he executed two powers of attorney in blank, one to receive and locate his scrip, the other to sell the land when located. A single touch of the pen is said to have sufficed for all the papers. The scrip or certificate was then obtained from the department of the interior; and, equipped with it and the powers of attorney, the dealer in timber lands was free to locate according to his knowledge and judgment. He naturally chose the finest pine timber he could find not already in private hands. Whether such blank powers of attorney were legally valid was a question not raised in the limited circle of persons engaged in the business. That at least one commissioner of Indian affairs received "a considerable portion of scrip," and that he refused issues when a division was not accorded, is a matter of record.[9]

The game went merrily on and in the sixteen months following the issue of the Borup scrip 564 pieces were issued. Then came a discouraging intermission. James Harlan became secretary of the interior under Lincoln's second administration in 1865. On June 9 of that year he sent back to the Indian office the application of Antoine Roy with a statement

[8] *Chippewa Half-Breeds of Lake Superior*, 12–14, 55–62, 66–79, 110–133.

[9] *Chippewa Half-Breeds of Lake Superior*, 59–62. On March 11, 1870, William P. Dole, United States commissioner of Indian affairs, sued Joseph P. Wilson of St. Cloud, Minnesota, to recover the sum of $6,720 for twenty-eight pieces of half-breed scrip sold by him to Wilson. To the complaint answer was made that twenty-four pieces had been delivered, but that they were of no value, because the commissioner had received them for services in issuing like worthless certificates from parties not entitled to them, in violation of his duty as commissioner and with the intent to defraud. The investigating commission reported that it was "well advised that the averments of Mr. Wilson's answer are correct and true."

that the treaty of La Pointe in 1854 did not "contemplate the issuing of 'scrip,' but patents, for the land . . . when selected and described." The commissioner was directed to instruct his agents that no more scrip would be issued to Chippewa half-breeds.[10] This firm and just decision remained in effect for three years, one month, and two days, during which time no issues were made. It is conceivable that some insignificant number of mixed-bloods entitled had been balked of their rights by negligence. It is certain that a clique of operators who had acquired applications were hoping for some turn of affairs which might enable them to recover their expenses and add to their fortunes. Whatever influence they commanded was brought to bear at Washington. Early in October, 1867, the junior United States senator from Minnesota requested the secretary of the interior to inform him as to the "proper method" by which an honest claimant under the treaty might obtain his rights. The matter was referred to the Indian office, which responded in a long communication on the twenty-fifth of the same month. It contained a recommendation that to mixed-bloods who should prove their claims, certificates be furnished entitling them to select eighty acres of land from any of the vacant public lands, whether surveyed or unsurveyed. The department took time to consider and on July 11, 1868, approved a form of a so-called "certificate of identity." The claimant fortunate enough to obtain one of these was authorized to present it at a local land office, to select his land, and to receive a patent for it. The new certificate was as convenient for the employment of blank powers of attorney as those issued in 1864 and 1865.[11]

No time was lost in getting the new machinery into operation. A man long resident in Minnesota, but then domiciled at Georgetown, in the District of Columbia, promptly laid before the Indian office 111 applications for scrip. These were examined so expeditiously that on August 15 they were forwarded to the secretary with a recommendation that certificates be issued. On the twenty-seventh such order was made. On the thirty-first the full number of certificates was issued to the attorney of the "scrippees." On the day following the same industrious agent filed 202 applications. Action on these was delayed while consideration was given to a request submitted soon after by the same person that mixed-bloods entitled to land should not be required to select their tracts from the area ceded by the treaty, but might be permitted to make their locations "upon any of the territory acquired from their own people." Obviously the scrip bearing this generous construction would be better property for the deserving mixed-blood or his assignee. The secretary of the

[10] *Chippewa Half-Breeds of Lake Superior,* 5, 40.

[11] *Chippewa Half-Breeds of Lake Superior,* 6–9, 40–45; H. L. Gordon to the author, June 8, 1904, Folwell Papers.

interior became convinced that it would be but equitable to concede that privilege, and in communications to the Indian office on October 28 and 29 he directed that certificates thereafter issued should bear such privilege. On December 17, the man from Georgetown received 196 more pieces. The two issues, aggregating over three hundred pieces, were Red River applications of 1865 which remained in the hands of the operators after the bars were put up by Secretary Harlan.[12] Another batch of 122 applications, filed by the same attorney, did not receive the same dispatch, however.

Under the new construction and orders, the search for Chippewa mixed-bloods who might be entitled to claim land under the treaty was renewed with great ardor. As the lists of applications swelled, the authorities at Washington evidently became apprehensive that some of them, at least, might not be meritorious. Suspicion deepened into conviction, and on August 11, 1869, the secretary of the interior informed the general land office that no more Chippewa half-breed scrip would be issued under the treaty of 1854, but that parties entitled could make their selections in person at land offices from surveyed lands. This ruling did not dishearten the diligent searchers for "half-breeds entitled." In the three years following large numbers of applications were accumulated and those of former years not granted were carefully preserved. The attorneys for the holders were active in demanding relief. The representative in Congress from the third district of Minnesota on June 15, 1870, represented to the secretary of the interior the hardships of half-breeds who had to travel 250 miles to a local land office to locate their tracts, and recommended the issue of scrip or certificates which could be located in person or by attorney. The Indian office approved this recommendation but the secretary did not act upon it.[13]

In the year following, under the ruling of August 11, 1869, which permitted locations in person, a notable variation of procedure took place. In the spring of 1870 Red River caravans, composed with few exceptions of mixed-bloods, came down from Pembina and points below for the usual trade. One, and perhaps another, bivouacked at St. Cloud. The members of the party were taken in gangs to the land office in that place, where they signed applications for patents for lands previously selected for them by benevolent persons. They also signed individual powers of attorney for the sale of their selections. Each received from the friendly citizens who had made known to him his good fortune a sum of money ranging

---

[12] *Chippewa Half-Breeds of Lake Superior*, 9, 45, 62. See also page 33 for forms of the certificates used. One of the certificates issued on December 17, 1868, on behalf of François Jondron, is in the Gordon Papers.

[13] *Chippewa Half-Breeds of Lake Superior*, 10, 47.

from fifteen to forty dollars. The register of the land office later certified that the applicants were mixed-bloods of the Chippewa nation, that
the witnesses were in most cases known to him to be reliable, and that he
believed the applications to be entirely accordant with the rulings of the
department of the interior.[14]

Doubtless in the hope that the government as in previous years would
relax the rigor of its rulings and instructions on behalf of deserving
half-breeds, the operators continued to accumulate applications; and the
Indian office was bombarded with demands for relief. On July 20, 1870,
the commissioner of Indian affairs recommended to the secretary of the
interior the appointment of a special agent to investigate claims, to take
evidence in the several cases, and to prepare a roll of those found by him
to be entitled to land under the treaty. The commissioner further proposed the name of a citizen of St. Paul as a competent person to perform
the service. The secretary approved the nomination and elaborate instructions were prepared for the guidance of the special agent. On March
11, 1871, the agent submitted a report of progress. He had been well
received by the mixed-bloods. They were almost universally solicitous
to obtain scrip free from embarrassing restrictions. A large number of
them had gone on their winter hunts and were found with difficulty, if at
all. He had rejected a large number of applications, was holding others
for further investigation or instructions, and thought that four or six
months' more time would be required to complete the work. Still, the
agent was able to show for his time and compensation a list of 135 claimants whose proofs of identity, with a single exception, he had found to be
"regular."[15]

The report was not satisfactory to Columbus Delano, the new secretary of the interior, to whom complaints had been made of frauds practiced
and contemplated. He decided to appoint a special commission to be
composed of men, well informed on Indian affairs, whom he could trust.
At the head he put his fellow citizen of Ohio, Henry S. Neal. The other
members were the two agents of the Minnesota Chippewa and the late
special agent. On September 4, 1871, the commission filed its report, the
essential points of which may be briefly catalogued:[16] (1) Of the 312
certificates issued in 1855, known as the "Gilbert scrip," 282 were unques-
tionably valid. (2) The 199 pieces obtained by the agent at La Pointe
were based on fraudulent or forged applications. (3) The applications

---

[14] *Chippewa Half-Breeds of Lake Superior*, 14, 64, 134–143. In some of the cases the
locations were sold by the operators before the applications were obtained. 43 Congress,
1 session, *Senate Executive Documents*, no. 33, p. 48 (serial 1580).

[15] *Chippewa Half-Breeds of Lake Superior*, 11, 47–52, 155.

[16] *Chippewa Half-Breeds of Lake Superior*, 12–15, 48. The report occupies pages 53 to
157 of this document.

collected by the St. Paul attorneys, upon which 261 pieces had been issued, were involved in fraud, and as a rule the mixed-bloods had received little or nothing for their claims. (4) The applications on which the Pembina trader had received 105 pieces were all fraudulent and in many cases the half-breeds had received nothing for their signatures. (5) Of the 310 applicants for whom "certificates of identity" were issued to the resident of Georgetown, "probably not one . . . had any claims under the treaty." (6) The locations, 116 in number, made in person at St. Cloud were every one fraudulent. (7) Of the applications approved by the late special agent, but one was found valid. (8) There remained for investigation some hundreds of applications, mostly accumulated after the ruling of August 11, 1868, submitted by attorneys few of whom cared to assist the commission in its investigations. Out of 495 entries but eleven are noted as approved. (9) Twenty-seven applicants appeared in person before the commission, and five of them were found entitled to land.

In the various lists of applicants the commission found numerous departures from the provisions of the treaty restricting the grants of land to mixed-bloods of the Chippewa of Lake Superior who were heads of families or single persons twenty-one years old or upwards. White persons had pretended to be mixed-bloods, duplicate applications had been made by the same persons by the use of different middle initials, husbands and wives had been treated as being each the head of the same family, persons who had received Sioux scrip had applied, many considerably under age had appeared as claimants, and the names of several who were dead at the dates of applications had been included in the lists. The commission recommended that all outstanding illegal scrip be canceled, that no new certificates be issued except by special act of Congress, that persons who had been guilty of perjury, forgery, and embezzlement should not go unpunished, and especially that no government officer should be allowed to enjoy the fruits of crime at the expense of his wards.

The revelations of the Neal commission evidently suspended the issue of patents for land which had been located with Chippewa half-breed scrip. This was embarrassing to persons who had paid good money for it. As innocent purchasers they felt themselves entitled to relief at the hands of a government which for years had tolerated, if not invited, trading in this scrip. A body of holders actuated by a common interest sought such relief. They had the good fortune to secure the intervention of the senior United States senator from Minnesota, the more cheerfully rendered, perhaps, because he had acquired an interest in some locations, and the more effective because he was at the time the chairman of the Senate committee on public lands. Upon his initiative, Congress on June 8, 1872, passed an act entitled: "An Act to perfect certain Land-titles therein described." The rapidity with which the bill was expedited to passage is noteworthy. The essential part of the act was that innocent parties who had acquired locations made in good faith by claimants under the treaty of 1854 might complete their entries and perfect their titles by paying such a price as the secretary of the interior should deem equitable, but not less than one dollar and a quarter per acre.[17]

On July 15, 1872, the commissioner of Indian affairs, under superior direction, appointed the Honorable Thomas C. Jones of Ohio and two others as a commission to investigate the claims which might be made under the act. They were instructed (1) to ascertain what persons were entitled to the benefits of the act and (2) to advise the secretary what would be an equitable "and proper" price. The Jones commission submitted its report on November 25, 1872. It found thirteen individuals, firms, or corporations entitled to relief as innocent purchasers in good faith of scrip notoriously fraudulent, and approved 262 entries of eighty acres each, nearly all of "the best quality of Government pine-land to be found in Minnesota." The Jones commission also concurred with the Neal commission of the previous year in the conclusion that all the so-called scrip except the Gilbert scrip and forty-five other pieces was so tainted with actual and clearly established fraud as to be of no value or validity. It found the persons whose claims it approved to be in no way implicated in these frauds. "Indeed, the testimony tends to show that these parties had very little knowledge, and made no inquiry on that subject." Those who had got up the scheme had managed it with such wonderful prudence and caution as to conceal its fraudulent features from these very capable men of affairs. They were, therefore, innocent purchasers in good faith, entitled under the act of June 8, 1872, to purchase directly from the United States the tracts designated by their worthless certificates. According to the testimony taken the value of the lands ranged from five to ten dollars an acre and was increasing at the rate of twelve per cent a year. The commission, however, advised the secretary that a price of two dollars and a half an acre would be "equitable and proper" for the reason that the government would never get more at a public sale. At any such sale "a combination of bidders" would hold the price to that limit.[18]

Although the commission was constrained to recommend relief to these innocent purchasers of fraudulent scrip, it declared that the testimony

---

[17] *Statutes at Large*, 17: 340; 42 Congress, 2 session, *Senate Journal*, 564, 904, 979 (serial 1477); *House Journal*, 1073 (serial 1501).

[18] 42 Congress, 1 session, *Senate Executive Documents*, no. 33 (serial 1580). The report of the commission (pp. 9–18) is followed by a minority report (pp. 18–24), the testimony taken by the commission (pp. 25–65), and a schedule of the approved claims with the names of the "innocent holders" (pp. 69–75).

taken revealed a "reckless carelessness in making large purchases, and . . . on the part of many claimants, guilty participation in an ingenious device to evade the orders of the Government, made under the law." Every piece issued bore on its face the statement that it was unassignable. The remarkable thing about this last phase of the business is that no more experienced or astute dealers in pine lands have been known in Minnesota than these "innocent purchasers." It is no pleasure to tell this story.

10. THE WATAB TREATY OF 1853[19]

An abortive effort to accommodate the dissatisfied Winnebago with a home more to their liking than that selected for them by Rice at Long Prairie is worthy of note. In the treaty of October 13, 1846, with these Indians it was provided that they should be removed to a tract of not less than eight hundred thousand acres north of the St. Peter's and west of the Mississippi, "suitable to their habits, wants, and wishes." The dissatisfaction of these Indians with their first Minnesota home, evidenced by the difficulties of removing them to and establishing them upon it narrated above, increased from year to year. In his report for 1852 Agent Fridley regarded as hopeless the idea of inducing any considerable portion of the tribe to reside on the reservation, covered as it was, he wrote, in greater part with swamps and almost impenetrable thickets, and swarming in the summer months with mosquitoes and other insects. In his report, for the same year, as superintendent of Indian affairs in Minnesota, Governor Ramsey approved the statements of Agent Fridley and expressed his own opinion in these words: "With their present location these Indians will never be satisfied. They continually urge that an imposition was practised in colonizing them upon it; that it is not the country they had in view in agreeing to the treaty of 1846." He had already, in January, 1852, recommended to the Indian office that the Winnebago be removed to a tract of some five hundred thousand acres, included in the late Sioux purchase and situated immediately north of the Crow River.[20]

When Willis A. Gorman succeeded to the governorship of the territory on May 15, 1853, he naturally accepted the views of his predecessor and asked for instructions from the Indian office. He was credited with a righteous resolution to inaugurate a new Indian policy in the territory, in which traders would play no considerable and no mischievous part. In a letter of June 7, 1853, the commissioner of Indian affairs recom-

[19] See *ante*, p. 318.

[20] *Statutes at Large*, 9: 878–880; report of the United States commissioner of Indian affairs for 1852, in 32 Congress, 2 session, *House Executive Documents*, no. 1, pp. 333, 342 (serial 673).

mended to the secretary of the interior that the Winnebago be removed to a new home on the Crow River at some distance west of the Mississippi, not nearer that river than the forks of the Crow. On the twenty-third of the same month the Winnebago submitted a proposition to accept (1) a tract adjoining the lower end of the Sioux reservations on the Minnesota, (2) a tract within the lower Sioux reservation, or (3) a tract on the Crow River. The department at once rejected the first two locations.[21]

On August 8, 1853, at a point on the Watab River, Governor Gorman and Agent Jonathan E. Fletcher concluded "articles of convention with the chiefs and head men of the Winnebagoes." It was agreed that the tribe should surrender the Long Prairie Reservation and accept a tract described as follows: "Beginning at the mouth of Crow River; thence up the Mississippi River . . . to the mouth of Clearwater River; thence up said Clearwater River to its head; thence directly west . . . to Crow River; and thence down said Crow River to the place of beginning." The Indians utterly refused to accept a tract which did not front on the Mississippi.[22] The Winnebago did not wait for the Senate to ratify this treaty but put it into operation on their part at once. Agent Fletcher in his report for 1853 stated that about three hundred Winnebago were at Long Prairie and a few were on the Watab Prairie; the larger remainder were on the Crow River, "which, since the late treaty with them, they consider as their home."[23]

Loud clamors of protest were soon heard throughout the territory and especially in the parts adjacent to the new reserve. The grand jury of Hennepin County presented the Winnebago Indians for depredations of crops and for other offenses and named Willis A. Gorman and Jonathan E. Fletcher as aiders and abettors.[24] The leading newspapers took up the controversy and, according to their politics, praised or damned the treaty and Governor Gorman. The *Minnesota Pioneer* and the *Minnesota Democrat* made elaborate editorial apologies. The *Minnesotian* of August 27, reviewing an editorial of the *Democrat*, characterized it as "a *leetle* of the tallest specimen of wholesale falsehood that has ever disgraced the columns of that disgraced and abandoned sheet." Objections were raised against the treaty as a whole, but it was particularly condemned because it brought the new reservation out to the Mississippi and did not

---

[21] *Minnesota Pioneer*, August 18, 1853. A somewhat different statement of the proposition of the Indians is given in the *Minnesota Democrat* for June 29, 1853.

[22] An account of the proceedings of the treaty council, reported by the editor, appeared in the *Minnesota Democrat* for August 10, 1853. A fuller account by "Jeromus Jayhawk" is in the issue of August 24. The description of the boundaries is taken from *Senate Executive Proceedings*, 9: 337.

[23] Report of the United States commissioner of Indian affairs for 1853, in 33 Congress, 1 session, *House Executive Documents*, no. 1, p. 309 (serial 710).

[24] *Weekly Minnesotian*, September 17, 1853.

confine the Indians to an area separated from that river by a considerable margin, as recommended by the Indian office.[25]

In his report for 1853 Governor Gorman asserted that, while the Winnebago were much pleased with their new home or at least professed to be, there were some persons who were dissatisfied because no difference in money had been allowed the Indians in the exchange to pay old debts. The same men, he added, complained against the treaty because they wished to "go on the west side [of the Mississippi] and make what they call claims, and thus cut the good timber off government lands . . . without being actual settlers." The exchange, "made without the *disinterested* interference of traders and speculators, some of whom have no other care for the red man than to fatten on his ignorance and frailty," ought by all means to be confirmed; he added, "I know what I say, and mean what I say." It was his judgment that, if the treaty should not be affirmed, the Winnebago would be "disintegrated forever, and must become shortly mere wandering trespassers, without hope, for all future time."[26]

The legislature of 1854 was no sooner organized than Representative Hezekiah Fletcher of Hennepin County on January 12 gave notice of his intention to introduce a "Memorial to Congress praying for the rejection of the late Winnebago Treaty." On the same day Joseph R. Brown gave notice in the Council that he would ask leave to introduce a remonstrance against its ratification.[27] A week later three councilors, of whom Brown was one, and seven representatives addressed a letter to Governor Gorman, in which reference was made to a conference held with him a few days previously in which he had expressed a willingness to unite in measures necessary to prevent the ratification of the Winnebago treaty, if its provisions "would materially conflict with the prosperity of our Territory, or a large portion of its population." They reminded the executive that the effect of the treaty, if ratified, would be to place a body of drunken and disorderly Indians within twenty-five miles of St. Anthony and the county seat of Hennepin County and less than forty miles from the capital of the territory. Disagreements with neighboring settlers and probable bloodshed would result. The governor replied on the same day that not till after he had written his report in September had he learned of any dissatisfaction with the treaty, unless by street rumor. He had no pride of opinion in the matter and no desire other than to promote the welfare of the territory. He would not, therefore, insist on the ratification

---

[25] *St. Anthony Express*, August 13, 1853; *Minnesotian*, August 13, 20, 27, September 10, 17, 1853; *Minnesota Pioneer*, August 17, 1853; *Minnesota Democrat*, August 17, 1853.

[26] 33 Congress, 1 session, *House Executive Documents*, no. 1, p. 297 (serial 710).

[27] *House Journal*, 1854, p. 42; *Council Journal*, 1854, p. 39.

of the treaty but would request the Indian office to withhold it from the Senate.[28]

The reasons for Gorman's change of position are not well known. The insinuation of an opposition newspaper that he desired to secure the support of Joseph R. Brown and the *Minnesota Pioneer* needs confirmation.[29] The same remark applies to a statement of Representative Fletcher, in a meeting of citizens in St. Anthony on January 21, that the governor preferred to request the withdrawal of the treaty himself rather than to have a legislative memorial go to Washington.[30] A reasonable rationale of his change of opinion is that a fuller knowledge of the situation had convinced Governor Gorman that the exchange of reservations for the Winnebago, which in September he thought should by all means be made, would not result favorably. But his tardiness in coming round to this conclusion had cost him a loss of prestige with his party. Henry M. Rice, expert in all Winnebago matters, was known to disapprove of the treaty, and his late election to the delegacy would give him vantage for opposing its ratification. The state of mind in one branch of the legislature, the House, may be inferred from the fate of two resolutions. One of them, introduced immediately after the reading of the correspondence above mentioned, which declared that the members had full confidence in the honesty, capacity, and integrity of Governor Gorman, was, after some futile badinage, upon leave granted, withdrawn. The other, introduced by Representative Fletcher, which approved of Governor Gorman's withdrawal of the treaty when officially notified of the just and reasonable objections against it and declared the withdrawal to be an assurance of his integrity as a public officer, was laid on the table by a vote of 12 to 5.[31]

The treaty was not withheld but was laid before the Senate on April 10, 1854. Either the Indian office approved of the exchange of reservations or the matter had gone too far to warrant administrative suppression.

[28] The correspondence was read in the House on January 24 and is printed in its *Journal*, 57–59.

[29] *Minnesotian*, January 28, 1854. In commenting on the correspondence between Gorman and the members of the legislature, which is printed in this issue, the editor states that, after Rice's election as delegate to Congress, "the Watab treaty was a dead cock in the pit." The governor is represented as saying to "Joseph the Juggler," "I don't want Rice — the villain — to have the credit of killing it; *you* can have the honor . . . if you will only promise to keep that memorial out of the Legislature; put a puff in the Pioneer . . . come down on the Indian traders generally, just a little; get your old Sioux trader friends to stand by me hereafter, and the Legislature to endorse me; keep Gov. Ramsey's Whig friends in good humor towards me, and not oppose me in flooring the Rice people." In a letter written to Ramsey on January 27, 1854, David Cooper alludes to a coalition between Gorman, Sibley, and Brown as a result of which Brown was to have one-half of the public printing. Ramsey Papers.

[30] *Minnesota Pioneer*, January 26, 1854. The *Minnesota Democrat* made no allusion to the proposed withdrawal of the treaty, but, on February 1, 1854, printed an apology for it.

[31] *House Journal*, 1854, pp. 60, 75.

When the treaty came up for consideration on June 19 the paragraph describing the new tract to be assigned to the Winnebago was struck out and replaced by another, assigning "a square of twenty miles high up on the southern main branch of Crow River . . . embracing two hundred and fifty-six thousand acres, or within the Sioux Reservation . . . with the consent of said Indians." A new article, permitting a change of the annuities if the policy of establishing farms for the benefit of the Indians should be decided upon, was adopted. Thus amended, the treaty was ratified unanimously. On July 10 the president at the request of the Senate returned the treaty. On the twenty-first another new article was added, which provided that, should the Winnebago prefer some other location, the president might assign them a tract of the same quantity "southwest of the Missouri River or elsewhere."[32] Up to September 30, the date of Governor Gorman's report for 1854 as superintendent of Indian affairs, the amended treaty had not been submitted to the Indians. Whether it was at any time formally submitted is not known, but on January 24, 1855, Gorman informed the commissioner of Indian affairs that the Winnebago had refused to agree to the amendments. The treaty of February 27, 1855, which gave the Indians the Blue Earth Reservation in exchange for that at Long Prairie, is discussed in the text. Gorman made a forcible protest against that concession to the Winnebago.[33]

11. SIOUX HALF-BREED SCRIP[34]

The liberality of the government in "exchanging scrip" with the Sioux half-breeds for the lands of the Wabasha Reservation granted them in the treaty at Prairie du Chien in 1830 for no valuable consideration whatever — lands which for a whole generation they had refused to occupy and settle and which they never intended to occupy — was perhaps admirable. Especially generous was the provision that the "certificates or scrip" might be located on any public lands of the United States. With childlike confidence Congress had enacted a statute which was to put it out of the power of anybody to defeat its benevolent purpose.

[32] *Senate Executive Proceedings*, 9: 336–338, 346, 348, 363.

[33] Report of the United States commissioner of Indian affairs for 1854, in 33 Congress, 2 session, *House Executive Documents*, no. 1, p. 256 (serial 777); *Statutes at Large*, 10: 1175, article 11; *Council Journal*, 1856, appendix, p. 2. The *Daily Minnesota Pioneer* for August 17, 1855, charged Rice with having informed the people of Rice and Stearns Counties that the responsibility for the location of the Winnebago in the Blue Earth region belonged to Governor Gorman, when, as a matter of fact, he, Rice, was responsible for it, or at least could have prevented it. The issue of August 22 contains Gorman's disclaimer of all responsibility for the removal. He had merely certified to the authenticity of the agreement made between General Fletcher, the Winnebago agent, and six Winnebago chiefs at St. Paul on May 25, 1855, at the same time protesting against it.

[34] See *ante*, p. 324.

"No transfer or conveyance of said certificates or scrip shall be valid," read the law. No land pirates could ever rob the deserving beneficiaries who had so long waited for justice, so-called.[35]

A year passed while the survey was in progress, and nearly another while the commissioners appointed for the purpose were making up a roll of the half-breeds entitled to participate in the distribution of the scrip. The survey showed an area of 320,819.48 acres in the reservation. The number of beneficiaries enrolled was 640.[36] It was decided in the interior department on November 24, 1856, to apportion to each claimant two pieces of 160 acres each, one of 80 acres, and two of 40 acres each— in all, 480 acres. The distribution was made in the spring of 1857 at Wabasha, Faribault, and other convenient places by General James Shields, who had lately become a resident of Minnesota and who was to be one of her first United States senators. The area thus disposed of, 307,200 acres, left a remainder of 13,619.48 acres of good land for the relief of any Sioux half-breeds who might have been overlooked in the general distribution. On October 12, 1860, the secretary of the interior recognized the claims of the convenient number of thirty-eight additional applicants and apportioned to each 360 acres, which exhausted the reservation. The whole tract was thus promptly opened to settlement, and it was rapidly taken up by desirable immigrants.[37]

The instances in which the beneficiary located his scrip personally on the reservation or elsewhere were rare. The sizes of some of the families of white men who had married Sioux women were truly notable.[38] Ten children were good for 4,800 acres. The provision of the statute declaring all conveyances of scrip invalid was evaded by the same device as that employed in the case of the Chippewa half-breed scrip. Two powers of attorney, one to locate, another to sell, worked a substantial alienation.[39]

[35] *Congressional Globe*, 33 Congress, 1 session, 1114; *Statutes at Large*, 10:304. It is interesting to note that Rice, who introduced the bill, made no remarks on it. An elaborate account of the numerous efforts to secure a division or the sale of the Sioux half-breed tract is in *Sioux Lands or Reservation in Minnesota Territory* (33 Congress, 1 session, *House Reports*, no. 138 — serial 743).
[36] In the debate on the bill the number of Sioux half-breeds was estimated at about two hundred, and no other number was suggested.
[37] 34 Congress, 3 session, *House Executive Documents*, no. 1, p. 214 (serial 893); 38 Congress, 1 session, *Senate Reports*, 62 (serial 1178); 36 Congress, 2 session, *Senate Executive Documents*, no. 1, p. 238 (serial 1078); Wheelock, *Minnesota: Its Place among the States*, 144; letters to Sibley from Shields, October 5, 1855, February 3, November 20, December 23, 1856, from Rice, April 7, 1856, from Dousman, April 9, 1856, from Welles, August 20, 1858, Sibley Papers. At land prices in the region in 1919 the reservation would have been worth over sixty million dollars.
[38] William L. Quinn of St. Paul, an Indian interpreter, and Francis J. Murphy of Los Angeles, California, both had lists to which the author has had access.
[39] See *ante*, p. 472. There are examples of the two powers of attorney on printed forms in the Steele Papers, under date of January 18, 1864. Joseph R. Brown granted similar

Where there were white relatives to counsel, some "breeds" got fair prices for their scrip. In some cases it went to pay old debts to traders on terms virtually dictated by them. But, as one of the distributees said, "the half-breeds mostly got cats and dogs for their scrip."[40] The framers of the act of July 17, 1854, had taken pains to have it provide that the scrip might be located on any public lands of the United States open to settlement, whether surveyed or not. Considerable quantities of it were taken to Nevada and California to be placed on forest and mineral lands.[41] It was peculiarly convenient at the time for the location of town sites in advance of surveys. Many Minnesota villages were laid out on sites thus acquired. Within five years, more than one-half of the whole area had been located in the territory, mostly "on town sites and their appendages."[42]

A later employment of Sioux half-breed scrip must here be mentioned. It could be located on forest as well as on agricultural lands, and no small proportion was so used. In instances notably numerous it happened that, soon after a "piece" of scrip had been located on a promising tract of pine land, the timber would be cut and removed. Thereupon the locator would go to the land office, allege some error in selection, and demand the privilege of abandoning the land thus devastated and of making a relocation for his deserving principal. What is remarkable is that the same thing would recur after no long interval, through the indulgence, not to say the connivance, of the land officers. It became chronic and general, and the operation came to be known as "the floating of scrip." It is, of course, not necessary to give the plain English for this method of acquiring pine timber from the United States. Whenever it happened, as it sometimes did, that pine land located by scrip in unsurveyed regions was covered by a survey before the timber could be removed, the operator would find an effective pretext for abandonment of the location, would then pay for it at the government price, on his own account, and would relocate the scrip. In 1872 the commissioner

powers in 1871. See Brown to his brother, February 16, 1871, in the Brown Papers. In a letter to Samuel J. Brown, dated September 16, 1870, Brown wrote: "The entry of that land requires care as much more than the scrip calls for can be obtained by management. . . . See ——— and get him to go to see the surveyor general with you." Brown Papers.

[40] In a letter to Brown, December 4, 1863, Sibley said, "I am in want of some *reliable* scrip for which I would be willing to pay $2.50." Rice wrote to Brown on December 7, 1863, "Purchase for me all the *adult* halfbreed scrip you can for $1.00 per acer." These letters are in the Brown Papers. In an interview with the writer on August 9, 1904, William Quinn, the interpreter, said: "Alexis Bailly was at the bottom of it [*the half-breed grant of 1830*]. Rocque and Cratte were also in it."

[41] Eastman to Sibley, February 20, 1854, Sibley Papers. See also the unpublished correspondence of W. S. Chapman with Franklin Steele and Henry T. Welles in the Steele Papers for 1850. Selections were made in many states.

[42] Wheelock, *Minnesota: Its Place among the States*, 166.

of public lands, in a circular, animadverted severely upon such use of the scrip.[43]

In 1884 iron ore was first mined in the "Triangle" north of Lake Superior, thus tardily verifying the predictions of geologists and explorers. Instantly there arose a demand for every possible means whereby control of, if not title to, lands in the ore districts still unsurveyed could be secured by private parties. None was more convenient or effective than the few pieces of Sioux half-breed scrip which, for one reason or another, had not been finally located and canceled. A considerable number of pieces were accordingly placed. But preëmptors on unsurveyed lands and homesteaders on surveyed lands appeared as rival claimants for title to certain valuable sections or fractions of sections and succeeded in securing favorable rulings at the local offices. Scrip claimants appealed to the secretary of the interior, Vilas, of Cleveland's first cabinet, who, to their surprise, sustained the local rulings against them. In an opinion of February 18, 1889, this officer held that the two powers of attorney could not convey title and that, in the case of unsurveyed land, improvements made by the half-breed or for his interest were a necessary condition precedent to patenting. The act of 1854 created only a personal right. The powers of attorney were but means to circumvent the law and to rob the real beneficiary. They were an "ingenious invention" to invest scrip with a quality of negotiability specifically denied by Congress. The same cases were reopened and reviewed in 1891 by the successor of Secretary Vilas, who sustained his rulings.[44] The scrip claimants now resorted to the courts and obtained an unbroken series of favorable decisions culminating in that of January 13, 1902.[45] In all the decisions it was held that the secretary of the interior had erred in his rulings, that the two powers of attorney, if genuine, did work a conveyance to the holder for value, and that improvement by the original "scrippee" was not essential to patents on unsurveyed lands. The supreme court of Minnesota remarked that for years after the passage of the act of 1854 such locations had been made without the thought that improvements were contemplated.[46] It

[43] Interviews with Caleb D. Dorr, pioneer lumberman, on May 20, 1904, and with Judge William Lochren on March 9, 1904. A copy of the circular is in the library of the department of the interior at Washington.

[44] Allen *et al.* *v.* Merrill *et al.*, in Department of Interior and General Land Office, *Decisions* (Public Land Decisions), 8: 207; 12: 138.

[45] Midway Company *v.* Eaton, 183 *United States Reports*, 602, 619. This case was popularly known as the "Section 30 case."

[46] Midway Company *v.* Eaton *et al.*, 79 *Minnesota*, 442. See also Bishop Iron Company *v.* Hyde *et al.*, 66 *Minnesota*, 24, for a description of the property involved. Two other cases are of interest in this connection: Thompson *v.* Myrick, 20 *Minnesota*, 205 (99 *United States*, 291), and Felix *v.* Patrick, 145 *United States*, 317.

may be surmised that the courts, considering that the whole matter had almost passed into history, deemed it impolitic to render decisions which might, by beclouding the titles of holdings, create loss and inconvenience. Statesmen and judges do well upon occasion to conform to an ancient principle of law known as *quieta non movere*. These decisions quieted title to mining properties worth many millions. After the beginning of the twentieth century only occasional pieces of Sioux half-breed scrip, mostly reissues of originals lost or destroyed, were used.

12. THE BOUNDARIES OF MINNESOTA[47]

The southern boundary of Minnesota was determined with the establishment of the northern limit of Iowa by an act of Congress of August 4, 1846. All the area between the Mississippi and the Missouri rivers north of the state of Missouri was made part of the Territory of Michigan in 1834. Two years later, after the organization of the state of Michigan, the Territory of Wisconsin was formed to embrace all the remaining area. Another two years passed, and in 1838 the Territory of Iowa was formed west of the Mississippi, and Wisconsin Territory was restricted to the eastern residue.[48]

The settlement of Iowa was phenomenally rapid, and as early as 1840 agitation began for the organization of a state government. Content with a government supported out of the United States treasury, conservative majorities defeated two referenda on the question, and it was not till 1844 that a convention was called. It met in the old stone Capitol in Iowa City on Monday, October 7, 1844. On the afternoon of the fifth day the convention, having completed its organization, took up the report of its committee on boundaries. The northern boundary at once became the leading issue. The report proposed that the northern boundary should run from a point on a branch of the Big Sioux or Calumet River "to the St. Peter's River, opposite the mouth of the Blue Earth, and down the St. Peter's to the Mississippi." This line was too far south to suit some of the more ambitious delegates and a variety of substitutes were at once proposed to secure a larger empire. One of these was the latitude of 45° north; and, when this failed, that of 44° was suggested. After first rejecting and then accepting a motion to run the northern boundary from the mouth of the Big Sioux River "to the Mississippi, opposite the mouth of the Little Sac or Wahtap River (above St. Anthony's Falls)," the convention in committee of

[47] See *ante*, p. 236.
[48] *Statutes at Large*, 4: 701; 5: 49, 235; Gannett, *Boundaries of the United States*, 120–125 (United States Geological Survey, *Bulletins*, no. 226).

the whole decided to lower the eastern end of that line about ten miles
to the latitude of 45° 30'.   The advocates of these distant bounds particularly desired to have the Falls of St. Anthony included in the new
state.   They would, said one delegate, "add wealth and power.   We
could not have too much water power."   Said another, "The water
power there was almost incalculable.   It would run machinery of every
description, and before many years it would be one of the most important spots in the Western country."   Delegates with more moderate
views thought it unwise to make the state too large.   Ex-Governor

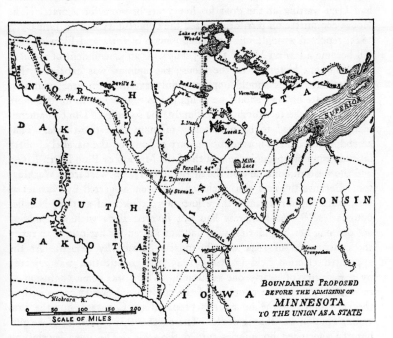

BOUNDARIES PROPOSED
BEFORE THE ADMISSION OF
MINNESOTA
TO THE UNION AS A STATE

Lucas pointed out that the extreme north line proposed would make a
state of more than 120,000 square miles and would "include the country
of the Sioux Indians, the title to which would hardly ever be extinguished."
There was a suggestion that such a "creeping up on the North" would
not be "in good faith to the South."   The moderate element prevailed
in the end and secured the acceptance of a report from a select committee
which recommended as the northern boundary of Iowa a line running
from the mouth of the Big Sioux River to "the St. Peters river, where
the Watonwan river (according to Nicollet's map) enters the same" and
then down the St. Peter's to the Mississippi.   This action met with

wide approval. The *Iowa Capitol Reporter* of November 9, 1844, voicing such sentiment, said of this boundary, it "gives us the majestic Mississippi for an entire eastern barrier, and carries our empire north to the St. Peters, and far west to the dark, rapid waters of the Missouri."[49]

The Iowa constitution of 1844 was transmitted to the Twenty-eighth Congress, which began its second session in December of that year. It had the usual references in both houses. The admission of new states into the Union in pairs, one free and one slave, had by this time become a part of the unwritten national constitution. The Territory of Florida had been waiting at the door for five years or more for a mate. The House committee on territories seized the opportunity and on January 7, 1845, reported a single bill for the admission of Iowa and Florida. The bill became a law on March 3, 1845, but with an amendment of moment in Minnesota history. In the House the opinion was expressed that new western states should not be unduly extensive in area, and that the new state of Iowa should be so limited as to leave room for two more free states in the territory. Accordingly, the so-called "Duncan amendment" was agreed to by a majority of more than two-thirds. That amendment fixed the northern boundary of Iowa on the parallel of north latitude running through the mouth of the Makato or Blue Earth River, and the western boundary on the meridian of 17° 30′ west from Washington. Because the area thus included had been suggested by Nicollet as a suitable one for a state, these lines were spoken of as the "Nicollet boundaries."[50] As Congress had not favored Iowa with an enabling act defining her boundaries, so it had not waited for her people to ratify the constitution of 1844 with boundaries chosen by herself. At the appointed election held in April, 1845, the constitution was rejected by a majority of nearly one thousand. There was some confusion as to whether or not the adoption of the constitution would carry with it the acceptance of the boundaries proposed by Congress, but the prevailing opinion was that it would. There were other objections of weight, but the shortened boundaries turned the scale. The Iowa legislature, by an act passed over the governor's veto on June 10, 1845, resubmitted the same constitution to a viva voce vote of the electors, with a proviso that its ratification should not be deemed an acceptance of the congressional boundaries. In the debate on the bill one member declared the interference of Congress to be "a glaring fraud, and a palpable and

---

[49] Benjamin F. Shambaugh, *History of the Constitutions of Iowa*, 234–240, 256 (Des Moines, 1902); Shambaugh, ed., *Fragments of the Debates of the Iowa Constitutional Conventions of 1844 and 1846*, 22–24, 29, 33, 135, 225 (Iowa City, 1900). The convention did not wait for an enabling act.

[50] Shambaugh, *Constitutions of Iowa*, ch. 12; *Statutes at Large*, 5: 742, 788–790; *Congressional Globe*, 28 Congress, 2 session, 274; Nicollet, *Report*, 73.

scandalous violation of an implied contract." In spite of the proviso many voters appear to have believed that the best way to reject the proposition of Congress was to defeat the constitution; the Whig press voiced the inflammatory appeal, "Strike against the Constitution — strike for big boundaries"; and the people struck, at the election in August, but by a reduced majority.[61]

The Twenty-ninth Congress had hardly convened when the Iowa delegate introduced into the House a bill to repeal so much of the act of March 3, 1845, as prescribed the Nicollet boundaries and to restore the St. Peter's line of the Iowa convention of 1844. The bill went to the committee on territories, of which Stephen A. Douglas was chairman. When he reported it on March 27, 1846, it was with an amendment fixing the northern boundary on the latitude of 43° 30'. The bill did not come up for consideration until June 8. Meanwhile the Iowa legislature had provided for a second convention, which met on May 4 and which, in the course of two weeks, turned out a new constitution, resembling in general structure that which had been twice rejected. By the time the article on boundaries was reached the probable action of Congress was known, and the advice of the delegate was to conform. After first voting to adhere to the St. Peter's line, the convention finally agreed to adopt that of latitude 43° 30', and the article was drafted accordingly Congress adopted the description and by act of August 4, 1846, settled the coterminous boundary of Iowa and Minnesota. The electors of Iowa gave a reluctant consent, as shown by the vote of 9,492 for and 9,036 against — a majority of 456.[52]

The existing eastern boundary of Minnesota was determined with the admission of Wisconsin to the Union by an act approved on May 29, 1848. The Wisconsin enabling act, approved on August 6, 1846, had prescribed the same line; but, in the meantime, the Wisconsin constitutional conventions had proposed two other lines. The original bill to authorize the people of Wisconsin to frame a constitution preparatory to admission as a state into the Union, introduced into the House by Delegate Morgan L. Martin, included in the proposed state the whole area of Wisconsin Territory. The amended bill reported from the committee on territories presented the St. Croix–Mississippi line as the western

---

[61] Shambaugh, *Constitutions of Iowa*, chs. 13, 14; Shambaugh, *Debates of the Iowa Constitutional Conventions*, 228–313.

[52] *Congressional Globe*, 29 Congress, I session, 86, 562, 938–941, 948; *Statutes at Large*, 9: 52; Shambaugh, *Constitutions of Iowa*, ch. 17; William Salter, *Iowa, the First Free State in the Louisiana Purchase*, 267 (Chicago, 1905). The survey of the Minnesota-Iowa boundary line is discussed in a letter from Nathan Butler to the author, January 14, 1908, in the Folwell Papers.

boundary. In the course of the consideration of this bill the Wisconsin delegate obtained the insertion of a proviso authorizing the Wisconsin convention "to adopt such northern and western boundaries in lieu of those herein prescribed, as may be deemed expedient, not exceeding, however, the present limits of the said Territory." No member suspected at the moment the intended operation of the amendment to be to allow Wisconsin to include the whole remnant of the Northwest Territory bounded west by the Mississippi and north by the international boundary. The House passed the bill with this proviso, but before the day was over a member surmised its natural and hoped-for effect and moved a reconsideration. This the House accorded on the following day, and it then rejected the exceptionable proviso by a very large vote and repassed the bill. The House was not disposed to allow the people of a new state to extend its limits at their pleasure.[53] The claim thus surreptitiously injected into the Wisconsin enabling act by the delegate was no novelty in Wisconsin. During the years when the question of assuming statehood was agitated, it had been taken for granted that the new state would include the whole extent of the territory. In February, 1842, a committee of the territorial Council submitted a report in which it was argued that under the Ordinance of 1787 Wisconsin had the right to become the fifth state authorized to be formed out of the old Northwest Territory whenever the population should reach sixty thousand. This "solemn compact entered into between the thirteen original States, and the people and future State of Wisconsin," argued the committee, Congress could no more repeal than it could repeal the Constitution itself.[54]

The first constitutional convention of Wisconsin met at Madison on October 5, 1846. On the twenty-ninth the committee on boundaries submitted a report which embodied the Council report of 1842 and

[53] *Statutes at Large*, 9:56–58; *Congressional Globe*, 29 Congress, 1 session, 196, 789, 941, 949, 952.

[54] Wisconsin Territory, *Council Journal*, 1841–42, pp. 279, 656–662. A more elaborate report of similar tenor submitted to the Council in December, 1843, was adopted by both houses the next month and was sent to Congress. It contains the following passage: "We could . . . take for ourselves and our state the boundaries fixed by that ordinance [*of 1787*], form our state constitution . . . apply for admission into the Union with those boundaries, and if refused, so that we could not be a state in the Union, we would be a *State out of the Union*, and possess, exercise, and enjoy, all the rights, privileges and powers of the *sovereign, independent State of Wisconsin*, and if difficulties must ensue, we could appeal with confidence to the GREAT UMPIRE of nations to adjust them." An accompanying address is even more truculent. Five hundred copies of the report and address were ordered printed. *Council Journal*, 1843–44, pp. 13, 55, 117, 128, 167, 169, 183, 187, 238, 240, 261, 263, appendix, 6–28; *House Journal*, 205, 209, 233, 242, 243, 245, 249; *Report of Select Committee on the Infringement of Boundaries, Made in Council of Wisconsin Territory December 18th, 1843* (Madison, 1843. 44 pp.). See also Reuben G. Thwaites, "Boundaries of Wisconsin," in *Wisconsin Historical Collections*, 11:451–501, in which the successive divisions of the Northwest Territory are happily stated and illustrated.

reasserted the irrepealable right of Wisconsin to the true boundaries fixed and established in the Ordinance of 1787. This long-standing pretension met with immediate dissent. Account has already been given of the enterprise of Joseph R. Brown in laying out the town site of Dakotah on the St. Croix in 1839, of the creation of St. Croix County, and of the location of the county seat at Dakotah. It has become traditional that it was Brown's ambition to secure the formation, from the area of Wisconsin Territory, of a new territory and state of which the capital would appropriately be located in the St. Croix Valley. There is some slight extant proof that Brown induced Morgan L. Martin, the delegate from Wisconsin, to introduce into the House of Representatives his bill .of January, 1846, for the creation of a new territory to be called Minnesota. William Holcombe, the delegate to the convention from St. Croix County, evidently came prepared to champion the project of carving a new territory out of the area of Wisconsin. On the day following that on which the committee on boundaries reasserted the claim of Wisconsin to her "fixed and established" limits, Holcombe obtained the appointment of a select committee to propose a line for the equitable division of the existing territory. The report of this committee, submitted on November 12, argued that the existing territory ought to be divided on account of its large extent and irregular shape, a fact attested by the enabling act itself. The people about the head of Lake Superior and in the St. Croix Valley were separated by a vast wilderness from the settled parts of Wisconsin and had different interests. The line recommended for an equitable division was one running from a point in the Mississippi River near the present railway station of Trempealeau — about twenty miles above La Crosse — northeastwardly to the headwaters of the Montreal River, the small stream which forms part of the western boundary of the upper peninsula of Michigan. This line would have cut off fourteen whole counties of Wisconsin and parts of five others.[55]

The convention first rejected the Holcombe proposition; but, when renewed in the form of a proposal to Congress as the preference of the state, it was accepted by a vote of 49 to 37. Upon a reconsideration it was defeated by a vote of 35 to 68. After a variety of proposals for asserting the claims of Wisconsin under the Ordinance of 1787 had been rejected by close votes, Holcombe moved to propose to Congress a line running

[55] Wisconsin Constitutional Convention, 1846, *Journal*, 133–146, 147, 154, 242–245 (Madison, 1847); Holcombe, in *Minnesota in Three Centuries*, 2: 350. There is a sketch of William Holcombe, by Mrs. Andrew E. Kilpatrick, in *Minnesota Historical Collections*, 10: 857–861 (part 2). The Minnesota Historical Society has a manuscript copy of a speech of his on the boundary question presumably delivered to the convention.

from the mouth of the Burnt Wood (Bois Brulé) River to the head of Lake Pepin. This line met with no greater favor than his former one. It would have added to the imaginary Territory of Minnesota four whole counties and parts of six other counties of western Wisconsin and would have given the hoped-for capital in the St. Croix Valley a comfortable margin to the eastward. The article on boundaries then went back to the committee of the whole, which on December 7 recommended a proposal to Congress of a line running from the first rapids of the St. Louis River southwardly to the center of Lake Pepin opposite the mouth of Clearwater Creek. The vote thereon was in the negative but the majority was so slight that Holcombe was encouraged to make another attempt at equitable division. On December 9, just before the final passage of the article, he proposed a line which should start from the same first rapids of the St. Louis River and run "thence in a direct line southwardly to a point ———— miles east of the most easterly point in Lake St. Croix; thence due south to the main channel of the Mississippi river or Lake Pepin;" and on down the main channel thereof. The convention adopted an amendment expressing a preference for this line by a vote of 49 to 38 and later filled in the blank with "fifteen miles." This line would have thrown large parts of five Wisconsin counties into Minnesota.[56]

Congress presumed the ratification of the constitution framed by the Wisconsin convention and by an act approved on March 3, 1847, provided for the admission of the state into the Union with the preferred western boundaries described in Holcombe's last proposition. But Congress presumed too much in the case. When submitted to a vote on the first Tuesday of April, 1847, the constitution was rejected by a notable majority for reasons which do not relate to the present narrative. The boundary question seems to have had no prominence in the campaign.[57]

The legislature of Wisconsin on October 27, 1847, authorized an election for delegates to a second convention, and the election was held on the twenty-fifth of the following month. The convention assembled on December 15. The article on boundaries which came from committee within a week accepted the boundaries of the enabling act but included a proviso expressing a preference for a western boundary running from the first rapids of the St. Louis River direct to the mouth of the Rum River and thence down the Mississippi. This line would have retained in Wisconsin all of Ramsey and Washington counties, nearly all of

[56] Wisconsin Constitutional Convention, 1846, *Journal*, 349-351, 361-365, 368-375, 378-383, 424, 444, 449.

[57] *Statutes at Large*, 9:178. Strong, *Wisconsin Territory*, 550-557, contains a résumé and a table of the vote.

Chisago, and considerable slices off the east parts of Anoka, Isanti, Pine, and Carlton counties. William Holcombe was not a member of the second convention, but St. Croix County found an equally vigorous champion in the person of George W. Brownell. At the earliest opportunity he presented a minority report and followed it with a motion to amend the proviso by substituting the Holcombe line from Trempealeau to the head of the Montreal River. In his report and speech he represented to the convention that his constituents on the St. Croix and about Fond du Lac were separated from the settlements of Wisconsin by a vast stretch of wilderness, which he declared to be mostly a low, flat region, "characterized for its pine barrens, lakes, tamarac swamps and marshes," and not worth the cost of surveying. This statement was vigorously disputed. But the Wisconsin delegates were not much concerned about the lay of the lands and their value for agriculture. Fenton of Prairie du Chien told the convention that the Rum River line would give to Wisconsin an immense pine region, the best probably in the world, and "the splendid water power on our side of St. Anthony's Falls." It would also secure a good route for a railroad soon to be built from the head of navigation on the Mississippi to the head of Lake Superior. He was supported by a colleague who expressed the belief that "the true cause of this movement was, that the people in that region were aware that the valley of the St. Croix was susceptible of a dense population, and that if set off into the new territory, the seat of government would be located somewhere in that valley." The amendment was rejected by the committee of the whole, but Brownell, undaunted, renewed it in convention, where it was defeated by a vote of 52 to 5. He then offered the second Holcombe proposition, the Bois Brulé River line, to be submitted to Congress as an alternative for the Rum River line in case that should be unacceptable; this was negatived by a vote of 53 to 2. At this point he ceased from troubling, and the article on boundaries, with the Rum River proviso incorporated in it, was adopted by the convention by a vote of 53 to 3.[58]

But a strong minority which had been outvoted on the question of asserting the right of Wisconsin under the Ordinance of 1787 to the whole remnant of the Northwest Territory was not disposed to surrender without

[58] Wisconsin Constitutional Convention, 1847–48, *Journal*, 3, 62, 79–84, 241–251, 257–259, 265; Holcombe, in *Minnesota in Three Centuries*, 2: 343. Brownell was a geologist. One account states that he was employed as a mining expert by a Boston company of which Caleb Cushing, Rufus Choate, and Robert Rantoul Jr. were members. See William R. Marshall, "Reminiscences of Wisconsin — 1842 to 1848," in the *Magazine of Western History*, 7: 248 (January, 1888). On the interests of Cushing and his associates in Minnesota, see also Folsom, in *Minnesota Historical Collections*, 9: 295, and Stanchfield, in *Minnesota Historical Collections*, 9:327, 328, 333, 339.

a further struggle. On January 21 Delegate Biggs introduced a resolution reasserting that right and declaring so much of the enabling act of Wisconsin as related to boundaries to be null and void. A prolonged debate ensued, at the close of which the resolution, somewhat toned down by amendment, was agreed to by a vote of 38 to 26. This vote was followed by an appropriate one to reconsider the adoption of the article on boundaries. There was an outpouring of oratory in defense of the rights guaranteed by the Ordinance of 1787. At the close Morgan L. Martin, president of the convention, summed up the sentiment of the majority. He assured the convention that it was useless to insist on any considerable enlargement of area. Congress would probably consent to giving Wisconsin the St. Croix Valley. He, therefore, counseled adhering to the Rum River line. As for the claim of a right under the Ordinance of 1787, it had already been "altered by common consent" when Illinois was admitted to the Union. The power of Congress on the question of boundaries was, in his opinion, absolute and unqualified. At the conclusion of Martin's speech the convention, on January 27, 1848, decided by a vote of 46 to 12 to adhere to the article on boundaries previously adopted. Dousman of Prairie du Chien wrote to Sibley, his old partner in the fur trade, that he thought himself doing Sibley good service in voting for the Rum River line in the Wisconsin convention, as it would include St. Paul in Wisconsin and leave Sibley to be the great man in the territory which must soon be established west of the Mississippi. Sibley, however, threw his influence with the people of the St. Croix Valley.[59]

The pending action of the Wisconsin convention presently became known in St. Croix County through the Madison and Galena newspapers and created no little excitement, especially in the circle of prominent citizens who had been quietly laboring to secure the formation of a new territory which should include some large area east of the St. Croix. On January 24, 1848, three days before the passage of the Wisconsin article on boundaries, a public meeting was held in St. Paul to protest against the Rum River line. The objections to that line as set forth in a series of resolutions were, in substance: (1) that all the people of St. Croix County were opposed to it; (2) that it gave to Wisconsin an inordinate accession of territory; (3) that it cut the proposed new Territory of Minnesota off from every part of the south shore of Lake Superior and deprived Minnesota of all the eastern bank of the Mississippi below the Falls of St. Anthony, the extreme point of navigation; (4) that,

[59] Wisconsin Constitutional Convention, 1847-48, *Journal*, 245-247, 250, 259-262, 423, 454, 483, 504-512, 515, 542-548, 604; Dousman to Sibley, January 28, 1848, Sibley Papers.

since St. Croix County was separated from the settled parts of Wisconsin by hundreds of miles of uninhabitable country, its people had no interests in Wisconsin and no desire to be politically united with that state. A memorial, drafted by William R. Marshall, was signed by numerous attendants at the St. Paul meeting and by others. It not only protested against the Rum River line, but it proposed another more to the liking of the memorialists — "A line drawn due south from Shagwamigan [*Chequamegon*] bay, on lake Superior, to the intersection of the main Chippewa river, and from thence down the middle of said stream to its debouchure into the Mississippi." The memorial, presented to the Senate on March 28, was given the usual reference. In April, 1848, a pamphlet was published in Washington containing a summary of the boundary issue, Brownell's minority report on boundaries, and the report submitted by Holcombe to the first convention.[60] Congress appears not to have been convinced by the memorial of "citizens of the Territory of Minnesota" or the arguments set forth in the pamphlet concerning the desirability of excluding the entire St. Croix Valley from Wisconsin; but these documents may have had some influence, for the Rum River line proposed by the convention was not accepted and Wisconsin was admitted to the Union by act of May 29, 1848, with the boundaries prescribed by the enabling act.[61] The eastern boundary of Minnesota was thus finally established, and the prospect for the location of the capital of a new territory in the St. Croix Valley faded away.

The story of the northern boundary of Minnesota is part of the larger one of the international boundary between the Dominion of Canada and the United States of America, a story which, beginning in Revolutionary days, is still in some minute details unfinished. The cession by France in 1763 of all her North American possessions east of the Mississippi, excepting a small area about New Orleans, and her nearly contemporaneous alienation to Spain of all her holdings west of the

[60] The manuscript proceedings of the meeting in St. Paul, including the resolutions adopted, are in the possession of the Minnesota Historical Society. They are printed by Holcombe in *Minnesota in Three Centuries*, 2: 358. The memorial, signed by Henry H. Sibley and 345 others, constitutes 30 Congress, 1 session, *Senate Miscellaneous Documents*, no. 98 (serial 511). The Senate clerk, possibly in expectation of things hoped for, attributed the memorial to the "citizens of the Territory of Minnesota." See 30 Congress, 1 session, *Senate Journal*, 239 (serial 502). The pamphlet referred to is entitled *Boundaries of Wisconsin*, with the subtitle, "Reasons Why the Boundaries of Wisconsin, as Reported by the Committee for the Admission of that Territory into the Union as a State, Should Not Be Adopted." It was "Printed at the Congressional Globe Office" and bears the date "WASHINGTON CITY, *April* 20, 1848." Holcombe, in *Minnesota in Three Centuries*, 2: 359, attributes it to Brownell.

[61] *Statutes at Large*, 9: 233–235. An attempt was made in the House to substitute the Trempealeau line and a lengthy debate ensued. *Congressional Globe*, 30 Congress, 1 session, 742–754.

Mississippi have already been noted in this narrative. Mention has also been made of the Proclamation of 1763, issued by King George III, which established the government of Quebec with its western terminus on Lake Nipissing and relegated the whole region southwest of that lake to Indian country, in which all settlements were forbidden and trade was permitted only under license. Sufficient account has also been taken of the passage by the British Parliament of the Quebec Act of 1774, which extended the province of that name to the Ohio, the Mississippi, and the southern border of the Hudson's Bay Company territory, wherever that might be.[62]

The First Continental Congress of 1774, in employing such phrases as "cause of America," "Friends and Fellow countrymen," "liberties of America," and "welfare of our common country," voiced, perhaps unconsciously, a nascent sense of American nationality.[63] The Declaration of Independence in 1776 as the manifesto of a "people" announced the birth of a new nation under the name and style of "The United States of America." Two years later, in 1778, the Congress submitted to the states that imperfect constitution known as the Articles of Confederation. Defective and powerless as it proved to be, it was still a national charter. It may be assumed that the victory at Saratoga in October, 1777, and the successful affair at Monmouth a year later had inspired the Congress to assume more formally the character and state of a national legislature. The alliance with France, concluded in February, 1778, presumed the recognition by that power of the United States of America as an independent state. The time had come when the new government should ascertain the bounds of its jurisdiction. To this question of capital importance the members of the Congress presently addressed themselves. On March 19, 1779, they agreed to the following ultimatum: "that the thirteen United States are bounded" on the north by a line drawn from the northwestern angle of Nova Scotia to the head of the Connecticut River, down that river to the parallel of 45° north latitude, thence due west to the St. Lawrence River, thence "strait to the mouth of Lake Nipissing, and thence strait to the source of the river Mississippi." The other boundaries are not of present concern, and only the clause just quoted, "and thence strait to the source of the river Mississippi," calls for attention. The Congress resolved that all the territory within the boundaries claimed should be absolutely evacuated by the British forces. A notable proviso followed to the effect that, if it should be necessary in order to put an end to the war, a more southerly line might be accepted, but not below the latitude of 45°. The steel-arch bridge at Minneapolis is almost exactly on that parallel.[64]

The boundary question now lay in abeyance until the opening of negotiations for peace between the United States and Great Britain. In April, 1782, Richard Oswald, a British agent without official commission, obtained from Benjamin Franklin, then our minister plenipotentiary at the court of France, a memorandum in which it was suggested that the voluntary cession of all Canada would be the surest means, not merely of establishing peace, but of insuring reconciliation. "It [*reconciliation*] is a sweet Word," wrote Franklin. The British agent was so well satisfied that he promised to impress this reasoning on Lord Shelburne, the British premier.[65] The negotiations for peace and independence moved tardily. In June, 1781, the Congress had elected a peace commission consisting of John Adams, Jay, Franklin, Laurens, and Jefferson. The last named, for personal reasons, did not serve. Laurens was taken prisoner and was detained in London Tower. Jay was minister to the court of Spain and Adams was in Holland laboring to secure recognition of the United States and a loan of money. On June 23, 1782, Jay joined Franklin in Paris and the two took up "the skirmishing business" of the commission.[66]

The moderating influence of Jay may be inferred from an outline of conditions for a treaty of peace communicated by Franklin on July 9 to the British agent. The paragraph relating to boundaries did not call for the cession of all Canada, but only for "a confinement" of its boundaries to what they were before the Quebec Act of 1774. Nevertheless

[64] *Secret Journals of the Acts and Proceedings of Congress*, 2: 133, 138, 226 (Boston, 1821). In a code of instructions to a commission to treat with Great Britain, adopted on August 14, 1779, the Congress repeated the same lines and proviso. On February 23, 1779, a committee of Congress recommended a line from Lake Nipissing due west to the Mississippi. This line would have touched the south end of Mille Lacs. The reader will remember that La Salle's proclamation of 1682 gave to France, under the law of nations, only the lands drained by the Mississippi and its tributaries. The valley of the Red River of the North and the terrain drained by the streams emptying into it belonged to Great Britain by right of discovery, and were a part of Canada. It was a portion of this pocket which was granted to Lord Selkirk. After the acquisition of Louisiana in 1803, the location of the northern boundary was wholly a question between the United States and Great Britain. The reader need not necessarily concern himself about the extent of Louisiana in other quarters. Hermann, *The Louisiana Purchase*, 32; Langford, in *Minnesota Historical Collections*, 9: 500; Frank Bond, *Historical Sketch of "Louisiana" and the Louisiana Purchase* (Washington, 1912). See also the following correspondence in the possession of the Minnesota Historical Society: Fimple to Wheeler, December 21, 1903; Bond to Wheeler, December 21, 1903; Langford to Fimple, January 12, 1904; Langford to Bond, January 20, 1904.

[65] Franklin, *Writings*, 8: 471–473 (Smyth edition); Edmond Fitzmaurice, *Life of William Earl of Shelburne*, 3: 179–183 (London, 1876).

[66] *Secret Journals of Congress*, 2: 441–443; John T. Morse, *Thomas Jefferson*, 72 (*American Statesmen* series — Boston, 1895); John Jay, *Correspondence and Public Papers*, 2: 311, 313 (New York, 1890–93).

Franklin cleverly introduced into an appended list of articles which he as a friend would offer to England one providing for "giving up every part of Canada." The British ministry apparently gave little heed to this extreme proposition. On October 5 Jay, doubtless with Franklin's approval, handed the British agent a plan of a treaty. The article on boundaries provided for a northern line from the point where the forty-fifth parallel crosses the St. Lawrence to the southern end of Lake Nipissing and thence straight to the source of the Mississippi. This article was acceptable to the commissioner, who transmitted the plan to London.[67]

On the twenty-sixth of October Adams reached Paris, and the skirmishing came to an end. Upon the insistence of Jay the British cabinet had finally given Oswald a commission with full powers to treat, not with the thirteen colonies, but with the thirteen United States. It had also supplied him with two able advisers. On the fourth day after the arrival of Adams the commissioners began a series of formal interviews, which lasted till November 5. The British commissioners proposed that the United States should give up her claims to the area covered by the Quebec Act, which extended to the Ohio River. Franklin, writing to Livingston, secretary of state, on December 5, 1782, said, "They wanted to bring their boundary down to the Ohio, and to settle their loyalists in the Illinois country. We did not choose such neighbours." The American commissioners in their letter of advice of December 14, 1782, transmitting a copy of the preliminary treaty, remarked that "The court of Great Britain insisted on retaining all the territories comprehended within the Province of Quebec by the act of Parliament respecting it . . . and they claimed . . . all the lands in the western country and on the Mississippi. . . . It would be endless to enumerate all the discussions and arguments on the subject." On November 2 the American commissioners submitted two alternate propositions regarding the northwestern boundary: "one the line of forty-five degrees; the other, a line through the middle of the lakes." In the end, the boundary matter seems to have been easily adjusted; the American commissioners exerted themselves far more ardently to retain the Atlantic fishery privileges, and the British struggled for the payment of debts due their countrymen and for the protection of the Tories.[68]

[67] Franklin, *Works*, 9: 355 (Sparks edition, Boston, 1836–40); Fitzmaurice, *Shelburne*, 3: 343; George Pellew, *John Jay*, 200 (*American Statesmen* series — Boston, 1894); Francis Wharton, ed., *Revolutionary Diplomatic Correspondence of the United States*, 5: 805–807 (Washington, 1889).

[68] John Adams, *Works*, 3: 298, 300–335; 8: 18 (Boston, 1850–56); Franklin, *Writings*, 8: 633 (Smyth edition); Wharton, *Revolutionary Diplomatic Correspondence*, 6: 131. For the strenuous efforts of the French court to induce the Americans to allow Great Britain to retain the territory of the Quebec Act and to permit the Spanish to extend their protectorate

Any school atlas will show why the British authorities chose the line of the Great Lakes. The line of 45° would have added to the United States the fairest portion of Ontario. The text of the preliminary treaty of peace signed at Paris on November 30, 1782, described the international boundary from the mouth of St. Mary's River in these words: "thence through Lake Superior northward of the isles Royal and Phelippeaux, to the Long Lake; thence through the middle of said Long Lake, and the water communication between it and the Lake of the Woods, to the said Lake of the Woods; thence through the said lake to the most northwestern point thereof, and from thence on a due west course to the river Mississippi." In the choice of this line the commissioners were guided by the map of John Mitchell published in 1755 and by a tradition that the Lake of the Woods had its outlet in Lake Superior. They supposed they were choosing a line of unbroken water communication. In so remote a region, over which the British government and the Hudson's Bay Company maintained a tolerated jurisdiction till after the close of the War of 1812, there was no call for a precise delimitation of the northwestern boundary.[69]

In article 4 of Jay's treaty of 1794, provision was made for a survey of the Mississippi River from one degree below the Falls of St. Anthony to the source of that river. As declared by that article the object of the proposed survey was to ascertain whether the Mississippi extended so far northward as to be intersected by a line drawn due west from the Lake of the Woods. This survey was not undertaken. During Jefferson's two administrations abortive efforts were made by his secretary of state, James Madison, to secure a location of our northern international boundary. The unreadiness of the British cabinet and the unwillingness of the Senate to act on the available information prevented the consummation of a convention in 1803, and of a treaty in 1807.[70]

up to the Ohio River, see the summary in John Fiske, *The Critical Period of American History*, 19 and map (Boston, 1888). For details consult Wharton, *Revolutionary Diplomatic Correspondence*, vol. 5; John Adams, *Works*, vols. 3 and 8; Franklin, *Writings*, vol. 8; Jay, *Correspondence*, vol. 2; Pellew, *Jay*, 184; Fitzmaurice, *Shelburne*, 3: 246, 269–303, 323.

[69] *Treaties, Conventions, International Acts, Protocols and Agreements between the United States and Other Powers*, 1: 581 (61 Congress, 2 session, *Senate Documents*, no. 357 — serial 5646). The definitive treaty, ratified on January 14, 1784, was in precisely the same terms. See also John Adams, *Works*, 8: 20, 210, 392, 398, 518.

[70] *Treaties, Conventions, and Agreements*, 1: 593; *American State Papers: Foreign Relations*, 2: 584–591; 3: 90, 97, 162. The lines proposed in the abortive convention of 1803 and treaty of 1806 are described in a letter from Dr. Neill to Charles E. Mayo, February 24, 1866, in the possession of the Minnesota Historical Society. This letter embodies the results of a study of the material then available at the Library of Congress. A summary by Alfred J. Hill, "How the Mississippi River and the Lake of the Woods Became Instrumental in the Establishment of the Northwestern Boundary of the United States," may be found in *Minnesota Historical Collections*, 7: 317–327 (St. Paul, 1893). Survey maps of various

Allusion has already been made to the efforts of the British commissioners appointed to negotiate a treaty of peace at the close of the War of 1812. They submitted as a condition to be admitted without discussion before proceeding to other matters that there be a revision of the international boundary — impliedly proposing that the boundary line in the West should be drawn, not from the Lake of the Woods, but from the head of Lake Superior. They further demanded the military occupation of both shores of the Great Lakes with the right to maintain a naval force upon them, and insisted that the Americans should agree not to maintain armed vessels thereon nor to construct any fortifications within a limited distance of the shores. For these concessions the Americans were to have the free commercial navigation of the lakes. Nor was this all of the British *sine qua non*. They modestly asked the United States to unite in maintaining a permanent Indian territory in all the region westward of the Greenville line of 1795. The intended effect was to turn over to twenty thousand Indians nearly one-third of the territorial domain of the United States. The hundred thousand white inhabitants already in that region "might remove," said Henry Goulburn, one of the British commissioners; another, Dr. William Adams, said that "undoubtedly they must shift for themselves." The American commissioners did not for a moment entertain the British condition precedent.[71] It is highly probable that it was put forward to be waived in consideration of substantial demands to be later announced. Having served its purpose, it was at length withdrawn, and the boundary line in the Northwest was left where the treaty of 1782 had put it.

The treaty of 1814 did provide, however, for a joint commission to survey and definitely to locate the international boundary. It was not till 1822 that this commission, which for some years had been employed in efforts to determine the northeastern boundary, was prepared to consider that part of the northwestern boundary between the head of Lake Huron and the Lake of the Woods, as provided for in a separate article of the treaty of Ghent.[72] At a meeting in June, 1822, the commission

points along the northern boundary of Minnesota between Lake Superior and the Lake of the Woods, drawn by the author of this summary, are in the Hill Papers. Other aspects of the subject are discussed in Ethel J. May, "The Location and Survey of the Northern International Boundary Line," in *North Dakota Historical Collections*, 4: 179–234 (Fargo, 1913), and John B. Moore, *History and Digest of the International Arbitrations to Which the United States Has Been a Party*, 1: ch. 1 (53 Congress, 2 session, *House Miscellaneous Documents*, no. 212 — serial 3267).

[71] *American State Papers: Foreign Relations*, 3: 709, 710, 712. The documents and correspondence relating to the treaty of Ghent may be found on pages 695–726. See also Adams, *United States*, 9: chs. 1, 2, and Adams, *Memoirs*, 3: 19. For the Greenville line see *Statutes at Large*, 7: 49.

[72] *Treaties, Conventions, and Agreements*, 1: 614, 617. The correspondence between commissioners and the communications of the American commissioners to the secretary of state

did no more than to instruct the surveyors to survey "the chain of waters supposed to be referred to in the treaty." There seems to have been mutual acquiescence in assuming the Pigeon River route to be the intended line of division. The report of the surveyors was laid before the joint commission at Albany, New York, in February, 1824. At this meeting no question was raised as to the Pigeon River line, but at the instance of the British commissioner, who objected to the insufficiency of the surveys, the commission further instructed the surveyors to complete their surveys "from the mouth of Pigeon River to the most northwestern point of the Lake of the Woods." In October of the same year the joint commission met again in Montreal, and the surveyors reported on the operations of the summer. The American commissioner was ready to agree to the Pigeon River line, but the British commissioner was not. He had been informed of another route which might prove to be the one answering to the treaty provision of 1782. Observing that the boundary was to run "*through* Lake Superior," the British functionary claimed that it should extend to the head of that lake. He chose to consider a long estuary with a narrow entry into the St. Louis River as the Long Lake mentioned in the treaty. From that water the boundary should, he claimed, run up the St. Louis River and one of its tributaries, proceed by a portage to the headwaters of the Vermilion River, and follow it down to its mouth. He demanded a joint survey of this line. The American commissioner refused his assent. The British commissioner was, or appeared to be, so confident of his claim that he had the survey made at the expense of his government. Had this line been adopted the whole "Triangle" with its billions of tons of iron ore undreamed of at the time would have been added to the Dominion of Canada.

Two years now passed before the joint commission reassembled on October 25, 1826. In the meantime the American agent had got new light, and he now presented a claim for a third boundary line from Lake Superior as far as Rainy Lake. It should start from the mouth of the Kaministiquia River in Thunder Bay and ascend that river to Dog Lake, which it was pretended was the Long Lake of the treaty. From the Kaministiquia above Dog Lake, the line was to pass through Arrow

may be found in *British and Foreign State Papers*, 9: 530–619. The debates are in T. C. Hansard, *Parliamentary Debates from the Year 1803 to the Present Time*, series 1, 29: 367–383; 30: 209, 500–533 (1803–20). The international boundary west of the Lake of the Woods was fixed by article 2 of the treaty of 1818, which describes it as extending "from the most northwestern point of the Lake of the Woods, along the forty-ninth parallel of north latitude, or, if the said point shall not be in the forty-ninth parallel of north latitude, then that a line be drawn from the said point due north or south as the case may be, until the said line shall intersect the said parallel of north latitude, and from the point of such intersection due west along and with the said parallel . . . from the Lake of the Woods to the Stony Mountains." *Treaties, Conventions, and Agreements*, 1: 632.

Lake and River and Sturgeon Lake and River. This line would have included Hunter's Island and a considerable additional area in the United States. The American agent offered nine maps in support of his claim. The arguments presented by each of the two commissioners for his new-found boundary are given at length in the printed report. If the commissioners were blessed with a sense of humor there must have been mutual smiles. They good-naturedly abandoned their game of bluff. The American commissioner again expressed his willingness to accept the Pigeon River line. The British commissioner agreed, except that he wished to have the line shifted from the mouth of that river to a point about six miles to the southwest so that it might include in Canada the site of the old Northwest Company trading post and the Grand Portage road. He also demanded that the boundary should run overland, following the accustomed portages, and not be confined strictly to the most continuous water communication, as proposed by the American commissioner. They were unable to compose the difference at the time, and at their final meeting on October 22, 1827, they had no better success. It remained for each to make his separate report on the disagreement.[73] The boundary from Lake Superior to the Lake of the Woods remained undetermined till 1842, when the disagreements were composed by the Webster-Ashburton treaty of that year. The amiable and fair-minded plenipotentiaries easily agreed to the Pigeon River route, with the understanding that Grand Portage and all the usual portages should be open and free to both countries.[74]

[73] It is probable that an agreement might have been reached but for a more serious problem regarding the line through the St. Mary's River. The commission could not agree on which side of St. George's or New Encampment Island the line should pass. The reports of the American and British commissioners and other documents relating to the boundary question are published in 25 Congress, 2 session, *House Executive Documents*, no. 451 (serial 331). See especially pages 24–31. Portions of the journal of the commission are quoted in Moore, *International Arbitrations*, 1: 171–191. See also *British and Foreign State Papers*, 30: 360–367. The commission agreed upon the principle to be applied in locating the "most northwest" part of the Lake of the Woods. See *Reports upon the Survey of the Boundary between the Territory of the United States and the Possessions of Great Britain from the Lake of the Woods to the Summit of the Rocky Mountains*, 80–83 (Washington, 1878; printed also in 44 Congress, 2 session, *Senate Executive Documents*, no. 41 — serial 1719). The exact location, as finally accepted in September, 1874, is north latitude 49° 23' 50.28'', west longitude 95° 08' 56.7''.

[74] *Treaties, Conventions, and Agreements*, 1: 650, contains the text of the treaty. See also 27 Congress, 3 session, *Senate Documents*, no. 1, pp. 27–145 (serial 413). These pages contain a letter from Webster dated July 27, 1842, proposing the line in the exact words put into the treaty, and a renewal by Lord Ashburton of the British commissioner's demand to start the line from a point about six miles south of the Pigeon River where the Grand Portage commences. The *Congressional Globe*, 27 Congress, 3 session, 2–30, gives the text of the treaty and the correspondence. The appendix to the same, pages 1–27, gives the elaborate speech of Thomas H. Benton in opposition to the ratification of the treaty. It was ratified by a vote of 39 to 9. For Webster's defense of his action, on April 7, 1846, see his *Writings and Speeches*, 9: 78–150 (National edition, Boston, 1903). For the debate

13. THE SALE OF FORT SNELLING[75]

The reader is aware that the Dakota did not establish themselves on the reservations allotted to them on the upper Minnesota by the treaties of Traverse des Sioux and Mendota till late in 1853. Fort Ridgely was built in the following year in the extreme western corner of Nicollet County.[76] To it the troops at Fort Snelling were soon transferred, leaving there only a guard for military supplies. In 1857 Fort Abercrombie was established in the Red River Valley. With sufficient armaments and garrisons these forts could hold the Sioux in order, and Fort Ripley would protect the missionaries and traders among the peaceable Chippewa. Fort Snelling thus became nothing more than a place, and a very inconvenient one, for receiving and forwarding supplies to those advanced posts. No reserve of twelve square miles was needed for this purpose.

in the House of Commons, consult the index to Hansard, *Parliamentary Debates*, series 3, volumes 67 and 68, under the heading "American Boundary Treaty." Joseph Hume, mover of a vote of thanks to Lord Ashburton, said that the discussion on the bill had been "disgraceful to the House." Lord Palmerston, who opened the debate, considered it "a good treaty but a very bad bargain." An excellent summary of all the negotiations, with a bibliography, may be found in Alexander N. Winchell, "Minnesota's Northern Boundary," in *Minnesota Historical Collections*, 8: 185–212 (St. Paul, 1898). At the time of the completion of this article, portions of the line were as yet actually unmarked. Another interesting contribution to the subject is that by Ulysses Sherman Grant, "The International Boundary between Lake Superior and the Lake of the Woods," in *Minnesota Historical Collections*, 8: 1–10. This author was employed in the geological survey of Minnesota and traveled over the boundary many times. In his opinion the line between the two points mentioned runs for more than half of the distance south of the boundary line contemplated in the treaty of 1783 and adds more than a thousand square miles to Canadian territory. An excellent map of the region in question may be found on page 40 of the same volume in which these two articles are published. In an article entitled "Another Word about the Northern Boundary of Minnesota," published in *Science*, 26: 79–83 (July 19, 1907), Newton H. Winchell describes twelve maps bearing on the boundary question and mentions particularly another, that of Laurie and Whittle, London, 1794. On this map the international boundary, shown by a heavy red line, passes north of Hunter's Island, strikes the north end of Rainy Lake, and runs thence direct to the north end of the Lake of the Woods. The author concludes that "it is plain that through the inadvertence of the American commissioners of 1842 about 2,500 square miles of land were yielded to the British." Drawings of portions of the Laurie and Whittle map and of John Mitchell's map of 1755 may be seen in 25 Congress, 2 session, *House Documents*, no. 451, pp. 32, 120 (serial 331). If the reader comes upon the articles of James A. Baker in the *Pioneer Press* of September 9 and 12, 1877, he should see also a letter in the possession of the Minnesota Historical Society, from Ulysses S. Grant to David L. Kingsbury, March 28, 1895, in which numerous corrections are suggested. The letter is filed with a manuscript copy of Baker's articles and with page proof thereof corrected by Grant. A brief discussion of the negotiations occurs in Moore, *International Arbitrations*, 1: 191–195. In a final note Moore acknowledges indebtedness to Annah May Soule, "The International Boundary Line of Michigan," in *Michigan Pioneer and Historical Collections*, 26: 597–621 (Lansing, 1896). The writer of this article has assembled the sources and authorities with extraordinary diligence and has illustrated it with eleven maps. The history of the boundary dispute is also summarized in International Joint Commission on the Lake of the Woods Reference, *Final Report*, 133–140 (Washington, 1917).

[75] See *ante*, pp. 432–434.
[76] See *ante*, p. 353. Gresham, *Nicollet and Le Sueur Counties*, 1: 179.

Forty acres would be sufficient. The probability, therefore, that the reserve, containing, as roughly estimated, some eight thousand acres, would soon be in the market was no secret. It was in the minds of many persons operating in northwestern lands. Under the circumstances it required no little ingenuity to negotiate a sudden and clandestine sale.

Among those interested in the possibilities of the Fort Snelling Reservation there was none who had better reason for such interest than Franklin Steele, sutler at the fort for many years and a resident in the territory since 1837. He had been a large and skillful operator in lands, lumbering, and merchandising, and, it was believed, had already accumulated a large fortune. By permission of the military authorities he had erected a dwelling, a storehouse, and other buildings near the fort. While these improvements technically gave Steele no preëmption right, the sentiment of the frontier would have held infamous any competition for the purchase of the 160 acres surrounding them. On what ground may have rested the presumption that the remainder of the reservation might be disposed of by the war department at private sale is not known; but Steele, so presuming, made, through Henry M. Rice, on April 24, 1856, a proposal to buy the whole tract at fifteen dollars per acre, cash down. On May 6, Jefferson Davis, secretary of war, replied that, as the reservation was still needed for military purposes, Steele's offer could not be entertained. The quartermaster-general had advised him that the offer, though far below the real value of the lands, was probably more than they would bring at public sale on account of the banding together of speculators, and that if the lands should be sold, 150 acres ought to be retained. The authority for a sale was at the time of this correspondence believed to issue from the act of Congress of March 3, 1819, empowering the secretary of war to sell all such military sites as "may have been found, or become useless for military purposes." But a question arose in regard to the interpretation of this act. Obviously the power conferred by this paragraph, taken reasonably, had been exhausted long since — indeed the attorney-general so decided. It was, therefore, thought desirable by those interested that the authority should be revived and so extended as to cover the sale of reservations later found useless. Rice undertook to secure the necessary legislation and succeeded in having inserted in the army appropriation bill of March 3, 1857, a brief paragraph extending the provision of the act of 1819 to all military sites "which are or may become useless for military purposes."[77]

---

[77] *Sale of Fort Snelling Reservation*, 49, 72, 73 (serial 1372). It was assumed that the area of the tract was five thousand acres and that the sum to be paid would be seventy-five thousand dollars. *Statutes at Large*, 3: 520; 11: 203; *Fort Snelling Investigation*, 384 (serial 965).

But very few persons in or out of Congress could have known the immediate purpose of this obscure legislation. It was not long before those who did know, or who presently learned, began a series of exceedingly interesting movements. The Honorable John B. Floyd, former governor of Virginia, had been appointed secretary of war by President Buchanan soon after his inauguration on March 4. On April 7 Rice addressed a letter to the new secretary in which he recommended the sale of the Fort Snelling Reservation, with the exception of forty acres to be retained for a depot of supplies. He advised a survey into lots not exceeding 160 acres each and a sale at public auction at or above a minimum price. He urged that the equities of any residents be respected. Two days before, on April 5, Rice had written to Ramsey from Washington, "I now think I shall get [an] order issued for the sale of the Snelling & Ripley reserves — but this is for your ear alone."[78]

Early in April, when Dr. Archibald Graham of Lexington, Virginia, was visiting in Washington, he called on the secretary to pay his respects to him as a Virginian. In their conversation Dr. Graham remarked that he was going to Minnesota to make some investments and inquired whether the secretary might not have some public business that way which would pay expenses. That official replied that he had nothing to offer unless it was an agency for selling some old forts, mentioning Fort Snelling. The dutiful citizen had been in Minnesota three years before and possibly had learned something of the value of Fort Snelling and the adjacent property. The secretary's offer was declined after a few days' delay for respectful deliberation. If the real purpose of the call was to ascertain the secretary's intention in regard to the sale, it was satisfactorily accomplished. John C. Mather, a senator of the state of New York, who had seen a copy of the law of March 3 and had observed the provision for the sale of some useless military reservations, appeared in Washington about the same time as Graham, but on other business. The two men named met by accident in Brown's Hotel and fell into conversation about investments in the West. It was their first meeting. It is evident that the Virginian made a deep impression on the New York statesman and a tentative agreement was made looking toward an operation in the Fort Snelling Reservation. Mather had a neighbor, Richard Schell, a "regular speculator," in his own phrase, who had learned from the newspapers that some forts would be sold. It did not take long to persuade him to resolve to invest some of his wife's money, if upon further examination Mather, whom he trusted absolutely, should assure him that all was right. As the

---

[78] *Sale of Fort Snelling Reservation*, 77; Ramsey Papers. Writing to Steele on April 6, 1857, Rice said, "The Fort Snelling reservation will be sold very soon. . . . If any chance for my brother Ed let him know." Steele Papers.

result of a conference between Graham, Mather, and Schell in New York or Washington, "The New York Company" was formed by them in April. On the last of that month Graham traveled to Minnesota, where he saw Franklin Steele. On his return to New York in May his report was so satisfactory that the "combination" was content to proceed. The secretary of war evidently considered himself obliged to sell Fort Snelling, for in April he gave Major Seth Eastman verbal instructions to proceed to that post and make a survey of the reservation. He was instructed to ascertain its area and then to subdivide it into forty-acre lots. Major Eastman seems to have regarded as confidential the secretary's statement that when the survey was finished he would send an agent to sell the property, and he kept silence.[79]

William King Heiskell, a fellow townsman of the secretary of war, now came into the play. This man, a farmer, had served as a member of the Virginia legislature, as a deputy sheriff, and as a third corporal in a militia company. He had been somewhat of a trader in lands in his county and owed nearly all his fortune to such speculating. "A hard student of newspapers," he was generally well informed. Unable to bestow upon this crony a four or five thousand dollar place as desired, the secretary called Heiskell to Washington and offered him the business of selling the Fort Snelling Reservation. Although the pay fixed by law was but eight dollars a day and expenses instead of a five per cent commission, as Heiskell had expected, the agency was accepted. On May 25 he was duly commissioned and was also intrusted with the delivery to Major Eastman of a commission to act as his colleague. On the same date the instructions of the department were issued. The commissioners were first charged to ascertain claims to any portions of the reserve; next, to sell all the lands embraced, except portions justly claimed by settlers, if any, either at public auction or at private sale and either in forty-acre lots, so as to enable persons of small means to buy, or as a whole, according to their best judgment, but in no case for less than seven dollars and a half per acre; further, and as if an afterthought, the commissioners were to examine the fort with reference to its military use and, if their judgment so dictated, to reserve from sale the existing buildings and not less than forty acres of the surrounding land. On delivering the commission, Governor Floyd said to his townsman: "Old fellow, I want you to do the very best you can for the government. I want that sale to be the best ever made in the United States. You have got a parcel of sharpers to deal with, and you have got to keep your eyes open." While in Washington awaiting his commission and instructions Heiskell fell in with Dr. Archibald Graham

[79] *Fort Snelling Investigation*, 49, 89, 103–105, 108, 113, 162, 164, 169, 170, 176, 189.

— it might have been "upon the streets, or in the Capitol grounds, or anywhere else." The latter testified that he had never seen the commissioner before. Heiskell claimed an acquaintance with the medical man of some five or six years' standing. It was probably no accident, however, that these two men were soon traveling together to St. Paul, where they arrived on May 31. On the way the commissioner revealed the general, but not the particular, character of his business; the latter he "communicated to nobody."[80]

It is an interesting coincidence that Senator John C. Mather arrived on the same Sunday morning and accompanied Heiskell to church. The senator was not traveling at his own expense. On May 26 the secretary of war had commissioned him as an agent to examine Fort Ripley near the mouth of the Crow Wing River, with a view to the sale of the military reserve there. There was mystery around this appointment. It was never solicited. The appointee when questioned less than a year afterwards could not tell how he had happened to be selected, how he had learned of his appointment, or whether he had had any interview with the secretary of war on the subject. Secretary Floyd said that he appointed him as a slight indication of his regard and confidence.[81] It appears to have been Friday, June 5, when the two commissioners, Heiskell and Eastman, found themselves together at the fort for consultation.[82] There was a remarkable coincidence of opinion but nothing was concluded. They met again at the fort on the following morning and "got to talking." It did not take them long to agree that the entire reservation ought to be sold as a whole and at private sale, that ninety thousand dollars would be a fair price, and that the refusal should be offered to Franklin Steele. Before noon they inquired in writing what sum he would offer and received a reply stating that he would be pleased to pay the sum offered by him the year before, seventy-five thousand dollars. The commissioners declined this offer and asked if he would not pay ninety thousand dollars. On Monday, June 8, Steele accepted the proposal in writing. The formal contract was not executed till June 10, but it bears the date of June 6. This document, drafted by

[80] *Fort Snelling Investigation*, 50, 112, 304, 305, 307, 309-313, 317, 322-324, 398. Heiskell admitted that he had told the barkeeper at his hotel in St. Paul that he "was there to make a sale or something of that sort."

[81] *Fort Snelling Investigation*, 163, 453. Mather's report is on pages 446 to 449 of the same document. See also page 165 for his testimony that the land at Fort Ripley was later sold at four or five cents an acre.

[82] On Monday there was an election in St. Paul; on Tuesday Commissioner Heiskell drove over the reservation in a buggy; on Wednesday he had a "little business" at Stillwater; on Thursday he went to the fort and delivered to Major Eastman his commission, greatly to the surprise of that officer. Meantime Mather was making an excursion to Fort Ripley. *Fort Snelling Investigation*, 305.

Mather, who had returned from his rapid journey to Fort Ripley, was not materially modified by the commissioners. It should be related, however, that Heiskell testified that he spent two or three days in framing the agreement and that he used up nearly a quire of paper before getting a draft to suit. The contract, which is, of course, of record, was brief and terse. The United States sold the tract described to Franklin Steele, who bound himself and his assigns to pay ninety thousand dollars, one-third on July 10 proximo and the residue in two annual payments thereafter. A deed was to be given to the grantee after the first payment, and possession as soon as the government could dispense with the property. Although Eastman had not completed his survey, he estimated the area to be "between six and seven thousand acres." As the commissioners had not examined the law governing land sales, they were not aware that it gave no authority to sell on credit, and it did not occur to them to exact security or interest on the deferred payments. The rate on current loans at the time in Minnesota was two and one-half per cent a month or more. It was understood that Steele would waive all claims to preëmption and equities on his own account and would satisfy any other claimants. The report of the commissioners was drawn up and signed at Fort Snelling on June 10. On the seventeenth it was submitted to the secretary of war, who laid it before the president on the same day.[83]

On July 2, 1857, the Honorable Robert Smith, the pioneer concessionary on the west side of the Falls of St. Anthony, to whose letter of inquiry of April 21 no reply had been received, called in person at the war department to ascertain, if possible, whether the Fort Snelling Reservation would be sold, and if so, when and in what manner. When informed by an official that the sale had already taken place, he believed that person to be in error. He and other inquirers had to content themselves with the courteous regrets of the secretary that letters he had ordered written had not been received; that was no fault of the department. Smith had been in Minnesota in the first half of June and had inquired of everybody, including the surveyor-general, but had been unable to learn that any action had been taken for the sale. Not the

[83] *Fort Snelling Investigation*, 52, 89, 129, 166, 168, 228, 233, 305-307, 314, 325, 326, 399-412. Commissioner Heiskell explained (p. 314) that he did not consider that this was a sale of public lands and that since it was a military reservation, he considered that the secretary of war had power to regulate its sale. On September 5, 1857, Steele offered to give personal bonds or to deposit state bonds to any amount required to secure his debt. The government was content to withhold its deed. See *Sale of Fort Snelling Reservation*, 59. The issue of the *Daily Pioneer and Democrat* for August 26, 1857, contains a full apology for the sale. The traditional estimate of the area was eight thousand acres; the survey reduced it to 7,916 acres.

slightest reference to the transaction can be found in the St. Paul newspapers. No officer at Fort Snelling was taken into the secret. Colonel
Lorenzo Thomas, senior officer on the staff of Lieutenant General Winfield Scott commanding the army, arrived at Fort Snelling on August 1
and learned that the fort was likely to be sold or probably had been
sold. Major Eastman so informed him. In his report to his chief,
Colonel Thomas ventured to say, "I do not know under what circumstances the post of Fort Snelling was sold, but I am perfectly certain
that no military man on the spot, at all acquainted with the state of
affairs, would have recommended the measure." This report was submitted to the secretary of war on August 28. On the day following
that minister put on it an indorsement not calculated to cheer the heart
of the staff officer or that of his general. "The dissertation about
Fort Snelling," wrote the secretary, "its sale, and the importance of
it for a military depot, is a gratuitous intermeddling in a matter already
disposed of by competent authority. . . . When this department is
required to report to subordinates 'under what circumstances the post
at Fort Snelling was sold,' or any other act was done, the duty shall
be performed; but, until then, a 'military man' will probably understand that a superior in authority is not to be called on for an explanation
of any order."[84]

The sale was confirmed on July 2, but the first payment of thirty
thousand dollars, which had been appointed for July 10, was not made
till July 25. That sum was made up of ten thousand dollars contributed by Steele, eight or nine thousand dollars by Mather, and the remainder by Schell. Graham paid in no money but was obligated to
compensate the company for his undivided share of the property by
services as manager at five thousand dollars per year. On July 31
the secretary of war issued an order through the adjutant general to put
Steele in immediate possession of the property, excepting the fort and
other buildings needed for the use of the troops, as the military post was
to be continued until a later period.[85]

The silence that brooded over the sale of Fort Snelling was not to be
prolonged indefinitely. On January 4, 1858, Robert Smith of Illinois
moved in the House of Representatives that a select committee be appointed to investigate that transaction. Once appointed, the committee

[84] *Fort Snelling Investigation*, 132, 135, 137, 141, 143, 206, 268, 358, 370, 411, 418, 419.
It is interesting to note that Steele's testimony contradicted that of Colonel Thomas. "I
think it was a matter of public notoriety that the property would be sold. . . . I think the
officers at the fort all knew it. . . . It was a matter of general conversation among them."
Fort Snelling Investigation, 228.

[85] *Sale of Fort Snelling Reservation*, 2–5, 88, 103; *Fort Snelling Investigation*, 114, 121,
164, 170.

proceeded to its duty and on April 27 submitted its report. When printed, the report formed, with the report of the minority, the testimony, and documents, an octavo volume of 456 pages.[86] The testimony was conflicting and even bewildering. One group of army officers testified that Fort Snelling was necessary for military purposes and should have been retained indefinitely; another, that it was either wholly useless, or that a small remnant of land would be sufficient.[87] As to the value of the property, opinions were equally diverse. Robert Smith produced a copy of his letter of August 12, 1857, in which he declared to the secretary that if the lands had been properly sold they would have brought four times the price obtained. Another witness knew many persons who would have been willing to pay four hundred thousand dollars for the property. Henry M. Rice, whose experience in handling all kinds of real estate had been extensive, would not have given fifty cents an acre for the property for town site purposes, if compelled to grade streets; for agricultural purposes, he thought the land was worth from three to four dollars an acre. Charles H. Oakes, the St. Paul banker, had laughed at Steele for paying the price he did. Great pains were taken to establish the fact that, had not the sale been made as it was, a combination of buyers would have held the price down to a dollar and a quarter an acre; and much stress was laid upon the results of the previous sales of excluded portions of the reserve. Of this danger the two commissioners appear to have been in great dread, but each had caught it from the other. On the other hand, it was shown that when Fort Dearborn at Chicago was sold in 1839, after advertisement for sealed bids above a minimum, fifty-two and a quarter acres of land brought $106,042. One witness swore that a proposition had been made to him to let him have a one twenty-seventh interest for $25,000. Steele deposed that he had sold the same fractional interest for $6,666.[88]

The committee recommended the passage of five resolutions to the effect (1) that the sale of Fort Snelling was without authority of law; (2) that the action of the secretary of war in disposing of the post without the knowledge or advice of any military officer was a grave fault; (3) that

---

[86] *Fort Snelling Investigation.* The committee held forty-eight sessions and examined fifty witnesses. The expenses for witnesses were $14,830.25. The whole cost of the investigation was placed by a member of the House at approximately twenty thousand dollars. A list of the witnesses examined may be found on page 74. See also *Congressional Globe,* 35 Congress, 1 session, 183.

[87] Thirteen military officers testified. The personnel at Fort Snelling in 1857, according to the report of the adjutant general, was but one officer and nineteen men. Report of the secretary of war for 1857, in 35 Congress, 1 session, *Senate Executive Documents,* no. 11, vol. 2, p. 73 (serial 920).

[88] *Fort Snelling Investigation,* 141, 146, 196, 212, 243, 247, 290, 300, 342, 372, 376, 381, 435–444.

the agents appointed were "unqualified, inexperienced, and incompetent men"; (4) that the management of the sale induced a combination against the government, excluded competition, and caused a loss to the government; (5) that John C. Mather, a government appointee, violated his duty by participating in the transaction, that Schell, Graham, and Steele were aware of his official character, and that, therefore, the sale was then void and remained so. The minority of the committee also submitted a report of great length. Their contentions were that the power to sell had been properly conferred, that the reservation, being of no military use, ought to have been sold, that the manner of the sale was unobjectionable, and that the price was greater than could otherwise have been obtained. Their recommendation was to substitute for the resolutions proposed by the committee a single resolution declaring that the sale had been made in conformity with law, that the evidence had failed to impeach in the slightest degree the fairness of the sale or the integrity of any of the officers or agents concerned, and that there was no need of further action by the House.[89]

The reports came up for consideration on June 1. On that and the following day eighteen elaborate speeches, which fill 128 columns of the *Congressional Globe*, were delivered. The Republican orators did not conceal their elation over the opportunity of smirching the administration; the Democrats found in the evidence sufficient foundation for elaborate and dignified apologies. A New York representative came forward with a proposition of compromise embodied in four resolutions: (1) that the investigation had disclosed nothing derogatory to the secretary of war; (2) that the sale was, however, injudiciously made; (3) that the terms of sale be disapproved; (4) that the papers be referred to the secretary of war for such action as he, with the advice of the attorney-general, might deem proper. This proposition pointed, of course, to an understanding that, should the matter be thus remitted to him, the secretary would retain the reservation and adjust the equities of the purchaser. The compromise resolutions were severally adopted, the test vote being 133 to 60. On the question to substitute them for the resolutions of the committee, however, the vote stood: yeas, 88; nays, 108. The resolutions of the committee then came up, and the first, declaring that the sale of Fort Snelling was unlawful, because it was at the time and ever since had been necessary for military purposes, was voted down, 81 to 86. Whereupon a motion to lay the matter on the table prevailed — yeas, 83; nays, 76. This action, of course, settled nothing.[90]

[89] *Fort Snelling Investigation*, 38, 40–73; *Congressional Globe*, 35 Congress, 1 session, 2408.

[90] *Congressional Globe*, 35 Congress, 1 session, 2595–2658.

At some time during the progress of the investigation Secretary Floyd bethought himself of a procedure which he might properly have thought of and adopted before ordering the sale. He appointed a board of army officers who were to assemble at Fort Snelling and examine into the necessity of retaining the fort as a depot of supplies and of keeping a garrison there for protection against Indian invasions. The board spent the three last days of April, 1858, in an examination of the post; and, at an adjourned meeting in St. Louis on May 4, it agreed to a unanimous report to the effect that the fort was not needed for either of the purposes. The board recommended, therefore, that it be abandoned and that an agency be established at St. Paul for the deposit and transshipment of supplies for Forts Ripley and Ridgely, which could be done there at one-fifth the cost of handling at Fort Snelling.[91] Of this report, signed by seven reputable officers, it may be said that its finding and recommendation were, in view of the existing situation, altogether judicious. When the two forts mentioned were established it was understood that Fort Snelling would be abandoned. No opinion was ventured upon the value of the property or the manner in which it should be disposed of. It may be conjectured that the report had some effect in producing the small majority of votes which tabled the whole investigation. That outcome, however, may also have been facilitated by a batch of seven identical petitions, signed by over three hundred citizens of Minnesota, some distinguished and some less so, praying for the confirmation of the sale. The signers were referred to in the debate as the bone and sinew of the territory. It was alleged by them that Fort Snelling was no longer needed for military purposes, that the land was not worth more than eleven dollars an acre, and that the price to be paid by Steele was adequate and ample.[92]

The secretary, either out of deference to a request of the House committee of investigation for delay, or from an appreciation of the propriety of delay, did not require the execution of his order of July 31, 1857, to give immediate possession to Steele. He did not, however,

---

[91] *Fort Snelling as a Military Depot* (35 Congress, 1 session, *House Miscellaneous Documents*, no. 133 — serial 963).

[92] *Military Reserve at Fort Snelling* (35 Congress, 1 session, *House Miscellaneous Documents*, no. 134 — serial 963). Among the more prominent of the signers of the petitions were Charles L. Chase, acting governor; Henry H. Sibley, governor elect; William Holcombe, lieutenant governor elect; R. G. Murphy, president of the Senate; James Starkey, representative in the House; Charles E. Flandrau, associate justice of the supreme court; Charles H. Berry, attorney-general elect; C. H. Emerson, surveyor-general; C. S. Cave, Samuel E. Adams, and William Sprigg Hall, state senators; and William Lochren, Thomas Cowan, Norman W. Kittson, Charles H. Oakes, George L. Otis, and Joseph R. Brown — all apparently of Democratic persuasion. See also *Congressional Globe*, 35 Congress, 1 session, 2211, 2596.

long postpone action after his ambiguous acquittal by the House of Representatives. Under the secretary's instructions the quartermaster-general on July 9, 1858, ordered the immediate transfer of Fort Snelling to Steele. Ten days later the transfer was made by the post quarter-master. The flag had been hauled down and the little garrison had marched out on June 1.[93]

A long sequel to this narrative must be summarized. The evident expectation of the members of the combination was that the enterprise would require but a small sum of ready money, that sales of parcels would be promptly made, that the proceeds of the early sales would enable them to meet the deferred payments, and that the residue of the lands could be disposed of without haste and at advanced prices. A survey of a portion of the tract was at once begun and about 640 acres were laid out in lots of an average size of 50 by 150 feet. A street was graded and some buildings were begun, and lots were given to persons on condition of building on them. Steele's own expectations were modest. He would be content to double his money in two years.[94] A few sales were made at the rate of one hundred dollars a lot, and a contract was made with an army officer to sell twenty lots at the same rate. The great scheme was suddenly checked by the universal panic of August, 1857. Sales and improvements hopefully begun ceased. The congressional

---

[93] *Sale of Fort Snelling Reservation*, 5, 89.

A cloud of mystery, not likely to be dispelled, still hangs over the sale of the Fort Snelling Reservation in 1857. The explanations by the members of the combination of the way in which they severally became interested in the project are vague and discordant. Their simultaneous, not to say concerted, activity may have been initiated by influences not revealed by the congressional investigation. A possible source of initiatory influence is suggested by a letter which has lately come to light. Major Samuel Woods had been commandant at Fort Snelling and had acquired property in various parts of the territory. On October 3, 1857, he wrote to Franklin Steele from San Francisco, his station at the time: "I think you and Rice ought to have let me into that Fort Snelling affair, as we started the game together." But it should here be stated that Edmund Rice, brother of the Minnesota delegate, was meant. In a recent letter to the author, Colonel William E. Steele said that it has been understood in the Steele family that Edmund Rice was originally financially interested in the purchase, and that his failure to furnish funds expected of him was the occasion of the default on the second payment. See also a letter of September 3, 1857, from William A. Croffut to Steele, relating to a draft by Edmund Rice in consideration of the silence of a newspaper in regard to the sale of the Fort Snelling Reservation. Henry M. Rice merely undertook out of friendship to secure the needed legislation. His only pecuniary connection with the transaction seems to have been the exaction by him, as attorney in fact for Kenneth MacKenzie of St. Louis, from Steele of fifteen thousand dollars for the Baker stone house and the quarter section of land about it. On a day between the execution of the contract and the execution of the bargain Steele took Commissioner Heiskell to Rice's house, where, after an interview which was "not very pleasant," the demand was agreed to. Steele Papers; *Fort Snelling Investigation*, 306, 329, 363, 372, 379–381, 456.

[94] *Fort Snelling Investigation*, 233–237, 370, 372. A "Map of the City of Fort Snelling . . . Surveyed August 1857" is in the possession of the Minnesota Historical Society. It is twenty-four by thirty-two inches in size and is tastefully executed in lithography with views of Fort Snelling and Minnehaha Falls on the margin.

investigation in the following year left the matter in such an ambiguous situation that the combination was unwilling to make the deferred payments and defaulted. In 1860 the government brought suit, which was continued from term to term and in 1865 was suspended.[95]

When Governor Ramsey issued his call for the First Minnesota Volunteers in April, 1861, Fort Snelling was at once recognized as the appropriate rendezvous. Without objection from Steele, so far as is known, it was commandeered by the military authorities. It served the same useful purpose for the other regiments and battalions as they were recruited and was held in military use throughout the war. At "The Fort" the returning commands were mustered out and discharged. When the last of the Minnesota volunteers were mustered out in 1866 the state had no further use for the post. Steele's expectation of founding a city had been dissipated and he was naturally desirous of a recognition of his equities. It may have been upon his solicitation that Major General William T. Sherman, on May 26, 1866, wrote from St. Paul to Lieutenant General Ulysses S. Grant recommending a compromise with Steele and a retention of the fort. At almost the same time, on June 1, an inspector of the quartermaster's department advised his chief that an area of one square mile would be all that the government would need, and a fortnight later, on June 16, the quartermaster-general reported this opinion to the secretary of war and recommended that it be carried into effect. The approval of the war department was indorsed upon this report, and a series of orders followed which resulted in a survey and a map in September and, on March 4 of the following year, in a special order of the department commander establishing the military reservation, the same to embrace one square mile — subject to the approval of the secretary of war. Upon the letter of advice the secretary put the following personal indorsement: "The Secretary does not approve and directs the order issued by General Terry to be suspended until further orders and results of inquiry as to the Steele purchase." The manner in which Steele's interests had been ignored by the quartermaster-general could not have been consolatory to him.[96]

Early in the following year General Sherman, whose counsel had been further required, wrote to the war department that "Fort Snelling . . . should be held by the United States forever. . . . Should the site now pass into private hands, it would have to be repurchased at some future

[95] *Sale of Fort Snelling Reservation*, 4, 98, 104; *Patents within Reservation of Fort Leavenworth*, 6,89 (37 Congress, 3 session, *House Reports*, no. 56—serial 1173). The committee which investigated the situation at Fort Leavenworth was also charged with the investigation of the "present situation of the military reserve at Fort Snelling."

[96] *Sale of Fort Snelling Reservation*, 5–11, 98.

time at a vast cost." The sale by Floyd was a fraud but Steele was not a party to the fraud. A settlement ought, therefore, to be made with Steele on fair terms. He suggested the sale of the tracts reserved for the control of the two ferries and, if need be, a strip on the west part.[97]

On January 24, 1868, Steele, through his attorney, filed with the department a claim for $162,000 for the use and occupancy by the government of the reservation for eighty-one months beginning on April 24, 1861, and proposed to offset so much of the amount as would satisfy any claim the government might have against him. He asked that the balance be credited and paid him and that a deed be executed to him for the whole reservation. General Sherman's counsel made so much impression that the secretary of war referred the subject to the board of claims of the war department. The report of this board, dated September 26, 1868, gave a well-digested history of the transaction and concurred fully with the recommendation of General Sherman, but advised the secretary that further interference by the war department should await legislative action. But the odor of "Floyd's fly-blown contract" lingered long and it was not till May 7, 1870, that a joint resolution of Congress authorized the secretary of war to set apart at least one thousand acres for a permanent military reserve, quiet the title thereto, and settle all claims upon principles of equity. For that purpose he appointed a board of officers, which submitted a report on November 10. The board computed Steele's debt to the United States to be $68,200, estimated the value of the fort and buildings at $12,920, and allowed $17,250 for rent for nine years and seven months at $150 a month. It was thereupon agreed to retain land enough at $25 per acre to make up the balance of $38,030. The area was found to be 1,521.20 acres. Secretary Belknap at once confirmed the action of his board, and a deed on parchment was delivered to Franklin Steele conveying to him 6,394.80 acres.[98] In a late year the government repurchased a portion of the land.

[97] *Sale of Fort Snelling Reservation*, 10. It appears from two letters from Rice to Steele, May 12, 27, 1861, that Governor Ramsey made an ineffectual effort to induce the government to repurchase the fort at the beginning of the war. In the second letter he remarked, "Gov Ramsey sent to Cameron a very strong communication showing the necessity for the purchase of the Fort. The only way now that anything can be done is for you to be here in person & get Forney or some other 'friend at Court' to have the matter called up." Steele Papers.

[98] *Military Reservation at Fort Snelling* (42 Congress, 2 session, *House Executive Documents*, no. 72 — serial 1510); *Statutes at Large*, 16: 376; *Sale of Fort Snelling Reservation*, 93–105. The deed of the United States to Franklin Steele is in the possession of Colonel William E. Steele of Minneapolis. Attached to it and part of it is the beautiful map by Captain Seth Eastman, on which the boundaries of the retained lands are marked by a yellow line. The descriptions of the tracts are quoted in Warner and Foote, *Hennepin County*, 164.

INDEX

INDEX